TURBID RIVERS

D1202601

CH'AE MAN-SIK

TURBID RIVERS
A NOVEL

TRANSLATED BY KIM CHUNGHEE

DALKEY ARCHIVE PRESS

Originally published in Korean as *Takryu* by Bakmun Seokwan Publishing House in 1939.

Library of Congress Cataloging-in-Publication Data

Names: Ch'ae, Man-sik, 1902-1950, author. | Kim, Chung-hee, translator.
Title: Turbid rivers : a novel / Ch'ae Man-Sik ; translated by Kim Chung-hee.
Other titles: T'angnyu.
Description: First Dalkey Archive edition. | Victoria, TX : Dalkey Archive Press, 2016.
Identifiers: LCCN 2016039383 | ISBN 9781628971491 (pbk. : alk. paper)Subjects: LCSH: Korea--History--Japanese occupation, 1910-1945--Fiction. | Women--Korea--Fiction. | Domestic fiction.
Classification: LCC PL991.13.M3 T3413 2016 | DDC 895.73/3--dc23
LC record available at https://lccn.loc.gov/2016039383

LIBRARY OF KOREAN LITERATURE

Partially funded by the Illinois Arts Council, a state agency
Published in collaboration with the Literature Translation Institute of Korea

Dalkey Archive Press publications are, in part, made possible through the support of the University of Houston-Victoria and its programs in creative writing, publishing, and translation. www.uhv.edu/asa/

Dalkey Archive Press
Victoria, TX / McLean, IL / Dublin
www.dalkeyarchive.com

Cover design and composition by Mikhail Iliatov
Printed on permanent/durable acid-free paper

Chapter 1:
A Human Monument

THE RIVER GEUM-GANG!

Take a map, spread it out, and look at it closely; at around the midpoint of the course of the Geum-gang River, two widely divergent tributaries, one flowing northward, the other southward, unite to form a single river (as is also the case with the Han-gang and Yeongsan-gang rivers). Take an airplane, and fly along the river, you will see the same thing.

The rugged Sobaek Mountains run fast along the nape of Joolla province, as if attempting a long jump over to Jeju Island, then jump high once—and once again, leaving behind the two soaring mountains, Galjae and Jiri. The southern branch of the Geum-gang River starts by absorbing the waters from the valleys of those two mountains, and flows northward, passing from Jangsu to Jinan and then on to Muju.

When it reaches the Yeongdong area, gathering waters from the Chupungryeong Ridge and Songni Mountain, it turns toward the northwest and flows on along the borders between the eastern and western portions of Chungcheong province.

And as for the northern branch of the river . . .

Its course is rather simple; it starts as a narrow stream where the tail of the Charyeong Mountains is about to disappear, flowing through Jincheon, which borders Gyeonggi and North Chungcheong provinces, toward Cheongju; but as it passes Jochiwon it finally merges with the southern branch of the river, which it's been longing to meet.

United after long, separate journeys full of hardship, the river now turns toward the southwest and, circling around Gongju, flows down toward Buyeo, leisurely glancing at Gyeryong Mountain . . . Then it meanders around Buyeo, abruptly changes direction, heads southward, and in a flash reaches Nonsan, then Ganggyeong. Up to this point, the river is also called the River Baekma, White Horse, a name suggestive of purity and innocence.

To use the analogy of a woman, it's akin to a maiden as yet untainted by worldly affairs.

The River Baekma, starting from the Gom ferry at Gongju, flows along the faint traces of the dreamlike vicissitudes of the long gone Baekje kingdom.

There you can enjoy the beauties of nature along with clean and transparent water.

Such beauties continue on to Buyeo, but as it reaches Ganggyeong, where the shouts of haggling market crowds and the smell of fish come bustling up, the dreams floating on the tranquil water shatter.

The water turns turbid.

At this point, the river claims its proper name, River Geumgang, once again. The river, now heading west-southwest, continues its rather prosaic journey along the borders of Chungcheong and Jeolla provinces.

Its water, mixing with tidal waters, becomes more turbid and more abundant at the same time; the river is now much wider and looks quite grand.

Thanks to this river, the famous Ganggyeong fields never experience drought, and stay moist throughout the year.

Unlike the rivers Nakdong-gang or Han-gang, which bring about devastating floods every year, this river rarely floods high enough to cause disasters. That's one good thing about the Geum-gang.

Having meandered all the way from far-off mountains, this river has at last run its course when it dumps all its broken dreams and whatnot into the Yellow Sea along with its turbid waters; and on the hills along the south bank where the river ends, a city emerges.

This port city is called Gunsan, and our story unfolds here.

Despite the fact that it takes place in a harbor town, this story is not one of those sentimental tales you hear around harbors every day; it's not a romance about sailors who go out to sea leaving behind their one-night stands; neither is it a sad but sweet story of women who end up weeping in company with sea gulls, gazing after the white waves in the wake of the ships that take their lovers away.

Those with rolled-up sleeves who work hard to sustain a hand-to-mouth existence, either through farming or labor, are bound to have the feeling that even "today" is not so easily secured. But there are worse-off people who can envision neither today nor tomorrow. Such people are abundant all over Korea, and Gunsan is no exception.

Mr. Jeong, or Jeong Jusa as he is usually called, being a former clerk in a county office, fits neatly into such a category.

At present Mr. Jeong is undergoing total public humiliation, having been grabbed by the collar and being held up in the air by a young man—a fellow pseudo-speculator half his age—in the middle of the street in front of the rice exchange market.

It's half past two in the afternoon, one day in early May, right after the market price quotations of the second session have come in from Osaka.

The scene of the scuffle seemed rather isolated, as no one came near them. Among the speculators were people who knew them personally, but none of them had a mind to meddle.

A shop errand boy who was passing by on a bicycle stopped to watch the scuffle with one foot on the pedal, the other on the ground. The scene, accentuated by the boy's presence, took on the appearance of a landscape painting.

The old straw hat being worn by Mr. Jeong, who was swinging in the air, fell to the ground and rolled down the street in the wind that had just begun to rise.

Guffaws burst out among the crowd of people who were standing in front of the main door of the exchange.

The rice exchange was the heart of Gunsan City; wide thoroughfares such as Jeonju Street, Bonjeong Street, or Seaside Street were the arteries of the city. Here and there along the arteries were several banks clustered near the heart as if to protect each other, and there were also several brokerage houses, encircling the heart, connected with each other through weblike telephone lines.

Mr. Jeong's humiliation was taking place right in the heart of the city, of all places.

But scuffles like this in front of the rice exchange are nothing new. You see them break out at least several times per day.

They usually arise from what they call "shooting blank," that is, people betting without seed money, taking advantage of their credit; when they lose and can't pay the stake, quarrels start up between the losers and the winners. Such scuffles are as common as fights among cocks over hens in villages.

Thus, even when people who are fairly well dressed begin to fight on this wide thoroughfare, grabbing each other's collars, hardly anyone pays attention to them unless they're totally bored.

Those speculators who were acquainted with Mr. Jeong were far from attempting to interfere with the scuffle; rather they stood aside under the eaves of the brokerage houses or the exchange building and watched unsympathetically, gloating over the unforeseen adversity of this gray-haired man approaching fifty being thrashed by a youngster who could easily be his son's peer. They were even mocking him.

"Goody-goody! It serves him right! Daring to bet without any money, swindling other people, he's been at it too often, too long."

"Mr. Jeong or Mr. Whatever, he shouldn't be allowed to come near the exchange."

"That old guy may get killed!"

"What the hell are they up to, I wonder!"

"Leave them alone. They know what they're about. In time, both may end up in jail."

Mr. Jeong, dangling from the wrist of the young man, struggled to get free. As he choked, his face turned dark blue, and he coughed violently. His worn-out straw hat was already tumbling on the road, and the half-torn ribbon ties of his white cotton coat were flapping wildly as he swayed.

"Hold on, look now . . . !"

"Look! Look what? What's there to look at but a face that's still ugly? Stop your mumbling, and just give me my money."

"Well, look at you. You're making a shameful scene! Let me go, please, and let's resolve this matter through discussion. Let me go, please."

"Pshaw! If I let go, you'd run away for certain! No way . . . Pay me now. Or I'll strip you naked . . ."

"Look! Do you think the money I don't have will appear out of thin air if you do that?"

"You shameless scoundrel! Why, why then did you jump in when you had no money? You assumed you'd just jump in . . . and if lucky, you might get away with the money like a dog trader who sells without even having a leash, let alone a dog. You vain, greedy rogue! What did you say? A fifty-jeon stake is too small? It should be at least one won? What an empty braggart! My goodness! You'll see what I can . . ."

The youngster raises his right hand, the one that's not holding Mr. Jeong's throat, as if intending to slap his face, and threatens him with his wide-open palm. Mr. Jeong, to dodge the slap, holds back his head and covers it with his hands.

The scene is so pathetic that loud laughter bursts out from every corner.

Right at that moment, Go Taesu, a clerk in the checking accounts department of the nearby Gunsan branch of the 00 Bank, appeared. He was strolling along the street in slippers, with a pen stuck behind his ear. Perhaps he was refreshing himself by taking an afternoon walk. As he was passing by the rice exchange, he saw the scuffle and stopped. The hunchback, Jang Hyeongbo, a clerk at the Marugang Brokerage House, looked out from inside the rice exchange, saw Go Taesu and, with a smirk on his catfish-like lips, shouted,

"Your future father-in-law is about to be murdered. Go on, hurry over to them and stop the disaster. Or you'll be holding your wedding ceremony dressed in mourning! . . . Quick, quick, stop it at once, I say!"

Those who were nearby, whether they knew Taesu or not, exchanged amused smiles.

Taesu shot an angry glance at Hyeongbo, but nevertheless he joined in the smiles. Without doubt, he wanted to stop the fight, but as Hyeongbo, with his big mouth, playfully teased him, he felt too embarrassed to step forward. Before long, however, he grinned at Hyeongbo once more, and dragging his slippers, approached the scene of the scuffle in the middle of the street.

"What kind of behavior is this . . . It's ungentlemanly. Let him go."

Taesu roughly grabbed the young man's hand that was holding Mr. Jeong by the throat. His grip was much firmer than the tone of his words.

Ashamed, Mr. Jeong tried to turn his head away, while the young man, although a little disconcerted, wouldn't let go.

"No, I won't put up with this cheat. He's old enough to know better."

"I say let him go now!" Taesu thundered as he grasped the young man's wrist more forcibly.

"Right or wrong, it makes no difference. Don't you have parents yourself? Look, there can be no excuse for a young man to use violence against an elderly man."

The ferocity of Taesu's gaze was undeniable.

Overpowered, the youngster reluctantly released his grip and stood back.

"Still, it's not me that did wrong but him!"

"The hell with right and wrong! It's clear to everyone what's behind all this. You're fuming 'cause he shot blank, aren't you? . . . Hey, if you know what's right and wrong, then why don't you go to the police and ask them to get your money back!"

"Oh hell!"

The youngster, unable to sustain his case, turned back toward the main door of the rice exchange, still mumbling complaints.

Mr. Jeong, in turn, picked up his hat without uttering a word, either good or bad, and headed toward a brokerage house on the other side of the street. A couple of men who were standing in front of it, and who'd been mocking Mr. Jeong, changed their expressions when they saw the utterly desolate look on his face.

"Give me a cigarette, if you have one."

Mr. Jeong addressed no one in particular, simply stretching out his hand, and looking aside with a deep sigh.

At any other time, they would have refused his request, saying, "Did you leave your cigarettes with me?" But today, one of them quietly handed him one.

Mr. Jeong lit the cigarette and exhaled the smoke along with a deep sigh, absently looking up at the far-off sky.

With his protruding cheekbones above sunken cheeks, Mr. Jeong looked hungry even when his stomach was full. His coarse complexion looked shadowed even in the bright sun-filled day in May. His habit of constantly blinking his murky eyes made him look still more pathetic. On his chin were growing a few unsightly yellow strands of beard, which he nevertheless was wont to stroke from time to time.

The man who gave him the cigarette felt sympathy at the look of despondency on Mr. Jeong's face, and offered him a few consoling words.

"I urge you, sir, to go home right away. Once you enter this world of speculation, it's not uncommon to encounter instances of humiliation. See how your breast-ties are torn. Go home at once, I beg you, sir."

Mr. Jeong, suddenly coming to himself, looked down at his unshapely coat without saying a word. The kindly man went into the brokerage house to fetch a few pins and fastened back the ribbon ties of his coat.

Taesu had been standing to one side of the entrance of the rice exchange, talking to Hyeongbo, and when he passed by Mr. Jeong, he deliberately looked the other way. Mr. Jeong also turned his face away.

Mr. Jeong waited until Taesu was far enough away, and then with a dry cough, "ahem," to clear his throat, began walking slowly toward the 00 Bank. Mr. Jeong, who was only five feet tall, toddled along the street with his out-toed gait, his chest sticking out, and one of his hands resting on his back. Any observer would have found this image of him pathetic.

When you reach the blue-roofed 00 Bank, you come to a crossroads. At the intersection, Mr. Jeong should have taken the road to the right leading to Dongnyeong Hill, if he was headed for his home in Dunbaemi. But he turned left, heading for the pier.

"Does the old guy want to kill himself? Perhaps that's why he's going to the pier," a pseudo-speculator, who'd been watching Mr. Jeong, said, grinning either scornfully or with concern, and turned back.

Mr. Jeong's household is stuck in utter poverty with no way out in sight. And there are six mouths to feed. In addition to himself and his wife, he has no less than four children.

Chobong, who is twenty-one years old, is his eldest daughter, while another daughter, Gyebong, is seventeen, and then there are two sons, Hyeongju, who is fourteen and, Byeongju, who is much younger, being merely six years old.

Each of them is old enough to consume a full bowl of rice at every meal; thus even an eighty-kilo bag of rice can't last a full month; they need at least one hundred kilos of rice per month.

In addition, there are many other items they require to sustain their basic needs. For instance, firewood; and now and then a bag of bean sprouts or a dash of salted shrimps since, no matter how destitute they may be, they can't eat their rice simply with salt, like a peddler camping at the roadside; once in a while they need to buy some fabric for clothing; and then there's also the monthly rent to pay.

Madam Yu, Mr. Jeong's wife, is a woman with strong ambitions for her children. She forces them to study day and night, and somehow manages to give them all a school education. Chobong, the eldest, finished the three-year course at Girls' High School in the spring of last year; Gyebong is now a senior at the same school; Hyeongju, the elder son, will graduate from primary school next spring; he's already pestering his parents to send him to Seoul for further education when he graduates. Madam Yu was extremely vexed when she failed to send her youngest, Byeongju, to a kindergarten last April; she still nags her husband about it whenever she's reminded of it.

Although he's the head of a family with such an expenditure, Mr. Jeong provides barely one-tenth of the household expenses. He was born into a gentrified family of modest means and, following in the family tradition, he studied the Cheonjamun, the Thousand Character Classic, the Chinese poem used as a primer for teaching Chinese characters, starting with the characters for "sky" and "earth", before going on to memorize all the others and studying all seven basic Confucian texts. And when modernization began in the country, he was sent to primary school to get acquainted with modern studies, from which he also graduated.

Mr. Jeong's father gave him a decent education, "good enough for him not to be ashamed anywhere." But the family income was scanty. Although he was the sole heir, with no one to share the inheritance, there was nothing much to inherit.

About twelve years ago, when Mr. Jeong decided to move from his hometown of Seocheon, across the river from Gunsan, in addition to the house they lived in, all he had in his possession were a small mountain hill, where the family cemetery was, and about four acres of rice paddy. He sold all of his properties except for a small plot on the mountain for family graves. After he paid off all his debts, however, he had little more than one thousand won left, out of which he spent about eight hundred won to purchase a new house in Gunsan, leaving only two or three hundred won in cash.

His father believed that he'd provided his only son with a good education in both "old and new studies," befitting the son of a scholarly family, and died contented, trusting that the son was well equipped to lead a decent life.

In fact, a quarter of a century ago, when the Japanese colonization of Korea took place, anyone who had some education, even those who'd merely finished the four-year course of primary school, was sufficiently qualified to work as a clerk at a county office.

Mr. Jeong took the same path too. He landed a job at a county office when he was twenty-three and worked there for a full thirteen years until he was thirty-six. Mr. Jeong, however, remained a minor clerk the whole time until the day he was made redundant.

For a mere clerk without any background, no matter how experienced or competent at his work he might be, it wasn't easy to follow the full course of promotions—from a petty clerk, to a full-status clerk, to a section chief, to a manager of general affairs, and finally to the head of a county. Especially for a man like Mr. Jeong, who lacked tact and resourcefulness, it was almost impossible.

In the end, Mr. Jeong, having wasted all his youthful years confined to a junior position, was declared to have become too old for the job. When he summed up his long years of servitude, all that remained were the piles of debt that usually haunt waged men like demons.

Having been thrown into such an impasse, Mr. Jeong, in the heat of anger, decided to leave the town. He sold all his family property, which wasn't much anyway, and after paying off all his debts, moved to Gunsan City with a vague hope that he might find a new career there. And exactly twelve years have passed since then.

During the first seven years in Gunsan, he moved from one job to another some three or four times. He started in a bank, but moved to a rice exchange brokerage house, and then to a couple of small companies here and there. Finally, about five years ago, he was forced out of waged employment for good, due to his age. With nothing better to do, he then went into rice exchange speculation, as a regular arbitrageur at first, and then as a speculator in peer-to-peer betting.

Not a speck was visible in the May sky. It was late in the afternoon; although the day was nearing its end, the sunlight was still dazzlingly bright as if it would never grow old. A pleasant breeze was blowing from the center of the wide-open river. The breeze coming off the river was refreshingly cool despite the warm season. In contrast to the stillness of nature, the pier was full of hustle and bustle.

Wooden ships, big or small, each with high or low masts, were crowding into the pier, covering the water until it was almost invisible. Yellow croakers, the first catch of the season from the sea near the Chilsan Islands, were being unloaded. Silvery herrings were also pouring out, glittering in the afternoon sunlight. The shouts of the fishermen, bargaining and counting, and the noise of anchors being hauled up resounded from each ship. Porters with A-frames on their backs and women with baskets on their heads were bustling about, giving the place the appearance of a market.

Steam trains that looked like sparrows with their tails chopped off chugged furiously along the seashore, letting out high-pitched whistles in their haste. As if responding to them, a steamship, her huge hulk floating in the center of the river, let out an occasional low-key groan, seeming to be sending a secret signal.

A dredger on the shore was digging up blackish silt from the river bottom, laboriously raising and lowering a huge crane bigger than itself.

The harbor was busy, leaving the sailors little time for melancholy.

Mr. Jeong, forgetful of his surroundings, walked toward the river, his scanty beard blowing in the wind. A small steamboat was chugging along the middle of the river. Mr. Jeong's gaze, at first turned toward his hometown across the river, now followed the wake of the boat.

He suddenly recalled the time when he and his family crossed the river on such a boat from Yongdang twelve years ago. Remembering that they were much better off then, he felt nostalgic for those days. At length tears began to well up in his eyes.

Mr. Jeong's in-depth knowledge about the rice exchange was acquired while he was working at a brokerage office as a clerk. But his actual participation in speculation came much later.

When he first moved to Gunsan, he was able to own his own house. The three children were all very young then. He wasn't just earning a moderate salary, but also had two or three hundred won in idle cash left over after purchasing the new house. Thus his financial situation hadn't been so strained at the time.

Nevertheless, as the years passed, the children grew up and began to require schooling expenses. And his wage decreased each time he changed his workplace. Although today didn't seem worse off than yesterday, this year was definitely worse than last year, and last year was even worse than the one before that. His financial situation kept shrinking even before he was laid off for good from his last job. Having ceased to earn a regular wage, meager though it was, he once again found himself under the heavy mound of debts that had accumulated during the seven or eight years spent as a waged man in Gunsan, in addition to the burden of supporting a big family without any source of income.

He searched high and low for a solution to no avail. At last he sold the house that was already mortgaged to the bank, settled the debt with the bank, and managed to have about three hundred won left in hand. From this time on, he began to speculate at the rice exchange with that money.

His luck at the rice exchange kept fluctuating, as it was bound to. When he was lucky, the money he made went into his household expenses; on the other hand, when he was unlucky, the money he lost was paid off from his seed money.

As the saying goes, it was like "a horse chewing at its own mane until it's all gone." Mr. Jeong's seed money of three hundred won was all gone, little by little, within two years. The fact that it lasted for two years, however, doesn't mean that Mr. Jeong was indiscreet or wasteful. On the contrary, it lasted that long while he was making a living out of it only because his scale of investment was so small; he had very little self-confidence, unable to attempt big bets, nor was he bold enough to covet big money.

After his seed money was all gone, he began to rely on the so-called "good-will presents of the rice exchange," that is, money given away by winners. From time to time, he received money from friends he made at the exchange, or from his home-town friends who came up to Gunsan to speculate at the rice exchange. They sometimes allowed him to bet by providing him with some security money. If he was lucky enough, he got as much as fifty won in presents, with which he managed to make one to three won a day for about one or two months, and then with a spell of unlucky days, he lost all the seed money. Such a pattern of life continued for about one year.

But this "goodwill" lasted only one year. During the past two years, not a soul had offered him such a gift even in passing.

Perhaps his sheer destitution prevented him from inspiring any fellowship in his friends. Like incompetent retired high officials, who end up frequenting a club, Mr. Jeong, with no money, had to drop down to the level of a pseudo-speculator, whose only source of consolation was reciting stories of bygone days as an arbitrageur.

Whether the stakes are high or low, the inevitable ups and downs are present in the rice exchange as in any type of gambling. For instance, when he was able to squeeze one won out of his wife's sewing income, or when he was lucky enough to receive a one- or two-won tip from winners while snooping around in the exchange, he was bound to feel the itch to play. However lucky he might be sometimes, his luck usually ran out before his third bet, leaving him empty-handed again. A gambler usually continues betting until he loses everything, and the only courage one can attribute to rice speculators might be the fact that they continue playing, knowing they will lose it all in the end.

Even when he had no money, a speculator would still go to the exchange, with the vague hope he might receive a handout from a winner and be able to play with it. Like a person addicted to opium or tobacco, he has to go to the exchange every day, if only to gratify his own curiosity.

Mr. Jeong too, even without a dime in his pocket that day, couldn't help but go to the exchange as usual, hoping for some lucky windfall, and loitered around from early in the morning. But that day nothing came his way, and the closing hour was approaching. In desperation, Mr. Jeong decided to take a chance, saying to himself, "What the hell do I have to lose!"

He used the old trick of a dog trader who doesn't even possess a leash, let alone a dog. But bad luck never comes alone. As if to mock Mr. Jeong's rashness, the price of rice in the second session of the afternoon market in Osaka turned out to have dropped drastically, and as a result, he had to go through that outrageous humiliation.

Mr. Jeong looked down at the rushing water that was surging up under the pier at high tide. He felt like throwing himself into the water with his coat over his head, but only if he could be assured he would survive. It was disgraceful enough to have been grabbed by the throat by a young man in broad daylight, let alone all the insulting words thrown at him. What was painful for him right now was that he was at a total loss how to make a living, with or without shame, regardless.

"How can I live and support my young children?"

No ready answer popped into his mind no matter how hard he racked his brain. The only way out he could see was to die and vanish so that he could hear nothing, see nothing, and think nothing.

Indeed, whenever he saw no way out, he blurted out,

"I want to die," or "I'd better kill myself."

But such intention was never carried out; however, his determination had a consoling effect like prayer or religious chanting, and helped to relieve him of his acute anxieties and to resign himself to his reality. Having experienced such effects so often, it became a habitual practice for him to desire his own death whenever he felt helpless.

AS HE WAS standing by the riverside this afternoon, thinking about death again, the heat of his distress somehow began to cool down. Muttering to himself, "How pathetic, how ludicrous I've been," he at last turned back from the riverside and began to walk away. Yet, whether he liked it or not, he had no other place to head for but his home. Recalling his starving family, his footsteps became heavier than ever.

His family had skipped breakfast that morning, and their last meal the night before was a bowl of rice gruel mixed with bean sprouts. If he went home now empty-handed, how could he face the hungry faces of those who'd anxiously been awaiting the return of the head of the family? If only he could get seventeen jeon to buy a bag of broken brown rice, that would boost his own spirits as well as those of his family. But he could see no means of doing even that.

Mr. Jeong was passing by the corner of the 00 Bank, and he unwittingly looked across at the rice exchange. But he immediately turned his head away, muttering,

"See if I ever step foot in that damned place again."

Indeed, he knew full well that no one would welcome him there anyway. Regardless, he felt better as he spat out his resentment.

It wasn't the first time that he'd made such a resolution. He'd gone through it often enough, each time he'd been drawn into some shameful row after betting without any money. Often enough he'd been angrily reproached by young men and subjected to all sorts of humiliation—even having his scanty beard pulled this way or that.

After one such disgraceful incident in the autumn of the previous year, Mr. Jeong had determined to seek his living in a more honest way and attempted to work as a day laborer on the pier, carrying loads on his back. But he couldn't endure it for more than half a day. Although he had to summon all his courage to take on such menial work, his physical strength wasn't up to the job. After a half-day's work at the pier, carrying loads from barges, he was almost dead with exhaustion and was bedridden for the next ten days. His family thought that he had fallen ill through simple fatigue and never found out the sad story behind it.

Since then, never again would he dare try such day-laborer's work. Back at the rice exchange, snubbed by almost everybody, regardless of whether he earned anything or not, he remained a stubborn regular of the place, putting up with all kinds of embarrassment. On days when he couldn't get his hands on any money, he simply sat starving with his family. Such was the life of Mr. Jeong and his family.

A man who has a mouth, but no limbs with which to feed it—Mr. Jeong was indeed such a man.

The breeds of dog native to Jindo Island, the so-called ten thousand rocky ridges of Geumgang Mountain, or the birds singing in the woods of Samcheongdong area, are called "natural monuments" for their uniqueness of shape and characteristics. Then a man with a mouth but without any limbs must also be considered a kind of monument. Since he's a human, however, he can't be one of the "natural monuments." Perhaps he's considered a "human monument."

This monument, Mr. Jeong, trudged slowly with heavy, reluctant steps toward home. When he passed the Dongnyeong Hill, which was also called Jeonju Street, he reached the crossroads in front of the police station. There he stopped and hesitated for a moment. A bit farther down the street was the rice store that belonged to shaggy-faced Han Chambong with his bushy beard. If he wished to avoid him, he had to make a detour through Sinheung-dong to go home.

He was weighing his options. As he owed him some money for rice, he wished to avoid him for fear of being harassed. But on second thought, he decided to push his luck and see if he could get some more rice on credit.

Mr. Jeong walked along Sowha Street, which had only recently been constructed, starting from the train station and heading eastward, then turned to the right into the center of Gaebok-dong.

This was the area where the Korean residences were clustered. Gaebok-dong, incorporated with the adjacent Gubok-dong, is now called by Japanese-style names, "Sansangjeong" (meaning a town on top of a mountain) or "Gaeunjeong" (meaning a town changed for the better). But regardless of such fashionable names, the town itself looks much the same as it did in the past, and nothing there has changed for the better. There is one unpaved street, which stretches only about thirty meters in the center of the area, and on both sides of the street are small pieces of flat land with steep, hilly slopes beyond.

The hilly slopes, however, aren't visible to the eye. The hills on both sides are covered with thatched cottages, which look like crab shells, and run-down tin-roofed huts, standing densely together like bean sprouts in a pot, not leaving even a palm-sized empty space in between. One can only presume that the houses are standing on hilly slopes. The hilly passage between Gaebok-dong and Dunbaemi is called Bean Sprouts Pass, a name quite humorously adequate.

Out of the seventy-thousand-strong population of Gunsan, Koreans number over sixty thousand. And most of them live packed together in a small area located behind the train station, covering Gaebok-dong, Gubok-dong, Dunbaemi, and Gyeongpori. Moreover, in terms of modernization, this area looks at least one century behind, compared to the rest of Gunsan, especially the Park area, or the Japanese residential area down under Wolmyeong Mountain, or the areas around Bonjeong Street or Jeonju Street where you can see many of the features of a civilized city, such as modern buildings and well-developed social and sanitary facilities. Perhaps one century wouldn't be enough to catch up. It's unlikely that those people now living in the Korean district will enjoy such benefits of civilization even one century later.

When Mr. Jeong reached the Bean Sprout Pass in the middle of Gaebok-dong, he stealthily peeped into shaggy-faced Han Chambong's rice store. He was simply checking on how the wind was blowing inside the store, having no courage to intrude further and ask for rice on credit.

"Hello, there. How are you, Jeong Jusa?"

Shaggy-faced Han Chambong, who was weighing out some rice for a boy customer, cast a sidelong glance at Mr. Jeong, and spoke a greeting. His words, coming through his thick mustache, sounded broken.

"Well, how's business, Han Chambong?"

On being recognized by Han Chambong, Mr. Jeong decided to enter the store.

Whenever he met the owner of this store, he felt sick with jealousy. At the time when he'd first moved to Gunsan and lived in Daejeong-dong, this shaggy-faced man had a tiny store across the street from his house, selling small quantities of rice, barley, and other grains as if he'd got them by begging.

His business, however, quietly grew with the years, and last year he bought a big house attached to a decent shop on this street. He was now a wealthy merchant who even had a private phone installed in his place. According to his own claim, he had amassed ten or twenty thousand won so far, but considering his secretive and understated manner of speech, Mr. Jeong reckoned that his fortune might easily exceed thirty or forty thousand won.

Shaggy-faced Mr. Han had been promoted to Han "Chambong," or "Master Han," only because people began to address him with this title as he became rich, when in fact he'd never gotten close to holding the government position of Chambong.

Whenever he saw Han Chambong, who'd managed his business well enough to promote his social status to such distinction within a decade, Mr. Jeong was filled with inward resentment over his own downfall. Remembering that he had more than a thousand won in cash when he first moved to Gunsan, he bitterly regretted that he hadn't started a business with the money at that time.

He believed that if he'd started a business back then, he would have been successful. He never considered the difference between himself and Han Chambong; one had been chained to his desk with pen in hand, and the other grew up working for merchants from his boyhood.

"You must be coming from the exchange market? How was it today . . . ?"

Shaggy-faced Han Chambong turned to Mr. Jeong, rubbing his hands. The money he'd just received from the customer he dropped with a jingle into the slot of a wooden box placed inside the door of the back room of the store. Although he'd accumulated quite a fortune, he'd never wasted any money to buy a new portable safe. The hand-stained, shabby wooden box that had been with him ever since he started his own business still served well as his safe. He was rather proud of the box, as if it had brought him all the good luck.

"Have you had some luck today and would like to pay back some of your old debts?"

"Luck! Never mention it, please! . . . Oh my, my, what a horrible day I had today!"

"What . . . You missed the target again?"

"I've lost almost one hundred won!"

Mr. Jeong quickly fabricated a number, saying "oops!" within himself. To keep up appearances, he'd been deceiving Han Chambong all along, pretending that he was still playing the game, having quite a large amount of rice deposited.

"Dear me! Why do you go on losing money like that all the time?"

Han Chambong knew well enough about Mr. Jeong's impoverished situation, but had much tact hidden under his beard, affecting ignorance and allowing Mr. Jeong to deceive him. He knew well that there would be no harm in being deceived by words only, so long as he was aware of the deception.

Moreover, since Mr. Jeong had been a regular customer for over ten years, Han Chambong couldn't be as heartless as to press him for payment. In fact, Mr. Jeong hadn't paid for an eighty-kilo sack of rice he took last year, as well as for a quarter of a sack of rice he took during this year's first lunar month. Han Chambong, however, had almost given up on the money and put a cross mark against his name in his credit book. Nevertheless, out of merchant's habit, he sometimes mentioned it in passing, so that even if he couldn't have the old debts paid back, it might at least prevent him from asking for more credit.

"Gee! . . . If I'd hit the mark right today, I could've become a bit better off, and paid off my old debts to you."

Mr. Jeong clicked his tongue, blinking his eyes, and then resumed,

". . . Wait a tiny bit longer please. I'll clear off all my debts soon enough . . . I wouldn't forget, would I? Don't worry . . ."

Whenever his debt was mentioned, Mr. Jeong immediately became defensive, trying to preclude any further discussion. It wasn't that he was sorry or worried because he couldn't pay back. He simply felt embarrassed at his inadequacy, afraid of being harassed.

". . . What a world it is! If it goes on being as bad as this, I'll get quite fed up with it . . . That bloody speculation goes wrong every time and gives me endless troubles! What am I to do with so many children in such a situation . . .?"

"Well, you're still not without hope! You have all those lovely children growing up healthy and stout, what's there to worry about?"

"Nonsense! What's so good about a poor man having many children? It'd be easier to have none."

"You mustn't say that. I'd be much happier if I had a couple of children, even if I didn't have money."

"No, no. I don't think so. I know from experience what a burden they are."

"What pleasure is there for a man without children?"

"You don't know what's involved . . ."

"What, it's you who don't know what's what! Suppose you had no children right now."

"Well, well . . . Han Chambong, suppose you're very poor, and have hordes of children waiting to be fed . . . It's only when you can feed them that you can say that."

Each of them was saying what was true from his own perspective. Each of them was sure that the other party was ignorant of the real plight he was in.

Shaggy-faced Han Chambong was nearly fifty, but had no children whatsoever. During the past two or three years, he'd been squandering money on one concubine after another, providing them with separate houses. But still he had neither a healthy nor an unhealthy child, while he was getting older every year.

"Well, do you feel like having a game? It's been so long since we played."

Shaggy-faced Han Chambong, who was standing there blankly, saw his errand boy come back into the store and, awakened from his troubled reverie, suggested a game of Janggi to Mr. Jeong.

"Why not? But I hope you've learned some new moves, Han Chambong."

Mr. Jeong gladly accepted the offer as he was thinking of suggesting a game of Janggi himself, with the hope that while playing he might find an opportunity to coax Han Chambong into giving him some rice on credit.

"Your skills in Janggi are still at a beginner's level, Jeong Jusa."

"I only hope that you won't beg me to cancel one of your moves in order to save a dead chariot."

The two men, both boasting of their skills, moved to the back room of the store.

At that moment, the back door to the living quarters opened, and Madam Kim, Han Chambong's wife, entered.

"Ah, Jeong Jusa! How are you?"

A smile that started in her eyes spread over her pretty, vibrant face. Jeong Jusa too greeted her with a smile and glanced up at her. She wore a fine flowing dress made of ramie fabric. She was much younger than her husband, being just over thirty. And her lovely face and slim frame, which had never borne a baby, made her look even younger, perhaps twenty-four or twenty-five. She knew how to dress to set off her beauty.

Thus, when she stood next to Han Chambong, who looked older than his age, she appeared to be his daughter-in-law or a young mistress.

"How's your wife? . . . Ah, by the way . . ."

Madam Kim, suddenly remembering that she had important business to talk to his wife about, stepped into the back room of the store.

"Oh Jeong Jusa, I'm enchanted by your eldest daughter. How is it she's grown into such an elegant beauty! I've been wanting to express my admiration for your daughter to you."

"Well, she's just . . ."

Mr. Jeong, though rather pleased, mumbled in embarrassment, and Madam Kim continued her animated praise.

"Oh, by the way . . . her name is Chobong, isn't it? Yes, it's Chobong . . . I mean she was pretty even when she was a little girl. But how beautifully she has blossomed, just like a flower! The other day she greeted me while passing by our store, but can you believe it? I didn't recognize her at first! She was so enchantingly pretty that I wanted to hug her and pat her on her shoulder. If I had a son, I would have compelled her to become my daughter-in-law by any means, ho-ho-ho . . ."

As she chatted away, laughing gaily, both Shaggy-faced Han Chambong and Jeong Jusa laughed along with her.

"So it would've been good if you'd had a child sooner, wouldn't it?" Shaggy-faced Han Chambong teased his wife with a laugh, while continuing with the Janggi game.

"Sooner is not early enough. Even if I gave birth on the day of my wedding, the boy would be only fifteen now. How old is she? Twenty? Isn't that right?"

"Twenty-one now! . . . She's grown only in height; she's still childlike in many ways."

As he responded to her, Jeong Jusa picked up Han Chambong's pipe, filled it with tobacco from the pouch lying on the floor, and started to smoke.

"Ah, I'm dying with envy! I'd give anything to have her alone, far more than four or five children together from another family!"

"Watch out Jeong Jusa. If she continues that way, she might very well end up stealing your daughter, ha-ha-ha."

"Ha-ha-ha . . ."

"If it's at all possible, I would steal her by any means . . . Indeed I would."

"If you feel so strongly about it, go ahead and steal her. I would pardon you and overlook it, ha-ha-ha."

"Ho-ho. I know you're joking. But I'd volunteer to do some matchmaking and find her a decent bridegroom."

"Oh, please do! While our situation is quite strained, she is getting older . . . When we're alone, my wife and I worry about how to get her married off."

"Of course you do!—Who wouldn't if they have grown-up daughters? I assure you, I'm not just saying this in passing, I'll definitely choose a bridegroom who suits her perfectly."

"That busybody wife of mine is jumping into hot water . . .," said Han Chambong, placing his Janggi piece down with a thump.

"They say bad matchmaking brings three slaps on the cheek!"

"But they also say good matchmaking brings three glasses of wine."

"Do they? Then when you get the drinks, give them to me, and if slaps are due, take them yourself. How about that?"

"You can have both, my dear. All I can do is find a good match . . . It's definitely unlike other matchmakings. I'm going to do it just because I adore her so much. Ho, ho, I really fell in love with her. That's why I'm volunteering to be a matchmaker. Don't you agree, Jeong Jusa?"

"Well, well, regardless of why you want to do it, I beg you, just find a suitable young man for her."

"Come on, we've had enough of that talk. Let's play on. It's your turn, Jeong Jusa."

Shaggy-faced Han Chambong, anxious to get back to the game, urged Jeong Jusa on.

"He's mad about Janggi! I'm going out, Jeong Jusa. Have a good time, and trust the matter to me."

"All right, I'll wait for good news from you."

"Since you're going out anyway, how about dropping by the market, and getting a good sea bass for Mr. Go? These days our dishes don't seem to please him."

Shaggy-faced Han Chambong mouthed the words automatically, as his mind was already absorbed in the *Janggi* game. Mr. Go, a lodger in the house, worked at the 00 Bank.

At the word "sea bass," Jeong Jusa felt hungry anew and gulped down the saliva that filled his mouth.

Chapter 2:
Lesson One in Everyday Living

IF YOU COME from the train station and head for Yeongjeong, you meet a three-way intersection. On the right corner of the intersection stands a pharmacy called Jejungdang, meaning "a place to save people."

It's an ordinary-looking pharmacy, the kind you find in any city. Its scale too is not at all remarkable. Its name, Jejungdang, however, is well known throughout Gunsan, and carries special significance due to the extraordinary characteristics of its owner and pharmacist, Bak Jeho. He's not only competent enough to serve as a doctor, diagnosing the simple diseases of country people and prescribing for them, he also has many remarkable personal attributes; he has a long face like a horse, and that strikingly long face looks even longer because he's been quite bald since his thirties; although he speaks with a stutter, his speech, in fact, is glib and eloquent, and each of his utterances, without exception, is punctuated with "damn it!"; he has unyielding perseverance and stout nerves, enough to argue that a crow is white and make people believe it. Thanks to these particular features, Bak Jeho has left a strong impression on his customers throughout the last ten years, and has become quite famous in Gunsan. People don't forget him so easily, just as they can't easily forget a one-eyed man or a face with a huge mole on it. Thus his pharmacy stands out as much as its owner, enjoying many privileges.

In the pharmacy now, the long face of Bak Jeho was nowhere to be seen. Chobong, sitting alone on top of a table, was browsing through an old issue of a women's magazine.

Chobong was somewhat restless, worrying about her family. She was anxious, as she had no means of obtaining ready money. She attempted to read a story in the magazine, in order to distract her thoughts from her worries, but she was unable to concentrate.

The clock hanging on the pillar struck four. "Is it already four o'clock?" she sighed, looking up. At that moment a peasant wearing shabby clothing and a summer hat woven of wood shavings entered cautiously, taking off his hat.

"Hello, may I help you?"

Chobong stood up instantly and walked toward her place behind the counter. It was the ordinary greeting of a sales clerk to welcome a customer, but her delicate voice with a sweet trailing vibration was so amiable that the country bumpkin felt almost dizzy.

Chobong's father, Jeong Jusa, often clicked his tongue at the sweet and delicate tones of his daughter's voice, out of the belief that it was a sign of a short life, like her small ears. Not only her voice, but her facial features, too, often made him feel uneasy about her future. Being of the opinion that a plump face brings happiness, he found Chobong's face too elegant and shapely. Her sharp, high nose looked more remarkable on her spotless complexion. Her oval face narrowed down toward her chin. Her eyes were big and round, but their corners retained a slender line, giving the impression that a few secrets were hidden there.

With these contours and her fair complexion, she looked as delicate as a wild chrysanthemum, producing an uneasy and anxious feeling in onlookers. Her mouth and chin, however, made up for the frail impression. Her tiny, well-defined mouth, and her round but slightly protruding chin, especially when she unconsciously put on a faint smile, made her look coyly coquettish.

She was always dressed simply, wearing a modest black skirt and a white blouse, but as her slim figure, like her face, was blossoming with youth, she was an excellent advertisement for the pharmacy, which also sold cosmetics.

Since last February, when Chobong first began working here, the general sales of the place, especially the sales of cosmetics, mouth fresheners, and nutritional supplements, items that men purchase without any particular reason, had increased threefold.

Jeho valued Chobong highly for this, of course. In addition, Chobong came from Seocheon, which was also his own hometown, and was the daughter of Jeong Yeongbae (Jeong Jusa's full name) who was a long-standing friend of his. For these reasons Jeho felt obliged to pay Chobong special attention. Even disregarding all the profits and connections, Jeho couldn't help but adore her simply because she was very pretty.

The peasant customer began to explain the symptoms of his seven-year-old son, who had sprained his leg, as if he'd come to a hospital. Chobong gave him a bottle of iodine for twenty jeon. The store was empty again. Chobong knew that between three and four o'clock in the afternoon was the least busy time in the day, unless it was a market day.

Chobong, feeling disinclined to return to the table and go on thumbing through the magazine, leaned back on the drug cabinet, and stared vacantly out at the street.

She'd been watching out for her mother from morning. She was still waiting. None of her family members had eaten any breakfast that morning. If by chance her mother had found the means to prepare a meal, she would have brought a lunch box for her. But having no news of her so far, it seemed almost certain that her family was still starving.

If it were a matter of feeding herself alone, she could have ordered something from a restaurant using the telephone in the store. But she had no mind to eat alone while all her family members were starving at home. She'd been waiting for her mother's lunch box primarily because she wanted to be assured that her family had procured something to eat.

As she stood there listlessly, images of her family—the shabby and despondent appearance of her father, her mother with her back bent from constant needlework, and her pitiful siblings, crestfallen with empty stomachs—hovered in the air. Her eyes began to ache with tears welling up. She had two ten-jeon coins jingling in her hand, which she'd gotten for a bottle of iodine.

On days when her family went without food at home, if she got some money from sales at the store, she always suffered from a strong temptation to send the money home. She now anxiously looked down at the jingling coins, preoccupied by the same wish, the wish that they were her own and that she had the power to dispose of them as she wished.

If one of her siblings, either Gyebong or Hyeongju, happened to drop by with a hungry face now, Chobong would have given them the coins without a second thought. Eagerly hoping for such a coincidence, Chobong kept looking out at the street to see if her sister or brother by any chance might pass by.

It wasn't that she didn't have other ways to send the money home. But she couldn't be reckless when the money wasn't her own. She had qualms enough not to dare to go that far.

Chobong saw Haengwha cross the street from a small alley on
the opposite side and walk into the store with a beaming smile.

"It seems you're all alone now? . . . Is the owner out somewhere?"

"Do come in please. He went out this morning, and still
isn't back . . ."

Chobong, with a smile, welcomed her in a manner suited
to a friend rather than a customer. Chobong, of course, had no
occasion to know or associate with a *gisaeng*. But as she worked
at the store, she often met such women as customers, and if they
were regular customers, she got acquainted with them.

Haengwha was a regular customer, who came by every now
and then to buy powdered milk or cosmetics, or to use the telephone. Whenever she came by, Jeho, the owner of the pharmacy,
jested with her, calling her by her name, Haengwha. That's how
Chobong got to know her name.

Chobong liked Haengwha best among the few regular *gisaeng*
customers. Her face with a few freckles around her nose made
an amiable impression. Chobong liked her brisk and easy way
of talking, using a Yeongnam dialect. But most of all, she was
attracted to Haengwha's ingenuous personality, devoid of any
pretense or the affected sweetness common in *gisaengs*.

Chobong's good feelings were reciprocated. Haengwha too
was attracted to Chobong's graceful figure and demeanor, as well
as her soft voice, which seemed to come from her good nature.
Thus even when she had no business, she enjoyed stopping by at
the store to engage in some idle chatter with Chobong.

"Whom do you buy the milk for so regularly?" Chobong
asked in passing as she handed over a can of dry milk, having
chosen a newly stocked one. She'd been curious about it for
some time.

"What? For whom, did you say?" Haengwha asked, holding
up the can and waving it at Chobong, at the same time laughing
like a mischievous girl.

"Of course, it's for my son! . . . My son, ha-ha-ha."

"Your son? You have a son?"

Chobong thought it odd for a *gisaeng* to have a child, but
soon nodded her head reasoning that a *gisaeng* certainly had
more chances of having a child.

"Why? Is it strange a *gisaeng* has a son? Ha, ha, ha. It's easier
to have sons and daughters when you're a *gisaeng*, isn't it? We
have plenty of seed providers, ha, ha, ha."

At such a forthright comment, Chobong blushed while
laughing.

"Look! What a lovely mouth you have! Look at the line of
your chin, too. They're really enchanting, though you're pretty
all over . . . How old are you, may I ask?"

"Twenty-one."

"My goodness! I thought you must be nineteen, or my age
at the most . . ."

"What's your age then? Twenty?"

"Yes."

"What! You have a son already?"

"Ha, ha, ha, I've been teasing you. He's not my son, but my
little brother."

"A brother? . . . What a good sister you are!"

Chobong was quite moved. She'd assumed that being a
gisaeng was a job for extravagant or vulgar women, and found
it astounding to see such warm-heartedness in a *gisaeng*. She
regarded Haengwha once again with more admiration.

As she thought it over, she recognized that compassion must
be universal.   Although Haengwha was looked down on for
being a *gisaeng*, the fact that she could support her family at such

a young age suggested she was a better person than Chobong herself.

At that moment, Jeho's wife, Yunhui, came into the store through the door behind the prescription room, and Haengwha abruptly walked out, with a slight frown around her eyes.

"Isn't he back yet?" Yunhui peeped around the door with her bony face, her long neck craned at the same time.

"Where on earth has he gone! How annoying! Has he got killed, hit by a car? Or is he tumbling about with his mistress?" Yunhui's outburst was surely a portent of a huge storm ahead.

Yunhui met Jeho about ten years ago when she was a student at a girls' junior college. Jeho, about eleven years her senior, was then a married man with a wife and children, working for a pharmaceutical company. They fell in love and married after Jeho got divorced from his first wife. It was Yunhui who provided him with the funds to open the Jejungdang pharmacy in Gunsan. The sweetness of their married life, however, had lasted for only two or three years. Now Yunhui had nothing left but her bitter, hysterical reproaches, while Jeho had reached the point where he was ready to welcome her death as a blessed emancipation from her harassment.

Chobong's coming to the store as a sales clerk had only made matters worse. Since then, Yunhui's nerves had stretched tauter, and she kept harassing her husband, connecting everything to Chobong.

Chobong wasn't totally unaware of what was going on. Though she found Jeho trustworthy due to his easy-going and happy personality, and wished to remain in the pharmacy until she was prepared to take the qualifying exam for pharmacists, lately she'd become quite uneasy because of Yunhui, and felt that she wouldn't be able to remain in the job if this continued.

"How come you don't know where he's gone?" Yunhui shouted at Chobong, gasping for breath, unable to control her anger.

"It's true, I don't know. He never tells me where he's going when he goes out," Chobong responded gently, though she felt mortified at being the unfair target of Yunhui's outburst. She knew she wasn't in a position to freely express her emotions.

Just then the phone rang. Yunhui started at the ringing sound, but soon moved toward Chobong who had picked up the receiver, demanding, "Give it to me if it's him."

"Hello, this is Jejungdang," Chobong answered, ignoring Yunhui.

"Pardon? . . . Yes, Mr. Go Taesu? From the 00 Bank? Oh yes."

"You remember Go Taesu of the 00 Bank, I hope?" the voice at the other end asked kindly.

"Yes, I do."

Chobong knew his name since he often made telephone orders for drugs and cosmetics, but she didn't know him in person.

He, however, was asking her whether she remembered him "in person," since he visited the store to buy things more often than he made telephone orders. Taesu took Chobong's affirmative response as a sign that she knew the "real person," Go Taesu.

"Well, do you have any nice perfumes?" the voice at the other end of the telephone asked, assuming a familiar tone now.

"Ah, perfumes? Yes, we have various kinds. What brand do you want?"

"Whatever's good will do. Perhaps something like Original."

"Original? Yes, we have it. But it's not one of the high-quality products . . . though many people use it . . ."

"Ah, is that so? Then . . .," the other side mumbled with embarrassment and said, "Then instead of Original, you choose something good for me, please."

"Well, how about Heliotrope? That's not the best either, but still . . ."

"OK, I'll have it. Can you send me one bottle of that perfume, Hel, Helio . . . right away?"

"Sure, I'll send it to you. You said you're Mr. Go Taesu of the 00 Bank, right?"

The other side was not a little disappointed when Chobong reconfirmed his identity. Thus his "yes" sounded a bit annoyed. Chobong, however, didn't notice it at all.

"Oh by the way, I forgot to mention . . ."

Chobong was suddenly reminded of something.

". . . I can't send it immediately since our errand boy is out on another delivery. Do you mind if it's delayed a little?"

"Well, then . . .," he hesitated a moment. "Since I won't be here for long, is it possible to send it to my lodging? If you send your errand boy to my place, there'll be someone to pay for it, even if I'm not there."

"All right, I can do that. Where's your place?"

"It's Han Chambong's rice store on the way from Gaebokdong to Dunbaemi, just before the hill. It's easy to find."

"Yes, I know the place. I'll send it there."

Hanging up the phone, Chobong said to herself, "Ah, that's who he is." She recollected that someone at home had once mentioned a bank clerk lodging at shaggy-faced Han Chambong's house.

Chobong kept herself busy to avoid being harassed by Yunhui, who was still in the store. She took out the last remaining bottle of Heliotrope from the display cabinet, packed it in wrapping paper, and wrote the bill. The phone rang again just then. Yunhui followed her, demanding she hand over the phone if it was Jeho. Paying little attention to Yunhui, Chobong picked up the receiver.

"Hello, this is Jejungdang."

Chobong recognized the voice coming from the receiver, and a smile spread over her eyes and mouth, while a deep blush instantly spread over her face and around her ears.

"This is Chobong."

Moving closer to the telephone, Chobong unintentionally looked back. Yunhui had been watching all this and, with eyes flaring, thundered out, "Get away, you slut!" She violently pushed Chobong aside, snatched the receiver, and shouted into it.

"What kind of hoax are you playing now? Huh?" she shouted at her highest pitch without confirming who was on the other side.

"What?" an embarrassed voice came back from the receiver.

"What bloody nonsense do you mean with your 'what?' You've made me terribly anxious waiting for you all day long, and now through this damn phone, you flirt with the slut you placed in the store. You surely want to see me burn down this damn store, don't you? Huh? You are the dirtiest scoundrel in the world . . ."

She would have continued pouring out her curses, but being out of breath, she stopped. Taking advantage of the pause, the voice on the receiver cut in.

"Who is this please? . . . Why are you so angry?"

The low, confident voice with its deep vibration was, without doubt, quite different from that of Jeho, who always stuttered in haste.

"What's that you're saying?"

Yunhui shouted in the same threatening tone, although she was now fully aware that this wasn't her husband, Jeho. She was too annoyed at her mistake to change her tone. She'd been certain that it was Jeho, and seeing Chobong becoming coquettish while talking on the phone, had lost all patience, burning with jealousy. Now that she realized this wasn't Jeho but a total stranger, she couldn't help but get furious at the odd situation.

"So you're not Bak Jeho, you say?"

Though her voice was still overbearing and quarrelsome, it was obvious that she was flustered and at a loss as to what to do. As she looked back, Chobong, whom she thought was bound to help her, was looking away as if she hadn't noticed anything. Yunhui hated Chobong all the more for that, if it was at all possible.

"Hello . . ."

The stranger began to speak, but in a kind and undisturbed tone, which curiously aggravated Yunhui's spitefulness.

"I'm not Mr. Bak Jeho. This is Nam Seungjae, working as an assistant at the Geumho clinic. I'm calling to order drugs . . ."

Yunhui saw no way out of this muddle. Instead she chose to bawl him out, if only to make herself feel better.

"What the hell is this? Damn it, such wicked luck . . ."

Yunhui threw down the receiver and turned away, glaring at Chobong, as if she were about to devour her. "You should've told me it wasn't him . . ."

Chobong, unable to put up with this anymore, straightened up, thrusting her chin out to confront her, but her words stuck in her throat, and uninvited tears welled up in her eyes.

"Are you here as a puppet on display? What the hell are you doing, for goodness' sake? Standing aside, watching me get into a mess . . . Is that all you do, flirt on the phone?"

Yunhui suddenly recalled Chobong's coy attitude on the phone and began to imagine her behaving the same way when Jeho was on the phone or when they were alone in the store. Yunhui pictured Chobong trying to seduce Jeho, and an enraptured Jeho ogling her with lustful eyes.

Yunhui, who'd been shooting spiteful glares that could have frozen Chobong, shuddered violently, grinding her teeth. If Chobong had done even something trivial at that moment to provoke her, she would have exploded and gone for her, eager as she was to savagely scratch and bite Chobong's infuriatingly pretty face, especially her devilish mouth and chin.

Just then the errand boy returned from his delivery. He got off his bike, and walked into the store. But perceiving the murderous, icy tension in the store, he sluggishly moved to a corner with a frightened face.

"Do you know where your master's gone?" Yunhui thundered at the boy.

"I'm sorry, but I don't know, ma'am." the boy responded cautiously, hoping not to aggravate her anger.

"You'll pay for this, all of you . . .," Yunhui spat out a threat as if talking to herself, and with loud thumping steps walked back to the residential quarters, passing through the dispensary.

The boy, who'd slunk into the corner, stuck his tongue out at Yunhui while repeatedly winking at Chobong in comradely fashion. Chobong didn't pay any attention to him. She felt mortified anew at having been such a fool as to endure all the insults without even attempting to confront Yunhui.

Supposing that she did start arguing with her, she would probably have ended up losing her job. She knew that it wouldn't be easy to find a new job, and moreover, even if she could land a new job, it might not offer the kind of good prospects she was enjoying now, the prospect of becoming a professional one day.

On top of that, if she lost the job now, she would lose the monthly salary of twenty won. However meager that might be, her family would suffer that much more. In her situation, enduring Yunhui's hysteria quietly seemed rational enough. Being rational, however, is more likely when you're not infuriated.

Even if you have to repent after messing things up, thinking to yourself, "I wish I'd been more patient," while anger is surging up inside you, you are apt to think you have strength enough to declare, "What's the problem! I can quit today." With head held high, Chobong almost shouted that back at Yunhui.

The truth, however, was that she couldn't do it. It wasn't just in this case. She was a timid woman who could never speak her mind in the face of conflict, whether big or small. Nor did she have the willpower to stand up against others or to insist on having things her way. It wasn't that she didn't feel resentment, anger, or disappointment. The problem was that she couldn't put into words what she felt inside; her thoughts usually sank deeper inside her, making her choke up, and her eyes fill with tears.

The more excited she got, the worse her symptoms became.

As for today, she'd done nothing wrong to provoke Yunhui, and she had plenty to say to defend herself. Yet she couldn't utter even one word and was crying before she knew it, as though she were the guilty party.

The receiver was still dangling from the phone after Yunhui had flung it down in her temper. If it were anyone else on the line, Chobong would have left it as it was. But she picked up the receiver, as she was concerned in case Seungjae was still on the phone waiting for her.

"Hello?" Chobong managed to say after clearing her throat.

"What a spectacular fuss that was . . .," Seungjae responded instantly.

"Forget it please. The mistress here thought it was her husband."

"Hmm! It was really grand."

She sensed her anger begin to melt away, and a smile appeared on its own around her mouth and eyes as before.

". . . Well, do you have any Rosinon calcium in stock?"

"Yes, we do. Shall I send it to you?"

"Yes, please. Send one box immediately."

"Sure, I'll send it right away."

"Thanks, just one box please."

Chobong continued to hold the phone for quite a while, long after she heard the click at the other end. She wanted to keep on talking with him whatever the subject might be. If she really wanted to, she could call him again, or she could have started a conversation while he was still on the phone. Chobong, however, didn't know what in particular she wanted to talk to him about. It was her vague desire to keep talking to him that made her reluctant to put the phone back on its hook. She always felt something was missing whenever Seungjae hung up the phone.

In fact, Chobong and Seungjae lived under the same roof, as he was a lodger in her house. Since they encountered each other every morning and evening, there was really no need to seek opportunities to talk on the phone. Moreover, her parents wouldn't have minded if the two conversed.

But neither of them talked much at home unless there were practical necessities to discuss. It wasn't that they were shy with each other, either. Simply that was the state of their relationship.

If someone asked Chobong, "You must have a crush on Seungjae, don't you?" she would flatly deny it with a blush on her face. Seungjae would have the same reaction if asked the same question. No one could say they were lying; they simply didn't know their own minds yet.

Chobong packed the box of Rosinon calcium and attached a bill to it. She gave it to the boy for delivery along with the package prepared for Go Taesu earlier. While she was explaining the location of Taesu's lodging house, the boy grinned playfully, stealing glances at Chobong.

"You mean Mr. Go from the 00 Bank?" The boy obviously had a mind to tease her.

"What's the matter with you? What about Mr. Go?" Chobong asked, unwittingly laughing along with him.

"Nothing's the matter, he-he."

"What's the problem with the boy, I wonder."

"No, no problem at all. I just wonder why he's having things delivered today instead of coming to the store himself . . . He, he, he."

"What's so odd about it?"

"See . . . Miss Chobong, how you affect innocence!"

"Look at him! What do I affect, you say!"

"Are you sure you don't know him? How can you say you don't know Mr. Go when he comes here almost every other day on the pretense of buying some stuff. You must know him . . ."

"Whatever you say, I don't know him. That's definite. How can I remember the face of every customer?"

"Yet, I say Mr. Go is special! Why else do you think he comes here so often and buys so many unnecessary things?"

"How should I know?"

"It's impossible not to know! He comes only to see you, Miss Chobong, he-he. No doubt he's in love . . ."

"You naughty boy!" Chobong shouted at him with embarrassment but her face heated up as if she were on fire. As she was listening to the boy, however, vague images of a man among the many regular customers popped into her mind.

He must be the tallish, slender man who usually wears a well-fitted suit. An oval face with a fair complexion, a handsome high nose, round lips with an amiable smile, all these made him look attractive. His eyes, however, shaped like those of a hawk, gave a ferocious impression. Chobong now conjectured he must be the man who worked at the 00 Bank, the man who lodged at shaggy-faced Han Chambong's, and the man who, as the boy said, frequented the store to see her.

As she tried to work out who he was, Chobong noticed that her heart had begun to pound. While going over each of Go Taesu's features, she was led to compare them with those of Seungjae and found Seungjae, in both appearance and situation, rather inferior to Taesu. Putting herself in Seungjae's shoes, Chobong felt jealous of Taesu.

Feeling angry with herself, she thought she should despise Taesu. Instead, she couldn't help but see his superior merits. Incredulous, she compared the two men one more time. Seungjae, of course, had a promising future if he actually became a qualified medical doctor one day. Right now, however, he was a mere assistant working at a clinic, not his own, whereas Go Taesu had already started a full career as a bank clerk.

As for appearances, though Seungjae was not at all bad looking, Go Taesu's sleekness, his most charming aspect, was something that Seungjae didn't have. Compared to Taesu's well-balanced features, Seungjae looked rather crude and disheveled. Seungjae was much taller, stouter, with wide, muscular shoulders. His thick face was wide and flat, together with his forehead. With all these features, he certainly looked weighty and dependable, but there was no trace of subtle delicacy.

His face, with brows, eyes, nose, and mouth all in the right proportion, protruding or set back as intended, had some of the aspects of a good sculpture, but he lacked the soft quality of an elaborate drawing easy to find in Go Taesu's features. Still, his eyes were far better than Taesu's. They were as pure and tranquil as the water of a deep lake in a mountain. They seemed to contain everything good in the world, and more than fully made up for any potential defects of the rugged haphazardness of his face.

When comparing their eyes, Chobong felt deeply satisfied, as the scales definitely inclined toward Seungjae. In a happy mood, Chobong kept tracing Seungjae's merits: his sturdy shoulders, which seemed to invite people to ride on them, as if on horse-back, or like someone dozing comfortably on the back of an ox; his rock-hard body, which seemed strong enough to withstand whatever blows it met, without so much as a wince; the distinctive features of his face with its broad forehead, and such calm and transparent eyes. She thought of these, one by one or as a whole, and succeeded in driving Go Taesu completely from her mind. She felt secure and happy at the simple fact that Seungjae existed in this world.

Even in the matter of future prospects, Chobong now realized that Taesu was no competitor with Seungjae, who had already passed half the doctor's qualifying exams when he went to Seoul last October. He would take the rest of the exams this coming October or May, or next year at the latest. In other words, if he passed one or two more exams, he would be a fully qualified doctor. When that day came, he wouldn't need to envy any mere bank clerk.

When her thoughts went that far, Chobong breathed a sigh of relief, and placed her hands on her breast, confirming her sense of security.

Curiously enough, despite her satisfaction with Seungjae and the sense of security she got from him, she somehow couldn't shake the image of Go Taesu engraved in a corner of her mind; it persistently refused to leave her alone. It drove her to set the image of his elegant face and stylish figure beside the ungainly figure of Seungjae, and seemed to tease her with a challenge, "Well, what do you think of the comparison?"

Annoyed, Chobong cast a reproachful glance at the image of Go Taesu, who, however, grinning complacently, refused to go away.

At that moment, Jeho bustled into the store at last.

"Oh ho, my dear Chobong is all alone, carrying the entire burden, damn it."

Beaming with a smile on his long face, Jeho made a fuss about nothing.

"So you've been working all alone, Chobong. Where's the boy gone? . . . Ah, he's out on a delivery, right? . . . Uh—hoo—hoo, it's hot. It's getting too warm already, damn it."

The way he chatted on seemed to suggest that something wonderful had happened to him.

Smiling along with him, Chobong took his briefcase off him.

"Good, good. Throw it down there, please . . . By the way, you'll be in trouble, Chobong, you're getting prettier every day! You will, indeed, ha, ha, ha. Damn it. What nonsense! Being pretty is good, isn't it? Ha, ha, ha. You know what? Something good in a big way has happened to me. I say, in a big way, you see? . . . And it'll be good for you in a big way, too, Chobong, ha, ha, ha. Damn it. I'm happy that it's all done!"

It was Jeho's usual way of making a fuss about everything, but today, he seemed much more excited, saying one thing this moment, and another the next, making a fuss in a much more exaggerated way.

Chobong grew curious about what "the good thing," which had made him so talkative and exhilarated, might be.

Jeho sat down in the chair in front of the table on which Chobong was sitting, took off his hat and began fanning his face and his glossy baldhead with it. He looked around the store before he noticed Chobong still holding his briefcase in her hand.

"Ah, it's there . . . I was worried I'd left it somewhere else. Damn it. Please take good care of it and put it somewhere safe in the dispensary."

Only a short while ago, he himself had told her to throw it down somewhere, and now he was asking her to take good care of it.

"There's something important in it, I say, in that bag . . . I had a great success today, a wonderful one, indeed! It will be good for Chobong, too. Well, well, shall I tell you right away? Let's see, I want to smoke a cigarette first. Oh gosh, I'm out of cigarettes . . . Where's that rogue got to? Ah, right, he's on a delivery. Damn it, I wish I had a bowl of shaved ice. Are they selling it now? Perhaps not yet. It's too early in the season, isn't it?"

"Well, I'm not sure . . ."

"I don't think they are. No, no, damn it. It's one of the troubles you have when you're married to the wrong woman. How nice it would be if she brought out a glass of cold water with honey when I'm so thirsty. I mean instead of having so many fits of hysteria day and night, ugh? Am I not right? Ha-ha, damn it."

"Your lady has been waiting for you so anxiously!"

"My gosh . . .!" Something flashed into his mind. He went blank for a moment and scratched the back of his head.

". . . Wow, I'm in big trouble! I'd forgotten the two o'clock appointment to attend the sixtieth birthday party of one of her friend's parents. I totally forgot about it! Well, even if I didn't, I couldn't possibly have left the place in the middle of a deal . . . What did she say when she came out?"

"Nothing in particular . . ." Chobong refrained from telling him the whole story, although she felt like talking for a moment.

"Didn't she make a scene?"

"She came out twice, checking to see if you were back . . ."

"No! I know what a scene she must have made. I know for certain. So she's gone after making such a big fuss? Am I not in trouble? How can I put up with all her harassments! Damn it! I wish someone would carry her away. I'd be happy to give him one hundred won into the bargain. Damn it, ha, ha."

"My goodness! What a terrible thing to say!"

"No, I mean it. Chobong, when you get married, don't ever attempt to nag your husband like that. That's really a bad thing to do. If that bloody wife of mine wasn't like that, I would've been a wealthy man with as much as ten thousand won twenty years ago, right?"

"It doesn't make sense, sir! You yourself said you've only been married to her for about ten years or so. It's impossible . . ."

"Aha, it is, isn't it? I'm out of my mind. Nevertheless, you know how exasperating that shrewish hysteria is! I wish I could get a divorce or something. I can't endure it any longer. As it is, nothing ever goes right!"

"That's just idle chatter."

"No-ope, marrying freely, then being able to divorce freely too is in order. What's the use of a woman who's full of hysteria but can't conceive even one child!"

"But your lady seems to think you're more at fault."

"Fault? I know I have some. She blames me for being a womanizer, and being indifferent to her hysteria. But isn't that why we've got to be separated? Regardless of which of us is at fault, the simple fact that we can't get along with each other is a solid enough reason for separation, don't you think?"

"I really don't know."

Although Chobong tried to respond to Jeho's idle chatter as best she could, her mind was somewhere else. She had her own concerns. In fact Chobong had been waiting for Jeho almost as anxiously as Yunhui, for she had a favor to ask of him. But, once Jeho was back, Chobong, as usual, was having difficulty in bringing up the subject now she was face-to-face with him.

It was something she should have mentioned earlier in the morning, before Jeho went out. But while Chobong kept hesitating, reluctant to bring it up, Jeho had abruptly rushed out on some business. Consequently, she had to wait anxiously for his return all day long, full of regrets for her lack of courage.

Now that he was back, it was time to bring up the matter, but Chobong found it so difficult to open her mouth and wished she could avoid it. It was impossible, however. Her family was starving right now, and there was no hope of things getting better tomorrow. Perhaps they would have to starve for days until they found some money. At last, Chobong summoned up every bit of her courage and began,

"Well, sir, I have . . ."

Chobong squeezed out the first few words, and looked up at Jeho to read his face. Jeho was busy looking for a cigarette he didn't have, poking his hand into his pockets here and there. But at Chobong's words, he looked up.

"What did you say? . . . How come I don't have one single cigarette! Damn it. Well, what is it? You have something to discuss?"

"Ye-es . . ."

"Well, what is it?"

"I'm so sorry, but . . ."

Though the word sorry was far short of what she felt, she did feel sorry, indeed awfully sorry. It was only ten days ago that she'd received an advance of ten won from her monthly salary. Her family had barely lived through the last day of the last month and the first day of this month. On the second day of the month, as soon as she got to the pharmacy, she had to ask for an advance, despite her embarrassment. Now that left her only ten won for her monthly wage, and payday was the twenty-fifth, more than ten days to go. That she had to ask for another advance payment was a circumstance she really wished to avoid. Jeho might say it was all right, but Chobong couldn't help feeling embarrassed.

Chobong kept her mouth firmly shut, unable to continue.

"Oh, my dear! You're impossible! . . . I know what it is, I know!" Jeho could read her mind.

". . . You need money, don't you? . . . Is it so difficult to say that? How innocent you are!"

"Yet it's something to be sorry about, isn't it?"

"Sorry for what? If there's anyone who should feel sorry, it's me. I brought my friend's daughter here, and keep her worried by not paying her well enough. I'm the one who should feel sorry, right? Ha, ha, damn it . . . Let's see, how much do you need? . . . Ah, let's do this. You don't need to ask me each time you need money. The money's in the safe, why don't you just take as much as you need, and keep a record in the book. There, the portable safe is there. Take the money. Oh, confound it! I took the key with me . . . Such forgetfulness! How troublesome, damn it!"

Jeho took out a bundle of keys, put the safe on the table, and it opened with a clink.

As she got to know him better, Chobong grew fonder of him for his free and easy temper. Though he wasn't related to her by blood, she liked him better as a kind of uncle, for he was a friend of her father. She sometimes wished he really were a relative, either of her mother or her father, thinking that he would then be a truly dependable guardian for her.

She sometimes wondered what there was about Jeho to make Yunhui harass him so when he seemed to be such a nice man in her own eyes, and concluded that marriage was an enigma.

". . . So, how much do you need? Five won? Ten won?" Jeho asked, taking out three different notes: a one, a five, and a ten-won note from the safe.

"Well, I'm not sure . . ."

Chobong wanted the ten-won note if she was borrowing anyway, but the words, as usual, didn't come out easily.

"Look at her! You say you don't know when you're the one who needs the money? Huh, huh, damn it. Here, take the ten-won note. Let's make it a round figure."

Chobong swallowed a sigh of relief and she took the bluish banknote that looked so pretty to her from Jeho's hand. Its touch felt quite different from those ten-won notes she received from customers—this one, which she held in her hand as her own after much difficulty, felt crisp but at the same time unusually soft and lovely as well.

Once the money was in her hands, Chobong became anxious to get back home. It was only four-thirty now . . . she had to wait another one and a half hours until six, her usual quitting time.

What should I do? Should I make some excuse to leave early? Or wait till the boy gets back and ask him to take the money to my house? She wished one of her siblings would turn up.

Jeho, who had gone into the dispensary in the meantime, was arranging some documents in his open briefcase. Looking at him thus busy, Chobong recalled the fuss he'd made earlier, bragging about a wonderful windfall that would be good for him as well as for her.

For those who feel helpless and hopeless about the future, the news that something good is coming, even if it turns out to be an empty promise, is a pleasant consolation. Now that she had solved the problem at the top of her list, Chobong became genuinely curious about the good thing Jeho had talked about. She even felt tempted to broach the subject with him.

After sifting through the papers, Jeho put them in a tidy stack into the big safe in the dispensary and came out into the store.

"Well, it's time to tell Chobong about it . . ."

Sitting on the chair next to the table, Jeho began.

"I've sold it. The pharmacy I mean, he, he. I got a wonderful deal to boot, damn it."

"What!" Chobong was stunned and remained silent, not knowing what to say.

Jeho, however, was beaming happily.

"What! Why are you so surprised? Ha, ha, ha, ha . . . Not to worry, there's nothing to worry about."

As she digested the news, Jeho seemed to be suggesting a new owner didn't necessarily mean a new sales clerk, whence his reassurance that she needn't worry. Chobong thought it reasonable, and felt awkward for having been alarmed too soon.

"Who bought the place?"

"Well, I found a lady who's very eager to buy it, ha, ha, ha. Damn it."

Jeho changed the topic.

"By the way my dear . . ., why don't you come with me to Seoul? How about that?"

"To Seoul?" Chobong heard his words, but was still in the dark as to his meaning.

"Yes, to Seoul."

"How?"

"Why, by train, of course. Do you think I would ask you to walk to Seoul? Ha, ha, ha, ha. Damn it, girl."

"Still I don't understand what you mean."

"What is it you don't understand? I mean you can come up to Seoul and work for me as you do now."

"Ah, I see!" Chobong nodded, grasping his meaning at last.

"You understand now, don't you? . . . I say let's go to Seoul together. In Seoul, I'll pay you better. There you'll be an office clerk, doing real office work, instead of a sales clerk as you are now. And what will I be? I'll be the manager-in-chief, you see? Ha, ha, ha, ha. Bak Jeho will be sailing with a fair wind thanks to the propitious location of my ancestors' graves. Damn it, ha, ha."

"What business are you going to start?"

"Nothing less than a pharmaceutical company. The plan's been brewing in my mind for many years. It's the kind of business that defies logic. See, if you create a medicine costing only thirty or fifty jeon, and put huge advertisements in newspapers, bragging about its effects with all kinds of spectacular words, people get taken in so easily and they would gladly pay even ten won for it. I say, even ten won. The ignorant know nothing about medicines. You make profits, ten, twenty times what you invested. I'm sure I'll make more than three hundred thousand won in savings within ten years. Trust me, three hundred thousand won!"

"How strange!"

"Isn't it wonderful? Look now. I found someone who'll invest in the business. He's going to invest forty thousand won, and I, twenty thousand. And we'll launch a pharmaceutical corporation. Well, well, the starting capital, three hundred thousand won, and the president, Mr. So-and-so, the managing director, Bak Je-ho. How about that? Ha, ha, ha, damn it. That's why I sold this place, and sold it for a huge profit. I started it with two thousand won, and I've earned almost ten million won over the past ten years. Now I've sold it for five thousand won. What a deal, huh-huh-huh, damn it. The world is still full of gullible people. There's a lady who's naive enough to pay five thousand won for this store. And think of all those people who happily purchase drugs at exorbitant prices, the drugs we offer with huge advertisements, when they're worth only thirty or forty jeon. They're paying for the advertising expenses as well. Businessmen like us deserve to be damned. Come to think of it, we couldn't complain even if we were to get struck by lightning. Ha, ha, ha, ha. Damn it all."

As he rambled on, Chobong couldn't figure out what he was driving at, although she could at least sense that he wasn't at all displeased.

"Well, Chobong, you'd best come with me to Seoul. A girl so pretty and so amiable shouldn't be buried in this lousy town, Gunsan. You'll have nothing much to look forward to if you remain here . . . When you're in Seoul, it'll be easier to find a good man to be your husband, he, he. Well, if your father, by any chance, opposes this plan, I'll run to him, and force him to change his mind. And if your parents feel uneasy about sending a grown-up girl to Seoul, I can assure them that I'll take good care of you by having you stay in my house. So when you get home, tell your parents about this. If you can come with us, remember that we'll be leaving for Seoul in about two weeks."

"I see."

Chobong responded in such a way as to suggest that she was accepting the offer. That she could go to Seoul with Jeho was indeed an event she was glad about, whichever way she looked at it.

On the other hand, for Jeho, who had finally seized the opportunity to fulfill his long-cherished dream, and who was about to launch a grand scheme that would drastically change his life for the better, it was an event that was bound to make him dance with joy. Facing such an exciting turning point, Jeho didn't really have to concern himself about a pretty girl.

For example, suppose that Chobong was in the way, hindering his path, or was the cause of trouble, Jeho would have no scruples in totally renouncing her. It wouldn't be beyond him. Luckily, however, Chobong didn't seem to conflict with his success. She would simply be a pretty flower that evoked genuine smiles in him.

As he lived under the duress of his wife's constant nagging, finding no comfort at home, it was a big consolation for him to have pretty Chobong near at hand, and to be able to watch her as he pleased.

Of course there were several reasons he wished for her development to be arrested: first of all, she was the daughter of a friend, or rather an acquaintance; secondly, she was young enough to be his own daughter, being half his age; and above all, she was an unmarried virgin. In general, most middle-aged, married men harbor strong curiosity about unmarried girls. Unless such a man is a notorious Casanova, however, he rarely acts on his lust, feeling somewhat intimidated by the fact that she's a virgin.

Jeho's behavior toward Chobong was of that kind. Nevertheless (or rather because of that), Jeho wanted to keep her near him rather than lose her outright.

Finally, Chobong left the store when it was six o'clock. The late afternoon sun was sinking idly toward the west. The sky was clear blue. It was too clean and pure to be left alone. It would have been better if there were a few patches of cloud.

The poplars around the station and the lowly heights beyond the streets were a lush shade of green. It was as though she was seeing them for the first time, when in fact they were like that this morning and yesterday and the day before that too.

She felt inclined to idle if she could find some soft turf on which to lie down. Despite the languid feelings coursing through her, Chobong walked rapidly toward her home in Dunbaemi, passing the Jeil Primary School. In the schoolyard a few kids were playing. Chobong looked through the wire fence to see if Hyeongju was among them. He wasn't, of course.

From the acacia trees that soared high above, a sweet fragrance was oozing, permeating the air she breathed. Seduced by the fragrance, Chobong looked up at the thick clusters of white flowers hanging on the trees and smiled at them.

Only a short while ago she had been anxious and restless, but now she felt quite relieved, relaxed enough to smile at flowers.

She had definitely made up her mind to go to Seoul with Jeho. She was sure that her mother would willingly permit her to go. If there were anyone who might oppose it, it would be her father. But she didn't worry about him either. If she explained the circumstances to him in detail, and if both her mother and Jeho would offer some support, her father, she was sure, would finally give in.

Jeho said her salary would be doubled. Out of the forty won, she might manage to send thirty to her family, and if things went well, it might be possible to bring all her family up to Seoul eventually.

Seoul! Seoul! The place she had always longed to go.

She had visited Seoul once on a school trip in the fourth grade. But she still harbored fantasies about the place as she had caught only glimpses of it at the time. She still believed that Seoul would offer more beauties and more delight than she had experienced then.

To Chobong, with such fantasies, going to Seoul meant a happy opportunity for something new and better—though what that something might be was still vague and indefinite.

In the middle of such happy reveries, Chobong suddenly recalled Yunhui, who might very well spoil all this dreaming, and she felt disheartened.

She knew that she couldn't go to Seoul if Yunhui opposed it. She tried to calm her anxious heart by assuming that somehow or other Jeho would find a way to silence his wife, and kept alive her hope that she would be able to go with him.

Another thing that bothered her was the prospect of losing the opportunity to be with Seungjae or to talk to him on the phone. That too, she managed to disregard. Seungjae would come up to Seoul from time to time for his exams, and she would have the chance to meet him on such occasions. As for telephone conversations, even though they might lose them, they could start writing letters to each other instead. And trusting that Seungjae would eventually come to Seoul for good assuaged her anxiety.

Chobong, who'd been walking toward her home deep in such thoughts, stopped and looked up at the acacia trees once again. She smiled her sweet smile at them, breathing in the fragrance deeply.

Chapter 3:
A New Version of the Heungbo Story

IT WAS ALMOST seven o'clock when Jeong Jusa left shaggy-faced Han Chambong's rice store. They'd played three rounds of *Janggi* and Jeong Jusa won twice. Though he was victorious, his hunger couldn't be vanquished by the victory.

Moreover, as he refused Han Chambong's plea in the final round to allow his move of a chariot to be cancelled, causing him displeasure, Jeong Jusa never got to ask for some rice on credit.

Jeong Jusa was now slowly walking toward the Bean Sprout Pass, pulling in his growling stomach with his belt. He pondered on the matchmaking offer Madam Kim had made earlier and consoled himself with the expectation that she might indeed find a proper bridegroom for his daughter. Though he was hungry and had no prospect of supper ahead, he felt greatly encouraged by Madam Kim's offer.

Jeong Jusa even relished the preposterous possibility that the talk of marriage might materialize sooner, say, tomorrow, for instance, and that he could marry off Chobong within the month.

Then he began to worry about his inability to come up with any money for the wedding expenses. Moreover, when Chobong got married, he would lose the twenty won she brought home every month.

Despite these worries, he acknowledged he could not sit idly by and watch a twenty-one-year-old girl grow old and remain unmarried. If it must happen one day anyway, it might be his duty to hurry it along if a good catch came his way.

Duty or not, how could he manage it when his family members were starving day and night? Unable to find any answer to that, his heart felt heavy, as if it were pressed down with a big stone.

Then an idea flashed into his mind. They say if the sky falls, we shall catch larks. So it was with Jeong Jusa.

"Perhaps? . . . Well, well . . . it's possible!"

He knew he wouldn't be able to come up with the money himself, regretfully. But it might not be impossible to find a bridegroom who'd volunteer to pay all the wedding expenses.

What a shameful idea! But he could see no other way out.

"Oh no! That can't be!"

He might say that to the matchmaker or to a member of the groom's family, in order to save face. And if they insisted, he would assent, pretending that he was conceding to them against his will. Then he would be able to marry off his daughter, empty-handed. Good, good!

Once the marriage is celebrated, if the bridegroom is generous, and has a fortune at his disposal, who knows, he might even offer some money to him, say a few hundred or a few thousand won, suggesting something like,

"I'm sorry to see you idling away your time with no money at hand. Perhaps you'd better start a small business with this money, just for a pastime?"

It wasn't beyond the realm of possibility. Since Chobong was wise and caring, she might even persuade her husband to do it. Who knows, it could happen.

So if the couple came along and offered him the money, he'd pretend to be embarrassed.

"Oh, no . . . I couldn't accept it!" And then he would remonstrate with them with a stern expression on his face, "Wouldn't it make me look like a greedy father who married off his daughter for money?" But surely there'd be people around who would urge him to accept it until he yielded to them. Then he would accept the money quite reluctantly and . . . start a business with the money . . . and if things went well, his family would be completely free from all the burdens of poverty!

Jeong Jusa's daydreams soon led to a feeling of hopefulness, which in turn hardened into a firm belief, as all desperate hopefulness does.

Dunbaemi sits on a hill steeper than that of Gaebokdong. It's filled with cottages as small as swallows' nests. The small alley leading to it is so steep that one may easily scrape one's nose while climbing it.

Adjoining this village was once a wide stretch of rice paddies amounting to tens of acres. On this field, houses began to rise, and in the middle of the area, they built a wide road that contrasted with the shabby houses in the neighborhood. One day, they say this road will stretch as far as Sinheungdong through a tunnel under the hills of Dunbaemi. If they actually construct the tunnel, Jeong Jusa's house will stand atop it. He sometimes worried the house might fall down if something went wrong with the tunnel. He didn't worry about the house itself, since it was a rented house. He worried that his family might get hurt.

As he got nearer to home, his daydreams about Chobong's marriage vanished into thin air. Instead, his mind filled with anxiety about how to face his starving family. He became as despondent as a bird without wings.

When he entered the house, pushing open the half-closed gate, however, he met a quite unexpected scene. In the kitchen, Chobong was scooping steamed rice, not the usual gruel, into a bowl, and Gyebong was carrying bowls filled with rice onto the *maru*, the wooden deck leading to the rooms.

The day that had been full of bad fortune seemed to have ended up a day that wasn't entirely lacking in good luck. No matter how they'd gotten hold of it, Jeong Jusa's shameless belly began to growl loudly at the sight of warm rice, while the pain of hunger grew acute under his thin chest. And from his molars, the saliva, urging the food to rush in, began to well up and filled his mouth. At the sound of the clicking gate, Gyebong looked back and said, "Ah, Papa's coming . . ."

Welcoming him with a bright smile, she shouted into the room,

"Hey, Byeongju, Byeongju, Papa's back, Papa's back!"

Gyebong's bobbed hair bounced around her face as she swayed along. Jeong Jusa frowned, as he always did when he noticed his younger daughter's short hair, and her plump, naked legs under her short skirt.

Chobong too welcomed her father, coming out of the kitchen.

"Ah, Father . . .!"

Seeing his haggard face, however, Chobong cut her greeting short, and her face clouded over.

". . . You must be really hungry!"

"No, dear, I'm fine," Jeong Jusa responded, blinking his eyes repeatedly, and stepped out onto the stone terrace.

The youngest boy, Byeongju, scampered out from the inner room through the open sliding door.

"Daddy, boo-hoo . . ."

Byeongju threw himself into the arms of his father, whimpering and playing the baby with a face smeared with tears and snot.

"Dear, dear, you've been crying and fretting again, haven't you?"

Jeong Jusa wiped Byeongju's runny nose with his fingers, and cleaned them carelessly on the edge of the *maru*.

Byeongju began to prattle on about the presents he'd been promised, rubbing his face on his father's shabby coat, the only coat he had, and smearing it with his snot.

"Dad, dad, my new suit, my hat, my shoes, my bicycle, my bananas . . ."

Byeongju could see none of those in his father's hands and renewed his whimpering.

"Woo-hoo, you haven't bought them, boo-hoo, woo-hoo . . ."

"Dear, dear, I'll buy them tomorrow for sure. I couldn't make any money today. There, there, Byeongju, let's go back inside. You're a good boy."

To soothe his son, Jeong Jusa held him in his arms, and walked into the room. Hyeongju, who'd been lying on his stomach doing his homework in the other room, stuck out his head to meet his father, but seeing him empty-handed as always, didn't feel obliged to come out and greet him.

Near the back door, Madam Yu was bent over, engrossed in her needlework. She was wearing her reading glasses. She was in fact too young to wear them, but without them, she couldn't do even a single stitch of her needlework properly.

"Where've you been, wandering around on a hungry stomach . . .?" said Madam Yu, without looking up, simply raising herself slightly in greeting to her husband. Besides, her question was meaningless, for she knew too well that her husband had been to the rice exchange market.

"What happened?"

Jeong Jusa, unable to imagine that Chobong had managed to get another advance payment, assumed that the rice for the supper came from some prepayment for the needlework his wife was doing now.

"I bought this fabric to make a new dress for me to find a new husband," Madam Yu blurted out with a straight face, even without a smile.

"See, Byeongju, what your mom says! . . ." Jeong Jusa, taking off his cotton outer coat, said to his son, who was hanging onto his legs and hassling him.

"You see, Byeongju? Your mom wants to leave us, because you behave like this."

"No, you're lying. You're a liar, you've promised again and again that you'd buy me a new suit, a hat, shoes, a bike, bananas, and rock candies, but it's all lies, boo-hoo-hoo."

"I'll buy them tomorrow, for sure."

"No, I don't believe it. That's just another lie. You lie all the time."

Byeongju crawled up onto his father's lap and pulled his yellow beard.

"That hurts, you rogue! Ouch, ouch, you little rogue . . .," he exaggerated the pain, sticking out his chin.

"Trust me I'll buy them all tomorrow. Certainly I will."

"That's a lie."

"No, I'm not lying. I'll buy them without fail."

Jeong Jusa resolved once again to hasten Chobong's marriage, if only for the sake of his little boy.

"I've heard Jeho's going to Seoul."

Chobong had told Madam Yu, and mother and daughter had already agreed to accept Jeho's offer.

"Jeho's going to Seoul?" said Jeong Jusa nonchalantly, unsurprised.

". . . On what business?"

"To start a big business in Seoul. I've heard he's already sold his store . . . And he's asked Chobong to go with him."

"Our Chobong?"

His tone clearly suggested that he wasn't happy about it.

"Chobong's been offered double pay, forty won a month. And if we're uneasy about sending our daughter alone to a place far away from home, Jeho can accommodate her in his house, Chobong says."

"What! That won't do . . ."

Jeong Jusa was in a state of mind far different from a few hours ago. Now that he had a handsome plan for Chobong and was full of hope, he had no interest whatsoever in things like Seoul or a monthly pay of forty won.

"I wouldn't like it even if the pay was four hundred won instead of forty. Sending a grown-up girl to a strange place— would any decent family do that? Staying in a friend's house isn't a good enough security. I'm not comfortable even with her working at the store as she does now, although she lives with us."

This wasn't a completely empty excuse he'd invented. Although his mind was fixed on getting Chobong married, he would've opposed it regardless, because he was an old-fashioned man who was bound to have serious reservations about sending a daughter away to Seoul.

"I think it'd be better to let her go with Jeho. What's the use of keeping her at home? She'd just starve all the time."

"That's why we should find a good spouse and get her married."

"It's easy to say . . ."

Madam Yu threw a sideways glance at him over her glasses.

"How ridiculous it is to consider a marriage when we can barely manage one meal a day?"

"But we don't want her to become a spinster, do we?"

"Who said she'd become a spinster? If she goes to Seoul, she'll save some money to be able to marry one day, and if she continues working for Jeho, she can learn enough to pass the exam for whatever they call it. Once she passes it, she says she can make much more money. Isn't it something good in many ways? I don't understand why you're so stubbornly opposed to it."

"You're too optimistic. If things turn out as we wish, there'll be nothing in the world to worry about. But no one knows what obstacles await us in the future."

"What sort of obstacles do you mean? You must remember how much trouble we've gone through to send her to school for ten long years despite our utter poverty. We should allow her the opportunity to prove that it was worthwhile. Why do you insist on holding her back in this poverty-stricken house? Though you're a man wearing a hat and a long coat, you're nowhere near as enlightened as me, a woman in a skirt."

"I don't envy you if that's enlightenment—a woman who pretends to such immature enlightenment is good for nothing, if not outright bad."

The couple bickered over the issue of sending Chobong to Seoul for a while. It was nothing new for them. Whenever they had disagreements, they both stuck to their own opinions to the end. Such arguments, however, eventually ended with Madam Yu as the winner, no matter how long it took.

In this case too, if a new problem hadn't intervened later, in the end Chobong would have gone up to Seoul with Jeho as she intended.

Chobong filled the last bowl with steaming rice for Gyebong and put the remainder, which was less than half a bowl, into a shallow aluminum bowl for herself. Then she poured some water into the large pot to make a watery porridge with the burnt rice stuck to the bottom.

"My, my, how little! How come you're having so little, Sister?" said Gyebong. But Gyebong was really saying that because she was afraid the half-full bowl might be for her.

"Why, that's not at all little . . .," said Chobong, placing the lid on the pot and standing up.

"Gyebong, did you put a lid on father's bowl? I'm afraid it may get cold."

"Why do we need to do that, when he's going to eat it right away? Come on, let's ladle out the soup now."

"The soup isn't quite ready. I need to put more wood on the fire to boil it a little longer . . . Go out now, find a lid, and cover the bowl properly, in case the rice gets dry." Chobong put more wood into the furnace, and the fire flared up again.

"Oh my goodness, I'm starving to death. You must be hungry too, Sister?"

"I'm all right."

"What! I know you're hungry . . . Sister, let's share my rice together later, OK?"

"Don't worry about me. I'll have the burnt rice too if I'm hungry. I want you to feel full and never say that you're hungry."

"You know what Mom would say. She'd scold me, 'You, shameless hussy, how come you take a full bowl of rice and eat so greedily, while your sister has only burnt rice like a servant!' I know that's what Mom would say. It seems she hates me all the time and it's only you that she loves. Don't you think so, Sister?"

"You're naughty! What nonsense!" Chobong smirked at her younger sister. Gyebong ran out of the kitchen laughing loudly and went into the room.

Chobong, sitting in front of the fire, wondered how her mother was managing the discussion with her father about her plan, when the gate creaked and there followed the thumping sounds of heavy shoes. Even before looking out, Chobong recognized Seungjae's footsteps.

Chobong and Seungjae's eyes met. Seungjae usually walked straight to his room at the back of the house, giving only a faint

smile to her. But today Seungjae lingered there, poking his hand
into the pocket of his jacket as if looking for something.

Although she turned her head away, Chobong waited for
Seungjae to start a conversation. If he did, she'd gladly continue
the conversation, and talk about the absurd incident that had
taken place at the store. She thought it might be fun.

But they rarely talked to each other face-to-face, unless it
was unavoidable. It wasn't because they were shy of one another.
Nor that someone was prohibiting them. It was simply because
neither of them could readily start talking. It had been like this
ever since Seungjae moved into the house. When either of them
had a message to pass on or something to give to the other,
for instance, if Seungjae wanted a glass of water, or Chobong
wanted to give him one, it was always delivered through one of
the younger children, who were readily available in the house at
any time. A habit they became quite accustomed to.

Though Seungjae had moved into the house around the
end of last year, it was only since February of this year, when
Chobong started working at Jeho's pharmacy, that they began
to talk to each other, if simply to say, "This is Seungjae" or "This
is Chobong," over the phone.

Chobong, unable to wait any longer, turned her head toward
Seungjae for a very short moment. Seungjae, however, giving
an embarrassed smile, quickly started to walk toward his room.
Chobong wondered what it was that he wanted to talk about
but couldn't. She thought he looked odd.

In the inner room . . .

Because all the children, apart from Chobong who was in the
kitchen, had rushed into the room, the argument between the
couple was forced into a truce without reaching a conclusion.
They had to keep their mouths shut.

Each member of the family, though they didn't say so, was anxiously waiting for the supper table to be ready. Gyebong was fumbling with the dark blue Bemberg silk fabric that her mother was pleating for a skirt. She stroked it with her hand for a while, then let it alone, and then started to stroke it again. Finally, in a pleading voice she said,

"Mom . . . can I have a skirt like this?"

But knowing too well that it was impossible, she lowered her head with a shy smile.

"What a thoughtless girl you are!" said Madam Yu, glaring at her over her glasses. Then remembering her elder daughter, she began to scold her younger daughter.

"What are you doing here, sitting idly and talking such nonsense, while your sister is working alone in the kitchen?"

"The supper is almost ready . . ."

Deeply embarrassed, Gyebong didn't know what to do with her hands that had been stroking the skirt.

"What do you mean 'almost ready' when the soup is still boiling? You're really hopeless . . ."

Gyebong moved to the far corner of the room with her back toward her mother, fuming with anger.

"You slut, get up this moment and go out to your sister."

"Oh, Mom, you hate me so much!"

Making a long face and blubbering, Gyebong walked out of the room and, stamping on the floor loudly with her heels, went to the kitchen.

Gyebong was quite different from Chobong in temperament as well as in features. She was plump, giving her an agreeable impression. Her fleshy nose made her look kindhearted, but her somewhat sunken cheeks suggested a certain grumpiness in her temperament. Her eyes and forehead were distinctively clear and bright. Her best feature was her mouth. When she laughed wholeheartedly, revealing neat white teeth, it made people around her feel at ease.

Even when she laughed, Chobong's mouth looked delicate and pretty, but Gyebong's laugh was carefree and full of masculine spirit like the ocean that boldly unfurls along the shore. So she looked much more dependable, even in appearance.

Gyebong hadn't yet fully bloomed. But she promised to grow into a woman with strong and sturdy features of feminine beauty, unlike her sister, Chobong, who had the subtle and elegant beauty of paintings of the Southern school.

Among the four children of the family, Chobong alone looked quite different; the other three, Gyebong, Hyeongju, and Byeongju had much in common in appearance. None of them, however, took after their parents. Chobong took after her paternal grandfather whereas the other three took after their maternal grandmother.

Chobong, who'd been crouching over the stove ladling out the soup, saw Gyebong walk in and asked with a smile, "Why such a sullen face again?"

"I must be a foundling. I'm always being abused and scolded."

Stopping her work, Chobong burst into laughter, triggered by Gyebong's long face mumbling complaints.

"You're heartless! Why do you laugh like that! I'm really upset."

"What's the problem with you? I didn't say anything . . ."

Chobong tried to coax her gently while retaining her smile.

"Stop your badgering, dear, and take the serving table in for Father now . . . He must be very hungry. You said you were hungry too. Go ahead, start eating first."

Chobong placed two bowls of soup on the small serving table for her father and Byeongju, and on another table that was for the rest of the family, put one big bowl of soup, because they had fewer bowls than the number of people in the family.

In addition to the rice and the soup, there were only two other dishes. A blackish, discolored radish kimchi and a small bowl of soy sauce. Nevertheless, the smell of the soup made with soybean paste and late-season mallow leaves was quite tasty to those who were hungry.

Under ordinary circumstances, Gyebong would have remained stubborn and unyielding for much longer, but as she was so hungry, she obediently carried the small serving table into the room for her father and came out again to take the other table.

In the meantime, Chobong had prepared a bowl of burnt rice water to give to Seungjae, and holding it in her hand, hesitated as to whether she should carry it to him herself or not.

Knowing that Seungjae was too humble to ask for a glass of water at night, however thirsty he might be, Chobong always prepared him a bowl of burnt rice water whenever she cooked the evening meal.

But tonight she felt inclined to carry it to him herself. While she was summoning up the courage to do so, Gyebong entered the kitchen. She gave a start as if she were a naughty child caught in the act of playing a prank, and handed it to Gyebong to take to Seungjae.

"No! . . . Why me . . . I don't want to."

Still under the influence of her vexed temper, Gyebong refused outright.

"Why not? Isn't it a good thing to take water to someone who might be thirsty at night?"

"What good will it do me? It's good only for you, Sister . . ."

"What?" Chobong was too shocked to respond and stood aghast, revealing her obvious embarrassment.

"You see? Ha, ha, ha, ha. Ah ha, ha, ha . . .," Gyebong laughed out loud, entirely forgetting her earlier anger, and continued her teasing.

". . . I caught you, right? Look at her face flushed to the ears! Ha, ha, ha, ha."

"You naughty girl!"

"There's no way to deceive me. Ha, ha, ha, ha. Well, I'll be kind enough to act as a messenger, ahem . . .," said Gyebong, taking the water from her sister, adding, "but be careful. Who knows, I may attempt to steal Mr. Nam away from you. Beware, Sister."

"Stop all this banter!" Chobong scolded, raising her hand as if to hit her, at which Gyebong quickly turned around and ran off to Seungjae's room, spilling half the water on the way.

Chobong picked up the remaining serving table and walked to the inner room, looking back once at Gyebong.

Standing in front of Seungjae's room, Gyebong called to him, mimicking a man's voice.

"Ahem, is Mr. Nam in?"

"Who is it?"

Gyebong opened the door after waiting till he responded.

Seungjae grinned, raising his eyes from the book he'd been reading at his desk. He was wearing the same clothes as when he returned from work. His clothes were simple enough, a tsumeeri stand-up collar jacket and trousers made of black serge.

If he put on an old felt hat in addition to this suit, it was only when he was on his way to and from the clinic in Jangjaedong and Chobong's house. If he put on a white gown on top of this suit, it was while he functioned as a doctor in the clinic. And if he carried his shabby bag of medical instruments in his hand, it was when he was going on free house calls to poor households in the neighborhood.

Since the day Seungjae had first rented the room last winter, his clothes hadn't changed, with the exception of the old overcoat he'd worn during the coldest months of winter. As his face had never changed, the black serge tsumeeri suit, too, had never changed. What would he wear when the weather got warmer? This question was the source of amused curiosity for many people around him, not excepting Chobong.

It wasn't that Seungjae was an unworldly man, who had transcended all worldly matters. Neither was it because he was eccentric. Rather he was too careless and untidy to take care of his appearance, or simply uninterested in such matters.

In addition, he was poor.

He was born in Seoul and had been left an orphan at the age of five. Then one of his distant relatives on the maternal side of the family, who was a practicing doctor, took him in rather reluctantly and raised him.

The doctor, who saw in Seungjae talent as well as an earnest desire to learn, provided him with the opportunity to go to school, partly out of compassion, partly out of curiosity to see what he would make of himself. Thus Seungjae was able to finish primary school and then junior high school.

During his school days, Seungjae spent most of the time when he was out of school at the doctor's consulting room or the dispensary. When he was in his final year at junior high school, knowing that he couldn't expect further education, he devoted himself to acquiring a practical knowledge of medicine.

After graduating from junior high school, Seungjae worked as his guardian's assistant for three years while preparing for the qualifying exams for medical doctors.

His guardian, in the meantime, had developed a genuine concern and affection for Seungjae, and did everything he could to help him pass the exam and become a licensed doctor. But he passed away without seeing Seungjae's dream fulfilled. Before his death, however, he wrote a letter of recommendation for Seungjae to Dr. Yun Dalsik, a friend of his who had the Geumho Clinic in Gunsan.

That's how Seungjae came to Gunsan.

Since coming to the Geumho Clinic two years ago, he's been to Seoul twice, in May and October of last year, and passed half of the exams that are required to become a general practitioner.

He would have to take exams in five more subjects, physiology and anatomy first, pathology and obstetrics second, and clinical practice third. He'd been putting off the exam for clinical practice since he was quite confident of his knowledge and experience in this area. Though he believed he wasn't fully prepared for the other four subjects, it was likely that he'd complete all the requirements by May of next year or by October of the same year at the latest.

It was true that since coming to Gunsan, his preparation for the exams had been progressing rather slowly because he had to work full time at the clinic, appropriate to one who was earning a wage of forty won a month.

Dr. Yun found Seungjae quite competent in clinical practice, so he entrusted most of the consultations to him. He also provided him lodging in his house attached to the hospital. As Seungjae was available at night as well, he had to take care of not only the inpatients, but also patients who visited at night, finding no time to study.

Dr. Yun felt sorry for him, especially when he considered his deceased friend's particular request to take good care of him. So in the end he suggested to Seungjae that he find a place to live away from the clinic so he could study at night. Therefore in the spring of last year he moved out of the hospital, and last winter, when he had to move again, he ended up finding a room in Chobong's house.

To tell the truth, however, living in the hospital was not the only cause of his tardiness in his preparation for the exams.

"What difference does it make if I delay the exams a bit longer?"

With such reckless thoughts, Seungjae put aside the medical textbooks and began to indulge himself in reading books and articles on natural sciences. Along the walls of his room, which had no furniture besides a desk, a big trunk, and a set of bedding, stacks of books were piled up to the ceiling, and almost two-thirds of them were on natural sciences.

Moreover, despite his determination to study at night away from the hospital, he found an extra job to do at night. Whenever he heard about sick poor people in the neighborhood, who couldn't afford hospital costs, he visited them for a free consultation and treatment, and even bought medicines for them with his own money. As the rumor of this spread, laborers in the neighborhood sent for him whenever they needed a doctor, regardless of whether it was midnight or the small hours of the morning, as if he were their family doctor. To respond to these demands, he saw about ten won of his wage vanish into thin air every month, let alone the precious time for study.

Out of the forty won of his salary, he spent about ten won for such purposes, twenty won on books, then with the remaining ten won, he paid four won for his rent, and used the rest for his personal expenses, which in fact mainly consisted of fees for the public bath and charges for a haircut. He never spent a penny drinking or smoking, and washed his underwear by hand. So if he had any leftover money, it usually went to bookstores, or as in the last few months, to Chobong's house as an advance payment of his rent. Such was the nature of his poverty.

Being a man who'd known nothing but poverty, however, his mind was quite at ease with this situation. He confidently trusted that he'd pass all the exams and become a doctor. He had a belief in the power of natural sciences. He enjoyed the opportunities of helping the sick poor people recover their health. Thus he had no anxiety or worry whatsoever.

"Though you're so big and burly . . ."

Gyebong teased him whenever she saw him smile with his eyes only, flaring his nostrils but with his mouth closed.

"What sort of a smile is that! Isn't that the way a cow smiles, rather than a man?"

Seungjae found Gyebong's bantering spirit rather charming and agreeable, and kept smiling with eyes that were full of benevolence.

"Look! You never listen to me! I say, if you're going to laugh, you should laugh loudly, ha, ha, ha, ha or huh, huh, huh, shouldn't you? You should laugh with a wide-open mouth and full heart. But what do you do? Hmm . . . you seal your mouth like this, and pretend to smile with your eyes and nostrils only . . . Shame on you! Such a good-for-nothing young fellow! Why can't you laugh aloud with a full heart, I wonder?"

"I may eventually." Seungjae rubbed the emerging bristles on his chin with his palm.

"When will that 'eventually' be? When your grandson has bristles on his chin, perhaps? Don't you mean that? Ha, ha, ha, ha . . ."

Looking at the laughing Gyebong affectionately, Seungjae thought, "You laugh wholeheartedly indeed."

Gyebong at last stopped laughing and pushed the bowl of water into the room.

"Well, here comes the burnt rice water for you . . . But you should know this isn't ordinary water. This is the elixir of life! Do you get it? The meaning of what I say, huh?"

Seungjae smiled awkwardly, a deep flush spreading over his face.

"Hah, why is that young man so embarrassed? Has he been caught stealing a radish in the field?"

Gyebong teased him like a child teasing a bear in the zoo. If she weren't hungry, she would have gone on teasing him as long as she liked, but being so hungry, she turned around to go back.

Seungjae hastily stopped her.

"Look, wait a moment . . ."

"You've got something you want to talk about?"

"Yes. But your supper's ready, right?" Seungjae asked awkwardly, and as he'd done earlier in the yard, fumbled with his hand in his pocket as if searching for something.

"Supper? Yes, they're having it now. So I'm about to go in and have it too. The basic physiological need is rather urgent now."

"Well, please take this and . . . you know . . . uh?"

He hesitantly pulled out a five-won banknote and handed it to Gyebong.

". . . Take that to your mother or father, and tell them I'm sorry I couldn't do it earlier, and that though I tried to get it in the morning, I got it too late."

Gyebong knew well enough that Seungjae was offering the money as he'd seen them having no breakfast again that morning. He was far from being behind in his rent payment; his rent for this month, May, had already been paid in April. And yet, he was giving money in advance again.

Gyebong felt very grateful for his thoughtfulness, perhaps not simply grateful but oddly delighted. Yet at the same time, she felt so ashamed that she was unable to hold her head straight.

"What's this money for?"

Instead of taking the money, she affected to question him sternly with her hands behind her back.

"Nothing in particular . . ."

"Nothing in particular? What do you mean by that? The rent can't be that much . . ."

"For rent or for whatever, I just thought your parents could use it . . ."

"I can't accept the money."

Her voice was too resolute to be taken as a joke.

Seungjae stared at her dubiously. She had the same mischievous expression on her face, yet he couldn't help but notice a certain difference in it, something that connoted an arrogant tenacity of spirit.

Though unsure, Seungjae began to suspect that she might have misunderstood his intention as something impure. He felt the weight of frustration and somewhat humiliated as well.

"Why can't you?" Seungjae asked in an indifferent tone, attempting to suppress his agitation.

"Because I don't want to forfeit my privilege as a beggar."

Looking at this young girl with her head high, her hands held tightly behind her back, haughtily pronouncing such a statement to a burly man, Seungjae couldn't help but be pleasantly surprised by her audacious spirit, not to mention the content of the statement.

Though Gyebong looked grave, in fact she wasn't serious. Having been vexed by her mother earlier, she simply wanted to vent some of her residual anger, and when the phrase she'd read in a magazine suddenly crossed her mind, she took advantage of it.

Seungjae, however, was innocently trapped by her performance.

He blinked his big eyes like a boy being scolded by an adult, and at last mumbled an excuse.

"I was just thinking . . . my familiar terms with your family, nothing else . . ."

He spoke falteringly, unable to clearly articulate.

"Nevertheless, you should know . . ."

Gyebong began to find fault with Seungjae again, assuming the dignified posture of an adult admonishing a child.

". . . Charity or pity can deprive the recipient of his pride."

"Am I not one of the poor, poor as poor can be?"

"Ha, ha, ha, ha. Ah, ha, ha, ha . . ." Gyebong burst into laughter, holding her sides. ". . . Ha, ha, ha, ha, ha. Look at his eyes. Just like those of a bull that's slipped on ice. Look at his eyes, indeed, ha, ha, ha, ha . . ."

Gyebong was greatly amused at Seungjae's perplexity, suppressing her laughter, pretending to be serious, only to see how he managed the embarrassing situation. But in the end she surrendered herself to a tirade of laughter.

It can't be denied that she and Seungjae were on friendly terms, yet, despite that, or rather because of it, she wished to maintain a certain level of appearances.

This seventeen-year-old girl was bound to feel ashamed of her family's utter poverty, poverty not in the vague sense, but the painfully palpable poverty that forced them to skip meals as often as they did. The fact that it was detected by Seungjae made the shameful situation all the more bitter for this adolescent girl.

Of course, it was self-inflicted shame.

Regardless, Gyebong now felt herself fully avenged. Though it was in jest when she said that "she didn't want to forfeit her privilege as a beggar," or that "charity or pity could deprive the person who receives it of his pride," Seungjae was definitely at a loss for words. Perceiving his awkwardness relieved her of her anger and uneasiness, allowing her to laugh heartily . . .

Seungjae too felt relieved seeing Gyebong laugh like that, though at the same time he also felt ashamed of himself for having been foolishly deceived by her clever trick.

"What a girl you are . . . I thought you were seriously upset!"

"Ha, ha, ha . . . But don't assume that it was simply a jest, either. It wasn't."

"All right, madam, I understand."

"Well, then . . ."

Gyebong looked down at the five-won bill that had been at issue. Although she laughed the issue away, she still felt uneasy about picking it up. But she knew she couldn't refuse it now. After some deliberation, she forced herself to take it.

". . . Then I'll deliver it to my mom."

Gyebong nodded her head once by way of farewell, and headed for her family's quarters. Seungjae followed her with his eyes, sensing that from now on he would see her from a new perspective.

So far Gyebong had been to him merely a girl who wasn't yet grown up enough to know the world despite being tall for her age. A girl always frolicking, boisterously quarrelling with her younger brothers, indiscreetly speaking her mind regardless of propriety, she had seemed a thoughtless, ill-tempered tomboy to him. But today he saw that she had surprisingly deep thoughts as well as the cleverness to express them effectively. He began to regard her with wonder and admiration.

It was the same with Gyebong, who now had more esteem for him as a result of what had just passed between them. With such mutual feelings, a more solid foundation for friendship and intimacy seemed to have been built between them.

The inner room looked like a wicker basket in which a bunch of silkworms were munching away voraciously at mulberry leaves; the five members of the family were busily devouring their food, each holding their own portions, scooping up bit by bit the precious rice, and slurping down the hot soup, making much noise. Who wouldn't when they'd gone without for so long?

"Where's Gyebong got to?" Jeong Jusa asked looking over at the other table. Perhaps he wasn't so hungry as not to notice when one of the children was missing.

"She took a glass of water to the outer wing," Chobong responded, wondering why it was taking so long for Gyebong to come back.

"She must be talking all sorts of nonsense there, that thoughtless kid."

Madam Yu always found fault with Gyebong and rarely talked about her in good terms. As Gyebong had claimed, perhaps she didn't like her younger daughter, though for no reason.

"Dear, why are you having only half a bowl of rice? It seems there isn't enough rice."

Looking over at Chobong's rice bowl, Jeong Jusa worried.

". . . Then, take this bowl, eat some more." He picked up Byeongju's untouched bowl from under the table.

Byeongju, who was eating from his father's bowl, reserving his own bowl of rice for later by putting it under the table, began to kick and scream, wielding his spoon in protest.

Just then, Gyebong rushed into the room, shouting, "Mother! Mother!"

". . . Please, Mother, if you give me fifty jeon, I'll give you five won!"

All of her family members stopped what they were doing; some were chewing the rice, others were in the middle of scooping it up from the bowl, while the rest were about to put the spoon into their mouth. They all stopped their movements, wondering what mystery Gyebong was talking about, and stared up at her.

At length, Madam Yu, casting a leering glance at Gyebong, threw out a rebuke.

"You hussy, if you have five won, I'll say I have a hundred won!"

"Really? Then I'll show you the five won, and you show me your hundred won."

"You're full of strange notions, girl. It must be money from Mr. Nam. I know she has no other way to get money."

"Heh, heh, heh, here you are, five won. Now Mother, you show me your hundred won, please?"

All the family members who had been in suspense, doubtful of Gyebong's words, were surprised at the sight of the money.

Chobong finally understood what Seungjae had been trying to do when he was hesitant, with his hands fumbling in his pockets earlier.

"You bitch, is it your money? Showing off with someone else's money!" Madam Yu rebuked her as she grabbed the money.

"But think, if I'd refused, you wouldn't have had it. You see . . .?"

Loudly protesting to her mother, Gyebong took a seat at the corner of the table.

"That girl is full of hot air! What do you mean, refusing money when someone has decided to give it out of good will?"

"Anyhow, why is he giving us that much money, I wonder . . . Well, well!" said Jeong Jusa with an expression of concern. His wife responded,

"He must've noticed that we had no breakfast this morning. He's always . . ."

"I know how obliging he is. Didn't he already pay this month's rent in advance? Yet still . . ."

"Indeed, that's what I'm also concerned about."

"What a man! He himself seems not very well off, yet I have to be so indebted to him . . ."

Jeong Jusa clicked his tongue as if he regretted the situation, when in fact he wasn't feeling regretful at all.

"Dad? Dad . . .," called Byeongju, alternating glances between his father and the money, and quickly enumerated the list of presents he wanted.

". . . My suit, my hat, my shoes, my bike, and bananas and oranges, you buy them all for me. You must, Dad, OK?"

"That boy always wants such vain things . . ."

Hyeongju, with a sullen face, joined in the talk, wishing that he might also benefit from the money.

"But I have my monthly school tuition overdue! Mother, my tuition for last month and this month, please! . . . And I need a notebook for my arithmetic class."

"You stinker! Damn you!" wildly waving his spoon, Byeongju challenged his elder brother.

"Why did you call me a stinker? You'll be sorry for it later, you're a stupid stinker yourself."

"You naughty boy!" Jeong Jusa shouted at Hyeongju, taking the side of his youngest.

Apart from being partial to his youngest, Jeong Jusa was usually displeased with his older son for no reason, just as Madam Yu was with Gyebong.

"Mother, I need to pay the tuition now. Otherwise, I don't know what I'll do!" Hyeongju insisted.

Now Gyebong challenged Hyeongju.

"Listen boy, do you think you're the only one with overdue tuition? Mine's overdue by two months . . . Well, Mother, the tuition can wait until the end of this month, I think, but please give me fifty jeon now, won't you? I need to pay my overdue fee for the circulating library. Please, Mother!"

"Why is that so important, Sister? I'm sure school tuition must have top priority."

"You stupid boy, it's quite all right to pay tuition late. Mother, Mother, please give me just fifty jeon."

"You're selfish . . . I need my tuition, really!"

"Dad, dad. You'll buy me my suit, my hat, my shoes, and bananas, won't you? And my bike too."

"Sure, sure, huh, huh . . .," said Jeong Jusa.

And then, after looking around the room blankly and feeling helpless, he uttered a concluding comment.

". . . Why, they're just like the children in *The Life of Heungbo*, the famous folklore story about a man who has a dozen children but no money. They're the children of Heungbo, exactly! . . . Only the one child that nags me to get him married is missing."

"Well then, you're like Heungbo exactly."

"Why am I like Heungbo? . . . What a senseless woman, to say such an impertinent thing!"

"You think I don't know what's in your mind?"

"Why, what is there?"

"Stop pretending. I know you want to coax me into giving you one won and six jeon out of this money, and you'll buy a pack of cigarettes with the six jeon and keep the one won for your seed money at the exchange market. That's what's in your mind, bah . . ."

"Huh, huh, huh, huh . . ."

His secret intention having been detected by his wife, Jeong Jusa had no other way to prevaricate than to cover his awkwardness with an empty laugh.

". . . Now that you know that already, why don't you give me that one won and six jeon, huh, huh . . .?"

Chapter 4:
Life is a Sheet of Calibrated Paper

THOSE WHO HAVE any dealings with it simply call this place "The Market," whereas other people call it "The Rice Exchange." The signboard, which is in effect a gambling house, reads "Gunsan Exchange Market for Rice Stock."

Though the building itself is a two-storied, run-down wooden structure with nothing remarkable about it, it is beyond question the heart of Gunsan.

It's a sort of outlying community, a settlement for gamblers, a shabby version of Monte Carlo. There are stories about places like Monte Carlo, stories about people who shot themselves after having lost all their money and, as if the gunshot was the starting signal for a race, joined others in the long journey to the other world. But in this rice exchange, no matter how quickly people lost all their money, none of them has ever attempted to hang themselves, leaving their body dangling on a rope. Some are proud of that, attributing it to the gentle, mild nature of Korean people!

There's only one instance in which people saw blood in the exchange, but even that wasn't a suicide.

It happened as follows:

A few years ago, an old fellow from somewhere down south who, in order to try his luck at the exchange, had collected about ten thousand won in ready cash by selling all his farmland and mortgaging his house, single-mindedly came up to Gunsan, to the exchange, carrying the money tied around his waist in a money bag.

He was completely inexperienced and ignorant about the operations of the exchange. He had simply determined to come up, cherishing an expectation of making a big fortune as he'd heard that the rice exchange was an easy way to make money.

He deposited all his money at a brokerage house and began to learn the science of the rice exchange from the very basic A, B, C, while dipping into the real game at the same time.

Whilst the palms of the speculators were turned outward and backward and the trend lines on the calibrated paper moved up and down, his ten thousand won vanished completely in the blink of an eye, even before he knew what ghost had carried them off.

The old man was left with nothing but his unpaid bills at the inn, and had no money to travel back to his home, even if he were brazen enough to do so.

The brokerage house, out of pity for him or something, gave him thirty won to cover his traveling expenses. Blankly staring at the money in his palm, the old man let out a deep sigh, and a moment later, fell to the ground, coughing up blood.

He died instantly.

This is the only record of bloodshed in the archives of the Gunsan exchange.

So the story went. However miserably they may end up, having lost everything, left with only a beggar's bowl, the worst people do is go to the pier and shed a few tears into the river. The Geum-gang River seems to have been fated to receive tears of despair ever since the fall of the Baekje Kingdom in the seventh century.

Certainly, the speculators at the rice exchange are apt to cry. There's a saying that the pond in front of Chukhyeon train station (now called Upper Incheon Station) became so wide and so full to the brim, because of the tears of exchange speculators. When country bumpkins, with a headband wrapped around their heads, and their ears hidden under the band, one day find their lives have somehow been reduced to poverty, they become so anxious that they look for an easy way out, and usually resort to vain or illusionary means. Driven by desperation, they sometimes trust themselves to some cult such as *Baekbaek-gyo* or *Bocheon-gyo*, and get swindled out of their last remaining farmland by religious tricksters. And those who claim to be smarter come up to Incheon, harboring a vain ambition to make a fortune overnight. But they all lose their money at the exchange and return with empty pockets.

They're not heroes like Xiang Yu the Great, who, after being defeated, killed himself on the battlefield. So they're thick-skinned enough to go back home, yet when they get to Chukhyeon Station to take the train home, they can't help but be overwhelmed by grief and despair. While waiting for the train, sitting beside the pond, they shed plentiful tears of remorse into it.

Because the same thing has happened to one person, two, ten, a hundred, a thousand people over the course of many years, the pond has been filled and refilled. Such is the story that has come to us, a story that sounds like something invented by the wandering bard and satirist, Kim Satgat.

Today is the second Monday of May, and the first market day of the week. Thus it is natural that people are cautious in entering their bids, but still, the exchange is quieter than usual, perhaps being the season of no consequence between spring and summer.

The transactions are mostly on a small scale, the biggest involving only five hundred or a thousand bushels of rice. The exchange is peopled mostly by groups of *mabaras*, small-fry speculators, clustered together, bidding for one or two hundred bushels.

Since the government began to control the price of rice, fixing the range of prices from lowest to highest, the market isn't as interesting as in the good old days. However enterprising one might be, there isn't much room for maneuver unless special factors happen to be involved, such as weather conditions during the summer or typhoons affecting the harvest, or political upheavals, or natural disasters like the Tokyo earthquake some years before. Such factors cause rice prices to fluctuate widely and supply much energy to the dealings of the exchange market, the scale of which otherwise resembles a grocery store.

Speculators hope to see hailstorms come pouring down on the Gimman fields, especially when they're filled with well-ripened rice crops, or wait for some natural disaster to destroy this or that field, just as some people, because of their profession, hope to see a murderous robbery, or trouble involving pistols.

Now it's time for the third session of afternoon trade . . .

The first floor is divided into two waiting rooms with picket fences between them, one for *badajis*, agents from brokerage houses, and the other for general customers. In the *badaji* waiting room about forty people are gathered, two badachis each from several brokerage houses and one *jotsuki*, or assistant, from each brokerage house.

In *Gakudamari*, the general waiting room adjoining it, about one hundred customers are waiting for the session to start.

Their appearances are quite varied, as if someone had deliberately collected them as unique specimens. There are people in traditional Korean costumes, people in Western-style suits, people in coats with bean-shaped sleeves, old men, young men, tall guys, small guys, bearded men, men with untidy hair, handsome faces, homely faces; each of them, however, is an individual, a sovereign entity, each a gambler carrying a unique name, Kim, Yi, *Nakamura*, or Choi, etc., etc.

But *Odae*, the so-called Big Hands, who deal with thousands or tens of thousands of bushels of rice, never come to the market in person. They have telephone lines installed in their homes by which they keep checking the market conditions, ordering to sell five thousand bushels, or bidding to buy ten thousand bushels. They make money sitting at home.

The people gathered in the *Gakudamari* are *habas*, pseudo-bidders who have no deposit money, or onlookers, or *mabaras* who, after bidding for one or two hundred bushels, anxiously watch out for the smallest change in price, as small as one jeon, as if it's a matter of life and death. But these *mabaras* along with the *habas* are the real veteran soldiers on the battlefield of the rice exchange.

Having hung around in the exchange for ten or twenty years, their lives are utterly dependent on the graphs drawn on sheets of calibrated paper as the prices go up and down, gaining a fortune one time and losing it another, following the same ups and downs repeatedly, and eventually reduced to the pathetic level of *mabaras*, or worse still, to that of *habas*.

Having experienced all those ups and downs, they've now acquired an ability to predict the movements of price, along with the guts to take risks. But they're like men whose appetite has returned only once they're broke, or soldiers with broken lances, who've lost the means to maneuver in a big battle.

To announce the start of the third session of the afternoon, someone from the gallery-shaped trading floor on the second floor claps the clapperboard loudly a few times and posts up a sign, "Deals for Current Month Payment."

This is a sort of summoning bugle.

At the clapping sounds, all the *badajis* instantly look up at the gallery, then look at the people in the waiting room. Out of the habit of their profession, they become alert to the signal, but only for a very short while, and soon return to their former relaxed posture.

In the general waiting section, people become alert and glance over the fence to study the movements of the *badajis*, who, however, show no signs of making orders. The customers too remain still.

Only the telephones on top of the picket fence are ringing incessantly, and the assistants from the brokerage houses alone are busy receiving the telephone calls and making notes.

In a corner of the gallery upstairs are clerks who handle the news correspondence. Hanging on to telephones, they're intent on noting down the price quotations from every market and posting them on blackboards.

On the trading floor, there are two *dakabas*, registry clerks, in addition to the clapper, each with a table in front of them, waiting for orders, looking down at the *badajis*.

For this "current month deals" no *badaji* makes a gesture, that is, no challenge for bids, or as they call it, *degimo-o*.

From the trading floor, the clapping sound echoes again, and the sign for "Deals for Next Month Payment" is posted.

In response to this, one *badaji* raises his hand and shouts, "*SengGoku yaro—*."

The hand he raises may appear to contain no meaning, just a hand raised at random, when, in fact, endless variations of subtle differentiation are involved in the shape of the hand raised up.

He has his thumb and forefinger folded while the remaining three fingers are stretched up and his palm is facing outward.

If you interpret it as if it were Esperanto spoken by a mute, the three stretched out fingers mean three jeon, and the palm facing outward means he wants to sell.

His shout, "*SengGoku yaro!*" means "selling one thousand bushels of rice." Taken as a whole, he is saying, "I want to sell one thousand bushels of rice at the price of three jeon (meaning thirty won and three jeon)."

To complete this deal, there must be another *badaji* who wants to buy. But no one appears, only a little stir sweeps through the place for a short while. In the *gakudamari*, puffs of cigarette smoke rise here and there.

Thirty won and three jeon isn't at all a tempting price: both badajis and customers look uninterested, as if saying in their minds, "Pah, who would want that . . ."

Thus, the "Deals for Next Month Payment" too gets aborted, ending up in *Sidenash*, that is, no response having come up.

In the quiet season, it's usual to have almost no deals made during the "current month deals" and the "two month deals." Moreover, when the price tends to go down, the buyers become more cautious. Despite the trend, the *badaji* offered thirty won and three jeon, that is, one jeon higher than the previous session. It's natural that no one responded to that.

A third clapping sound rings out, and a new sign, for "three month deals" is posted. A customer in the *gakudamari* waiting area instantly moves toward the fence, calls out a *badaji*, and begins to whisper into his ear.

The *badaji* listens to him, nodding his head incessantly, while looking through his ledger.

At last he turns back and raises his hand with his thumb, forefinger, and middle finger stretched out, and his palm facing outward. He shouts,

"*Goaku yaro!*" meaning that he wants to sell five hundred bushels of rice at the price of eight jeon, that is, twenty-nine won and ninety-eight jeon. The offer fills the place with excitement.

Another *badaji* in the other corner of the room, without a second's hesitation, raises his hand with his palm facing inward, and shouts,

"*Dotta!*" meaning he will buy that.

At once, many hands are raised here and there, with the shouts, "*yatta*," for selling, "*dotta*," for buying. As the bidding shouts crowd together, and the hands of *badajis* clash in the air, the place is full of hurly-burly, astir with the roaring and bustle of people.

While the *badaji* room is seething in uproar, the *dakabas*, or registry clerks, are busily recording the bids, their eyes shifting up and down like falcons' eyes.

The *badajis* and *dakabas* are excitedly carrying out the transactions, while the people in the *gakudamari* are naturally excited about the unusual trend of prices.

This morning the trade started at thirty won and twelve jeon, and the morning trade ended at nine jeon. When the afternoon trade started, the price was down to seven jeon, and by the end of the second session, it further went down by five jeon, being only thirty won and two jeon. And now in this third session, the thirty-won boundary is being broken, offers being made at eight jeon (= twenty-nine won and ninety-eight jeon), four jeon lower than the last session.

In the actual market for rice, the supply is in shortage, thus the prices are bound to go up. But contrary to this trend in the market for rice, the exchange market price keeps going down, causing a serious blow to the *suyoki*, the buyers, who have pushed their luck too strongly.

If the price keeps going down at this pace, by the time afternoon trading closes, it's very likely that it may go further down by another four or five jeon. In that case, the price might very well go down by twenty jeon today alone.

Since the system of standard rice prices came into effect, a daily fluctuation range of one or two hundred jeon has been a dream of bygone days. The fluctuation range has become so narrow, that this twenty-jeon difference in one day is indeed an event worthy of excitement, especially in this quiet season.

The facial expressions of the customers in the *gakudamari* are instantly divided into two opposite groups, as if a line has been drawn between them. Those who sold earlier assume a look of smug satisfaction, pushing up their chins, whereas those who bought assume looks of sullen despondence, pulling in their chins. Those are the only two expressions you can find in gamblers, who are bound to be either winners or losers.

As the price is plummeting, the hunchbacked Hyeongbo, a *badaji* of the Marugang brokerage house, and a friend of Go Taesu, frowns his tense forehead, flipping through his ledger.

The account with a G mark in a square box is Taesu's. Taesu bought one thousand bushels of rice paying six hundred won as deposit, a sixty-won deposit per one hundred bushels. If the price goes down by another ten jeon, that is, to twenty-nine won eighty-eight jeon, Taesu is fated to become empty-handed, losing all his deposit money, when he pays the charges for dealing.

Hyeongbo, after a little hesitation, waddles toward the telephone, swaying his hunchback. He dials the number for the Gunsan branch of the 00 Bank, cautiously watching out for the people around him. He's going to inform Taesu of the situation.

Both Hyeongbo and Taesu are cautious when they call each other, for, Taesu being known as an exemplary bank clerk, the rumor that Taesu is speculating on the rice exchange could be quite damaging to his career if it were known in the bank.

Go Taesu, who's sitting behind the checking accounts window of the Gunsan branch of the 00 Bank, is listlessly waiting for closing time, enduring the headache and nausea caused by carousing all night long the previous evening.

It's not yet three o'clock, so there's more than one hour still to go.

Swallowing yawns, he keeps looking at his wristwatch, when the office boy comes and tells him that he's wanted on the phone. Taesu goes to the phone, and answers languidly,

"*Hai.*"

"It's me, here."

Taesu recognizes Hyeongbo without asking. Taesu's heart begins to pound in expectation of good news that the market price is going up.

"What's up?"

"It crashed, really!"

Taesu understands that the thirty-won boundary has been broken.

All of his energy seeping away, he feels like collapsing on the spot.

"Hmm!"

Taesu simply utters a groan, being unable to ask any questions in the presence of his colleagues and superiors. He suffers like a mute who has much to say but can't speak.

"Hey, down to eight jeon now, you hear me . . .?" Hyeongbo says as if chewing the words in a cheeky voice.

". . . I say eight jeon now. We should let it go."

"Well . . ."

"What bloody 'well' is that? Ten more jeon down, and you'll be asi! You'll be in deficit! Do you follow me? . . . Why the hell are you so dumb and mindless?"

"But what's there to think about when the matter is . . ."

Taesu is quite averse to Hyeongbo's idea of selling, knowing that only fifty won will be left in hand if he sells now.

With vain hopes for a windfall of one thousand won, with which he might avoid imminent disaster, he had stepped into the speculation; now that the six hundred won he invested is about to vanish, let alone earn any money, he wants to see the end of it rather than rake in the mere fifty won dangling at the tail of his enterprise. Such a trifling sum would do no good in his desperate situation.

"Don't hesitate! . . . It's not the way you take in speculation . . . Listen to me, do as I tell you . . ."

At Hyeongbo's admonishing words, Taesu gets annoyed and cuts in.

"I don't want to hear your advice! . . . Stop there, but what I left with you yesterday, you still have it with you, don't you?"

"I do."

Last night Hyeongbo received from Taesu a check for two hundred won issued by a usurer called Baekseok from an account at Taesu's bank. Hyeongbo occasionally received such requests from Taesu to cash checks.

"Do the job today as I asked, please."

"You asked to do it tomorrow, didn't you?"

"No, do it today."

Taesu hangs up the phone, and returning to his seat, plops down. Now that the last glimmer of hope has vanished, Taesu feels utterly helpless.

It was a few days ago that Taesu left six hundred won with Marukang brokerage house as a deposit to buy one thousand bushels of rice on *nariyuki*, that is at his orders.

It was a Saturday, and the market was moving rapidly upward; the trade that started at thirty won seventeen jeon in the morning kept going up, to twenty-nine jeon at the second session, to thirty-six jeon at the third session, and to forty jeon at the fourth session.

Being informed of this, Taesu asked Hyeongbo to buy at the fifth session, confident that it would turn out to be his much-needed good opportunity. Hyeongbo, on the phone, tried to dissuade him, pointing out the risk involved, but Taesu turned a deaf ear to him, convinced that the market would keep soaring up, soon passing the thirty-one-won point and eventually giving him an easy one-hundred-jeon profit margin. The weather happened to have been dry for a long time, when it was the season for rice transplanting that required lots of water. Obviously it was one of the strong factors that might lead to a rise of rice prices. But it was simply one of many factors, or rather a superficial one, and Taesu's expectation of a one-hundred jeon profit was not only far-fetched, but overly greedy.

On the day he made the bid to buy through Hyeongbo, he was also using his bank's telephone, which prevented him from talking in detail. Seeing no reason to discuss with Hyeongbo, Taesu simply ordered him to do as he was told.

In about thirty minutes, Hyeongbo called back.

"I bought at forty-five jeon in the fifth session, and the price went up by four jeon again in the sixth session. The trade is at forty-nine jeon now . . . It's your decision to keep it or sell! I'm in the dark."

Hyeongbo was again equivocating on keeping a way open to evading responsibility.

After finishing his bank work at around one o'clock in the afternoon, Taesu inquired into the price, only to find that forty-nine jeon was the peak, and the price had gone down again to forty-six jeon at the end of the morning session. Taesu, however, consoled himself by interpreting that as a temporary reaction to a too rapid rise.

As if mocking his naive expectations, however, the market kept going down until it broke the thirty-won point. Now Taesu is facing a crisis, about to be in *asi*, having almost run out of all of his deposit money.

Near closing time, a stranger came to the bank to cash in the check Taesu talked about earlier. Hyeongbo never handled the matter himself, always having someone do it in his stead. Though Hyeongbo did errands for Taesu, he was always discreet enough not to be involved directly.

Taesu received the check, made a record in his account book, and passed it to the cash window. He didn't need to verify the handwriting of the check, nor compare it with other records, since it was a check he himself had falsified in the name of Baekseok.

When the time was up, Taesu cleared up his desk and left the bank. He was quite annoyed at being unable to overcome his worries. With his forehead deeply wrinkled, he walked so listlessly that someone, in amazement, might have asked him if he was seriously ill.

For Taesu, however, such anxiety never lasted long. He soon recovered his equanimity.

Whatever was at issue, he never mulled over it for long, nor did he allow himself to remain stuck in worries, for he knew well that worries never got him anywhere.

"What's the use of worrying? If the worst comes, death will be an end to it all!" He spat out desperate words to himself.

Since he began embezzling, he'd grown more daring every day. Now he was so reckless that he could envision death as a final resort. Whenever he abandoned himself to such thoughts, he felt quite relieved from his suffocating worries.

His crime was withdrawing someone else's money from the bank, driven by his own bankruptcy.

Since last spring, when he was transferred to the Gunsan branch from the head office in Seoul, Taesu had been indulging in drink and women.

He was handsome and looked like a young man from a well-to-do family. And in this small town a rumor somehow spread that he'd graduated from a junior college in Seoul, and that he was the only son of a widow whose estate yielded an annual crop of more than a thousand bushels of rice. Furthermore, that he was a man who began to work in a bank not for the sake of earning a living, but to idle away his time, and who somehow or other was transferred down to this city. Befitting the man in the rumor, he was easy with his money and well versed at playing the field.

As he had been squandering money like that, within six months, he was up to his neck in debt, too huge to handle with his salary of sixty won a month.

His position at the bank afforded him the opportunity to find a temporary solution to his problem; he enjoyed the total trust of the bank manager because he knew the bank operations inside out, and his position in the checking accounts department made embezzlement very easy for him.

So his embezzlement began last winter when he started to falsify the checks of Mr. Baekseok, a usurer.

Big-scale usurers or big account holders, whose businesses require a frequent inflow and outflow of cash, rarely notice any discrepancy in their account report when a few fake checks of not so great an amount have been cashed without their knowledge. Therefore, if the person in the checking accounts window, who was supposed to detect whether a check was fake or not, let the check pass, it caused no problem for the time being. Taesu knew very well how to take advantage of this secret weak point.

Taesu easily obtained a checkbook, had Baekseok's seal exactly copied, practiced imitating his signature, and finally was able to produce checks that looked no different from those of Baekseok. He gave the fake checks to his supposedly trusted friend, Hyeongbo, who in turn found someone to cash them at the bank. When the check came into the bank, Taesu processed it and passed it to the teller in the cash window, who without any suspicion paid the cash to the person. The money, a little later, returned to Taesu, having passed through Hyeongbo's hands. That's how Taesu played the embezzling game.

At the beginning of his fraudulent career, Taesu did the job with trembling hands and suffered from a violently pounding heart for a few ensuing days. As he grew familiar with such practices, however, he was able to issue the checks whenever required, as if issuing his own checks, and squandered the money as he pleased without any compunction.

He further expanded the target of his fraud, recruiting two more companies for his victims, the "Company for Agricultural Products Promotion," and "Maruna," a big rice exchange broker. It was from those three sources that Taesu had been drawing money for his personal use. During the past half year from around the end of last year, Taesu had embezzled three thousand three hundred won in total, including one thousand eight hundred won from Baekseok's account alone.

Out of the three thousand three hundred won, about four to five hundred won went to Hyeongbo as commission for his assistance in cashing the checks, and the rest was squandered in generous tips for *gisaeng*s, expenses for drinking parties at *gisaeng* houses, and speculative gambling at the rice exchange.

Committing such crimes, he was leading a life as risky as walking on thin ice. Yet the real crisis came around early in April when a rumor had it that Baekseok was having trouble with the bank and thus was considering changing banks. If that happened, Baekseok would take out all his money from the bank, and be bound to notice the missing one thousand eight hundred won in his account. On that day Taesu would be finished.

Taesu would have no option but to run away somewhere, or kill himself as he often said to himself.

If he were indeed the only son of a widow with an annual crop of one thousand bushels of rice, as rumor had it, he could have found a way to survive the crisis. But in fact, the rumor was totally groundless.

His widowed mother lived in a single rented room in the run-down neighborhood of Ahyeon-dong in Seoul, barely managing with the fifteen won Taesu sent her every month.

As a middle-aged poor widow, she had had to do all sorts of menial work such as sewing, laundering, or housemaid's work, in order to send her precious only son to school. But when Taesu finished primary school, she couldn't afford to give him any further education, as she was getting old and weak without any means other than her bare hands.

So Taesu found a job at the 00 Bank as an errand boy as soon as he'd finished primary school. While working at the bank during the daytime, he began to study at a night school as other poor industrious boys did, and graduated from a class B commercial school.

When he was twenty-one years old, he was promoted to being a regular staff member of the bank, thanks to several of his merits. His superiors were fond of him because he was a clever-looking boy who knew how to be useful. In addition, by the time he was twenty-one, he had not only acquired the relevant educational background, even though it was from a class B night school, but also extensive working experience at the bank. In consideration of all these merits, the head of his department assisted him in landing a bank clerk position.

In this new position at the head office of the bank, he worked for two full years. In the meantime, the department head, who had homosexual inclinations, was particularly fond of him and felt sorry for him as his colleagues seemed to look down on him for his past career as an office boy. He was looking out for an opportunity to send Taesu somewhere new, and at last, when an opening in the Gunsan branch became available, he arranged to have Taesu transferred there.

While he was at the head office in Seoul, he was an exemplary bank clerk, well versed in office work, clever and modest in his behavior, abstaining from women and drink, unlike other young men around him.

But he abstained from women and drink, not because he wanted to, but because he had grown accustomed to doing so as an office boy.

Thus when he came down to Gunsan, leaving behind his shadowy background, he became quite elated and self-confident. The first thing he sought out in Gunsan was the sensual pleasure that had been forbidden to him in Seoul. Opportunities to have women and pleasure were as wide open to him as if he were in Shanghai. Like a child who greedily devours candies that have suddenly become available, he gobbled up those profligate pleasures without any restraint.

His mother, having no knowledge of this dark side of her trusted son's life, was anxiously waiting for him to settle down in marriage so that she could come down to join him and comfortably enjoy the remaining days of her life. Such was her situation, and the rumor that she was a wealthy widow with an annual income of a thousand bushels of rice was ludicrous nonsense.

Last April, when his situation became quite desperate due to Baekseok's troubles with the bank, Taesu, after much deliberation, forged another check for six hundred won in the name of "Maruna" to invest in rice speculation.

He'd done this before, though on a smaller scale, three hundred or five hundred bushels and had lost money each time, but it was his first time to try his luck with a thousand bushels.

He had the vain hope that, should he earn a thousand won from this, he might somehow manage to collect one thousand eight hundred won and go to Baekseok to beg forgiveness on his knees, or muster the assistance of that department head from the head office to coax Baekseok not to make an issue of his fraud.

But as it turned out, far from making a profit of a thousand won he was about to lose all his seed money; he was a man who'd lost his net without catching a single crab.

One consolation was that, of late, Baekseok had showed no sign of changing his bank, having less trouble with the bank. But it was only a temporary relief from the imminent danger and there was no question the matter would come up again one day or another to seal his fate. Taesu, with no future to look forward to, was anxious and restless every moment of his day, only relieving himself by muttering,

"It'll all be over if I kill myself."

These magic words revived his spirit for the moment and he threw caution to the wind.

Taesu walked out to the street and hesitated for a moment as to which way to go. He wanted to go to a quiet, cozy café like those in Seoul to sit and daydream. He suddenly longed for such a café though he'd rarely gone to one when he was in Seoul.

Here in Gunsan, however, there were no such clean and cozy cafés. Instead, he considered walking toward the pier or a park, but his body, worn out by his overnight drinking, was not up to it. Then the idea of going to Jejungdang to see Chobong tempted him. When he visited the place yesterday afternoon, Chobong seemed to recognize him as she'd acknowledged on the phone; blushing deeply, she acted a bit awkwardly, at which Taesu was not a little pleased.

Even now, the mere idea of Chobong brought a wide smile to his face. He became unbearably happy by the simple fact that Chobong existed in this world. His final and one remaining desire in life was to marry Chobong and live with her happily even for one or two days. After that, he thought, he would have no lingering desire for life.

He unwittingly headed for the train station.

But recalling that it was only yesterday that he'd dropped by at the pharmacy on the pretense of buying some refreshing lozenges, pomade, and whatnot, he refrained from his desire, for fear that Chobong might show displeasure at his too persistent approaches.

Taesu regretfully turned his steps to Gaebok-dong, near the entrance of which was the house of the *gisaeng*, Haengwha. Her gate was wide open as if ready to welcome anybody. How wonderful it would be if he were so free to go to Chobong's place like this, Taesu thought.

From the inner room, Haengwha's singing voice echoed,

"The su—n is set—tiiing . . .," the voice trilled in a high pitch, ". . . and it's getting dark, alas, not a letter has come, though, ah . . . heh . . ."

The voice reverberated as it ended with a long trailing sound. It sounded so sad that it seemed to evoke all the sorrows of the world.

"Hurrah! . . ."

It was Hyeongbo's voice. He was already there waiting for Taesu. The two men usually met here these days, even when they had no prior appointment.

At the sound of footsteps, Haengwha looked out, and holding up her trailing skirt, stepped out onto the *maru* to welcome him with a smiling face.

As Taesu walked into the room, Hyeongbo, who was lying on a long cushion, affected to raise his head slightly for a greeting.

"Coming now?"

"The weather's so good! I'd like to go to Eunjeok Temple for a change."

Sitting down plump in the middle of the room, without taking off his hat, Taesu muttered as if talking to himself. That idea had been with him for some time now. On such a fine day, it would be nice to go on an outing and make merry, he thought. He couldn't think of any other way to deal with such a melancholy and oppressed state of mind.

"Sounds great!" Hyeongbo chimed in an agreement.

Taesu, however, was silent, thinking of something else. After a while he asked, "What was the closing price?" Though he'd given up on it, he still had some lingering hope that persisted like an obsession notwithstanding his attempts to forget about it.

"Nine jeon . . . It went down to six jeon but rebounded to nine jeon at the end."

Taesu was mute again. Hyeongbo, with his ivory pipe at a jaunty angle in his mouth, which was split all the way to his ears, remained lying on the long cushion, but looked up closely at Taesu's brow that was sloping downward. Hyeongbo's sunken, lustrous eyes were as large as saucers.

Hyeongbo looked even weirder when he was in the bath.

His legs looked like the hind legs of a gorilla, having thick knees and being bow-legged; on top of which sat his short torso with a hump on the back; then there was almost no neck between his torso and head; his hair being shaved off like a monk, his head looked like a big gourd; with this huge head and weird face placed atop such a body, on the whole, he exactly resembled the totem poles of American Indians you see in ethnographic pictures.

Because of such features, he looked over forty, when in fact he was only thirty now. He had no parents, nor any family, had worked here and there, hanging around speculative markets in Incheon, Seoul, or Andonghyeon. He came to Gunsan a little before Taesu, and though they were acquainted with each other in Seoul, it was in Gunsan that they became buddies when Hyeongbo began to act as an intermediary for Taesu's womanizing career.

Taesu, however, considered Hyeongbo to be a trustworthy and intimate friend rather than a mere intermediary and was prepared to stand up for him should things go wrong. On the other hand, Hyeongbo was a friend to Taesu only in appearances. He seemed to concern himself about Taesu, and gave advice to him, but that was only superficial affection.

Hyeongbo and Haengwha too were silent for some time, affected by Taesu's despondent mood. At last Hyeongbo spoke in a serious tone, sitting up abruptly.

"By the way, Taesu, my dear . . .," he began, looking at Taesu intently.

"I have a good way out to suggest. Do you have a mind to do as I suggest?"

"A good way out? Well, I'm not sure . . ."

Taesu understood him to be talking about the plight caused by his embezzlement of bank money, but wasn't very keen to listen to him, as he didn't expect anything short of a miracle could help him.

"What's on your mind, being so indifferent and listless, I wonder?" Hyeongbo began to scold him seeing him uninterested, as if he were quite worried about him.

"I know there's no way out . . .," said Taesu, leaning backward on his two hands, and stretching out his legs. He simply puffed out smoke nonchalantly.

"Then, put aside all your reservations, and do what I tell you to do, all right?"

"How?"

"Now including Baekseok, there're . . ."

As Hyeongbo started to talk, Taesu winked at him. Hyeongbo understood him and looked back at Haengwha.

"Haengwha, I'm sorry, but can you leave us alone and go to the other room for a little while?"

Haengwha, who was trimming her eyebrows in front of her dresser, killing time, stood up, grabbing her towel.

"I was about to go to the bathroom anyway . . . Well, is there going to be something wonderful?"

"Yup, something terrific is sure to come."

"Aha . . . It seems I can expect a treat thanks to you, Jang Jusa . . . But don't forget my share when your something wonderful comes true. You got it?"

"Of course! Even if I forget, there's always Go Jusa who will take care of it!"

"I don't know what that may be, but you two enjoy lots of good something."

Haengwha walked out of the room, mixing laughter with her words.

"Well, there are three clients . . ."

Hyeongbo waited until Haengwha was out of hearing, and resumed talking in a whisper.

". . . From those three, you draw out about three thousand won each, and get ten thousand won in your hands, then I assure you we can set off for something."

Taesu wasn't at all tempted by that and said shaking his head,

"What do you mean to do with that ten thousand won?"

"I mean, you and I go up to Seoul with that ten thousand won . . . And should you feel lonely going up alone, you may take Haengwha along with you."

"Pah!"

"Don't turn it down too hastily, and listen to the end . . . Once we get to Seoul, you seclude yourself in some obscure suburban place, say, for three years, or at the most four years."

"I haven't seen anybody who got away with embezzlement; they were all caught without exception . . . Even those who ran away as far as Shanghai or Beijing were eventually dragged back to Korea, and put in prison. No chance in Seoul!"

"It depends what you do and how you do it. They were caught because they weren't careful. If you lie low and sit tight as if you were a dead man, no one can find you even in ten years."

Taesu shook his head without saying anything. Regardless of whether he was caught or not, it was horrible even to think of being confined for three or four years. It seemed unbearable to him to be unable to go out even for one or two days.

A life without the liberty to go out and be merry, the liberty to spend money as he pleased, such a life seemed to him worse than death. That's why he was determined to choose suicide if things went wrong, rather than go to prison.

Hyeongbo, being unaware of Taesu's desperate mind, continued explaining his so-called project.

"So there's nothing to worry about, you just endure a secluded life for about three years, while I do the business of selling money with the ten thousand won. You get it? It's the business of selling money."

"The business of selling money? What is that?"

"Yup, the business of selling money! . . . It means getting advance interest when you lend money for promissory notes.

I'll explain the details later, but if I take a place in the Jongno area and make that ten thousand won work hard, I can easily make a fortune of forty or fifty thousand won within three or four years!"

"What unrealistic schemes are you talking about?"

"You say that because you don't know the secrets of such a business! Just try it, and you'll see . . . Well, when we have forty or fifty thousand won, you can take back to the bank the thirteen thousand won you stole, and beg for forgiveness on your knees. You know that defeated generals save their necks by begging. Once you return the money and beg, you may avoid imprisonment . . . And then you and I will begin our business again with the remaining money. Wouldn't it be a decent enough life? How would you like it?"

"Well, I know you're saying this as a caring friend. I thank you for that, but I'm not sure, though I'll think it over later . . ."

"Since you understand my good intentions, I tell you it's quite a risky venture for me as well! Should something go wrong, I too would end up being a jailbird, won't I? . . . But I suggest it simply because, as a friend, I can't sit still and watch you suffer in such a predicament. There are enough reasons to be cautious not only for you but for myself as well."

Hyeongbo's pretense that he was willing to put himself in danger for the sake of Taesu was an absolute lie. Moreover, he had no intention of doing as he just said, once the money was in his hands.

Hyeongbo had always cherished two projects in his mind.

The first was that, by whatever means, whether by his own tricks or by taking advantage of someone else, he would get hold of some big money, some tens of thousands or a couple of hundred thousand won, then with the money safely in his hands he would cross the northern border, and escape to China.

He was ready to steal money, even if it was the Queen's own personal money.

His plan was to go to Beijing, then engage in smuggling goods that were in high demand, or to go down to Shanghai, to run either a brothel or a bar, or the two combined.

Two years ago in the winter, he had wandered around China, from Shanghai to Beijing, for about half a year, before he came down to Gunsan. These "business items" were what he had earned through "the knowledge and experience acquired on the spot." Since then, he'd been intent on finding a victim from whom he could swindle about ten thousand won.

The other plan was lawful, unlike the first that would put him in constant danger of being pursued by the police.

That plan was to find and befriend a customer in the exchange who looked naive and easy with his money, and when the time was right, to coax or pressure him to give him the right to speculate on some of the rice, say, five hundred or one thousand bushels, out of his portion of the investment. The atmosphere of the rice exchange was not so hard and cold-hearted yet, people there still had some humane traits, so it wasn't out of the question to find such a simpleton.

Once he got hold of such a gift, he would maneuver it cleverly, selling and buying as the prices changed. If the wind turned in his favor, it wouldn't be that difficult to get his clutches on five or six thousand won.

If he made that much money perhaps within one or two years, he would wash his hands of the exchange, and go to Seoul to begin a money-lending business. He would start with buying small, postdated checks, say, one or two hundred, or at the most, four or five hundred won, taking advance interest for them. If he was prudent enough, he might easily make some tens of thousands of won within ten years. Once he had that much money in hand, he could be assured of being rich for the rest of his life.

Should he stay around the rice exchange too long without seeking a way out, he knew that he would end up joining the club of those numerous *habas*, that is, the penniless pseudo-speculators.

Unlike single-minded speculators, he'd had discretion enough to envision those two escape plans from the exchange, and had been on the lookout for the means to realize them. At such a juncture, he found Taesu deeply entangled in a huge predicament, which seemed to offer him an easy way out from the exchange, if he could manage to take advantage of it adroitly.

Should Taesu listen to him, and draw out ten thousand won, he was planning to grab the money, and take off for Beijing or Shanghai, leaving Taesu behind to face the music as best as he could.

With such fine plans hidden up his sleeves, he'd been waiting for an opportunity to lure Taesu into his plan through deception. To his dismay, however, Taesu seemed not at all interested when he casually mentioned it. When Taesu glossed over the idea, merely uttering kind words, Hyeongbo was so exasperated that he wanted to beat him to death.

You son of a bitch, wait and see what I can do if you keep refusing to listen to me. I'll make you pay for it dearly. This was what Hyeongbo muttered inwardly, harboring a deep, venomous grudge against Taesu.

As the talk was going nowhere, the two men sat glumly in silence when Haengwha entered the room.

"So have you finished enjoying your secret cabal?" said Haengwha, drying her face.

"Well, we have," Hyeongbo answered bluntly, disgruntled.

"Somehow, the air in this room is really bland and no free drinks seem to be coming my way!"

With this comment, Haengwha sat down in front of a mirror and began to put on makeup.

"Have you received an invitation to a party?"

"No, I haven't."

"Then why are you beginning your toilet already?"

"It's my business . . . I should be ready for a call. In case a rickshaw comes to fetch me, I have to be prepared to jump into it promptly! . . . Isn't that the way to earn more money, even if it's only a matter of a few coins?"

"You're really desperate."

While he was chatting with Haengwha, Hyeongbo suddenly recalled something and addressed Taesu,

"By the way, what are you going to do with it?"

He meant the rice Taesu had in the exchange.

"I'll leave it as it is!"

Taesu, who'd kept smoking, at last opened his mouth, which had remained tightly sealed.

"What do you mean, 'leave it as it is?' Isn't fifty or sixty won a big enough sum of money to care about? . . . If you feel that way, why don't you give it to me? . . . I'll handle it this way or that, get some money out of it for my tobacco."

"Tut! Do as you please!"

Seemingly annoyed, Taesu gave his prompt approval. Taesu had been vacillating between the two unwelcome options, whether to sell it or leave it. He wasn't at all inclined to sell it for such a small amount of money, neither did he feel like getting caught up in the enterprise, as Hyeongbo kept nagging him to do this or that.

But neither of them expected that the small remnant of money would be subject to a surprising turnover starting from the next day.

"Thanks a lot, indeed!"

Hyeongbo beamed with delight at Taesu's ready assent. If you look with hindsight into the future, Hyeongbo was right to be delighted, anticipating the surprising fate of Taesu's thousand bushels of rice.

In fact, as the saying goes, gambling is a game for hobgoblins, and the price on the rice exchange went right up by twenty jeon the next day, even before Hyeongbo had any time to sell. Hyeongbo turned it into an opportunity to make some seed money out of Taesu's rice, with which he eventually made a full thousand won within six months. And in one year's time, Hyeongbo had accumulated five or six thousand won, the amount he so earnestly desired to have in his hands in order to start a new career. Such an outcome was something neither Taesu nor Hyeongbo could even have dreamed of at the time.

Hyeongbo, however, never informed Taesu of those developments; Taesu never knew that the price of rice went up by twenty jeon, giving Hyeongbo a profit of two hundred won the very next day, and that the money kept growing as steadily as food piled up by an owl.

But this development was not a matter that could have been imagined that day. It somehow came about the next day, and Hyeongbo was as much in the dark about it as Taesu. Though Hyeongbo was delighted at the assent Taesu gave him, it wasn't because he was expecting such a development. Perhaps you may say that he was possessed by a ghost, and unwittingly led by it to feel delight.

"Hang it all . . . worldly affairs change with the flick of a wrist; life's nothing but a sheet of calibrated paper!"

Hyeongbo, raising his body with a groan, and squatting down again, began to sing the ballad with which speculators used to express their feelings whenever they were happy or despondent. Then he suddenly recalled something.

"My goodness! I've almost forgotten."

Hyeongbo took out a bulging brown envelope from his vest

pocket, and threw it to Taesu. This was the two hundred won cashed at the bank earlier.

". . . It's all there, untouched."

Hyeongbo hadn't forgotten about it, but had kept it, waiting for a chance to take out a few ten-won notes before giving it to him. Now that he'd gotten the remnants of the money left at the exchange from Taesu, he couldn't bring himself to take any money from this envelope as well.

Taesu thought it odd that Hyeongbo gave him the money intact, but took it and opened it.

"Look, Go Jusa, hello?"

Haengwha, who had been busy with her makeup, sitting with her back toward them, turned and accosted Taesu for fun, as he looked so sullen and quiet, though she wasn't seriously worried about him.

"Yes?"

Taesu answered absentmindedly as he was absorbed in counting the money, intending to give one hundred won to Haengwha. He'd slept with her about a week ago, but hadn't had the chance to reward her though he'd been visiting her every day since then.

"Listen to me, Go Jusa-ah!"

"What do you want?"

"Why are you sulking like that? Huh? . . . Is the father of your concubine across the water dead, or what?"

"You slut!"

"Well, the father of your concubine is . . ."

Hyeongbo chimed in,

". . . Isn't he the father of Haengwha?"

"My old man passed away long, long ago . . . he's gone to Heaven!"

"Does the father of a *gisaeng* go to Heaven as well?"

"I don't know! But I think he did. If not, he couldn't have sent me a letter from there, could he?"

"You must've mistaken it when in fact it's from Hell!"

"No, the address was from Heaven. Gosh, what was the street number? . . . It had the street number and was c/o God in Heaven."

"No, it can't be. He must've been called from Hell to Heaven for a short while to undergo investigation!"

"Hey, you, Haengwha . . .?" said Taesu suddenly turning around toward Haengwha.

". . . What would you say if I asked you to go to Heaven with me?"

"Heaven? . . . Why not, let's go together!"

"You mean it?"

"Well, I think you'll have to follow him to Hell instead of Heaven!" Hyeongbo cut in sarcastically, but Haengwha continued her pretense.

"I mean it. I can go with you right this moment."

Both Haengwha and Hyeongbo were making jokes. For Taesu, however, it wasn't at all a joke.

Taesu stared at Haengwha's face intently. His eyes, which usually looked sharp and harsh, were now glittering with a particular luster. At that moment, he was actually seeing Chobong's face while looking at Haengwha's face.

As he talked about going to Heaven with a girl, the words, "lovers' suicide pact" struck his mind, which in turn suggested the idea of "suicide with Chobong."

Though the idea was quite accidental, Taesu felt like slapping his thighs in exuberance, imagining that it might come true in the near future.

Taesu flashed a happy grin, and then suddenly sprang up, shouting loudly,

"Who the hell cares!"

Both Hyeongbo and Haengwha looked up at Taesu in sheer astonishment.

". . . Come on, let's move on. Let's call a cab and take an excursion to Eunjeok Temple," urged Taesu.

"Eunjeok Temple! Good, good!"

Hyeongbo at once welcomed the idea with excitement, and Taesu dropped the hundred-won note he was holding in his hand into the folds of Haengwha's skirt.

"Hurry up, and get dressed!"

"My goodness, what a rush!"

Haengwha put rouge on her lips without paying any attention to the money.

"Quick, hurry up!"

"Seeing you're in such a hurry, I'm sure you'll cry again tonight, Go Jusa."

"What madness! Why would I cry?"

"You'd better say nothing. Who the hell is this girl called Chobong? . . . Who is she? Perhaps, Jang Jusa, you know her?"

"I know of her, but I've never seen the bloody face of that girl."

Haengwha wasn't at all aware that the young woman at Jejungdang Pharmacy was called Chobong. She simply assumed that she must be a *gisaeng*.

"I wish we could call her to come over here today! . . . What sort of a *gisaeng* is she, I wonder, to delude Go Jusa to cry and whatnot like that?"

"Ha, ha, ha, ha."

Hyeongbo laughed loudly at Haengwha's mistake in supposing Chobong to be a *gisaeng* because the name sounded like one.

Taesu, too, put on a sour smile.

"Won't you tell me, Go Jusa? I won't be jealous when I too am a *gisaeng*, and you're a libertine; I can't expect to have you all to myself. But I'm simply curious because Go Jusa was so deluded that he called out the name, 'Chobong, Chobong,' while holding me."

"Stop your small talk!"

"No, no, I won't. You just have to let me have a look at her today. I want to see how she looks by any means."

"I say, stop acting so flighty!"

"My, my! It's the first time anyone called me frivolous in my twenty years of life . . . Anyway, Go Jusa, let's take her with us today. Where does she live?"

"She's not a *gisaeng*. Don't dare to call her that, or . . ."

"Hah, if not a *gisaeng*, is she a whore in a Sinheungdong red house?"

"Impudent slut!"

Taesu made as if to hit her, and Haengwha, giggling loudly, ran to a corner of the room.

"Bravo! Bravo!"

Hyeongbo danced a hunchback dance in his excess of mirth.

Having called for another *gisaeng* for Hyeongbo, the four men and women rode in a car, raising dust all over the street. The car passed through the park and the tunnel, heading for Bulichon.

On the right was the river mouth near the sea, on which a few sailing boats were floating; across the river was Chungcheong Province where dark mountain ridges were rising up, and with the clear blue sky of May hanging over them.

Under the soft sunlight, the boats on the river and the people in the fields looked as though they were dozing off, even though they were moving.

Taesu wasn't much interested in the scenery but recalled that the road also led to the public cemetery. He imagined that in the near future his dead body on a hearse would ride the same road, but not come back as he would today. Thinking about the empty hearse that would come back, he sensed bitter tears welling up in his eyes despite himself.

This sorrowful mood, however, was mingled with a certain pleasant anticipation that he would die and be buried with Chobong, and that it wouldn't be he alone but he together with Chobong, who wouldn't be able to come back.

The party dined with drinks at a restaurant near Eunjeok Temple, and came back downtown after dusk had fallen. There they went to another restaurant to have more drinks and didn't part until nearly two o'clock in the morning.

Taesu drank a lot, trying to get drunk, but his mind was as clear as when he was sober. Only his body was as weary and heavy as wet cotton.

Riding home by taxi, Taesu dropped Haengwha at her home near the entrance of Gaebok-dong. Haengwha urged him to stay at her place since it was so late, but, though inclined to do so, Taesu declined with kind words. He was under an "obligation" not to sleep away from home for many days in a row.

When he got home, hoping that shaggy-faced Han Chambong hadn't gone to his concubine but was staying with his wife, he stealthily pushed open the half-closed gate, passed the front yard unnoticed, and safely got to his room in one corner of the yard. But as he was taking off his jacket, he heard the sound of footsteps, and Madam Kim, the landlady, came into the room with sulking eyes. She abruptly ran into the arms of Taesu and bit his arm with all her might.

Chapter 5:
Chronicle of a Lady's Escapade

TAESU COULD TELL by Madam Kim's behavior that shaggy-faced Han Chambong wasn't at home; obviously he'd gone to his concubine's place. Like a soldier responding to a command, Taesu shouted without any restraint,

"Ouch, ouch, it hurts!"

With this exaggerated scream, Taesu ran off to the far corner of the room.

Madam Kim, having lost her grip on his arm, approached him with rasping breath, while Taesu, cornered and with no retreat, tried to dodge her, holding out his two hands to keep her at a distance.

"I won't do it again, never again . . ."

Taesu begged Madam Kim, acting like a child, and Madam Kim, trying to suppress her erupting laughter, which might cancel out her show of anger, renewed her attack with mouth wide open, saying,

"No, it won't do, no, no."

"I promise I won't do it again. Please, dear, I won't do it again!"

Unable to keep his weary body standing any longer, Taesu let himself flop down onto the floor, and implored Madam Kim's mercy, rubbing his hands together. The more Taesu begged, the more Madam Kim felt the desire to bite him just one more time. Now it wasn't because she still held a grudge against him, but because he was so lovable.

Biting was something Madam Kim very much enjoyed as a way of expressing either her love or her anger. She bit him whenever he looked adorable, or hateful. She didn't affect to bite him, but really bit him, that is, deeply and mercilessly.

When she bit him, she felt a strange, ecstatic pleasure; the tingling sensation inside her mouth spread throughout her body as if it would melt completely. This, for her, was the second greatest pleasure in the world.

So Taesu's body was full of teeth marks, on both of his arms, and on his chest and shoulders.

It had started as a way of settling their arguments quietly, because they had to be cautious about making any noise. Now it had become an essential part of the lovemaking between them.

It had become an enjoyable ritual even for Taesu who had to be bitten, let alone Madam Kim who bit; being bitten was painful enough, but Taesu also got from it a sense of sudden relaxation, the kind of sensation that came with being vigorously massaged.

Madam Kim was attracted to Taesu because he was young and handsome and had many other charming qualities, but on top of all that, she liked him best because she could bite him.

Sometime before, when she was sleeping with her husband who had stayed at home that night, she, out of her habit with Taesu, unwittingly attempted to bite his chest, which after all was not as plump or as firm as Taesu's. Shaggy-faced Han Chambong got scared out of his wits.

"What the hell is this, is this woman mad?"

With this outcry, Han Chambong knuckled her cheek. Ever since that unlucky blunder, Madam Kim had been extremely cautious when in bed with her husband.

At last, Madam Kim, with her mouth wide open, ready to bite, and her head bent forward, began to implore Taesu,

"Ah . . . let me bite you just one more time, please. Ah . . ."

"But I'm in agony!" Taesu complained like a whining child, rubbing the spot that was bitten earlier.

"You've got a crime to pay for, haven't you? . . . Please just one more time, please. Ah . . ."

"No, you can't!"

"You cute thing!"

Like the expert that she was, she swiftly managed to get in a bite at Taesu's shoulder before he realized it. She shuddered with a groan that sounded rather sinister.

"Ouch! This hag is killing me, ouch!"

Taesu pretended to blubber, throwing his body flat on the floor, and rubbed the bitten spot with his palm.

"Does it hurt?"

Madam Kim happily looked down at Taesu's face, and then embraced his head, to place it on her lap.

"Yup, it hurts awfully!"

"My poor thing! Come on, my little boy, I'll rub it with my healing hands, all right?"

She rubbed Taesu's shoulder with her palm, singing,

"Ups-a-daisy, ups-a-daisy . . . come magpie, magpie, it's my baby's birthday . . . Oh, my! What a stink! You had quite a booze-up, didn't you?"

"Umm, a big one, indeed . . ."

"Why do you drink so much when I keep telling you not to!"

"Because I was so vexed!"

"What makes you so vexed? What good do you expect if you drink every time you're vexed? It only harms your body. Shall I bring you a glass of honey and water?"

Taesu shook his head, and closed his eyes slowly.

His face was deeply shaded with anxiety.

While looking down at his face for a while, Madam Kim became infected by his anxiety and assumed the same weary look.

"Perhaps, I think . . ."

With a soft sigh, she began to mumble in a lamenting tone.

". . . I may have to help you get married and settled! Perhaps that's the only way."

"Marry? Bah! What marriage!" Taesu muttered unenthusiastically as if mocking at himself, but after a while added,

". . . if it's to my Chobong, maybe . . ."

"No way, that can't be!"

Madam Kim opposed it outright, changing her expression from that of a kind and amiable woman to that of a venomous and ruthless one.

"Why on earth do you gnash your teeth whenever Chobong is mentioned?"

Taesu, riled, abruptly sat up and cast a reproachful stare at her.

". . . Is Chobong some kind of a family idol you worship?"

"She's far too good for you."

Madam Kim, swiftly changing her expression back to her usual one, before Taesu noticed it, pretended to be dispassionate.

"Then I'll marry Chobong by any means, if only out of spite!" Taesu spat out his determination, and threw his body down onto the floor carelessly.

"Even if I try to thwart it?"

"What a bloody crooked and perverse mind you have! . . .
Tell me, who was it that started talking about our separating,
arguing that our relationship is too risky to continue. Didn't
it come out of your mouth? . . . And who said that I should
get married and settle down in order to reform my life? Who
was it that volunteered to take care of the whole process of my
marriage, from matchmaking to getting the home ready for the
newlyweds?"

"Well, right! I assure you I'll find a bride for you and do
everything to get you married decently!"

"Then why would you try and prevent me from marrying
Chobong when I say I like her so much."

"Chobong won't do! If she marries you, I'll feel really sorry
for her. She's too good a girl to ruin her life by marrying a good-
for-nothing wretch like you. It can't be."

"What bloody gibberish!"

Taesu turned his body toward the wall in protest, fuming
with rage.

No doubt Taesu was entitled to get peevish and angry, but
this conversation made Madam Kim angry with Taesu too. This
anger led Madam Kim to regret that she'd started this relationship at all, which was typical for a woman.

IT WAS IN the summer of last year that Taesu had moved into
her house as a lodger. One of his acquaintances recommended
the place to him; he'd been staying at an inn at the time.

It wasn't that shaggy-faced Han Chambong needed extra
money. They were too well off for that, but Madam Kim
thought, since the extra room was unoccupied anyway, it might
be good to have a respectable man stay there, and mentioned it

in passing to one of her neighbors, who happened to know Taesu had been looking for a family house as lodging.

Though they were total strangers to each other at first, and met as the landlady and the boarder, their relationship soon developed into something more intimate than merely giving and receiving twenty-five won a month.

Taesu was pretty good-looking and affable in personality; he not only called shaggy-faced Han Chambong his uncle, but acted like a good nephew, sometimes bringing home a bottle of good quality sake to drink with Han Chambong at table.

Shaggy-faced Han Chambong, who had no children of his own, took much consolation from Taesu's affectionate behavior. He developed paternal feelings toward Taesu as if he were his son or nephew, and paid much attention to Taesu's meals. That he asked his wife to prepare a special dish of steamed sea bass was only one instance of his growing affection for Taesu.

"The cuckold is the last to know."

As this proverb suggests, he couldn't even dream of the possibility that his wife and Taesu could become lovers, let alone the possibility that an affair was already going on between them.

Women tend to grow attached to someone more easily than men. Madam Kim grew as fond of Taesu in three months as her husband was after one year. As Taesu called her "Auntie, Auntie," behaving so affectionately, Madam Kim, even in less than three months, began to dote on him, treating him like a nephew or a little brother, or even like a son despite his age, and even more tenderly than Han Chambong did.

Things being as such . . .

One night in early October last year, the moonlight was streaming down, it being a full-moon day, and the weather was cool, heralding the coming of winter; it was the kind of night that was apt to evoke melancholic nostalgia in a young man who was away from home.

Taesu didn't come home for supper that evening; he came back after midnight, drunk from a banquet at a *gisaeng* house. The semi-intoxicated Taesu had wanted to spend the night at the home of his favorite *gisaeng*, but somehow or other, he and the *gisaeng* had missed each other, leaving him no other choice but to go home alone.

Taesu walked on tiptoe toward his room because he didn't want to be noticed by shaggy-faced Han Chambong, who, whenever he came home late after drinking, would call him into his room, and, like a good elder in the family, begin a harangue on his intemperance. He would say that though a man can't avoid drinking a few glasses now and then, the habit of drinking too much every so often would indeed be harmful to his health, or something to that effect. In order to avoid such a lecture, Taesu was keeping his steps across the front yard to his room as light as possible, when Madam Kim opened her door and, looking out, said,

"Is that you, Master Go?"

"Yes, it's me . . . Are you still up?"

Taesu was obliged to turn back and step up onto the stone step leading to her room.

Madam Kim, with her long hair down, was looking out with a soft smile, trying to keep the front of her thin nightgown closed with her hand.

Though she knew that her husband's affection for her hadn't changed, she nevertheless was feeling lonely, being a young woman who had to share her husband with a concubine. Especially on such a cool night after the summer heat, feeling the chill seep into her body to the very bone, she couldn't get to sleep and had been fidgeting and tossing about on her bed.

"You're late? How about your supper? Do you want something to eat?"

"No, I've had . . . Is Uncle sleeping?"

"He's gone to the other house."

"Ha, ha, ha. I was afraid of being caught by him because I had a few drinks. I was trying to get to my room as quietly as possible. Ha, ha, ha . . . If he's not home, shall I hang around here a little, before I go to bed?"

Taesu, without any hesitation, walked into her room, passing through the *maru* with long strides.

This was nothing extraordinary or indecent, since he usually enjoyed the liberty of hanging around in the inner room, whether it was day or night, whether Han Chambong was in or not.

Tonight, however, Taesu was not unaffected by the disheveled appearance of Madam Kim, who had just arisen from her bed; he could sense something alluring in her figure. But neither was it the case that he had any particular scheme in his mind. He was simply responding to a sudden urge, an urge to have a little fun, at least at the beginning.

Madam Kim, too, had the same urge. If Taesu had turned back to go to his room, she would have halted him and invited him in for a little chat.

As Taesu entered the room, Madam Kim cleverly affected a start.

"Oh, my goodness!"

With a faked exclamation of consternation, she sat down and slowly pulled the purple coverlet over the lower part of her body, which was thinly clothed with a voile skirt.

"Sorry! I thought you hadn't gone to bed yet."

"No, never mind! Come and sit here. What's there to hide? You know, I'm old enough . . . Have a seat now."

As Taesu was hesitant, seeming to be about to turn back, Madam Kim, as if to force him to sit down, welcomed him with an expression full of delight.

The two exchanged a few words about Taesu's banquet, and then there was an awkward silence for lack of topics, a silence quite new between them.

"I think Master Go, you too . . ." Madam Kim at last found something to talk about, to break the odd silence in the room.

"You need to marry and settle down now! Living like this must be troublesome . . . And how lonely it must be!"

"Well, Auntie! How can I marry when I have no bride?"

"My, my! What do you mean, a young man like you can't marry for having no bride? I'm sure there are countless girls waiting out there for a chance to get at you, or rather, ready to hang themselves on a crossbeam, ho, ho, ho."

"No, I've never come upon one. I won't be able to avoid dying a bachelor, I'm afraid."

"What an ominous thing to say! . . . Do you think I would sit by without doing any matchmaking, when you want to marry?"

"Will you indeed?"

"Why yes, of course!"

"Well then, please look for a good match for me. I'm willing to buy you, not just three glasses, but three hundred glasses of wine, if you do that."

"No problem! . . . But come to think of it, how sorry my husband and I will be, when you move out after you're married. Ho, ho, what am I saying, such a selfish thought! Ha, ha, ha, ha."

"Ha, ha, if that's the problem, I can continue living in the room in the yard after I get married, ha, ha."

"Ho, ho."

Madam Kim laughed along, but soon changing her expression, said wistfully,

". . . Ah, I wish I had a son like you. How wonderful it would . . ."

Madam Kim stopped short, breathing out a deep sigh.

"You'll have one soon enough, I'm sure . . . You're still so young!"

"Am I young . . .?"

She affected to throw a sideways glance at Taesu, and then shook her head.

". . . No matter if I'm young or old; it's not possible anyhow!"

"Why not?"

"My husband isn't quite up to scratch! He's had so many concubines so far, replacing one after another, yet he's got no children at all."

"That's right! It's possible to have no children . . . when the man has a problem . . ."

"So this family seems fated to remain without an heir! . . . Why in hell's name isn't it possible for a woman to reproduce by herself?"

Madam Kim smiled at Taesu sweetly, and Taesu responded with a gentle smile.

Madam Kim, having no children, not only felt desolate, but insecure about her future as well.

She knew that should she end up having no children of her own, while one of his concubines produced a child, whether a boy or a girl, her husband's affection and property would be snatched away from her for the child and its mother, for sure.

When such a day came, she thought, she'd become a woman with no situation to count on. Out of this anxiety, she'd begun to prepare for her old age by saving some money of her own. A few years ago, she'd received a present of five hundred won from her husband, with which she had engaged in a private money-lending business. She now had about one thousand won that would be a good enough prop for her old age, or, so to speak, a cane to lean on when she got old.

The stronger this anxiety grew, the more intense was her desire to conceive a baby. She was desperate enough to do whatever was possible, if there were indeed a way to conceive a baby by herself, as she said earlier.

It wasn't that she'd determined to find another man or to abandon her chastity, about which she felt no moral compunction, but because her thought simply hadn't yet gone that far.

These days, as the affair with Taesu had begun to give her an uneasy conscience, she sometimes repentantly said to herself, "It happened only because I wanted to have a baby of my own." But strictly speaking, it was only an excuse she came up with to deceive herself.

In fact, she began to dream of having a baby from the very next day after she had begun to establish a relationship with Taesu for the first time. It was also true that she was still hopeful of having a baby now. But it wasn't true that she had started that relationship because she wanted a baby. The desire for a baby was an afterthought. Once the relationship started, she began to think that it would be nice to have a baby as a consequence of the affair.

Shaggy-faced Han Chambong always felt sorry toward his wife for his having concubines, though he had the justification that he needed an heir. His wife had lived through the good and bad days with him for fifteen years; they'd endured hardships together until he finally established himself as the owner of this prosperous store.

Her inability to conceive was the only flaw he found in her, and other than that, she was a trustworthy companion who was entitled to command true affection from him.

But Han Chambong, who was thirteen years her senior, was already on the verge of becoming an old man.

On top of that, he mostly slept at his concubine's place, except for three or four days each month, thus he had stopped being an adequate husband for her, even though his affection for her hadn't waned.

Madam Kim, on the other hand, was well aware of the unchanging affection of her husband, who trusted her and made much of her. Having maintained a good relationship with him for half her life, she too had as much affection for him, and was not unaware of her obligations to him.

Therefore, it wasn't that Madam Kim suddenly began to dislike her husband or had any intention of betraying him.

In her mind, it was simply that this was one thing, and the other was something else; she was like someone who was hungry but also tempted to have a bowl of cold noodles for a change besides the main dish.

It was not at all improbable, considering that Madam Kim was rather young. She was even younger in her heart than her age. And Taesu, who was around in the house, calling her "Auntie, Auntie," was so affectionate and treated her so well like a little brother or a nephew or even a son, that she felt confident she could control him as she pleased. Such a dutiful *enfant chéri* who also happened to be a handsome guy, robust in body, full of vigorous charms like a sheepdog.

That sheepdog was now crouching right in front of Madam Kim's lap that night, when she had been sitting alone in her room, with her husband away with his mistress; and the chill air of early autumn precipitated her desire for an embrace. That was the true picture of the dangerous situation she'd been placed in that night.

Her blood was circulating vigorously, making her gasp for breath, when the clock on the wall of the *maru* struck twice.

At the sound of the clock, Taesu thought he should leave, but somehow he couldn't stand up: the amorous ambience that filled the room was too alluring for him to leave.

"Master Go, how about a game of cards?" Madam Kim with much difficulty managed to bring out her suggestion after calming her trembling voice.

"Sure, why not!"

Readily consenting, Taesu stood up, went to the chest of drawers to take out a pack of Korean cards, and then sat close to her, shuffling the cards.

"You must be tired, Master Go?"

"No, I'm fine."

"Then let's play just one round . . . But are we having bets?"

"Yep, that sounds good. What bet shall we have?"

"Well, what do you want? . . . You choose it, Master Go."

"I don't have any preference. Whatever you choose, I'll follow."

"I have no preference either! . . . Come on, Master Go, you decide."

"Then, how about a smack on the wrist?"

"That's too uninteresting!"

"Then, what should it be?"

"Anyhow, we must decide before we start!"

To determine the first player, both picked up a card from the pack, and Taesu said,

"I'm the first . . . well, how about this, the loser must do whatever the winner demands?"

"Good, good. Let's do that. Whatever is demanded, it must be done exactly, right? . . . Master Go, you mustn't try to get away without doing it."

"Never worry about me. I'm the one who may have to urge you to stick to the rule. I hope you'll do as agreed."

The two began to play, but both were uninterested in the game; being bored, they were making mistakes, taking a black bush-clover card for a red one, or miscounting the winning points.

For both of them, it didn't matter who won or who lost; but somehow or other, Taesu turned out to be the loser.

"Now that you've lost, you should do as you're told!"

"Sure, just give the order, I'm ready."

"Let me see . . . What should I make you do?"

"Whatever you feel like . . ."

"I wonder what I should like . . ."

Madam Kim pretended to mull over her choices, and then abruptly blurted out,

"Oh, I don't know!"

With this outcry, she threw herself down on the floor.

"How silly you are!"

"Then, you want to hear what I have in mind . . .?"

Madam Kim suddenly bounced back up, and whispered in Taesu's ear, pulling it to her mouth:

". . . uh-umm, let me have . . . a baby . . ., would you?"

While whispering this, she embraced Taesu's shoulder with her hands.

Ever since that night, their intimate relationship had continued to this day. It had been continuing for eight months now, nearing one year.

Shaggy-faced Han Chambong almost always slept at his concubine's, so deducting the nights Taesu spent with other women, they had about fifteen nights in a month at their disposal, that is, the freedom to be the master and mistress of the house.

The kitchen maid and the servant girl were handsomely paid off for their silence with money or clothes; they knew they should treat Taesu as the master of the house when night came. So the couple was free to act as they pleased. Just as Han Chambong had a kept mistress and was free to go there as he pleased, Madam Kim, too, in the same manner, had Taesu in the house as a gigolo and was free to enjoy Taesu's company.

When Taesu first moved into the house last summer, he had nothing but a set of cheap bedding, an old suitcase, a wicker trunk in his room.

After that, however, his room began to fill with presents from Madam Kim. On the third day, he found a new set of pure silk, fluffy bedding and cushions sitting in his room. Since then, the room began to fill with furniture, starting with a cabinet for clothes, then a desk, then a pier glass mirror, and then even things like an ashtray and a chamber pot.

In addition, there came traditional Korean suits, one for each season, followed by herbal medicine for stamina. Taesu now enjoyed Haetae cigarettes, the top quality brand, keeping the stock in boxes thanks to Madam Kim.

All these luxury goods were purchased by Madam Kim with her own money, but she didn't forget to pretend to her husband that she was doing errands for Taesu, with the money he'd given her.

The boarding charge was agreed at twenty-five won a month at the beginning, but was increased to thirty won to give Madam Kim the pretext of making Taesu's meals more sumptuous. Taesu, however, had paid the boarding charge of twenty-five won only for the first three months; since then neither Taesu nor Madam Kim expected to pay or receive the charge.

In the meantime, Madam Kim contracted a venereal disease from her husband who got it from one of his mistresses, and she, in turn, passed it to Taesu.

Thanks to this unwelcome gift, Taesu suffered tremendously. Though he had medical treatment, the stubborn disease didn't go away completely, recurring whenever he drank too much or took poor care of himself, forcing him to frequent the hospital.

Taesu hadn't yet fulfilled Madam Kim's order given him on the night they had played the card game. Whatever might be the cause, Madam Kim showed no signs of pregnancy yet.

"Perhaps, I'm destined to be childless!" Madam Kim muttered whenever the thought came into her head when in company with Taesu, partly as a complaint, partly as a lament.

Nevertheless, their affection for each other had ripened and grown deeper.

Despite his relationship with Madam Kim, Taesu continued sleeping with *gisaeng*s from time to time. Of late he'd been obsessed with Chobong and was earnestly looking for a way to marry her. Regardless of these other concerns, Taesu was strongly addicted to the sensual enjoyment of Madam Kim, whose attraction to Taesu was even stronger.

No matter how strongly they felt for each other, they tacitly understood the condition attached to their relationship, that it was bound to end one day.

Madam Kim, moreover, was a fairly clever woman; she had no intention of ruining her whole life for the sake of the transient pleasures of an affair.

She was well aware of the inevitable catastrophe that awaited her, if she maintained the relationship with Taesu for too long.

With this anxiety hanging over her, she'd been racking her brain to find a smooth way out of this relationship ever since last March.

Without doubt, it was a matter of great sadness for Madam Kim to think of separating from Taesu. At times she was tempted to keep going until she had a baby, as she was already involved.

Last March had marked the sixth month since the affair started. If she couldn't conceive, despite what she'd been doing for the last six months, it wasn't very likely she would, even if she prolonged the affair. On top of that, her dread was growing more intense day by day, as she was fully aware of the probability that the longer she cheated on her husband, the higher the chance of being caught, and the more imminent her disaster.

Once the dread grabbed hold of her, she indeed became fearful and anxiety-ridden, even to the extent of thinking it unbelievable that she had been so carefree and unworried about their affair so far. Moreover, even if there were no such danger for the time being, it was certain that there was no possibility of keeping Taesu beside her for the rest of her life. In that case, Madam Kim thought, it might be better to stop the affair right now.

Despite such thoughts, Madam Kim couldn't easily bring herself to act on what she had determined. Her next thought was to get him married to someone, which might be an easier way for her to be detached from him. When she conveyed this idea to Taesu, however, he simply turned it down with a snort, saying that he had no intention at all of getting married, though he'd go along with her resolution to get separated, if the situation demanded it.

So the D-day kept being postponed, until the following incident.

It happened in early April, that is, about one and a half months ago. That afternoon, Taesu was having an idle conversation with shaggy-faced Han Chambong in his rice store, having come back from the bank, when a young girl who looked like a student passed by the store. Taesu was at once struck by her graceful appearance despite her simple clothing. She was indeed dressed rather poorly; though she was wearing a mid-length skirt, with her hair coiled up neatly, her rubber shoes and traditional socks gave the impression that she might be a girl working at a factory or a rice mill.

Taesu thought, if so, it was a great pity for such a pretty girl. While he was staring at her, deep in enchantment, the girl saw shaggy-faced Han Chambong and greeted him with a low bow.

It was Chobong.

"Hi! How's your father? Is he well?"

Shaggy-faced Han Chambong responded to her greeting in a rather familiar manner.

"Y-yes."

Her soft voice was almost inaudible, but Taesu, looking at the sweet smile that spread across her mouth, almost felt like fainting, thrown into a sudden paroxysm of admiration.

No sooner was Chobong out of sight, than Taesu hurriedly asked Han Chambong with a gasp,

"Who is she, please?"

"Why?"

Han Chambong gave him a meaningful smile.

". . . Well, she's the daughter of one of my acquaintances who lives in Dunbaemi over the other side of the hill . . . I heard that she's been working at Jejungdang Pharmacy downtown since graduating from school . . . So, do you fancy her?"

Under his shaggy mustache, he smiled a rather insidious smile.

"No, no. I'm just . . ."

Taesu scratched the back of his head, feeling embarrassed at his forwardness.

"Ah, hmm, I see that you like her, don't you? . . . She certainly looks smart and clever. If you like her so much, why don't you ask my wife to act as a go-between? Just say that she's the eldest daughter of Jeong Jusa over at Dunbaemi. She should know her better than I do."

"No, Uncle, don't bother."

From that night on, Taesu kept harassing Madam Kim; he claimed that although he'd been indifferent to marriage so far, he now really wanted to marry soon, and beseeched her to act as matchmaker for him and Chobong.

Surprised at Taesu's sudden change of attitude, especially at the name of Chobong, Madam Kim was overcome by an abrupt eruption of jealousy; she was at a loss as to what to do, as her body trembled wildly, and her vision darkened completely.

It was true that she herself had suggested that Taesu should marry, and had even volunteered to find a decent bride and to engineer the whole process of his marriage. While she was offering such services, she'd never felt even a shred of jealousy. She now realized that it was possible only because the bride was then an abstract concept, not yet having materialized into an actual person.

Now that Chobong, a living girl, whom she knew very well, whom she hadn't seen since last year, and who had looked so neat and pretty then, was about to snatch her beloved Taesu away from her, jealousy stoked her fire and was about to engulf her with its flames. She kept this feeling hidden from Taesu, however, and made an excuse to refuse his entreaties by saying that Chobong was far too good for him.

But in the end, she was forced to change her mind.

Chapter 6:
A Small Enterprise

GAEBOK-DONG IS A slum area where small huts cluster together like fish-scales. Atop a steep slope sits a low mud cottage.

Myeongnim's family was renting this house, which had only two rooms, at five won a month, subletting one room to pockmarked Meokgombo and his family at two won a month.

In this small house, the total surface area of which was only twenty-four square yards, were living six people, three in the main room, and another three in the second room.

In the second room now, neither Meokgombo nor his wife was visible. A one-year-old sick baby was lying on the warmest part of the floor and at the other end was sitting an exorcist chanting verses to drive out the demons causing its illness.

The warm *ondol* floor was overheated with too much firewood and the stale stink of poverty filled the room, heated up by the warm air.

The baby had been suffering from whooping cough for a long time, and had been reduced to a mere skeleton, with a face as pale as a candle and lips scorched black. In addition to the whooping cough, the baby was now also suffering from pneumonia.

Its tightly closed eyes and motionless limbs suggested that the angel of death had already arrived and was about to shroud him in its pall. Its life was barely hanging on by a thread, its chest heaving up and down rapidly and gasping for breath. Perhaps its life had only seconds left rather than minutes.

Facing the wall, the exorcist, fully dressed in traditional garb, wearing a top hat made of horsehair and a long cotton coat, was intent on reading the chants in a quite detached manner, sitting on the floor with his legs folded.

In front of him was a small table with its corners chipped away, serving as a ritual altar. On it were offerings, consisting of a bowl of steamed rice, a dish of cooked bean sprouts, a dish with a few chestnuts, jujubes and dried persimmons, and three dried pollacks. In addition to these, there were also two one-won notes, about two measures of rice, three folded sheets of white paper for burning, and a bowl in which a one-jeon candle was burning. And on the floor next to the table were three pairs of loosely knit straw shoes. These offerings meant that the ghosts haunting the sick baby should eat the food, put on the straw shoes, and set off to a faraway place using the money for their travel expenses.

The exorcist, sitting in front of the table with the offerings, rather solemnly read out his chants, beating his drum at the same time; the low beat of the drum echoed, and his chant, keeping pace with the beat of the drum, went on and on in a subdued and trailing voice.

"For—the son—of Mr. Jeong Gweon—family—on a—hilltop—in Gunsan city—Jeolla Bukdo—Ko—rea—Far East—and..."

Blah, blah, blah, blah . . . he rambled on for a while and then, clearing his throat after a pause, began to address the guardian deities in a dignified voice.

"Spirits of the generals who each guard the five directions, south, north, west, east, and center . . ."

And then speeding up both his drumming and chanting, he began to summon all kinds of ghosts, perhaps all the ghosts in the world he could think of. Not only were their class and status varied, but their stories too were diverse, amusing, and popular. Perhaps the exorcist was well versed in matters of the modern world as he even evoked "the ghost of the one who drowned himself while on a date on the railroad bridge over the Han-gang River."

As the ghosts he summoned were so numerous, enough to form a legion, the offerings on the table seemed preposterously little if they were all truly to respond to his summons. They might very well have engaged in a bloody battle to get their hands on what little food lay on the table first. Ghosts are, however, known to be invisible, so there was no blood-spattered spectacle to watch.

After summoning up this legion of ghosts, he suddenly raised both his drumbeat and his voice to the highest pitch, with his buttocks rising and falling, thrashing his arms up and down, and began to scold them severely.

"You unfortunate ghosts! . . . Hasten to take the offerings, and leave the baby this very moment. Unless you obey this command instantly, I'll have the spirits of the guardian generals seize you all and exile you to a far, far away region, tens of thousands of leagues away, absolutely forbidding you ever to come near, even simply to smell the soy sauce . . . and to all eternity . . ." The exorcist's biting commands poured forth like thunder.

Having thus finished one chapter of his ponderous incantation, the exorcist was about to resume it from the beginning. Just then Meokgombo's wife rushed in through the wood-paneled gate of the hut, gasping for breath, followed by Seungjae with his worn-out doctor's bag, and Myeongnim.

Even when they entered the room, the exorcist paid no attention to them and kept on reciting.

"My poor baby, Eopdong!"

Meokgombo's wife ran to the baby, and crouching down to embrace it, looked at its face.

The little baby showed no reaction whatsoever, no opening of its eyes, no trembling of its lips, not even a wiggle of its fingertips, all remained cold and pale.

Seungjae could tell at once what to expect, but nevertheless he approached the baby, donning his stethoscope, when the mother, opening her eyes wide, shouted in panic,

"Oh, heavens! He must be dead!"

Seungjae opened the baby's shirt and listened with the stethoscope; the pulse was gone, a faint gurgling sound was barely audible. Seungjae, taking away his stethoscope, sat back with a deep frown on his forehead.

"I'm sure it's still alive . . . come, my baby, take a suck at your mom. Oh, my God, what's to be done! Please doctor, do something, for God's sake!"

"It's no use. He's already dead!"

If Seungjae had been attentive to the pity he felt for the mother, who seemed beside herself in desperate grief, he might have injected a stimulant into the baby's heart. It would have been useless, but at least it might have given the mother a few less regrets. But he refrained from doing that, as he knew it was better to stay passive in such cases than take useless measures driven by pity, because that would certainly get him mixed up in nasty trouble later.

When he had first started his charity practice, he went wherever he was called for, and didn't hesitate to give emergency shots even to patients who were almost dead, regardless of their efficacy, if the family hung on to him pleading. In most such cases, it was too late to do anything for the dying patient. The shots prolonged their life for just a short while, but soon the effect of the drug wore off, causing the patient to succumb. When things turned out like that, the family changed their attitude, and claimed that it was Seungjae's fault that the patient died. Sometimes they even pursued him to his house, using violence and threatening him.

The worst had been about a month and a half ago; the family of the deceased grabbed Seungjae by the collar and dragged him to the police station. He was held in a police cell that night and was released the next morning only when Dr. Yun, his employer, came over to help him. But it wasn't a discharge, he was booked for interrogation without physical detention.

Although the charge was eventually dropped, as he was proven innocent, that experience taught him a valuable lesson, that until he was in possession of his full medical license, he should try to avoid visiting critical and hopeless patients, and if he was forced to visit them, he should take care not to administer any medical treatment to hopeless cases.

That day he went home from the hospital around seven o'clock in the evening and found Meokgombo's wife and Myeongnim waiting for him. Myeongnim had come along to help her neighbor find his house.

The wife explained that her baby, who'd been suffering from whooping cough for some time, had begun to experience complications about three or four days ago; it was suffering from extreme shortness of breath, barely breathing, its throat often clogged-up by mucus. Seungjae knew that things went irrevocably wrong. He didn't want to involve himself in this case, but being unable to close his ears to her repeated tearful imploring, he reluctantly came long.

When he entered the house, he felt aversion to the performance the exorcist was putting on. And then when he saw the baby already dead, he was angry at the mother rather than taking pity on her, as he thought she could have saved the baby's life had she come to him two days earlier, instead of making such a fuss with this exorcist.

"But still, isn't it possible to do what's called . . ."

Meokgombo's wife touched the body of the baby again, calling its name and begged Seungjae earnestly.

"Is it called shots or injections? I heard that you gave a shot and revived the dead. Can't you do that, please?"

"It's too late now."

"But still, people say those shots give life back, isn't that true? Please, save its life, please! . . . How can I let it die, oh, my goodness, how can I . . . For heaven's sake, try to do something please . . ."

"I told you, it's no use!" he replied bluntly, annoyed at their astonishment.

". . . Why didn't you come to me earlier? See what you've done. You've given your child an untimely death . . . I'm sure he can't be saved even if the Chinese 'Divine Doctor' Bian Que were to come here right now."

Fueled by anger, Seungjae lashed out at the mother, and picking up his bag, he left the room.

Meokgombo's wife clutched the dead body of her baby to her bosom and began to wail, lamenting her hard fate.

The exorcist, in the meantime, was still absorbed in his chanting, maintaining his posture quite detached from the commotion around him, as if he wouldn't budge even if the sky fell down on him.

"Stop that damn chanting or whatever that cursed nonsense is!" Meokgombo's wife thundered at the exorcist.

"Eh . . .?"

The exorcist immediately stopped his chanting and turned his head toward the mother, showing that he was in fact conscious of what was going on around him despite his utterly detached appearance. He must have been pretending to be absorbed in his chanting.

"I'll stop if you say so!" he bluntly responded, snatching up his drumstick and standing up. Then mumbling something to himself, he collected the offerings on the table, including the money, and placed them into his shoulder bag.

". . . We're all born to die at a destined time! That's beyond human control. Tut-tut!"

"What about getting your hands tied behind your back and being damned? Is that destined too? . . . If life and death is a matter of fate, why did you lure me into believing my child would be cured if you did the chanting, eh?"

Meokgombo's wife was bawling at the top of her voice, and Seungjae, hearing the shouts trailing behind him, left the house with a grave face.

Seungjae was already repenting his hardness toward the mother; he could have given an injection whether it was useless or not, the injection the mother so desperately desired for her dead son. Perhaps he should have given in to her plea, even if he would have to risk whatever might happen to him later, since it might have given some consolation to the mother who was despairing in her grief.

Seungjae had begun to recognize that these poor people were doing their best to save their children as much as any other parents; what they did determined whether the child lived or died, but their fault lay not in indifference or lack of care, but in their ignorance. Through this experience, he confirmed that ignorance contributed to people's misery as much as poverty; people indeed were in need of food, but at the same, they needed to acquire an adequate level of knowledge as well.

With that conclusion, Seungjae nodded as if reassuring himself.

Seungjae, who was left an orphan at the age of four and raised by a distant relative, who was almost a stranger to him, could claim that his life had been unfortunate. But the hardships that dotted his path of life so far had been rather simple.

He had rarely had any opportunity to be exposed to "the world," let alone the necessity to grapple with the complications of human emotions or conflicts in life; he had had almost no occasion even to observe such complications in his surroundings.

Having spent most of his life in a clinic, he'd dealt only with sick people, and his contact with them had been primarily clinical. He observed them through various clinical instruments: thermometers, stethoscopes, x-ray machines, or by checking their pulses; and when he determined the nature of their troubles, he wrote prescriptions and gave them injections and medicines.

He surely knew that disease was one of the great causes of human unhappiness, but his thought went no farther. For him life meant physiological life, which existed as a separate entity, without being entangled in a web of human relationships.

However, since he moved to Gunsan, he began to see life in a new, more comprehensive way.

While he'd been in Seoul under the old master, he'd rarely seen patients who were turned back for having no money; but at the Geumho clinic in Gunsan, he witnessed such scenes often.

He sometimes even cried when faced with such scenes. Being well aware of the severe pain of disease, he became infuriated at the world, in some corners of which a certain group of people were denied access to basic medical services, when they desperately needed them.

One day he saw a girl, whose face and chin were greatly swollen because of an inflammation of the sublingual gland, walk into the clinic, led by a middle-aged laborer, who seemed to be her father. The man asked the receptionist how much the charge might be, and learning that the charge would be more than ten won, the father and daughter turned back without a word, and walked out in dismay.

They were Myeongnim and her father, Mr. Yang. Unlike other poor people, who begged for free treatment or pleaded to be allowed to pay later, giving their assurances that they would pay when they earned some money, the father and daughter simply asked the charge then walked out. Greatly touched by the quietly retreating father and sick daughter, who seemed so crestfallen and disconsolate, Seungjae hastily followed them to the door of the clinic and asked their address.

In the evening, Seungjae borrowed a few basic surgical instruments and medicines from the clinic, went straight to Myeongnim's house, and performed surgery on her. He was at that time already living at a boarding house, having moved out of the room in the clinic, so was free to do as he pleased in the evening. Prompted by Myeongnim's case, he purchased some basic equipment and medicines and started a small enterprise as a doctor ready to respond to emergency calls at night. He provided his services without receiving any money, while supplying drugs out of his own pocket though he'd been poor even before beginning such an enterprise.

Seungjae thought of this as a private enterprise that rewarded him with some sense of satisfaction and joy. Other than that, he expected nothing more, being devoid of any vanity to attach any serious meaning to it or to see it as something that would contribute to his self-esteem.

He continued his night work with this selfless attitude, but this evening he was immensely annoyed by the preposterously stupid people who, instead of seeking reasonable assistance, drove their little baby to premature death by resorting to the superstitious practice of hiring an exorcist. That outburst of anger he'd directed at Meokgombo's wife was something quite unprecedented in his experience.

However, as he came to realize that this stupidity was the result of their ignorance rather than the lack of a caring mind, he began to suspect that even if there were charity hospitals on every street corner, they'd be of no use so long as people remained ignorant. He indeed felt helpless in the face of that ignorance, as if he'd bumped into a gigantic obstacle while pursuing a way of his own.

As this thought began to weigh heavily on him, he seemed to lose all the excitement and enthusiasm he'd enjoyed in his enterprise.

When he walked out of the gate of the house in this dispirited mood, there, right outside the gate was Myeongnim, waiting for him.

"Oh, you've been waiting here?"

Despite his distracted frame of mind, Seungjae was glad to see Myeongnim.

"As I couldn't see you in the room, I wondered where you'd gone. Both your mother and father seem not to be at home."

"Right . . ."

With a shy smile, she stretched out her hand toward him.

". . . Give that to me please. Let me carry it for you."

Myeongnim felt very grateful to her "esteemed Master Nam, sir," who always doted on her, doing many kind and considerate things for her. She was happy to see him in her house and really wanted to carry the bag for him. Seungjae, at first, tried to decline, but knowing her mind, soon gave in and passed the bag to her.

"Then, just until we get down there, all right? . . ."

"All right." Happy with the chance to do a small service for her dear Master Nam, sir, Myeongnim trotted down the steep hill ahead of Seungjae.

"Is your father out to work?"

"Yes."

"How about your mom?"

"She's gone out to do some laundry work."

"Then you must be having a few meals these days?"

"Yes . . . luckily we are . . . but we don't have lunch. Still, I don't want to have lunch, I'm not hungry at all." Myeongnim added this last bit in anticipation of what Seungjae would say next.

"What do you mean you don't want lunch! You're hungry, aren't you? . . . The days are so long lately."

"Still I'm not hungry."

"Shall I buy you your favorite Chinese dumplings? Shall I have them delivered to your house?"

"No, don't bother, please! I'm fine!"

Myeongnim, however, stopped walking and with a delighted look, turned back toward Seungjae.

Seungjae said Chinese dumplings because he suddenly recalled a scene from the past. After operating on Myeongnim, Seungjae visited her house every day for treatment; one day, when she was almost cured, he happened to see her being scolded by her parents for having pestered them to buy her some Chinese dumplings. It was only natural for a child who was going through the recovery stage to desire some nutritious food.

Seungjae quietly left the house and went to a Chinese restaurant, to order three dumpling dishes to be delivered to her. The next day when he went to Myeongnim's again, the whole family was full of gratitude. But Myeongnim's happy look especially made him beam with delight.

After she was fully recovered, Myeongnim often visited Seungjae's place to take home his dirty underwear, and socks. She almost forced him to give them to her and returned them clean and tidy after she and her mother together washed them and mended where necessary. This service was the only way for them to express their gratitude.

Seungjae, well aware of their motive, gradually began to accept their services, appreciating their simple but kind hearts. He in turn found a way to express his affection for them; he often dropped by at their house and enjoyed the opportunity of leaving some money for rice if there seemed to be no signs of cooking in the house. From time to time he even bought some fabric for Myeongnim, with which her mother made clothes for her, like a yellow top or a blue skirt.

Seungjae doted on her for being a smart and amiable girl, but above all she was his agent of pure joy. He attached this particular feeling to her, because she was the very first patient of his small enterprise. Of course Seungjae had had many patients at the clinic, some of whom were critically ill, poised between life and death, and who were saved through his efforts. But Seungjae had tremendous joy when he succeeded in performing the operation on Myeongnim and then saw her completely recovered afterward, despite the fact that her case wasn't serious, nor was the operation at all complicated. The joy he tasted in this case was incomparably greater than for any patient he'd cured in the clinic.

Thus Myeongnim stood for a particular joy for Seungjae; but on the other hand, she was also the cause of some grief to him, that is, since he'd learned that her parents were intending to give her away to a *gisaeng* as a foster daughter.

Whenever he got to thinking about her future as a girl selling her body, he fell into a deep grief, feeling anxious for her as if she were his little sister. Ever since he learned about this prospect for her life, whenever he met her, he couldn't help but be overwhelmed with sorrow, while smiling with the pleasure of meeting her.

Because of this situation, Myeongnim became an example of harsh reality through which Seungjae examined the nature of human life as well as a mirror in which the world was reflected. It had been this way for Seungjae so far, and surely it would be so in the future.

Seungjae unconsciously sighed as he watched her back recede into the distance, walking down the slope ahead of him.

"She's thirteen already!"

With her long hair fluttering down her back, her features seemed to suggest she would soon reach adolescence. Noticing that the child had grown so plump and healthy, his anxiety too grew almost unbearable.

"Hey, Myeongnim?"

Myeongnim looked back at him swiftly in response.

"Are your parents still urging you to go to, well, you know, um! . . . to that place?" Seungjae asked hesitantly, feeling awkward to name the place. "That place" referred to the *gisaeng* house to which Myeongnim was destined to be sold.

"Yes . . . But . . .," Myeongnim answered in a faint voice, lowering her head.

"Well . . . but what?"

"I told them I don't want to."

"So . . . what did they say?"

"Then they said I can wait until I grow a bit older."

"Did you say no because you still want to suck at your mom's breast?"

"No, no! Oh my goodness . . ."

But Myeongnim took it as a joke and said,

"You want to tease me, don't you?"

"No, I'm not teasing you, but . . ."

"Nevertheless, I'm not sure how I can live in a stranger's house; I'd miss my mom very badly."

"Then, do you think you wouldn't miss your mom when you grow a bit older?"

"They say I won't. Mom says I won't, and Papa says the same . . . So they say I should go there when I grow a bit older."

"Humph, when you grow older!" Seungjae muttered to himself, looking into the distance.

Seungjae saw an analogy between Myeongnim's situation and that of piglets and calves; country folk wait until their young cattle grow old enough to be weaned before they sell them, because, if not, they would make a lot of trouble, refusing to be taken away from their mother.

What difference is there between such country folk and Myeongnim's parents? One set of folks waits for their baby cattle to grow a bit older, when they can run around on their own and feed themselves, counting the days before selling them at the market, while the other set waits for their daughter to grow a bit older, when she no longer misses or needs her parents, when she's a bit taller and her breasts are a bit rounder, counting the days before selling her to a *gisaeng* house as a foster daughter.

With a scowl on his face, Seungjae coughed as if something was blocking his throat, and spat before realizing it.

Soon after, however, Seungjae recalled the mild and good-natured faces of her parents, and his anger at such vile practices was transformed into a deep pity for them.

Seungjae sent Myeongnim back to her house and, going via the Bean Sprout Pass, he returned to his room at Chobong's.

He could hear the clatter of spoons from the main room; perhaps they were having their supper now. As he entered his room, he found a bowl of warm water neatly placed just over the threshold of the door.

As Gyebong often boasted, this bowl of rice water for the night might indeed be the precious drop of life.

Though not at all thirsty, Seungjae picked up the bowl and drank the water in one gulp. He felt he'd drunk not a bowl of water, but a bowl of happiness because it had come from Chobong.

The next morning . . .

Seungjae got up from his desk, where he'd been reading a new book, *Studies of the Stratosphere*, for some time. Seven-thirty was the time for him to go to the clinic. When he got there, he would clean up the place and have his breakfast. And then it would be eight-thirty, the time for him to be ready for patients in the consulting room.

Seungjae, wearing an old felt hat, as was his habit, was sitting on the small wooden deck attached to his room, when loud shouts came from outside the gate.

Paying no attention to the noises, Seungjae walked across the yard to the gate when, all of a sudden, Meokgombo rushed in, wildly pushing the unlocked gate open.

Seungjae halted, realizing that trouble lay ahead. He recognized Meokgombo as he'd visited Myeongnim's house frequently. He was also well aware of Meokgombo's reputation as a badly behaved drunkard, as well as an aggressive and quarrelsome street fighter.

Behind Meokgombo was his wife, and a couple of passersby were peeping in through the open gate, their curiosity roused by Meokgombo's shouting.

"There you are, you scoundrel!"

No sooner had he spotted Seungjae, than Meokgombo, shouting wildly like an angry bull, with his eyes goggling, ran at Seungjae like a swift arrow, and grabbed him by the collar, lifting him up into the air.

With his eyes rolling wildly in his head, Meokgombo pressed his dark, pockmarked face into Seungjae's face. To Seungjae, Meokgombo's face, like that of a rotten fish, made even darker by excessive drink and frenzy, was more abominable than his threatening words.

Seungjae was amazed; he couldn't have anticipated such a rough and violent attack from Meokgombo. While Seungjae was thus taken aback and bewildered, Meokgombo, grasping his collar with one hand, slapped him on the face with the other, shouting,

"You rascal!"

Seungjae, rather than feeling pain, merely became much more embarrassed and confused.

"Oh, my goodness! What's he doing!" Gyebong, who was stepping down from the maru to go to school, saw the scene and cried in astonishment, stamping her feet.

All her family members ran out of the room to see what was going on.

"Listen, you rascal!"

Without budging an inch as the Jeong family came crowding out, Meokgombo began to enumerate Seungjae's crimes.

". . . You rascal, you think you're somebody because you carry needles in your bag! How dare you abandon my dying son, when you claim you know something about medical practice! Not even giving a dose of medicine, mercilessly refusing to give a shot when my wife begged and begged . . . You drove my son to death, how dare you! . . . you shameless wretch!"

Grinding his teeth, Meokgombo once again slapped Seungjae across his cheek with full force.

Seungjae simply stared at him, at a loss as to what to say in the face of such stunning ignominy.

Then Meokgombo's wife slowly walked toward her husband, and holding his arm, pretended to dissuade him from violence, saying that he should try to settle things by conversation. But her manner and facial expression suggested that she was gloating over the slaps on Seungjae's face.

Jeong Jusa, dragging his shoes, belatedly rushed to the scene and roared,

"What the hell is this violence . . . Off with your damn hands, take them off right this instant!"

Meokgombo glanced at Jeong Jusa, sizing him up, and then not at all impressed by his shabby appearance, contemptuously replied,

"Who's this person? Stepping in where he's not wanted!"

Madam Yu and Chobong were too scared to do anything but tremble. As for Gyebong, she looked around as if searching for something, and ran into the kitchen.

". . . You rascal, let's go to the police station right now. I'll have them teach you how fearful the law is."

Meokgombo tried to drag Seungjae toward the gate, roaring loudly. Just then, with a whack, Meokgombo's side was struck with a piece of firewood. It was Gyebong.

Gyebong, clenching her teeth, was about to strike Meokgombo again, this time aiming at his arms, when Jeong Jusa, scared out of his wits, grabbed her hands and pushed her aside, rebuking her for her audacity.

More passersby gathered around the gate, a few of them sneaking inside the gate to watch the spectacle.

Jeong Jusa, who didn't dare to fight, only repeated his threatening shouts, keeping his distance from Meokgombo, whereas Gyebong, overcome by indignation, spitting angry, stared furiously at the man.

"Tut, tut, what the hell is this!"

Seungjae at last looked back at the spectators, and after giving an awkward smile to no one in particular, suddenly grabbed Meokgombo's wrist that was tightly holding his collar and twisted it roughly.

Unable to withstand the sudden counter-attack, Meokgombo

instantly released his grip. Both were strapping young men, but Seungjae was especially sturdy and brawny whereas Meokgombo was boozed up, so he was no match for Seungjae.

Seungjae alternated his glance between Meokgombo's twisted wrist and his face, and then pushed him toward his wife.

". . . You take him away! . . . Was it me that killed your baby? It was the two of you who killed the baby."

On being pushed, Meokgombo almost fell down, but with great difficulty managed to keep his balance and shouted,

"Come on, you rascal, how dare you hit me, when you're the one who did wrong, not us! What a shameless rascal you are to hit me . . ."

Meokgombo staggered up, ready to resume his attack, plucking at Seungjae's nerves with his nonsensical cries, but his wife held him back, embracing him from behind. At that moment Myeongnim's father, Mr. Yang, ran into the yard, gasping for breath, followed by Myeongnim.

"Are you out of your mind? How dare you make a scene here?"

Mr. Yang severely reprimanded Meokgombo and pushed him roughly toward the gate.

"Oh, elder brother!"

"Stop wheedling with that damn brother business and get out this instant! You listen to me, and if not . . ."

Mr. Yang once again pushed Meokgombo away from Seungjae and then, approaching Seungjae, attempted to make a plea on Meokgombo's behalf; he entreated Seungjae to ignore him and forget the foolish things the wretch was doing, saying that Meokgombo was a drunken dog who'd gone mad after losing his only son. Mr. Yang, however, only spoke for Meokgombo because he didn't know that Seungjae had been slapped twice in addition to being grabbed around the collar.

Without mincing words, Seungjae readily acquiesced to Mr. Yang's request and suggested he should take Meokgombo home.

Meokgombo no longer attempted to go for Seungjae, but he continued swearing at him while endeavoring to control his staggering body.

"Damn you. You, who claim to be a medical man, you are less than a man; how was it possible to turn your head away when my son was dying? Moreover, you rascal, you even dared to scold my wife for not seeking help earlier, how dare you? Damn you, you deserve to be beheaded. Before the devils take you, bring my son back to life, you scoundrel!"

"Eopdong's dad is falsely placing blame on him, when in fact there's nothing to accuse him of . . ."

Myeongnim, who'd been trying to speak for some time, at last interceded, her face flushed hot with anger, speaking loudly for all the others to hear.

". . . The baby's condition was absolutely hopeless; he wasn't breathing at all. How can you expect an injection to bring a dead baby back to life? . . . If he gave a shot to the dead body, wouldn't he be rather subject to a wrongful accusation, as if he'd really killed the baby? . . . Don't forget that there were witnesses, if you persist in blaming someone unjustly. I mean it . . ."

Jeong Jusa had expected as much as that, but as he became clearer about the actual state of affairs from Myeongnim's eloquent account, his indignation at Meokgombo grew more intense.

What infuriated Jeong Jusa more than anything was the contemptuous bullying Meokgombo had exhibited earlier. The more he thought about that, the more upset he was. Now that Meokgombo's spirit seemed to have calmed a bit, Jeong Jusa's spirit began to puff up.

"What a vile man that is!"

Blinking his eyes and stroking his yellow beard, Jeong Jusa

began to reprimand him severely in a dignified voice.

". . . It's not as if he was doing it to receive any money; you know he was doing it purely out of sympathy. You should be grateful he came over to your place at all. If he didn't touch the baby, it must have been because he knew full well that nothing could be done . . . You ungrateful vile man! . . . Even though you're one of those reckless racketeers, what you did was way beyond what such men do."

The severity of Jeong Jusa's reprimand seemed likely to be followed by a strong action, but he simply stamped his feet.

Seungjae and Mr. Yang, standing aside, were conversing with one another. Seungjae was giving Mr. Yang an account of what he'd gone through the night before, while Mr. Yang was giving Seungjae an account of Meokgombo's pitiful situation of having repeatedly lost his babies within a year of their birth. The baby that died last night he had got when he was over forty and after repeated misfortunes, thus to him it was more precious than all the treasures in the world. It was only natural that Meokgombo had lost his mind and gone mad when he lost the baby, who might very well be the last child he could ever have. And it looked like his wife had given him quite a distorted report, aggravating his fury. Mr. Yang, with these words, was begging Seungjae to close his eyes to Meokgombo's outrage and provocation.

Meokgombo, totally exhausted now, collapsed to the ground; sitting there with his legs outstretched, he continued mumbling inarticulate words.

Jeong Jusa began to talk about Seungjae's past troubles, partly intending the spectators to hear, saying that Seungjae had been embroiled in similar cases a few times, and had even been arrested by police once, although he was soon released because he hadn't done anything wrong, but was only doing what was right and praiseworthy.

He then turned to Meokgombo and began a new round of rebukes.

"You, unworthy man, you must thank Heaven that he's an extremely gentle and mild-natured man. If he had even one drop of hot temper, you would have been in deadly trouble! . . . And if I were younger, I would have taken a stick to you on his behalf, and thrashed your bottom at least thirty times, to teach you to give up that outrageous behavior of yours. No decent man would ever imagine abandoning himself to such madness! Wicked, wicked man! . . . Get out of my place this instant!"

Jeong Jusa roared out his final command, stroking his scanty yellow beard to embellish his dignified posture.

His thundering command, however, didn't have much effect on the "wicked man," who, nevertheless, supported by his wife and Mr. Yang on each side, was dragged out through the two-pillar gate. Chobong, in relief, smoothed her hand over her heaving chest.

Gyebong, however, was quite annoyed on seeing the "wicked man" leaving the house without being punished, or as her father suggested, without being thrashed as he deserved.

"That rascal, I won't let him . . .," she looked around, hissing with burning anger and, picking up the piece of firewood once again, started to head for the gate.

"You slut!"

Jeong Jusa snatched the firewood from Gyebong and threw it to the kitchen.

". . . What vulgarity! Behaving like a slut with no breeding!"

"But how can I let the wretch go free . . . the wretch who beat up our Master Nam . . ."

Unable to contain her exploding anger, Gyebong stamped her feet wildly, and large tears began to run down her cheeks. At last, noticing that Seungjae had picked up his hat off the ground and was shaking the dirt off, she rushed to him and punched his chest repeatedly with her clenched fists, as though she were pounding starched clothes on a fulling block. At the same time she poured out her dissatisfaction with him.

"You fool! Master Nam is a fool. How is it possible you let the wretch slap you in the face, and not just once but twice, and still not do anything? . . . Why did you do that? Why? . . . Oh, I'm so upset! I hate Master Nam!"

Although she stepped back after this exclamation, she still squirmed with vexation.

Jeong Jusa and his wife, looking at each other, smiled away their daughter's show of fury. Chobong, who shared Gyebong's sense of indignation, felt rather relieved by her sister's outburst, and dropped her head as tears welled up in her eyes. Seungjae too was touched. He even felt like patting Gyebong on her back as her behavior was so endearing, like that of a little sister who was upset for her big brother.

"Never mind! What's the big deal if I was beaten a bit. It didn't hurt at all. You must hurry, get going to school now, huh?"

"It's not a matter of getting hurt or not! You know that . . .," Gyebong snapped at him, wiping away her tears with her fist.

Chapter 7:
Piles of Money Out There

"I WILL NEVER so much as set one foot inside that damn place again. Wait and see, damned place!"

Feeling hatred toward the exchange market out of a sense of shame and embarrassment, Jeong Jusa spat out that curse, shooting a sullen glare at the place as he left. But it was only a momentary resolve. He went back there again the very next day, and then he kept going there day in and day out, and as usual, gambled, speculating though he had not a penny in his pocket, or strolled around, peeping into this corner and that. That day too he'd been there all day long, and on his way home, he decided to drop by at shaggy-faced Han Chambong's rice store.

Unless he had the awkward business of asking for some rice on credit, Jeong Jusa usually avoided the store by taking a detour, to prevent being seen by Han Chambong and being asked to pay his old debts. But today, he mustered up his courage to visit the store on a special errand.

Chobong and her mother were bustling about in preparation for her departure for Seoul, which was scheduled for the next day; they were busy making new clothes or buying necessary things and suchlike. As for her going to Seoul, he could stop it if he had a mind to exercise his authority as her father and the master of the family (so Jeong Jusa believed); but rather than quarrel with the mother and the daughter, it might be easier if he came across a decent man to whom he might marry her off, he thought. With such a convenient excuse, he should be able to dissuade her easily from going to Seoul; but more than anything else, he really wanted a marriage that would bring a breakthrough for him in many ways. Remembering that Madam Kim had been so eager to find a match for Chobong the other day, he decided to stop by at the rice store to see how things were moving on. And he wasn't disappointed . . .

Madam Kim, who happened to be in the store, greeted him with a welcoming smile and told him that she'd visited his home earlier that day and discussed the matter with his wife, and that she'd been waiting for him in case he happened to pass by, to have a face-to-face discussion with him about Chobong's marriage.

At the mention of Go Taesu of the Gunsan branch of the 00 Bank, Jeong Jusa recalled the assistance Taesu had rendered him when he was being harassed in front of the exchange a few days ago. He couldn't help but flush deeply; on the other hand, he thought it might be the work of providence that the very man who'd been so kind to him should reappear now as a candidate for his daughter's hand.

"So, Mr. Go has been . . .," Madam Kim chattered away like a sparrow, "Mr. Go has been boarding at my house for nearly a year now; the more I see of him, the more I find him to be well mannered and gentle. I think it would be hard these days to find another young man like him!"

"Yes, I also find him quite decent and he seems so well-bred." Jeong Jusa recalled the amiable features of the young man who'd been so obliging to him and readily agreed with Madam Kim.

"He also said you were acquainted with each other. When I mentioned your name, he said that though he hadn't had the opportunity to be introduced to you, he'd seen you a few times and he knows who you are."

"Anyway, I wonder where he's from originally."

"I heard he's from Seoul. He's the only son of a widow, and he's of noble birth. He has a house with a lofty gate in Seoul and his mother's a lady who does nothing but order her servants to do this or that in and out of the house . . . That's what I heard. His family fortune seems to be well over one thousand bushels of harvest rice . . . So his monthly salary only goes toward the expenses for his cigarettes, and he receives money every month from his mother to cover his other expenses. I've often seen the money order delivered to him. And his work at the bank, from what I've heard, is a kind of pastime, as well as a means to learn something before he begins his own business . . . But I've never heard about these things from his own mouth. These stories are what I've heard in bits and pieces from his friends."

"So how old is he? Is he about twenty-six or -seven?"

"He's twenty-six . . .; that is, born in the year of Eulsa, the year of the snake. From what I've heard, he graduated from a junior college in Seoul the year before last and began to work for the bank, at the Seoul office, and was transferred to the Gunsan branch last year."

"I see," he answered rather absentmindedly as his thoughts wandered elsewhere.

When he was from such a good family and pretty good-looking as well, why was he still unmarried at the age of twenty-six? As is usual with young men these days, wasn't it possible that he already had a wife back in Seoul or was divorced, and wished to have a new wife again?

Those suspicions arose in his mind, and he felt like asking Madam Kim about these possibilities.

But he soon dismissed those suspicions. He was too fearful to ask in case they might prove to be true.

There's no way that can be true . . . Of course it isn't possible, Jeong Jusa told himself silently, pushing away those suspicions. Yet traces of doubt lingered in a corner of his mind. So he tried to rid himself of those suspicions for the time being by arguing within himself that, "although I'm on familiar terms with the matchmaker, it would certainly transgress the code of honor if I asked such frank questions . . . Eventually, I might be able to probe into the facts some other way."

"Well, well . . ."

Jeong Jusa at last began to express his opinions to Madam Kim, saying that he appeared to be a smart man, and judging from what Madam Kim said about him, he must be well educated and come from a good, well-to-do family. And since he believed everything she said about him, he would have no objection to the match. And then he added, starting with a however,

". . . However, as you know well enough, my financial situation is so strained that I'm not sure how I can take up such an excellent offer of marriage. Indeed I'm at a loss as to what to do! Huh, huh . . ."

Sensing that everything was going according to his wishes, Jeong Jusa expressed this reservation to see how Madam Kim would respond. But once again, Madam Kim said exactly what he desired to hear, as if she'd been waiting for the opportunity.

"Sure, sure, Jeong Jusa, as a matter of fact, I was about to talk about that . . . You needn't worry about it. I've already informed him of your difficult situation and he doesn't care about it at all. As he doesn't want to be a burden to you, he says, he'd be pleased to take care of all the wedding expenses . . . Can't you see how wise and considerate he is? Ho, ho."

"Huh, huh. It can never be so! Even if I have to fast for several days to make money, it can't be so . . ."

Contrary to his remarks, Jeong Jusa was so happy about the way things were going that his lips were curving into a smile despite him. It seemed too good to be true.

"What! You seem to be too scrupulous about appearances, Jeong Jusa!"

A bright smile spread over her face. Madam Kim urged Jeong Jusa not to worry about such formalities and resumed talking, to give him an outline of what he could expect:

The wedding ceremony will take place at a church or community center following the modern fashion; the reception too will be at a big restaurant; so Jeong Jusa's family needn't prepare any food, not even a bowl of noodles; Taesu says his mother has given him full license to become his own master not only in choosing the bride, but in arranging the ceremony also; his mother will come down only on the wedding day. Being the only son of a wealthy widow, he's been allowed to do everything as he pleased ever since childhood, so it's only natural that his mother allows him to do as he likes in the matter of marriage too. Therefore, Taesu has asked his uncle (Han Chambong) and auntie (Madam Kim) to take care of all the wedding arrangements. So, as far as the marriage proceedings are concerned, it has been left to the two families (Mr. Han's and Mr. Jeong's) to consult and decide between them.

So it seemed the wedding would proceed easily and smoothly.

"In addition . . .," Madam Kim lowered her voice as though she was about to give some inside information and whispered to him in a conspiratorial manner,

"I may not need to talk about it now, as you will find out about it by and by. But perhaps I may as well give you a hint in advance. This is what he said while talking about paying all the wedding expenses; he was really sorry to hear that you had so many difficulties in everyday life. He became quite concerned about your having no ready money, even if you wanted to start something new. So eventually he said that once the wedding ceremony was over, he would find an occasion to offer you some money, to set you up to start some business! . . . I was amazed at his thoughtfulness! So considerate at his age! My, my . . ."

Jeong Jusa, who had been listening in silence to her sweet talk so far, found himself unable to remain calm and composed any longer; he felt so tickled all over with joy that he longed to jump up and dance in excitement or express his joy through a loud peal of laughter.

Shaggy-faced Han Chambong had been busy selling rice on the other side of the store, but now that the store had become quiet, he came toward them, clapping his hands to shake off the rice dust.

"Jeong Jusa, I think you'd better accept that marriage offer. He appears to me a worthy young man too . . . though at times he's inclined to drink, it seems . . ."

Shaggy-faced Han Chambong recommended this marriage not because he wanted Taesu married, nor because he felt like a father with the prospect of gaining a daughter-in-law. He was rather an upright man, who didn't like to beat around the bush or make up stories. He simply recommended that Jeong Jusa should accept the offer while at the same time talking frankly about Taesu.

"What do you mean? When and where did he take to drinking, for God's sake!"

Madam Kim seemed really upset at her husband's remark and strongly reprimanded him.

"Hunh, I don't understand why you react like that."

"It's because you're talking nonsense!"

"When he drinks, I should say he does drink. And moreover, is it such a big deal if a young man enjoys a few drinks occasionally? I don't think Jeong Jusa would mind that. Am I not right, Jeong Jusa? . . ."

"Oh, well . . ."

"No, Jeong Jusa . . . I know he doesn't enjoy drinking. I've never seen him drinking."

"Well, whether he drinks or not, it's . . ."

"But I say he doesn't drink!"

"I saw him drinking!"

"When was that?"

"Ah, I saw him the other night walking in an alley off Jangjae-dong rather drunk."

Jeong Jusa left shaggy-faced Han Chambong's rice store, thinking that he wouldn't mind one bit even if (in fact) Taesu drank a hundred barrels of wine.

Before he left, he gave Madam Kim his word that he would let her know his decision as soon as he'd discussed the matter with his wife, as well as finding out what Chobong herself thought about it.

But he only said this out of courtesy; he in fact didn't care at all what his wife or Chobong would think.

He rather wanted the matter settled that very instant, on the spot, if he could.

Instead of consulting his wife, he wanted to tell her outright the moment he got home, "Come, dear, everything's worked out perfectly; let's get them married. Let's tell them to have the letter from the groom's family for the bride's family prepared, and we should choose the lucky day for the wedding right now. Bring the calendar here." He wanted to have it settled quickly, without any delay.

He saw no reason to hesitate or to feel uneasy about it. As for his wife, since Madam Kim said she seemed favorably inclined toward the match when she'd visited her earlier, there'd be nothing to worry about. He had some doubts about his daughter's response, the person directly concerned, but he was also confident that she wouldn't oppose him even if she wanted to. Chobong had been an obedient girl all along, who did what her parents asked her to do regardless of whether she liked it or not.

On top of that, he wasn't going to impose an unworthy man as a spouse on her; what a top-notch bridegroom Go Taesu would make!

"On the contrary, he would rather be overqualified for her."

When Madam Kim first brought up the name of Go Taesu as a match for Chobong, he had a very vague image of him in his mind; none of those excellent qualifications, which he now had in a very clear form, had been attached to the image then.

As Madam Kim chattered away, one story after another, the picture of Taesu began to bloom. It was like a faint painting on a canvas that grew into a distinct portrait as the painter added colors, shades, and lines with his brush.

The image of Taesu underwent a magical transformation in Jeong Jusa's mind; the initial vague image turned into something quite clear and bright when he was identified as a graduate of a junior college, and then the image was completed in perfect beauty when his intention to give some seed money to Jeong Jusa was revealed.

Jeong Jusa felt that he was dreaming; how fortuitous for him was each aspect of Go Taesu's qualifications as a bridegroom! Where had he been hiding all this time, to pop out so suddenly when he really needed him! Taesu seemed like a man made-to-order for Jeong Jusa.

Once he'd made up his mind to accept Taesu as his son-in-law, he began to consider Taesu's qualifications once again like an examiner who puts a red tick next to each positive item.

Well, the result was full of red ticks.

He skipped over and ignored everything that might be shady about him, such as the reckless glint around his eyes, a somewhat snobbish and impudent trait in his manners, and above all the possibility that he might intend to commit bigamy, or to take part in a flawed marriage.

Having put only red ticks next to the items on the exam paper, Jeong Jusa was jubilant about his good luck in finding a candidate with full marks, disregarding how and by whom the red ticks were given out.

Parents are usually delighted when they see good grades on their child's report card, despite their knowledge that he's really no good at all in studies. This might be understandable viewed as the foolishness of loving parents. Jeong Jusa, however, couldn't claim even that for an excuse, as his foolishness wasn't activated by his love for his daughter.

Nevertheless, Jeong Jusa, exuberant with happy prospects, was clambering up the Bean Sprout Pass. It was only a few days ago on this very pass that he'd fantasized about Chobong's marriage and its subsequent benefits for him. Now that the fantasy was about to turn into reality, almost exactly as he'd dreamt, the idea that this pass might have some magical power struck him, causing him to look at it afresh.

"Let's see, when I get hold of the money . . .," Jeong Jusa leisurely deliberated on how he would use the money, walking slowly toward his house.

How much would he give me? About five hundred won? Five hundred won would be either too little or too much to find an appropriate business for myself . . . Perhaps he'd manage to offer me a thousand won. Or, who knows, he may even turn out to be so generous as to offer a few thousand won.

But what type of business should I start? . . . a rice retailer? . . . a textile merchant? . . . a general merchandiser? . . . No, these businesses would have too little profit margin . . .

How about jumping straight into rice exchange speculation? I may make a fortune out of that.

No, no. I shouldn't do that. If I slip and fail, I would completely lose face. Not only that, this is a rare chance, one for which I've waited a long, long time; no, I shouldn't do anything imprudent with it.

Then what should I do? How can I find the sort of business that's easy and smooth to run, but brings in a good enough profit?

Chobong wasn't back from work yet. Gyebong and Hyeongju were sent away to the other room. Byeongju, the youngest, had fallen fast asleep in the room soon after his supper. Jeong Jusa and his wife, sitting face-to-face alone in the room, were intent on discussing Chobong's marriage.

"Ah, I saw him a couple of times at Han Chambong's house," Madam Yu added abruptly while ironing a collar she'd attached to a voile blouse for a customer.

"He appeared to be smart and clever, but his eyes were somewhat strained, giving the impression of a stern man."

"No, I don't think he has the eyes of a stern man . . . If you pick up faults like that, dear, you'd better look for a custom-made son-in-law. I wonder how you can . . ."

Jeong Jusa seemed quite at ease and relaxed, sitting with his legs crossed, rocking his upper body right and left, poking at the gaps between his bare toes with his fingers, and blinking his eyes. His wife, following suit after him, added,

"I didn't mean to say such eyes should be taken as a fault. I just said his eyes looked hard. That's all . . . Anyway, I too thought he was pretty good."

"Of course he's very good! More than good enough . . . By the way, from what I hear, he seems to enjoy drinking now and then?"

This time, Jeong Jusa pretended to find fault with him, at which Madam Yu hurriedly jumped in to defend Taesu, as if the couple were obliged to take turns in their roles.

"What silly things you say! . . . Where can you find a young man who doesn't enjoy drinking? It's rare to find one out of a hundred these days. As a matter of fact, it's quite all right for youngsters to enjoy a few drinks. It's no problem unless they drink too much."

"Come to think of it, you're quite right. I think it's better for a young man to enjoy a few drinks with his friends; such socializing would help him advance in the world. Surely that's better than keeping to himself, staying sober and sullen all the time."

"That's exactly what I mean."

Then Madam Yu began to criticize her husband, after giving him a sidelong glance over her reading glasses.

"So you just realized that now? . . . Where on earth is there a man as sullen and gutless as you are? You've never been bold enough even to think about having a few drinks; you always take care to remain sober and petty, too much concerned with small things, and now what's the result? See, you've ended up as wretched as can be."

Jeong Jusa had no words to respond to her, so he let out a loud, empty laugh, and then with the fingers that had been poking between his toes, he began instead to twist his ungainly mustache upward on both sides. But it kept falling down, unable to attain the posture of the Kaiser mustache.

"Ah, by the way! . . . That lad . . ."

Jeong Jusa brought out another story in order to get away from his sense of embarrassment. Curiously he was already calling him "that lad," a term of endearment.

"That lad has known our Chobong since early spring! . . . He's been madly in love with her ever since, and desperately sought ways to get near her! Huh, huh."

"These days it seems young men usually marry the woman they fall in love with. They want to date before they marry. But our Chobong is a solid, modest girl, never allowing men to approach her. I know she's never even glanced at a young man. Anyway, there's one thing I can never understand—how come his mother allows him to do everything he pleases! Although they say, those so-called fashionable, enlightened families tend to do so . . ."

"Oh dear, can't you see that it's not at all unusual? . . . Being the only son of a widow, from a well-to-do family, he must've been raised to indulge all of his whims. Isn't that the reason why he's still unmarried? He must've insisted that he'd marry only when he found the right woman. Accustomed to his stubbornness, his family may have given way to him, saying, 'Tut! I don't care. Do as you wish, but hurry up and find a bride and get married.' Isn't that the way it stands? Doesn't it make sense to you?"

Both wife and husband were reluctant to touch on topics about Taesu's personality or any shady aspects of his life that might make them have reservations about the marriage. And if such topics happened to be mentioned, both of them were eager to cover them up or to justify them from Taesu's point of view. It was as if they were afraid to touch inflamed abscesses for fear of aggravating them and making things worse.

The truth was that they would never be so bold or reckless as to plot a scheme to sacrifice one of their daughters in order to secure a livelihood for the rest of the family. Schemes, for instance, such as giving a daughter to a rich man as a concubine, or worse, making her a *gisaeng*, or selling her to a brothel, those things were beyond them.

They had their own sort of moral refinement, however shabby and run-down it had become. By force of habit, they were bound to it, and so long as they were under its influence, they daren't be as honest as animals; instead, they had to be cunning and sly, in the mode typical of humankind.

Having been enticed by this good fortune, a seemingly good fortune that would open up the door to financial security, if only they could marry off Chobong to Taesu, they couldn't afford to entertain any doubts about Taesu. They evaded the parental duty of standing back a little to examine whether this marriage might not bring miseries upon their daughter, or to confirm Madam Kim's stories by investigating here and there until their doubts and reservations were all cleared up. They had to be evasive because they were frightened of the possibility that once their doubts turned out to be facts, they wouldn't dare proceed with the marriage.

They thus pretended that they could smell nothing fishy when in fact their nostrils were besieged by bad odors. If one happened to say,

"Doesn't it smell a bit stale?"

The other would promptly come up with a reassuring reply,

"No, not at all, it smells rather savory to me!"

If one of them again pointed out,

"But somehow it smells a little rotten, I think!"

The other would rebuke such unreasonable doubts in a rage,

"What a fuss! It's only fragrant to me!"

Thanks to their cautious ploy and self-deception, wife and husband reached perfect agreement to proceed with the marriage.

Picking up the socks lying on the floor and putting them on again to go out to the drug store down the hill, Jeong Jusa gave instructions to his wife: when Chobong came home, she should let her know that they would never allow her to go to Seoul, and then tell her about the marriage offer, to find out how she felt about it.

"They say even sages follow current trends. Isn't it the done thing to ask the person concerned how she feels about it?"

With this concluding comment, Jeong Jusa stood up, ready to go out, having finished tying up the bottom of his traditional-style trousers.

"Well, when you say we should ask her opinion, is it because you have a mind to give up on the idea of the marriage if Chobong says no?" Madam Yu asked as if it was merely a passing joke, but in fact she had a mind to test his conscience. And perhaps she blurted out this cynical remark because she too felt a deep compunction.

"What reason would there be for her to say no, when she knows nothing of the world? . . . She should trust her father and mother and know that we must have chosen the best man for her spouse."

"Then what's the point of me asking her about her opinion?"

"Such a chatty woman! . . . Just ask her, and if she likes it, that will be superb, nothing more to wish for. But if she seems displeased, it's your job to talk her into complying, isn't it?"

"Don't you worry, I'll do the job well enough without your prompting. You're the one who was chatty first . . . Anyway, just get going to where you need to go."

Jeong Jusa walked out of the room, amused by his wife's retort.

Just then the sound of the gate was heard. Madam Yu listened carefully, expecting it might be Chobong, but instead heard the voice of Seungjae exchanging greetings with Jeong Jusa.

"Ah, Seungjae! I almost forgot about him!" Madam Yu suddenly said to herself for some reason.

She'd noticed for some time now that Chobong had unusual feelings toward Seungjae.

That wasn't the only reason though. She'd also been watching him carefully as a candidate for Chobong's spouse. She liked him especially because he was extremely compassionate, warm and good-natured, though he was rather taciturn and seemingly blunt. Once she got to like him, everything else about him looked favorable to her.

His grave, taciturn disposition made him appear more dependable and trustworthy in her eyes. He was very poor at present, but she'd heard that he would become a fully licensed doctor in autumn next year, at the latest. When that happened, she was sure that he would make a lot of money and become capable of living well, proving eligible to take her daughter as his bride.

There was, however, one reservation about him; he had neither parents nor relatives, being a man adrift in the world like a piece of radish kimchi. His obscure family background was something that kept bothering her, like a flaw in a piece of beautiful jade.

But they say, there's always a way out when one is desperate. As was the case with Madam Yu; she was able to find a way to ease her mind, by adopting the commonplace sayings that surrounded her.

"In this modern world, what signifies whether one has a good family background or not?"

"What on earth is the essential distinction between gentry and commoner these days?"

"Money and ability alone determine whether one is gentry or not."

Armed with such logic, which catered to her own convenience, Madam Yu gave a favorable verdict to Seungjae despite his obscure origin.

It wasn't that she had already determined to take Seungjae as her son-in-law in the autumn of next year. She just kept eyeing him as a potential good candidate for Chobong's hand.

Unlike Madam Yu, Jeong Jusa had never thought of Seungjae in that capacity.

He was not unaware of Seungjae's good qualities; he had had many opportunities to observe Seungjae's very gentle and compassionate heart, lying hidden under his crude appearance, as well as his being very discreet and prudent both in words and behavior.

For all that, what Jeong Jusa saw before him was the shabby and poor Seungjae, who fell far short of his expectations regarding a son-in-law. Perhaps Jeong Jusa might change his mind if Seungjae were to transform into a totally different man, when he became a fully licensed doctor, wearing nice clothes, making a lot of money, but Seungjae as he was now would never strike him as a suitable candidate.

Jeong Jusa didn't even try to imagine the successful, prosperous Seungjae of the future, as his wife did.

Therefore, if by any chance Jeong Jusa noticed that Chobong had more than usual feelings toward Seungjae, or if his wife had tried to see his reaction, suggesting Seungjae as a proper candidate for Chobong, he would certainly have jumped with anger, shouting,

"What an absurd idea that is! How dare you even consider marrying the daughter of our decent family to such a low-class nobody? Who knows what his ancestors were up to?" Twisting up his yellow mustache, he would bark at his wife with many callous and dismissive words, although he would eventually end up being showered with as many hard words himself by his wife.

Madam Yu, who well knew her husband's character, had never given him even a remote intimation of her sentiments, and kept her thoughts strictly to herself until now.

Then that day, out of nowhere, a new candidate suddenly emerged in the shape of handsome Go Taesu, carrying a heavenly wedding gift.

Madam Yu was instantly enamored of Taesu's outward appearance as well as that lavish wedding gift promised to them. She had no time to recall Seungjae in order to weigh him up in comparison to Taesu, but simply cast her vote in favor of Taesu, considering him the sole candidate.

Seungjae hadn't come to mind until she heard his voice greeting Jeong Jusa. Once Seungjae entered her mind, Madam Yu began to compare the two young men as if they were a pair of rainbows. Soon it turned out that Taesu was the brighter and more distinct rainbow up front, whereas Seungjae remained the dim and vague rainbow in the background. Or to put it another way, the manner in which people used to distinguish a double rainbow, Taesu was like the daughter-in-law rainbow in front, and Seungjae was like the mother-in-law rainbow in the background. The comparison didn't require much debate within herself. A smile stole over her face as she was quite satisfied with the verdict, in which Taesu far outshone Seungjae.

But at the same time she wasn't devoid of a sense of regret at losing such a young man, whom all along she had considered to be a decent, promising contender for Chobong's hand.

This sense of regret, however, was soon replaced by a desire to reserve him as Gyebong's spouse. Seungjae was twenty-five, a bit too old for Gyebong, but an eight-year difference seemed to her not to signify much. So she determined to keep him around and watch for the future, feeling satisfied with the good luck that allowed her to settle for two sons-in-law in one night.

It was around nine o'clock when Chobong came home.

Madam Yu was quite astonished at how she looked.

"Are you ill?"

Her sunken eyes, pale face, and colorless lips made her mother quite uneasy.

"No," Chobong gave a short answer, but her voice was very weak and faint. She sat down on the floor, seeming about to collapse.

Madam Yu stopped her needlework and looked at her anxiously.

"Are you really not ill? . . . Hyeongju brought you your supper, didn't he? You had it?"

"Yes, I did."

"You look exhausted because you've been working late and got hungry, haven't you?"

"No, I'm not hungry."

"Then, why is your face so pale? . . . You must be ill? I'm sure you're not well!"

"Aw, Mom, I'm all right."

Chobong tried to force herself to smile, but it didn't look like a smile at all.

". . . What makes you so concerned, Mom? I'm fine, nothing's wrong with me."

"What do you mean 'nothing's wrong?' You really look like someone who has a serious disease . . . Just tell me if you're not feeling well! I'll get some medicine . . ."

"Seriously, Mom, I'm not sick. I told you nothing's wrong with me."

Chobong frowned a little, as if feeling annoyed.

When she left home early in the morning, she had been merry and full of energy.

She had told her mother that the pharmacy would be passed over to the new owner in the evening, and tomorrow she would rest at home all day, and then the next day she would take a night train to go to Seoul. Though she hadn't been talkative, being always a prudent girl, it had been obvious that she was quite happy and excited at the prospect of her new life in Seoul.

For these last few days, whenever she had a chance to be alone with her mother, she kept asking her to intercede with her father and persuade him not to stop her going to Seoul.

This morning again, she called her mother to the kitchen and asked the same favor. And when her mother said not to worry, she was beaming with a happy smile, covering it with her hand as she left for work.

As Chobong, who'd been as merry as can be in the morning, returned in the evening with a dismal, dejected face, Madam Yu naturally assumed that she must be very ill.

But, after examining her face for a little while, Madam Yu could see that it wasn't sickness that troubled her, as Chobong had told her, but some sort of anxiety or disappointment that was affecting her.

Madam Yu now began to suspect that Chobong might have encountered some problem that would prevent her from going to Seoul. She knew that it wasn't possible for her daughter to have obtained any information about what had been going on at home . . . Then she must have come upon some trouble . . . What could it be? . . . With such puzzles floating in her head, Madam Yu quietly kept on with her needlework.

Chobong, who'd remained silent for some time, abruptly said,

"Mother, I won't be able to go to Seoul, as it happens!"

She said this as if she were passing on someone else's unpleasant news.

"Uh? Why?"

Though Madam Yu had already guessed as much, she assumed a surprised look. While affecting surprise, she was in fact very pleased with the news, which would make her task easier.

Madam Yu, who'd been supportive of Chobong's plan to go to Seoul up until this morning, even assuring her not to worry about her father, had been not a little embarrassed with the necessity to persuade her to give it up. To contradict one's own words within a single day was quite an awkward job even between mother and daughter, no matter how justifiable it might be.

So the news that Chobong's plan to go to Seoul had miscarried even before her intervention was quite a relief to Madam Yu, without a doubt.

Chobong sat blankly for a while, forgetful of both what she had said and what her mother said. At last she reluctantly opened her mouth.

"Uncle says I shouldn't come to Seoul."

"You mean Bak Jeho?"

"Yes."

"Why? On what account?"

Chobong did not answer, but kept her head down.

"What on earth is this . . .?"

Madam Yu furiously began to blame Bak Jeho.

". . . Wasn't it Jeho himself who began the plan, and asked you to come along with him? Now he tells you not to come, what kind of damn caprice is that? . . . Where can you find another story as ludicrous as that?"

Madam Yu, who was supposed to make Chobong quit her plan, had no reason to get angry, but had many reasons to be thankful. However, quitting a job was one thing, and being forced to quit was another. The more she thought about it, the more she got angry at Jeho for his unreasonable behavior.

What kind of a man is he, who, after coaxing Chobong with sweet talk to prepare this and that for her move to Seoul, now furtively takes back his words, asking her not to come? He is indeed a vile man, who made her daughter so disheartened and sick at heart. Those thoughts were searing Madam Yu's mind.

If she hadn't already made up her mind not to send her to Seoul, she would have run to Jeho with her fists clenched, and vented her fury at him, demanding him to admit who was right and who was wrong. Considering her temper, she could very well have done that.

In fact, Madam Yu still felt that temptation off and on, while observing Chobong's pitiful state. She felt inclined to rush over to him, thrust her fists in his face, and pour out words of reprimand: "How could you do that, uh? How on earth is such chicanery possible? Well, I don't care! We don't need to send her to that bloody Seoul. I'll show you she's much better off by not going with you. You'll see how she marries to her advantage; we'll surely get her married to an adorable man who has both money and status."

She indeed wanted to see Jeho stunned and aghast, with his mouth wide open.

"Don't you think he's doing this because he looks down on us? How come he told you not to come, after having asked you to come with him? I can't understand it at all. Just tell me what's behind it, please?"

"I don't know either . . . as he just said not to come . . ."

Chobong, unable to give an honest answer, gave an equivocating one, pretending that she didn't know either.

She was too ashamed to talk about what she'd gone through earlier this evening, be it to her mother or to anyone else.

It happened sometime after five o'clock in the evening.

Jeho always kept himself busy even when there was nothing important going on, but these last few days, he'd been really busy, and today too, the whole day from early in the morning he kept walking in and out, holding his long face up high. Around five o'clock, he came back again and was taking a short rest, when his wife, Yunhui, summoned him into their house next door to the pharmacy.

A little while after he'd gone into the house, loud shouting started.

Since the couple usually fought every other day, Chobong didn't pay much attention to the shouts at first, assuming it was one of their usual quarrels.

"So you insist on taking that slut with you by all means?"

Yunhui's howling voice, as if it was meant for Chobong to hear, was too loud and clear for Chobong to miss. Chobong's ears instantly perked up.

"What is it to you if I take her with me? Why are you so upset?"

It was the voice of Jeho who responded rather roughly.

"Did you say why? You think I don't fathom what's on your mind?"

"You fathom what? What's there to fathom?"

"Hah, you talk well! . . . That slut is so pretty and you hunger for opportunities to satisfy your desires, I know that . . ."

At Yunhui's frantic bawling, Chobong felt all the blood rush into her face, making it flush hot. Although she was sitting alone in the store since the delivery boy was out on errands, she couldn't hold up her face, overwhelmed by shame. She was also full of rage, feeling as if Yunhui had flung mounds of filth onto her pure and innocent maiden heart.

"Learn behavior befitting your age!" Jeho spat out half scolding, half mocking.

". . . You're old enough to know right from wrong. But how come you're getting worse and worse? . . . Even if I'm desperate for women, how can you imagine I would touch a girl who's not only young enough to be my daughter, but is the daughter of my friend who entrusted her to me with confidence? . . . However hysterical you might become, there must be some limit. What groundless jealousy!"

"My my! What a sleek tongue and big mouth you have! With that mouth as big as a hamper, you babble away sly things so well! . . . It's no use to keep talking. Just tell me—are you taking her along with you or not? Huh?"

"I'll take her!"

"Really?"

"Yes."

"Then I'll also do as I want . . ."

Yunhui's venomous voice stopped for a while and then resumed.

". . . You know what these are? This is acetic acid, and this is potassium cyanide. I'll splash the acid over that slut's face first, and then I'll swallow the cyanide. Well, how would you like that? You'd feel relieved and happy, wouldn't you?"

The moment Chobong heard Yunhui threaten to throw acid over her face, she shuddered with horror, her blood freezing, her limbs trembling like an aspen.

Sounds of banging and shouting kept coming from the house, and by the time the sounds got closer to the store, Chobong had already run out onto the street.

But Chobong was too frightened and too paralyzed to know what to do. Then she saw Jeho walking into the store carrying two bottles, one in each hand, panting for breath.

In the house Yunhui was bawling and crying wildly, abandoning herself to fits of rage, and Jeho was looking around the store till he found Chobong standing on the road. He beckoned her to come in with his hand, nodding his long face as well.

"Damned things!" Jeho grumbled, looking at the bottles, as he picked them up again from the table where he'd put them.

"I wonder when that mortal enemy of mine stole these and kept them on her? We could have been in a horrible mess! Damn it! . . . I think I should drink it myself, and be dead! . . . By the way, Chobong . . ."

Though he spoke her name, he was too embarrassed to continue. After much hesitation, he managed to begin again,

". . . I'm awfully sorry, Chobong, um, . . . but I think it might be better if you didn't come to Seoul with us, I mean not at this time . . . Stay at home for a while, I'll contact you to come up when things have cooled down. All right? I'm sure you understand my awkward situation right now . . . Damn it, this cursed world!"

Too embarrassed to wait for Chobong's response, Jeho quickly turned back when he finished his words, and carried the bottles to the drug cabinet with the sign, "Deadly Drugs and Poisons."

The situation having been such, and feeling too ashamed, Chobong couldn't disclose the whole story even to her own mother.

"Nevertheless . . .," Madam Yu decided to drop the subject rather than inquiring into it further, and at last began to bring up the topic of Chobong's marriage in the following manner.

"I think it's better this way. To tell the truth, what good can you expect even if you went to Seoul? I'm sure it would be the same either here or there . . . You'd better forget about it completely and get married."

Chobong, however, didn't attach any significance to the last sentence, as she assumed it was just one instance of her usual talk, mentioned in passing.

Her parents had often talked about their eagerness to get her married, worrying that she was growing old fast, whenever they had the occasion to sit face-to-face, regardless of whether she was around or not. So this evening too, Chobong didn't pay any particular attention to the words, "get married."

Madam Yu, on the other hand, was weighing her options, whether she should give Chobong the whole story about Taesu tonight, or wait until later and give her just a small hint.

She thought it might be inconsiderate to talk about it now, when Chobong was so confused and disappointed, having been frustrated in her plan to go to Seoul.

But on the other hand, it might also be possible that the news that a good marriage was ready at hand would help her forget her disappointment, drawing her attention to something else.

While Madam Yu was thus weighing her options, Gyebong, who'd been in the other room, quietly came over and sat down near her mother.

Gyebong had noticed, since early in the evening, that something unusual was in the air, and having guessed that it concerned her sister, had been quite anxious with curiosity.

"Let me learn some sewing, Mom, he, he . . ."

She made up an excuse, so as not to be sent away and looked at both her mother and sister, trying to read their minds.

"How sly you are!" said Madam Yu, giving Gyebong a side-long glance over her glasses, with a look saying that she knew what Gyebong was up to.

". . . You really want to learn to sew? . . . If that's true, I'm afraid you're about to turn into a different person, that is, a good person, aren't you?"

"My goodness, Mom . . . Do you think you'd be happy if my husband's family sent me back for being no good at sewing?"

"Nice talk isn't it? . . . That girl's good only with that sleek tongue of hers!"

"He, he, he . . . Still, that girl's a daughter of yours, isn't she?"

"I wonder how I conceived such a vixen!"

"But for me, Mom, the question is how come a girl as good as myself came out of my mother! That's what's strange to me!"

"You slut, you're full of foolish notions! . . . If you're going to be so facetious, go back to your room this instant!"

"OK, I'll sit quietly and meekly, and just watch you sewing."

Although she rebuked Gyebong, Madam Yu was pleased with her playfulness, since the atmosphere in the room, which had been quite tense, became more relaxed thanks to her. She thought, now it would be easier to talk about Chobong's marriage.

"Chobong, my dear?" raising her head, Madam Yu addressed her elder daughter in a voice full of affection and earnestness, staring at her for a while.

Chobong too raised her head in response, wondering what urgent matter her mother had in her mind to make her change her voice and expression like that.

". . . Since you're already over twenty-one years old . . ."

Though she'd begun talking, once again she remained silent for some time. And then she resumed at last,

". . . It's not empty talk, but we wouldn't have left you still unmarried, if we'd been without worries about everyday living as we used to be back in the old days in our hometown. Neither would we have sent you to work for such a paltry wage, nor caused you to suffer such ludicrous inequity at the hands of that presumptuous Bak Jeho. I think he must have done that as he thought us easy prey . . . I'm afraid all these things are happening because we've become so rundown and poverty-stricken!"

Starting with this introduction, she kept chatting on, lamenting in a similar vein, perhaps for almost thirty minutes, until she ended with the real issue at hand, which she'd been discussing with her father earlier this evening, how to get her married off before it was too late.

Now she readjusted her voice once again, assuming a very persuasive tone.

"You know Han Chambong of the rice store over there? Have you by any chance seen the young man called Go Taesu, the one who lodges there, and works at, oh, what was it, ah, at the 00 bank branch office?"

Madam Yu stopped and looked up at Chobong.

Chobong was surprised at hearing the name of Taesu, trembled a bit, guessing that he must have started to attack her family at last.

She'd been engaged in a hard and desperate battle with herself, in order to ward off Taesu's powerful, unrelenting spirit creeping into her heart; sometimes she was taken by it, and sometimes she succeeded in defeating it.

Ever since she'd found out who Go Taesu was, and what he was up to, her heart had been agitated despite herself. On the day when she first figured out Taesu's identity, she'd been unconsciously drawn into comparing his face with that of Seungjae, and she had become angry because Seungjae was not as good-looking as Taesu. That was indeed an inauspicious sign from the start.

Since then, however hard she tried to push it away, the image of Taesu had stuck in her mind like a leech, having taken its seat right next to that of Seungjae.

The more Chobong tried to boost up and protect Seungjae's image, the more powerful Taesu's image became, the latter outshining the former, forcing its way deep into her heart.

Taesu was like a colorful flower or a perfume with strong scent that affected her nerves. Feeling the ache in her eyes and the sting in her nostrils, Chobong tried to close her eyes so as not to see the flower, and turn her head aside so as not to smell the fragrance of the perfume. Nevertheless, as though it were fated, she couldn't get over Taesu completely.

In this odd situation, Chobong had often felt like crying, extremely annoyed at her inability to shake him from her mind.

But she'd had one consolation, if she went to Seoul soon, she'd escape from such conflict, and be clear and free of the alluring Taesu.

Taesu's name in her mother's mouth was indeed a shock to Chobong, who'd been walking precariously on a tightrope because of him, especially after the disappointment of learning she wouldn't be going to Seoul after all!

It seemed that Go Taesu had at last come right up to her face, augustly escorted by her own mother, and having neatly pushed Seungjae aside into a far corner.

She was oblivious of her mother's question, absorbed in a kind of reverie, the net thrown by Taesu in which she was caught and entangled, feeling totally helpless. And then she saw herself offering her hand to Taesu with a timid smile. This vision made her suddenly tremble all over again.

"According to what I've heard, he said he was acquainted with you, you too must know who he is, I assume."

Madam Yu was bringing up the topic again, when Gyebong interrupted her mother and cut in.

"Oh, that man? . . . I saw him a few times . . . But he seemed too slick, like a dandy!"

"What do you know? Just sit quietly, stop being so nosy! Presumptuous girl!"

After severely reprimanding Gyebong, Madam Yu turned to Chobong again.

". . . Well, as your father also said, he seemed to be very neat and intelligent in my eyes too . . . He's twenty-six now, and I heard he graduated from a school in Seoul, what do you call it, ah, a college university, right . . .?"

"My goodness, Mom!" Gyebong cut in again, risking a scolding from her mother, because she could not let it pass for shame.

". . . What in the world is a college university, Mom? It must be either a college or a university."

"You little chit. Then it must be a more advanced school, anyway!"

"My, my, I can't bear watching you make such a fuss about him! You've absolutely fallen for him even before the wedding. I don't like that sort of man! Too glossy in my eyes!"

"You hussy, how dare you!" shouted Madam Yu, glaring at Gyebong as if she might attack her suddenly. She was afraid of Gyebong, who seemed to know her vulnerable point, and was poking the tip of a knife into that very point which she'd been so hard at work and anxious to keep safe and untouched. At that moment, Gyebong seemed to her not a daughter but a mortal enemy, hateful enough to kill.

Chobong remained quiet with her head lowered; Madam Yu withdrew her eyes from Gyebong and turned them toward Chobong to study her reaction. Madam Yu at last began to give a full account of the story.

"From what I've heard, his hometown is Seoul; he's the only son of a widow of a noble family; they harvest more than a thousand bushels of rice a year; he works at the bank only because he wants to get some training for the business he plans to undertake in the future; he wants to have the wedding ceremony at a church or a public hall in the modern style; the wedding feast will be offered at a big expensive restaurant; when he heard that we were too poor to afford a wedding, he offered to cover all the expenses for the wedding anyway. To speak frankly, I don't think we'll find another like him anywhere. In our situation, to find a bridegroom as good as Taesu, who is competent, good-looking, and has a good family background, and is prepared to satisfy all our requirements into the bargain—I think that's due to providence. So after a good deal of discussion your father and I have decided to accept this marriage offer. And you should know that things are settled. Your father told me to ask you your opinion, but as you are already acquainted with Taesu, I expect you'd like him as well, whether I ask you or not.

Madam Yu thus closed her long story, and taking a breath, looked up at Chobong again to study her reaction.

After her mother's explanation, the image of Taesu grew more splendid in her mind, eclipsing the already dim and obscured image of Seungjae. Fretful at such shifts in her mind, Chobong felt like shouting in protest, writhing in agony and desperation.

The mother and two daughters sat quietly for some time, and when Madam Yu was about to speak, Gyebong began first, winking knowingly at Chobong,

"Isn't it superb, Sister? He's good enough for an instant OK. What do you have to think about? Ha, ha, ha . . . Now my sister's going to ride around in a chauffeured car! Ha, ha, ha, ha."

Laughing loudly, Gyebong mischievously made fun of her sister, seeming to insinuate something more than what she said.

Chobong glanced sharply at her, but soon dropped her head again.

"Hey, Sister. From tomorrow morning I'll cook, all right? He, he . . . I should start offering services to you . . . As a reward, would you help me go to a school in Seoul, when you're married and live there? You should, uh?"

Chobong kept silent.

"Why won't you give me an answer? . . . I don't expect much, just let me finish pharmaceutical or medical college."

Though she said this in jest to her sister, Gyebong had in fact cherished this dream of becoming a professional in pharmacy or medicine all along, often talking about it.

"Dear, dear! . . . what impudence!" Madam Yu snapped at her.

". . . You little chit, what good would there be if a dull girl like you gets more education? It would surely be a complete waste of money and effort to educate a girl who's got no potential to become an honorable person."

"Well, well, Mom . . . whatever you say, I'll also take a share of the bounty of my sister's marriage, for sure . . . I know Father's expecting a big chunk of the bounty from his rich son-in-law . . ."

"What should I do with that damned mouth of yours!" Madam Yu started up as if about to hit her.

"I won't say that again, Mom! Never again, I promise, Mom! . . . But, mother . . . have you made any enquiries about him?"

"Oh, impudent girl, what's there to enquire about?"

"Things like if he's really rich, of a noble family, and graduated from, as you called it, a college university, and so on . . ."

"That maiden won't walk under a castle wall if she's carrying rotten eggs!"

"Ha, ha, ha, ha . . . Then is my sister nothing but a rotten egg?"

"What a cheeky girl! You're asking for a whipping. Your father and I are certainly capable of knowing what we're about! How dare you step in and tell us to do this or that? Such an impertinent girl!"

"OK, if you say so . . . I'm saying that simply out of concern for my sister."

"You may as well say you care as much as a cat cares for a rat!"

"Well, well, my sister who was a rotten egg a moment ago has become a rat now! . . . She's going through a hell of a lot of metamorphoses tonight!"

"You damn hussy! Stop it!"

Madam Yu picked up the ruler lying next to her to threaten Gyebong, who swiftly ran from the room, and escaped to the other room.

"You wait and see. I'll thrash you until you're black and blue . . . What a wicked girl!"

Despite her anger, Madam Yu felt quite relieved when Gyebong left the room. She was afraid of bringing up the last bit of her story in the presence of "that vixen," Gyebong, because her big mouth, without fail, would meddle and drive her mad (. . . the truth is, it wasn't that she was afraid of being upset, but she was frightened of her younger daughter's penetrating insight).

Madam Yu kept on with her sewing, trying to cool down her temper. After a while, she brought up the last bit of her story in a very soft voice.

"And there's something I haven't told you. Perhaps you needn't know about it just yet, but since I've already started to talk about it, I may as well tell you . . . This is about what Taesu is going to do for us . . . He's not only going to pay all the wedding expenses, but he's also offered to help us out in a substantial way; when he heard from the matchmaker that we were destitute, he said he couldn't let that be. In other words, soon after the wedding, he'll provide your father with a few thousand won (she enunciated 'a few thousand won' clearly) so that he can start a decent business. That's what I've heard! . . . I'm afraid you might think your mother and father want to take advantage of a son-in-law, wishing to live in luxury thanks to him, and force you to marry a rich man against your inclination. But think what you will, if the bridegroom had any faults, or if there were something shady or uncertain about him, we wouldn't do such a thing, not for the world or even for any precious jewels. May lightning strike us if we did. How can your father and mother even consider forcing you into such a marriage? Your happiness is our first consideration. First of all if you marry and live in affluence without having any difficulty, we will be happy. And then, perhaps, it may not be bad either if we can start our own business with his assistance. Don't you think?"

Madam Yu stopped her speech for a moment with the pretense of threading a needle, and carefully examined her daughter's reaction.

"Alas, dear!"

Resuming her needlework, she suddenly switched her tone into a sorrowful one.

"As you yourself have always shown concern about . . . the kind of figure your father is becoming these days, is it that of a proper human being? The other day he came home at night with the ribbon ties of his coat all torn and asked me to mend them! It appears someone had grabbed him by the collar, though he said not a word about it . . . Ah, poor man, dragging his frail body around, going here, there, and everywhere, doing whatever comes to hand, whether good or bad, and who is then subjected to all sorts of humiliations and outrages, yet still endeavoring to find a way to bring home one penny more in order to feed his little children . . . Alas, when I think of him, as pitiful as he is, I can't help but shed tears."

Madam Yu, who claimed tears for her husband, had dry eyes, whereas Chobong shed a flood of tears, with head bowed. They must have been tears of sympathy for her father. But it's also true there were more complex reasons for her tears.

The moment she heard about Taesu's intention to provide her father with several thousand won for his business, Chobong's mind was definitely inclined toward Taesu, leaving no room for reconsideration.

But supposing that there'd been no agitation in her heart caused by Taesu in advance, Chobong would've fallen for him anyway, since the offer itself, as it was revealed to her now, was too good for her to decline.

Chobong, however, retained strong inclinations toward Seungjae in addition to some stubborn regrets over losing him.

Those feelings of regret were so strong that she wished to console and justify herself by closing one eye to the real state of her mind, and allowing herself to believe that she was going to marry Taesu, not because she was attracted to him, but solely because he was offering such a good gift to her family. Her need not to face her divided heart was that desperate.

Even if she didn't resort to such a lame, make-believe strategy, her affection for Seungjae, being the tender bud of first love, was indeed stronger than that for Taesu. Therefore her sense of regret for Seungjae was potent enough to make her cry. But added to that was the touching performance of her mother, who resembled an actress in a tragedy, and though unable to cry herself, was a good enough actress to provide her audience with ample material to weep over. And the final element that could be considered as a defining factor in her weeping was her girlish realization that she was about to sacrifice herself for the sake of her poverty-stricken family and father. Chobong shed floods of tears, overwhelmed by those diverse causes jumbled all together.

Five days passed by, and the auspicious day of the engagement celebration for Taesu and Chobong arrived; the ceremony was to take place at Han Chambong's house.

Taesu had his own reasons to rush the engagement, and Jeong Jusa, who was anxious to get his hands on the funds for his business, gladly went along with Taesu's haste.

From the bride's side, Chobong, her father, and her brother, Hyeongju, were present, and from the bridegroom's side, Hyeongbo, who was invited by Taesu as his best friend was present, along with shaggy-faced Han Chambong and his wife, who also acted as the host and hostess of the ceremony.

The ceremony was slated to begin at five o'clock, but it was around six o'clock before all those invited gathered.

Having seen her only for the first time, Hyeongbo was stunned by Chobong's beauty.

In a paroxysm of admiration, he looked over at Taesu, muttering to himself, "Ah, that sly rogue!" And he instantly felt jealous of Taesu.

In Hyeongbo's eyes, Chobong looked as fragile and as pure as the crescent moon, as tender and soft as willow twigs in the spring breeze. At that moment, Hyeongbo's desire for Chobong was much more intense than anything Taesu had felt when he first saw her.

Craving to hold her in his arms, Hyeongbo sighed to himself, *Ah, ah, that pretty thing, I wish I could hold her in my hands, and bite her. She wouldn't give out even the smell of blood!*

Hyeongbo swallowed his saliva.

She's too good to be given away to that rascal who's destined to end up in jail before long. Too precious! Far too precious!

As he mumbled thus to himself in his mind, a wicked light shone in his deep-set eyes, and rolling those eyes, he looked at Chobong and Taesu alternately.

He even began to elaborate schemes to go behind Taesu's back and sabotage this engagement by exposing his cheating and treachery.

Just at that moment, Madam Kim, who'd been busily coming in and out preparing the feast, wearing a pretty apron, opened the front window wide and looked into the room to see how to arrange the table.

Taesu took out the box with the engagement ring from his pocket, and holding it in his hand, waved it at Madam Kim as a reminder.

Though they were gathered here for the engagement ceremony, none of them knew how to proceed, so the ring had remained in Taesu's pocket until the feast tables were ready to be brought in.

If it were a wedding, they could have invited a man of high rank or a priest to officiate, but since it was an engagement, they didn't know what to do, other than that it wasn't necessary to bring in anyone of rank.

So the guests were left sitting in the room doing nothing in particular for more than one hour. The atmosphere was rather dull for everyone in the room. Chobong, who had to keep her head lowered all the time, was feeling stiff, and her eyes became bloodshot; Hyeongju had become impatient sitting still for so long and wanted to move around; Taesu was hankering for a cigarette as he'd had to abstain in the presence of his future-father-in-law; Jeong Jusa, on the other hand, even though his tongue was aching, kept right on smoking as the expensive Haetae cigarettes were available free of charge. He was giving shaggy-faced Han Chambong an account of a Korean envoy in the old days, who astonished people in China with his amazingly clever literary talent. At the same time, Jeong Jusa was gloating over the fact that Han Chambong couldn't bring up the matter of his old debts because of the special occasion of the day; shaggy-faced Han Chambong, growing bored at sitting idly, wished either to return to the store left under his errand boy's charge, or to play *Janggi* with Jeong Jusa; Madam Kim couldn't avoid feeling jealous and was full of rancor at the sight of Chobong and Taesu sitting together right on the spot where she and Taesu had enjoyed intimacy so many times, but she couldn't indulge in such feelings for long as she had to move in and out of the room to prepare for the feast. And as for Hyeongbo . . .

Hyeongbo had indeed been tempted to sabotage Taesu's marriage at first, but on second thought, he realized that not only would it be very difficult to accomplish, but could be risky and damaging to him as well, it being like an attempt to provoke a sleeping tiger with a hot iron rod.

If the engagement were broken off, "this girl" would return to her parents and would soon be married off to some other fellow. Hyeongbo knew that there wouldn't be the slightest chance for him to touch her, considering his situation or his background. On the other hand, if Taesu succeeded in marrying her, he was confident that many opportunities would open up for him to play tricks of his own.

Well, well, go ahead and get married to each other. Once that's done, I'll wait, watching out for my chance.

Hyeongbo resolved to be patient, and not to hurry. For him, it didn't matter at all whether Chobong was a virgin or not.

Having set aside his desire for Chobong for the time being, he began to chat idly with Taesu, as if nothing had been going on in his mind; he recounted the rumors he'd heard that Janghang on the other side of the river was about to be developed into a big harbor, and that if it happened, Gunsan's business would suffer a severe setback, and so on.

So, each one in the room was far from having a good time, either feeling uneasy or totally bored.

Madam Kim alone was putting all her efforts into keeping the "ceremony" going, acting as a kind of moderator from the beginning. She had arranged the seats and tried to make her guests feel comfortable, talking to this one or that. Busy with such work, she'd totally forgotten about the ring until the ring began to dance in Taesu's hand, as if shouting to her, "Hey, let me be a part of this ceremony. I want attention!"

Feeling embarrassed, Madam Kim hesitated a bit, unsure what to do with it. But soon she spoke aloud, though in a manner suggesting she was talking to herself.

"Well, well, what does it matter one way or another!" With these words of reassurance, she walked into the room, snatched the ring box from Taesu's hand, and took out the ring as if it didn't really matter either way. She then held the ring high up in the air, addressing the audience like a magician on stage.

"Look here please, this is the engagement ring."

With this introduction, she moved toward Chobong.

"See, I'm putting it onto the bride's finger!"

With this proclamation, she held Chobong's left hand and put the ring onto her third finger. The thin eighteen-carat gold ring, embellished with a red ruby, looked very pretty on her slender white finger.

Chobong's hand trembled faintly as it received the attention of all eyes in the room, each of the guests watching it with distinctly different emotions from the others.

When the performance was over, Madam Kim sensed something was missing, so she raised Chobong's hand up into the air and declared, "Now the engagement is complete!" She looked like a referee in a boxing ring raising the winner's hand up.

Chobong thus got engaged to Taesu, and the next day, a box of wedding gifts was delivered to Jeong Jusa's house, containing a few articles of fabric and two hundred won in cash, supposedly from Taesu, but in fact from Madam Kim.

From that day on, there began a heated hustle and bustle in her house, and everyone in the family except Chobong was either smirking or beaming. The wedding was to take place within six days, but there were so many new dresses to be made, one for each member of the family, and a few for the bride.

So the house, where all the sewing done so far had been for customers alone, grew busy sewing for its own members; from that evening on, seamstresses were brought in from outside, a sewing machine was hired, and women were bustling about cutting fabrics, stuffing padding into clothes, or pressing the fine textured ramie clothes, creating a great hurly-burly in the house.

And Gyebong, standing in front of the room in the outer wing, teased Seungjae with a sinister suggestion that he was like a dog staring blankly up at the hen it had been pursuing for some time, which had flown up onto a roof . . .

Chapter 8:
On a Single-Log Bridge

GYEBONG WASN'T AT all pleased that her sister was going to desert Seungjae to marry someone else. Moreover, she didn't like Go Taesu.

But oddly enough, she felt a vague sense of relief knowing that Seungjae would now be left alone, although she also felt sorry for him; he was sitting idly in his room, seemingly unaware of what was going on outside, while the whole house was frantically busy, making the wedding wardrobe of his beloved, fated soon to be the bride of another man.

Gyebong not only felt pity for Seungjae but couldn't bear to see him stay in the house under those circumstances. She wanted him to move out to some other place so that he wouldn't witness the preparations for Chobong's marriage.

After supper, she went to Seungjae's room on the pretense of borrowing a book from him. She began to talk about this and that in order to find out whether Seungjae was indeed unaware of it or feigning ignorance; but as she'd expected, it turned out that he knew nothing about it.

So Gyebong conveyed the news under the guise of inviting him to the wedding; she told him that her sister would be married on the twenty-third of the month at the Public Hall to a man called Go Taesu working at the 00 Bank, and asked him to attend, even if he had to miss his work at the clinic.

Seungjae was visibly surprised, but the agitation lasted only a few moments, and he soon recovered his composure, simply saying, "Is that so? I'll try to attend it if my work permits."

Gyebong was rather disappointed; she had expected that, being struck by the news, he'd be embarrassed, disappointed, and depressed. If that had been the case, she would have admired him more, and enjoyed the tension it created. But Seungjae's reaction was simply too weak and undramatic.

As he seemed to have been hit by a mere cotton ball, her pity for him evaporated, and instead, she felt quite annoyed. So she tried provoking Seungjae with the sinister analogy of a dog that failed to catch a hen when it flew up onto the roof; she challenged him, "Go ahead, and just look up at the roof in vain."

Pointing her finger at Seungjae and clucking her tongue, she rattled on,

"My, my, how could you . . . Well, there you are, sitting, blinking your eyes, just like a dozing cow, . . . totally unaware of your lover's engagement and impending marriage to some other guy, . . . and then when I bother to tell you about it, . . . my goodness, you respond just like a spineless man . . . You don't deserve the manly appearance you happen to have!"

For all her rash provocation, Seungjae simply kept grinning, seemingly not at all affected by it.

"Who wants to laugh with you? . . . You think you've been in love? Well, well, what sort of love is that? Can you call it love when you never even had a clue that your lover was marrying someone else? . . . It serves you right that you're losing her, doesn't it?"

"Tut, tut! . . . but there's nothing I can do about it!"

Swept up by the rapid stream of Gyebong's jeering, Seungjae forgot his dissimulation, and had to admit his feelings in spite of himself while attempting to defend himself.

". . . Whether I knew it or not, I can do nothing about it either way. It would've been the same all along . . . regardless."

In fact Seungjae had neither a reason nor the resourcefulness to do anything about it, whether he'd known about it or not.

It wasn't as if he and Chobong had had a romantic relationship, let alone a promise to marry. Even if they had, Seungjae being who he was, there still wouldn't have been anything he could've done; he would simply have assumed that she had changed her mind or guessed that there must have been some unavoidable circumstances. But the truth was that nothing particular had taken place between them, their relationship having been at that stage where one could perhaps say at most that there was some unusual attraction between them.

Of course Seungjae was in fact experiencing serious emotional turmoil deep in his heart, but it didn't surface easily, because his inner world took the spiral form of the snail shell.

When he had first moved into the house, renting a room in it, Chobong, the eldest daughter, had caught his attention. And as he got to know her better, he sensed, through the way she raised her eyes, or the way she turned her face, or things she said in passing now and then, or many other signs, tangible or not, that she had some special interest in him as well as some good feelings toward him. At the same time, he also realized that the feelings were mutual, and he felt drawn to her more strongly as the days went by.

Then since February this year, Chobong had begun to work at the Jejungdang Pharmacy, which happened to be the supplier of medicines for his clinic. To order medicines Seungjae needed to talk to her on the phone a couple of times a day, which soon became a delightful daily routine for him.

Then a few days before, a stranger had come to the clinic to inform him that he was taking over the Jejungdang Pharmacy and hoped that he could continue to supply medicines to the clinic. He called the pharmacy a few times to confirm it, but Chobong wasn't in. Having guessed that Chobong must have quit as the owner was changing, his disappointment was beyond description.

Ever since that day, his foremost concern had been that Chobong should soon find a new job . . . even wishing that his clinic might have an opening for a nurse! . . . And that night, when Gyebong came over and informed him out of the blue of Chobong's upcoming marriage, Seungjae, who'd been worried about Chobong, couldn't help but feel stunned, as if he'd been suddenly struck on the back of his head.

The moment he heard the news, his heart began to pound so violently as to surprise himself, and it was impossible not to show it, despite himself. However, he soon felt quite embarrassed at his own reaction, especially in the presence of Gyebong, and forced himself to hide his agitation and affect indifference.

But not because he suddenly became a magnanimous saint or a superman with strong will power. Just as Gyebong had reproached him for being spineless, he was indeed the sort of timid and introverted man who could rarely assert himself in the face of frustrations. Always having been a man with neither the self-confidence nor the versatility to maneuver his situation, he instantly thought when he heard the news, "Ah, dear me, I've been presumptuous, misunderstanding Chobong's mind; what a shameful embarrassment!"

Chobong wasn't interested in me at all; she just seemed to be, simply because she was a kindhearted and amiable person. To be truthful, what basis do I have to think she has favorable inclinations toward me? The things Gyebong said the other night when she brought me a bowl of water might have been one of her jests to tease me. Or Gyebong herself may have misunderstood her sister. So I was the one who was overstepping the mark, and delighted with such a false assumption, when it was only my one-sided affection for her! And then to get astonished by news of her wedding!

He longed to find a big cloth to cover his humiliation, and managed to act like a dispassionate man while Gyebong was around, though not as deftly as he desired.

After Gyebong left him, having poured out her mockery to her heart's content, Seungjae sat at his desk, leaning his chin on his hand; his heart was wandering in a maze of sorrows, tortured by confusion. He remained in the same posture without realizing the passing of time, while the night got deeper and dawn came again. He felt an aching void, as if his whole body had abandoned him; he began to feel utter loneliness, while his yearning for Chobong was growing more violent; then he began to be haunted by fierce jealousy toward Go Taesu, the unknown man who would take his beloved away from him . . . All these feelings produced an excruciating agony he'd never before experienced in his life.

Having passed the whole night without a wink of sleep, Seungjae walked into the yard when dawn was breaking, full of odd emotions about the house. He quickly rushed out of the gate, sensing a ticklish feeling on his back, as if someone was pointing a finger at him in derision. He felt that perhaps he would never again be able to step back into the house with his head held high.

Walking down the hill with heavy steps, Seungjae thought he should look for another place to move to. But if he suddenly moved out of the house, the family members who hadn't guessed at his heart might find out his feelings for Chobong, and then everyone, including Gyebong, would think of him as a petty, narrow-minded man. That certainly would be an embarrassing situation. Still, no matter how embarrassing that might be, he knew that remaining in the house would be much more unbearable. So he concluded that he'd better move out anyhow . . .

No sooner had he arrived at the clinic with this determination than he sent for a rickshaw man he was acquainted with and asked him to look for a room for rent in the neighborhood of the hospital.

Luckily he found a small Japanese-style *tatami* room available on the corner of the road leading to Gyeongpori, a few bus stops from the clinic. The room was in the back of a rubber-shoe shop run by an old couple.

Seungjae decided at once to take the room, which was secluded enough and had a small gate of its own so that he could go in and out without being noticed by the old couple. The room itself seemed better than the one in Chobong's house, especially for him to study at night quietly or to be called out to visit his own patients.

It was a little past four o'clock and he was about to leave the clinic in order to make arrangements for the new place when he was held back by a patient.

It was a new patient. In the case of new patients, Dr. Yoon, the owner of the clinic, usually took the first consultation, but when he was out on a sick call or for some other reason, Seungjae did the job.

The patient, ushered in by a nurse, sat on a round stool next to the desk in the consulting room, and Seungjae, putting back on again the gown that he'd taken off a moment ago, gave a professional glance at the patient.

Seungjae instantly guessed he must have a venereal disease, as he had the normal appearance of a gentleman, wearing an expensive Western-style suit. Other than a professional one, Seungjae had no interest whatsoever in the patient.

"Your name, please?"

Sitting on the swivel chair behind the consultation desk right next to the patient, and looking at the tip of his pen and the chart on the table, Seungjae asked, simply following procedure. But the answer was as startling as thunder in a blue sky.

"Ah, Go Taesu."

Seungjae almost jumped up in astonishment as if someone had poured cold water over him, and jerking his head up reflexively, looked into Taesu's face intently.

Uh! This is the man!

Seungjae groaned silently to himself, nodding his head slightly, when he succeeded in calming down his thumping heart a little.

At this sudden, unexpected encounter with Go Taesu, the man he'd thought about so much all day long, Seungjae was utterly dumbfounded, not knowing what to say. Oblivious of his job, he kept looking at Taesu's face.

The fair-skinned, oval-shaped, rather plump face of Go Taesu was very handsome with well-defined features. The face was instantly ingrained in Seungjae's mind, making him feel he would never forget it even in a hundred years.

Humph! So you're Go Taesu!

Seungjae again silently muttered to himself as a more clearly defined hostility began surfacing in his mind.

While taking this meeting as a rather amusing and interesting coincidence, at the same time, Seungjae felt a strong urge to hit Taesu's handsome face with something hard.

Being stared at so insolently by the so-called doctor, Taesu at last got irritated and said with a frown,

"What? Do you know me?"

Anyone would have demanded as much.

"No, no, not at all!"

Seungjae, suddenly coming to himself, looked down at the chart at once and began to scribble with his pen.

Taesu was extremely displeased with this weird behavior of the doctor.

He'd suffered the relapse of syphilis a few days ago, and had been receiving treatment at another clinic until now. Although he was well aware that it wouldn't get cured easily once it had started up again, he wanted to try a new clinic. First of all, the pain was unbearable, and secondly, the wedding was only a few days away. So he'd come to the Geumho Clinic to see if they could do any better than the clinic he used to visit.

Once he entered this clinic, the doctor who came out to examine him made a bad impression. In fact, he didn't look like a doctor at all; he seemed to be perhaps a pharmacist at best or a hospital orderly. His build and face were such as to make him afraid of meeting him in a quiet alley, especially if he had money with him. That was the first impression Seungjae made on Taesu.

And then when Taesu, who was already feeling very uneasy, gave his name, this doctor became even weirder than before, staring at him for a quite long time with an enigmatic expression on his face. Taesu was so upset that he felt like starting a fight with him, despite his being a doctor.

"What is your complaint, please?"

Seungjae at last asked, turning around on his swivel chair to face Taesu, when he'd filled in the chart with the necessary information, such as age, address, and occupation. Seungjae was afraid to ask this question. He thought Taesu's problem must almost certainly be venereal, but he also eagerly hoped his guess would turn out wrong. He anxiously waited, hoping to hear that Taesu had come in for a checkup before his wedding.

"It's a venereal disease . . ."

Despite his sullenness, Taesu had to answer, full of embarrassment and shame. Though it wasn't the first time, he still felt hesitant, as anyone would, to name the vile disease especially in the presence of a young nurse.

"You say a venereal disease?" Seungjae shouted, unlike a doctor, though he'd guessed at it already, and he inwardly exclaimed to himself,

You, who are marrying Chobong within a few days, you who would marry my precious Chobong, you say you have that vile disease!

Seungjae gnashed his teeth with indignation.

Taesu, who was already feeling embarrassed, became even more confounded at the doctor's shouting and began to suspect this man might be a madman rather than a real doctor.

"How long have you suffered from it?" Seungjae at last asked, resuming his role as a doctor.

"It first started sometime around last fall. It cleared up after some treatment, but it recurs again and again . . ."

"I think the root of the disease hasn't been eradicated. In such a condition, you mustn't be careless . . . You mustn't! You should've been more careful."

Seungjae was giving this advice out of concern for Chobong, who would soon marry this man. Taesu felt annoyed by this advice, but being in need of Seungjae's assistance, he answered meekly.

"Well, I know I should have, but as it is . . ."

After mumbling a little, he brought up the issue in his mind.

"To tell the truth, there's some urgent matter coming up . . . Is there any way to be cured within four or five days?"

Seungjae thought to himself,

You rogue, you really are desperate, aren't you?

With this thought, Seungjae felt quite elated as if he'd caught a mortal enemy and had him kneeling at his feet.

"No, I don't think it's possible."

After a violent shake of his head, Seungjae added,

"Anyway I need to examine you first, but I know it's very difficult to cure it even when it's in its first stage, and in your case, it seems to have entered the chronic stage, I wonder how . . ."

"But I'm in a desperate situation, so I came over to consult, and . . ."

"What's the occasion? Are you planning a trip? Traveling will be very harmful with that disease," Seungjae dissimulated, to add pressure on Taesu.

"No, it's not traveling . . ."

"Then, what is it?"

Seungjae perversely nudged him, and Taesu, after some hesitation, said with a grin,

"I'm about to get married, heh, heh."

"Ma—rried?" Seungjae shouted, affecting astonishment, and deliberately shook his head.

". . . Getting married! That can't be! I think you should rather postpone the wedding, making some excuses."

This was reasonable advice on the part of a doctor. But Seungjae was giving this advice not at all for the sake of Taesu, but to put him in a predicament; or rather out of spite, wanting to see his marriage aborted somehow or other because of this delay.

Taesu being Taesu also shook his head wildly. To postpone the wedding! What a preposterous idea that was!

"No, that's impossible! Absolutely not . . ."

"Still, you shouldn't go ahead with your marriage. First of all, it's harmful to you, the patient, and then to your future wife . . ."

When the last word came out of his mouth, Seungjae became full of odd emotions, almost bursting out an exclamation, "Oh, my goodness!" But with much effort, he restrained himself.

He was full of rage, thinking of Chobong about to be ravaged by this rogue, and who would get infected by his filthy disease to boot. For Seungjae it was no less than sacrilege. He was so heated that he wanted to smash the rogue's head.

Being totally unaware of Seungjae's mounting rage, Taesu began to implore him,

"That's why I'm here consulting with you. Though complete eradication might not be possible, you could try to free me of the pain temporarily, and prevent contagion . . . for instance, by stopping the oozing pus . . ."

"Well, if I can do as much as that, that of course will be a great relief to you and good for all concerned, but I'm not sure . . ."

Seungjae smacked his lips. If Taesu alone were involved, he would've sent him away with a rap over the knuckles, exclaiming, "Stop your nonsense." But when he thought about Chobong, despite all his reluctance, he couldn't help but see that he should do his best to find even a temporary way of dealing with the disease as Taesu had asked. He thought he owed that much to Chobong.

Taesu, on the other hand, was very much vexed at this begrudging answer of the so-called doctor, who'd been unpleasant from the beginning, so much so that he even felt like springing up and storming out of the place at once.

Taesu saw himself as a man living on a knife's edge, reckless enough not to care a whit about such a paltry disease. It even seemed ridiculous to him that he should be so eager to cure it, feeling sorry for Chobong who might get infected too.

Am I not determined to choose the last day of my life? That day is so near! . . . So is Chobong's last day . . .

Mumbling to himself inwardly, he determined to leave the place at once if this man exasperated him one more time.

"Nevertheless . . .," Seungjae finally said, standing up decisively from his chair, "I'll do as much as I possibly can. Now then, let's see . . ."

As Seungjae stood up, the nurse, without waiting for instructions, began to prepare an injection, picking up a 500 cc syringe
with a pair of tongs.

*Injection first? Am I not going to test the germs first? . . . Well,
it's all right to give the injection first . . .*

Seungjae said to himself, his mind jumping from one thought
to the next with confusion. And he came back to Taesu carrying
a microscope slide.

The nurse was skillfully drawing up the yellowish liquid from
a bottle of Thiarabine with a syringe.

As if hypnotized, Seungjae stood still, staring at the liquid,
his face gradually turning into an odd scowl.

He was imagining Taesu dying an excruciating death, his
limbs writhing with agony. As he saw the syringe, he began to
fantasize about adding a few grams of potassium cyanide.

The usually meek and docile eyes of Seungjae were now
bright with a murderous glint when he looked back at Taesu,
who in his ignorance was idly looking at something else.

Seungjae awoke from his fantasy with a start when the nurse
handed him the syringe.

Holding the syringe in his hand, Seungjae looked down at
Taesu's naked arm under the rolled-up sleeve. It was a plump arm
in which blue veins were clearly visible. His skin was unusually
fair.

Seungjae imagined that this arm would soon embrace
Chobong's soft shoulders, and it suddenly looked like a huge
snake, giving him shivers. Unable to look at it any longer,
Seungjae closed his eyes.

Having closed his eyes, he was tempted to push the needle
at random anywhere in the arm so that Taesu would jump in
pain; he thought that would certainly give him some satisfaction.

But the nurse, who'd been waiting for Seungjae to administer the shot after cleaning Taesu's arm with a sterilized cotton ball, urged him by poking his side, and he finally opened his eyes and managed to give him a shot.

He then collected some pus on the glass slide. He knew the disease was too obvious to require a microscopic examination. He was simply following routine procedure, which was intended to give an impression that their clinic was very thorough and cautious.

Seungjae heated the slide over an alcohol lamp, which turned the color of the pus brown, and examined it through a lens, magnified 900 times.

As the lens focused, there appeared bluish spots in the shape of a kidney, proving it to be syphilis.

Seungjae beckoned Taesu, who was sitting blankly, and stepping aside, made him look into the microscope.

"Do you see? The kidney-shaped, bluish things . . ."

"No, I don't . . . Well, but it seems there're some rather murky things."

"How about now?"

Seungjae readjusted the lens.

"Ah, yes, yes. I can see. I see them clearly now. Hah! So these are the bacteria?" Taesu asked, surprised by the novelty of what he'd just seen; Seungjae felt rather amused and, suppressing a grin, said,

"Yes, right. They're a sort of bacteria. They're syphilis germs."

"Hah-ah! They are indeed!"

Taesu raised his head after looking into the microscope for quite some time. This experience was totally novel to him as he'd never seen a microscope, let alone looked into one.

"Hah-ah! So they are!"

Standing beside the microscope, Taesu, with a tilt of the head, asked a question that exposed his ignorance,

". . . so are they magnified by about ten times? I thought bacteria were very small . . ."

"They're magnified by 900 times!"

"Nine hundred times? . . . My goodness! Nine hundred times . . . Ha ha, indeed . . . I see . . . how interesting . . ."

Enchanted by the novelty of it all, Taesu looked into the microscope one more time.

Despite his hatred for Taesu, Seungjae sensed that Taesu could be affable at times, as he now looked as naive and blithe as a child.

To be precise, this thought of Taesu's being attractive was not something that suddenly struck Seungjae's mind out of nowhere. It began in his mind as an embryo at the moment he recognized him as the man who'd stolen Chobong from him; he was hateful because he would take away Chobong, but at the same time, he could be attractive because he would be her spouse.

This embryonic good feeling toward Taesu, however, had been utterly smothered by the intensity of his hatred, until this trivial instance of his naivety opened up a small outlet for it to surface in his consciousness.

The embryo didn't disappear again, but somehow grew stronger. Seungjae struggled hard to get out of the vortex that the two contradictory feelings had created in his mind, but he found himself still submerged in it, unable to get free.

After standing near the microscope for some time, utterly perplexed by his strange mixture of feelings, Seungjae at last moved to the bookshelves in the corner of the consulting room. While Taesu was still busy looking into the microscope, Seungjae took out a thick book from the bookshelf and leafed through it until he found the page with color illustrations of magnified syphilis germs, and then placed it open on the consulting desk.

Seungjae waited for Taesu to come over, and pointing at the illustrations, he began to explain all the details regarding the disease; beginning with the shape of the germs, their progress, their routes of infection, their latent period, their activity and propagation, the pathology of the disease, its impact on patients and their partners, their offspring, and on the general public as well; and finally about the treatment of the disease and the recommended diet for patients. Seungjae explained all these very carefully and kindly.

Taesu looked up at Seungjae with a new sense of respect.

Everything Seungjae said sounded probable and convincing. In the other clinic where Taesu had been treated, from the first day they just did the pumping and then gave some injections. And there had been no microscope viewing or detailed explanations, which he was receiving now in this clinic. Though the doctor at this clinic looked at first like an orderly or a bandit and was unpleasant in manners, Taesu received all the necessary information here and obtained a very clear view of how to manage his disease. The unpleasant doctor gradually transformed into a seemingly meek and gentle person. Being a man of no long lasting vindictiveness, Taesu began to trust Seungjae as if he were a renowned M.D. or an old friend.

Seungjae wrote a prescription.

After writing down the powder medicine, he was about to prescribe the liquid medicine, and just then the temptation to add one gram of potassium cyanide to the liquid (no, a mere half a gram would be enough) recurred to his mind. Taesu would swallow the liquid medicine two hours after his supper, and soon after, he would have convulsions, as well as difficulty in breathing, while exuding a sour smell from his breath, his eyes sunken and losing focus, and his whole body falling into lethargy. Within three minutes of these symptoms, Taesu would breathe his last.

Absorbed in this fantasy, Seungjae paused for a moment in the middle of his writing, but he soon came back to himself with a shudder and resumed writing the prescription.

At the end of it, he wrote,

"Water, 100 grams."

But a little space above the final line kept luring him to write there, "Potassium cyanide, one gram."

Possessed by this temptation, he sat still, holding the pen in his hand, and began a dialogue with himself.

What will the pharmacist say when he sees it?

He'll make a great fuss, calling me a madman!

Suppose the pharmacist has already left the clinic . . .

Well, perhaps, I should wait until tomorrow . . .

Seungjae, however, was glad when he found the pharmacist still there, no matter what the other half of his inner-self desired.

When he finished writing the prescription, Seungjae began to give careful instructions to Taesu: he should come to the clinic every day for injections until the night before the wedding; he shouldn't forget to take the medicines on time; he should apply a plaster to the affected area as often as possible; he should keep away from women and wine; he should avoid spicy food and excessive exercise; and finally, he should follow these instructions without fail, in which case there might be a chance of getting cured. But Seungjae added,

"Even if the pus stops, the mycelia, which are also contagious, will continue to come out. So I'll find a makeshift measure to handle that and administer it on the last day. You shouldn't by any means let your disease pass over to the woman you're marrying. That would be not only an unforgivable sin against an innocent woman, but a deadly crime toward the offspring you may have in the future. I hope you keep that in mind."

As he was giving such advice to Taesu, Seungjae felt as if he were his own younger brother, whom he should take good care of with a kind heart.

Though Seungjae was in fact a year younger than Taesu, in appearance he looked older, more mature, and more composed, like a senior, whereas Taesu looked junior to Seungjae, being more youthful, and more inexperienced.

After Taesu left the clinic, Seungjae went to his newly rented room, carrying a broom, a duster, and a mop to clean the place.

Now that he'd met Taesu, pretending that he knew nothing about him at all, he thought, would be very embarrassing should Taesu visit Chobong in his position as her fiancé, say tomorrow, and bump into him in the house. So Seungjae thought it best to move to the new house that night as he already had the room available.

Covered with dust, Seungjae cleaned the room thoroughly, even mopping the tatami mat floor and the inside of the large, built-in closet that occupied the whole wall on one side of the room. Upon returning to the hospital, Seungjae sent for a cart to come over to Chobong's and left for Dunbaemi.

As he walked into Chobong's house, a house he was both happy and sad to see at the same time, Seungjae felt awkward, as though he were entering a house that he hadn't visited for a long time, having fallen out with the family who lived there.

The house seemed full of excitement and bustle, perhaps because he expected it to be so.

In the kitchen, Gyebong was busy preparing the meal with a woman who was a total stranger to him. Gyebong welcomed him with a bright smile.

The smile was rather faint, but was innocent and good-natured; it seemed to suggest to him,

"I'm glad to see you, though I gave you hard time last night. That teasing was nothing but a meaningless prank. You can see that when I smile like this, can't you?"

Seungjae was extremely thankful for Gyebong's welcoming smile, even to the extent that the sense of gratitude seemed to shoot through his whole body. But soon realizing that this would be the last occasion to enjoy such a sense of pleasure or gratitude, he became quite pensive. He had enjoyed her company as if she were a mischievous but delightful little sister, allowing her to indulge in her whims as much as she pleased in his company. Recalling that such pleasures would no longer be his, he felt an intense sadness about the prospect of moving out, and combined with the dark twilight that was approaching, he felt as gloomy and as helpless as a lost child.

While walking through the yard, despite his fear of meeting Chobong, Seungjae unconsciously turned his head toward the inner quarters, driven by an instinct contrary to his will, hoping that he might catch a last glimpse of Chobong. But there was no sign of her anywhere in the inner quarters, which were crowded with unfamiliar, ungainly women moving around busily.

Seungjae was packing up his books, which he'd taken down from the bookshelves, when Gyebong quietly approached him.

"Wow, oh my goodness! . . . What a lot of fuss . . .?" Gyebong shouted, with her eyes wide open in surprise.

". . . Why have you taken down all of your books?"

"Well, uh . . ."

Seungjae stopped moving his hands that were busy packing the books together, but was hesitant about what to say. He gave an awkward smile. Gyebong soon understood the situation.

"Are you moving out?"

"Yup."

"Moving? Out . . . ?"

Gyebong was about to frown, but soon burst out in loud laughter, saying,

"Ha, ha! . . . All right! Bravo, good Master Nam!"

Seungjae looked at her blankly, unable to grasp her meaning. Gyebong, not paying any attention to his puzzled expression, was merry and full of excitement, nodding her head over and over again.

". . . Right, Master Nam? . . . I too hoped you would move out to someplace else . . . Because I felt so sorry seeing you. I was afraid you might become sulky, misunderstanding me! . . . Nevertheless, it's definitely a good step! . . . You've escaped being a bovine. Ha, ha, ha . . ."

Gyebong burst into loud laughter with this last bit of mockery and then began to talk softly, moving closer to him.

". . . And, please let me know the location of your new place, then I'll visit you from time to time, all right? . . . I have things to report to you too . . ."

Seungjae wrote down his new address on a piece of paper, and gave detailed directions to the house as well as to the separate gate to his room. He also asked Gyebong to give the directions to his new abode if anybody came looking for him for emergency patients.

"I'll see if I can visit you tomorrow, maybe around six o'clock in the evening . . ." Gyebong said, looking at the address, and slipped the paper under the waistband of her skirt.

". . . Our Master Nam . . . Ha ha ha ha . . . Wait for me tomorrow, won't you?"

It was good to see him moving out since she wouldn't need to feel sorry watching him sit helpless and uncomfortable in the house. But more than that, she liked it better because she'd be able to visit him whenever she wanted when he lived somewhere else.

The next morning, upon his arrival at the clinic, he put a small portion of potassium cyanide into a small bottle, kept it in his pocket, and anxiously waited for Taesu. He knew Taesu wouldn't come until late in the afternoon, yet still he had to make himself ready from early in the morning. At around eleven o'clock, however, he threw the bottle away, and then when it was one o'clock in the afternoon, he again got a bottle ready, then at three o'clock he threw it away again; he became fretful and grew restless. When he heard the clock strike four, he again got a bottle ready, but this time he didn't put it into his pocket; instead he laid it among the other bottles of medicine in the consulting room.

Taesu came around at half-past four and walked into the consulting room wearing a flowery smile, with his upper lip half curled up on one side.

Seungjae also welcomed him with a smile. He was glad to see Taesu, though he didn't know why, nor had he time to think about the reason.

"How did you get on overnight?" He waited until Taesu was seated before asking, not out of his habit and duty as a doctor, but with genuine concern and interest.

"Well, I've noticed . . . no particular difference yet!"

"That's right, not yet . . . But if it didn't get worse, you'll get better by and by."

While they were talking like this, the nurse was preparing the injection. Seungjae instructed her to prepare a different kind of injection, one that they didn't have at the clinic. He told her to call Jejungdang Pharmacy or some other to find it and with this excuse sent her away to the far end of the hall where the telephone was.

That injection was also used for the same disease, but was a hypodermic one, not as effective as the other. It was hard to get because it wasn't widely used these days. Seungjae deliberately ordered it because he knew that fact.

Once the nurse was away, there were only the two men left, he and Taesu, the two alone who were needed for what he was about to do. Within two or three minutes, he would be able to finish it. At last, Seungjae stood up.

The thought that Taesu was attractive returned to Seungjae as he looked at the man sitting like a straw effigy, not only in ignorance of what was about to happen, but also with absolute trust in the man who was about to harm him.

Seungjae picked up the syringe the nurse had left on the table, and holding it in his right hand, drew up the liquid from a pretty glass ampoule containing Thiarabine. The yellow liquid reached the 20 cc mark.

He then took out the bottle he'd left among the other bottles, and holding the bottle of poison in his left hand, he squeezed out its cork stopper.

"Pop," . . . the sound wasn't at all loud, almost inaudible, but Seungjae winced. The room was that quiet.

Seungjae tilted the bottle with poison and, placing the syringe into the bottle, slowly pulled up the inner cylinder of the syringe.

The poison in the bottle decreased little by little, while the liquid in the syringe increased . . . by 1 cc . . . 2 cc . . .

When the liquid reached the 25 cc mark, he took the needle out of the bottle. From the tip of the needle small drops of poison fell drop by drop, nervously trembling.

Seungjae, standing still, stared at the syringe for a while, holding it far from him up in the air.

Taesu couldn't see what Seungjae was doing since his huge back obstructed his view. Furthermore, Taesu wasn't paying any attention to that corner but was simply sitting in the chair waiting for the doctor's return.

Seungjae, turning his head, looked at Taesu who was sitting blankly in the chair, and then he glanced at the syringe, and then back at Taesu, and so on alternately.

When I push the needle into his blue vein . . .

In one, two, three minutes, his face will turn deadly white, and he'll pluck and tear at his chest, writhe, tumble down, turn his eyes up, and gasping in agony, breathe his last!

Yes!

At this moment of his resolve to make a man's body go rigid, a light smile rather than a tense grimace spread over Seungjae's face.

Seeing Seungjae approaching him, Taesu rolled up his shirtsleeve, and stretched his naked arm toward Seungjae.

Seungjae cleaned the injection spot on Taesu's arm with alcohol cotton.

"Clasp your fist tightly."

With this instruction, he tilted the syringe and placed the tip of the needle right on top of the bulging vein. From the tip some liquid oozed out and spread over the skin.

Now if he pierces the needle into the vein and slowly pulls back the cylinder, the dark scarlet blood will begin to flow out into the syringe. Right at that moment, if he pushes the cylinder back in, it will be over.

Seungjae, however, stood still, doing nothing further for some time, simply holding the needle tip on top of the vein.

Taesu, anticipating the needle piercing his skin, closed his eyes. As always, he couldn't stand to watch as the prick would cause him to shudder.

With his eyes closed, Taesu waited for the needle prick. But somehow it didn't happen.

He waited for at least thirty seconds. Impatient, Taesu opened his eyes and found that Seungjae, instead of giving him the shot, pulled back the syringe, and then turned away with a grin.

Taesu stared at Seungjae's back in amazement.

Pushing the cylinder, Seungjae emptied the poisonous liquid from the syringe. A thin stream of liquid, which looked like a pretty, silver thread, flowed out and fell to the linoleum floor, drawing a meaningless curve on it.

Seungjae truly wanted to kill Taesu and had gone as far as almost attempting to do so.

The truth was, he had simply wanted "to attempt to kill"; but he didn't actually "intend to kill."

You may call it a game of nerves. Being a doctor, Seungjae wanted to prove to himself how thin the line between killing and saving a man was; he proved it to be as thin as a strip of celluloid.

The goal he'd set himself from the start lay on this side of the strip; keeping that precise goal in mind, he prepared the poison, sucked it into the syringe, looked alternately at the syringe and at the victim for comparison, placed it on the vein, and drew a breath as if about to pierce the skin. He approached the task of murder as if walking up a set of steps one by one.

But the final goal of his game was right up to the line.

Approaching murder step by step, and stopping right in front of the threshold, leaving a distance the thickness of a strip of celluloid—the process thus far was only a game of nerves, one that would generate a pleasant tension for the player.

Seungjae fabricated an explanation, saying that the injection seemed to have gone bad, and Taesu bought it . . .

When Seungjae brought out a new syringe and gave him an injection from a new ampoule, Taesu was quite pleased, taking it as evidence of the careful and kind practice of the hospital.

When the treatment was over, Taesu started to leave, but turning back, asked Seungjae to attend the wedding if he wasn't too busy.

Seungjae felt some qualms at the invitation and was standing hesitant, unable to answer.

"I know you must be very busy, but please just drop by . . . To tell the truth, I'm somewhat ashamed to invite you as the wedding will be so modest. Anyway, I'll send you the invitation card, and hope you can come by. It would be a great honor for me."

"Yes, I'll try . . . if I'm not too busy that day . . ."

Sensing that Taesu could be persistent, Seungjae gave a prevaricating answer.

Seungjae anxiously waited till it was six o'clock then left the hospital for his new house. When he arrived near the shoe store at the corner of his street, he found Gyebong waiting for him, looking around.

"Ah, Master Nam!"

"Hi, Gyebong!"

The two called each other, smiling broadly. They were glad to meet as if they hadn't met for a long time.

But it was only the night before that they had last met, so there was nothing much to talk about.

"Well . . ."

"Yep . . ."

Each gave a monosyllabic greeting that had no particular meaning, but was enough to convey each other's mind.

"Welcome!"

"He-he."

"Let's go inside."

"Yup."

The two went through the gate, which was left unlocked, and walked along the long, narrow passage under the eaves until they reached Seungjae's room.

"It's not as easy to get in here . . .," Seungjae said, looking back at Gyebong with a smile, while unlocking the door of his room.

Gyebong, not attempting to sit, stood in the room looking around; the books were already on the bookshelves, and all of his paltry household goods, other than his desk, were stored in the built-in closet. With the signs of his shabby bachelor life all stashed away, the room looked neater and cozier than the one in her house.

Gyebong was pleased with the tidy room and happy to be alone with Seungjae away from her house, where she'd been somewhat cautious, minding her parents. But at the same time, she felt more uneasy and uncomfortable than back in her house, sensing something awkward in the air.

Gyebong tried to figure out what that something might be, but being unable to come up with anything, she grew more puzzled.

"Why do you keep standing? . . . sit down somewhere . . ."

At Seungjae's insistence, Gyebong sat down on the same spot where she was standing with a shy smile on her face.

Seungjae was very pleased to see Gyebong in his place, but couldn't think of anything to talk about.

Talking about social or political events or discussing scholarly matters would be far too absurd. That left her family matters as the only topic that was natural to discuss in this situation, and Chobong's marriage might be the only thing interesting to both, yet he couldn't bring it up.

Seungjae wished Gyebong would behave as casually and frivolously as she used to do, then, he thought, they could more easily start a conversation and get rid of this awkward atmosphere. Gyebong, however, unlike her usual self, was very quiet and well behaved tonight, only exchanging casual smiles from time to time. Her attitude contributed to Seungjae's uneasiness.

"I wish I had some snacks or fruit in the house . . ."

At length, Seungjae stood up muttering to himself. He thought he should go out and get something to eat.

". . . I'll go out for a moment, and soon . . ."

"What? You want to buy something? . . . No, don't bother for me, I don't want to eat anything!"

Gyebong hurriedly got up too as if she would hold him back.

"Whether you want to or not, you'll have to eat when I buy something for you! . . . That'll make you a good little girl."

Although he normally lacked glibness of speech, as Seungjae began to take on this teasing tone, Gyebong too began to feel relieved from the awkward tension in the room.

"What! You're trying to bully me!"

'Hmm, if I am, am I at fault? . . . Incidentally, what's happened to you overnight? You've suddenly changed into a modest girl, shy and discreet."

"Ha ha ha, do I look so to you, Master Nam?"

"Yep."

"Oh, my, my! . . . Even I feel as though I've changed in that way, so I was about . . ."

"Uh-huh! If you've indeed changed, that's big trouble, isn't it?"

"What a sourpuss you are! . . . Is one's becoming a good girl a cause of big trouble to you?"

"Yes, it is."

"How come?"

"Because I like the capricious . . . no, not capricious, but mischievous, and carefree Gyebong better than the prudent Gyebong."

"Then you want me to remain a child and a little hussy forever?"

Gyebong somehow grew sulky, which was something new and unfathomable for Seungjae.

"Being a child, isn't it good?"

"What good is there about it? It means falling short of being an adult."

"There's nothing enviable about being an adult . . . But listen, Gyebong?"

"Yes?"

"Um, Gyebong . . . How would you like being a little sister to me?"

"A little sister? You mean calling each other brother and sister . . .?"

Gyebong stared at his face for some time, and suddenly blurted out,

". . . I don't like that idea!"

She flatly refused, and Seungjae's face flushed with embarrassment at such an unexpected response.

"You don't?"

"Nope, heh heh," Gyebong replied with a soft smile, regretting her abrupt and unfeeling response.

"I wonder why you don't like that idea?"

"Why? . . . Umm, I just don't."

"What do you mean? There must be a reason."

"A reason? Well, no . . . no reason at all."

"I know there has to be a reason. Perhaps Gyebong dislikes Master Nam. Isn't that the reason why you don't want to be a sister to me?"

"Who said I dislike you? That's not true."

"Yes! . . . You do dislike me, that's the reason."

"No!"

"I'm sure you do!"

"I said no. Why do you insist! You don't know what's in my mind . . ."

Gyebong at last got testy and reproached him.

Seungjae, finding no words, quietly went out of the room.

Walking along the street, Seungjae began to mull over what Gyebong had just said, the accusation that he didn't know her mind, and the sullen and irritable temper with which she protested.

He knew that Gyebong hadn't said it on a whim or to tease him; it was something unusual that came out of her inner self, which was as deep as that of an old man.

Seungjae loved Gyebong's frivolous and carefree behavior, and felt amused by it as simply and innocently as if she were his real little sister; and he all along had wished to cherish that relationship for a long, long time.

But having seen the new Gyebong moments ago, he felt that that wish now belonged to the dim past of an old legend.

The eyes that intently stared at him when he suggested she might become a sister to him, the eyes that grew narrow while she complained that he didn't know her mind, the eyes that seemed almost dangerous as they glittered with strong passion, despite her innate intelligence that could have hidden it; recalling those eyes, Seungjae worried he might never be able to see her face-to-face again.

So precocious!

Seungjae muttered to himself with a deep sigh of regret.

When he came back with some fruit and cookies, however, Gyebong seemed quite oblivious of what had happened earlier. Seungjae was both pleased and relieved at the return of her usual self.

"You'll bully me again, if I don't eat, so . . ."

Gyebong opened a bag of cookies and began to eat with Seungjae. Then out of the blue she asked,

". . . Master Nam, you must have been very curious?"

"Curious?"

"Yep. I mean about my sister's marriage."

"Ah, I wondered what you were talking about! Well, I'm just . . ."

"Don't pretend! You were really curious . . ."

"What if I don't get to know about it? It's the same either way . . ."

"If you don't really care, that's perfectly all right with me . . . But nevertheless, I really want to tell you just one thing, all right?"

"Well . . ."

"You know what? It seems my sister can't forget you!"

"What idle talk!"

Contrary to his dismissive reply, Seungjae's face blushed deep red. He couldn't hide his delight at the report and was almost in tears, overwhelmed by it.

"Yes, I'm telling the truth!"

Gyebong related to him everything she had heard from her mother while she was in the room with Chobong the other night.

As he listened to her story, Seungjae began to understand why her parents were so strongly drawn to the marriage. As Taesu was reported to be from such a noble and wealthy family, and not only well educated but decent in himself, it was only natural that both Chobong and her parents should want to have him as her bridegroom.

On the other hand, however, another part of his mind was howling in protest at the same time,

Still, how could it be!

He became rather bitter, feeling rejected, concluding that he'd lost Chobong because he wasn't as highly qualified as Taesu, and his delight earlier at the news that Chobong was still missing him evaporated into thin air.

He felt some resentment and anger toward Chobong, though not as intense as Suil's who lost his lover because of his poverty.

At the same time, a suspicion about Taesu's true identity arose in his mind; he thought especially fishy the story that he'd graduated from a college or university, judging from what he'd seen at the hospital.

Earlier, at the hospital, because he didn't know anything about Taesu's supposed educational background, and because he was preoccupied with his own conflicts, he didn't pay much attention when Taesu was so amazed by the microscope, as if it were a magic box. Now that he came to think about it, it seemed quite preposterous for a college graduate to think the germs under the microscope were magnified only by ten times. If he'd attended even a junior school, let alone a college, he wouldn't have said that!

There must be some deception involved . . .

How was it possible to have such a disease if he were indeed a decent, well-behaved man? Even conceding that it was possible to get infected by bad luck or mistake, he couldn't have been so reckless as to have it recur so often and for so long if indeed he were who he was reported to be. A decent man would have got it cured completely and behaved more discreetly afterward.

It was obvious that he was deeply addicted to the pleasures of women and drink . . .

Seungjae became suspicious of his supposedly noble background and his reputed wealth. Perhaps those stories too might have been made up by a trickster. Isn't it possible that he has a wife back in Seoul, and is about to ruin Chobong's life . . .?

When his thoughts reached that point, Seungjae was scared out of his wits and wanted to run to Jeong Jusa to share his suspicions with him. He felt obliged to persuade him to stop the marriage.

In spite of such anxieties, however, Seungjae couldn't bring himself to act, as other possibilities surfaced in his mind.

Even if his conjectures were correct, it was doubtful whether the marriage would be actually cancelled. Moreover, if Taesu's reputed background turned out to be true after Jeong Jusa investigated it (or according to what he had already learned), Seungjae would be spat at as a malicious and jealous man who'd slandered Taesu out of spite at having lost Chobong. That would be too shameful to endure; he might have to kill himself by taking the poison with which he had wished to kill Taesu.

He also questioned his own conscience as to whether he wanted to thwart the marriage purely out of concern for Chobong's happiness. Wasn't it possible that he was prodded by his own desire for Chobong, even if it was unconscious? Regardless of whatever answer he might get, he was too ashamed to ask that question seriously of himself.

Then, should he let it go, and sit on his hands?

That would leave him full of anxiety and regrets.

Should he stand up and interfere?

There were too many factors that held him back.

How on earth should he handle this odd situation?

He repeated these questions to himself, without coming up with an answer. He was as restless, you might say, as a dog eager to piss.

"So, I was forced to leave the room . . . and then, you know what . . .?"

Gyebong resumed her story after quietly peeling the fruit. She'd been reading his face for some time, as Seungjae seemed absorbed in thought, his face changing color and his lips smacking from time to time.

"Since then, my sister has become quite crestfallen, letting out deep sighs all the time! . . . I had no idea that she would consent to the marriage on the spot! . . . Well, it's true that she couldn't have said no, when my parents told her that everything had been decided and that she should come along with them. I know she couldn't say no, even if she disliked it . . . My sister has such a frail heart . . ."

Gyebong stopped her story as if waiting for Seungjae's consent, while giving him a piece of fruit. Seungjae remained silent after taking the fruit, and Gyebong continued.

". . . So, the other day, ah, I guess it was the eve of the engagement . . ., when we were together alone, I asked her, 'Why do you allow yourself to be driven into marriage if you don't want it? However hard our parents urged you to do it, I'm sure that if you refuse, that will be the end of it.' And you know what she said? She told me, 'You can say that because you don't know the whole story. If I marry him, he's going to give our father a few thousand won so that he can start a business of his own. Knowing this, how can I refuse the marriage?' I was so upset by the story that I hated everyone. So I shouted, 'What an absurd story? Am I reading the old folktale of Simcheong who sacrificed her life for her blind father? Or is this some sleep-talking nonsense from *Janghanmong*? . . . Nothing like that should happen in this modern world.' And I raised my voice much louder so that my parents in the other room could hear. 'Why did they raise children if they want to sell them? Isn't it better for them to raise pigs and fowls to sell at the market?' . . . I was shouting like this, burning with anger, when my sister started to cover my mouth and to pinch me! I'm sure they heard it all . . . They must have felt some pangs of conscience . . . He, he, he."

Gyebong burst into loud laughter, recalling the gratification she had felt that night with her outspoken accusation against her parents.

Seungjae, however, remained silent, staring straight at the wall ahead and breathing deep sighs. He now forgot all his anxiety about how to stop the marriage, or the bitter feelings he had harbored against Chobong a little while ago. His countenance was now full of admiration and seriousness.

He was deeply touched by the sacred soul of Chobong, who was willingly throwing away both herself and her love for the sake of her poor parents and siblings.

Seungjae had once criticized Myeongnim's parents for waiting until their daughter had grown a bit older so that they could sell her to a *gisaeng* house. He too had compared Myeongnim's parents with farmers who wait for their piglets to grow up (using the same metaphor Gyebong used in her outrage against her parents).

Seungjae, however, didn't feel the same resentment toward Chobong's marriage (which, after all, might be even more inhumane than Myeongnim's case). To be precise, it wasn't that he didn't feel such resentment; rather, he couldn't feel it because he wasn't listening to Gyebong when she mentioned the metaphor of selling pigs; he was too absorbed in his own thoughts to be able to think about anything else.

Seungjae, who'd been staring up in the air in silence, began to assume the expression of a man lost in reverie. He was fantasizing, seeing a sacred painting, in the middle of which stood the merciful Chobong in the shape of an angel, while to the left and right and behind her stood her pitiful family members, whose faces received a dim light and vague comfort thanks to Chobong's halo.

"What an admirable deed!"

Seungjae let out this exclamation as tears came welling up in his eyes; he was so deeply moved.

"Uh—h . . .," he groaned after a while, pursing his lips slowly, and nodding his head repeatedly.

He now saw how ugly and shameful his thoughts had been, when contrasted with Chobong's pure and beautiful soul; the resentful thoughts he had against Chobong, the fretful anxiety he suffered in hoping to prevent the marriage, the jealousy and hatred he harbored against Taesu, all these feelings seemed now too mean-spirited.

"How holy!"

His admiration for Chobong's sacrifice was undergoing a transformation into an active intention to emulate her holiness; for a start, he wanted to throw away all his mean thoughts against Taesu and devote himself wholeheartedly to the cure of his disease. By doing this, he might consider himself devoted to Chobong indirectly. That would be a deed worthy of praise, he thought.

Once this resolution was firmly ingrained in his mind, Seungjae felt as comfortable as someone falling into a sound sleep after severe exhaustion.

Gyebong, on the other hand, with an amused smile on her face, enjoying the fruit and cookies, had been observing the strange state of Seungjae, who seemed entranced and lost in some sort of reverie as though he had suddenly become a somnambulist. When Seungjae uttered the second exclamation, "How holy!", however, Gyebong changed her expression into one of mockery and, staring up at him closely, snapped,

"What a scene! . . . Well, what about a rat's horn, isn't it holy?"

"Why? . . . Things holy and beautiful, aren't they good?"

Seungjae's voice sounded hollow, and he stared with a rather dimwitted expression on his face, as if he were still dreaming.

"Oh-ho, I see! . . . So if you have a daughter in the future, you'll give her away to anybody who offers to supply you with business funds, will you, Master Nam?"

"Pish! I'm just admiring your sister Chobong's beautiful mind, that's all!"

"Is it beautiful? No, it's just a very old, outdated mind!"

"That's a mean thing to say! . . . You'd better learn to see the beautiful as beautiful . . . Isn't your sister's heart indeed beautiful?"

"She's doing that simply because she's foolish."

"Look at you! Nonsense again!"

"You stop your vain gibberish now. Or I'll scold you . . ."

"Gyebong, you'll be a good-for-nothing!"

"Humph! You watch and wait!"

"What, wait and find a spoiled brat?"

"No matter how spoiled I might be, I still have eyes to see right from wrong . . . Look, Master Nam . . . Let's assume that she marries this man and lives happily ever after. Nonetheless, isn't it still unjust and vile to offer a man a girl with the intention of getting money for business? . . . I say what's wrong is wrong even if it's my parents' doing . . . Don't they have virtuous pretenses that sound good and plausible? They say the man is good-looking, smart and clever, educated at a college university . . . Ha, ha, ha, ha, that's what my mother called it! So I snapped at her pointing out there's no such thing as a college university, and you know what she said? . . . She shouted at me, claiming that the school then must be a more advanced one! Ha, ha, ha, ha. My, my . . ."

Seungjae too was drawn into laughter by Gyebong's contagious hilarity.

". . . According to what I heard from my sister, my mother insisted that she was urging this marriage primarily for the good of Chobong since the man had so many good qualifications, blah, blah, blah, assuring her that the business fund was nothing but an added benefit attached to a good marriage . . . My goodness, I wish I'd stayed in the room to hear all that nonsense, and caused a spectacle there to expose her."

"Listen, Gyebong, supposing . . ."

Seungjae began to suggest a hypothesis to see how she would respond to it.

". . . Supposing that it's bad for children to sacrifice themselves for their parents, is it also bad for parents to take all sorts of trouble to raise their children, sacrificing themselves?"

"No."

"Why not? By what logic is it not bad?"

"Because parents have the responsibility to educate and take care of their children until they're capable of living independently. So even if they have to sacrifice themselves, it's right that they have to fulfill their responsibilities . . . You know if you don't fulfill the responsibility of paying your taxes, the bailiff comes and confiscates your household goods such as kettle, pots, and spoons . . . As a matter of fact, our family also experienced such a turmoil some time ago. Ha, ha, ha."

Seungjae was impressed by her logical argument, wondering how a girl of just seventeen, a third-year student of a girls' school, could be so mature and articulate. Seungjae again felt intimidated by her, though in a different way from what he'd felt earlier when she refused to be a sister to him.

The next day, Seungjae racked his brains to find ways to cure Taesu by any means before his wedding day. And at the same time he made a vow to himself that he would never again hate Taesu.

But when the evening came, and Taesu walked into the clinic, the vow he'd made to himself wasn't as strong as he intended it to be.

He was again agitated by violent feelings the moment he saw Taesu. Exerting self-control, however, with the utmost effort, he tried to be impartial toward him; he asked as kindly as possible how his symptoms had been overnight and didn't forget to remind him one more time of all the usual precautions, such as abstaining from drink, or avoiding spicy food, and so on.

Chapter 9:
Haengwha's Vindication

TAESU WENT STRAIGHT to Haengwha's house in Gaebokdong after his treatment at the clinic.

As usual, Hyeongbo had preceded him and was lying on a fancy futon, his head resting on a square pillow. Haengwha was plucking on the strings of a gayageum, for her own amusement.

"Hey, I've heard you rented a house. How many rooms do you have in it? Any spare ones?"

The moment Taesu stepped up onto the maru, Hyeongbo questioned him through the open door of the room.

Hyeongbo was hatching a scheme to squeeze his way into Taesu's house after his marriage.

"Don't worry. I've already thought about that . . ."

Walking into the room, Taesu took off his jacket and looked around the room before he threw it on top of Haengwha's *gayageum*, and then taking off his hat, placed it on Haengwha's head, pushing it deep down.

"What a fuss! I'm sure you're acting like this because you're marrying a girl student, a thing no one has ever done before, aren't you? "

Haengwha, without flinching, sneered facetiously.

"Ha, ha, ha, yes, yes. I'm indeed full of mirth these days!"

"My, my, I can't stand it! . . . How long ago was it that you were walking around looking so glum because you couldn't get hold of that bloody student girl? And is this the same man, I wonder, twirling and frisking about with excitement as you are now?"

"Ha, can't you imagine how I feel? I'm a man who's just accomplished his lifelong dream! . . . But you needn't worry . . . However great my new love might be, in no way will I forget my old love either, trust me!"

"Hurray! I was about to go up to Seoul and jump off the railroad bridge into the Han-gang River, but I'll give that up and trust your words, all right?"

"Sure, sure . . . I say you need never worry!"

Though Haengwha was speaking in jest, Taesu was expressing his true intention in a flippant mode.

Ever since the engagement, Taesu's mind had been as clear as the autumn sky, all his worries and anxieties had been washed away.

Before the engagement, of course, Taesu had been stranded between two desires, the one being to kill himself, and the other to somehow survive. Whenever he felt overwhelmed by worries and anxieties, he spat out a resolution, "Well, what the hell, I'll put an end to everything by killing myself." He used to repeat that just like Christians praying or Buddhists chanting. Though that resolution relieved him of his anxieties temporarily, deep in his mind, nevertheless, he was still harboring a desire to escape from his troubles without killing himself. Because of this tenaciously lingering desire within him, he'd always been restless and fearful of his situation.

While his anxiety had been escalating in anticipation of the inevitable day, for the day when his crimes at the bank would be exposed seemed imminent, he suddenly found himself about to possess Chobong. Having secured this gift for himself, Taesu's resolution to kill himself became quite firm and final.

Thus he acquired absolute emancipation from the agony of constant worries and a heavy heart.

Once he'd fulfilled his foremost, final wish by marrying the student girl, Chobong, there'd be no further lingering desire for life. Then until that final day—whenever that day might be, the day he would take his life with composure and dignity—he should make each moment of his life grand and magnificent, savoring its pleasures to the full.

First of all, he should adorn the dream days spent with Chobong with the highest luxuries imaginable. On the other hand, he had no intention of giving up the other kinds of pleasures he'd been accustomed to. He would debauch himself in the grandest manner, reveling in drinking parties with music and dancing, and enjoying as many women as he could possibly get his hands on. Therefore Haengwha too would have to stay with him.

As for money, he'd get it by any means possible—stealing, borrowing, cheating, or embezzling—he didn't care which, as long as money came into his hands.

In order to enjoy all these things happily and merrily, he must be free of pain. So he would continue going to the clinic to get medical treatment.

Taesu was thus making meticulous plans for his remaining days, as if he were preparing for a ceremonial ritual.

So Taesu was genuinely merry and cheerful that night, not at all pretending.

While Taesu and Haengwha were exchanging jests, Hyeongbo was deep in thought lying in one corner of the room, and at long last, he sat up, reached for the pack of Haetae cigarettes lying next to Taesu and began to smoke. He then joined in the conversation.

"Though Haengwha says she's not affected by Taesu's marriage, I'm sure she feels bitter about it."

"Why should I?"

"Why, because you're losing that pretty lover . . ."

"Hah, was Master Go pretty for no reason? He was pretty because he gave me money . . ."

"That wench knows no better way to talk even in jokes!"

"What jokes? I meant what I said . . ."

"All right. I grant that what you said was nothing but the truth. Even so, isn't it also true you feel sorry since Go Jusa is getting married?"

"Pish! Would Go Jusa by any chance marry me if he remained single? . . . I've no ambition to become a lawful wife to him."

"Well, well, that wench seems destined to be a woman of pleasure!"

"What childish nonsense you talk, Jang Jusa!" Haengwha retorted sharply, but was neither upset nor in a jesting mood.

"A *gisaeng* needs to act like a *gisaeng*, content with making money when she can. I'm sick of those girls who lament their bad fortune, wishing that they were lawfully wedded wives, hating their situation as concubines. Damn such sentimentality!"

"Humph!"

"I don't like that . . . And I have even more difficulty putting up with those girls who rashly venture into what they call true love or some such nonsense, which is quite unbecoming to the profession of a *gisaeng*. They really get on my nerves."

"Why? Is there a law against a *gisaeng* having a romantic relationship? You demean yourself too much . . . I fear you'll earn a beating from your fellow *gisaeng*s soon enough . . ."

"What has love got to do with a *gisaeng*? If a girl, in spite of being a *gisaeng*, steps out of her role and claims she's in love, she must be a good-for-nothing slut; in the same sense, an idle bum who ventures into a love affair with a *gisaeng* is the most good-for-nothing rogue in the whole world."

"What, why is that so?"

Taesu, who'd been enjoying the chit-chat between the two with an amused smile, broke in at last, and continued in a provocative tone to see how Haengwha would respond,

". . . Heaven forbid! Instead of you, I should be the one to go up to Seoul and commit suicide as you said . . . because now it turns out that I've been happy in vain, foolishly assuming that we've been in love with each other all along. I was a foolish rogue, as you called it!"

"Ha, ha! Whatever you two say, I won't budge an inch . . . Never even try to change me! Do you think having so-and-so for money is love? . . . This body has been a plaything to all sorts of men. Syphilis germs have come swarming into me, and part of my body is decaying now, eaten up by them. In this condition, what does love have to do with me?"

"Huh! . . . I still think I've had a love affair with Haengwha, haven't I?"

"No more of that nonsense . . . As for you, Go Jusa, you've been sleeping with me, but in the mean time you fell in love with that young maiden, Chobong, and are going to marry her soon . . . I'm not saying this out of jealousy, I have not an ounce of it, to be sure. But I know you're doing it because it isn't possible to be in love with a *gisaeng*. Am I not right, clueless young Master?"

"Humph! But still as I see it . . ."

While Taesu hesitated, unable to find words that could be a match to what she said, Hyeongbo cut in.

"I know some *gisaeng*s who are openly involved in love affairs, that's a fact."

"Is it really a love affair? Isn't it just the debauchery of a man-about-town? Or a *gisaeng* being debauched by him? You're childish if you call it love when you see some long-standing whore-customer relationship. Don't you get it, Jang Jusa, my honorable sir?"

"That thing keeps calling me childish! Good heavens, really . . . Nevertheless, Haengwha, isn't a *gisaeng* also a human who's bound to fall in love and go along with it at times? Why do you so detest a *gisaeng* who's in love?"

"Does making love entitle everybody to be human? Didn't I see dogs making love over there the other day?"

Taesu burst out laughing along with Hyeongbo at her sharp comment. After a while, he picked up his cigarette pack, saw that it was empty, and then taking out some money, began looking out into the yard.

"What?"

"Cigarettes . . ."

"No one's out there . . . smoke my Pigeon cigarettes."

Haengwha took out a pack of cigarettes from a drawer of her dresser.

"Didn't you say the other day that you would get a girl? What happened to her?"

Taesu recalled having said this, and feeling the inconvenience caused by the absence of an errand girl, asked her casually,

"What? A girl . . .?"

Before Haengwha had time to answer, Hyeongbo abruptly broke in, excited by the prospect of having a girl he could dally with at his pleasure in Haengwha's place, where he felt quite at home.

". . . How did you find her? What does she look like?"

"Why are you so excited even when there's no side dish coming? . . . I wanted to take a girl as a foster daughter, but she's still too young, so I decided to wait until she's a bit older. Well . . ."

"My goodness, a daughter at your young age?"

"Hah! Am I not turning sixty?"

"Sixty for a *gisaeng*, you mean?'

"No matter by what standard, I know I'm old enough to need a daughter, and if I raise her well, she might perhaps feed her aging mother with the rice she earned somewhere. Doesn't it make sense to you?"

"Oh, no, knock it off! . . . I wonder how much you're paying for the girl in order to be able to squeeze her right down to the marrow in her bones? . . . Tut-tut."

"What bone marrow? . . . It's all for her own good as well as mine!"

"But tell me, how many coins were you going to pay for her?"

"Goodness me! Jang Jusa, you have an odd notion of the cost . . . It was set at two hundred won, that is, two huge coins of one hundred won each. But when the deal was settled, the girl was unwilling to come, and I was in no hurry to take her either, so we've decided to wait a little longer. Are you satisfied, now?"

She was talking about Myeongnim, Mr. Yang's daughter. But neither Taesu nor Hyeongbo knew her, never having heard of her.

"I wonder how the wallpapering is going on . . .," Taesu muttered to himself, standing up and picking up his jacket off the floor.

". . . I think I should go and see."

"Where's the house?"

"It's over at what used to be called the Big Well Street . . . Why don't you come along with me? You can get acquainted with the place today, and move in soon after the wallpapering is done."

"You mean I move in before you do?"

Hyeongbo took down his long coat from the wall and put it on while inwardly rejoicing at the way things were working out exactly as he had wished.

"The maid's already living in the house. As I'm going to furnish it now, I'd feel more secure if you were living there, rather than entrusting everything to the maid. Since you're going to live with us anyway, you may as well move into it before us."

"Well, if that's the case . . ."

"Haengwha, won't you come along with us? Perhaps you need to know the location of my place in advance. And since I want to have dinner with you and Jang Jusa afterward anyway, you may as well leave with us now . . ."

Taesu was casually taking Hyeongbo and Haengwha to his new house, unaware that, at the same time, Chobong was heading there with Gyebong.

The house, like most of the other preparations, was being taken care of by Madam Kim, who had not only found it, but had made the contract for rent on behalf of Taesu.

For his marriage preparations, Taesu gave Madam Kim five hundred won, which he'd acquired through his usual forgery of checks, and trusted her to handle all the time-consuming and difficult matters; he himself was taking care of only simple things such as printing the wedding invitation cards, making phone calls to the Public Hall and the restaurant for reservations, and ordering the food for the reception at the restaurant.

Madam Kim, however, was as earnest and enthusiastic in handling the matter as though she were preparing to receive her own daughter-in-law.

As a matter of fact, the five hundred won Taesu had given her had almost run out already; two hundred won in cash was sent to Jeong Jusa; about sixty won went to buy clothes and other presents for Chobong; the rest of the money was used for buying rings, the bridegroom's ceremonial suit, renting a house and furnishing it, et cetera.

For any further expenses that might arise, Madam Kim

would pay out of her own purse.

However, she was quite happy and excited at the prospect rather than begrudging it.

After securing the house, Madam Kim informed Madam Yu that Taesu had wanted to purchase a house but couldn't find a desirable one, so he'd rented a house for the time being with the intention of buying or building a new house in the near future. And giving the address of the rented house, she also suggested that Chobong might have a look at it to see whether she liked it or not, if she had some occasion to come out to that area.

And then this morning, when Chobong was going out to a public bathhouse with Gyebong, her mother repeatedly urged her to stop by the place and take a look.

Chobong was quite indifferent as to whether she saw it or not, but nevertheless, she went there on her way home from the bathhouse. She thought that she might come across as too stubborn if she didn't go and see the place after Madam Kim had advised her to do so and her mother had also urged her so strongly.

The house was located in the middle of Big Well Street, which was behind the newly made Sowha Boulevard.

Seen from the outside, the house didn't look old, having clean and well-maintained eaves and pillars. Once inside the gate, she found the yard spacious and with a ledge for earthenware crocks filled with sauces and condiments in one corner.

The house was crescent-shaped and faced the east; the kitchen faced the gate. Next to the kitchen was the main room, and to the left of the main room were the maru and the opposite room.

Another room in the outer wing of the house was on the right-hand side of the kitchen.

There were three wallpaperers busy with their work; the house looked messy with scraps of paper and lumps of mud scattered all over, but Chobong liked it immediately.

She liked it, not because she thought it magnificent, but because it was brighter, more spacious, and with higher ceilings in comparison to her house in Dunbaemi.

Though Madam Kim had mentioned that she'd hired a maid, Chobong couldn't see her anywhere. Only the men who were doing the wallpapering were peeping out from the opposite room.

Chobong was about to turn back to leave the house, when Gyebong exclaimed with delight,

"Oh my! There's a flower bed!"

There was indeed a small flower bed in a corner of the yard, hinting at the former tenant's caring mind. There were crepe myrtles, balsams, and nasturtiums, all beginning to bud; a few cosmos were also growing strong there; and along the sides of the flower bed were some moss roses that had bloomed in the morning but were withering now under the afternoon sun.

But having been left unattended for some time with no one living there, the flower bed was in a very bad condition; some flowers were bent at the neck, while others had been trampled down by uncaring feet. On the far corner under the wall a few morning glory plants were growing, but for lack of any support to climb, they were crawling haphazardly over the ground.

Chobong felt like attending to the flower bed that instant, at least to try and straighten some of the flowers that had bent or to tie the morning glory stems onto something so that they could climb. But she dissuaded herself from doing it and resolved to take care of the flower bed the very next day, after she moved into the house.

Just as she turned to leave, a group of people entered through the gate with loud footsteps.

Taesu entered the yard along with Haengwha, followed by Hyeongbo at their heels.

Both parties were taken aback.

Chobong dropped her head very low, Gyebong stood by nonchalantly, Hyeongbo grinned in amusement, Haengwha was puzzled, and Taesu was flustered, thrown into utter confusion. He looked back once, and glanced over at Chobong, seemed about to scratch the back of his head, gave a dry cough, and then made an awkward grin. He looked pathetic. The five men and women were all agitated, but each in their own way. Each of them wore distinct expressions on their faces.

Chobong wondered what brought Haengwha to this place, but she had no time to pursue that thought, as she was too overwhelmed, feeling deeply shy; she simply stood there with her back toward Taesu's group, her face blushing like a beetroot. Gyebong recognized Taesu; but seeing Hyeongbo for the first time, she was amazed at the hideously ugly features of the man; and then at the sight of Taesu accompanied by a *gisaeng*, she tightly knit her brows, construing that he must be a flighty womanizer.

Hyeongbo was gloating over Taesu's discomposure, thinking to himself,

You rogue, you had it coming!

How uneasy you must feel!

Marrying such a pretty girl, yet with a gisaeng by your side all the same! Heaven must have noticed what you are!

But Chobong, you will be mine no matter what, ha, ha.

Haengwha didn't know Chobong's name and had no idea that Chobong was the girl whom Taesu was about to marry. Thinking of Chobong simply as the friendly young woman she used to meet at Jejungdang pharmacy, Haengwha ran to her quite pleased to see her unexpectedly, though she thought it rather odd to see her here.

Taesu was utterly at a loss to know what to do, and was so confounded that he was almost ready to cry.

Haengwha was so glad to see her that she was about to clasp Chobong's hand.

"My goodness! It's been so long since we met!"

With this greeting, she looked into Chobong's lowered face.

Unable to say anything, Chobong greeted her only with eyes that showed pleasure in seeing her.

". . . But what brought you here, I wonder?" Haengwha asked.

That was the very question Chobong wished to ask her, but keeping her mouth shut, she simply stroked her chin while showing her pretty smile.

At that moment, Hyeongbo saw fit to step in. He toddled over toward where the three women were standing, and began to intervene rather pompously.

"Ah, do you two know each other already?"

"Gracious me, of course! We've been on friendly terms for a long time! Ha, ha."

"I never imagined that! Heh, heh, heh, heh . . . Well, incidentally, speaking of Haengwha, she's, well, let's just say, she's an intimate friend of mine, you know, ha, ha . . . And Haengwha, Miss Chobong is the lady Go Jusa is marrying, you get it?"

"Oh my goodness! Really?"

Haengwha, surprised at the strange coincidence, kept nodding her head, and turning toward Taesu, gave him a wink.

"I'm glad to hear that you two ladies are acquainted with each other. Ha, ha . . . I was passing by with Haengwha on our way to her house, and happened to meet Go Jusa right in front of the gate."

Hyeongbo thought he was doing well enough to clear any suspicions Chobong and Gyebong might have about Haengwha.

To tell the truth, however, unlike Gyebong, Chobong had no suspicion about Taesu's relationship with Haengwha, nor was she displeased at their being together. She simply thought it rather strange.

Chobong made a slight bow to Taesu's group and walked toward the gate with Gyebong, when Haengwha ran after them with a smile, sending an amused glance back at Taesu.

Taesu, who was feeling quite relieved thanks to Hyeongbo's quick wit, became anxious again when he saw Haengwha run after Chobong; he cast a reproachful glance at her, for fear that she might say anything unwelcome to Chobong.

"Well, goodbye now! . . . I'll be at your wedding to get a bowl of ceremonial noodles, all right?"

Haengwha bid farewell, standing at the threshold of the gate.

Chobong nodded to Haengwha with a smile instead of saying that she'd be welcome at the wedding.

Haengwha stood there alone, looking at the backs of Chobong and Gyebong, who walked side by side along the street. After a few steps, Gyebong swiftly looked back at Haengwha and began to say something intently to her sister, so Haengwha assumed that they were talking about her . . .

From the first moment she saw Chobong at Jejungdang, Haengwha, for whatever reason, had liked her very much, that's to say, she'd been strongly attracted to Chobong even before their relationship developed into a friendly one.

A couple of days ago, when Haengwha stopped by at Jejungdang, instead of Chobong, a stranger had greeted her; she asked him about Chobong and learned that she'd quit her job when the pharmacy was sold to a new owner. Haengwha was quite disappointed at losing a good friend with whom she'd always felt comfortable. And this evening, she not only met her quite unexpectedly, but learned that Chobong was the very person whom Taesu was marrying.

The more she pondered on it, the more interesting and strange it seemed to her. Taesu's marriage had been an event for her to observe rather indifferently, but now it turned out to be an extraordinary event for her after coming upon the inside story.

Haengwha, however, was simply amused and amazed by such a turn of events, feeling no jealousy whatsoever toward Chobong, as Madam Kim did.

Not only was Haengwha without jealousy, she also felt no real concern or interest in the marriage (which Madam Kim had in abundance, shouldering all the responsibilities related to the marriage, despite the excruciating pain caused by her strong jealousy of Chobong).

The only feeling Haengwha had about the situation was a mild sort of regret and pity for Chobong.

In Haengwha's eyes, Taesu had nothing much to boast about except that he appeared to be from a well-off family, had some money at his disposal, and had a sleek and handsome figure; in short, he seemed to be a man with few prospects for the future.

Despite that, Haengwha didn't think badly of him or anything like that.

For Haengwha, none of her customers was either good or bad; they were merely men with some money who came for fleeting moments of pleasure and left.

She neither had any particular liking for Taesu, nor harbored any obstinate dislike for him. So it was none of her concern whether Taesu had any good prospects or not.

Her concern had nothing to do with Taesu; rather, it was due to the affection and pity she felt for Chobong, who looked so fragile and tender, almost brittle enough to be shattered by anybody's touch. And yet, she was still bound to become the spouse of Go Taesu, that good-for-nothing womanizer, who seemed to be wasting his days in debauchery, his body ravaged by venereal disease.

Well, what the hell can I do about it! . . . *Why should I meddle in the business of others* . . . *Tut-tut! Perhaps sitting aside to watch a shaman ritual and getting a share of the rice cake afterwards is all I may have to do.*

Muttering to herself, Haengwha turned back into the house after the two sisters had at last disappeared around the bend of the street. At that moment Taesu and Hyeongbo came toward the gate, giggling noisily at whatever they'd been discussing.

Chapter 10:
A Typhoon

THE WEDDING CEREMONY of Taesu and Chobong was over at last, without any major trouble. It was a very dignified event that went off smoothly.

One untoward "incident" was that there were many uninvited female spectators, who created additional problems, making the hall too crowded, whereas Taesu's mother, who had every right to be there, never showed up.

Madam Yu had been prepared to show the highest respect to that supposedly grave and important lady and anxiously awaited her arrival, but she failed to come down on the promised day, that is, the day before the wedding. There was just a telegram from her, which was among the few congratulatory telegrams that arrived at the wedding hall on the day of the wedding.

It said she had suddenly fallen ill and couldn't make it.

The truth, of course, was that Taesu's mother, who resided alone in a small rented room in Aeogae on the outskirts of Seoul, had never been informed of her son's marriage. The telegram was not from her; one of Taesu's friends in Seoul had sent it at Taesu's request.

Madam Yu expressed profuse regrets and concern about the sudden illness of Taesu's mother, and her sympathy for the lady's severe disappointment at missing the joyous event of her precious only son.

Madam Yu, however, was not uneasy or uncomfortable, since the lady's absence didn't in any way hinder the wedding, nor did it threaten to erode any critical part of the promises attached to the wedding.

Seungjae too was present at the wedding.

Seungjae made up his mind to attend, forgetting his own heartache in a spirit eager to emulate Chobong's noble self-sacrifice, and because he wanted to sincerely celebrate the wedding of the woman who was almost "holy" in his mind.

But his well-meaning expectations were thwarted, and he came back from the wedding burdened with a new sorrow; for he saw that Chobong looked extremely sad and distressed.

Chobong was wearing a white dress and white veil, and holding a bouquet of white lilies. Dressed all in white, she herself was more than white; she looked extremely pale. She walked very slowly toward the rostrum with her head lowered, and it seemed as if she were taking unwilling steps, one step and then half a step, forced by irresistible fate; the tranquil serenity surrounding her seemed so sad that Seungjae felt as if he were listening to a silent elegy. Overwhelmed by the sorrow surging up in his heart, Seungjae imagined that Chobong must be in tears and his own eyes began to well up. He lowered his head, unable to watch the scene any longer.

But what Seungjae imagined he'd seen was entirely the creation of his own mind. Chobong, in fact, was far too nervous, as any bride might be, to be feeling sad or happy, while Seungjae, steeped in his own sadness, projected his sentiments onto Chobong, imagining that he was taken hold of by her sadness.

This sudden rush of sadness led him to disillusionment. It wasn't that Seungjae had expected a happy, smiling bride. But he didn't think far enough ahead to anticipate a sorrow-laden bride either. When he saw the unexpected scene of Chobong looking sad and restless, more like a young widow mourning at the funeral of her spouse than a bride, while all her family members except for her were full of happy smiles, full of satisfaction, he began to feel strongly disillusioned about what he assumed to be Chobong's noble sacrifice.

The sacred picture he'd drawn in his mind and admired the day before was transformed into a bitter picture in which her happy, contented family members were highlighted in front, while Chobong receded into the dim background, pitifully standing almost invisible.

Seungjae unconsciously closed his eyes to avoid seeing this disgusting picture that was too clearly and too distinctly visible to his open eyes.

When he closed his eyes, however, there appeared "the great spirit of sacrifice" in black clothes; blocking his way with a cane wand, and stroking his beard rather mischievously, the spirit said,

"I will allow you to pass only if you are enlightened about the true nature of what I am."

No sooner was the wedding over than Seungjae rushed out of the wedding hall. From the start, he'd had no intention of attending the reception, but now he was so upset that if someone had tried to drag him to the restaurant, he would have exploded with anger.

From that day on, Seungjae could no longer sustain his admiration for Chobong's beautiful mind, as his grief for Chobong, who had looked so sorrowful at her wedding, got the better of him.

Finally, he began to have a premonition that Chobong's destiny might not be easy and smooth, and that she was destined to encounter misfortune in the future. Along with this presentiment, there arose a strong feeling of antipathy toward Jeong Jusa and his wife, who had pushed the marriage through for their own wicked aims.

Nevertheless, Chobong had thus got married without a hitch, and about ten uneventful days passed.

June ushered in the summer season, but it was still cool and pleasant early in the morning.

Too—oot.

At the sound of the first siren at five-thirty in the morning, Chobong woke and abruptly sat up, as she used to do in her own house.

She looked around the room, which was still unfamiliar and strange to her eyes. The dim light of dawn began to infiltrate the room through the open shutter of the front door and the back window, but the lamp with a blue shade was still turned on.

The lime-plaster walls looked sedate and composed despite their stark whiteness; an armoire and three-tiered dresser stood side by side in the upper part of the room, showing off their glossy magnificence; a long, single chest of drawers was by the bedside, on top of which were lying stacks of bedding, a gramophone, and so on; everything in the room looked quite unfamiliar, yet they were the same things she'd seen the night before when she went to bed.

The woman who was now sitting in a loose nightgown, with the lower portion of her body covered with an indigo-blue silk coverlet, was the same Chobong she'd known all along. Taesu, sleeping right beside her, covered with a maroon silk coverlet, was indeed a stranger to her, yet he was also the same husband whom she'd seen before she fell asleep last night.

Finding everything unchanged when you wake up in the morning is nothing unusual. Yet still it seemed weird and marvelous to Chobong.

Thus, Chobong felt surprised again this morning with the new reality revealed to her as she awoke and opened her eyes. She even muttered in wonder, "Is everything here indeed real again?"

The next moment, she realized that she'd been rather foolish in asking such a silly question and muttered again to herself, "Did you expect that everything might have disappeared overnight?"

Amused by her own childishness, Chobong felt like laughing aloud.

Chobong, who'd been laughing to herself for a while, at long last began to tilt her head sideways, marveling again, "Yet still . . . can it be real?" . . . and with wonder in her eyes, she alternated between looking at Taesu and herself.

After what they call the "marriage" was celebrated, I moved over to this place alone while all my family members, my mother and father, my sister and brothers, remained in the old house; and now I'm living in this house as the wife of this man—the man who's sleeping here—what on earth is this man to me? Why does he make so much of me, why is he so excessively fond of me day and night, happy just to keep me company, and what am I who go along with whatever he wants to do?. . .

What has been going on for the past ten days seems to me just a laughable farce, the cause of which I shall never fully understand.

Am I not the Chobong who lives in "Dunbaemi" over the hill, the daughter of my parents, the sister of Gyebong, the big sister to Hyeongju and Byeongju? Why am I living like this in this house with this man? However far I stretch my imagination, the real Chobong still seems to be somewhere else, and the Chobong here in this house seems to be a total stranger to me.

A stranger? . . . Yes, a stranger! Not I but someone else . . . Chobong enjoyed this schizophrenic division of self that allowed her to see herself as someone else.

Yes, yes, I am—the real Chobong is—still over at my house in Dunbaemi. I still get up earlier than anybody else and sweep the front yard with a worn-out broom; I go into the kitchen and prepare the meal; Byeongju, the youngest boy, pesters father in the main room to buy him candies; my mother scolds Gyebong, who's still asleep, for not helping me in the kitchen; the door of the outer room opens, breaking the silence, and after a while Seungjae's big body emerges and walks toward the gate, making heavy thumping sounds. The phone rings, clang, clang; but it's not Seungjae; after a few other calls, at last it's Seungjae's call; the voice says, "This is Seungjae calling." "Ah, this is Chobong." "Uh, please send us a box of OO syringes . . ." "Yes, I'll have it sent right this moment . . ." I wish he would talk a little longer. He too seems to wish that, as he hesitates in silence. At last he hangs up. The gate clicks open and Seungjae walks into the house in big strides. As our eyes meet, he nods, giving an awkward smile, and I too smile back and bow . . .

Her smile in this fantasy became infectious in reality and caused her to smile sweetly. At that moment Taesu turned over in his sleep, and Chobong suddenly woke up from her daydream and came to herself.

Her smile at once disappeared and in its stead an agonizing anguish began to shroud her face.

For quite some time Chobong sat still; at long last, she let out a heavy sigh, reluctantly adopted a composed expression and began to change her clothes.

Vain thoughts! Idle distractions! I should forget bygone days as well as bygone people and put them out of my mind completely. From this moment on, right in this spot, I should nurture a new life; wasn't that what I determined when I first moved here? . . . No matter how this marriage came about, the fact that I am married to this man is irreversible. My life, my behavior, must be based on that fact . . . the fact that can never be disregarded—and it should never be affected by the motives involved in it or by any lingering regrets about someone else. Moreover, wasn't I myself already a little inclined to him even before I heard about his intention to give some business funds to my father, a piece of information that enabled me to envision a better life for my family, and eventually confirmed my preference for him? The situation being as it is, how can I let myself be swayed by lingering regrets for another man, who is a man of the past? Isn't it a foolish and even sinful double-dealing against this husband of mine, to whom I should entrust my whole life?

After this rationalization, Chobong felt pretty much at ease with herself, and began to fold and put away her bedding.

This wasn't the first time Chobong suffered from so many distracting thoughts about her marriage. It had been the same when she woke up early yesterday morning, and the day before that. In fact she had repeated it every morning ever since the first morning after her marriage. In a sense, it was an inadvertent effect of having been abruptly transplanted into a new environment.

Though Chobong wasn't entirely free of anguish in not being able to forget Seungjae, she didn't have any complaints about the new environment. Rather, she was gradually discovering new pleasures in it, spending cheerful hours, as she tried to get on with her new life. But it was the certain kind of pleasure that a sacrificial victim in a shaman ritual enjoys, enraptured by the beauty of the altar, in total ignorance of the fate awaiting them, destined as they are to be destroyed in the process of the ritual . . .

Chobong changed into a yellow top and a long indigo-blue skirt and swiftly put a white apron on over the skirt, after which she quietly opened the door and walked out onto the maru.

Once out of the room, the clean and fresh dawn air of the early summer caressed her face as if it had been waiting for her, and she felt quite braced by it. Instinctively, she drew in a deep

breath of the fresh air and then breathed it out in one long
breath. As she repeated the deep breathing a few more times,
she felt like all the fatigue of her body, which had been subjected
to unnatural torment overnight, as well as the fuzziness of her
head caused by the warm, humid air in the room, were cleansed
away at once.

It was still very quiet both inside and outside; she heard no
noises of passersby or peddlers yet, Taesu was still asleep, and the
maid would come out to the kitchen only around six o'clock. It
would be another hour before she heard the sound of coughing
and spitting that Hyeongbo would make in the opposite room.

While Chobong was leaning on the front pillar of the maru,
thinking, or rather thinking of nothing in particular, the dim
dawn light was growing brighter and brighter, until it suddenly
became vividly bright.

As if enchanted, Chobong put on her shoes and stepped
down into the yard. Though the night had been dispelled by
the bright dawn, the house was full of quietness, with no one
stirring yet; ever since her marriage, Chobong had savored the
short period of time before breakfast as something precious,
taking a walk around the yard, or attending to the flower bed,
or wool-gathering, looking up at the sky.

"Oh my, how beautiful!" Chobong exclaimed in a whisper as
she absentmindedly looked up at the sky while stepping down
into the yard.

The clouds in the sky looked like innumerable flower buds
in a peony flower bed, buds that would fully bloom as the day
advanced.

In the middle of the blue sky were numerous small patches of
grayish clouds, the tips of which were tinted with a pretty pink
color like a peony bud.

It was too splendid and too varied a sight to be simply
described as beautiful.

She watched the peony buds in the sky for quite a while without sensing the ache in her neck and then, suddenly remembering her flower bed, ran to it hurriedly.

Chobong had been taking good care of the flower bed since the day after her marriage, keeping the promise she'd made to herself when she first saw its neglected condition a few days before her wedding. Not minding her hands getting dirty, she'd invested all her efforts day and night into keeping it neat and full of healthy flowers.

Soaked with morning dew, the flowers looked fresh, their leaves and stalks were very strong and hale. A couple of crepe myrtle buds were beginning to bloom. The moss roses were creeping over the ground, showing off blooming flowers in motley colors—in pink, yellow, red, and white. Morning glories were climbing up the strings that Chobong had tied to the wall for them, as though they were engaging in a climbing contest.

Chobong walked along the flower bed, examining each of the plants, and smiled her morning greeting at each of them. She gave the flowers her affection since she still found it hard to proffer affection to the people in the house.

She noticed half a dozen empty flowerpots lying beside the flower bed and decided that she would ask Taesu to buy some chrysanthemum seedlings. The moment she turned back with this thought, Taesu's voice came from the room.

"Ho—ney?"

His tone was as mellow and soothing as that of an old man calling his wife who had aged with him over several decades. It had been so from the first night of their marriage.

The way Taesu doted on Chobong was, to borrow Hyeongbo's expression, too obnoxious to watch as it set every fiber of his nerves on edge.

Taesu should have taken her on a honeymoon, to a place like a spa, but he gave up on the idea as he was worried that his absence might offer the bank the opportunity to discover his chronic embezzlement; if he were away from the office for several days, a colleague would have to take up his work in his stead, and would eventually notice something was wrong. Therefore he took a leave of absence just for the wedding day alone and returned to work from the very next day.

Although the bank manager encouraged him to take a few days off, Taesu declined the offer, pretending faithfulness to his duty at the bank.

Though they couldn't go on a honeymoon, Taesu did everything he could to make the first ten days of his marriage as amusing and pleasant as possible.

He had intended to continue his debauchery despite his marriage, to have drinking parties, to frequent Haengwha's place, or to have more *gisaengs* in his arms than he used to.

But these were only intentions; ever since his marriage, he in fact had never gone out to drink, never visited Haengwha's place, and even avoided his colleagues' demands for a drinking party in celebration of his marriage. So both his drinking friends and colleagues all lamented that marriage had ruined him.

Regardless of what they said, Taesu went straight back home the moment his work hours were over, not even casting a sideglance at anything.

The worst victim of this new habit was Hyeongbo, who had to endure a dry spell, having no sponsor for his drinking parties other than Taesu.

The resentment Hyeongbo had begun to harbor against Taesu when he refused his proposal to make ten thousand won in forged checks and run away to Seoul was now doubled as Taesu no longer treated him to drinks.

These causes of his hatred for Taesu could have been ignored or tolerated but for one thing; Chobong was the strongest cause of his hatred for Taesu, one that spurred him to plot a vicious scheme to harm him.

While Taesu had that deliciously succulent Chobong all to himself day and night, indulging in every kind of pleasure, Hyeongbo had to endure solitude in the opposite room, groaning with jealousy, and imagining what was going on in the other room through the sounds he could hear. It was truly the worst form of unbearable torture for him.

Ah, that pretty little thing, she's bound to be mine!

Hyeongbo smacked his lips at such thoughts day and night.

May that mortal enemy of mine soon be arrested and thrown into prison!

This was a sort of prayer that had been often in his mind since he moved into the house.

The truth was that Hyeongbo had been waiting for the moment the police would come and arrest Taesu; he expected it would happen soon, today or tomorrow, or at any moment, even if he had no hand in it; he imagined that the moment Taesu was taken away, Chobong would be his.

But the anxiously awaited moment never came, making him increasingly impatient. "That enemy" Taesu, who seemed to have been in real danger, whose situation seemed so precarious it might not even allow him to go through with his wedding ceremony, having escaped being detected, was still safe.

At this rate, who knows how long it would take for him to get arrested . . . a few months, half a year, or even a whole year . . . Hyeongbo thought, he might die of impatience, or waste away with unfulfilled desires.

No, that can never be!

Hyeongbo had finally begun to search for other ways to achieve his aims.

A two-jeon postcard would be enough to do the job. Either
to the bank, or to the Baekseok Company, or to any one of the
other firms that had been swindled by Taesu, he would simply
send a postcard, reporting what Taesu had been doing and suggesting they should investigate the matter. Since he knew that
Taesu had been prepared for this, expecting it could happen any-
time, it wouldn't make much difference whether he got caught
today or tomorrow, or one or two years later.

And then recalling that Taesu had repeatedly said, "It'll all
be over if I kill myself," Hyeongbo thought it would be best if
Taesu actually committed suicide.

Hyeongbo definitely preferred Taesu's suicide to his being
imprisoned; if Taesu were arrested, he would violently claim his
wife back once his prison term was over; if he died, however,
he would be able to live with Chobong with much more ease,
sleeping at night comfortably with his legs stretched out.

Once his thoughts went that far, Hyeongbo determined not
to snitch on Taesu. If he did, Taesu would probably be arrested
in his office, with no opportunity to kill himself. The best way,
one worth a million won, he thought, was to goad Taesu one
way or another into a situation in which he would anticipate
the imminent exposure of his crimes and have enough time to
commit suicide.

Yet Hyeongbo couldn't simply wait for a miracle to drop from
the sky; he couldn't just sit by under a tree with his mouth open,
waiting for a ripe fruit to drop in by itself. Such passive waiting
would shrivel him up, he thought.

With what magical move can I hasten it? Hyeongbo had been
racking his brain for the past two days; he needed a skillful
move that would expose Taesu gradually rather than making
everything come out at once. It was essential for Hyeongbo to
make Taesu realize what was coming, for instance, through his

colleagues' whispers or gossip, well before the actual arrest took place.

Taesu had no clue whatsoever about the vicious scheme that was hatching in Hyeongbo's mind. Though he was often tormented by frightful nightmares, when he woke up, he at once became quite gay and cheerful.

This morning when he opened his eyes, still half asleep, he couldn't find Chobong in the room, and missing her, called aloud for her in the sweet tones of an old husband.

Chobong answered him, and dragging her feet, went into the room. Though outside it was bright, inside the room was still dim.

Rubbing his eyes, he looked up at Chobong and smiled a happy smile.

Chobong, who still felt shy in his presence, smiled back, turning her head aside abashed.

Taesu smiled and Chobong smiled, then the first order of the day was over for Taesu; he confirmed Chobong's presence; he saw her smile; and he returned a smile again, asking,

"What time is it?"

"It's five-thirty."

"Are you making breakfast?"

"I haven't started yet . . ."

"He-eh."

For the past ten days, Taesu had repeated the same ritual of calling her into his presence for no particular purpose both in the morning and in the evening. Having grown accustomed to this, Chobong wasn't at all surprised and was about to turn back to go out. But this morning, Taesu called her back again in a somewhat serious voice.

"By the way, Honey?"

Chobong stopped, and waited.

"Well, what do you think? I guess at least one thousand won will be needed."

At this remark out of the blue, Chobong was rather bewildered.

"I mean, for your father. You know, for him to start a business . . ."

Chobong at last understood, but she simply smiled. From the beginning, Chobong had assumed that Taesu would fulfill his promise as a matter of course, so she hadn't been concerned about that at all. She took it for granted, as naturally as day follows night.

". . . Come dear, and sit by me here. Let's have some talk about the matter as I'm reminded of it now."

Taesu beckoned Chobong to his pillow, picking up a cigarette and lighting it.

Chobong sat beside him as she was told, and Taesu putting his hand on her knee said,

". . . What do you think? Would a thousand won do? Or wouldn't it be enough?"

"Well . . ."

"What do you mean, 'well?' It's a matter we two should decide."

"But still . . ."

Chobong felt too awkward to say anything about it. It was one of the conditions attached to the marriage from the beginning; yet still, if she promptly responded by demanding this or that, it would make her feel she was negotiating the price of her body. She was quite averse to such a conversation. On the other hand, the figure of one thousand won was so vague and unfamiliar to her that she couldn't have any concrete idea as to how much it amounted to.

Though she'd heard from her mother that Taesu would provide her father with a few thousand won, she couldn't point out the discrepancy when Taesu said one thousand won. She knew that such talk would make her an object of bargaining.

Chobong wanted to avoid any sort of discussion about the money. She was sure that Taesu would give money to her family regardless of whether she joined in the discussion or not, so it seemed to her much better to leave the matter to be settled between her father and Taesu, rather than embarrassing herself by being drawn into it.

Taesu had suggested some seed money for Chobong's father's business simply as a decoy when he first proposed to her, without any serious intention of keeping the promise. But as he came to think it over now, turning the lie into a fact didn't seem to be a bad idea at all.

First of all, having embezzled so much already, taking another thousand won from someone else's account wouldn't make much difference, he thought. He also thought it worth attempting, as it would make him look like a magnanimous man who kept his promise.

Moreover, in case he left Chobong alone, having failed to take her life along with his when he committed suicide, she'd be spared penury if her father was provided with some means of independent living. That was another positive motive that encouraged him to decide on this plan of turning his empty promise into a real one.

Look now! As I bring up the subject, Chobong seems to be pleased though she acts rather coy about it. Making Chobong pleased is what pleases me. If I can only please her, even ten thousand won would be cheap let alone one thousand! Ten thousand won is only a piece of paper for me . . . Pshaw! Even if I swindled a million won rather than ten thousand, who would dare to violate my corpse? How inspiring! How thrilling it would be! . . . Yes, I'll take out a few thousand won at the earliest opportunity, I will surely do that within a few days . . .

Taesu was exhilarated as he thus confirmed his resolution. However, he wasn't thinking far enough ahead to realize that any money he gave to Jeong Jusa would be confiscated once his embezzlements were detected, since the money would certainly be traced, and they would find out that the money was given to Jeong Jusa.

"What do you mean—'but still?' It's a matter we two should discuss and determine . . ."

Taesu pressed Chobong, holding and shaking her knee.

". . . Isn't that what we should do?"

"I have no idea whatsoever!"

With these words Chobong started to get up.

"Dear me! Then what should I do?"

"Well, I think . . . you should consult with my father."

"Ah-a, with your father? . . . I know that, but . . ."

"Then it's settled, right? . . ."

"Nevertheless, I still want to consult my lady first, he-he."

"Oh, my!"

Chobong startled at the word, "my lady," blushed crimson.

"Ha, ha, ha. Aren't you my lady?"

"I don't know! I must get on . . ."

As she reached for the sliding door, she turned back and asked,

". . . Please, don't forget to buy a few chrysanthemum seedlings today."

"Chrysanthemum seedlings? Sure, sure, I won't forget."

"Five seedlings please . . ."

"Only five? . . . How about a dozen?"

"When there are only five flowerpots?"

"We can also buy more flowerpots."

While carrying on such sweet talk, Taesu was thinking to himself, *for whom are you going to plant chrysanthemums?* Looking at Chobong, who seemed as innocently happy as a child, in utter ignorance of the real state of affairs awaiting her, Taesu felt deep compassion for her, and he once again looked up at her with a new sense of regret.

After Chobong had gone out to the kitchen, Hyeongbo in the opposite room made sounds of spitting as if to announce that he was up, and called out,

"Are you up now, Go Jusa?"

At this usual signal from Hyeongbo in the morning, Taesu called out his unenthusiastic response.

"Yah!"

Hyeongbo, flapping his bathrobe, walked into the main room, confirming his resolution to scare Taesu in a sly manner this morning.

Chobong, who heard Hyeongbo's voice from the kitchen, shuddered unconsciously. Chobong had felt Hyeongbo was rather creepy and ugly when she first saw him. That feeling of dislike hadn't diminished at all during the past ten days. She still felt frightened, as if a huge snake was stationed in the opposite room.

At such moments, she tried to persuade herself that it was a foolish thought. She had maintained decent manners toward him, treating him with kindness as she was supposed to do. But as the days went by, her fear of him grew rather than subsided.

Of course, Chobong hadn't detected the sly, vile intentions lurking in him. She was simply frightened by his physical appearance, especially by his deeply sunken eyes.

Taesu, still wrapped in the maroon bedclothes, stretched out his body to the full when Hyeongbo walked into the room. Hyeongbo, sniffing like a hound at the oddly mellow and sensual scent of a woman's boudoir, a compound of perfume and the smell of flesh, sat down next to Taesu. Hyeongbo relished this scent every morning as it allowed him to visualize the body of Chobong. This association of the scent with Chobong aroused in him an excitement that was simultaneously painful and delicious. For this reason Hyeongbo made sure to visit the room early in the morning even when he had nothing particular to talk about to Taesu, afraid lest that special scent should vanish as morning progressed.

"I went to Sinheung-dong brothel last night, damn it."

"So that's why you came home at dawn . . . you damn rogue!"

"Why am I a damn rogue? How do you expect me to stand all those crazy things you two do in this room? . . . Being a man neither too old, nor too young, what torture do you think it is for me to be crouching in the room opposite?"

"If you did, you could have saved some money, ha, ha, ha, ha."

"You wretch! . . . Huh, huh, huh, huh. What a thing to say!"

"Ha, ha, ha, ha."

"Huh! Stop your nonsense . . . by the way, Taesu, old friend . . ."

Hyeongbo's expression abruptly changed from one of jest to serious concern. The change was so abrupt that it seemed almost unnatural. Wondering about the cause of this sudden seriousness, Taesu stared at Hyeongbo and waited for his next words.

Hyeongbo lit a cigarette and putting it into his mouth began to whisper to Taesu affectionately.

"I bring up this topic as no one is around, but I'm really concerned about how you could be so easygoing and carefree. Do you have any strategy to deal with your imminent disaster?"

"What are you talking about?"

Taesu immediately understood what Hyeongbo was driving at; but with a frown he pretended not to understand him; he was very displeased with Hyeongbo for introducing such an unpleasant and unwelcome topic early in the morning, which seemed to portend bad luck for the day.

"Don't you get it? I mean the checks . . ."

"Ah, that? . . .Tut-tut! That can't be helped!" Taesu spat out in annoyance.

"What do you mean, 'that can't be helped?' Do you mean you're going to sit still and let them do as they please with you? Are you prepared to face it? That nasty business . . ."

"Who said I'd sit still and suffer? Don't worry, nothing will happen to me."

"Nothing? You wouldn't suffer . . .?"

Hyeongbo, quickly wiping the startled expression off his face, said,

". . . Well, if that's true, nothing would make me happier! . . . Does that mean that you have some clever schemes to avoid trouble? . . . You really have something up your sleeve?"

"Tut-tut! You might say I have or haven't, either way."

Annoyed and irritable, Taesu blurted out his answers haphazardly without any serious interest in the conversation; Hyeongbo, who had no way of knowing his real state of mind, assumed that Taesu was indeed free from worries, having some definite means to avoid trouble.

He seemed to have found a way out. What had he been doing to have such an underhand scheme? How and where had he found it?

Ah-hah! Right, right. Ten to one, he got it from that source . . .

Hyeongbo slapped his knee in his mind.

The wife of shaggy-faced Han Chambong suddenly flashed across his mind. He knew all along that she'd been deeply involved with Taesu and that she had a lot of money.

If she's gallant enough to marry off her playmate Taesu to another woman, taking full charge of every preparation for the marriage, who knows, she may also be capable of paying off his debts of several thousand won to save him from imminent danger.

Having arrived at that conclusion, Hyeongbo realized that his plot was a bubble that had burst. How foolish and thickheaded he'd been to dream of a day when Taesu would be taken away. No, Taesu shouldn't get away like that.

Tilting his head this way and that as if trying to figure out an answer, Hyeongbo sat silently for a while and at last he asked,

"Hey, man! Stop equivocating and open your heart candidly. Won't you tell me the truth now? . . . I'm dying to know . . ., tell me please?"

"What's it matter to you? . . . Isn't it also a good move to kill yourself when you're stuck with no way out? . . . Isn't rat poison readily available? Or sleeping pills? . . . It's good that the rivers are deep enough and the railway tracks are cool enough to lie on."

"Fiddlesticks! . . . It's not everyone that can commit suicide. You're not the type."

"Humph! Anyone can if pressed hard enough."

"If that's true, who would endure a prison term when he has to wear a sad-colored prison uniform, fettered with iron chains, and carrying the dung pot placed right next to him? . . . It's only because suicide is not so easy that people endure all that shame and hardship in prison."

"Shut up!"

Taesu shouted in anger and turned over in his bed. He could indeed imagine a vivid picture of his own self in the sad-colored uniform, fettered in chains, lying next to the dung pot against the background of the redbrick prison wall, just as Hyeongbo described it.

Hyeongbo's suspicions weren't yet allayed, but being unable to ask any more questions, he fell to mulling over the matter more deeply.

After breakfast, Taesu went to the bank as usual. But he was uneasy all day long as what Hyeongbo blabbered about in the morning kept returning to his mind; it was as inauspicious as the sound of crows cawing early in the morning before a business transaction.

He barely managed to sit at his desk, frowning all day long until it was almost time to close. It was two minutes to four when he received a phone call from the Farm Produce Promotion Company.

It was one of the three companies from which Taesu had embezzled money. Taesu jumped as though by reflex action when the office boy announced a phone call for a clerk in charge of checking accounts from the Farm Produce Promotion Company. All his blood rushed to his heart while his face turned pale, and cold sweat oozed down his back and dripped from his forehead.

All these symptoms were only the reflex reactions of his body, independent of his will.

The day has come at last!

Taesu thought rather nonchalantly, taking it as something that was bound to happen or rather as something he was well prepared for. Therefore his head remained as clear as crystal and the heart that had beat so violently soon calmed down to normal.

"They want me . . .?" Taesu casually muttered to himself, while he was deliberately continuing to put away the account books. His voice was a bit cracked but not distinctly so.

". . . Did they ask for me? Was it for the checking accounts clerk?"

"Yes, sir. They asked for someone in the checking accounts department."

"How annoying! Just when it's time to close . . . What do they want?"

"I don't know. They just asked for your department . . ."

"Let me see!"

Taesu lingered on until it was past four o'clock and then picked up the phone after sending the office boy away by asking him to get some fresh water.

"Yes, can I help you?"

"This is the Farm Produce Promotion Company . . . I'm calling because there's something irregular in our checking account that we can't understand . . ."

The tone of the voice wasn't at all urgent or imposing, but rather polite and inquiring.

Taesu thought that it must indeed be what he'd expected, but lowering his voice said,

"Ah, is that right? . . . Um, well, the person in charge of checking accounts has left the office as it's past closing time. I'm not sure what your problem is, but if it's not too urgent, can you call again early tomorrow morning . . .?"

"I see, that may be all right, but . . . has the bank manager also gone?"

"Yes, he has."

"Ah-ha! . . . Then I'll call again tomorrow . . . I don't think it's very serious, yet I wanted to confirm as there is something unaccountable."

Taesu heard the sound of him hanging up and turned around as he too hung up the phone, just as the office boy brought in the water he'd asked for.

Taesu drank the full glass of water in one gulp with relish, returned to his desk and began to sort out his thoughts, which were all about what he would have to do from now on in order to prepare for his final day.

First, he would buy one packet of rat poison, then buy some fruit and cookies, and return home as cheerfully as usual.

Chobong would welcome him with a smile; he would spend some pleasant time with Chobong until the evening; after supper he would leave home and visit Haengwha's place and then Madam Kim's; if shaggy-faced Han Chambong wasn't at home, it would be nice to stay there for a couple of hours, renewing his old intimacy with her. That old saying is never wrong; they say new love is never as good as old love, and indeed he felt he was missing the old love. Yes! He should enjoy some intimacy with her to keep the promise he'd made before his marriage. If the shaggy-faced man was at home, he wouldn't be able to do it. Well, that couldn't be helped. He would simply pretend to be making a courtesy call, as it would be his first visit since his marriage.

What the hell. How wonderful would it be if he could take all three women together on his journey to the other world, not just Chobong, but Haengwha, and Madam Kim as well? Wouldn't it be exciting? Well perhaps that would be a rather vain indulgence, he thought.

On his way home from Madam Kim's, he would buy a bottle of the best quality sake and ask Chobong to prepare something to accompany the drinks, and while waiting for the table of drinks, he would destroy the seals and checkbooks with which he had forged the checks. After all it wouldn't matter whether he did that or not, but it wouldn't be bad if he left no evidence behind him.

When the food was ready, he would drink a glass of sake, having Chobong sit at his side; he would have Chobong drink as well, and enjoy the drinking party until twelve o'clock and then go to bed. At three o'clock in the morning, he would wake

up and confess everything to Chobong. And then he would ask
Chobong to die with him.

What if Chobong refuses?

Well, he can pretend with a laugh that it was a joke to test
her, and set her at ease. If she falls asleep again, he would attempt
with a belt or something . . .

Wait! He'd forgotten to provide his father-in-law with some
seed money for business. He felt sorry for him. He should have
drawn at least one thousand won for him. What a pity he hadn't
thought about it a bit earlier.

It was all a matter of the past, something he couldn't help at
this stage.

Had he thought everything through?

*Confound it! Ah! . . . My mother! What should I do with my
mother? That poor, forlorn mother of mine!*

I'm a thief, a vile man, and an undutiful son to boot!

Taesu let out a long sigh, overcome by the unexpected surge
of remorse in his mind.

Having stashed the rat poison in his pocket, Taesu resumed
his normal self as if the poison had nothing to do with him, and
holding a basket of fruit and a packet of cookies in each hand,
rushed helter-skelter back home.

"Honey?"

The moment he stepped over the threshold, a broad smile
spread over his face as he called out for Chobong. This wasn't a
forced smile to counteract his consciousness of it being the last
day of his life. A smile naturally emerged in spite of himself.

Chobong was cleaning the flowerpots in the yard, her hands
all smeared with soil like a child playing with mud. Hyeongbo
too was beside her, sweating as he helped.

Chobong sprang to her feet and took the fruit and cookies
from Taesu with a smile.

"You're rather late today, Go Jusa?"

"Working hard, Jang Jusa?"

Taesu looked down at Hyeongbo who was squatting on the ground, his bent knees rising to his shoulders.

"Nothing hard here! . . . I couldn't sit still while your lady was busy, getting her delicate hands all dirty . . ."

"Then I'll also join in."

Rolling up his sleeves, Taesu looked back at Chobong and sent her a big smile. Chobong, who was returning to the yard after placing the fruit and cookies on the maru, suddenly noticed that Taesu had come back without chrysanthemum seedlings. She stretched out her tiny dirty hands toward Taesu and said,

"The chrysanthemum seedlings . . ."

"Oh, darn it!"

Taesu slapped his knee and darted his tongue in and out. The tiny hands stretched out toward him were so endearing that he would have fondled them if Hyeongbo weren't around. Even the dirt on her hands looked lovely.

". . . Oh, dear, I forgot! What can I do now?"

"You should've asked me to buy them," Hyeongbo cut in to assert his presence there. "You should know that he's prone to forgetting such errands even before he crosses the stream."

"Then you buy them tomorrow on your way home, Uncle."

Chobong called Hyeongbo "Uncle" as Taesu had suggested she use that title for him.

"No, I won't forget to buy them tomorrow for certain, ha, ha, ha, ha."

Taesu's reply ended with loud laughter. But no one guessed at the cause of his empty laughter. Hyeongbo, as if in jest, threw a sneer at Taesu.

"See, what an exemplary husband you're trying to make yourself!"

"Stop your nonsense, you wretch!"

"Stop being so openly affectionate! Seeing you two like that makes me quite jealous and depressed."

"Why don't you begin your own family, Uncle?"

"I have neither money nor a woman, even if I wanted to."

"What about Haengwha?"

"Haeng? Wha? Huh, huh, huh. Uh-huh, huh."

At Hyeongbo's excessive laughter, Chobong blushed right up to her ears, afraid she might have said some seriously inappropriate thing. Taesu turned aside so as not to face Hyeongbo.

At that moment, the maid from shaggy-faced Han Chambong's house walked into the yard rather cautiously.

"Oh, is that you?"

Taesu guessed that Madam Kim had sent her to ask him to come over. If that was the case, it would be a very timely call for him, Taesu thought.

After bowing to Taesu and Chobong, the girl conveyed the message that Taesu was asked to visit Han Chambong's house after supper as they had some business to talk about with him.

"All right, is the message from your master Han Chambong?"

"Yes, it is."

The girl responded in the affirmative as instructed by Madam Kim.

So Chobong bore no suspicion, paying no particular attention to the summons.

Even if Taesu and the maid hadn't fabricated a lie, Chobong would have thought Madam Kim simply had something to talk about with Taesu, because she'd had no reason to suspect their relationship.

Hyeongbo's situation, however, was different.

He was confident that Madam Kim surely wanted to discuss measures to solve Taesu's problems at the bank, or that she'd already prepared a few thousand won and wanted to give the money to Taesu tonight. Recalling Taesu's indifferent reaction earlier this morning when he'd expressed his concerns about Taesu's monetary problems, Hyeongbo had no doubts whatsoever about his conjectures as to the nature of Madam Kim's summoning of Taesu.

In case my guess turns out to be true?

Go for it, snitch on him right now! What do I have to lose?

Hyeongbo nodded his head repeatedly as he kept thinking to himself.

A little after seven o'clock, when he'd finished his supper, Hyeongbo went out, saying that he had some business to attend to, and a little before eight o'clock came back again. On ordinary nights he usually intruded into the main room, uninvited, where Taesu and Chobong were enjoying themselves, listening to the gramophone while eating.

But that night he came back with an unusually pale face and went directly into his own room, alleging that he wasn't feeling well. Then he soon turned off the light and went to bed.

While they were having supper, Taesu told Chobong that he would go out after the meal and wouldn't be back until midnight, as he would stop by at the rice store, and then meet a friend who was visiting from Seoul. So Taesu asked Chobong not to wait up for him.

After supper Taesu spent some time with Chobong as usual and around nine o'clock he left home wearing a Japanese-style bathrobe and wooden clogs. As he left, he told Chobong one more time to go to bed without waiting up for him.

Haengwha wasn't at home because she'd been summoned to a party. He felt more relieved than sorry, as he was quite impatient to submit to the ecstatic caresses of Madam Kim, who must be anxiously waiting for him.

When he arrived at shaggy-faced Han Chambong's house, he inspected the store first. The shutters were drawn down and locked. He looked through the cracks, but all was dark within. He was sure that Han Chambong wasn't at the store.

Having thus confirmed that the field was all clear, Taesu began to feel that he'd been foolish and laughable.

Why have I been so careful? When she sent for me, she must have made certain that no obstacles were in the way.

Though he reasoned as such, he wasn't feeling as secure or as relaxed as usual; he couldn't help feeling uncomfortable in a corner of his mind.

Therefore, when he passed through the inner gate, he announced his arrival, calling for Han Chambong.

"Ahem! Are you in bed, Uncle?"

No sooner did she hear Taesu than Madam Kim opened the sliding door of her room, revealing her upper body covered with a light green coverlet; she simply smiled without saying a word.

Taesu thought she looked exactly the same as the night in the early autumn of last year when they'd had their first encounter. He walked into the room in big strides, filled with nostalgia for their first intimacy. Madam Kim tapped on her futon a couple of times to beckon him to sit next to her, and brightened up with a sweet smile.

Taesu carelessly plumped down on the spot she pointed to, baring his hairy legs under his robe. Taesu felt a little tension along with a sense of relief, as if he'd returned to his first wife after some absence.

The sensible maid came out of her room, locked the gate, and removed Taesu's wooden clogs.

"Well my boy, how are you enjoying your new life as a married man?" Madam Kim said as if fondling an infant, stretching her neck forward to stare into Taesu's smiling face.

"Why do you treat me like a boy when I'm an adult now that I'm married?"

"Oh, you impudent thing!"

Madam Kim pinched Taesu's cheek and shook it softly and then drawing him toward her, she————.

She wanted to bite him as her lips were already on his face, but decided to forbear for the time being.

"Since your marriage, you've become better at doing cute things!"

"Heh, heh."

"Well, you look haggard though. That's one bad consequence when you help youngsters get married! . . . Don't do it too much, it's harmful to your health."

"You should have sent me some herbal extracts for my health!"

"Sure, sure. I'll get them ready for you tomorrow. But still you should be more careful about your health! . . . Is she that lovable?"

"Yup."

"Ha, ha, ha! You rogue! . . . But tonight, you're absolutely mine, aren't you? You haven't forgotten your promise? Never to fail to come to me at least twice a month."

"Yes, dear. But it's only until midnight, right?"

"Is anybody going to kick you out?"

"By the way, how did you know in advance that your shaggy-faced old man would be away tonight and . . .?"

Taesu had been curious about that, feeling strangely uneasy all along.

"How did I know that? . . . I knew very well since it's his slut's birthday. Isn't it obvious that he would go to her place on this special day? That's why I sent word to you, way in advance, and got myself prepared . . ."

"Is that so? I was foolish enough to check the store before I came in here; I was afraid he might be in! Heh, heh."

"Don't worry about that and relax whenever I ask you over. You know I can handle matters quite smoothly."

Shaggy-faced Han Chambong had in fact been lying crouched in the room attached to the store for nearly an hour in total darkness, anxiously waiting for the tedious time to pass.

He'd left his concubine's house at around ten o'clock, so it should be almost eleven o'clock by now, but the clock hadn't struck yet.

He was half curious and half nervous, and he himself felt laughable too when he thought about the pathetic thing he was doing at this moment. On the other hand, it was also true that he was frightened as well. He stretched out his arm and touched the heavy laundry bat that he'd placed right next to his head as he lay down.

Shaggy-faced Han Chambong had received a strange phone call earlier in the evening around seven o'clock.

Assuming that it was a rice order, he answered it casually, but the voice on the line was bold and imposing.

"Hello, is this Han Chambong?"

"Yes, speaking."

"Are you sure you're Han Chambong?"

"I said I am . . . Who's calling please?"

"Well, you don't need to know who I am. Even if I gave you my name, you wouldn't know me . . . But I know you very well."

"I see . . .," Han Chambong answered in an absent sort of way, blinking his eyes.

He was afraid that it might be one of those threatening calls demanding he bring money to a certain place. His heart fell. But the voice was too polite to be one of those calls. Moreover, the time of social unrest when political blackmail was high in the air had been over for quite some time. Nowadays it was hardly possible to find such cases of blackmail.

"Well, go ahead and tell me your business . . ."

The caller cleared his throat once and began,

". . . I'm calling you to warn you of a big disaster that will befall your family tonight . . ."

"Di—sas—ter?"

"Hush! Don't speak so loud, please . . . Just listen to me carefully . . . Is there anyone beside you in the store?"

"No, there's no one here!"

"Then I can talk freely . . . By the way, I understand you're going out to your mistress's tonight, aren't you?"

"What?"

Han Chambong gave a start.

"Haha! You don't need to be so surprised, I assure you . . . Well, later tonight, after you've had your supper and closed the shop—pay close attention to what I say now, please!—you must go to your mistress's as planned, acting naturally. Make sure your wife and servants know that you're on your way to your mistress's. Do you get it?"

"Ye-es!"

It was more a groan than an answer.

"Then you go to your mistress's and stay there for a while. But at around eleven o'clock, you should leave the place on the pretense that you have to stop by somewhere, and then go back to your house. But no one should know that you're back. Perhaps you should leave one of the side doors to your store unlocked and come back through it, or you could jump over the wall. Whatever you do, your return mustn't be detected by anyone. Understood?"

"Ye-es!"

"Once you're secretly back at your house, head to your wife's bedroom without making a sound, not even the sound of your footsteps. And then . . ."

"And then?"

Shaggy-faced Han Chambong hurriedly urged him to go on, overwhelmed by the tension that had been gripping him.

"Well . . . when you stealthily get to the door of your wife's room, just open the door quickly, and then you'll know everything."

"Hey, Mr! What the hell!"

"Don't ask anymore. Just do as I say, or if you're doubtful, forget about it . . . But I hope you won't regret it later."

"Hey, listen!"

"I don't need to listen to you, and I have nothing to add, except that . . . I've nothing to gain or lose by informing you of this. Remember that I'm totally disinterested in this, please."

With this final word, he abruptly hung up the phone. Shaggy-faced Han Chambong at last regained his composure, but he still blankly stared at the phone, flabbergasted by what he'd heard.

Needless to say, it was Hyeongbo who made the call from a payphone near the bus stop.

Hyeongbo was expecting an outcome similar to what he'd often read in newspapers—both the wife and her gigolo get killed by the husband at the scene of their secret affair. If the tide turned in his favor, the same thing might happen to Taesu. In addition, he was scheming to take care of Chobong while Taesu was away at Madam Kim's.

That was why he suggested eleven o'clock to Han Chambong instead of earlier in the evening, when Taesu was supposed to receive a few thousand won from Madam Kim.

Even if things didn't turn out as he expected, Hyeongbo had nothing to lose and he was confident that there would be numerous ways to have Taesu fall into the hands of the law in the near future. However, if Taesu were killed tonight, it certainly would be a great windfall for him.

Shaggy-faced Han Chambong at last put the phone back on its hook and slowly turned around.

The story he'd heard was too preposterous to be true. For a moment he thought it had to be a prank being played on him. If it was a prank, however, it was of a serious nature; moreover, he couldn't think of anybody who would dare to play such a prank on him. Then it seemed obvious to him that it couldn't be that.

It suddenly occurred to him that it might be a vicious conspiracy on the part of his concubine, who wanted a rendezvous with her secret lover tonight by inventing a sham situation to send him away. It seemed reasonable enough to suspect a concubine of having another lover.

On the other hand, he recalled that his concubine was going to have a birthday party with a few of her friends at her place, having made plans to party all night long. Moreover, she had sent her maid three times already, asking him to close the store early and come over to her place sooner than usual. She wouldn't have done that if she wanted to keep him away.

He had to admit that especially for tonight there was no reason to suspect her of a conspiracy.

Then in due course his suspicions should have switched to his wife, but his trust in her faithfulness had always been so strong and firm that he couldn't even imagine infidelity on her part.

"Then what sort of catastrophe could it be?"

Tilting his head this way and that, Han Chambong racked his brains, trying to figure out the cause of this odd call, but in vain. Neither could he ignore the warning, feeling too squeamish to simply do nothing about it.

Who was that guy on the phone, who knew the intimate details of his domestic situation? How could he know that he (Han Chambong) was going to visit his concubine tonight when it was only his intention, not yet discussed even in his house? Unless that guy was a ghost, he couldn't have been so accurate.

"A ghost!"

Indeed, it might well have been a ghost's prank. Once he arrived at that thought, he suddenly felt a chill run down his spine and had to look back.

However, like any stouthearted man would do, shaggy-faced Han Chambong always mocked those people who claimed that they saw ghosts or that ghosts did this or that; he'd never believed in the existence of ghosts from the days of his youth. So long as he was in a sober state of mind, he couldn't explain the strange event as something staged by mischievous ghosts without mocking himself.

"Damn it! Tut! What a fuss, when it was only some mad nonsense uttered by some crazy jerk!"

He gruffly vented his disgust, though there was no one to respond, and shook his head wildly while stamping his foot, as if reassuring himself not to pay anymore attention to the weird things he'd heard.

Nevertheless the strange telephone call had exerted a hypnotizing force over him and had him fully in its grasp, even though he was as clearheaded as possible. First of all, when he was closing the store around eight o'clock, he left one of the shutters unlocked as if he were spellbound.

After closing the store, he carried the cash box into his room, put it into a closet and locked it. And then with the usual instruction to his wife to keep the gate well secured, he reluctantly headed toward his concubine's house.

Once he arrived at the place, he found it full of pretty young women, and the sumptuous feast was no less inviting. It was like sitting down in a charming flower bed. For all the festivity, he couldn't enjoy it, even the wine was bitter to his taste. The bold and daring voice over the phone that had warned him of an impending disaster kept returning to his mind.

He became too anxious to wait until eleven o'clock. He left the place even before ten, having decided to be there in advance and wait for the time, hiding somewhere in the store.

All the women at the party, not only his concubine but her drunken friends as well, tried to detain him. But he told them that he had urgent business to attend to on the outskirts of the town and would be back again by midnight. And then he got hold of a laundry bat and took it with him, explaining that he'd need it to protect himself as rabid dogs were roaming the streets. He took it because he felt insecure without any weapon, and then he also intended to beat indiscriminately any suspicious man in sight in his house, whether over the shoulders or the hips.

He cautiously walked home, careful not to be seen by anybody, and examined the house; the gate was well locked, and no one was astir within the house. He could find nothing unusual on the outside, either.

Feeling relieved, he entered the store through the door he'd left unlocked. Once inside the dark store, he felt himself shrink in fright, fearing something might emerge from the darkness. He groped for the door of the room in the store almost crawling, and the moment he sat down in the room, he breathed a long sigh of relief.

Now he was anxiously waiting for the time to pass, blinking his eyes.

Shaggy-faced Han Chambong, alone in the dark room of the empty store, where some inauspicious aura seemed to be thickly afloat, groped for the bat and felt somewhat reassured when he touched it. It was, however, not reassuring enough to remove the anxiety, terror, and restlessness that were building up in him with every moment.

It wasn't just his mind that was being tortured. Though the room wasn't too cold, lying on the bare floor without any blanket underneath made his body ache to the bone with chills, for he was already in his fifties.

The clock on the wall was idling along tick-tock, tick-tock, refusing to strike eleven.

No matter how wide he opened his eyes, there was nothing to see except for sheer darkness. He desperately longed for a cigarette, but he didn't dare to strike a match in case its light showed outside.

He became more and more annoyed at the situation, which denied him the pleasure of smoking at will.

You rascal! If you're a thief, I'll knock your . . .

He resolved to beat up whoever it might be, aggravated by his anger at not being able to smoke.

Though he thought for a moment the man might be a thief, on second thoughts, it seemed obvious that the man could by no means be a mere thief. If he were a thief, he would break into the store instead of into his wife's room. It was true that there was some cash and jewelry in her room. If that was the case, however, the guy on the phone should have told him to sit in his wife's room and guard against any intrusion. But he told him to sneak into the house and open the bedroom door at eleven o'clock. It could be nothing but a plot to catch a gigolo red-handed.

A gigolo? My wife's gigolo?

Gosh, what nonsense!

As his suspicion finally turned toward his wife, he quickly forced himself to dispel it as something too outlandish. His trust in his wife had been so deeply rooted for so long that he even trembled in fright at the mere suggestion.

The more he tried to deny it, however, the more reasonable it appeared; an old husband, a kept mistress, a young wife, a gigolo—it seemed too plausible for him not to have considered that possibility sooner.

"However it looks, it just can't be, no way . . ."

It was the most likely scenario, and at the same time, the most disgusting and inauspicious thing to imagine, which forced him to struggle to the utmost not to believe.

"In all probability, my wife would never, never . . ."

He tried to convince himself that, even if all the women in the world were unfaithful, his wife wouldn't be one of them.

"Right, didn't that guy say a disaster?"

Disaster, it might have been an attempted rape he had tried to warn him against.

It still didn't seem to make sense. If he meant that, he wouldn't have suggested an abrupt intrusion upon the scene at eleven o'clock; instead, he would have told him to beware and keep guard in his wife's room.

All of a sudden he felt an itch in his throat, a cough was about to erupt.

As he tried to suppress it, the itchiness moved up toward his nose, making his nostrils ache. This sneeze was hard to control. He couldn't help but let out a sneeze, though he attempted to muffle it as best he could. It seemed he was catching a cold now.

Right at that moment, he heard loud footsteps outside the store. He listened carefully, but the sounds soon trailed away toward Bean Sprout Pass. When he felt a bit relieved by the fading sounds, the sudden thought came to his mind that he, like a puppet, was faithfully following the absurd instructions of that wretched fellow, when it might really turn out to be a prank after all, played for fun! What a fool! In that case, that guy on the phone must be laughing his head off at the moment. With these thoughts, he felt quite embarrassed at his folly, although no one was watching him.

At the same time, he also earnestly desired that this would indeed turn out to be an idle trick, no matter what a laughing-stock he might become.

The old clock on the store wall at last began to make a screeching sound as if clearing its throat and then wearily struck eleven times. Han Chambong was happy to hear it; it sounded like a lifesaving signal, and he unwittingly let out a long sigh of relief.

He stealthily crept out of the small room and stepped onto the floor of the store. Standing upright in his bare feet, he listened carefully for any unusual sounds. He could hear only a few footsteps passing by in front of the store, but no sound at all from the inner quarters.

Seizing the bat tightly with his right hand, he tiptoed toward the paneled door leading to his house.

Worrying that the damn thing would make a noise, he tried to push the door open little by little. Not surprisingly, the door, which had moved smoothly at first, soon gave out a creaking sound, confirming his worries. Startled, he withdrew his hands and listened for a while. Still there was no sound of movement from the inner quarters. He cautiously began to push the door again, trying to make an opening large enough for his body to get through. His forehead and back were soaked with sweat.

He thrust his head through the opening and looked around. Light was on in both the main bedroom and the room opposite, but there were no signs of movement. Neither could he sense anything in the yard though it was very dark.

Attempting to calm his rapidly beating heart, he stepped into the yard and once again looked around, but he could see nothing unusual. With cautious, light steps, he approached the inner yard and saw in the dim light coming from the room only a pair of his wife's white rubber shoes lying alone on the stone terrace.

He pictured his wife lying alone, having fallen asleep while waiting for his return. Suddenly struck by pity for his wife, he began to admonish himself for his own foolishness.

"Oh dear me! I must have been bewitched by a goblin. What groundless suspicion it has been all along . . ."

For a moment he debated with himself whether he should turn back and leave the place. Intruding upon his wife's innocent slumber all because of one weird phone call seemed way beyond decorum, useless and embarrassing to him, and insulting to his wife.

On the other hand, he was averse to the idea of just turning back now he'd come this far. He stepped onto the stone terrace, having determined to go all the way through as instructed by the weird phone caller, if only to prevent any qualms that might bother him later. Moreover, even if he turned back now, he wouldn't be able to go back to his mistress, leaving the store unlocked all night, as there was no way to lock it from the outside. He thought it might be better to take the risk of becoming a victim to a bad prank than spending the whole night in the cold room in the store.

At last he stepped up onto the maru and put his hand on the jamb of the sliding door; his hand was trembling, but he didn't sense it.

"'Without saying a word, just open the door of the main bedroom.'"

The words he'd heard on the phone rang vividly in his ears and made his hair stand on end. He unwittingly clenched the fist that was holding the bat. Although he wasn't conscious of it, his mind and body were preparing to strike.

He took a deep breath and opened the door in a flash, instantly thrusting his head into the room. The scene before his eyes was startling but not unexpected.

The room was in disarray, and in the center of the room lay two half-naked bodies that had just fallen into a light sleep, legs and arms tangled together, not even having separated after riotously indulging in pleasure . . .

It took less than a second for him to take it all in, to recognize the meaning of it, and to explode with wrath. It was true that he almost froze at the sight at first, but that also passed within that short moment.

"Uh-ung!"

Bellowing like a mad bull, he rushed forward, trembling all over, holding the bat high above his head. The fierceness of his rage was like that of a wild boar struck by burning embers haphazardly thrown by kids on New Year's Day. His face, covered with bristles, flushed with anger, his eyes rolling and blazing as if about to shoot flames, the sight was frightful enough to make anybody tremble. The first to awake from light sleep was Madam Kim. The moment she opened her eyes, she tried to spring up, but she froze, completely unable to move. Taesu awoke a moment later. Perhaps he had just a hair's breadth of time to gain his composure.

The frightening mass of wrath, which seemed powerful enough to bring down a mountain, dashed toward them like a landslide.

"You, who-o-ore!"

With a ferocious growl, he slammed down the bat.

It landed on Madam Kim's head with a dull thud.

"Oh my G—"

Even before she finished her scream, she fell on her face, leaving behind the sound of her last breath.

Taesu took advantage of the moment when the first strike landed on her head. He flew toward the open door. If it were a race, he would have established a new world record in the short-distance dash. His speed was almost superhuman.

Taesu dashed between Han Chambong's legs and ran for the maru, letting out a scream,

"Help! Help!"

He'd planned to commit suicide a few hours later, but his cry for help was genuine. Of course he had no time to recall that he wanted to kill himself. Nevertheless, even if he had recalled it, he still would have shouted for help, running from the scene as fast as lightning to save his skin. Was it because he wanted to take his life honorably in his own good time rather than being brutally killed in disgrace? No. He acted on pure animal instinct.

He had barely got out of the room, when the roar, "you villain!" thundered from behind his back. Despite his intention to run out into the yard, he had no time to do it, and he had to run toward the room opposite. His body might be able to break through the thin lattice door, and there might be someone in that room; he was desperately counting on these two possibilities. In order to charge at the door properly, it was necessary for him to turn about thirty degrees to the right, but the stubborn laws of inertia wouldn't allow it. Although he saw where he was headed, he couldn't avoid striking his chest hard against the large rice chest that was standing on the corner to the left of the door.

"Ough!"

With this cry, Taesu flew up into the air and fell backward with a thud. The impact of the collision was in itself nearly enough to render the rat poison he had previously purchased superfluous. But there followed repeated blows from the bat on his head. The sounds of Han Chambong's curses and the thumping were intermixed with Taesu's screams of pain: "You, wretch!"—"Whack!"—"Uugh," this set of three sounds repeatedly rang through the house.

The cook and the maid stood in the room opposite, looking out through the half-open door, trembling in fright, shouting out frantic cries of, "oh, God!"

Madam Kim's body was stretched on the bedding with her face down; slight shivers at the tips of her feet and hands were the only perceptible movements her body made. The first blow from her husband, who exploded in extreme fury, had been sufficient to smash the skull of the cheating wife to pieces.

The site of vain pleasure was soaked in the blood that was flowing profusely from her head, transforming it into a spectacular crime scene.

Laundry bats made of birch wood from Mun-gyeong Height are known for their hardness; the folk song "Arirang" celebrates this quality, noting that all the birch trees there are turned into laundry bats. That bat, however, sometimes functions as a messenger of bloody death.

The hysterical shrieks of women mixed with the thunderous roars of a man in the dead of night were enough to draw the attention of passersby. At first one or two of them stopped to see what was going on, but the number gradually increased to three, then four, and so on until they formed a sizable group of people. Once they realized that the situation in the house was far from normal, they could no longer remain as mere spectators. An alliance was forged on the spot in silence, and they began to shake the gate, and then to shout loudly.

At the sound of the gate being shaken wildly, shaggy-faced Han Chambong at last came to his senses and stopped beating Taesu. As if awakening from a delirium, he looked down at the body of Taesu that lay senseless at his feet.

Taesu was lying on his side, breathing intermittently, but his limbs and body were totally motionless. Blood was flooding down, drenching his face and bathrobe.

Shaggy-faced Han Chambong stared down at Taesu's body for quite some time, as if he were seeing something weird and unbelievable. Then he turned around and hurried toward the main bedroom.

Madam Kim's body was still lying face down, the slight trembling of the tips of her limbs had already stopped, she was clearly lifeless.

Shaggy-faced Han Chambong approached his wife's body and stared at it for a while, then he slowly lifted his eyes skyward, muttering,

"So this is how it ends!"

He seemed unable to accept the strange outcome of his fit of wrath.

With his own eyes, he saw two dead bodies, killed with his own bare hands, but somehow he couldn't believe that he himself was the murderer.

He feebly dropped the bloodstained bat he'd been holding and stood there vacantly, as if in a trance. He remained standing like that until the police came and shackled him.

Hyeongbo on the other hand . . .

When he'd completed his mission of tipping off Mr. Han about Taesu from a public phone, he went back to his room, with a feigned air of innocence. As he was lying on his back, his heart palpitating, he felt relieved, anticipating that his long-drawn-out task would reach an end shortly.

While listening to the amorous play between Taesu and Chobong in the room opposite, Hyeongbo was able to grin, muttering to himself,

Well, well, it's the last chance for you, so play on to your heart's content.

When Taesu left the house at nine o'clock with the clatter of his Japanese clogs, Hyeongbo was again beaming with a happy smile, muttering to himself,

Well, kiddo, it's down the road to hell you're going.

At the sound of Chobong locking the gate after seeing her husband off, Hyeongbo's exuberance grew wild, and he was busy talking to himself,

So now you'll be mine, for sure!

Certainly . . . no doubt whatsoever!

Then, as of today, I'll make you absolutely mine!

Of course I have to seal it tonight . . . then no one would dare to step in to claim her!

Even if he hadn't preplanned it, Hyeongbo wouldn't have been able to endure leaving Chobong to sleep alone, the woman, who in his mind, was destined to be his.

He waited until Chobong fell asleep. It was tedious to wait, but mustering all his patience, he forced himself to wait for the right time.

At last the clock on the wall struck ten and Hyeongbo determined it was the right moment; Chobong must be sound asleep by now, and even if Taesu managed to come back safely, he wouldn't be able to do so within an hour.

What if he shows up unexpectedly right now? . . . What if he runs mad later when he gets to know of it?

You damned boy! Don't you dare try anything; I'd fix him with a stern glance, wouldn't I? . . . Even if he manages to come back safe tonight, he's destined to be taken away in a few days, for sure.

Hyeongbo trusted that even if Taesu got arrested and investigated, he wouldn't divulge his name as the accomplice who'd cashed the forged checks on his behalf. Hyeongbo counted on Taesu's solemn vow not to get him into trouble, but more than that, he somehow had total trust in Taesu's loyalty to him.

This shows that Hyeongbo, though vicious and wicked, was neither clever nor meticulous in laying down his plans. Feeling quite comfortable with himself, Hyeongbo adjusted the flaps of his bathrobe and cautiously opened the door of his room. The maru was quiet and still.

"Are you asleep, Missus?"

He called out in a low voice in case she might be awake.

No response was forthcoming, and Hyeongbo, on tiptoe, approached the sliding door of the main bedroom and listened. He could hear the even sound of breathing of someone sound asleep.

Hyeongbo, his heart wildly pounding, slid the door open slowly and thrust his head into the room. A fifty-watt light bulb covered with a light blue shade cast a dim light in the room. Chobong, wearing a sloppy nightgown, was sleeping peacefully, with her white thigh thrown on top of the dark blue coverlet, and a few strands of hair scattered around her face. Being a spectator of this scene alone was a feast of unequalled delight for Hyeongbo.

Chobong had fallen asleep early in the evening, right after Taesu had left. Being alone in bed for the first time after a long while gave her an unusual sense of comfort, being able to stretch out her limbs as she pleased, and feeling unconstricted. That's why she fell into a sound and peaceful slumber so easily.

Chobong's mother, Madam Yu, who was very tough and determined in giving a school education to her daughters, had somehow never even thought of teaching Chobong about the precautions a woman should take when sleeping alone.

Hyeongbo grinned once, walked into the room, and closed the door behind him without any noise. He was fully prepared for dealing with the fuss if Chobong woke up and started to give him trouble. Despite that, he approached Chobong very cautiously and grabbed the light switch.

He savored her beauty one last time before turning the light off.

Frightened enough to kick up a storm, Chobong struggled to escape, but before any sound could emerge from her mouth, Hyeongbo's strong palm had sealed it tight. Then gasping, he whispered into her ear,

"Hush! If you make a sound, Taesu will be killed . . . Right now he's lying in bed with Han Chambong's wife at the rice store . . . The moment I go out and inform Mr. Han of it, Taesu will be beaten to death. If you don't want him dead, be quiet and lie still!"

Taken by total surprise, Chobong had no time to work out the precise significance of what Hyeongbo said, though her astonishment was certainly doubling by the moment. Although she was extremely stunned, nevertheless Chobong tried to move her body, but to no avail. She had absolutely no idea how to deal with such a horrible situation.

Aware of the urgency of her situation, for a short moment Chobong thought of her mother, who would surely know what to do in such a predicament. But she was nowhere near. Although she sensed that no effort whatsoever could save her, she couldn't stop trying to wriggle her body to free herself, only to find that she couldn't move at all.

She was somehow too frightened to shout, though in fact even if she had attempted to, she couldn't have done so to good effect, her mouth being tightly covered by Hyeongbo's hand. But driven by her exasperation at the inconceivable situation, she gathered up all her might and twisted her body while she tried to shout. The sound that came out was no more than a groan. Barely making the sound, "ugh," Chobong stopped short in her struggles and fell into a swoon.

The clock was striking twelve when Chobong finally came to her senses. Everything that had happened earlier was like a dim dream—she couldn't believe its reality. Imagining that it really could have been a dream, she momentarily came alive. But however dim her memory might be, she couldn't deny it wasn't a dream. It was real enough to have left her feeling permanently disgraced, turning her body into something filthy, covering it with a stain that could never be ignored or washed out. It had happened in the blink of an eye, in an almost unbelievably vague moment, but its result would be nothing near vague or momentary.

She shuddered to the bone as if she could see her body even in the darkness. Faced with that abominably tainted body, she felt like throwing up. She wanted to throw her body into a seething cauldron, add tons of caustic soda, and boil it for a long, long time. No, that wouldn't do the job well enough. She thought she should rather get a sharp knife and carve out the tainted part from her body. Then she realized that, no matter what she did to her body, it would be to no avail, the harm had already been done.

Then, what on earth should I do?

A swift answer to this searching question popped up as if it had been lying in ambush.

You should die!

Right, that's it; other than death, there could be no way to forget or endure that horrid ignominy. This thought sprang purely out of her pathological fear of contamination, but right away, another reason for suicide struck her mind and reinforced her determination.

That's it! I should die! she cried, biting her lips hard, recalling that she was a wife who had lost her chastity, a wife utterly dishonored.

Chobong groped for her clothes at the bottom of the bed. When she was dressed, she sat hunched up, resting her chin on her hand. Once she began to think about death (she wasn't determined to die, but believed she should), a myriad of indignant emotions began to surge up.

To have been outraged by that horrendous monster, Jang Hyeongbo! And then to die a vain death! She was possessed by a desperate urge to run to that hideous rascal right then and there, and cut his abominable snake-like body into pieces.

But if she did that, the infamy she had endured would be made known to everyone, even after her own death. She didn't want that. Exasperated by her helpless situation, which wouldn't allow her to be avenged to her heart's content, she wanted to pound her heart until it was crushed.

What on earth is Taesu doing now? Is he really at Han Chambong's doing what that rascal claimed? How could it be? It's probably a fiction that rascal fabricated. If so, why did I feel so intimidated that I couldn't exert my full force against him!

How exasperating it would be if I were to die without being avenged! What grief and shock it would give my parents and siblings if I died in silence?

With such thoughts, tears welled up in her eyes, and she was about to burst into sobs, when she heard the sound of wild knocking at her gate.

Chobong jumped up instantly, swallowing back her tears, but she couldn't move her feet. She stood still, not knowing what to do; she was too ashamed to face her husband.

Full of regrets, thinking that she should have done away with herself earlier or run down the street to the pier instead of crouching here in the room, she looked around for something with which to hang herself.

Someone was shaking the gate repeatedly, shouting, "Hello, hello, open the gate, please!" She knew instantly that it wasn't Taesu's voice. Though relieved, Chobong's heart filled with new misgivings.

Perhaps that rascal Hyeongbo's story was not completely unfounded; something terrible might have happened to Taesu. Weighed down by this apprehension, Chobong could no longer hesitate. She slowly walked toward the gate.

"Who is it please?" She noticed her voice was quivering.

"This is Go Taesu's house, isn't it?"

The voice that came through the gate sounded like a policeman's. In addition, Chobong could hear the clinking sound of a sword. Now she could no longer doubt what Hyeongbo had said, and felt sure that something really bad had befallen Taesu. But how could it have happened?

Had that wretch Hyeongbo gone out and worked some sort of wicked scheme while I was rendered senseless? But how could he dare to do it when he'd already violated me like that? It was inconceivable, even though it involved that shameless wretch.

Who knows, it might indeed be Hyeongbo's doing, who else could it be?—Still, was there enough time for him to do all those things and come back? The interval seemed to have been only a short while.

Befuddled by doubts, Chobong nevertheless opened the door. As expected, a policeman in black uniform was standing under the sole streetlight.

"Go Taesu, is he home?"

"Well, uh . . ."

"Then, tell me please, did he go to Mr. Han's house in Gaebokdong this evening, er . . . I mean, to his residential quarters?"

"Yes."

"Right, I see . . ." The policeman nodded his head, seeming to have understood the whole story, and added,

"Uhm . . . Then you'd better go to the Provincial Hospital at once."

"Wh—at?"

Chobong barely squeezed out the sound as she staggered out into the street, but the policeman had already turned his back on her and was walking away. A young girl, who had been standing hidden behind the policeman, suddenly appeared. It was Han Chambong's maidservant.

"Ah, you! . . . So?" Chobong gasped, and the girl dashed toward her.

"Oh, the master, your husband . . .," the girl began in a quivering voice, but stopped short, looking at the policeman, who, without looking back, drew away into the distance.

"What?"

"Your husband is, er . . ."

"Yes? What is it?"

"Er, he's about to die . . ."

"Wh—at?"

Chobong reeled, barely maintaining her balance. She leaned on the gatepost. She felt as though someone had poured hot water over her head, and just stood there full of pain, totally dumbfounded.

"My goodness, what's going on . . .?" Hyeongbo asked, running out with the clattering sound of his clogs, approaching her from behind. Though he seemed to be in a flurry, he was merely putting it on, because he'd been awake all the while since leaving Chobong's room, and had been listening to what was going on at the gate. He had a pretty accurate grasp of the situation.

". . . What are you doing here?"

Hyeongbo, shooting a sideways glance at the dumbfounded Chobong, approached the maidservant.

"Er, the master of this house was about to die, er, so he's been taken to the hospital . . ."

"What? How?"

Hyeongbo cried out, feigning extreme astonishment, while inwardly he couldn't be happier as he confirmed things were going just as he'd planned.

". . . What are you saying? . . . What on earth really happened?"

"Uh, my master . . ."

"Yes, your master, what . . .?"

". . . left the master of this house . . ."

"Well, well . . . You mean, left him almost for dead?"

"Yes, sir."

"You say yes? . . . What the devil . . ."

"And my mistress passed . . . passed away right on the spot . . ."

The maidservant started sobbing.

He wasn't prepared for the unfortunate news about Madam Kim, but he thought it a likely consequence.

Chobong was already running toward the main road.

"Now you go back home, I'll take the lady to the hospital . . ."

After sending off the maidservant, Hyeongbo rushed out, the skirt of his night-robe flapping, trying to catch up with Chobong. Chobong seemed not to be running toward the hospital, but hastily running away from Hyeongbo, who was chasing her with the loud clattering of his clogs.

You villain, the most wicked villain under the sun! You've got to pay for the violence you've done me . . . and my husband . . .

Chobong wanted to turn back and curse at him, enumerating the crimes he'd committed. If she did, a crowd, not only of passersby, but of all her neighbors would throng around, and they would probably beat and kick Hyeongbo to death . . .

Though he was wearing clogs, being a man, Hyeongbo was

fast enough soon to catch up with Chobong and began walking abreast of her.

"Let's find a car!" Hyeongbo said, looking around to see if there was a car passing by.

Chobong ignored him completely and kept accelerating her already fast steps.

"Huh, what a disaster!" Hyeongbo mumbled as if to himself, trying to keep pace with her.

". . . How could it be! . . . What a blow! . . . Well, it looked too dangerous all along! I wonder why he did such a dangerous thing, when he was already married. He's been rather too bold, I guess . . . With that boldness, he was rushing head on into it!"

While it was true that Chobong was quite worried and anxious for her husband's life, she was, at the same time, not at all free from curiosity about how all this had happened.

"By the way, in any case . . ."

This time, Hyeongbo started to address Chobong directly.

"Mr. Go was bound to die pretty soon, regardless of what's happened . . ."

What?

Chobong pretended not to hear him, but she couldn't help but respond to him inwardly.

". . . He has embezzled several thousand won from the bank, forging checks from his clients' accounts . . ."

You rascal, how dare you!

"So he was expecting to be caught soon. He's been saying he'd rather kill himself when that happened than be locked up in prison. Even this morning, when you were in the kitchen, he again talked to me about such a plan. Haengwha heard him talking about killing himself all the time. Haengwha, to tell you the truth, is also one of Taesu's mistresses. I'm sure you've never guessed it, have you?"

What nonsense is that?

"That his family's very rich, that he's the only son of a rich widow, that he graduated from a college, all those stories were invented to trick you into marrying him. Yes, all fibs, falsities . . . Actually he barely finished primary school and had been merely an office boy for more than ten years at the main office of the 00 Bank in Seoul before he became a bank clerk, hmm!"

No, what are you talking about?

". . . and his family, having no place of their own, not even a piece of land, his mother lives in a rented room somewhere in Seoul. Remember how his mother didn't come down for the wedding? Let alone attending it, she wasn't informed of it at all."

Stop lying, you wretch!

"Ask around everyone in Gunsan, not a soul would know where his family actually lives. I'm sure he hasn't told you about that either."

You, rascal, who wants to hear such rubbish?

Chobong was shouting silently, but it wasn't only because she utterly abhorred him, but also because her situation was too deplorable to listen to such stories. Nevertheless, she couldn't totally disbelieve what he was saying.

". . . You see now, you've been tricked into marrying him and thus ruined your life, all for that deceitful man!"

What does it matter to you?

". . . I think you should forget what's past and try to calm your mind. So long as I'm near you, you don't need to worry about your future . . ."

My goodness, that rascal is becoming way too brazen as I let him go on talking . . .

Chobong could barely repress her urge to spit on Hyeongbo's shameless face, when he began talking as if she'd already become his own woman; she was too astounded by what he was babbling and couldn't even regard him as a human being.

". . . as the rent for the house has been already paid, and it's suitably furnished, perhaps we don't need to consider moving out, do we? . . . It seems as though everything has been perfectly made just for us . . ."

"Shut up!" Chobong at last cried out, stamping her foot, unable to bear him any longer. After that, she felt like screaming out curses.

If it means that I might have the chance of pulling out your liver and swallowing it in one gulp, then perhaps I might live with you, but I can't, not even for that reason. I'm simply at my wit's end.

If Hyeongbo were a bit smarter, he would have attempted to coax her, rather than exposing all Taesu's wrongdoings at this chaotic moment.

When they at last arrived at the Provincial Hospital, Hyeongbo stayed to answer police inquiries, identifying Chobong as Taesu's wife, himself as a companion and friend living in the same house, while Chobong went straight to the treatment room. As she stepped into the room, where Taesu's body was lying on the examination bed, a nurse was just pulling up a white sheet to cover his head.

Recognizing the white sheet as the signature of death, Chobong felt her hair suddenly stand on end while her legs went limp. Unable to walk, she stopped at the entrance. The doctor took off his stethoscope and, turning around toward the Japanese police officer who was sitting on a chair facing the door, said rather sluggishly,

"Mou, Damaedaes!"

With this announcement of Taesu's death, the doctor glanced at Chobong, but he simply gave a wide yawn as if he hadn't noticed her. The police officer, however, out of the habit of his profession, scanned Chobong from head to foot, and asked,

"Are you Go Taesu's *Ogami-sang*?"

"Ye-es."

Chobong's quivering voice emerged faint from the back of her throat.

"Well, you may . . ."

The police officer, nodding his head, pointed his chin toward the bed.

As though her brain were wrapped with a thick blanket, Chobong couldn't think clearly or measure the meaning of what she saw, but nevertheless she tottered in the direction the police officer had pointed at with his chin, like someone hypnotized.

The nurse lifted the sheet to let Chobong see her husband's face and gave Chobong a polite nod. In her nod was something more than mere professional etiquette, perhaps an expression of sympathy and condolence for a young and pitiful widow.

Taesu's left forehead, which had been smashed, was clotted with blood, his left cheekbone was swollen and had a deep blue bruise; the blow to the head had left traces of blood on his face, but the cut was invisible, covered by his hair. His blood-stained face as a whole was contorted and unsightly, with eyes and mouth half open. It was hideous enough to send chills down any onlooker's spine.

Chobong almost turned her head away automatically, but conscious of the eyes watching her from behind, she suppressed the urge, and instead covered her face with both hands. Then she dropped to her knees, burying her head on the side of the bed.

She couldn't feel anything, not even sorrow, but somehow tears poured down, making her shoulders tremble.

She began to cry, not even knowing why, yet with the crying there came surging into her mind this or that sorrow, and all things irksome and troublesome that she would have to face in the future in utter helplessness. Besieged by endless sources of grief, her crying grew ever more sorrowful.

She was overwhelmed by her own grief, without feeling any sort of sadness for Taesu's misfortune. She wasn't even aware of the sheer absence of any affection for Taesu in her mind.

Meanwhile Hyeongbo was exercising his skills in taking care of small matters in such a situation. For instance, he called a cab service and sent a car to Jeong Jusa's house in Dunbaemi, which had no access to a car.

About one hour later, Chobong's parents rushed into the hospital. Chobong was still crying, leaning her head on the edge of the bed. Her parents, having been informed that their son-in-law had died, were utterly confounded, unable to figure out what had happened.

Hyeongbo came and explained the details of the incident, according to what he'd heard from various sources, not forgetting to expose Taesu's recent misdemeanors, much the same way he had done with Chobong on their way to the hospital, including the forgery of checks.

Jeong Jusa and his wife were very reluctant to believe what Hyeongbo said, other than the fact that Taesu was lying dead in hospital. Although they were forced to believe Hyeongbo, they resisted because they wanted to avoid their own guilty feelings, at least for the time being, by discrediting what Hyeongbo was blathering on about. They couldn't forget that they'd given good marks to Taesu, seduced by the seed money for business they could get from their son-in-law, disregarding their doubts about the shady aspects of his character.

Regardless of whatever had happened, their main regrets centered on "the seed money gone up in smoke" and they felt as if heaven had collapsed when they realized the total futility of their inflated expectations.

"Huh! What a hideous incident!"

Jeong Jusa muttered with a deep sigh, looking up at the ceiling. It couldn't be denied that the sigh was a sign of his grief as a father-in-law over the death of his son-in-law as well as the concern of a father for the future of a widowed daughter. But the truth was that Jeong Jusa much more deeply mourned the demise of his expectations regarding the "seed money," and was inclined to lament,

"Huh! How vainly it has all turned out!"

Chapter 11:
In Search of a Refuge

IT WAS AROUND sunset the next day.

Taesu's body had been brought home, released after the autopsy.

Concussion of the brain was the cause of death. They found one part of his skull shattered, four of his ribs broken, and in addition there were more than twenty large or small contusions all over his body. But no problems were found in his internal organs other than the involuntary evacuation of urine and feces.

On the next day, while the family was busy preparing for Taesu's funeral, a number of policemen came over and searched the whole house. Taesu's check forgery had been discovered. The police took away some of the evidence of the crime, such as the fake seals, checkbooks, and letters that Taesu hadn't gotten rid of. Everything now came out into the open.

On the following day, amid all that fuss, Taesu's body found a final resting place—a sunny spot in a public cemetery.

His coffin was lowered into the pit and covered with the dug-out yellow clay until there was a small mound. And that was then covered with turf that was very green at that season. So a new grave came into being.

Leaving behind this grave covered with coarse grass and the fresh smell of earth lingering in the air, Chobong started to walk away; but after a few steps, she stopped and looked back as if drawn by something, then shed a new flow of silent tears.

Though it was surrounded by numerous old and new graves, Taesu's grave, under the slanting light of the setting sun, looked so lonely. Struck by the thought that it would soon just be one more unclaimed grave, Chobong felt a sudden burst of pity for Taesu. It was the first time that Chobong had shed tears of pity for her deceased husband.

Then, all of a sudden, Chobong realized that she was assuming she would never come back to the grave to weed it, not even once. The pity she felt on considering the grave as one that would soon be unclaimed implied that. She felt ashamed of the hardness of her heart.

Out of compunction, she determined that she would bring a bunch of flowers before nightfall and in future would hire someone to weed the grave at least once a year. Consoling her guilty conscience with that determination, she forced herself to turn away.

The house she came back to seemed deserted and unwelcoming.

Hyeongbo, who hadn't attended the burial ceremony, having been summoned to the police office, soon toddled into the house. At the sight of him, Chobong shuddered as if a snake had slithered across her body.

Hyeongbo stayed on in the opposite room and seemed determined not to move out of the house either. Luckily for Chobong though, her mother and her brother, Hyeongju, slept in her room with her at night, and during the day all her family members stayed in the house. And Hyeongbo himself was fully occupied looking after the funeral and police matters, and so on, and thus had neither the opportunity nor the free time to approach Chobong with evil intentions.

Instead, Hyeongbo made every effort to secure the goodwill of Chobong's parents; on behalf of Chobong and her family, he ran this way and that, dexterously dealing with matters as they arose as if they were his own.

No one ever mentioned the need to inform Taesu's mother of his death. On the day of the funeral, the thought struck Chobong and she begged her father to send her a telegram at least, but Jeong Jusa, who abhorred even the name of "that damnable wretch," flatly refused with the excuse that no one knew her address in Seoul.

Chobong, Jeong Jusa, Hyeongbo, and a few *gisaeng*s, including Haengwha, were summoned to the police station many times, but in the end, all of them were cleared of suspicion of any involvement in Taesu's crime. Hyeongbo was subject to particularly rigorous investigation, even being confined in a police cell for a few days, but he doggedly denied any knowledge.

The investigation on the check forgery case finally came to a close, leaving the identity of Taesu's accomplice who had assisted in cashing the checks a mystery.

ABOUT A FORTNIGHT had passed since the tragedy had taken place and it was late at night around the middle of June; summer was fast approaching. Madam Yu and Hyeongju were deep in sleep, but Chobong, lying next to them, was wide-awake, wrestling with the many thoughts floating in her head like clouds.

On the night she had been violated by Hyeongbo, Chobong had thought it was a fatal disgrace from which there was no way out other than by killing herself. But the typhoon that swept through her house immediately after the rape, the turmoil caused by the disastrous death of Taesu, took all her strength away and left her dull and unfeeling. It was as if she'd become an old woman overnight; she didn't have even the faintest ember of fire left within herself, let alone the strength to force herself to attempt suicide for the loss of such a high virtue as chastity or innocence. Somehow or other, Chobong was now able to face the things that had happened to her without any acute pain; they seemed like events that had happened to someone else. Nothing seemed significant to her.

Of course she felt annoyed, exasperated, or even resentful at times when she was alone, tracing back each of her false steps as well as the disasters that had befallen her—the vacillations and uncertainties she had experienced before her marriage, her half-hearted consent to marriage with Taesu, her life as a newlywed that lasted for ten not so unhappy days, the violation she suffered from that horrid Hyeongbo, Taesu's disastrous death that fell on her out of the blue, and the discovery of all those crimes committed by Taesu; at the end of such reminiscences, she was inevitably engulfed by a sickening sense of disillusionment at her early youth that had suddenly vanished like a beautiful rainbow. But after a few moments, all those feelings too became rather vague. She was in a frozen state, incapable of sensing anything other than the first dull ache when touched.

It was fortunate for her that she was unable to feel any acute pain or agony other than some blunt dullness; it helped her set aside everything she'd gone through as vain dreams, following the old saying that life is but a dream.

So she was convinced that she would be able to let bygones be bygones and forget everything. But what made her desperate was the uncertainty of her future, which she could in no way passively allow to flow on without worrying. While the past needed to be abandoned by changing her viewpoint, the future required of her the wisdom to plan and the willpower to act.

For the past ten days, she'd been sleepless, deliberating on how to carry on with her life, how to recover her precious youth that had been crushed and trampled on, and how to revive hope for a normal life.

Lying on her side, Chobong stared at the bright light of the fifty-watt bulb without blinking, unaware of time and space, fully absorbed in her haphazard wandering thoughts. Both her mother and her brother Hyeongju were deep in sleep, though at times they tossed and turned. She felt quite distant from them as if they were in another world.

At that moment, the clock on the wall of the maru began to strike and stopped after striking four times. As though awakened by the sounds, Chobong suddenly sat up and muttered to herself,

Then I must leave Gunsan!

The haste with which she spat out the words seemed to suggest that she was about to get dressed and set out immediately. The recent abhorrent memories had led her to not only hate herself, but to despise more than anything else the city itself, in which she would be constantly exposed to the mortifying stares of people. And moreover, it was a dangerous place because of that wretch Jang Hyeongbo; she sensed that he would never give up and would surely keep harassing her. It would be best to run far far away from him.

Seoul . . . Seoul might be a good place. She had no clear idea about what good it might offer, but she had a vague impression that it would be a good place.

She also had a certain trust in Jeho. But when she remembered his wife Yunhui, she knew that she wouldn't be able to work in his store or company. In that way, he might not be

someone she could resort to. On the other hand, she also knew
that Jeho was certainly a man of resources who had a wide range
of social connections, a man who not only would be able to find
a job for her, but would be willing to take care of her in many
ways.

Then perhaps I should leave tomorrow . . .

With this determination, she breathed a deep sigh of relief,
and putting aside all the worries about her future, mustered up
a daring spirit to face whatever came her way.

But there was still one matter of concern that remained
before she could move on—her parents and her siblings had no
decent means of livelihood, their house was as empty as any that
has endured a long succession of misfortunes. She became very
uneasy about her resolution to leave her family behind.

Nonetheless, she soon became aware of the futility of her
remaining in Gunsan, a place she abhorred so much, even if she
could find a job there. But in reality, she knew that she would
never be able to get a job in Gunsan, and that by staying on she
would simply be an extra mouth to feed.

*Maybe it would be better to go to Seoul and find a way to help
them from there . . .*

Thinking that the worries about her family would lead her
nowhere, she pushed aside the matter into one corner of her
mind, moved to her desk, and began to write a note for her
mother.

She wrote that she was going to Seoul to distract herself from
her gloomy feelings, and that though she would write again when
she was settled in Seoul, in the meantime her mother should
retrieve the deposit money for her house, which amounted to
fifty won, and sell any of her furniture that would bring in any
money to help her family. Then she earnestly urged her mother
to keep her whereabouts a secret.

As she finished writing, she took off her two rings and her wristwatch, and put them into an envelope along with the note.

When this was done, dawn was already breaking, so she went to bed and slept for a couple of hours.

The next morning, she waited until it was about eleven o'clock, then, accompanied by her maid under the pretense of shopping for groceries, headed for the station.

Her mother, who'd been vigilant at all times about her daughter's movements, for fear that she might act rashly on account of the recent misfortunes, had no suspicions whatsoever this time, as she was going out accompanied by a maid. Madam Yu simply believed that Chobong was going to the market as she claimed.

Chobong, who had worn her hair tied up on the back of her head since her marriage, rearranged it to look like a schoolgirl, and chose to wear a black skirt and a brand new white summer blouse. She took out a new pair of shoes she'd bought for the wedding as well as the handbag and parasol that Taesu had given her as wedding presents. Out of the one hundred and fifty won Taesu had left with her, one hundred won had been spent on funeral expenses, and from the remaining fifty won she took out thirty won and put it in the envelope for her mother.

On her way to the train station, Chobong couldn't help but cast a glance at the Geumho Clinic where Seungjae was working, and her vaguely lingering sense of regret darkened her heart.

When the 11:40 train was about to leave, she sent her maid back home, giving her the envelope for her mother and conveying her hope that she would soon find a good place to work and have a happier life in the future.

As the train began to move slowly, she felt she was bidding adieu to her nightmares and moving into a new phase of life. With this, a sense of relief and hopefulness was quietly emerging in her, yet still, when she was reminded of her forlorn situation and the uncertainty of her future, her overall feelings in departing from Gunsan were sad and melancholy.

Chapter 12:
An Easy Prey, Named . . .

CHOBONG GOT OFF at Iri to change trains for Seoul and was waiting on the crowded platform, when a loud, boisterous voice suddenly accosted her from behind.

"Well, well, if it isn't Chobong!"

The man, who seemed to have appeared out of nowhere, was Bak Jeho with that horselike long face.

"Ah, Uncle Jeho!" Chobong exclaimed in a high voice, pleasantly surprised.

She was so pleased by this unexpected meeting that she would have even embraced him if it weren't for the eyes of the public. Jeho too seemed very glad to see her. But his happy smiling face had a subtle tint of something odd. Jeho, while visiting Gunsan, had heard all about the disasters that had befallen Chobong. Chobong, who suspected as much, lowered her head in shame.

"Well, where are you heading?" Jeho asked, studying Chobong's appearance from top to bottom.

"I've just come out rather aimlessly," Chobong said, scratching the ground with the tip of her foot, her head lowered.

"Aimlessly . . . That's not bad at all. It's nice to wander around like a breeze and see new things. Damn it . . . Good move, really . . . Since you're already out, how about going to Seoul with me and seeing this and that? What do you say?"

Jeho spoke loudly, totally ignoring the crowd around.

"I was also thinking of . . ."

"Going to Seoul?"

"Yes."

"Good, good! Surely, that's the place you should choose. You're right . . ."

Chobong was weighing in her mind whether or not she should tell him at that moment that she was going to Seoul with the hope of getting help from him, for eventually she would need to tell him that. But Jeho started to talk about his own situation before she could decide either way.

Jeho told her that his plan to open a pharmaceutical company in Seoul had gone very smoothly, and that he would begin business within a few days. He added that he came down to Gunsan yesterday morning for business and was on his way back to Seoul, and that he had got on the train at the Gunsan port station, so he didn't know that she was on the same train. While he was rambling on like this, the train for Seoul arrived, and they hopped onto it together, one following at the heels of the other.

The train was very crowded. Though they walked through the aisles of every compartment, there were no empty seats that would allow the two to sit side by side.

Jeho, carrying a Boston bag in one hand, and a fruit basket in the other, was leading the way looking around, all the while grumbling.

"What the hell is this? The railroad people are only concerned about profits. They pay no attention to improving customer service. There are no damned empty seats anywhere! . . . Where's the conductor? Don't you think we should demand a discount on our fare? . . . Damn it all."

No matter how often he "damned it," no luck came their way allowing them to find two empty seats side by side. At last they went into the second-class compartment.

"Come on, let's take seats here. We'll make it a special occasion by treating ourselves to these higher-class seats. Neither you nor I dare to take the second-class train; the fare is too expensive, isn't it? Damn it."

Jeho placed his Boston bag and the fruit basket on the shelf and then carelessly took off his jacket and hat.

"Damn it. Give me your ticket. We'll exchange it for a second-class one by paying some extra . . . Well, how do you like it? The seats are more spacious and very clean here. Isn't it nice? It's what you can enjoy when you have money!"

At first Chobong had thought that they had come in only because the third-class compartments were all crowded, feeling uneasy in case the conductor came along and made trouble. Now that Jeho mentioned changing their tickets by paying extra, Chobong was struck with a different sort of worry, considering how little money she had with her.

Nevertheless, she reluctantly took out a ten-won note from her bag and gave it to Jeho with her ticket, at which Jeho, waving his hand said,

"What? Do you think I'm incapable of paying for your second-class ticket? It's a favor I'm more than willing to do for you . . . Well, well, put the money back into your bag, and just give me your ticket."

With an exaggerated show of generosity, Jeho snatched away her ticket.

When the train started to move faster, leaving behind all the bustle and vain show in the station, a cool breeze came rushing in through the window. As she looked out, she could see that the summer in its ripening splendor had turned everything green. In the rice paddies, the seedlings had already matured and covered the fields with fluttering leaves. On a small hilly path at the corner of a green mountain ridge an old woman was standing carrying a bundle on her head, vacantly looking at the passing train. All these were endearing scenes for Chobong.

Having run away from the unpleasant house where she could do nothing but lie huddled in despair, Chobong felt like a bird soaring freely, as she watched the lush scenery of early summer passing by through the window of the speeding train. She felt her heavy heart growing much lighter.

"By the way, I . . ."

Jeho, who'd been away in search of the conductor to change the tickets, returned to his seat, and taking down the fruit basket from the rack, began to talk.

". . . I finally sent that cursed wife of mine back to her family. He, he he, damn it."

"What? Oh, no! But why?" Chobong asked in surprise, unable to fathom Jeho's gleeful state of mind. Furthermore, that was good news for her as well, since it would be easier for her to get help from Jeho.

"What's the use of such a wife? She's at most fit to be kicked out . . . that confounded woman . . ."

That Yunhui had been evicted was his way of talking; the truth was that they had agreed on a separation for one year, something that had been coming for quite some time.

Yunhui was well aware that her physical and mental condition rendered her unsuited for married life; her hysteria and the general weakness that came with her gynecological ailments would only be aggravated so long as she continued living with Jeho, and she knew only too well that that wasn't good for her at all. So they'd discussed a plan to take a period of separation for one year, when they were about to move to Seoul. That was one of the reasons why Yunhui had so fiercely opposed Jeho's plan to take Chobong to Seoul as an employee. She had no trust in Jeho even if Chobong weren't around. But having succeeded in aborting his plan regarding Chobong, her immediate threat, she felt much relieved and was able to leave him with a relatively easy heart soon after they moved to Seoul. Once everything was settled in their new house in Cheongjin-dong, Yunhui went down to Sincheon where her family lived.

However, before her departure, Yunhui extorted several promises from Jeho—that he would not womanize, that he would never attempt to keep a mistress, that he would not indulge in riotous parties, that he would send her letters at least three times a month, in addition to sundry trivial and petty assurances.

Jeho, who was simply too happy at the prospect of her leaving, said yes, yes, yes, the moment each item dropped from her lips, assenting to all her demands whatever they were. He thought he had nothing to lose; if her hysteria subsided during the period of separation, that would be good for the both of them, and if it didn't, he would seek an opportunity to divorce her giving one excuse or another. On the whole, he felt he was saying goodbye to a smallpox germ while he saw her off.

This was the state of Jeho's marriage. But he didn't bring up the news of Yunhui with any ulterior motive of seducing Chobong, or with any intention of giving any unusual hint to her.

He simply happened to be reminded of Yunhui when he met Chobong, who not only knew Yunhui but was often persecuted by her groundless jealousy. He had no idea whatsoever as to how this would affect their future relationship, and was imparting it merely as a piece of news.

Chobong too was listening to it as an interesting piece of news, without attaching any particular meaning to it. Nevertheless, it was also true that Jeho's feelings toward Chobong couldn't be as innocent as they used to be. Somehow, his inner feelings were becoming more and more depraved now that he was sitting next to her.

While Chobong had been working in his pharmacy, Jeho saw her as the daughter of his hometown friend, a girl as young as his own daughter might be. The possibility of desiring this pretty girl had never surfaced in his mind, not only due to his wife's abnormal jealousies but also because of his prudence as a middle-aged man toward an unmarried young girl. Even if he'd harbored such a desire deep in his unconscious, it had never dared to emerge, let alone as any sort of reaction. But now there seemed to be no such obstacles to consider.

When he heard the stories about Chobong in Gunsan, which were on everybody's lips, he felt deeply sorry for her, and as a means of offering consolation even wished to visit her and ask her to go to Seoul with him.

But he desisted from that plan when he came to think of the feverish state her family must be in. Moreover he abhorred even the thought of meeting Mr. Jeong who would surely go on and on talking about his misfortunes and miserable feelings. So he gave up the thought, and instead, decided to write to her later, inviting her to come up to Seoul.

The situation having been such, Jeho's delight and surprise at seeing Chobong at the station were almost indescribable, even to the point of feeling that some invisible hand might have been at work.

From outside a feeling of great delight at this odd coincidence flooded his heart while from inside a consciousness that she was no longer a virgin but "used goods" surged up. The two met at an opportune moment, arousing a daredevil spirit in him.

She's already used goods.

On top of that, a woman who belongs to no one.

At such thoughts, he felt relieved from any of the constraints of a middle-aged man's prudence and reserve.

A woman who had been ruined by having made a wrong choice in marriage, a woman who, out of despair, was on her way to Seoul, a woman who could be anybody's prey—in the case of such a woman, isn't it true that anybody clever enough to catch her could be her owner? As the old saying goes, she was as open as an unclaimed piece of land.

She would be quite tempting even if she were a total stranger he'd never before seen. But in this case the woman was the same unforgettable Chobong for whom Jeho's heart had long pined. She looked as tasty as a rice cake seasoned with honey. And how opportune it was that Yunhui had gone away! Perhaps he could divorce Yunhui, or if he couldn't, why not take Chobong as a kept mistress. She's used goods and so am I.

Chobong was totally unaware of the sinister buildup in Jeho's dark soul. She was no less excited and happy than Jeho with this accidental meeting. Now that Yunhui was out of the picture, she would be able to seek Jeho's assistance without worrying about her, and if she could work at Jeho's company, she would be able to further her study in pharmacy and, who knows, she might even take the qualifying exams for pharmacists one day. If only she could pass the exam, she might dream of days living as an independent woman . . .

The train was speeding along. Through the window she could see the fertile fields with fast growing crops and the hills that were turning greener.

Bright sunbeams came through the window, highlighting the graceful elegance of the dark blue velvet seats; the few passengers in the compartment were either reading newspapers or smoking, not paying any attention to others.

"Come, have some fruit . . ."

After taking out an apple, Jeho gave the whole basket to Chobong.

". . . Help yourself to whatever you like. Here's a knife too."

He fumbled in his vest pocket, took out a knife, and gave it to Chobong. Then he simply rubbed his apple with his palm once or twice and took a big bite out of it.

"I like it this way, with the skin unpeeled . . ."

"Please let me peel it for you!"

Chobong thought his carefree rustic manners were pleasant, but was a bit embarrassed by the eyes of the genteel people around.

"It's all right, don't bother . . ."

Jeho waved his hand, biting at the apple.

"This damn apple is supposed to be good when eaten with skin and all, isn't it? Have some yourself, Chobong . . . They say you'll never need a doctor if you have an apple after each meal. Huh huh, if that's true, we who make a living selling drugs would starve to death. Huh, huh, damn it."

Chobong smiled too, taken hold of by this pleasant man. It was her first smile since her husband had died a fortnight ago.

Looking at the smiling face of Chobong, especially the tips of her mouth and her chin, Jeho once again felt a strong, renewed admiration for her beauty. Her face with a bright smile looked quite different from her earlier prim and cautious face, and was indeed enchanting.

"By the way, are you going to Seoul with any purpose in mind?" Jeho asked, casting a meaningful glance at Chobong's lowered forehead.

Chobong stopped peeling her apple and raised her head. But swallowing back the candid reply that she was in fact going to Seoul in search of Jeho, instead said,

"Just to look around . . ."

"To look around? Huh-uh!"

Jeho stared at her for some time, and nodding his head began to say,

"Well, well, I don't mean to intrude, but I'm asking because I heard about your situation, and knowing that . . ."

Chobong had guessed that Jeho knew about it, but once Jeho mentioned it, her face flushed and she had to lower her head.

"Hunh! Dear, dear. You don't need to feel embarrassed at all in front of me. I wouldn't have known it if a friend of mine hadn't mentioned it in passing . . . I heard about it, it was in the newspaper as well, but I haven't read about it . . . What an unforeseen calamity! . . . How could that happen! . . . It must have been a real calamity out of nowhere, a great calamity, indeed! . . . When I heard it, my heart really ached! Damn it, how could such a horrible thing have happened to you . . ."

Jeho stopped and stared for a while at the white line that parted her hair , and then resumed,

". . . But look Chobong, listen to me, Chobong, Chobong dear?"

He repeatedly called her name.

"Ye-es?"

Keeping her head down, Chobong was fumbling with the apple that was already peeled, unable to eat it.

"Well, what I want to say is . . . that you don't need to despair. It's really bad to despair . . . What's the problem? Anybody can take one wrong step in life, no, it wasn't your fault, it was a calamity that fell from the blue sky, but what does it matter that you had such a misfortune once? No, it's nothing, especially when you're so young . . . Just consider it as a bad dream that comes and goes, everything will turn out all right, won't it, Chobong dear?"

"Yes."

Chobong agreed with him quietly, but wholeheartedly rather than reluctantly. She was almost in tears out of gratitude for Jeho's kind words, which seemed to touch her wound and alleviate its pain.

After all, in Chobong's eyes, Jeho was, as he'd always been, a man of competence, successful in business, vigorous in manners yet kindhearted; Chobong saw in this middle-aged man a reliable and secure prop on whom she could lean with trust. She was like a helpless child who'd lost its way but happened to find a kind uncle on the road. Now all her shame and embarrassment seemed to have vanished.

Jeho too was offering genuine consolation out of an older man's compassion toward a younger person in misery. It wasn't mere bait used to lure her to him, despite the fact that he was actually harboring an impudent desire to take Chobong as easy prey, and was ready to take action in that direction whenever an opportunity was offered; at least at that moment, he was expressing his genuine concern for her,

"Well, well . . . what's there to worry about? Things will turn out all right . . ."

Then after lighting a cigarette, Jeho started again,

". . . It's good that you decided to go to Seoul. I was going to write to you once I got to Seoul! . . . Well done anyway . . . No matter how powerless I might be, I'm certainly capable of taking good care of you. Don't you worry. Put your heart at rest, won't you?"

Chobong was at last relieved of the burden of telling him that she was on her way to Seoul seeking his assistance, and thus felt quite easy and secure.

While they were absorbed in conversation, the train passed the rich fields and the lush mountains of early summer as well as small towns such as Hwangdeung, Hamyeul, and Ganggyeong.

Nonsan was a place she had once visited on a school trip to Buyeo. Chobong felt that the station and the people in it were somehow familiar and was glad to see them again.

When the train came out of a tunnel after passing the Red Bean Valley, Jeho looked at Chobong's hands folded on top of

her lap and noticed that her finger had only the faint mark of a
ring on it, but no ring itself.

"Oh, dear! You've taken off the ring? . . . Certainly you did
well. It's best to forget all about the unpleasant past, like cutting it off with a knife. And make a fresh new start all over, no?
Hunh, confound it."

Jeho had no way of knowing the real reason why Chobong
had taken off the ring, leaving it for her family to pawn if needed.
But when Jeho remarked on it, her face flushed, she feared it
might look as if she had taken it off cold-heartedly.

When the train reached Daejeon Station, they got off to
change trains. Stepping down onto the platform, Jeho saw a
tourism information board, and the words "Yuseong Spa" on it
especially drew his attention.

With a devious grin spreading across his face, Jeho muttered
to himself, *Yuseong Spa? . . . A spa?*, casting at the same time
a lewd glance at Chobong's pretty back. He suddenly saw an
opportunity to put his desire into action.

In any case, Jeho would've arranged an occasion before long,
if an opportunity hadn't come along by itself. But when he saw
an opportunity spring up within easy reach so soon, he couldn't
help but feel thrilled.

"Chobong, dear, have you ever been to a spa?"

They say, hoist your sail while the wind is fair. Jeho resolved
to make his move, in order not to lose the opportunity; he was
not without qualms, however, since Chobong was after all a
woman from a decent family, the kind he'd never attempted to
seduce.

Chobong, meanwhile, recalled the old days as she passed
by the board, which she'd seen on her school trip to Seoul and
admired as something very rare, and didn't hear Jeho's question
until he repeated it.

"A spa? You mean a hot spring . . .?" Chobong asked, and shaking her head replied, "No, I've never been to one . . ."

"Well, so much the better. There's Yuseong Spa not far from here. It's a place worth visiting . . . Since you haven't seen a spa, how about going there and you can experience it for the first time? We can discuss plans for your future in that quiet place as well. How would you like that?"

"But . . ."

"But what?"

At this unexpected hesitation, Jeho was taken aback, feeling rather embarrassed, but Chobong merely said,

"But I'm afraid you must be very busy . . ."

Jeho took it as the timid way of a shy woman saying yes, one who understood his hidden intentions but was feigning an air of reluctance. With this self-flattering interpretation, Jeho felt the field was left wide open for his attack.

"Gosh, I was a bit alarmed, not knowing the meaning of your 'but!' Huh huh huh, was that it? You don't have to worry about such things . . . Then it's settled. Shall we also have lunch at the spa?"

"Yes."

"You must be hungry?"

"I'm all right."

"Then hurry up. We need to take the bus to Yuseong."

Chobong had no way of knowing the hidden implications of going to a spa alone with a man. She simply assumed that a spa was a place like a bathhouse where men and women have separate spaces with huge bathtubs that people visit strictly for the purpose of taking a bath.

So Chobong was quite free of any alarm or suspicion, and instead felt happy at the prospect of visiting a hot spring for the first time as well as discussing her future plans with Jeho.

Jeho, who was ignorant of the innocent nature of Chobong's assent, felt somewhat disappointed at her yielding so readily.

The bus to Yuseong was waiting right outside the station. After about half an hour's bumpy bus ride together with only a couple of other passengers, they arrived at an inn in the newly developed spa area.

During the bus ride, Chobong wondered,

Why is it taking so long, when he said it's quite nearby.

How will we manage to return to the station in time, if we're taking a bath as well as having lunch?

Though she was somewhat worried, she didn't air her concerns.

The moment the bus stopped in front of the inn, a group of housemaids rushed out, opened the door, snatched the baggage from their hands, and shouted a welcome in Japanese,

"Iratshaimase!"

Upon entering onto the porch, a dozen more housemaids again made deep bows, shouting *"Iratshaimase!"* in chorus.

Chobong was stunned at this overly courteous welcome.

What a fuss they're making! Is it really a bathhouse? The bathhouses in Gunsan, as far as Chobong had experienced them, had only a dull or surly looking man sitting behind a curtain, who just threw a glance at customers and received the fee without saying a word, let alone offering a welcoming greeting. But what a place this was! Chobong was at a loss as to what to do, too flurried and overwhelmed by this ceremonial reception. She felt her shoulders slumping.

And how magnificent the bathhouse itself was, how numerous the serving maids were, how courteously polite they were; struck with these wonders Chobong thought the fee must be nearly one won, at least ten to twenty times higher than the seven jeon she used to pay in Gunsan.

Chobong, who'd never experienced such luxurious service, not even in her dreams, was feeling intimated and uneasy rather than excited.

She looked around at the entrance, wondering why they didn't have signs for men and women, whether they would provide towels, where she could purchase soap. Jeho, who in the meantime had stepped up onto the wooden floor, looked back at Chobong with a grin and urged her, "Why don't you come up?"

At this solicitation, Chobong at last took off her shoes and stepped up onto the floor. Then a woman swiftly brought a pair of leather slippers and, kneeling down, placed them right in front of her feet. Utterly embarrassed, Chobong really wished they would stop making this fuss.

Jeho was already going up the stairs to the second floor, following a woman who was carrying his luggage. Chobong wondered again for a moment how it could be possible to have a bathhouse on the second floor, but soon followed Jeho for fear that she would look like a rustic country lass if she kept on hesitating.

The maid led the way along the lengthy carpeted corridor and on reaching a room squatted down to open the door. And there a spacious room with a Japanese-style tatami mat floor came into sight. Chobong knew nothing about the size of a room being measured by the number of mats; so instead of thinking of it as an eight-mat room, she simply thought it very spacious.

Soon after, a maid came in and placed two silk cushions on the floor facing each other and opened the windows to let in some fresh air.

"Where are we now?" Chobong, who couldn't understand why they were ushered into a room where no bathtub was in sight, at last asked Jeho.

"Where? We're at the hot springs."

"Where's the bath?"

"The bath? Of course we'll soon have it . . . Let me see, we should change our clothes before we have our bath."

"Clothes?"

"Ha, ha, you don't know anything because you've never been to this kind of place before? . . . At a hot springs, they provide you with yukada bathrobes. It's more comfortable to be in one of those."

Chobong thought that made sense, and nodded her head.

Just then, two maids came in, one carrying the tray with a tea set, the other holding neatly folded *yukada* bathrobes. Each time they came in and out, first they always squatted down at the door. Chobong felt too embarrassed to watch their subservient manners.

While the maid poured tea into the cups, Jeho nonchalantly began to take off his clothes and change into a *yukada*.

Chobong turned her face away, flushing deep red in amazement, wondering how Jeho could be so rude and so different from the way she'd previously known him to be. She even felt affronted.

The maid who brought in the two bathrobes unfolded the remaining one and, holding it up with smiling eyes, signed to Chobong to change into it. Chobong was too dumbfounded to say anything.

Jeho, who'd finished changing into a *yukada*, saw Chobong's unease and burst into a guffaw, explaining to the maid,

"My wife has never been to a spa, and on top of that, Korean ladies are never comfortable taking off their clothes in front of their husbands or strangers. It's against their code of behavior. Just leave it there please . . ."

Who is he calling his wife?

Taken aback, Chobong was furious at Jeho. But withholding her urge to contradict him, instead she gave him a fierce reprimanding glare. Jeho, while understanding the meaning of it, was unable to grasp why she was so upset.

He wondered how she could behave like this when she had acquiesced to his invitation so willingly earlier at the station. Perhaps she was acting like this out of shyness, right, that must be it, what else could it be . . .

"Huh huh, confound it, Chobong, what's there to be so shy about? But try not to behave so awkwardly . . . in front of those women. They might suspect I've lured someone else's wife and brought her here."

Jeho's hint at the possible misunderstanding sounded plausible. Chobong too thought it might be better to pretend to be his wife than be taken for a woman seduced into an extramarital affair. At least it would be less shameful, she assumed.

"Well, let's see, what shall we do first? Shall we have a bath first? Or perhaps we should eat something first since we're hungry now?"

"Well, I'm not sure . . .?"

Chobong felt hungry, but she didn't feel like expressing her opinion either way.

"Then let's eat after the bath. We'll feel refreshed after the bath and enjoy our lunch much better. Though we're hungry, we can wait a bit longer . . . can't we?"

On his way out, Jeho gave several instructions to the maid who was waiting outside: that they should have a *domburi* or some kind of Japanese lunch prepared while they were taking the bath, and that since his wife never took a bath with him even at home, they should guide her to a private bath. Then throwing over his shoulder the towel the maid handed him, he strode out.

Compelled by the presence of the maid attending her, Chobong at last changed into her *yukada*. But she really abhorred the fussing of the maid, who obsequiously tried to serve her this way or that, with, "Madam, Madam," dropping constantly from her lips.

Once inside the private spa, she felt very relieved on being left alone. Though she felt a bit sad and sentimental with no one around, the quiet and tidy place with its faint smell of sulfur felt very cozy and pleasing.

The transparent water, reflected on the blue tiles of the bathtub, looked deep blue like the water in a pond, and the tub was brimming over with water, giving her the sense of indulging in some sort of luxurious extravagance.

As she stepped into the tub, the water felt very hot, but once she immersed herself in the water fully, stretching out her legs, the fatigue that had accrued in her body over many days seemed to leave her and be washed away.

Gazing at her white body through the transparent water, she was struck anew by a deep sense of mortification on recalling that that pure and clean-looking body had actually been ravished and stained. It was hard to believe that her body carried the stigma of shame, actually not just one shame, but two . . . the shame of having lost face in the eyes of others and the secret shame that was gnawing at her heart for having lost her chastity.

That such filthy, invisible shame was engraved into that pure-looking body, never to be removed for the rest of her life! Once she came to that realization, she desperately longed to scrub her body clean until her skin peeled off. She hurried out of the tub, wildly scrubbing at her body with her hands. But her body, which had soaked in the sulfurous water, was too slippery to have any dirt come off. She looked around to find some soap, but there was none. She thought it odd that a spa with such good facilities and service didn't provide a bar of soap.

Later on when she mentioned it in passing, Jeho mocked her, saying no one uses soap in a sulfur spa.

When she came out of the bath, Chobong couldn't find her way back to the room. As she was standing in the aisle wondering, a maid who was passing by came over and took her back to her room. Jeho was waiting for her, sitting at a small table, with his long face flushed all the way up to the top of his bald head as a result of his hot bath. The moment Chobong entered, a maid brought in another small table for her. She was glad that she didn't have to sit face-to-face as at a Korean-style table.

"How did you like it? Don't you feel great after the bath?"

Fanning himself continuously, Jeho beamed with a big happy smile.

". . . Come, come, let's eat. You must be really hungry! I'm sure you haven't eaten properly for the past few days, engulfed in worries and troubles."

As Chobong sat in front of the small table, the maid briskly scooped rice into a bowl and then handed it to Chobong with both hands. Chobong too received it with both hands.

"Come on, eat now. Eat heartily as much as you can. From now on, I hope you'll stop worrying and keep your heart at ease. Since you've just had a bath, you've washed out all the bad memories of your past, haven't you? Huh huh huh, damn it all . . ."

Chobong smiled inwardly, thinking that she couldn't even wash her body properly because there was no soap.

". . . Well, well, enjoy your meal, dear . . . How is it that such a pretty person became a victim of such a horrible fate! Pitiful it is indeed! . . . I can't even look at you straight, I get overwhelmed by pity. Huh huh huh, damn it . . ."

Jeho was behaving as if he were trying to coax a child, Chobong thought, and she couldn't even laugh, feeling that the whole situation was too pathetic.

"Well, I'll have a glass of beer now . . ."

Jeho pushed his glass toward the maid.

". . . Love is a pleasant thing, and a drink surely makes it more pleasant, doesn't it? Huh huh, damn it."

Chobong frowned at him and her heart, which had calmed down somewhat, was enraged again. Muttering to herself, how could this man be so flighty?, she cast a stern glance at him.

But Jeho, disregarding her look, emptied the glass in one gulp, drinking the beer along with the froth, a smile of contentment spreading over his face.

"Uh huh, it's really refreshing! . . . Won't you try a glass?"

Jeho, rubbing his foamy lips with his palm, handed the glass to Chobong, who turned her head aside after giving him a reproachful glare.

"You don't like beer? . . . Uh huh huh."

Jeho turned toward the maid, chuckling, and looking like a madman in Chobong's eyes.

Chobong, full of fury, felt like throwing down her spoon and storming out of the place.

How dare he mention love right in front of her, how dare he offer her a drink! It wasn't simply casual rudeness, but a deliberate transgression intended to disgrace her. She now began to suspect dubious intentions on Jeho's part, that he must have brought her to this place in order to seduce her. All the things that he'd said and done came back to her, carrying new meanings. For instance, soon after they met, he kept bragging about having sent his wife away and his plan to divorce her; he pretended deep compassion for her misfortunes, referring to them as unavoidable disasters that had befallen her out of the blue; he'd also assured her that he would take care of her future—all of which must surely have been overtures to his dark scheme. When he said the words "husband and wife" in front of the maids, he wasn't simply lying but was insinuating at a relationship he intended to forge with her.

Having traced back Jeho's dark schemes so far, Chobong was totally stunned as well as frightened by the prospect of what was awaiting her.

What a treacherous liar he is!

For Chobong it didn't matter how disgusting the man was. Even if he weren't a mere liar but a traitor to the state, that wouldn't be an issue for Chobong. Her critical concern was the dangerous prospect that suddenly began to loom up. While being naively off-guard, she had been unwittingly drawn into a fatal snare from which she could hardly see a way out.

With this realization, she began to feel as if she was sitting on a big pincushion. She desperately wanted to muster up all her willpower and run away from this wicked place. No matter what the cause, however, instead of resolutely stomping out of the room, Chobong felt the power seep out of her body. Sitting still, she merely let out a deep, long sigh.

Nevertheless Jeho was the same man to whom she had wanted to entrust her future when she left home. She'd believed that once she found him in Seoul, he would help her find a way to become independent. Leaving Jeho, who had been such a reliable resource for her, and setting off into the unknown world was a frightening prospect. The idea of it made her feel lost and helpless, like a child abandoned on the side of the road. She tried to reprimand herself for giving way to such a sordid and shameful situation, but she couldn't bring herself to move, to attempt an escape.

The truth was that Chobong wasn't so much frightened of the uncertainty of her future without Jeho as she was overwhelmed by Jeho's domineering force, as he sat there nonchalantly facing her. His huge stature emitted a strangely overpowering force that seemed to proclaim, "No matter how hard you struggle to escape, you're bound to follow my lead." Although Chobong wasn't conscious of it, she was yielding to that force even before attempting to resist it. That domineering force of Jeho's was nothing but his innate ability to push and shove. Though he appeared lighthearted and frivolous on the surface, he was capable of achieving what he desired, by overpowering others if necessary, and all the while obstinately persevering in his will. On top of that, Chobong had cherished an image of Jeho as a competent man who could save her from the misery that had befallen her. Whether that image was a vain illusion or not, Chobong wasn't able to call forth a fighting spirit in front of her supposed idol. It might be more accurate to say that she had never been confident or aggressive enough to pursue what she thought good for herself, and now she had lost the last vestige of self-esteem since she had totally failed in her first choice of life, her marriage. A sort of self-abandoning disposition shrouded her mind, precluding her from taking any actions for herself, though she wasn't clearly conscious of it.

Sitting there, she was quietly lamenting her fate of becoming easy prey, and condemning her own helplessness that was forcing her to surrender to ignominy as if her hands and feet were bound.

I've never once done anything I pleased, ever since I grew old enough to consider others!

That I let myself marry Go Taesu was the product of my weak mind, and that I was violated by that rascal Jang Hyeongbo might also have been the result of my seeming too soft and easy. The reward of my being such a person is to have both my body and youth ruined beyond repair.

And now, faced with a critical moment in which my future is at stake, I simply remain dull, unable to utter even a single sharp word of protest. What on earth is the matter with me?

Although she couldn't forgive herself, through her laments she could at least give herself a sort of outlet through which her stifled heart could breathe; she offered a few soothing caresses of self-pity to her troubled mind. Finally, she let out a long, deep sigh, tears welling up in her eyes.

But to look deeper into the issue, Chobong's laments were ill-grounded and out of focus. From the start, she didn't question the moral aspect of succumbing to Jeho's will and eventually becoming his mistress. She just let that detail pass by without question. She was totally ignorant as to whether becoming Jeho's mistress was morally acceptable or not, let alone the thought of how detestable it all might be. To use an old saying, she was like the servant in an old story who cried all day long without knowing which of his master's wives had passed away.

The situation being such, Chobong had no appetite, so she just made a few gestures of eating and let the maid take the table away.

Jeho, who was still drinking beer, made a big fuss, urging her to eat some more. Chobong forced herself to reply, saying that she'd had enough, though she didn't want to converse with him at all, and then she removed herself to the verandah behind the big glass window.

The view outside was rather monotonous, showing a few Western-style houses and Japanese-style restaurants here and there against a background of paddies full of rice seedlings and the empty fields where barley had been harvested.

Sitting on a comfortable cool rattan chair, she looked out blankly at the fields, filled with a sense of utter helplessness.

Jeho was at the table for nearly an hour, consuming as many as five bottles of beer, while talking about this or that with the serving maid. When he'd finished several bowls of rice, he stacked a number of cushions on the floor, and laying his head on them, fell into a deep sleep, snoring loudly. It was as if he'd forgotten Chobong's presence. Sickened at the sight of Jeho lying asleep on his back, his bare legs covered all over with black hair fully exposed, Chobong drew the curtain of the window to hide herself.

But before long, succumbing to the lure of sweet slumber, she too fell asleep, resting her head on the tea table. Before she fell asleep, she reassured herself with the resolve to fight back with all her might, and avoid the worst at whatever cost, a resolution she herself was not so confident of being able to carry through, but which was soothing for her at the time.

They had a late supper around eight o'clock and went to the spa one more time. When they returned, the maid had spread out the bedding and placed two pillows side by side in the middle of the room.

Ah, things have come to this after all!

Muttering to herself, she stopped at the door and closed her eyes, as if wishing to deny its reality.

How on earth have I been driven to this?

When she left her home in Gunsan that morning, she hadn't even dreamed of anything like this. She'd been hoping for a life of independence at the start of the journey. Overwhelmed by the absurdity of the situation, she felt as though she had suddenly fallen into a bottomless pit while walking leisurely along the road. That she was about to sleep in the same bed with Jeho was something utterly beyond her imagination, something that left her too confounded to seek a rational explanation.

The maid, who had finished making the bed, retreated from the room, obsequiously bowing and wishing them a good night's rest after a long day of travel.

Jeho, who was sitting on the verandah, cast a glance at Chobong, who was standing near the door full of embarrassment. With a smile spreading over his face, Jeho at last accosted Chobong, nodding his head at her.

"Why are you standing there like that . . .? Come over here, Chobong, dear, and let's have a talk."

At the words "a talk," Chobong reluctantly went to the verandah and sat down in a chair opposite Jeho.

"By the way . . ., what shall we do about our residence?" Jeho blurted out without any preliminaries, lighting a cigarette.

"Our residence?" Chobong raised her head, unable to understand his meaning.

"Yes, our residence . . . a house for us to live in together . . . Huh huh huh, damn it."

Chobong wished she had the boldness to reply, "When and where and with whom have you reached an agreement to talk about such things?" But it was merely a wish.

Jeho began to expound his plans.

"I shall certainly divorce Yunhui one day, but as you know, it won't be an easy task. Since she's an intractable, wayward woman, she would oppose the divorce much more stubbornly out of spite if she got to know about our living together. Therefore it would be best to keep it secret until the divorce comes through. That's why I can't take you straight to my house in Cheongjin-dong. I hope you don't mind. I'll rent a proper house for us somewhere in Seoul for the time being.

"Once you live like that in a house of your own, you'll be able to settle your restless mind and be free from everyday worries. Even if you get a job and make something like twenty or thirty won a month, you would never be comfortable enough. I assure you that with me you can live a far better life, many times better off than you can manage if you live alone.

"If you can put up with that life for some time, I'll solve the problem with Yunhui completely and bring you into my

Cheongjin-dong house as my wife. In addition, if you want, we can have a wedding ceremony as well.

"So relax and trust me. You may still have some misgivings, but consider how I, a man of this age, a man who has maintained a good relationship as your family's friend for a long time, a man who has always been kind and affectionate toward you, could possibly harbor an evil intention of taking you as a mere plaything? I can by no means be a villain who would play with you for some time and then desert you. I'm sure you know well that I'm not such a ruthless scoundrel."

The above is a rough approximation of Jeho's lengthy explanations. He was sincere, earnest, and cordial all the way through as he talked for nearly an hour, sitting in the chair in a serious posture. He didn't even scatter his customary "damn it" over his speech, not even once.

He was fully preoccupied with his one ardent desire to make Chobong his own and at least, for the moment, Jeho really meant what he said.

It may not be correct to say that Chobong believed Jeho's words and attitude to be truthful, but she at least wanted to believe him and allow herself to take them as such.

Now that things have gone this far, what else can I . . .?

Chobong resolved to force herself to take things as they came, but as reluctantly as someone who had no other option but this unless she chose to die.

She was pretty much satisfied with the details of Jeho's future plans. She even wanted to get some assurance from Jeho about providing for her family in Gunsan, but at the thought that it might look too greedy and businesslike, she didn't dare bring up the issue.

Jeho, grinning from ear to ear, suggested a celebration for their first night together and summoned a maid to bring some more beer.

Chobong at last came to consider how she liked the idea of becoming Jeho's wife. Oddly enough though, however hard she thought about it, all her feelings seemed numbed. She didn't even want to think about whether it was right or wrong.

She simply kept alternating her glance between Jeho and herself and kept muttering to herself,

Me, the wife of that elderly man?

That man, my husband?

The idea seemed simply too laughable to be a reality. It sounded more like a joke or a prank. She tried to recall how she'd felt when she was about to marry Go Taesu, but she could find no memory of ever having thought about it.

Around two in the afternoon the next day, Chobong, now really Jeho's so-called "woman," got on the bus heading for Daejeon, leaving behind Yuseong Spa, the place that would become her honeymoon site in retrospect. Mulling over the new development in her life, Chobong wondered how she could have gone through so many vicissitudes in life within one month. She felt as if all these things had happened to someone else, and that she had only been acting on behalf of that person for the time being.

Now was the fourth day since her arrival in Seoul. Chobong, who'd been staying at an inn, was moving to her new house in the afternoon. Jeho came by in a car loaded with miscellaneous household goods to pick her up. Now their car was passing through the center of Jongno heading east of Seoul.

"My company's in that building . . . I'm renting the second floor temporarily, it's very spacious and in a very convenient location . . ."

Jeho pointed at a two-story brick building on the corner of the street near Donggwan Pajugae, the historic building right outside the East Gate.

"And, over there is a movie theater . . . I chose this area to give my kitty good access to something to enjoy, heh heh."

Jeho had begun using the pet name "my kitty" on the bus from Yuseong Spa.

When they got out of the car near Donggwan Pajugae and entered an alley on the right-hand side, there came into view a clean, newly built house overlooking a back alley. The house was very new, still emitting a scent of pine resin and had a high gate from which two lamps were hanging on each side. Seen from the outside, the house looked nice enough to catch Chobong's fancy.

When she entered through the gate, on the right was the servants' quarters and through the inner gate, which had glass windows, there appeared the kitchen and the main bedroom on the left, connected to the maru and another bedroom on the right. Though it looked nice from the outside, once inside, the house was rather small and cramped. The yard was so small you might hit your nose on the walls of the houses on the front and to the side unless you walked cautiously. In that small yard had been set up something like a ledge for earthenware crocks filled with sauces as well as a tap for water. As the house was facing southeast, there would be plenty of sunlight coming in during the winter, but for the upcoming summer, it would be rather stuffy for lack of ventilation, since the west side of the house was blocked by another house.

Chobong wasn't quite satisfied with the house and was most surprised when Jeho said the rent amounted to thirty won a month in addition to a two-hundred won deposit. Jeho had said that he would leave the servants' quarters unoccupied, since tenants might mess up the premises. But as they were entering the main quarters, a young woman with a rugged-looking face and rather dark skin came out from the room opposite the main room, and greeted them very courteously.

So it seemed that Jeho had already hired a maid; in addition, he had had the house fully furnished, with a wardrobe, a kitchen cupboard, a wooden rice chest, and small kitchen utensils. Seeing the house so well furnished, Chobong couldn't help but be reminded of the day when she had first entered the house Taesu had prepared for her as fully as this house. This memory somewhat dampened her mood.

Jeho was as meticulous as could be; the rice chest was full of rice; the kitchen was fully stocked with firewood; he even had brooms ready standing in the corner. The most welcome item for Chobong was a sewing machine, which seemed to have been taken from his house in Cheongjin-dong. Chobong felt a bit uneasy because it might have been used by Yunhui, but recalling the hard time when she and her mother had sewed clothes for customers by hand until their backs hurt, she could easily dismiss her uneasy feelings toward Yunhui.

All in all, Chobong was pretty much satisfied, except that the yard was too small to yield a space for a flower bed. But she consoled herself with the thought of buying a few flowerpots instead.

The next morning, once Jeho went to work after breakfast, Chobong sat down at a small table and began to write a letter to her mother.

She said that she had arrived in Seoul safely; that fortunately, she had found a comfortable lodging and the means to live independently; that, as she had suggested to her in the letter she had left on her departure, her mother should somehow manage the family budget for the time being by getting the deposit money for her house reimbursed, as well as by selling whatever was in the house, such as all the furniture and other small items she had left behind, including her watch and rings. She also promised her mother that she would find a way to help her family before long. Her letter was brief and to the point.

She surmised that her family would be able to collect nearly two hundred won by doing what she had suggested, on top of the small amount of won they had left over from the funds for the wedding expenses from Taesu. She felt relieved by the thought that her family would get along at least for three or four months with that money. She thought she would soon open her heart to Jeho and ask him frankly to help her family with twenty to thirty won a month, assuring him that she would cut back on her own living expenses, or else that he would find a means for her to help her family.

She was even harboring a plan to bring Gyebong and Hyeongju to Seoul for education as soon as they finished the schools they were attending now in Gunsan and ask Jeho's support for them.

She hesitated for a while, holding the pen in her hand, before concluding the letter. She wasn't sure whether or not she should mention the fact that she was now Jeho's "woman." She knew that she should, but she also knew that her parents would be greatly upset at her imprudent behavior without understanding the lengths to which she had gone before arriving at her decision. So she decided that it was too early, and sealed the letter without hinting at anything of the kind.

In the evening around sunset, Jeho returned home, bright with happy smiles, and laid five fresh ten-won bills in front of Chobong.

"This is the monthly allowance for my kitty. Huh huh huh huh, Bak Jeho must be the only guy in the world who pays a kitten a salary, surely? Damn it, hah hah hah."

"But so much?"

Chobong smiled back with delight. Fifty won for a monthly allowance seemed way too generous even before considering that the monthly wage she would make, if she worked, would probably amount to between twenty and thirty won at the most.

"Uh-uh, that's nothing much . . ."

Jeho gave a pinch at Chobong's cheek affectionately and said,

"Do you think fifty won is enough for you? It depends on how you spend it . . . With this money you'll pay for such things as groceries, electricity and water bills, the maid's wage . . . But the rent I will pay myself, and I'll supply the firewood and rice separately. You see? . . . And in case you need extra money, I mean when you need to buy large household items or fabric, just ask me for more."

Listening to him, Chobong was busy in her mind calculating the expenses she would need to cover; perhaps ten won would be enough to cover the electricity and water bills as well as the maid's wage. And even if she had to prepare quality meals for Jeho, grocery expenses wouldn't exceed twenty won.

She was sure she would have at least twenty to twenty-five won saved each month from Jeho's allowance. Then she thought she would send those savings to her family, instead of asking for Jeho's help. Perhaps she might have to tell Jeho about it one day. But for the time being she would handle it by herself, because making a request for her family to Jeho seemed an awkward and embarrassing task for her.

She indeed had twenty odd won left over out of the fifty-won allowance when she counted the money on July 15, the day her first month with Jeho was over. It was possible because she was very frugal in her expenses. But she didn't send the money to her mother outright, as the letters from home indicated that her family's finances weren't yet too tight, having done what she had instructed in her letter. So she stashed the money away for future use.

Chobong, who had been quite unsettled and restless at the beginning of this new life, began to feel more secure and accustomed to it. At first her new situation seemed too unreal to accept, and she even had some premonition that fate would sport with her again, giving her new trials within a few days.

But as time passed, ten days, half a month, a month, then two months went by without any momentous incidents, she found her mind quite calmed down, as she settled into her new way of life.

In her life with Jeho in Seoul, just as in her life with Taesu, Chobong poured all her energy and affection into good housekeeping. She kept her house clean and tidy by sweeping and mopping day and night; she enjoyed arranging her furniture this way or that; having bought a few flowerpots, she tended the flowers with great care; she spent much time sitting at the sewing machine making this or that. Chobong's touch was visible in everything in the house, from the grains of sand in the yard to the lampshade. She was absolutely devoted to maintaining the house in good shape.

Jeho at times tried to dissuade her from her absorption in housekeeping, jokingly suggesting that such an obsession with cleanliness might scare the good luck away from the house. But for Chobong, it was the only source of pleasure and satisfaction, having nothing else to feel attached to.

Though she kept herself busy all day long while Jeho was away at work, the moment Jeho returned, she turned herself into a most devoted companion. If Jeho laughed, she laughed too. If he wanted to converse, she became a very attentive listener. Utilizing her innate skill at cooking, she prepared each meal for Jeho with the utmost care. Even before Jeho asked, she always had a few bottles of beer ready for dinner, cooled in ice . . .

In view of all this, she could well be considered a loving mistress, or an affectionate wife, or even an exemplary housewife.

However, she wasn't performing this role out of any affection for Jeho. The truth was that she acted as a loving wife only as a part of her housekeeping duties, not unlike those chores such as cleaning the house, tending flowers, polishing the surface of the wardrobe to make it shine, or quilting a patchwork, which she really enjoyed.

Thus, except for those occasional moments when Seungjae came into her mind, she was leading a pretty much contented life. She had no occasion to be excited, but neither did she have anything to complain about. She followed her routine faithfully day in, day out, almost like a robot.

Chobong had called Jeho "Uncle" when she worked at his pharmacy in Gunsan and she liked and trusted him as if he were a real uncle. So she still responded to his affection without any reservations. But she found it impossible to have strong emotions or attachment such as are normal between lovers or husband and wife. She had not even a hint of such feelings in her heart.

Rather, her longing for Seungjae deepened. She felt lonely and empty as though she had lost something very precious long ago, and in its place was left with immense sorrow. Such feelings were, without exception, a portent of her falling into vague longing for Seungjae. Whenever she felt lonely and empty, the next moment she thought of Seungjae.

This, however, was the only source of joy and comfort she could have—perhaps a painful comfort, but a pleasantly painful comfort. If she hadn't had such emotional reveries, her life would've been no different from that of a woman in her fifties who worked as a housekeeper. It was the only sign that she was still a youthful woman.

Jeho, on the other hand, was utterly enamored of Chobong. Once he got home in the evening, he always made sure that she was at his side. If he could have time off, he would've taken Chobong to some summer retreats like Sambang or Seokwang

Temple. But he couldn't be absent from his office even for one day as the company had just started trading.

Instead, he took Chobong downtown or along Jongno for a stroll almost every night. While walking down the street, if something caught his eye, he would instantly buy it for her, whether it be clothes or something for the house. He was doing his utmost to win her heart.

It was on the third day of their living together, when Chobong was bringing the dinner table into the room, that Jeho blurted out,

"Dear me, I wonder how this came about. Do you have any idea, Chobong?"

As it was totally out of context, Chobong was blank for a little while, unable to understand his meaning, but when it struck her that it might have something to do with Hyeongbo, her heart dropped.

"To be sure, I've never . . .," Jeho, holding up his spoon, began to explain in a casual manner, ". . . had any relationship with another woman ever since Yunhui left. Huh huh, what the hell is this then? It's really odd . . . I have symptoms of VD, huh huh, damn it all. Isn't it a shame for an old guy? It seems that guy, Go So-and-So, did all kinds of evil deeds to you before his death!"

Chobong was still in the dark, having no idea what VD was. Jeho had to give her a long lecture explaining what it was. Chobong dropped her head, engulfed in shame. She sat motionless for quite some time, her head down.

She recalled that a few days after her marriage to Taesu she had had some of the symptoms Jeho just explained.

"What's done is done. Let's not worry about it. The thing we need to do is to get treatment for it. Huh huh huh huh, damn it . . . It's all right, dear, no problem!"

Whatever was in his mind, Jeho, in appearance, was laughing away the matter lightly. He even tried to extinguish the fire of Chobong's shame, almost regretting bringing up the matter.

From the next day on, he brought home all the necessary medicines and injections for VD, and skillfully administered the treatments for both himself and Chobong. Though the process couldn't be called pleasant, nevertheless, the man and the woman sat together and went through it all, even making jokes about it at times.

Jeho took great care to offer every comfort to Chobong. He'd been fed up with his domestic life for quite some time due to Yunhui's hysteria and ill health. Unable to get even an ounce of pleasure from his family life with Yunhui, he was often left with a sour taste in his mouth. In the eyes of such a man, who'd been utterly unhappy in his home, Chobong, who now provided him with a snug and happy home, was truly endearing and precious. On top of that, Chobong was the woman he'd longed to have in his embrace.

It was true, however, that from time to time he felt uneasy because Chobong was somewhat reserved, never giving him her full heart, which he couldn't fail to notice. In fact, he wasn't sure how long he could endure this distance Chobong was maintaining. It was as if he were living with a doll carved out of plaster. If this lack of enthusiasm and full affection on the part of Chobong should continue for long, he was pretty certain that he would have to give her up one day.

Nevertheless, he was still hopeful. Surely sooner or later I'll win her heart completely; isn't she a human, a woman? The more I shower her with my true affection, the more likely she will respond to it in earnest. With such determination, Jeho did all he could to steal her heart. When he found Chobong rather prim and aloof, he would throw in a joke with the intention of amusing her.

"My kitty's in a bad mood, isn't she? . . . Come on, dear . . . come over here, my kitty, I'll give you a fish head."

He would beckon her with his hand, thinking that he was making a joke to amuse her.

But Chobong would cast a sharp glance at him, calling him "Horse head, horse head." At times she would really turn into a cat, rush at him and scratch the back of Jeho's hands or his forehead mercilessly, even throwing in abusive language, which she had never used before.

She would explode in discontent, triggered by the idle teasing of the man whom she could never love, especially when she was in a low mood. Such teasing simply annoyed her rather than amuse her. Jeho, who couldn't see through her, would feel disconcerted at such behavior, being reminded of the early stage of Yunhui's hysteria. He even had a fleeting premonition that Chobong might be following in Yunhui's footsteps.

Chapter 13: A Seed Already Sown

JULY AND AUGUST had passed with nothing significant taking place. As the hot days of summer began to retreat, September came bringing a foretaste of autumn.

The narrow patch of sky visible at the edge of the eaves was transparently blue, having been washed clean during the rainy season. In a few of the flowerpots in the yard chrysanthemum buds were beginning to sprout. Giant dahlias, whose tubers Chobong had planted with much difficulty by digging up one corner of the yard, were as tall as she was, and blooming in full.

As the *Chuseok* holidays were approaching, Jeho was making plans to take Chobong on a trip to the Geumgang-san Mountain to enjoy the colorful autumn leaves. So it was a joyful season, if one had a mind to enjoy it. Chobong, however, was too uneasy and restless with a darkening heart to be excited over the coming of the new season or to look forward to the blooming of dahlias, anticipating whether they would be red or yellow or white.

She had her last period in May, the day before her marriage to Taesu. She should have had it again around the end of June, at the latest, but she didn't. She had never missed before.

When she skipped her menstruation in June, she attributed it to her hectic state of mind as a bride who had just started a totally different sort of life. Recalling that someone had said marriage could cause such irregularity in women's periods, she hadn't worried too much about it.

But when she missed her period again in July, her heart sank. Dismissing this sign of pregnancy, she anxiously waited until August was over.

When September started, Chobong began to have symptoms of pregnancy. She recognized them instinctively, as well as through her memory of her mother's pregnancy with her youngest brother Byeongju.

One of the first symptoms was a craving for something sour. She especially had a craving for apricots, those unripe apricots that had a strong, sour taste. Since apricots weren't in season, she instead bought tons of mandarins and ate them to her heart's content until her mouth felt numb.

One day she suddenly wanted to eat bean curd, which she didn't care for much. She had her maid buy ten cakes of tofu, shallow-fried them after sprinkling a bit of salt over them, and ate them all. The maid, who was watching her with amazement, teased her saying,

"Madam, you must be pregnant?"

Chobong scolded her to stop such nonsense.

When the odd cravings for food had passed, she began to experience nausea, feeling queasy all the time, as though she had an upset stomach. She lost her appetite, and her body, which had been bothered by the warm, humid weather of summer, became more listless because she couldn't eat at all. But such bodily discomfort was not the source of Chobong's concern.

She had married Go Taesu and lived with him for ten days, and on the last day of her marriage she was raped by Jang Hyeongbo, and then fifteen days after that she began to live with Bak Jeho. So whose child might it be? She agonized over that question.

If it was Jeho's seed, nothing could be better. If it was Taesu's, it would simply be sad and unfortunate. But it wouldn't be so disastrous, for Jeho was generous and open-minded, and would understand the situation. But she couldn't discount the possibility of it being Hyeongbo's. If such a horrid thing happened to her body, what, what . . .?

She couldn't help but be terrified of that possibility. She felt a cold shiver run down her spine when she imagined a being exactly resembling Hyeongbo might be growing inside her belly.

Whose child might it be?

No matter how anxious she was to know the answer, there was no way to find out. It was all just speculation. It could be the seed of Go, yet it might not be; it could be the seed of Bak, or not; it could be the seed of Jang, or happily it might not.

She would be able to tell only after it was born. If, when it was born, it looked like Jeho or Taesu, she would be relieved. But if it took after Hyeongbo, it would be nothing short of a thunderbolt for her; she would feel as though she had given birth to a snake. She would be too ashamed to face Jeho. How on earth could she raise such a monster, let alone breastfeed it. She would rather die than do it, she thought. Perhaps it might not be bad if it looked like no one but herself. But then it would be impossible to know who its father was. Even if Jeho, unaware of the uncertainty, would love and cherish the child as his own, it would be wrong and unbearable for her to let that pass.

What would be worse for her conscience was allowing the child to grow up thinking of Jeho as its father when in fact there would be no certainty as to who its father was. She knew she wouldn't be able to bear it.

Then how on earth should I handle this dilemma?

Chobong usually ended up muttering this question rather helplessly, after tormenting herself by desperately probing all the possibilities. With no clear-cut solutions coming up, she was often drawn toward a more dreadful option.

Though it was a life only three months old, it seemed a mortal crime to kill it. Knowing all that, she still began to think that it might be best not to give birth, if she wanted to avoid future predicaments. She shuddered with fright when her thoughts reached that point. Yet she would still rather confront that fright than risk the troubles that would follow its birth.

She became more and more anxious that Jeho might find out about her pregnancy, so she strengthened her resolve to end the pregnancy as soon as possible. However firm her determination, putting it into action wasn't easy. Hesitant all the while, she was physically exhausted, mentally desolate; on top of that, she was so nervous that she couldn't pay any attention to her household duties or to the exciting aspects of the upcoming season.

It took Chobong half a month to find out that Sabina was the best medicine for an abortion, although she mobilized all her commonsense knowledge as well as all the knowledge acquired through her meager three-months' work experience at Jejungdang Pharmacy.

As soon as she found that out, she purchased some. After that, she resolved every day to take it, but never actually took it. She continued delaying for about ten days.

It was already October 10. Her belly was pretty much round and she could feel the difference even when she touched it through her clothes.

That day, at the breakfast table, Jeho began to inquire with a meaningful smirk at the corners of his mouth,

"You don't look so well lately! Aren't you well?"

Chobong was taken aback, but said casually it must be because she'd had a stomachache for the last few days, perhaps caused by roundworms.

"Roundworms? That can't be! . . . Anyway I think I should take you to the hospital or have Dr. S come over for a checkup."

Alarmed, Chobong shouted in a loud voice despite herself, "No, I won't!"

"Hunh! What's this about? How odd that you respond so sharply when it's only a suggestion for a medical checkup? Huh huh huh huh, don't be so stubborn, dear. Finish your meal, and doll yourself up, dear. On our way back from the hospital, I'll treat you to some fancy food at Chosun Hotel."

"I said I don't want to go!"

"What obstinacy! Huh huh huh huh . . . If you really don't want to go to the hospital, just come over here and let me feel your pulse . . ."

Jeho stretched out his hand toward Chobong, putting down the spoon on the table. Chobong, retreating from the table, said in a rather coquettish tone,

"No! I won't! I'd rather scratch you mercilessly, I would, really . . ."

"Huh huh huh huh, what drives my kitty into such a temper! Hah hah hah hah, all right, I'll stop. For I know it all now . . . huh huh huh huh."

"What do you mean you know? How unbearable you are!"

"Well, well. You don't need to try to hide it, do you? . . . Damn, damn, my kitty's soon to be a mother! Huh huh huh huh."

"You must be out of your mind! . . . Goodness, what an idea!"

"Damn it! I'm going to have a child at my age, thanks to my Chobong, am I not?"

"Stop your nonsense. You must be playing a joke on me out of boredom . . ."

"No joke! It all came out of my happy excitement."

Jeho's being happy was empty words, and his gaiety was a joke. He had suspected it for some time, but it was last night that he became certain of it. And now seeing Chobong wildly denying it, Jeho became quite uncomfortable. It must mean that she was carrying the seed of Go Taesu, otherwise she wouldn't have tried to hide it so desperately. Indeed she came to him only half a month after her husband died, thus there was no assurance that the child in her body was not Taesu's.

If it were Taesu's, Jeho would be like a cuckhold, raising someone else's child conceived by his woman. It would not only be an "unwelcome burden" but a reminder of unpleasant memories for him. Despite all that, Jeho forced himself to accept it like a man who swallows a bitter pill; so long as he lived with her, there would be no choice but to accept the baby as well, he thought. On the other hand, it would be a magnanimous act of charity if he were to raise as his own the child of a man who, despite having met an untimely and unhappy death, had the extraordinary luck to leave behind his own flesh.

Whether or not she saw through the complex state of Jeho's mind, Chobong became only more anxious to get rid of the child, and reinforced her determination to carry out on that day the abortion that she had delayed for so long.

The moment Jeho left for work, she took out the drug she had stashed away among her clothes in a drawer. She had not had any breakfast, so she asked her maid to bring just a bowl of cold water. She had a box of twelve capsules ready in her hand. For normal use, that was three days' dose. Taking them all at once might prove fatal, she thought. She took out only ten capsules and put them on her left palm.

Squatting down on the floor with a firm resolution, she held up the bowl of water with her right hand. Her hand was trembling and she couldn't help but look down at her belly.

For the past ten days, she'd reached this point every day, but each time she'd been overwhelmed by a fearful sense that Heaven was looking down at her and that the life within her was wriggling, so she couldn't go on.

She tried to lift her left hand holding the capsules to her mouth, mesmerized by the sparkling grains within the capsules, but soon her trembling hand dropped as if weighed down with heavy stones. She repeated the same process a few times and finally stopped, emitting a deep, heavy sigh.

She put the water bowl in her right hand down on the floor and stared intently at the capsules in her left palm.

"Just throw these into your mouth, and drink one or two gulps of water, that's all that's necessary . . ."

As she kept gazing at the capsules for some time, she began to feel an odd fascination.

I know swallowing them is a very hard step to take, although it seems deceptively simple and easy. However, just think of the myriad troubles it will save me; just close your eyes tightly, hold your teeth firmly together, and swallow them as though your life is at stake. Once they pass down your throat, there'll be no turning back, of course; no matter how scared you are, no matter how afraid of Heaven you become, when you expel the lump growing inside your body, it will be irreversible. If I only manage to take that last step, I'll be able to avoid all sorts of agonies and unpleasant anxieties that will follow if I give birth to the baby and raise it. What a great relief that will be!

When her thoughts went that far and she stared at the capsules again, shaking them in her palm, instead of heavy-heartedness, she felt a strange excitement mixed with fear, as if she were about to engage in a game of chance, fraught with suspense.

She must have been struggling with her irresolution for over an hour. The wall clock began to strike clang, clang, incessantly.

She counted the sounds though she knew it was eleven o'clock without counting.

Then she urged herself on with the thought,

Before long, he'll come for lunch, I have to finish it quickly . . .

Yet still, propelled by the desire to linger a bit longer, she looked around, searching for excuses. The cabinet for storing bedding came into her sight. She stood up and brought down a set of bedding and spread them on the floor. Then to facilitate the cleaning up process after the abortion, she changed her underwear to something easier to manage.

She looked around one more time to see if she'd missed anything. But soon she realized that she'd been doing that in order to delay the critical moment rather than to be more thorough in her preparation. She instantly held up the bowl of water, scolding herself severely for shilly-shallying.

Holding up the bowl, she tightly closed her eyes and opened her mouth wide, tilting her head back, for fear of hesitating again. She wanted to clench her teeth as well, but she couldn't do that because it was a matter of swallowing something.

She knew she couldn't swallow all ten capsules in one gulp, so she threw about half of them into her mouth and drank some water.

It was hard to swallow them all at once, but somehow they managed to pass down her throat.

You see now!

Confirming the simplicity of the task, she threw the other half of the capsules into her mouth and drank some more water.

You see, I've done it!

Swallowing them with some difficulty, she kept pressing down on herself.

Now that it was all over so quickly, Chobong began to reproach herself for having made such a fuss over such an easy task, having so often urged herself to do it, then hesitating again and again, while constantly looking for excuses to delay.

Well, a violent commotion should start up in my body now, and eventually I shall be relieved of that disgusting lump growing inside me. Taken up by these expectations, Chobong forgot to put away the two capsules remaining on the floor, and hurriedly laid herself down on the bedding.

She anxiously waited for the symptoms for about thirty minutes, when she began to feel nauseous. Taking it as a good omen, she patiently resisted without throwing up. But the nausea grew unbearable, accompanied by severe pains in the stomach. She reckoned her womb had started contractions.

Her ears were ringing loudly, her head was swirling, and everything in sight was turning yellow. The dizziness, the nausea, the pain of the twisting stomach all grew worse and worse.

Though delirious, she desperately struggled not to throw up, clenching her teeth, but the struggle couldn't go on for long.

The maid rushed to Jeho's office in a flurry, and called to him.

"The madam, my lady is dying, sir! She's talking gibberish! She's delirious!"

It was around noon when the maid reported this.

Jeho instantly knew that Chobong had taken drugs for an abortion. Although he was in a hurry, Jeho remembered to call his friend Dr. S and ask him to come over immediately to his house and not to forget to bring a stomach pump. Dr. S was an obstetrician, but being one of Jeho's best friends, he was like a family doctor who used to visit Jeho's house even for small troubles such as a cut on a finger or a headache. The moment he finished what he had to say, Jeho threw the receiver down, rushed down the stairs, taking two steps in one stride, and hurried to his house.

Whatever he thought about Chobong's pregnancy, Jeho was not a man who would agree to an abortion, especially one that would risk the mother's life by taking dangerous poison, when a life had already begun in her womb.

It was true he would rather Chobong not give birth to a child whose father could not be determined, but never by means of an abortion. Moreover, regardless of whether the abortion worked or not, he was truly flustered because it was Chobong's life that was in danger.

When he got home, he rushed to the kitchen first, grabbed the dishwater bucket, and ran to the room with it.

Chobong appeared to be in a critical condition as she was barely breathing, almost unconscious.

Jeho looked around to find what she'd taken. When he found two Sabina capsules in a box on the floor, he felt a bit relieved. He'd been really worried, suspecting she might have taken Ergotin instead, which was much more dangerous.

She must have thrown up a lot, for the floor was still covered with residues of her vomit, though the maid had mopped most of it up. So Jeho didn't make Chobong drink the water he'd brought in. Instead, after examining her pulse, he sat down next to her, and anxiously awaited the arrival of Dr. S.

Twenty minutes later, Dr. S ran into the house accompanied by a nurse. First of all, he pumped her stomach, but there was nothing much to be pumped out since she'd already thrown up most of the drugs and the rest had already been absorbed into her body. The doctor injected two shots, one a heart stimulant, the other a detoxicant. Now there was nothing else to do but wait for her body to recover on its own.

"How is she? . . . She's not dying, is she? Damn, damn," Jeho asked worriedly the moment Dr. S put down his stethoscope.

"'Damn?' What is it that you damn?"

Dr. S, ignoring Jeho's question, started to joke as he came out onto the maru following Jeho. The conversation between the two men was always spiced with jokes. They had long been accustomed to enjoying that way of talking.

". . . Well? One may either live or die, as it happens. What's there to be damned?"

"Why on earth did she take so many of those damned Sabina pills! She's a damned nuisance."

As Dr. S started to joke, Jeho could breathe easily at last, and they began to smoke, facing each other. Jeho's cracked, dried-up lips revealed how much anxiety he'd felt during that short time span.

"They say the trouble in a blacksmith's house is having no proper knife in the house. In your case, Jeho, on the contrary, 'the trouble in a pharmacist's house is having too many drugs in the house.'"

"What a pity that she's so ignorant!"

Jeho was endeavoring to fend off the possibility of Dr. S's getting to know of Chobong's pregnancy. However intimate their relationship might be, Jeho didn't want him to know that Chobong had attempted an abortion.

"That's called a retribution for crime . . ."

Enjoying Jeho's uneasiness, Dr. S continued to provoke him with more banter, seeming to have forgotten all about the patient.

"I say it's all a sort of retribution for what you're doing. Make a quack medicine costing fifty jeon or so, and sell it at ten to twenty times the price by placing big advertisements here and there. It's a punishment for that."

"So you quack doctors give a shot worth two won and charge twenty won, don't you? How about that?"

"In addition, you've another crime to answer for. Where 'ein' should be enough, you have 'zwei' or 'drei' all to yourself, haven't you? Why on earth do you need two or three when one alone can overwhelm you?"

"In the old days, you know, men used to enjoy playing with as many as eight fairies, damn it."

"By the way, how many of those 'damn its' of yours do you spit out each day?"

Giggling sounds came from the main bedroom where the nurse and the maid were attending to Chobong; the nurse burst into giggles, and the maid was making a tittering sound, trying to repress her laughter.

After a while, Dr. S stood up to go back into the room with his stethoscope in his hand and looking down at Jeho, blurted out with a meaningful grin on his face,

"I hope she won't have a miscarriage."

Jeho scratched the back of his head in resignation and simply said, "Huh! Damn you."

CHOBONG WAS DELIRIOUS for nearly two days. Hanging onto a consciousness as thin as a hair's breadth, she was floating in the air, then plummeted to the ground, or was chased by Hyeongbo, who in a moment transformed into Taesu, or was carried to the gate of the netherworld to be investigated by the King of the Underworld, but soon the King of Death assumed the figure of Jeho, who, grinning with his long face, approached her, or at another moment, Hyeongbo emerged from her womb, slashing his way out of her belly with a knife. She spent the whole night and the next day beleaguered by these hellish nightmares.

When she regained full consciousness around the evening of the next day and realized that she was still alive, the first thing she did was reach out to her lower abdomen. Upon finding her belly still round, she breathed out a deep sigh, feeling both a sense of relief and a sense of despair at the same time.

Her attempt to miscarry, which had almost cost her her own life, had proved to be a failure. In about three days, she recovered enough to sit up while Jeho was having his supper.

"Stay lying down, dear! . . . It's all right, just stay down there."

Jeho quickly admonished her to stay in bed and cast a look at her pale, haggard face, which looked like a listless flower that had been shaken by merciless gusts and storms for some time.

Chobong stopped short of an attempt to smile and turned her face aside, overwhelmed by a sense of shame and awkwardness. As Jeho continued to remain silent about what she had attempted to do, a tense uneasiness fell between them, which prevented Chobong from facing him calmly.

Jeho, however, wasn't intending to keep silent about the matter, he was simply postponing his talk with her until her full recovery.

"How thoughtless you were!"

Jeho at last opened up about the issue with a kindly smile on his face.

"What were you trying to do? It could very well have killed you, didn't you know that? Weren't you afraid of that?"

With her face turned aside, Chobong kept silent, just twisting the ties of her top around her finger.

"Weren't you afraid, Chobong?" Jeho repeated his question, looking at the silent Chobong.

"My dear Chobong, you shouldn't have done that. It was wrong. Aren't you the mother of the living thing inside you? You're the mother . . . but you attempted such a horrid thing, and aren't you feeling some remorse?"

As Jeho reproached her with the word "mother," Chobong realized that she should feel remorse. Though it seemed appropriate to feel that, somehow she couldn't really feel guilty or remorseful.

If it were her second or third pregnancy, she might have had such a feeling of remorse like a good mother. Or rather she would have felt that even before anybody pointed it out. Or perhaps she would never have attempted the abortion, nor have thought about it. Chobong in fact had never been a mother in the full sense. Therefore her maternal instincts hadn't yet developed sufficiently to function for the four month old fetus within her body, even if it had been conceived in normal marriage rather than being a troublesome product of unidentifiable origin.

Her aversion to taking the medicine had been caused by the general weakness of a human or a woman, fearful of committing a crime, rather than from any particular maternal instinct, which, still remaining in a vague and underdeveloped stage, couldn't have any effect on Chobong.

Chobong barely had such instincts or affection as a mother because she knew of them only through the words of others or through observing others' experience. In her case, it was something inchoate, being "prior to physiological reality," not yet experienced by her own body. Therefore, when she heard Jeho say, "Aren't you the mother of the living thing within you?", though the harsh reminder made her ashamed of herself in the eyes of others, she didn't actually feel any pain or pang for the child.

"And Chobong, dear, you should know . . ."

Jeho resumed admonishing in a soft and gentle tone, to avoid the impression that he was criticizing her.

". . . it's not right to go willfully against the ways of Nature. Going against the grain is bound to end in failure . . . Do you get it, dear? Whatever you call it, it was a sort of destiny, which reflects the will of Heaven. Do you think we, weak and abject creatures, can resist the divine will through mere human power? No, we can't! The ways of Nature are the best guides we have, a precious gift we have to cherish. Right? You got it, dear?"

"Ye-es."

Though Jeho's words were too vague and incomprehensible to grasp, Chobong grudgingly said yes, when pressed by him.

"As for me, this Bak Jeho, it would be no problem at all. I don't mind it at all. Why? . . . Because it would be the child my Chobong gave birth to. What's the problem with raising someone else's child? There are lots of people who are happy while fostering foundlings! . . . I don't mind that at all, no problem whatsoever . . ."

Jeho was talking with a firm belief that the child in her body was Taesu's. When he considered the risk Chobong had taken, that was the only assumption he could possibly have.

". . . Therefore, Chobong, you too must think again . . . Are you listening, Chobong?"

"Yes, go on, please."

"Don't think of it as giving birth to the child of someone you hate, Chobong. Just think of it as fostering a child, a human, regardless of who the father is . . . Think of it as just a human, all right? . . . And never again attempt such a foolish thing, dear. You got it?"

Jeho urged Chobong to answer, leaning his head closer to her.

"Ye-es."

Chobong nodded, confirming her assent to Jeho; in fact, she was feeling no temptation whatsoever to repeat the risky business, even if Jeho hadn't dissuaded her from it so assiduously.

"Right, right . . . that's the right thing to do . . ."

Jeho nodded his long face repeatedly while resuming his meal, and added,

"There you are, that's my good Chobong! Aren't you indeed? Huh huh huh huh!"

"Dear me! You'll spit the rice everywhere!" Chobong blurted out, repulsed by the sudden change of manner adopted by Jeho

who, having stopped being serious, began to laugh rather frivolously.

"Uh? Never mind . . . What's the problem? Who cares whose
child it might be? I don't mind at all. It's nothing but having a
child born, then raising it. It's as simple as that. But see what
kind of trouble you caused. Perhaps that's why people say that
one half of the human race who wear skirts are narrow-minded!
Huh huh huh huh, damn it."

After that, whenever anxiety about the baby arose within her,
Chobong tried to repeat the mantra that Jeho had taught her,

*Who cares whose child it is? It's nothing but having a child born,
then raising it. No more idle sweating over it, it's all right.*

This incantation gave her relief from her anxiety by enabling
her to resign herself to what was coming, but the effect was temporary, like an "Amen" or the Buddhist chant of "*Namu Amita
Bul.*" It lasted no longer than the effect of a narcotic.

As the autumn ripened, Chobong's pregnancy also ripened.
By the time the New Year arrived, her belly had become as big
and as tight as a drum. Around the middle of March the midwife
announced the baby was due in about five days. So Chobong
was taken to Dr. S's clinic and waited there for labor to start.

On March 20, deep into the night, the baby began to struggle tenaciously to come out into this world. As spring had just
started to arrive, it would at least have its birthday in a good
season, no matter how unwelcome it was to its mother.

*If you knew who you were, if you knew what sort of world you
were entering, you'd hang on to your umbilical cord instead and
struggle not to come out into this world, shouting wildly in tears, "I
don't want to be born."*

This was what Chobong thought during the pauses in her
labor pains. Her pangs, however, grew tremendous when the

baby, who'd been upside down, turned around and began to push its way out with full force.

Chobong had never expected the pain would be so extreme. If someone had pressed her belly till it burst, or thrashed it with a cudgel, or tore it open with something sharp, once the deed was over the acuteness of the pain would decrease before long. But labor pains were persistent, becoming more excruciating without any let-up. It was far beyond anything Chobong could endure.

Chobong's eyelids were closed, she was slowly losing consciousness. Though the doctor, the nurse, and Jeho were talking beside her bed, she had no ears to listen to them. Being a woman accustomed to self-restraint, she clenched her teeth and lips in order not to cry out, but repressed moaning sounds kept leaking out through her teeth.

They say all lives, from that of an emperor to that of a homeless vagrant, are equally precious. At least half the justification extends from the enormous pain and risk endured by the mother in the delivery of each life.

In addition to being her first childbirth, it was really a very difficult delivery. Having experienced extreme pain for two full hours, Chobong had reached the limit of her endurance. She could see nothing and she could do nothing except drop her jaw in agony.

Finally Dr. S found it inevitable to administer a scopolamine injection. Its anesthetic effect was very swift, and the baby was delivered without any further complication.

When she finally came to her senses, Chobong felt empty and dull, as though a big part of her lower body had been taken away.

Ah, have I given birth? I must have.

The first thing that came to her mind was a sense of relief, a sense that came out of nowhere as if it had been waiting somewhere ready to be called.

What does it look like?

The next thing that came to her mind was curiosity about the baby, which also was something unexpected.

Before her delivery, she had been gripped by persistent terror and anxiety, thinking to herself, *What if it looks like Hyeongbo?* But after her delivery, pure curiosity overtook her, though the terror soon followed, only this time in a very diluted form of slight fear. Such a change in her mindset seemed very odd to Chobong.

"Hah, hah, have you recovered consciousness, my dear?" Jeho approached, beaming at Chobong.

Spineless man! What is there for him to be so happy about?

Chobong closed her eyes, not simply because she was exhausted but mostly because she didn't want to face Jeho. Just then she heard the sound of a baby crying, coming from the other side of the room. The sound was so pretty and enticing that Chobong suddenly opened her eyes wide despite herself. She became quite tense with an eager anticipation of something marvelous.

The whimpering sound of the baby rang out as though it was calling someone. Enchanted by the piteous sound, Chobong could think of nothing but the wonder of a new life. Something that had lain dormant within her suddenly stirred, and she was engulfed by a strong desire to meet the baby who was emitting such pretty sounds. She thought she wouldn't even mind if it took after Hyeongbo.

"Heh, heh, it's a girl, a girl!" Jeho said, standing up and nodding in the direction of the baby.

A girl? Chobong was more pleased that the baby had the same sex as her.

The nurse, who noticed Chobong's wish to see the baby, ran to the other side of the room and brought the baby wrapped in

a cotton flannel sheet. Chobong, as if drawn by a magnet, leaned
her head in that direction and anxiously waited.

"What a pretty baby you have!"

Presenting the baby to Chobong, the nurse kept making
compliments.

"She looks exactly like you! She's the very picture of you!"

As Chobong looked down at the baby, her mouth unwittingly broadened into a smile. The baby's skin was quite transparent, showing blood vessels underneath, but too reddish to be
pretty; its eyes were closed so tightly as to crinkle its nose, but
her hair was quite dark. Overall the baby didn't look as piteous as
her crying suggested. Chobong, nevertheless, took it as a happy
miracle that she looked exactly like her, feeling quite relieved by
the fact that she didn't at all look like Hyeongbo.

"A child whose father will never be identified!" she lamented,
but this time, it wasn't as heartrending as it had been during her
pregnancy. She found it even amusing that she'd given birth to a
girl who resembled her, a girl who was exactly like her.

"Look! How exactly alike . . .," Jeho joined in with a mirthful
expression, looking alternately at the baby and Chobong. "How
could you produce a girl that's exactly like you? It's certainly
what comes of your nasty temperament, isn't it? Damn it."

"Then, would you rather the baby looked like you instead?"
Dr. S said in a bantering tone.

At that, Jeho was startled, and thought to himself, *That can
never be. You don't know its father!* But Jeho only said,

"Sure, sure, it should look like the father!"

"That long face would be troublesome, to be sure! Perhaps
she would have to leave half of it behind when she marries,
wouldn't she?"

"Huh, huh, that would certainly be inconvenient. Huh huh
huh huh, damn it."

Despite the painful heritage of the baby, Jeho was able to chat on about the baby in an amused manner, satisfied to a certain extent. Though he'd assured Chobong that he wouldn't mind having someone else's child, in actuality he'd been rather uneasy about the possibility of its resembling Go Taesu. He would have been displeased if it had. But when the baby turned out to resemble Chobong alone, he felt relieved, thankful to fair providence.

Late in the evening the next day, Chobong held the baby in her arms and breastfed it for the first time. At that moment, Chobong felt that she had truly become a mother. She was carefully examining the baby's face, looking for signs of beauty, with a happy smile spreading all over her face. Though it wasn't so beautiful, being a newborn, still in her eyes it seemed to have many beautiful features.

The baby, whether it could see or not, opened its eyes and began to suck at her mother's breast after a little hesitation, as though already taught by someone. Chobong was only too happy watching it sucking so vigorously.

Other than the aftereffect of the scopolamine, Chobong had no postpartum trouble. After two weeks, she returned home, fully recovered.

Jeho suggested that Chobong should hire a nurse. It was a suggestion to help Chobong as well as not to lose her too much to the baby. But Chobong, who'd already fallen utterly in love with the baby, refused firmly.

To find a good name for the baby, Chobong obtained a Chinese-Korean dictionary, and studied it for over ten days. At last she chose the name Songhui. She wasn't fully satisfied with it, but she couldn't find anything better.

Though she gave it a name, the problem was what to choose for its surname. Among the three surnames, Go, Jang, and Bak, it might belong to any one of them. But she had no way to determine which. In that sense, the baby was entitled neither to a surname nor to a father. Chobong felt the deep sorrow of the mother of a fatherless child penetrating the marrow of her bones, a sorrow much more specific and concrete than any she had felt during her pregnancy.

She became entirely engrossed in caring for the baby, oblivious of the colorful beauty of spring and then even the humid heat of summer. Now it was autumn again and October had passed its mid-point already.

In the meantime, Songhui was growing fast without any serious troubles thanks to Chobong's care and devotion. By the time Songhui was about two months old, and her features had begun to take shape, it became more obvious that each and every feature of her face was the exact copy of her mother.

Though she was only seven months old now, Songhui had already begun to crawl around from one room to another and was able to sit up by herself. She snatched at everything within her reach, whether a sewing box or a dinner table, and put everything she grasped into her mouth. She even began to utter the word, Mommy, when she crawled toward her mother's lap. Chobong at times tried to train the baby to stand up on her own. When helped by her mother, Songhui managed to remain standing for a few seconds, but soon her plump body plopped down on its bottom. Then Chobong and her maid burst into happy laughter, and the baby responded with a pretty smile.

To borrow a phrase from the popular song, "Stork-down Song," other than the absence of "balls and a dangling chili-like penis" from Songhui's crotch, she was capable of doing everything cute and lovely.

As the days passed by, Chobong became more and more enamored with Songhui, finding each and every one of her fea-

tures and acts adorable. Raising an infant who behaved more or
less like an animal could, of course, be troublesome. Chobong
too was annoyed or embarrassed at times and had to resort to
smacking the baby's bottom or scolding her severely from time
to time. But she always repented immediately after, feeling sorry
for the helpless baby.

While she was engrossed with Songhui's charms, she sometimes recalled her attempted abortion. That memory made her
ashamed to face the little innocent one. She often imagined to
herself, what if she'd succeeded in the abortion, and felt a chill
run down her spine. At such moments, she would cuddle the
baby, and kiss her repeatedly, patting her buttocks. And she
would also reprimand herself for her rashness,

"To this lovely and precious girl of mine, what did I try to
do? . . . Oh my gosh, what a damnable mother, what a wicked
mother I've been to my dearest! Truly!"

Whenever she was reminded of the fact that the baby had
been given neither a surname nor a birth record yet, her heart
ached. But she had become quite free of the anxiety surrounding
the question of who the father might be. She no longer minded
whether it was Taesu, or Hyeongbo, or Jeho. Neither did she
need to force herself to repeat the mantra, "it's nothing but
having a child born, then raising it . . . " The only thing that
occupied her mind was the simple fact, *the baby is mine, one I
gave birth to.*

Chobong showered all her attention and affection on Songhui
alone. She had no desire other than what was related to the baby.
Awake or asleep, she always thought of Songhui. Her only hope
was that she could somehow continue living with Jeho and get
the financial support from him to raise and shelter Songhui
adequately. She believed she could live the rest of her life totally
dependent on this sole source of happiness.

She even forgot about her earlier devotion to good house-keeping, not to mention the pleasures of flowerpots or the sewing machine. She was also forgetful of her own family back in Gunsan who had been the object of her constant worries and concern. She still sent down twenty won a month to her family, but she sometimes delayed the remittance for a few days because she was preoccupied with some work for Songhui as trivial as making quilted socks, or that sort of thing.

Even her vague yearning for Seungjae had disappeared. It didn't mean that she'd forgotten him completely. He certainly came to her mind occasionally. She sometimes let her fancy run wild; in her imagination, Songhui was Seungjae's daughter, who would babble, "daddy, daddy," and she and Seungjae would watch Songhui's cute tricks full of blissful amusement.

She imagined this not for the sake of Seungjae, nor to comfort herself. She did this out of pity for Songhui who would have to live fatherless.

All these changes in Chobong also affected her relationship with Jeho. She became openly indifferent to him. She almost forgot at times that Jeho was her husband, or even that she had a husband. Whenever Jeho wanted to have her in his bed at night, she would try to avoid it, making up this or that excuse.

It was true that Chobong was too tired, having spent all her mental and physical energies on Songhui, and that she didn't mean to neglect Jeho. Regardless of whether Chobong had any justifiable excuses or not, Jeho was bound to feel hurt, which had become more serious since the start of summer.

Jeho was a shrewd man, who wouldn't display resentment at petty instances of neglect; he never complained, yet still it didn't mean that he didn't actually feel it. What he felt remained deep inside him, and that inside was as convoluted as a snail shell.

During that sweltering summer, whenever Jeho returned home after a long, exhausting day, he could find nothing comforting at home. Chobong, busy cuddling the whimpering baby or doing whatever she'd been doing, would glance at him the way a gardener looks at a bitter-tasting, useless cucumber. Was she doing something that important as to have to ignore her husband when he had just returned home from work? Well, it was important things like changing the baby's diaper. During those days, she never once brought out a cold towel for him as a welcoming gesture. The best Jeho could get was a bucket of water set in front of him by the maid for him to wash his face and hands. Though Chobong knew how much he enjoyed cold beer, she stopped having a bottle ready for his return. She simply forgot about that. As for serving Jeho his meals, she left it totally to the maid, who reeked of the stench of sweat, ruining his appetite. The food itself was meager and simple. Diapers were littered all over the house, and wherever he turned, the fishy smell of milk met his nostrils.

At night, Chobong usually acted like a crusader's wife who had to protect her chastity. Even when she yielded, it was to him no better than sleeping with a prostitute at a brothel.

As the night deepened and it grew cooler, Jeho would drift off into sound sleep, and Chobong would close the windows for fear the baby might catch cold. Moreover the baby's loud wailing would often interrupt his sleep at any time of the day or night.

If the baby were his own, he would have endured all those troubles without complaining. But the fact was that the baby girl was totally unrelated to him, and he couldn't help but be annoyed. What was worse was that when he sat at the breakfast table, Chobong would start pressing him,

"We should do something soon about Songhui's birth registration!"

Then Jeho would be befuddled. Since he hadn't yet divorced Yunhui, it wasn't possible to put Songhui in his family register. So Jeho would mumble this or that to appease Chobong, but at that she would start nagging him, losing her temper. On such days, Jeho would feel bad all day, and things would go wrong in all his business transactions as if an unlucky spell had been cast in his office.

Things being like that, Jeho felt like a foolish cuckold who was being imposed upon with all the burden of taking care of the baby and its mother when they actually belonged to someone else.

As for Chobong, she didn't have what it would have taken to keep Jeho's affection alive, even if she weren't preoccupied with Songhui. On the surface, she was Jeho's mistress, but in actual fact, she didn't act like one, as she offered no genuine affection to him. It was already a year and a half since they'd begun living together. Enough time had passed for his love to be exhausted. His enthusiasm for her beauty and the novelty of having her as his woman had also waned. Whatever others might call her, she was after all a mere mistress . . .

In such a situation, the only remedy to keep Jeho's affection alive might have been Chobong's own affection for him. But from the beginning, Chobong had never felt any at all. So to put it metaphorically, Chobong became to Jeho something like a wild apricot, pretty to view, but too sour to eat. Chobong thus became useless, having been unable to satisfy the forty-year-old man's full-blown desire for the caresses of an affectionate companion.

The relationship between the two, therefore, was sure to end sooner or later, but Chobong, like someone who perversely wears a sun hat on a moonlit night, was doing everything unpleasant and unpalatable to Jeho, dampening the embers of his already ebbing passion.

Beginning from September, as summer was cooling down, Jeho's heart too began to cool down rapidly. By the time October started, he had begun to reveal clear symptoms of his wavering heart. Almost every two or three nights, Jeho slept away from home. When he returned the next night, he would try to make excuses, saying that he'd slept at the home of some guests or that he'd had to go to Incheon on business, anticipating Chobong's nagging. But seeing that Chobong was not at all interested in what he did, or didn't do, Jeho would sit around awkwardly for a while and then stomp back out into the night.

Chobong, however, didn't mind the difference in Jeho's behavior at all. She thought it convenient, since she wouldn't be bothered by him. She simply thought he must be busy as he claimed, trusting firmly in the promises Jeho had made at Yuseong spa. She didn't even think about doubting him.

Then Jeho stayed out for three consecutive days. She paid no heed to the fact, sitting on the *maru*, happily feeding Songhui and enjoying the baby's cute tricks.

It was around five o'clock in the evening. The autumn sun was setting in the west, shedding its thin rays on the wall of the neighboring house. The maid was washing something under the tap next to the gate.

Songhui, sucking at one breast while playing with the other with a tiny hand, was about to fall asleep, her eyes half closed, but she abruptly opened her eyes at the thumping sound of footsteps that came from the gate.

Jeho walked into the house rather hesitantly, as if he were entering a stranger's house, looking this way and that with his long face.

"Are you coming into a place unknown to you? What need is there to look around?" said Chobong, sitting on the floor with Songhui in her arms and not getting up. Despite what she said, Chobong felt a bit awkward, as if she were greeting a visitor.

"Well, no, nothing, nothing."

Jeho with an evasive smile on his face flopped carelessly down on the edge of the maru. He tried to behave casually to give an impression that he felt at home, but he still appeared distant and out of place.

He sat there like that for quite some time, then after looking around aimlessly, his eyes settled on Songhui.

"Come on dear, let me see you!"

Jeho stretched his thick hands toward Songhui and flapped them. This was a gesture intended to rectify the awkward situation, but Songhui, after briefly looking up at Jeho with sleepy eyes, turned her head aside and continued poking her mother's breast. Chobong frowned, annoyed by Jeho's disturbance.

"Ah ha! She's taking me for a stranger . . . Huh huh, damn it, what a failed dad I've become, huh huh huh huh, damn it."

Jeho burst into an exaggerated laughter that was somewhat different from usual. Chobong paid no attention to this; she was only eager to lull the whimpering baby.

"There, there, she's got her mother's temper as well as her features, hasn't she?"

"Never mind that! . . . I won't exchange it for your easygoing temperament."

"Huh huh huh huh, damn . . ."

"Can't you be quiet, please! Why do you make such a noise when the baby's about to fall asleep? I can't . . ."

"Hah ah, what the hell!"

Having been pushed aside, Jeho was silent for a while and lit a cigarette. In the meantime Chobong went into the bedroom holding the sleeping Songhui. She laid her down and covered her with a quilt, patting her quietly. She looked back several times before she finally came out onto the maru.

"How's your stock of rice?" Jeho asked, looking up at Chobong who was pacing around. Aside from the monthly stipend, Jeho had been providing an eighty-kilo bag of rice whenever it ran out. Since he couldn't know when it ran out, he used to order it only when Chobong asked for it. But now, Jeho asked first.

"I still have enough in stock," Chobong said casually, remembering that a bag had been delivered only a fortnight ago.

"Still it could run out before long . . . Isn't our rice chest big enough? I could order a bag tomorrow."

"No, don't do that! I would rather wait until the new crop of rice comes out onto the market. I don't want to store the old stale grains in hiding like the Catholic believers used to in the old days."

"Hah hah, the new crop of rice! That makes sense. It's already time to talk about new crops, damn it . . . This year's almost gone by while I've earned only a little money! All right, let's forget about rice, but what about firewood?"

"You could order a cartful tomorrow or the day after . . ."

"Then I'll have it delivered tomorrow."

Jeho brought out his wallet and took out five ten-won banknotes.

"Now that I come to think of it, the stipend for this month is already two days overdue! Huh huh huh, this minister is getting forgetful these days."

"Give me thirty won more, please."

"Thirty won? OK . . . You've got something to buy?"

Jeho took out his wallet one more time, and thought to himself, *well, well, this might be the last time you ask for money. Ask for as much as you wish.* With this magnanimous turn of mind, he further thought, perhaps he should give a few hundred or a thousand won to Chobong when he actually broke up with her.

Chobong put the eight ten-won banknotes Jeho handed over into her waist pocket, thinking to herself,

He indeed is a good and kind uncle.

Whenever she received the money or household goods that Jeho so generously provided, she truly felt grateful, and her trust in him increased as much.

"By the way, was it yesterday morning or the day before, I'm not sure, but . . ."

Jeho, putting his wallet back into his pocket, started to talk rather casually, as if he were mentioning a piece of news about someone else.

". . . Yunhui came up."

"Yu-unhui? Why?"

Chobong jumped up, startled. It wasn't that she'd always been consciously thinking of Yunhui. But it was true that she hadn't been free from some anxiety as she was living with Yunhui's husband. When Jeho mentioned Yunhui, that dormant anxiety suddenly awoke in Chobong.

"Huh, what do you mean 'why?' How would I know? I don't have a clue!" Jeho responded bluntly, maintaining his casual tone.

His tone obviously suggested that he was being dismissive. It could mean either that he didn't give any significance to Yunhui's showing up in Seoul, or that he was annoyed by Chobong's sensitive reaction, acting like a jealous mistress who couldn't tolerate any mistress other than herself. Chobong couldn't decide which of the two might be the meaning of Jeho's dismissive manner. As she had solid trust in Jeho's affection for her, she tried to choose the meaning favorable to her and to feel at ease.

"She's my wife all right, so perhaps she came back to live with her husband."

At this reply, Chobong at last came to her senses. If Jeho took it to mean that, what could his intentions regarding Yunhui be? Chobong wanted to believe that Jeho's words implied, "what's the use if she came back. I wouldn't change my mind, no matter what." On the other hand she couldn't exclude the possibility that Jeho might be implying, "her return is only natural; she's back, so she'll live with me. It's pitiful that you're pestering me with questions about why or how." In fact, this interpretation seemed more credible than the other.

In that case, the situation was quite critical for Chobong.

Verbal promises between a man and a woman, as in treaties between nations, can be broken. The one who for reasons of inconvenience breaks the promise usually has the upper hand whereas the one who is betrayed ends up with no place to appeal for a remedy. Chobong, who had no knowledge or experience of such realities, was leafing through the old, moth-eaten promissory notes she had received at Yuseong Spa, having recovered them from deep down in her memory. She thought inwardly that perhaps she should reconfirm them with Jeho item by item.

Don't you see what's written here? You promised that you would get a divorce within a year at the latest, and have me registered in the family register as your wife, didn't you? You've been dilly-dallying, delaying it for no obvious reasons. And now you say Yunhui has come up; what do you mean by that? What are you going to do with her? Are you going to divorce her? If you can't, what do you want me to do? Besides, what should I do regarding Songhui's birth registration?

Chobong wanted to argue and press him into keeping his promises. To do that, she should be prepared to make a scene perhaps. She would even have to meet Yunhui face-to-face, fighting with her in an ugly manner over who had the right to claim Jeho. She thought she wouldn't recoil from such a fight. She was mustering up her courage to believe she could do that, when in fact she was merely a cowardly woman who would rather retreat quickly than run head on into a fight when the situation actually called for that.

Was Jeho a man so dear and precious to Chobong that she couldn't bear to lose him at any cost? No, he wasn't. He was, in a sense, rather a burden, who often stood in the way, interrupting her devotion to Songhui. Perhaps it might be best to separate from him at this occasion. Once she made up her mind to become independent, she thought, she was confident she could find a way to raise Songhui on her own, whatever hardships she might have to endure. But that was for when there would be no other way she could turn. She wanted to raise Songhui, her precious flower, in a sheltered conservatory; she wanted to avoid the necessity of facing the harsh winds of reality carrying Songhui in her arms. For the sake of securing a safe shelter for Songhui, she wanted not to lose Jeho to Yunhui.

If you saw into Jeho's mind, however, the picture was quite different to what Chobong imagined. Jeho didn't want to divorce Yunhui now. Even if he wanted to, the prospect was too grim for him. Let alone a divorce, even Yunhui's learning about his living with Chobong would cause a great storm in his life, ruining his business, since he had coaxed Yunhui into persuading her own family to buy shares in his company some time ago. All things considered, it would be best for him to end the relationship with Chobong.

It was now not a matter for him whether or not to separate from Chobong, but only a matter of when and how to do it.

He could very well have settled the issue then and there, giving sundry excuses, primarily the fact that he no longer enjoyed life with her and that she herself seemed not to savor life with him so much. He could very well have said, "It might be best for us to separate, you go your way and I go my way."

He really wished he could. But he couldn't do that so abruptly unless the situation became very urgent. He knew that he wouldn't be able to hold up his long face, if he discarded Chobong like a worn-out pair of shoes. Chobong was not only a young girl when he took her in, but the daughter of Jeong Jusa, his hometown friend. So far she hadn't done anything seriously wrong, at least in appearance, whatever was taking place in her inner world. So he couldn't find a decent justification for an abrupt separation.

Being unable to dismiss the burdensome plaster figurine heartlessly, he'd been waiting for an occasion that would offer him a justification for separation. In case nothing came up, he thought, he would have to do it gradually like an opium addict in the process of curing his addiction.

"So, what are you going to do?" Chobong asked at last, breaking the long silence into which both of them had fallen, absorbed in their respective thoughts.

"What?" Jeho replied, staring at Chobong, for at first he couldn't grasp the meaning of Chobong's question, which seemed to come out of the blue because of the time that had lapsed. But he soon understood it from Chobong's expression and answered with an awkward smile.

". . . What's there to do? . . . Perhaps there's nothing I can do other than take things as they come . . . Things are pressing in on me wherever I turn! Damn it."

Jeho faltered, trying to avoid the situation, but Chobong, preoccupied with her own thoughts, interpreted Jeho's words as she wished, that is, as meaning he didn't care whether Yunhui came or went since the issue with Yunhui would be over before long, except that he was annoyed by how things were proceeding. Once she understood it as such, she felt it was ridiculous that she'd quibbled over Yunhui just now. She also felt secure enough at having such a good man as a guardian, not at all threatened by the fact that Yunhui had come up to Seoul.

"Ah, it's already five-thirty! I've got to go out again, damn it," Jeho muttered as he put his watch back into his pocket and stood up, stretching.

Watching Jeho stand up, Chobong felt uneasy and somehow was reluctant to let him go, because she imagined he was going to Yunhui. It wasn't simply out of material greed that she desired to keep him near her. As the saying goes, people tend to grudge giving away their food, even if they don't particularly like it. Chobong, having lived with Jeho for nearly two years, was averse to the idea of seeing him go back to his legal wife. She felt threatened by his wife, as any mistress living in the shadows would do.

"Why? Why don't you go out after supper?"

Chobong, who hadn't shown such kindness to Jeho in many months, flushed as she said this as if her inner thoughts had been revealed.

Pah, you must be afraid now . . . you shrewd girl!

Jeho, however, hiding what he thought, responded casually.

". . . I have an appointment to meet someone at six o'clock."

"But please have a quick supper before you go out . . . I want to . . ."

Chobong put on a pretty smile that she hadn't shown to Jeho for a long while, and continued in a luring tone.

"I want to prepare a special feast for you to celebrate my payday. I'll cook your favorite dishes, how about grilled ribs and beef tartare?"

"Ribs? Beef tartare?"

Jeho was tempted to have a drink along with those special dishes that Chobong would prepare with her excellent skill in cooking, while thinking to himself that the offer would be much more appealing if she put on some makeup and a nice dress to boot.

"It sounds very tempting indeed . . . By the way, how is it that I'm being showered with such excessive kindness tonight?"

"It's to celebrate my payday, I said . . ."

"Huh huh huh huh, they say you need to live long enough to see all the surprises in store for you. But I don't have time . . ."

"The rice is already done. I can quickly have the meat and drink purchased."

Chobong began to make a fuss, calling the maid, but Jeho took out his watch again, and stepping into the yard, said,

"No, wait a while . . . I'll come back before six-thirty or seven after meeting the person. So take your time and prepare whatever you wish for me. On my way back I'll buy a few bottles of drink. Wouldn't it be better?"

"Well, do as you please. Six-thirty or seven? You'll keep your promise, right? Don't make me wait for you until my eyes are sore, please. You won't go to a drinking place with the person, right?"

"Of course not. Never worry."

Jeho walked out toward the gate with a swaggering gait.

Chobong went into the room and put the money Jeho had given her into a drawer of her wardrobe. She was planning to go out to a department store the next day with Songhui strapped on her maid's back and buy a cradle and a pram for the baby. With such happy thoughts she looked back down at the sleeping Songhui whose lips were making sucking motions.

Chobong sat next to Songhui, engrossed by her cute motions, and even forgot to send the maid to the butcher. At that moment someone shouted loudly at the gate,

"Hello, is anyone in?"

The voice was shrill but daunting. It was a voice that resonated in the listener's ear for quite some time. Even before her mind registered the voice, Chobong's heart knew it at once, and began to pound violently. She unconsciously raised her hands and clasped them to her chest.

Chapter 14:
A Sad Acrobat

CHOBONG STEPPED STEALTHILY out onto the *maru* while the maid, who was in the kitchen, ran out to the gate. A little later, as the maid came back, there appeared behind her the hunchbacked Jang Hyeongbo, the man Chobong would never be able to forget.

The maid was walking toward her, looking back at Hyeongbo, seemingly arguing with him, while Hyeongbo too was saying something, telling her not to worry. They somehow looked as though they weren't total strangers. It should have looked odd to Chobong, but she was too flustered to notice that. The moment she saw Hyeongbo, or even before that, she was in utter consternation.

All her blood seemed to have rushed into her face, her temples were about to explode, and her body was trembling beyond control.

The maid, stopping in front of her, said, "This man wanted to see you, Madam, so I told him to wait, but he wouldn't listen, forcing his way into the house like this."

Chobong couldn't hear properly what the maid said, as though her voice was being drowned out by the thumping of her heart.

Chobong inhaled deeply, held her head straight up, and forced her fluttering heart to calm down; she scolded herself for being frightened, and tried to persuade herself that there was nothing to be scared of about the man. Yet still, her chest was heaving, and she couldn't help but shiver all over.

Hyeongbo's clothes were as dirty as usual, indicating that he was still a bachelor with no one to take care of him. His unstarched cotton coat was shabby; his trousers drooping under the coat looked grimy. The only difference from the past was that he was now carrying a smart new briefcase.

Despite his squalid appearance, Hyeongbo held his head upright and boldly walked up onto the step, swinging his hunched back. With a mocking grin on his face, he said,

"Excuse me, please. Uh, how have you been?"

"How on earth can a man unrelated to this house intrude into the women's quarters without permission?"

Chobong, who'd been staring down at Hyeongbo for a while with eyes filled with repulsion, at last protested sternly, though in a trembling voice.

"But the thing is, I have some business to discuss with you . . ."

As if he didn't give a damn about what she might say, he sat down on the edge of the *maru*.

". . . I hope your family has been well; the thing I'm particularly concerned about is the little one. Is she well these days?"

At such impertinent remarks from Hyeongbo, who apparently looked down on her, Chobong should have been more taken aback than angry, but the moment he mentioned the little one, her mind, which had become a little more composed, began to lose control once again, and she became utterly terrified.

"What is it to you whether the baby's well or not? You certainly have nothing to do with it. Leave the house this instant!"

Any contest between a calm and an agitated person is bound to end in favor of the one who stays calm. Chobong was on the losing side from the beginning of the fight.

"By the way, I also need to see Mr. Bak Jeho. As I understand it, he's expected back by seven, isn't he?"

Chobong was even more astounded at this; the maid who was peeping through the kitchen door was also scared out of her wits and shrank her head into her neck like a turtle.

For the past two months or so, Hyeongbo had been sneaking about outside the house and had bribed the maid from time to time to give him some information about the family situation. The maid, who was ignorant of Hyeongbo's dark schemes, gave him all the details of the family for the sake of the money he so freely gave away. She had virtually acted like an informant for Hyeongbo, though she had had no intention of harming her mistress. Then this evening, he had knocked at the gate loudly as a visitor, asked the whereabouts of the master, and even walked into the house boldly. The maid, who'd been anxiously watching Hyeongbo's odd manners in dealing with her mistress, became even more frightened when she heard Hyeongbo mention the information about Jeho she'd given away, for fear that her past dealings with Hyeongbo might be exposed.

Chobong, on the other hand, was frightened when he announced his intention to meet Jeho, because she instantly interpreted it as a plot to take Songhui away from her. Even if she could keep Songhui in the end, the one old secret Jeho hadn't known about would be disclosed. In addition, Jeho might want to give Songhui away to Hyeongbo, supposing him to be her real father. In that case, Chobong, determined not to lose Songhui, would have to fight against both men.

Chobong knew she would be overcome, not knowing how to confront them. As she looked at Hyeongbo, he seemed quite at ease, enjoying his cigarette.

"Why are you lingering here, when I told you to leave? . . . Get out at once before you get into trouble. What an annoyance this is . . ."

Her voice betrayed intense nervousness, despite her efforts to display firmness.

"There's no need to hurry. Let's have a talk first. How about that?"

Hyeongbo, crossing one leg over the other, turned around to face Chobong.

Chobong was even angrier when she asked herself why on earth she had to endure such torment at the hands of this obnoxious man. In a fit of rage, she felt like shouting out for the neighbors to help or call the police and have him beaten. She really wished she could. But she was too afraid of what might ensue if she did; it wouldn't only arouse an uproar in the neighborhood, but also might bring public shame on her; considering the malicious and reckless character of Hyeongbo, there was no knowing what might emerge from his mouth when he was aggravated. She couldn't risk that. She knew she had to subdue her resentment, in order not to risk that. She further thought that the best way of sending him away without too much trouble might be to give him an opportunity to talk as he wanted. The stain she wanted to hide was making her hesitant and weak willed. She had no idea that she was taking the first step into an evil trap Hyeongbo was deliberately setting for her.

"Hey you, Chobong . . .?"

Hyeongbo, all of a sudden, leaving off the seemingly polite and respectful manner of talking he had adopted thus far, began to address her in a manner better suited to a minor or an inferior. But he kept his voice low, in case the maid should hear.

Chobong felt a great lump of resentment lodge in her throat at such rude and audacious manners, but she swallowed it, determined to hear him out.

"Ahem . . .," Hyeongbo cleared his throat, flicked the ash off his cigarette, and then started to talk.

"What I want to say is as simple as this. You see? The thing is . . . that the baby in there is mine . . . So you listen carefully . . ."

As if to maximize the effect, he stressed the end of each sentence, as if he were crushing the words with his heels. Then he bent his head sideways to look up at Chobong, who was standing a few steps away from him leaning on one of the pillars of the maru. His nostrils flared, and his lips puckered, as if he wanted to insinuate, "Well, how about that?"

So that's what you're after then! With that thought, Chobong's heart began to thump again, but determined to conceal her inner turmoil, she defiantly stared back down at Hyeongbo for a little while and soon turned her face aside, saying dismissively,

"What a crazy fellow!"

"No matter how hard you resist, it'll be no good in the end. Listen carefully . . . Not only is the baby mine, you too are mine, my woman . . . So you must come with me, carrying my baby in your arms . . ."

Chobong almost burst into laughter, stunned by such a preposterous statement. Chobong had no basis for denying Hyeongbo's claim of being the father of the baby with any confidence, but when he claimed her as his woman, she became simply aghast. And then, when he demanded that she come with him, along with the baby, Chobong could take it only as a madman's joke if not a silly outburst, a childish tantrum.

"So, is that all you wanted to talk about?"

Chobong looked down at Hyeongbo with contempt.

"That's right. So you pack up the diapers and all, put the baby on your back, and leave the house with me."

"Stop that absurd talk, and get out this very instant. If you keep on pestering me, I'll call the police . . . What right do you have to walk into the inner quarters of somebody else's house, and babble such nonsense? Aren't you afraid of the law?"

"Law? Haw haw, the law?"

Hyeongbo repeated the word with a grimace as though he found it ridiculous.

". . . Law? That sounds good! How about this? How about I myself go out and bring back a policeman right this moment? Do you want to settle this dispute in front of a policeman?"

"Hah! You think the police would take your side? Stop dreaming!"

"Hey Chobong! You make me sick! If I were afraid of the police, I wouldn't have come here to start with. Call the police right now, if you wish! For simply breaking in, it could hardly be more than a twenty-nine day prison term, couldn't it? I don't mind that, or not even if it's several years. I know it can't be life imprisonment or the death penalty. Once I've served out the term and come back to you, you see what would happen? You understand? . . ."

Hyeongbo glared his frightful eyes and ground his teeth, making audible sounds.

"At a pinch, I'll stab the baby to death right in front of the policeman and be arrested willingly. Go on, call the police, if you dare, call them in!"

Chobong shuddered all over. She had said she would call the police only to intimidate him. But the situation was now growing urgent enough to actually require the police, seeing as how Hyeongbo had escalated his threats to this extent. If she brought in the police, however, she knew what disaster to expect at the hands of that rash and impudent, crazy man. Chobong could only feel extremely anxious and desperate.

Hyeongbo, in fact, wasn't as reckless as Chobong imagined. He was just as daunted as Chobong was, for he had some sense of discretion. He spat out rash and violent words only to intimidate Chobong, considering her easy prey. If Chobong could hide her frightened inner state, and pretend to be calm, dismissing his threats as a mad dog's barking, even if she didn't have the firmness to fight back at him, she wouldn't have been so easily entangled. But the fact was that Chobong betrayed her agitation too obviously, overwhelmed by Hyeongbo's perverse demands and threats. It was evident that the odds were turning entirely against Chobong, and it looked as though she would end up losing the fight quickly.

"Perhaps you, you may have assumed . . ."

After a while, Hyeongbo opened his mouth again, but this time with a softer, more convincing tone.

". . . the little one is the child of Go Taesu. That's entirely wrong. You know, Go Taesu had had relations with so many women, either prostitutes or ordinary women, but he never got any of them pregnant. It's impossible for him to have made you conceive when he lived a mere ten days with you, you see?"

Chobong was speechless.

"As for myself, regardless of the circumstances, it's true that you slept with me once; moreover, Go Taesu, when he was alive, asked me to take care of you. He used to say, 'Hey, Hyeongbo, after my death, you must become Chobong's guardian, or rather take her in as your wife.' I have a witness to that who's still living."

Chobong thought it wasn't so improbable for that cowardly Taesu to have said such a nonsensical thing. Yet she said defiantly,

"Hah, am I the offspring of your slave, to be traded between the two of you?"

"What? Are you really refusing my offer?"

"Why should I comply with your demand?"

"Are you sure?"

"So what?"

"Then give the child to me."

"You'll have to cut off my head first!"

"You mean you won't give away the child?"

"You bandit, shameless villain!"

"Are you sure you won't give her up?"

"What if I don't?"

"I see. So the child is really precious to you . . .?"

Without replying, Chobong stepped back onto the threshold of the room where Songhui was sleeping. She was unwittingly trying to protect the baby.

". . . If the child is so precious to you, it is even more so to me. Because of my deformity, do you assume that I don't have feelings as well? Pah! Just think of this. What kind of heartless son of a bitch would just sit still with eyes wide open and let his child be taken away by its stepfather? Huh? . . . Hell no, no way. Pah! . . . Look at this."

Hyeongbo paused for a moment to fumble in his pocket and brought out a short wooden object. It was curved and flat with a white line drawn on one side. Even at first sight, one could see it was a Japanese dagger.

Chobong got scared, but though she knew what it was, she turned her head aside, feigning ignorance.

"You . . . you know what this is?"

Hyeongbo unsheathed it halfway with one hand and raised it high.

"So be it, kill me now! Even if you kill me . . ."

"Kill you? Why, do you think I'd kill you? . . . No, you'd better wait . . ."

Hyeongbo pushed the dagger back into the wooden scabbard and then put it back into his pocket.

"You're not the first target. It's for the one in there, the baby. Right in front of your eyes, I'll stab the baby through and through. I mean it . . ."

Chobong stretched out her two arms to obstruct the door into the room as if Hyeongbo was really rushing into the room with dagger drawn. Having seen the knife in Hyeongbo's hand, Chobong thought he was not merely threatening but actually intending to do it.

She no longer had any strength left to argue or confront him; crestfallen, she shuddered like an aspen while her eyes grew blank and lifeless as if she were about to lose her mind.

Looking up at Chobong's ashen face, Hyeongbo appeared to grow more elated. He pressed on with added viciousness in his voice.

". . . Pah! If I have to lose it to a stepfather, it would be far better to kill it and get rid of it myself. Did you dream I would just sit on my hands and let it go? Far from it . . . If it's only to get back at you for your rejection of me, I'll do something right before your eyes that will surely drive you to kill yourself in shock and desperation. See? I'll hold the baby like this and thrust the knife right into . . ."

Hyeongbo abruptly stopped the gesture in the middle of the demonstration, because a sudden thought had struck him; what if Chobong were to actually bring out the baby, give it to him, and say, "Here, take your child and go away." If Chobong did that, either out of fear or contempt for his harassment, he would be in big trouble.

All he had played out so far was only in pursuit of Chobong. He had no interest whatsoever in the baby, especially a baby whose father could never be identified for certain. Even if it were his, a child was something he'd never dreamed of having. So if he got hold of the baby instead of its mother, what would he do with it? It would be like scaring away a live rabbit to grab a dead one.

The realization that he had been heading in the wrong direction confounded him, and he was now busy figuring out a way to correct it. Contrary to his supposition, however, the staging of an imaginary infanticide was effective with Chobong in the way he desired.

Chobong almost screamed out in sheer terror when Hyeongbo staged the climax, in which the gestures of his hands, his eyes, and his body all collaborated perfectly with his threat, "I'll hold it like this, and thrust the knife right into . . ."

Chobong closed her eyes tightly. Despite that, she saw the vivid scene in which Hyeongbo, his eyes glaring like a madman, held a bloody knife high, while the bleeding Songhui was stretched out on the floor, face down in a pool of blood, quivering fitfully. With a shudder, she opened her eyes and looked back. She found Songhui peacefully asleep. She breathed a sigh but the sense of relief was short-lived. Soon her heart was beating with wild agitation. She couldn't scream out for help for fear that Hyeongbo, at that very moment, should rush into the room, wielding his knife. She wanted to run out of the house holding Songhui, but she knew she would be caught even before she reached the gate.

What on earth should I do?

No answer was forthcoming.

I wish I could make that rascal . . .

She thought to herself that she would have shot him dead on the spot without hesitation, if she'd had a gun.

As she looked up, she saw the thick crossbeam above his head. If only that beam would break and drop down on top of his head, he would die instantly without letting out even a final shriek. She silently prayed in desperation that would happen. The beam, which in her fancy appeared ready to fall at any moment with a thundering sound, was still there, intact, when she looked up again.

"By the way, you should know that . . ."

Hyeongbo, with a new set of words ready in his mouth, resumed his speech.

"Even if you give up the baby and hand it over to me, I would still have to kill it here in front of you. I'd have to kill it anyway . . . because there's no way for a bachelor to raise it. It still has to be breastfed, so it would whine and fret day and night. What else could I do? . . . Not only would I not be able to raise it, but also I wouldn't be able to endure it, for I'm such a bad-tempered, wild guy. So what else can I do but kill it, though I might feel pity for its sparkling dark eyes. Would there be any other option, for God's sake? It's only rational according to human nature . . . Ask yourself if it isn't rational . . . Well I know an old story—about how, when a wife once ran away abandoning her husband and their baby, the husband salted down the body of the baby like a fish and roamed all over the countryside carrying it on his back in search of that bitch. It sounds very probable, considering how the deserted man must have felt."

Hyeongbo paused for a moment, lighting a new cigarette.

Chobong stood by motionless, her face turned aside, as if no sound of his words came into her ears.

Now she rather wished that Jeho would walk into the house at that moment. As things had gone so far, and there being no prospect of her sending Hyeongbo away on her own, she wished the sturdy Jeho would take over the matter, kick the rascal in the teeth and throw him out of the house. She thought Jeho was generous enough to ignore the stain she had suffered, even if the old secret was revealed. Moreover she would rather endure the shame in front of Jeho than be tortured by Hyeongbo like this.

When she looked back, Songhui was waking up; stretching out her arms, the baby looked around and called out for her mommy in a weary voice. Mom was who the baby always looked for, the moment it woke up. Confirming that afresh, Chobong had a moment of happiness, but soon her eyes welled with tears.

Songhui was suckling, snug in Chobong's bosom. With one hand she held onto one breast as if warding off any potential intruders, while with the other hand she grabbed at her own foot. Watching the innocent, carefree Songhui, Chobong felt herself becoming carefree too. Both the impending danger and the predicament she was facing at the moment seemed like something happening to someone else somewhere far away.

It was nearly seven o'clock when Jeho walked into the house, carrying wine bottles in his hand. Having anxiously awaited his return, Chobong, for the first time since she met him, viewed him as an extremely precious person, and heard his footsteps as the most welcome sound in the world.

"Uh-huh, am I late . . .?" Jeho said casually as he entered the inner quarters, but stopped in his tracks on seeing a stranger.

Hyeongbo made a few dry coughs, standing up from the edge of the maru and stepping down onto the yard. Jeho glanced at the stranger with suspicious eyes and turned toward the maid, who was peeping out from behind the kitchen door. The maid, having no idea what to say, instantly lowered her head to avoid Jeho's eyes.

Jeho moved forward and met the eye of Chobong, who gladly stood up and leaned upon the pillar, holding Songhui in her arms. Jeho, casting a glance at Hyeongbo, asked Chobong with his eyes who the stranger was. Chobong's eyes lit up as if she was about to say something, but soon turned her head aside with a sulky expression.

Jeho grew more discomposed, feeling as though he wasn't fully awake from a nap. He wondered who that hunchback might be, and why the woman was so tense and reserved. The situation seemed to suggest that Chobong and the monstrous stranger must have had some sort of heated quarrel. Over what sort of problem?

Is she being harassed over a debt? It's unlikely that she needed to borrow money from anybody. Even if she'd had to, her face wouldn't have turned so deadly pale over some debt . . . What could the cause of the hostility be then?

Unable to figure out the cause of the strange atmosphere, Jeho hesitantly approached the *maru*.

Hyeongbo took off his hat, and leaning backward, rather arrogantly said,

"Well, you must be . . . Mr. Bak, sir?"

"Yes, I'm Bak Jeho . . ."

Jeho responded awkwardly to Hyeongbo, who made a polite bow to him after his greeting. Jeho didn't like the presence of the ugly stranger, who seemed to have introduced an air of heavy anxiety into his house. Despite his hostility to this intruder, Jeho had to respond with decency, for to his surprise Hyeongbo showed very decent manners.

". . . but may I ask to whom I have this honor?"

"Ah, my name is Jang Hyeongbo, I forgot to introduce myself first . . ."

"Mr. Jang Hyeongbo? Mr. Jang Hyeongbo? I see."

"Well, I've come to see you, sir. Though you were out, I heard you were expected back soon, so I took the liberty of waiting for you. And moreover . . ."

"Ah, in that case . . ."

"As for lady Jeong Chobong, your wife, I've known her well for a very long time, so I thought it permissible to wait for you in your absence . . ."

"I see, I see. In that case, you should have waited sitting over there on the maru . . . Come on up, please."

Jeho felt there was something revolting about Hyeongbo, but observing his consistently polite manners contrary to his appearance, Jeho was beginning to feel less hostile toward him.

Following Jeho who led the way, Hyeongbo took off his shoes and stepped up onto the *maru*.

"Hey, dear, shouldn't you bring out a cushion when we have a guest?"

Chobong, with an offended look in her eyes, stared at Jeho who was making a fuss over Hyeongbo and just turned her face away.

". . . Huh uh, what the hell is this! Where have all the cushions gone to in the house? She should've brought out some cushions and asked the guest to come up and take a seat . . . Perhaps she couldn't because the baby wouldn't leave her alone . . . Let me see, where's the cushion . . ."

Mumbling to himself, Jeho stood up and walked around looking for cushions. Chobong wanted to appeal to Jeho for help the moment he walked into the house. She was glad to see him and was about to report that this rogue had come in with a knife and threatened to kill our Songhui. She thought she'd feel avenged to a certain extent if she did. But on second thought she grew fearful the rogue would go wild and wield his knife, or that a violent scuffle might ensue between the two men. It might make matters worse and deprive her of the opportunity of solving it calmly. So she thought it best to leave the matter to Jeho and watch how things evolved rather than cause more trouble by exciting Hyeongbo's anger. It could be as perilous as waking a tiger from its slumber, she thought.

In her calculation, Jeho was much sturdier and bigger than Hyeongbo; Jeho would be able to deal with Hyeongbo without much difficulty, and perhaps have things settled in one stroke. In case Jeho found him invincible, she could join in, and together they would surely vanquish him.

After searching here and there for some time, Jeho at last came out with a couple of cushions. The master of the house and the visitor, facing each other, took seats on the cushions. Probably without intending to, Jeho took the seat facing the bedroom whereas Hyeongbo took the seat with his back toward the room.

"Here, have a cigarette please."

As he took out a pack of Haetae from his pocket, Jeho stood up again, and brought back an ashtray from a corner of the *maru*.

Chobong too took a seat right inside the threshold of the bedroom, but in a squatting posture without realizing it herself. It showed how intensely strained she was by the situation, which seemed to hold her life at stake. Though she was somewhat relieved at having Jeho nearby, she was still very tense and eager to see how things would develop.

"Uh, I understand you too were in Gunsan a couple of years ago, Mr. Bak? Was it Jejungdang pharmacy you had . . .?"

Hyeongbo started talking in a leisurely manner, taking out a cigarette from his own pack of Pigeon.

"Yes, that's right. Were you in Gunsan as well?"

"Yes, I was. I lived there for more than three years . . . no, it was over four years that I resided in Gunsan. It was last summer that I came back to Seoul to start a business. I run a small business here, though it's too trifling to mention . . ."

"Do you? Well, that's good to hear."

Jeho nodded his head repeatedly, not to compliment Hyeongbo on the business he didn't want to hear about, but because he thought he could figure out the nature of this man's business in his house; since Hyeongbo mentioned that he'd known Chobong from Gunsan, he might be visiting on an errand from Chobong's family. Chobong was sullen and depressed because that man had brought an unwelcome message from home. It must be that, as always . . .

Hyeongbo continued with a much more dignified poise.

"By the way, though I didn't have the pleasure of meeting you in Gunsan, I was quite familiar with your success. I regret that I wasn't bold enough to pursue an opportunity to be introduced to you earlier, sir."

"Don't mention it please! The regret is mutual . . . Anyway, since you say you were in Gunsan, I'm glad to see you as though I am meeting a friend."

"Yes, I'm glad to see you too . . ."

Hyeongbo took his time before getting to his main point. He was paving the way with leisurely chitchat.

Hyeongbo knew that he made an unpleasant impression on others because of his hunchback. He also knew the big disadvantage he had in the initial stages of any meeting because people usually treated him with contempt. Therefore he always assumed a dignified pose when meeting people, as if it would somehow or other compensate for the despicable impression he was bound to make on them.

Even before they got to know him, people despised him for being a hunchback, and for being ugly on top of that. Hyeongbo grew up with contempt, had lived with contempt, and was still enduring contempt.

"The hunchback . . ."

"The deformed . . ."

"That bloody loathsome face . . ."

"That frightful horrid mug . . ."

Most people, except those very few who happened to develop a close relationship with him like the late Go Taesu, usually insulted him with such name-calling, either behind his back or to his face.

Especially during his childhood, he had been severely abused and mocked. It wasn't just his playmates, even adults who had nothing to do with him did the same.

The tender innocent mind of the young boy had had no opportunity to grow up sound; it became twisted and warped like a hook or a snake. He became perverse, sly, and vicious.

Even in his adult days as well, he couldn't make a living in normal ways, because people tended to ostracize him for his obnoxious appearance.

All right, I'm a hunchback.

All right, I'm deformed, and ugly as hell.

But is there a law that such a person should perish? I too have the right to live, and I will.

Turning the whole world into his enemy, cultivating deep-seated rancor within himself, desperate, Hyeongbo trudged his way through the hostile world and somehow or other maintained his four-and-a-half-foot tall body alive.

As he'd been struggling like that for thirty odd years so far, his fiery, rancorous frame of mind had settled down and solidified into his nature, having been heated and hammered constantly like metal in a blacksmith's forge.

On the surface, he concealed his curses and his rage against the world. Instead, he calmly exercised a murderously polite art of living, guided by his perverse and reckless fortitude. He performed this art as naturally and nonchalantly as drinking a glass of water. Therefore even if he assumed an extremely polite and civil manner, it wasn't at all out of respect for others. He simply performed it out of his vicious nature in order to protect himself, as well as to take advantage of others more effectively.

The golden oriole changes its color to gray when autumn comes. If this is a natural phenomenon, the transformation of Hyeongbo's mind into a wickedly crooked state might also be considered a natural phenomenon. The only difference is that the former is physiological whereas the latter is psychological.

Only consider the contrast between Hyeongbo and Jeho: Hyeongbo's sitting height was less than three or four spans from the ground, whereas Jeho was three times as tall as that . . . Jeho's face was very long and looked even longer with his bald head, but Hyeongbo's face was rather short and square shaped . . . Hyeongbo's facial bone structure was rugged enough to suggest that of a cannibal, whereas Jeho's was as refined and graceful as that of an aristocrat . . . Jeho was well dressed in a clean and sophisticated homespun suit, whereas Hyeongbo was wrapped in a dirty and shabby cotton coat . . . Hyeongbo swung his body from side to side as if to assert his confidence, whereas Jeho swung his body to and fro out of curiosity for what would come next out of Hyeongbo's mouth.

The two men sitting face-to-face presented a queer contrast in every respect, a spectacular contrast.

Dusk was deepening and the lights in the house were already turned on. The distant din of the city drifted in now and then like the accompaniment of an orchestra to the sounds of the two men's talking.

"I wanted to see you, Mr. Bak, because . . ."

After the short silence that followed their leisurely chitchat, Hyeongbo at last began to bring up the real issue for which he had come by.

". . . Well, it's regarding the lady Jeong Chobong, your wife."

"I see."

Jeho responded without any strain as he thought his surmise was probably not far off the mark.

"But I'm hesitant to bring it up, for you may find it very awkward and unpleasant to listen to. It's an uncommonly weird story, but I think it's inevitable to discuss it. I hope you can understand . . . huh huh."

"Yes, yes, it's all right. Though I have no idea what it is, I think I can understand . . ."

"Then I'll begin with an easy conscience. Hem, hem . . . You know Go Taesu, the one your lady was married to. He was a very close friend of mine. Even blood brothers couldn't have been as affectionate and intimate as we were. When the bride and the bridegroom set up a new house, I lived there with them. So much trust we had in each other."

"I see."

"Nevertheless, you know how Go Taesu, that unfortunate fellow, met a sudden and tragic death, don't you?"

"I've heard that he did!"

"To tell the truth, he had intended to kill himself for a long time . . . A suicide! That had been in his mind even before he married."

"Really! Why?"

"As already revealed to the whole world, it was because of the fraud he'd committed at the bank. He didn't want to face the world when his embezzlement was found out. Rather than endure the shame of being handcuffed and imprisoned, he preferred to die by his own hand. When I happened to mention prison, he became wildly furious, leaping and running. He hated jail that much."

Jeho wanted to spit out a "humph!" but instead he simply said, "I see!" For Jeho it sounded too improbable, that a man who had determined to kill himself would take the trouble to marry someone.

"And then, as it happened, the incident befell him. To put it another way, he was bound to die either way, except that the death he actually met was too shameful. It was a real pity! Ah, by the way . . . he asked a sort of favor of me when he was determined to commit suicide. A sort of last will as it were."

"Did he!"

Jeho realized his assumption that this fellow had come on an errand for Chobong's family was wrong when he started to talk about Go Taesu. He'd been reluctantly listening to his tedious story regarding Taesu until Hyeongbo mentioned a last will. Now Jeho had to assume that this man had come to claim Go Taesu's posthumous child. He nodded to himself, taking it to be a reasonable assumption.

"Let me tell you the long and short of how I came to learn of his last will. He'd often told me how badly he wanted to end his life. One day he said, 'Look, Hyeongbo, I don't want to live in this world for long. I'm determined to end it. But there're a few things that hold me back. There's one thing that especially won't allow me to be free to die. I don't think I can close my eyes unless I've taken care of it.' On a few occasions he said something to this effect. Then it was two days before that horrible incident. It was May 30 that year, as I remember it, at the house of Haengwha, a *gisaeng* Taesu had been intimate with . . ."

Taesu, in fact, had completely stopped visiting Haengwha after his marriage. Anyone who heard what Hyeongbo said would know that he was fabricating a sheer lie now. But not only Jeho but Chobong as well had no way of discerning it as a lie. Perhaps even if they did, it wouldn't have made much difference to Hyeongbo, to tell the truth.

". . . So at such weakness in my friend . . ."

Hyeongbo continued his narration.

"I began to scold him severely, 'Stop talking such crazy nonsense! You can come out after serving your time, it'll only be three or four years at most. How come you keep talking such crap?' I tried to change his mind, but shaking his head, he at last said, 'No, no, you don't understand. You shouldn't take lightly what I'm going to say. Take it seriously and do as I ask you word for word . . . The thing I implore you to do is this. When I'm no longer in this world, please take Chobong as your wife and take good care of her. I can't leave her in poverty without any protection. Don't take it the wrong way or as strange; I entrust you with this because I know I can trust you.' That's exactly what he said, I'm afraid!"

"Indeed!"

Jeho inwardly was so elated at this story that while he went on nodding his head he was almost ready to slap his thigh in excitement. *Oh, I see it now, you've come, not for the posthumous baby, but to carry away the grown-up mother, Chobong, on your back. You have indeed! . . . That's why Chobong is so sullen and angry . . .*

Jeho took it as the most welcome and opportune thing that could happen.

Wasn't Chobong a burden now? Though he wanted to get rid of her, it wasn't so easy for he still had a shred of loyalty to

her and her father. At such a juncture, a stranger comes walking
into his house out of the blue, demanding the burden as his own.
What a lucky good riddance it would be for him! He even felt
like giving him some money as a token of his gratitude.

Ah-hah, isn't that a windfall! Good, good.

Jeho had been exuberant at the prospect of making Chobong
his woman a couple of years ago. He was just as exuberant and
happy now at the prospect of getting rid of Chobong and hand-
ing her over to this stranger.

As he cast a glance over at Chobong, he saw her biting down
hard on her lower lip, with her eyes downcast. She was gasping
as if her breath was caught in her throat, and her nostrils were
flaring.

At that moment, Chobong was furious with wild resentment
at Taesu, taking it for granted that that cowardly guy could have
made such a bizarre request to Hyeongbo. Jeho, however, interpreted her agitation as a sign of her strong protest, her aversion
to the idea of going to that monstrous man. It seemed quite natural for Chobong to react like that when he tried to put himself
in her shoes. Who would want to be this unnerving man's wife?
Jeho felt some pity for Chobong.

But Hyeongbo hurriedly resumed his talk.

"Ah, there's one thing I have to mention . . . I imagine Mr.
Go had no opportunity to reveal that he'd prepared a will to his
wife. He couldn't have expected his sudden and untimely death.
He must have been on the lookout for the right moment, but
never had the chance, for he met with tragedy so unexpectedly. So I presume that he left the world without expressing his
wishes to his wife. The nature of his will was such that he could
never discuss it with his wife well in advance of his death. It's
something he could only talk about right before his suicide or
after taking the drug for his suicide. Therefore, I'm pretty sure

your lady Jeong Chobong never heard about it from Go Taesu. But I'm not the only one who heard it. Haengwha, the *gisaeng* who was there, heard it as well, and she's very much alive, if you need a witness."

Hyeongbo was making the same point repeatedly because he was anxious to prevent Chobong denying that she had never heard of it.

Whatever Hyeongbo's anxiety might have been, Chobong in fact had no intention of interrupting the two men yet. Moreover she was quite ready to believe that Taesu could have been as reckless as to say that, and had no mind whatsoever to argue about it.

Hyeongbo waited for a while for a counterattack from Chobong, but finding none forthcoming, was relieved enough to congratulate himself for being such a clever and tactful manipulator. Soon he resumed his talk in a higher pitch.

"So what do you think? However awkward the request might have been, isn't it right to act on the wishes of such a dear friend if you had been asked to before his death? Should I execute the friend's last will faithfully, or should I just ignore it? Well, please tell me your opinion . . ."

"Well, well, I don't know what to say, but . . ."

Jeho, casting a sideways glance at Chobong, equivocated. He in fact wanted to agree with Hyeongbo enthusiastically; he wanted to chime in, "Sure sure, there's no doubt, it's only right to do as your friend wished," for he thought things were moving exactly in the direction he wanted. But the moment he saw the deadly despair at work in Chobong's face, he had to swallow the words and instead utter something evasive.

Hyeongbo, who was carefully observing Jeho's face, began to talk again without waiting for Jeho to finish his response.

"It's all right if you're reluctant to give your opinion. You don't need to answer now, for there'll be time enough soon for you to give an answer with one word. So, please just hear me out . . ."

He cleared his throat one more time and continued,

"And then, as you know, that friend of mine met such a miserable death. Because of that, I felt more pity for him, and was engulfed with deep sorrow for him . . . I couldn't sleep for several nights, for God's sake, searching for ways to do something for that poor fellow, till I came to the conclusion that the least I could do for him would be to put his last will into action, however unreasonable that might be. I was a bit reluctant at first, to tell the truth, but regardless of what others may say, I think it's my duty to do as instructed by him, considering how sweet and endearing he'd been as a best friend . . ."

Jeho almost broke out into laughter, as he thought what a ridiculous duty to a friend that was. It wasn't because Jeho was ignorant of Hyeongbo's dark motive that he could listen to him quietly. He knew well enough that the weird-looking man was spinning a yarn in order to take away the pretty Chobong. It was a scheme that appeared extremely disgraceful to him. But he didn't bring up any argument as to whether it was right or wrong, because Hyeongbo's scheme would fulfill what he himself wanted. In other words, one man's dark scheme, in effect, corresponded with the other man's dark scheme very opportunely.

"And there's one more point, a very important point I must convey to you, I'm afraid. However, it's awkward to bring it up . . ."

"Please, it's quite all right. Speak up please."

"Then I'll make bold, if you please . . . That important thing is, uh, the very night Mr. Go had the fatal disaster . . . that night, between me and Chobong . . . there was, let me say, there happened to be, something, uh a relationship, uh huh."

Jeho instantly felt rage spreading like fire over his face. With an angry questioning look, he stared at Chobong. Having found a good excuse, he was about to discard the woman and he had no business concerning himself with how many men she had had relations. But somehow he couldn't help but be strongly provoked when it came to the issue of a woman's chastity.

Chobong, however, had no courage to examine Jeho's expression; she kept her eyes lowered, afraid to meet his gaze. Totally mortified, she wanted to shout out, "that bastard raped me by force!" but the words were stuck in her throat, unable to find a way out. First of all, she could by no means look Jeho straight in the eye, and secondly, she suspected it might be useless and serve no purpose even if she tried to vindicate herself at this point. So she swallowed the words that had reached her throat.

Jeho had no other option but to interpret Chobong's lowered head as proof that she had no excuse to offer. He felt deeply offended at the realization that Chobong indeed had been an easy lay. He also recalled how easily she had been lured to go to Yuseong with him at the train station, and then at Yuseong Spa how easily she had yielded to him, without much hesitation. Convinced that Chobong had been an easy woman all along, Jeho began to look down on her.

Once he began to think of her in that way, he considered himself a brainless fool, for he had always rated her virtue higher than her physical beauty, never doubting it or ever testing its solidity.

Hyeongbo was delighted at Jeho's altered expression, interpreting it to mean the tide was flowing in his favor. So he began to press his point.

"Not only did we have a relationship one night, but a child happened to come of it. Perhaps it was the work of providence, the baby over there, I mean."

Hyeongbo pointed at Songhui with his head. That Songhui was the seed of Hyeongbo was quite unexpected news for Jeho. But soon he nodded his head, taking it as probable. He could understand now why Chobong had been so desperate to abort the baby last year.

He had simply assumed that the baby was Taesu's, but as he saw it now, she had taken the drugs to miscarry the product of her immoral, extramarital affair . . .

With his eyes squinting, Jeho repeatedly nodded his long head in silence. Hyeongbo too was silent, smoking his cigarette and watching the impact of the bomb he had just dropped.

As utter silence prevailed, the *tick tock* sound of the wall clock grew louder, breaking the silence. The night was growing darker. The lights from the rooms facing each other, with the *maru* in the middle, cast long drawn-out, monster-like shadows of the two men sitting on the *maru*. The silence that wrapped itself about them was heavy and stifling like the silence of people waiting for a death.

Chobong's lowered gaze was blankly fixed on the sweet little hands of Songhui, who was innocently sucking at her bosom. Though curious about how Jeho took the story, she didn't dare to look up. Despite her old stigma that had been freshly revealed now, Chobong was pretty confident that Jeho would pass it over, without making an issue out of it. Nevertheless, she couldn't free herself of a deep sense of shame either, because she was totally ignorant of Jeho's hidden plan to discard her soon.

Therefore, even if she had noticed at that moment that Jeho wanted to abandon her, she would never have taken it to be the result of Jeho's long-hatched plan; she would have believed that it was purely the outcome of her mortal enemy, Jang Hyeongbo's wicked interference. Because of that mistaken understanding, she might have attempted to win Jeho back by explaining the circumstances behind Hyeongbo's ridiculous claims.

As for Songhui, I can't deny that there's the possibility that she may be that rogue's child. But on the other hand, there's no certainty of that either. As for my attempted abortion, it wasn't because the baby was the outcome of an immoral relationship, but because it might be the child of that hateful enemy. I also didn't want to give birth to a fatherless child.

And she would have continued,

As for what Hyeongbo presented as a one-night relationship, it happened while I was asleep when he violently raped me. It happened not because I wanted it, but despite my utmost resistance. And as for that so-called will of Go Taesu, you know it's utterly senseless and absurd. Even if he did ask Hyeongbo such a stupid favor, am I some chattel that can be sold to someone else as he pleases? Is he a judge and I a criminal who must obey if he commands? . . .

Chobong could have made such protests if she had detected Jeho's dark intention. But since the cause of Jeho's impending betrayal came from somewhere else, thousands of such protests would have been useless. Therefore her new destiny that would unfold in a few minutes could not be attributed to the fact that Chobong kept silent without offering any explanations.

The vines of her destiny were intricately entangled.

The origin of this new destiny might be traced back to her maternal love for Songhui—an exorbitant love that was nearly maniacal—or rather her crime was to have become a devoted mother.

But, if traced further back to its provenance, the vine stretches out from human nature, or the sad law of nature that doesn't allow humans to pretend to love for long when there is no real mutual affection involved. And if you probed further, you would encounter the social customs of the time at the root of Chobong's harsh destiny. A young woman whose marriage went wrong was bound to seek a living either through prostitution or by becoming the mistress or concubine of a married man; such women had no voice with which to claim their rights even though they were abandoned without any advance notice. Once thrown into this dangerous cycle, such a woman had no asset but her body that could help her, and was prone to be led into selling her body. Women had no chance or ability to stand firmly on their own feet in the world, because they were forced by society to remain frail beings dependent on others. The original root of Chobong's warped destiny started from the sin that she was born one such frail woman in this society.

If you pulled out the whole of Chobong's destiny from below ground, you would find two huge rhizomes dangling at the end like sweet potatoes—one being the custom of the world, and the other human appetite.

Those rhizomes were magic pouches from which many kinds of adverse fates might emerge.

Hyeongbo's story could be roughly summarized as follows.

"Mr. Bak, you don't think the baby is your own. As a matter of fact, it can't be. If you say it's Go Taesu's, that might be more probable. But I know it can't be Mr. Go's either. Taesu slept with many women for several years before his marriage, but never once made any woman pregnant. Therefore the mere ten days of his married life would never have produced a child. So the baby can't be Taesu's, to be sure. Who's left then? I'm confident that it's mine. I saw earlier that the baby looked exactly like its mother. I know it's not easy to determine the father by its looks. Yet still, I'm sure if we search carefully, somewhere in her features or her feet or hands, we can definitely find something that resembles me."

(Seeing Hyeongbo so outlandishly eager to prove the baby was his, should we assume that he had read "The Toes Resemble Mine," a short story by the author Kim Dong-in in which an impotent protagonist endeavors to believe the baby his wife has given birth to is his own? Probably not.)

"Soon after Taesu's death, Chobong came up to Seoul, as you know. I could have come up to Seoul after her, and taken her back down to Gunsan or lived with her in Seoul. But at that time I didn't have enough money saved, so I couldn't assume such a responsibility. I was worrying myself to death until I heard that she had settled down to live with you, and the news somewhat relieved me of my worries about her for the time being.

"Since then, I have labored like a desperate beaver, grinding my teeth constantly. In the end, I got lucky enough to lay my hands on several thousand won. I think I managed that because I was totally devoted to the sole desire of fulfilling my dear friend's ardent request.

"And when I learned that a baby had been born, I sought out the relevant information about it and could confirm that I must be the father. The determination to get my child back and a sense of responsibility as a father also spurred my efforts to make money.

"So last summer, with the several thousand won in my pocket, I came up to Seoul to start a business in which I had much experience. As expected I'm making a good profit, good enough to start a family and to support them well. If you doubt it, I can show you the evidence. The bills in my briefcase are the evidence, for I'm in the business of discounting bills.

"I am now fully equipped to take the mother and the daughter and have more than enough to provide them with a comfortable life. Today is the day I have been so anxiously awaiting to visit you, and claim the mother and the daughter."

Hyeongbo paused here, wetting his dry lips with his tongue, and relit the cigarette that had gone out. He was mustering his strength in order to bring up the critical point with more emphasis. He soon resumed talking without much delay,

"You see, therefore, I'm here to take away the mother and the daughter. I absolutely have to do that by whatever means. The reason is because I have no other purpose in life but to fulfill my dear friend's last wish in the first place, and then to take custody of my child and raise it properly. Those two goals will be the only source of pleasure and hope for me for the rest of my life. You can understand the nature of my position, can't you? In other words, it's a matter of life and death for me, life and death, indeed . . . I hope you'll take it into consideration too, before you answer, please . . ."

Hyeongbo spat out his resolute intention word by word in a very articulate voice, and then looked straight at Jeho, holding his head upright.

Jeho knew that it was time for him to give an answer; but he kept his mouth tightly sealed, pretending to be deep in thought, biting his lip, and embracing one knee with two hands. He took that posture, not because he was hesitant about what to say. His answer was already phrased fully in his mind; only he was too embarrassed to bring it out.

Chobong was anxious and her suspense grew agonizing as she had no access to Jeho's mind.

She knew that Hyeongbo's tricks were nonsensical and incongruous by any standard. He was simply pushing his way through at whatever cost. Chobong, however, was frightened of that willful, irrational driving force. If she lost the protection of Jeho by any chance, she knew she would end up becoming a prey to Hyeongbo's vicious manipulation, however hard she struggled to get out of his grip. She sensed she was at the very edge of a dangerous precipice.

What a disaster! She was trapped and bound by such absurd tricks with her eyes fully open, and was about to cry bitterly, when in fact she should laugh and dismiss them as pure lies that deserved no proper response. She felt like choking at the sheer absurdity of the situation.

To avoid that disaster, she needed Jeho. It wasn't that she thought Jeho was untrustworthy. Yet still she wasn't completely free from some misgivings either. So she was waiting for the words to emerge from Jeho's mouth, feeling as frightened and anxious as someone awaiting the words of an oracle.

Suddenly the wall clock started to strike, breaking the prolonged silence. As if startled by the sound, Jeho sprang up from his seat. Hyeongbo and Chobong were also startled at Jeho's sudden movement, and both looked up at Jeho with puzzled looks. He looked as though he'd been frightened by something.

"I've understood your meaning . . ."

Jeho started to talk, but without continuing, he slowly bent over to pick up his hat that was lying on the floor and put it atop his head. He moved very slowly this time because he was somewhat ashamed of the suddenness with which he had stood up.

". . . But I can't understand how things have got tangled up in this complicated way. Having listened to your story so far, I see that the situation is indeed quite convoluted. It seems not at all simple to handle. By the way, as for me, I'm the kind of man in both temperament and habit, who is not at all inclined to be involved in problematic conflicts. I tend to avoid any situation that requires judgment on who's right or who's wrong. It's not just that I hate such confrontations; my personality is also quite unfit for such things, I'm afraid, huh huh . . . Therefore . . ."

Jeho fumbled for words for a moment, but Hyeongbo, who had stood up following Jeho's example, immediately understood the drift of Jeho's statement, and his face, which had been tense all along, instantly brightened up. He had expected strong resistance from Bak Jeho. Though he had intended to threaten him further, he wasn't hopeful of success at all. He was almost prepared to meet defeat and perhaps to turn back, scratching the back of his head. Despite that unfavorable expectation, he'd been bullying his way through, calculating that he had nothing to lose. But as it turned out, Bak Jeho was so easily retreating from his position, that Hyeongbo almost regretted having squandered his strength in the face of such an easy opponent.

" . . . Therefore . . ."

Jeho reopened his mouth, trying to turn his face toward Chobong, but he didn't dare to.

" . . . I'm going to wash my hands of this situation right now. Out of my ignorance—it wasn't out of knowing willfulness, you should know, I've been intruding upon someone else's right, so to speak, huh huh . . . Please settle the matter between you two. From now on, I'm a third person who's got nothing to do with it."

Though it was to Hyeongbo Jeho was speaking, he obviously was intending Chobong to hear. With the final words of withdrawal, Jeho prepared to step down into the yard. He seemed to be conveying with his movements the firmness of his mind, as though he had already said all he needed to, and he had no more need to linger in this place.

The thought of his being a third person made him feel at a loss as to what to do with his long awkward body in this embarrassing situation. However, when he tried to leave the place, he felt more embarrassed.

The thought struck him that it would be utterly disgraceful if he ran away like a coward, without giving a word of explanation to Chobong.

After all, Chobong was the woman he'd picked up and lived with for some time because he'd had a crush on her. Of course there were some aspects that might alleviate his guilt; recently their relationship had cooled down significantly, and then there popped up this opportune situation that offered a good excuse for him to abandon her. Yet still, as a man who had a face twice as long as others, he couldn't deny that it would be shameful if he so mercilessly (as a matter of fact, so brazenly) grabbed at the first opportunity to escape, especially when he knew well enough that that opportunity had been presented to him by a reckless and untrustworthy rascal. On top of that, he himself seemed to corroborate the rascal's morbid lies only in order to take advantage of those lies.

He was totally at a loss in his mind as to what to do. Right at this point, the senseless hunchback came forward, rendering his tricks even more abominable. Hyeongbo, assuming the posture of the master of a house sending off a guest, bowed deeply, and said,

"My, my, I really appreciate your full understanding . . ."

Jeho, appalled by this presumptuousness, hurriedly stopped Hyeongbo, waving his hands.

"Understanding! No, it's nothing like that! For heaven's sake, no, I'm in no position to understand it or not. I'm, so to speak, a defeated soldier that's retreating. That's it, a defeated soldier!"

Jeho attempted to pronounce the words, "a defeated soldier that's retreating," rather dramatically, but finding it didn't come out quite as he'd intended, he repeated it one more time like an actor anxious to emphasize it. He was in a way an actor in a play.

Jeho had wanted to end his relationship with Chobong in an amicable manner, without exposing his sly schemes. He had wanted to handle the matter tactfully and leave the place as swiftly as possible, avoiding any scuffles with Chobong. He needed such shrewdness so that he could save face in front of Chobong or her father Jeong Yeongbae, even if he would have no occasion to see her again after leaving. Thus he had determined to sneak away after leaving behind a few equivocating remarks. While he was exercising every precaution not to set off Chobong's temper, as if she were the smallpox germ, Hyeongbo, the hunchback, came forward and screwed up his scheme with such flippant remarks.

He couldn't leave just like that when he heard Hyeongbo say, "your full understanding," which without doubt would lead Chobong to interpret his stance improperly. It would've looked as if the two men had put their heads together and were making a friendly deal regarding Chobong, one saying, "that's my woman, give her back to me," and the other responding, "all right, take her please. It's a good riddance, for I was beginning to get sick of her." Jeho sensed that it could very well be seen as a friendly game between the two men, one man taking off a burden and dumping it onto another man. Jeho needed to play a role in order to prevent that suspicion. Thus we saw Jeho nervously denying Hyeongbo's words, "full understanding," aiming at Chobong's ears. Then he introduced the concept of "defeated soldier," to present himself as someone who had been vanquished in the battle for Chobong, as well as to solicit her sympathy for his pathetic situation. That made-up pretext, however, having no authentic basis in his mind, sounded too hollow to move anybody's heart. Instead of conveying the disconcerted despair that should be apparent in such situations, his speech was only dry and awkward, turning his act into an utter failure. Jeho had lost the opportunity of departing from the scene casually, without incurring disgrace. It was now imperative for him to talk with Chobong and clarify his position one way or another.

Putting together the words he would say to Chobong in his mind, he hesitantly turned back and approached the bedroom with faltering steps. He looked like a child trying to swallow a bitter medicine with his eyes tightly closed. Although his eyes were open, he couldn't hold his head upright, or look straight ahead, but moved toward the bedroom door like a crab moving sideways. When he reached the door, he reluctantly forced himself to turn his head toward Chobong.

The moment their eyes met, Jeho shuddered all over, a chill running down his spine. An eerie light was shining from her eyes. Her eyes seemed full of blue flames and the moment Jeho came face-to-face with her, the fire began to shoot out. It looked like a beam of light burning with an extreme intensity of desperation, something beyond mere anger. It clearly held murderous intent.

Jeho had never imagined it might be possible to see such murderous fire beaming from a woman's eyes, or from any human eyes. The words he had prepared instantly froze in his throat, and Jeho was left just standing there, not knowing what to do.

Normally Jeho was capable of doing what he needed to do, callously ignoring the opponent's anger or excitement. But in this case, facing such an eerie beam of ferocious light, he felt as if his whole body was shriveling up.

In fact, Chobong was at a loss as to what Jeho meant when he finished the first part of his speech. It was only when he had finished the second part that she understood what Jeho was on about. It was truly a bolt out of the blue.

As she had been so desperately beleaguered by Hyeongbo, her expectation of Jeho's support was equally high in proportion.

The moment she understood Jeho's intent, the high expectations she had been clinging to were cruelly dashed at a single blow, so unexpectedly that she felt that she was falling from a high cliff into a bottomless pit. She was utterly astonished, almost out of her mind. Her despair at having no way out was soon transformed into vicious resentment toward the man she had trusted.

Chobong never imagined that Jeho could turn his back on her so heartlessly. The worst she had expected was that he would ask her advice or at least try to consult with her about accepting Hyeongbo's demand, if he couldn't handle the situation by himself.

The rage arising from having her desperate hopes betrayed was insurmountable. She would have chewed him up or torn him apart if she could. Her wrath against Jeho was that intense.

She couldn't even think about Hyeongbo. Her fury at Hyeongbo had receded into the background and now she could see only Jeho.

He must be the worst rascal in the whole world. Where is the man who had been so kind and generous, pretending to be eternally loyal to me? Now that Bak Jeho is attempting to run away after dumping me into the hands of that abominable Hyeongbo! What a two-faced hypocrite this rogue is! Hasn't he been cheating me all along, using me as his toy?

The more she thought about him, the more bitterly rancorous she became. Her sense of resentment was pouring oil onto the fire of her rage. She was quivering, overwhelmed by a flaming indignation.

It was a natural response for Chobong, who had had no idea about Jeho's recent change of heart. But Jeho began to suspect the cause of Chobong's extreme rage.

She seems to be furious at my sudden change of heart. Then is it simply because she doesn't want to go to Hyeongbo? As for that, she

can refuse and order him out if she doesn't want him. Then why is
she so mad, particularly at me . . .?

Is it possible that she had deep affection for me despite the way
she seemed indifferent?

As this thought passed through his mind, Jeho briefly felt
slight remorse.

Soon, however, Jeho shook his head, dismissing the thought
as vain and groundless. He couldn't recall even one moment in
which Chobong had acted with genuine love, however thoroughly he searched through the days they had been together.

Although his love for her had cooled down now, he had loved
her with all his heart, doing all sorts of things to win her heart
in return. In other words, she was the woman toward whom he
had had ambivalent feelings, contradictory feelings of love and
antipathy intermixed.

As his earnest desire to win her love was never fulfilled, his
love for her had also cooled. Hyeongbo appeared at the right
moment, when he had become weary of the relationship, and
offered a good opportunity to get rid of the burden. Although
he grabbed the opportunity gladly, he couldn't be completely
free from a lingering trace of affection for her, either. This remnant of affection, of which he was not conscious, unexpectedly
surfaced now as he stood face-to-face with Chobong, and made
him fall into a sentimental doubt about his earlier verdict on
her indifference.

That doubt, however, didn't last long. He rebounded to his
usual rational self soon enough. Oddly enough, the short interval of doubtful reflection about their past, instead of renewing
his love for her, reinforced his antipathy toward her, as well as
his determination to abandon her.

Pshaw! What good has she ever done me to glare at me so furi-
ously? It's revolting! I'm not a man to be frightened of a mere woman!

What's the problem? Is deserting an old flame as atrocious as high treason against the state?

With sudden bravado, Jeho deliberately took a step closer to Chobong.

Chobong kept glaring at Jeho without any movement. She was gasping for breath. Her face was ashen, drained of all color. She was biting her lips so hard that they were also pale and trembling. The tips of the fingers of her left hand, which was hanging over the chest of Songhui as she sucked at her breast, were also trembling visibly. Words were about to burst out but they seemed blocked by her overpowering rage.

"Uh, during all the time we've been together . . ."

Jeho, having determined to disregard whatever posture she was taking, began to say nonchalantly what he had prepared. Nevertheless, he avoided her murderous eyes, fixing his gaze on her lips.

"I know how much trouble you've had, living with this poor, unworthy man. I'm indeed sorry for that, I don't know how to express it in words . . ."

Chobong showed no response, as if she heard nothing. Jeho resumed after pausing a moment for breath.

". . . And, uh, you should know my personality from having observed me this far. You know that it's not because you've done anything wrong or because I'm finding fault with your past that I'm going to leave you. It's not that. It's only because I'm a fool, by nature incapable of confronting any severe conflicts. In this case too, I can't come up front and quarrel with that man, not by any means! . . . But don't get me wrong, as if I am asking you to go to Mr. Jang. That's not at all what I mean by leaving you now. I think that's something that must be settled between you two as far as circumstances allow. As I don't want to be a factor in your decision, neither am I in the position to dictate this or that . . ."

Jeho said all this in one breath. Although the last sentence was unfinished, he couldn't think of anything else to add. So he started to say his farewells.

"So, therefore, I'm . . ."

But no sooner had he started to speak, than Chobong suddenly thundered out,

"You rascals, both of you, get out this instant!"

Shouting at her highest pitch, she jumped up as if she had gone mad. As she did so, Songhui was thrown down onto the floor and began to cry wildly, as though she had been burned by something. Yet Chobong was totally unaware of it.

From her eyes shot murderous blue beams of light, which seemed sharp enough to rend anything they touched. A thread of dark red blood trickled down from her lower lip, which she had bitten, making a clear line on her chin. As the pin that held her chignon came loose, her disheveled hair fell down over her shoulders. The face that had been so beautiful and shapely was gone and there appeared an ugly, distorted face that seemed about to explode at any moment into violent spasms. These couldn't be the eyes and face of a human being. Perhaps it might be more correct to call it the face of a frail animal pursued by a predator into a dead end and that turns back to face its predator in utter desperation.

Quite appalled by this outburst of fury, Jeho stared at Chobong with eyes wide open. He thought she must have gone insane or become a totally different person.

Chobong gasped heavily after that one outcry.

Hyeongbo, his back toward Chobong, couldn't see her face, yet he was callously smoking as if he were deaf to it all.

Jeho hesitantly took a few steps back and then sneakily turned his back on Chobong.

Songhui was wailing piercingly, holding onto Chobong's skirt and trying to scramble up, but Chobong didn't even glance at her.

". . . You, ruthless, relentless, brutal scoundrels!"

Chobong at last shouted at the top of her voice, stamping on the floor and tightly clenching her fists.

"You're not afraid of thunderbolts because the sky is blue? You're the most vicious, worthless ruffians in the whole world . . ."

Chobong's voice was now choking and her wild howling was turning into a mournful lament.

"What have I done to you to deserve such persecution? You ruthless rascals! . . . I've done nothing wrong, I didn't offend anybody, I've lived without making so much as a sound. How on earth can you dare to cause me such pain? Such cruelty . . . You damnable brutes!"

The storm of her rage and bitterness, which seemed as though it would never pass, somehow subsided into an insuperable sorrow over her own fate after she spat out only a few curses. She soon lost all her words of protest, abandoning herself to wild outbursts of loud sobbing.

Jeho quickly moved to the gate as if he was being chased by someone, and Hyeongbo followed him with a tottering gait to see him off.

"Oh well, I'm really sorry!"

At the gate, Hyeongbo bowed to Jeho, saying he was sorry, but without specifying for what or wherefore.

"No, no, don't mention it!"

Jeho, who rushed out without looking back even once, felt obliged to respond reluctantly, then hurriedly stepped out of the gate.

Jeho felt a heavy weight had been lifted off his shoulders, and Hyeongbo too felt the same way. Both men felt relieved and easy.

Chobong was sobbing, the top half of her body thrown forward, and her face covered with her hands. Songhui was nudging her way into her mother's armpit, bawling desperately.

The maid, stunned by this mayhem, stood blankly at the door of the kitchen.

Hyeongbo, on his way back from the gate, cast a glance at the maid, and commanded,

"Why don't you go to the lady and hold the baby for her?"

His tone already sounded like that of the master of the house. The maid, disregarding his order, didn't move, remaining awkward and hesitant. She knew it was her duty to calm the baby in this situation. But as the whole house was shaken and in disorder, she too felt as though even her usual duty was someone else's work.

"Ah, by the way, listen . . ."

Hyeongbo began to coax the maid, who seemed to be keeping her distance from him like a stranger.

". . . You'll see soon enough, but from today on, I'll be the master of the house . . . You need to know that . . . And though there's been some disturbance in the house, all will be fine pretty soon. So you needn't worry about your position or anything else. Do you understand that? You'll take good care of the household work on behalf of your lady, won't you?"

Hyeongbo was about to take charge of the lady and the house at the same time. It was true that Jeho had withdrawn, leaving both in his hands.

At Hyeongbo's words, the maid almost burst into a fit of laughter, sensing the pathos of the absurd situation. It may not be so odd, if a new concubine moves into the house the same day the old one moves out. But here, a man moves out and another man moves in. She thought it too preposterous.

Chobong, who was exhausted by her wild sobbing, which had continued for some time to express her endless sorrow, at last raised her head to hold the fretful Songhui. At that moment she caught sight of Hyeongbo boldly stepping up onto the maru.

That sight triggered once more the rage that had been subdued by her overwhelming sorrow, and it surged up once again with double force.

"Here, take your child, you knave!"

Jumping up suddenly, with a fierce howl, she held up Songhui and, like a madwoman, threw her at Hyeongbo's feet.

Hyeongbo somehow caught Songhui as she was falling to the floor. Chobong instantly clasped her hands against her own chest, recovering her senses and recognizing what a hideous act she had just committed. Frightened out of her wits, she felt as though she had seen a glittering sharp blade in Hyeongbo's hand. The baby, in shock, cried desperately as if it were dying. Amazed by her own cruelty, Chobong became more helpless, and could find nothing better to do than thunder out her wrath with curses.

"Damn you, you damnable wretch! A woman's rancor brings frost even in the summer. You wait and see. I'll make you pay for your wicked evil that's ruined my life! Just wait, you wretch!"

Grinding her teeth, she glared fiercely at Hyeongbo through her disheveled hair. Her eyes, however, were soon lowered to focus on Hyeongbo's hands, for fear that he might harm Songhui with his knife.

"Would you really treat me like this?"

Hyeongbo shouted back, rolling his eyes at her. If he picked up his knife and pointed it at Songhui while shouting at her, Chobong would have plumped down (instead of rushing at him to save her daughter, being too frightened) and begged his mercy, rubbing her palms together incessantly, on her knees.

Hyeongbo held Songhui by the back of her clothes like a kitten, swinging her as though calling Chobong's attention. The baby was floundering, its limbs hanging in the air, crying desperately, and shouting for Mommy all at the same time.

Chobong momentarily felt relieved on seeing that Hyeongbo wasn't attempting to use his knife, but she was so upset to see Songhui mercilessly harassed. She suddenly turned back, walked into the room and flopped down in the corner. She knew it meant surrender but she didn't care. If her surrender could save Songhui from harm at the hands of Hyeongbo, she would surrender to Hyeongbo as many times as necessary, she thought.

"If you keep on being obstinate, you'll certainly witness a bloody scene, I assure you!"

Hyeongbo spat out the threat, rolling his eyes. Despite his braggadocio, he didn't know what to do with the little thing that was crying so wildly. He tried to embrace her in his bosom, but being totally inexperienced in such things, he felt awkward and annoyed.

He felt like throwing the baby onto the floor, regardless of the danger of her getting killed or injured. Yet he knew he should pretend to be fatherly, affecting his love for it for the time being. The baby kept on shrieking frantically like an alarm clock. His head was aching, driving him crazy. It was a perfect punishment for him. If the situation continued like this for one hour, he would go mad, for sure.

The maid at last approached and held out her arms. Hyeongbo gladly put the baby into her arms, saying,

"Soothe her well, and try to make her fall asleep . . ."

Hyeongbo then added with a sigh,

"You suffer because you have the wrong mother! You'd better die soon if you want to avoid suffering!"

Rather than being inflamed by this provocation, Chobong simply despised the mouth that spat out those words.

Songhui kept floundering in the maid's arms, calling for her mommy. Chobong wished the maid would bring the baby to her, but the maid was too witless to do that. Instead, the maid was doing everything she could to soothe the baby; bouncing her up and down in her arms, or making sounds by knocking on the door. When these had no effect, she went down to the yard and then to the gate, jumping around.

As all her efforts were in vain, the maid at last brought Songhui into the room. The moment she was in her mother's arms, Songhui stopped crying, and began to suckle vigorously, giving out clear smacking sounds. Having cried so long, Songhui made a few hiccup-like sobbing sounds while sucking. Overwhelmed by pity for the baby, Chobong wanted to pat her bottom, saying "Oh, dear dear! Who made you suffer like that! My poor poor baby!" But she couldn't express her emotions, being all the time conscious of Hyeongbo, who was watching them from the maru.

Songhui's eyes and cheeks were still wet with tears. As her mother gently dried them with her hands, Songhui stopped sucking, stared up at her mother, and was on the verge of crying again, calling "Mommy," as if asking for consolation from her mother.

"Sure, sure, I'm here, my dear baby!"

Chobong too was on the verge of tears. She no longer minded Hyeongbo's stare, and patted the baby's bottom affectionately. Reassured, Songhui resumed her suckling.

Chobong couldn't even imagine being separated from this precious little baby. Moreover, it was not only beyond her imagination, but also an infamous crime for a mother to leave a baby exposed to horrible dangers.

Because of the storm that had just swept through the house, Chobong's affection for Songhui grew more intense. While looking down at Songhui, Chobong felt unprecedentedly strong courage surge up within her.

That courage, however, wasn't enough to help her seek a way out; she simply remained passive; it wasn't the will to live, but the reckless abandonment of not fearing death. Considering that Chobong had been that way since birth, expecting her to become suddenly aggressive or positive about herself would have been nearly impossible.

Songhui's panic had now all evaporated; having suckled to her heart's content, she was happily lying on her mom's lap, staring at her mom and babbling something that no one could understand but herself, either a song or a story. Whenever her mom was nearby, Songhui never cried, nor felt bored. She was happy and comfortable. She could sing or tell a story. If she felt hungry, the sweet milk was right in front of her. If she sucked, the milk was plentiful. Her eyes enjoyed watching her mom's face. It was fun to watch it. Her mom's nipples were right there for her hands to play with. If her feet needed something to do, her hands reached out and played with them. Everything seemed fine and snug for Songhui when her mother was around.

Chobong knew that. Tonight she felt even more keenly how much Songhui needed her.

Despite the horrible situation she was in, Songhui feared nothing, totally at ease in the bosom of her mother. At whatever cost, she should protect Songhui, ensure that she would go on living this easy and contented life. Chobong resolved that if she could only do that, she wouldn't care what befell her.

She wouldn't mind being slashed by a knife, or being burned by a red-hot poker, so long as no one touched even a strand of

Songhui's hair. Nor should anyone pose a threat to Songhui, either with their eyes or by shouting in a loud voice. She wouldn't allow it, no matter the cost to herself.

For Songhui's sake, my body will be a sturdy shield, or, if that's not strong enough, I can even become a gigantic rock. A warm, cozy blanket on a cold winter's day, an umbrella on a rainy day, a windbreak against gales, a bright lamp on a dark night, a bowl of warm rice when Songhui's hungry—my body will function as each and all of those for Songhui's sake.

My body's already rotten and ruined. This body has already had three men including two husbands so far. What's left for this rotten body to do besides keeping danger away from Songhui? Should I be reluctant to defend Songhui in order to spare this rotten body? Never! Perhaps I should feel lucky that I can use this rotten body for a good cause.

Hyeongbo? Why not? I would take a man even more abominable than Hyeongbo. One worse than a mortal enemy, for that matter. I wouldn't mind it if only I can protect Songhui and raise her in comfortable circumstances and without giving any hardship to her.

Chobong shuddered with astonishment when her thoughts reached that point. *When did I make up my mind to become Hyeongbo's woman?* Unaware of it, she must have determined to accept that fate at some point, or she wouldn't have had such a thought.

Whew, a deep sigh rose from her heart. She seemed too frivolous, too much like a weathervane, even in her own eyes. At that moment the sound of Hyeongbo's dry cough drifted into the room. A shiver ran through her body as though she could feel Hyeongbo's flesh, like a snake, sliding over the top of her bare feet.

Hyeongbo, who had been sitting idly on the *maru* like a stuffed owl, at last stood up at the sound of the clock striking ten, and walked into the room. Chobong, having anticipated everything, resolved to get the most out of Hyeongbo.

All right, come on you villain, I've figured out what to do, if things go in that direction . . .

Hyeongbo couldn't free himself from embarrassment, so with an awkward grin, he moved to a corner of the room where he sat and sneakily cast glances at Chobong to study her expression. After a while, finding Chobong sitting still with her face turned aside (contrary to his expectation that she would scream at him with fury), he began to try to trick her. His talk, however, was completely free of intimidating threats. He tried to use only kind and gentle words, sometimes in a tone of imploring supplication, and at other times in a tone of coaxing admonition.

"As things have come this far, there's no other option now, I'm afraid. So please change your mind. If you stop being so stubborn, everything will turn out all right in the end; good for you, good for the child, and good for myself as well. Everyone can be happy together, I assure you.

"As I said earlier to Bak Jeho, I've started a business with a fund of five to six thousand won, which brings me a considerable income now. I can afford to provide you and the child with a modestly luxurious life. So trust me on that.

"One other advantage is that you can live as a legal wife from now on for I'm a single man, whereas you've lived as the concubine of Bak Jeho so far. In addition, you can get rid of that bastard tag for the child, if you marry me."

Hyeongbo continued talking in this vein for nearly an hour, smoking from time to time, and adding a few embellishments to what he had said as they came to his mind. All the while Chobong sat still beside her Songhui, holding her knees with clasped hands, showing no sign whatsoever whether she was listening to him or not. But toward the end of that hour, Chobong at last changed her posture by turning her body toward Hyeongbo, and looking straight at him, she began to speak,

"All right, I will be your woman if you wish. But . . ."

She gave this assent, not because of his entreaty, but because she was determined to exploit him.

The moment the words of assent emerged from her mouth, Hyeongbo, excited, beamed with a huge grin, which made his already large mouth stretch to his ears. Mumbling, "Sure, sure, that's the right way to go, you should've done that from the beginning, without giving me so much trouble, good, good," Hyeongbo began to move toward Chobong, hesitantly shuffling forward on his knees. Startled at his movement, Chobong burst out,

"What are you doing? . . . Stay where you are, I have a long way to go before I finish talking. You stay there till I've finished."

"Yes, yes, ma'am, huh, huh."

"Pshaw, don't be delighted too soon! Do you think I'm giving in to you because I want to become your woman? Rubbish! . . . I only want to avenge myself on you. Vengeance, that's what I want . . ."

"Uh-huh! What nonsense!"

"You wait and see! Do you expect me to act like a docile wife to you, the man who has utterly ruined my life? Oh no! . . . I'll make you shake that head of yours in disbelief and dismay. Wait and see, I warn you!"

Chobong shouted out haphazardly whatever came to her lips, yet still she felt not one iota of consolation. Although she talked about vengeance, she couldn't think of any viable method. She might slash his belly while he was asleep; or she might put some arsenic in his soup. These were indeed things she could do. But she knew that such vengeance would never bring back her innocent youth; she would only end up staining her hands with blood in vain. The more she thought about it, the more helpless and distressed she became in the face of her fate, which would certainly lead her deeper into the swamp. Tears welled up in her eyes.

"Dear, dear, let bygones be bygones, please . . ."

Swinging his back this way and that, Hyeongbo was restless, not knowing what to do. He stood up and squatted down repeatedly. At last he resumed in a cajoling voice,

". . . Get rid of all your anger, please? . . . And then we can start a new family, filled with happiness, a family no one would dare to look down on . . . Huh huh"

"Well, dream on! How revolting you are!"

"No, no, dear. I beg you to stop being so unrelenting, dear!"

"You were boasting of your money? How much do you really have?"

"About six thousand won . . ."

"Really?"

"For sure! I can show you right at this instant!"

Hyeongbo picked up the briefcase he'd been carrying

". . . I have about two thousand odd won in my savings account and nearly four thousand won's worth in bills I have received from my customers. You can see them now if you want. Would you like to?"

"Wait. You can show them when I ask to see them . . . Then, listen, will you do everything I demand of you?"

"Sure, sure. I would even pick a star from the sky if you demand it. Just name it please, lady!"

"Then, first of all, get an insurance policy for Songhui. One with your name and another with mine, and Songhui as the beneficiary. Two life insurance policies . . ."

"Insuring for how much?'

"One thousand won each."

"One thousand won? Let me see, two policies for one thousand won each, how much would the monthly premium be?"

Hyeongbo did some mental arithmetic, blinked his eyes and nodded.

"All right, no problem!"

"That's settled then . . . the next thing is to provide for me just as Bak Jeho has been doing. He purchased the firewood and rice from his own pocket, and paid the monthly rent, in addition to giving me fifty won as a monthly allowance for household expenses. You'll do the same, won't you?"

"If I did . . ., it would cost far more than one hundred won a month . . . But how could I not do that! It won't do if I can't provide as much as Bak Jeho did. Then, that's also settled!"

"And you should also give me one thousand won."

"One thousand won? In cash?"

"Yes."

"That might be a bit difficult for me . . . It's not that I don't have that much money. I have, but the cash I have is the seed money for my business. If I take out one thousand won, my income will also be reduced. At present I'm conducting my business with a fund of six thousand won, earning about two hundred won a month. Deducting one thousand won from the fund would cause me difficulties, I guess. What on earth do you need that much money for?"

"I should help my family back home stand on their feet, shouldn't I?"

"My, my! You'd beat a *gisaeng* in dealing with a man!"

"What! Am I any better than a *gisaeng*?"

"How formidable you are!"

"There's one more demand. You should bring my brother and sister to Seoul and pay for their education!"

Chapter 15:
Methods of Coping with Appetite

ANOTHER YEAR PASSED and May came round again.

If you counted from the day Chobong quietly left Gunsan, exactly two years had passed. It was also the second anniversary of the tragic deaths of Go Taesu and Madam Kim, who had been brutally battered to death by Han Chambong.

However, the port city of Gunsan had forgotten the scandal long ago. The city was a small giant into which all sorts of goods, money, and people drifted, providing a dynamic spirit full of vitality. It was too vibrant a city to remember or mourn the small, bloody incident that had taken place years ago, or the fact that a young woman had her life ruined due to the tragedy.

The sun still rises from the east and sets in the west; when the season changes, the landscape of the city also wears new colors as it has always done; uniform turbidity currents incessantly flow into the estuary of the Geum-gang River, where the water heaves up and down according to the ebb and flow of the tide. In the meantime the small giant keeps going, fueled by the momentum of the mechanism produced by the combination of people, money, and goods; the goods move following the money and the money moves along with the goods and people flock in and disperse according to the movements of money and goods. Thus the heart of the giant never ages, always beating robustly. So too the speculation at the rice market continues day in and day out.

Our Jeong Jusa, too, was the same as ever. His beard still looked like that of a catfish, still yellowish and drooping downward. He still blinked his eyes constantly. His main pastime was also the same as ever. At the rice exchange, where huge sums of money were transacted, and the rise and fall of many people's fortune were determined by the flipping of palms this way or that, our petty "speculator," Jeong Jusa, was hanging onto his bet of fifty jeon, agitated at every single scrap of news from the Osaka Exchange.

One surprising development in Jeong Jusa's life was that he now never ran out of funds, even if it amounted to only a few score jeon. Wherever the money came from, he now paid off what he owed to his fellow speculators, so never "shot blank" as they called it. It truly was a big improvement, if it was an improvement at all. Since the previous autumn, he had been clean in all his dealings, never drawn into scuffles or grabbed by his collar or subject to verbal abuse.

This improvement was a result of the five hundred won Chobong had sent down from Seoul the previous autumn. Her mother opened a small grocery store with the money, and thanks to the income from the store, Jeong Jusa had become an honest speculator at the exchange market. An old saying goes, "The shadows of Suyang Mountain stretch a full eighty li in the Gangdong area." Likewise, if we trace back the origin of Chobong's five hundred won, it goes as far back as Taesu. The money came from Chobong, but Chobong got the money from Hyeongbo, who'd made a fortune amounting to between five and six thousand won using the money left over by the late Taesu at the rice exchange. It was a welcome realization of Jeong Jusa's dream; he'd always hoped for a windfall from a son-in-law through Chobong, and both Taesu and Hyeongbo were his sons-in-law. So Jeong Jusa in the end took full advantage of having a pretty daughter.

Madam Yu ended up running the store, for she had to stay home to do her sewing work at the same time, while Jeong Jusa took responsibility for supplying the goods for the store. He would go out early in the morning to the bus stop, where he could meet farmers to buy vegetables, and then move on to the public market to purchase fruit and cookies. He would also go to the fish market in Ansure from time to time to purchase some fish for the store. When this responsibility was over, Jeong Jusa had the whole afternoon to himself, having nothing else to do. To tell the truth, he could have stayed at the store, helping his wife who was always shorthanded, doing the needlework as well as serving the customers. But Jeong Jusa never felt like sitting there, waiting for customers who would leave only one jeon or half a jeon profit for each salted mackerel, or for children who would come in carrying one jeon or so for cookies. He felt stifled staying in the store; moreover, he knew he could make at least fifty jeon or one won in one afternoon if he played well or got lucky at the rice exchange. It certainly would be more profitable to go to the rice exchange than keeping the store, he thought.

The horses from the northern countries get excited at the north wind, and the birds from the southern countries build nests only on the south-facing branches of trees. Jeong Jusa, though degraded now to a cart-pulling, scrawny horse, still believed that he had once been a vigorous steed that could gallop a thousand li in a day. So he wanted to continue betting at the rice exchange even if it was only for fifty-jeon stakes.

When his wife scolded him, asking what would happen if he lost everything, he always bragged that would never happen.

This in fact meant that he had the nerve not to care even if he lost everything.

Today Jeong Jusa was as arrogant as can be, having a whole three won to play with at the exchange market. His wife had given him the money to buy a couple of dozen dried pollack at the fish market.

A hungry tiger doesn't care if its prey happens to be a village magistrate, and Jeong Jusa was the same. He didn't care what the money was for, and moreover he saw a dragon in his dream last night. Confident of his good luck, he was having much fun playing with big money, three won, all day long. He alternated between winning and losing streaks, and in the end was left with only one won and fifty jeon in hand when the market closed for the day.

As he left the market along with the other speculators, he at last began to feel bitter about the lost money that had been meant to purchase pollack.

The dazzling glare of May sunlight poured down over the street, where all sorts of speculators from the rice exchange were streaming out. They all looked rather wilted, like plants that had grown in the shade but were suddenly exposed to bright sunlight.

Those who'd won some money had their chins sticking out, bearing complacent smiles. Their gait was also light and gay, which, however, looked rather unnatural, having nothing to do with the sunlight.

In contrast, those who had their noses instead of chins sticking out, their heads down, and their shoulders drooping like roosters with broken wings, were the people who lost money, ranging from a couple of tens of jeon in the case of off-the-market speculators to several hundreds or thousands of won in the case of in-the-market arbitrageurs. Some of them, unable to contain their vexation, blurted out, but to no one in particular, "Damn bloody day!" And then they usually raised their hands to scratch the back of their heads but stopped short. It was obvious they wanted to cry. They tried to put on smiling faces, but could only laugh out of the wrong side of their mouths. They were all the more out of place, like aliens under the gay sunlight of May.

Jeong Jusa, who'd lost one and a half won out of the three won for pollack, was of course one of the latter group. He walked out onto the street among several people and stood there clicking his tongue. Now that the market was closed for the day, there was no way to recover the lost money. He felt like grabbing someone and playing the rock-paper-scissors game for a stake of fifty jeon.

"Jeong Jusa!"

As he was standing there blankly, someone touched his shoulder, calling out his name from high above. It was his fellow petty speculator, the "Utility Pole" guy. People needed to look up quite high to see his face. Hence he got this nickname from his extreme height.

"What are you staring at? Come on, get a move on."

In this world of speculation, so long as they haven't "shot blank" at someone, everyone is friends with everyone. It's also a custom in this world to urge someone to "get a move on" when they're lagging behind, even if it's just for one block.

"All right, let's go."

Jeong Jusa reluctantly began to walk beside him. His head was on a level with his companion's waist. Those who were walking behind them began to giggle, amused by the contrast, but Jeong Jusa didn't notice that.

"Jeong Jusa, I believe you've had a pretty good day?"

"No, not at all. Quite the contrary!"

"Don't whine like that . . . I remember you won fifty jeon of my money earlier today . . ."

"Still I lost one and a half in the end! What a luckless day . . ."

"Bullshit! Stop pretending to have been unlucky. Just buy me a noodle soup with the money you've won. I'm starving to death!"

"Same here, I'm starving too!"

Jeong Jusa was really hungry. Since the previous autumn, he'd never been forced to miss a meal and usually went back home for lunch around noontime. But today, he was having so much fun with the three won at the exchange market, alternating between winning and losing streaks, that he even forgot about lunch. Now that it was all over, he began to feel hungry, while being annoyed at himself all over again.

"Damn, damn. If I'd had lunch with the money, at least I'd have a full belly now!"

"You see . . ."

The "Utility Pole" took the lead in the conversation at the end of Jeong Jusa's lament.

"If you treat us poor guys to a bowl of noodles at times, Heaven will notice it and bless you with luck!"

"Heaven would notice it? Huh huh, what the hell. Well, why not. Let's go and have some noodles then!"

"My, do you really mean it?"

"Do you take me for a liar? . . . But it'll only be a bowl of noodles for each of us, you got it? No wine to accompany it, to be sure!"

"Of course not! We know the size of each other's purse, no wine for sure . . ."

In the past, when the off-the-market speculators also played for high stakes, those who earned money usually treated fellow speculators to a big party involving drinking and revelry. The remnants of such gallantry still survive; on days they win one or two won, they usually invite one of those who hang around at the exchange for a bowl of noodles and a bottle of strong wine and to unburden their sentiments as petty speculators. But Jeong Jusa was going to treat the "Utility Pole" to a bowl of noodles, not out of such gallantry, but out of anger at his situation.

While his lingering sense of frustration for the lost money was aggravated by his hunger, the "Utility Pole" was plying him with flattery, goading him into buying a bowl of noodles; he certainly felt it would be great if he could gulp down a bowl of noodles without leaving even a drop of the soup. In a "what the hell" mood, he allowed himself to be cajoled by the "Utility Pole." In the past he wouldn't have dared to give in to such coaxing, knowing that the money for two bowls of noodles could purchase two bags of half-crushed rice. But these days, he had a pile to lean on, and thus felt bolder to do as he pleased at times.

His grocery store was still located in the Dunbaemi area, but not at the top of the hilly village where they used to live in the past. The store was on a street corner on the flat patch of land cluttered with small cottages at the foot of the steep hill, an ideal location for a small grocery store. The store also had a two-room house with a kitchen annexed to it, which served as a living area as well as sewing space.

Investing three hundred won out of the sourceless five hundred won Chobong had sent down last autumn, Madam Yu set up the store and the new living arrangement. She spent one hundred twenty won for a sewing machine, and about forty won evaporated for moving expenses and for treating the starved family to sumptuous feasts. The remainder of the money, forty won, she stashed away to run the store. Jeong Jusa did everything he could to wheedle the money out of his wife in order to invest at the rice exchange—he could have played with as much as a hundred bushels of rice if he had forty won in deposit—but his wife was too obstinate to listen to him.

Nevertheless, the store yielded about thirty won or so profit every month, and in addition, Madam Yu made ten odd won a month with her sewing machine. Overall she now made enough money to feed the four members of her family. Thanks to this improved financial situation, Jeong Jusa could afford to lose a few won at the rice exchange or have the boldness to treat a fellow speculator to some noodles.

It was a further advantage that they had fewer mouths to feed. Last fall, Chobong, who'd left home nearly two years before, summoned her sister Gyebong to come up to Seoul. Hyeongju too could have gone to Seoul at that time, but having been admitted to the Agricultural School in Iri in April last year, he decided to finish that school first before moving to Seoul for higher education. So Hyeongju was commuting to Iri from home.

Now that there were only four people in the family, Madam Yu, being a tough and thrifty woman, could have saved some money out of the monthly income of forty to fifty won and expanded the store bit by bit, if it weren't for the way Jeong Jusa was squandering her petty cash at the rice exchange day in and day out, as if he'd become the father-in-law of a king. Because of this "big extravagance" of his, the family was having more squabbles now than in the days when they had had to skip meals so frequently. Moreover, as Madam Yu was going through menopause, her hysteria was truly spectacular.

It was early May, and the days were already quite long and warm, causing people to doze off. Madam Yu was fighting against sleepiness, trying to concentrate on her sewing, sitting in front of her treasure, the sewing machine, her old magnifying glasses with broken rims hanging off her nose.

The buzzing sound of the sewing machine was lulling her into sleep. She longed to doze off, but she couldn't, because no one was there to watch the store even if she could delay the sewing work. She couldn't even count on her husband's return, having given up on him long ago. She knew he'd be back when he had nothing else to do. Yet, she stored up her anger to unleash it on him the moment he got back.

Her youngest son, Byeongju, who was a first-year student at primary school, usually came home around two in the afternoon. But today he was late, causing her to miss her nap. She was quite annoyed at him.

An elderly woman carrying a baby on her back walked into the store and, after looking around, unwittingly aggravated Madam Yu's ire when she said,

"It seems you don't have any dried pollack . . .?"

Madam Yu, who was about to stand up to greet the customer, sat down again. It was the third time that she'd failed to sell a pollack. Thoroughly vexed, she felt like preparing some boiling water for her husband's return, and throwing it in his face the moment he walked into the store.

"Well, if you don't have pollack, I may have to go to the other store over the hill," the elderly woman mumbled to herself, and turned away.

"My husband will come back soon with the pollack . . ."

Thinking of the lost opportunity of selling pollack—if she could sell five pollack, she would have earned five jeon—she put it down on the list of items she would use when reprimanding her husband.

"How can I wait for him? I have guests at home waiting with wine glasses in hand."

"How about taking some dried cod instead?"

"I have dried cod at home, but they specifically asked for dried pollack."

Just as the old woman left the store and turned the corner of the alley, Byeongju rushed in gasping for breath. He always breathed with his mouth open, gasping, because his nose was filled with mucus that constantly ran down.

"Mom."

Calling his mom once, he took off his hat, throwing it along with his school bag into the room, and ran to the wooden plate on which candies were displayed. That was Byeongju's usual routine. But Madam Yu, who was sharply glaring at him over her glasses, shouted like thunder,

"You rascal!"

Byeongju turned his head around toward his mom, utterly startled at the unexpected shout.

"What were you up to, getting home so late?"

She stormed on, ready to have a go at him with the ruler in her hand. She was raging now, not for the sake of correcting her son's behavior, but to vent her anger at her husband, as well as for her missed nap. The thought that her anger was misdirected never entered her mind.

Byeongju hissed and his cheeks drooped at the first sign of his mom's scolding, resentful of it.

Being the youngest, Byeongju had at first enjoyed all kinds of indulgence at the hands of his parents. Even when he pestered them with absurd demands or acted willfully or stubbornly, they always embraced him with amused faces. But as he grew up, they began to realize that he was no longer a babe-in-arms; he resented their scolding, never fearing anybody. So since last year, a rod had begun to be used to correct his behavior. But the only one who actually used it was Madam Yu, for Jeong Jusa being of milder temper only verbally scolded the boy. Jeong Jusa even begged for forgiveness when the boy got angry and began to cry.

From Byeongju's point of view, he was entitled to get angry because it seemed his desires were always thwarted, and everything always went contrary to his wishes. It was especially annoying since it was so different from what he'd been used to. Unlike the days when he had always been cuddled and indulged in his every whim, his parents suddenly became stern, often harshly scolding and even beating him at times. As for his coming home late, it had never been noticed by anyone, but today, his mother was unexpectedly furious. So what was the problem with her, Byeongju wondered. He felt fully justified in resenting his mother's abrupt scolding.

"Don't act so sullen! . . . You, bad boy, how dare you be so obstinate!"

Madam Yu, fuming with anger, rushed out of the room, holding the long ruler aloft. Byeongju didn't even flinch, and just looked the other way.

"You no-good rascal!"

The moment she hit him with the ruler, Byeongju burst out in a loud cry, as though he'd been waiting for it. The cry was louder than necessary to call for the assistance of his father.

"What's this shouting! Why are you bawling like that? How dare you, you rogue? Stop it!"

The ruler came down upon Byeongju again each time she ended a reprimand. Byeongju flopped down on the floor and kept bawling louder and louder, wriggling wildly.

"You rascal, such a stubborn no-good! Are you still wet behind the ears? How dare you, you naughty boy, how come you have nothing but resentment in that little body? Naughty, naughty thing!"

Madam Yu kept beating him mercilessly. As the pain grew too severe to endure, Byeongju at last shouted out, "I won't do it again."

But he didn't say it in a pleading tone; he hollered it at his highest pitch, as a sort of angry resistance.

Byeongju had learned to shout "I won't do it again" when his parents first began to beat him. But the words came out of his mouth because his parents forced him to say it while beating him. He said it without recognizing the real meaning of the words.

"Not again?'

"No, I won't."

"Not again?"

"Ouch, ouch, I won't, ugh!"

Madam Yu finally stopped her beating, gasping for breath.

Byeongju stood up, still sniffing, with his nose dripping snot as far down as his navel. He showed no sign of repentance despite the beating, he only grew more sullen and petulant because of it.

"What's that sound you're making?"

Madam Yu, who was about to go back to her room, shouted once again, turning back. Byeongju lowered his sniffing sounds a little.

"Won't you blow your nose?"

"Hsss!"

"What? What do you mean by that?"

"Hsss!"

"You wait, I'll show you!"

Seeing his mother start to turn back to go for him, Byeongju blew his nose with his fingers and flicked them to shake off the snot onto the floor, then wiped his hand on his clothes.

"You're a hopeless piece of work, you never study at home after school, yet you've learned well enough to be as stubborn as an ox. What a no-good lout you are . . ."

"Hsss."

"Always craving for sweets at that . . ."

"Hsss."

"You must study hard if you want to grow up and never have to worry about feeding yourself!"

"Hsss."

"If you keep developing such bad behavior, never studying, not a jot, what's your future going to be?"

"Hsss."

Byeongju's grumbling sounds grew louder and louder. None of his mother's words of admonishment was agreeable to him, so the sound was a way of expressing his defiant complaints.

"Will your mom and dad live a hundred years? No, we won't for sure. However young you are, you must know that much. Don't you know you'll end up a bum if you don't study hard?"

"Hsss."

"You see how your old mom works her fingers to the bone in order to feed you and to send you to school. You must keep that in your mind, and follow what I say and study hard, so that you can succeed and make lots of money when you grow up."

"Hsss, but I know my dad doesn't make any money . . . hsss."

Though spoken by a child, it had enough truth in it to make Madam Yu feel a chill pass through her heart, if she considered it carefully. But she didn't. Instead she just cast a wild glare of vexation at the boy.

In fact, it had been customary for her to blame Jeong Jusa for having failed to provide a living for the family despite all his years of study. She used to scold him viciously, "What's the use of all your scholarly achievements? You boast that you studied classics at the village school for a full fifteen years and on top of that you also had the benefit of the new education in the modern school system at primary school. Well, for all that, you're still starving your family, sitting there idly with your eyes blinking all the time. For all your pretensions of being an educated gentleman, you're certainly worth much less than a woman with no education, a woman wearing a skirt." Having heard such harsh denunciations all his life, Byeongju had formed the opinion that his father hadn't proved to be a good man for all his education, and thus made no money. Therefore, he believed studying hard had nothing to do with becoming a good man or making a lot of money. That was what he saw and it was indisputable.

Because his opinions were such, he couldn't understand why his mother nagged him all the time for not studying hard. Not only did he have no idea how to study hard, but he could also find no motivation in himself to do so, knowing already that he wouldn't become a good person, or a successful man, no matter how hard he studied, as proved by his father's case. In addition, his mother never tried to cajole him into studying hard with gentle words. She always used violence, either abusive words or harsh beatings. Considering all that, he couldn't help but conclude that his mother was ill-treating him only out of spite or hatred for him. So he kept resenting his mother's scolding, hissing his complaints.

Madam Yu had no reasonable reply in store to refute her young boy's apt retort that almost left her feeling defeated. But because she had no inclination to self-examination, all it did was aggravate her anger. She just thought the boy was too bold and shrewd for his age.

"You're such a perverse boy!"

She started to scold him again, glaring at him.

". . . Well then, do you mean to imitate such a hopeless man as your father? What an impossible boy you are! Despite all my constant efforts to make a good man out of you, you're only taking your example from that man, who is no use whatsoever

in the world and is as unmanly as can be . . . You useless seedling
of a rogue!"

Muttering her reproaches, which had at last turned toward
her husband, and clicking her tongue at the same time, she went
back into the room and sat in front of her sewing machine. At
that moment, Jeong Jusa walked into the store.

"What's the problem? Why are you crying again . . . ugh?
What on earth is all the shouting for?"

Jeong Jusa imposed his authority as the master of the house
while assuming an affectionate fatherly tone when talking to his
youngest son.

Jeong Jusa found the situation quite opportune, allowing him
to circumvent his wife's attack on him as he could start finding
fault with her first. Byeongju too was quite elated now that he
had an ally, grunting louder and more frequently.

Madam Yu cast a sidelong glance over her glasses at her husband and returned to her sewing with a disgusted expression
on her face.

"Won't you stop making that sound!"

Jeong Jusa reprimanded the boy first, as if clearing his throat
before starting his real business with his wife, admonishing her.

". . . Why do you make such a racket all the time, when you
could scold the boy quietly?"

Blinking his eyes and stroking his yellow beard, he spoke
sternly with a dignified posture, but Madam Yu, inwardly siz-
zling with anger, muttered to herself, *My, my, what a shameless
thick face that man has!* And then, as if too overwhelmed to say
anything, she just glared at him, shaking her head.

"You know that our place now faces the street, so you must be
more discreet . . . Think what a spectacle you're making. Doesn't
it make our place look like the residence of vulgar, ignorant
people, now?"

"My, my! How great your pride is to be sure! Take it, your damn honor . . . Pshaw! Honor indeed!"

Madam Yu at last shouted back at her husband in high-pitched, contemptuous tones. Jeong Jusa too made his voice rough as he firmly confronted her.

"What good is it when you totally ignore the good name of our family?"

"As if you alone take care of the family! . . . We were on the brink of becoming a bunch of beggars until I was tightfisted and hardworking enough to open this store and keep it going. Now that we manage not to worry about skipping meals, do you think you're entitled to be arrogant like that? . . . You're in your fifties now, so isn't it time you learned the difference between right and wrong? Yet you're still only idling away your time day and night. Do you think the whole world is yours because the eastern sky is bright at sunrise? Because your belly is full and warm, you take your reality to be just a dream, don't you?"

"My goodness, what have I done to deserve such nonsensical complaints?"

"Am I complaining now? Am I really hurling needless, non-sensical complaints? . . . To buy that damned dried pollack, have you traveled all the way to China? . . . Or was it India, that faraway country in the West? And then when it's almost evening, you come back swinging empty hands. What nerve do you have to talk big like that? How dare you, for heaven's sake? Am I doing this only for my own sake?"

"Certainly, that's one thing and this is another. Is it really because I didn't bring back the pollack that you're making this weird scene? And sitting right in the middle of the main street at that? What disgraceful behavior for a woman! Darn it, it's outrageous!"

The couple's squabble was heating up. Seungjae, who'd arrived some time ago, was standing outside the store, hesitating to enter. Seungjae knew the origin of the money that had allowed the family to make their modest living. Gyebong, who'd gone up to Seoul last fall, had written him a letter, filling him in on her sister's life in Seoul for the past two years.

Seungjae interpreted everything Chobong had done as acts of pure self-sacrifice for her family, beginning with her life as Bak Jeho's mistress to her life with that abominable man Hyeongbo after she was abandoned by Bak Jeho. Having come to that conclusion, he couldn't help but harbor strong resentment toward her parents, who could be so shameless as to maintain their livelihood by recklessly sacrificing their own daughter.

He'd assumed that, despite his poverty, Jeong Jusa would be different from Myeongnim's father in that he was a so-called man of culture. This made him all the more angry at Chobong's parents, whose ugly behavior he deemed reprehensible. He was strongly disillusioned by what he'd considered good breeding or being cultured. When men of culture were poor, they tended to utilize their knowledge cunningly to exploit ignorant people rather than to maintain their goodness, he thought.

Since Gyebong had left home last fall, Seungjae had almost stopped visiting Jeong Jusa's family, having no one in particular he wished to see, and because of his resentment toward them. But that day he had come as he was soon to leave Gunsan for good. In addition, Gyebong had written eagerly asking him to observe how her family's business was going and report back in detail for the sake of her sister Chobong, who was always uneasy and anxious about her family back home. So Seungjae came over, dragging his reluctant steps toward the store.

Upon arrival, Seungjae felt even more offended, having found them bickering despite the financial security provided by their daughter's self-sacrifice. He hesitated there because he could neither turn back nor walk into the store while a heated quarrel between husband and wife was going on. He recalled an old story about two beggars.

Two beggars were living together amicably at a humble shrine for the mountain spirit. They not only cared for each other, but never forgot to offer food to the mountain spirit first whenever they brought some back with them.

The mountain spirit had enjoyed their offerings for several years, however meager they were; one day the wife of the spirit suggested giving them some sort of reward, like a treasure, for their unwavering loyalty. The mountain spirit declined the suggestion, arguing that treasure would make them rather unhappy. But as the wife kept pleading, the spirit placed a jewel on the offering stand, saying, "Wait and see what this brings them."

The beggars jumped and danced with delight when they found the gem. Declaring that their lives would be lived in quite a new way, they wanted to celebrate their good fortune and offer a drink to the spirit to express their gratitude. One of them went down to the village to buy some wine.

The beggar who remained on the mountain longed to possess the jewel all to himself, and had a club ready for his friend. When the friend walked into the shrine carrying the wine, he beat him to death. Delighted with his success, he drank a glass of the wine his friend had brought. The friend, who also wanted to have the jewel all to himself, had added poison to the wine, so the beggar who drank the wine died of the poison.

Having watched all the proceedings of the two beggars, the mountain spirit told his wife, "You see what fate the jewel brought to the beggars." The wife nodded in silence.

The story he recalled made Seungjae shudder with a premonition that this couple too might kill each other like the beggars.

The battle between the wife and husband was becoming more heated.

"Yes, I am indeed vulgar in my manners . . . So what? . . ."

Madam Yu shouted and jumped up, pushing back the sewing machine. With that, the machine and its wooden stand fell to the floor. Though she had pushed the machine in a towering rage, she didn't expect it would fall so easily. She flinched out of fear that it might have broken.

Although the sewing machine was not an expensive model, but one produced locally and worth only one hundred and twenty won, it was still a most treasured means of living for her. For her it was much more precious and endearing than a daughter such as the troublesome Gyebong, who always got on her nerves.

If it weren't such a treasured item for her, she would have picked up the sewing machine and smashed it on the floor out of the anger raging inside her, rather than be scared out of her wits at the fall of the machine.

Surprised at the loud clattering sound of the falling sewing machine, Seungjae rushed into the store without hesitation.

Jeong Jusa was happy to see Seungjae, not because he really liked him, but because he could end the losing battle with his wife, thanks to Seungjae's sudden appearance. Jeong Jusa quickly changed his expression and offered an exaggerated welcome to Seungjae. As for Madam Yu, she had enough stored-up anger to continue the fight for quite some time. But she thought it best to stop the fight, for she knew she could no longer continue making a scene in front of Seungjae, who was a welcome guest to her after all.

Hiding their awkwardness, the wife and husband quickly put on smiles, and welcomed Seungjae. It was Seungjae who was embarrassed in the face of the sudden change of the couple, who seemed to have washed away all traces of their fight.

Seungjae had rushed in at the sound of clanking and rattling, for he thought they were having a violent and dangerous confrontation, throwing household items at each other, instead of having a mere verbal squabble. So he couldn't help but feel awkward at the smiling faces of the couple, who seemed to have performed the magic trick of obliterating all traces of what they had been up to.

"How come it's so hard to see you lately? Come and sit over here, please . . ."

Jeong Jusa was doing his best to show his welcome.

"No, thank you, I have to go soon . . . How are Hyeongju and Byeongju doing these days? Are they doing well at school?"

Uttering such words of greeting, Seungjae glanced at the couple and looked around the store. Byeongju was nowhere to be seen, perhaps having fled after stashing away a couple of candy drops.

"Well, it seems they're only pretending to study . . . By the way, I heard that you passed last fall, what do you call it, was it the exam to become a doctor? How wonderful! Congratulations!"

Jeong Jusa looked up and down at the outfit Seungjae was wearing; he still looked like a hireling in an office. He wanted to ask him why he still looked so shabby, but he couldn't. Instead he nodded his head and rephrased his question in a euphemistic way.

". . . Then perhaps you plan to start your own clinic now, I guess?"

"Yes, as a matter of fact, I'm about to start . . ."

"Indeed! You're going to open a clinic? Well, well, isn't it something to be proud of!"

"But it's not something grand at all . . . It's only . . ."

"I don't think so! It must be great . . . You're opening it in Gunsan, aren't you?"

"No, not in Gunsan, it's going to be in Seoul; a friend of mine in Seoul . . ."

"In Seoul?"

"Yes, right. A friend of mine is about to open a clinic in Ahyun-dong that offers low-cost medical care and asked me to run it . . ."

"A clinic for low-cost medical care?"

Jeong Jusa repeated in a disappointed voice. He seemed to think it not worthy of compliment, but something befitting Seungjae whose clothing was still so shabby. Jeong Jusa was inwardly confirming that Seungjae had never been good enough for a proper hospital. But he said,

"Whether a low-cost clinic or what, it's good to hear after all!"

"Oh! It's wonderful news indeed!"

Madam Yu, who'd been waiting for an opportunity to interrupt her husband and start a conversation with Seungjae, cut in.

". . . Then is it all settled like that?"

"Nothing's settled yet. That friend of mine doesn't have a doctor's license yet, so he asked me to run the clinic on his behalf. I'm going to go up to Seoul tomorrow or the day after tomorrow, and discuss the matter in detail before deciding either way . . . Nevertheless, it's possible that I may not come back to Gunsan, so I wanted to say goodbye to you both . . ."

"Oh, that's the reason for this precious visit of yours after such a long absence! I'm grateful you remembered us like this, but how sad that you're leaving the town for good! You've been so obliging to us all along, and we owe you a lot . . . By the way, please come on up into the room. Please take a seat over there for the time being while I clean the mess. We'll miss you so very much . . ."

Making a fuss, Madam Yu hurriedly went into the room and was busy putting the fallen sewing machine back in its place and tidying up the things cluttering the room. Seungjae sat down on a nearby wooden box in the store while Jeong Jusa squatted down on the doorsill and faced Seungjae, resting his chin on his palm. Jeong Jusa wanted Seungjae to stay until sunset or hopefully deep into the night, so that the unfinished fight with his wife would fizzle out. Madam Yu also wished to keep Seungjae around, although for reasons different from her husband's.

Whenever she saw Seungjae, Madam Yu was always reminded of Chobong, and was always swamped with regrets. Now that Seungjae had become a fully qualified doctor and was about to leave for Seoul to open a clinic, she felt inclined to beat her breast in self-reproach.

She hadn't missed the signs that Chobong's heart had been inclined toward Seungjae; and she could tell too that Seungjae had deep affection for Chobong, guessing that from the way he so hurriedly moved out of their house when her marriage to Go Taesu was decided. If only she had allowed them to marry, Chobong's fate would not have been so warped. Moreover Chobong, as the wife of a doctor, would have enjoyed all the benefits of Seungjae's success, and her family too would have benefited from such a son-in-law. But having been swindled by that evil man, Go Taesu, she had not only made her precious daughter the victim of a horrendous debacle but saw her fall into an even more shameful situation. Madam Yu knew her regrets wouldn't be diminished even if she kicked herself repeatedly for having made such a terrible choice for her daughter.

She couldn't deny that her family had all along been taking advantage of her daughter's misfortunes. Through Chobong's marriage to Go Taesu, they had quite a big sum of money at their disposal; and after moving to Seoul, Chobong punctually sent twenty won a month to her family for their livelihood; on top of that, they received as much as five hundred won last fall from her, with which they could open this store and become free from worries about everyday living. Those benefits could never be considered insignificant. At the same time, however, she couldn't forget that in one way or another she had greatly contributed to ruining her daughter's life.

What if she had suppressed her greed and seen the situation from a different perspective at that time? What if she had listened to her second daughter, Gyebong's advice, and looked into Go Taesu's background, instead of hating and scolding Gyebong for her interference? If she had, she would have downright rejected Go Taesu's proposal and perhaps eventually accepted Seungjae as her son-in-law. If she had, although the family's poverty might have been prolonged for two years, Chobong would now be living a happy life as a doctor's wife, happy enough to envy no one. In addition she would be proud of her son-in-law, and receive his assistance without any guilty conscience.

On the other hand, although full of such regrets, Madam Yu was scheming to devise another plan.

Madam Yu, who at first had viewed Seungjae as Chobong's suitor, had begun to see him as a potential husband for Gyebong when she accepted Go Taesu as her first son-in-law two years ago. That's why she closed her eyes to Gyebong's frequent visits to Seungjae and her intimacy with him. If not, she would have sternly forbidden Gyebong to have any form of communication with Seungjae, without doubt.

And then last fall, when she heard that Seungjae had passed the final exam for his doctor's license, she became rather anxious to push through the marriage between Seungjae and Gyebong. However, much to her disapproval, Gyebong went up to Seoul for further study, and since then Seungjae had abruptly stopped visiting her family, causing her deep disappointment.

But today, Seungjae had not only visited them after a long time, but informed them of his plan to move to Seoul and open a clinic. This indeed was auspicious news for Madam Yu, who now wished to find out how he felt about Gyebong, and to encourage him to approach her. She determined to orchestrate chance encounters between Seungjae and Gyebong, which might develop into a romantic relationship. Once she succeeded in that, she thought, things would work out as she desired . . .

Seungjae, sitting face-to-face with Jeong Jusa, began to ask questions, as if in passing, such as how well the store was going, how much money they made every month, and how they managed their living, to which Jeong Jusa replied they were doing fine, and even though they couldn't expect much from the store, the income was enough for them not to have to worry about everyday living, and in addition the earnings from sewing were also pretty good. Seungjae felt he'd gotten enough information to relay to Gyebong, and the aim of his visit was well accomplished.

Toward the end of their conversation, in a tone suggesting he was complaining to himself, Jeong Jusa added that nevertheless, he was really bored at having nothing he could call his own work, and that he really wanted to have the means to start some sort of business, even if it was only to pass his time away. He said this for his wife's benefit, hoping that she would understand why he went to the rice exchange and why he didn't bring back the dried pollack, that is to say, that all his faults were caused by his having nothing to do.

Seungjae, however, understood it as an indirect appeal to him to convey his difficulties to Chobong when he went up to Seoul, in order to solicit more financial support from his unhappy daughter. Utterly disgusted with Jeong Jusa, Seungjae cast one more glance at his ugly face.

At that moment Madam Yu, putting on her apron, stepped out into the store, having cleaned up the room that was cluttered with her sewing material, with the intention of inviting Seungjae into the room. Though it was a bit early for dinner, she wanted to cook something and treat Seungjae.

"By the way, do you know what my second daughter is doing?"

Before walking toward the kitchen, she began to strike up a conversation.

"She went up to Seoul saying that she would pursue further studies. You know what? Instead of getting into a school, she got a job at—ah, what is it? I keep forgetting, though I've heard it so many times—oh, a department store, right, she's working at a department store. I can't understand what trick she's intending to play . . ."

Seungjae, who already knew Gyebong's situation, nevertheless pretended he didn't know.

"You recall how she kept going on about getting into further study. Then whatever whim took hold of her, I don't know. Her sister would have willingly supported her if she wanted to study. Shouldn't she have done that?"

Seungjae kept silent not knowing what to say.

". . . I'm sure she's changed her mind because she's flighty. No doubt she is . . . but despite that, she certainly has many talents. In addition, she's always eager to work hard . . . So all in all she's a pretty promising girl. As to her being frivolous, that too will pass as she grows older and more discreet."

It was the first time Seungjae had ever heard so many good words about Gyebong come from Madam Yu's mouth.

"More education for a bad girl like Gyebong would be a waste of money. It would only add more burdens to her sister!"

Jeong Jusa, ignorant of his wife's covert scheme, cut in and muttered impertinent words.

Madam Yu, angered by his ineptitude, shook her head hard and retorted,

"What do you mean? She's not at all a bad girl. You don't know how mature she is in discerning what's right and wrong!. . . I only wish everybody was as good as she is!"

Giving her husband a sharp rebuke, she pursed her lips. Jeong Jusa, though embarrassed in front of Seungjae, forbore from responding to his wife, for fear that it might rekindle the dispute they'd been having a few moments ago, and instead calmed his temper by twisting his scrawny yellow beard.

"By the way, I have a serious favor to ask of you, Mr. Nam . . ."

Madam Yu took some time to transform her countenance from one of displeasure into one full of affection, and began to address Seungjae again.

". . . When you go up to Seoul, would you kindly admonish or persuade Gyebong to quit her job and resume her studies? Do whatever you can, I'm sure she'll listen to you. I know I can count on you."

"Well, I'm not sure if I can do . . ."

"Yes, yes, you can influence her! I remember how she liked you so very much and looked up to you! So please keep the matter in your mind, and lead her onto the right path, I implore you. And it's not just Gyebong that I'm worried about. You know it's been two years since her sister left home, but I know nothing about what and how she's doing in Seoul. If you live in Seoul and visit them occasionally on your way to work or back home, they'd feel very secure and protected, I think. We, their mother and father, too, would feel quite relieved. So, Mr. Nam, when you go up to Seoul, please . . . no, I think this would be even better, how about asking Chobong to empty one of her rooms and you live in it? How wonderful that would be . . . Shall I write a letter right away?"

"No, no, please don't bother. I don't want to impose . . ."

Seungjae hurriedly shook his head. He was assuming that this talkative and shrewd lady was scheming to bring him and Chobong back together by arranging occasions to renew their old feelings and relationship one way or another. However, for Seungjae, that was totally out of the question.

It was true that since she was his first love, he still felt some vague longing for Chobong and was deeply sad about her disastrous fate, feeling deep compassion for her. But he'd never even dreamed of the possibility of rekindling the old feelings, let alone the possibility of taking her as his wife. On the contrary, his heart at present was strongly inclined toward Gyebong.

Gyebong, at last, had succeeded in capturing Seungjae's heart. Seungjae himself hadn't been aware of it until she abruptly left for Seoul. In her absence, Seungjae felt as empty as if his own body had flown away, and so came to realize how strongly he felt attached to her. Now he had determined to go to Seoul, not just to run a clinic, but mainly drawn by the force of Gyebong; perhaps even "one strand of her hair" would have been strong enough to pull him to Seoul.

Politely declining the couple's ardent invitation to stay for dinner, Seungjae left the store and, making his way through the Bean Sprout Pass, hurried to the night school held at S Girls' School. It was already half past five, and he had to rush to get there on time. Moreover, he would have to skip the plan to visit Myeongnim's place on his way to school because he had wasted too much time by overstaying at Jeong Jusa's place. He felt bad about that.

The night school had started in the spring of the previous year, initiated by a few people residing in Gaebok-dong and Dunbaemi. They obtained the permission of the school to use the classrooms during the late afternoons and evenings in order to teach basic numeracy as well as basic Korean and Japanese writing to those kids who worked during the day or couldn't afford to go to primary school. One among those who started the school was an acquaintance of Seungjae, who had asked him to teach arithmetic for one hour every evening.

Seungjae, who at that time was very enthusiastic about all kinds of activities tending toward enlightenment, had promptly accepted that assignment and had been teaching there for over a year.

Just as he arrived at the foot of the hill where the school was located, the school bell began to ring and by the time he entered the school, the students were all gathered in the class-room, already making a loud noise. Seungjae headed directly for the classroom without stopping by the teachers' room.

As the kids saw him enter, they stopped talking abruptly and sat up straight. It was as if a hawk had passed through a bamboo grove where sparrows were squawking. There were only fifteen or so students in the room. When the school started, there had been as many as eighty students, but as time went by, they dropped off one by one, leaving a small group of only fifteen or so in the class.

Seungjae sent the monitor to the teachers' room to bring the roll book and looked around at each of the students' faces, who were all staring at him with their heads up. It was customary for him to look around the classroom before starting his lesson. But today, knowing that it would be the last time he would see them, he looked at them more intently with a special feeling.

They all looked rather pathetic. Although he'd been quite enthusiastic about the night school at the beginning, it wasn't long before he lost all interest in it. Since the winter of last year, he began to feel disillusioned about so-called enlightenment or educating people; he sensed that it could at times produce dysfunctional people and even reached the skeptical conclusion that it in fact could poison them rather than offer benefits, considering the extremely difficult reality that surrounded the students. As such skepticism overshadowed his mind, he lost all his initial eagerness and was often tempted to quit the work.

However, he couldn't reveal what was in his mind, he couldn't say that he wanted to quit, since he had no justifiable excuse to present to the other teachers or students. So he halfheartedly continued teaching at the night school. But now that he was going to Seoul, which gave him a good reason to quit, he wouldn't need to feel ashamed of leaving the school.

Though he saw no good purpose in educating them, he wasn't totally devoid of some affection for them. Especially when he thought he would be leaving those pitiable kids behind in order to seek his own way, he couldn't help but feel a certain sense of regret.

They all looked as though they would still feel hungry even after devouring a full bowl of rice; some looked pale and others looked yellowish. The kids with a darker complexion were the better nourished ones. Nearly half of them still had the thick grime that had accumulated during the winter caked on their necks, on the back of their hands and behind their ears. Their clothes were in perfect harmony with their looks; some were still in their winter clothes, the shabby tops and trousers padded with cotton; some had changed into unlined tops and trousers; and some were wearing tattered Western-style suits, which were something to be proud of in those days.

Seungjae had visited all their homes at least once or twice. And in those where there were sick people, he had visited innumerable times to treat the patients. So he knew very well how bad their circumstances were. Whoever he looked at, he could recall and visualize every feature of their homes.

Mostly they lived in run-down huts whose roofs were leaking. If there were two rooms, there were two families, and if three rooms, three families, and so on. Rarely did just one family occupy the whole house. When you opened the door, you would find the room full of a bad stench; in the darkness would be lying a woman with a belly as round as a drum and a face as yellow as a cucumber flower, or a man with black spots on his face like fermented malt because of jaundice, coughing heavily.

Or in another room you would find a baby fiercely crying with its face all smeared with tears and snot; like a piglet, the baby's waist was usually bound with a string, tethered to the lock of a chest in the corner of the room. In this case, both the mother and the father would be out at work. Or in some other cases, you would find both the man and wife squatting among their children, indicating that they were out of work, and probably had starved for a couple of days.

Whenever he visited those houses, Seungjae felt distressed, but especially when he found a family starving with no food to eat, he always gave away all the money he had in his pocket to the family. If he didn't have any money about him, he always sent them a few won later. In addition, for those students who came to school with drooping shoulders and hungry stomachs, he usually bought some pancakes or rice cakes, which were certainly much more welcome and necessary gifts to them than learning.

Because of this charity work, Seungjae spent all his money left over after paying for his everyday necessities. In the autumn of last year when he had passed the exam for the doctor's license, the owner of the clinic raised his monthly salary by forty won, doubling his pay. Out of the eighty won, he spent about twenty won on the medicines for his free medical care, and about ten won for his living expenses. The remaining fifty odd won was always sucked into the bottomless pit of charity. However, unlike earlier days, he no longer felt any satisfaction or pleasure in his charity work. Rather his discontent and melancholy mood grew more intense every day, as he was overwhelmed by the enormity of the ongoing poverty, feeling helpless when facing it.

The rumor that Seungjae sought out the poor and sick people and treated them without receiving any fees had spread to every corner of the city, whose population was over sixty thousand. So at any time throughout the year, on average he had more than ten patients under his care, though he took on only those who were seriously ill with no money for treatment.

In addition, innumerable people flocked to seek his help, complaining of boils, heartburn, or other troubles. Even if he had a general hospital, he couldn't have provided sufficient treatment for all of them. On top of that, he had to work at his clinic during the day, so he could offer free medical care only after his working hours, that is, only in late afternoons and at night. It was indeed too much for him to handle alone.

Putting that aside, Seungjae had an additional problem, that of feeding starving people. He could invest only forty odd won for this every month, but considering the number of needy people he had to support, it was just like distributing a grain of rice to each starving person, giving no one any real satisfaction.

He was often dumbstruck when he considered how many starving people there must be throughout the nation if there were so many in this small city of Gunsan.

Seungjae, who had begun to help the poor people he happened to meet out of pure sympathy, was now turning his attention to the wider reality in which unfortunate people were an integral part. This might be a sign of his intellectual growth.

He had begun to be aware of the size of the problems, but not the nature of the problems pervading society. He had come to the realization that there were many people who were unfortunate because of their poverty, sickness, and ignorance, but he was yet to discover the fundamental causes of their misery or how to tackle those problems.

Therefore Seungjae, whose humanism was only naive and simple, could feel nothing but despair over the social problems he encountered every day. He knew only too well that a few individuals, no matter how clever they might be, could never save the infinite number of needy people. Giving money or offering free medical care to those who stretched out their hands for charity could be done more to ease the donor's conscience than to help the unfortunate.

Having reached such an understanding, he usually asked himself what the right path to pursue would be; he found no answer, or not much of one. Feeling frustrated and helpless, he just wanted to go to Seoul where Gyebong was. Just at this juncture in his life, he was offered an opportunity to move to Seoul.

So Seungjae's move to Seoul would be a sort of escape from this deadlocked situation; Gyebong, of course, was the strong loadstone that drew Seungjae to Seoul, but he also imagined that once he got to Seoul, where he could breathe fresh air, he might find new ways to tackle the social problems.

"Well, today . . .," he nodded his head a couple of times meaninglessly before he started to address the students.

". . . Let's put aside our study, for I want to have a conversation with you."

"Yeah, yeah!" the students chorused with glee.

The classroom was abuzz with noise as the boys were busy putting away their books and notebooks.

"Tomorrow I'm moving to Seoul . . . so I won't be able to meet with you any longer . . ."

At this surprising news, the students were speechless for a moment, but soon each of them began to chatter about what was uppermost in their mind.

One expressed his regrets for losing their teacher, another pleaded with him not to leave, yet another asked the departure time of the train, saying he wanted to see him off at the station, and the rest of them were saying this or that to each other, creating a noisy commotion in the classroom.

Seungjae, who was staring at them in silence, at last hit the table with his teaching rod.

"Stop talking and be quiet please!"

The students stopped at once and turned their heads to look at the teacher.

". . . Well, I will ask each of you a question, and you must answer, standing up one by one as I call your name, all right?"

"Yes, sir."

Though he'd said he would have a conversation with them, he knew he couldn't make up stories of rabbits or tigers as he used to do, on the day they were parting. Having pondered for a while, he came up with an interesting topic.

"You, Chang-yun . . ."

Seungjae pointed at a boy in the middle of the room with his rod, and a wiry lad of about fifteen stood up instantly. He was wearing tattered black trousers that had few intact parts and a cotton flannel shirt with varicolored patterns. On his forehead was an ugly scar, and his eyes were sparkling, looking audacious.

"Uhm, Changyun, what do you want to become when you grow up after studying here?"

The boy responded promptly to the question Seungjae put to him in a rather slow tempo.

"I'll become a teacher like you, sir."

"Like me? Why?"

"Because I like you, sir."

Seungjae smiled, thinking to himself, this indeed was a shrewd boy.

"And next, how about you?"

The tallest boy in the class stood up in the last row. His slack features made him appear rather thickheaded, though his eyes were big and deep set.

"You, what do you want to do after studying here?"

"Sir, I, I want to become the Japanese Government-General in Korea."

The students looked back at him and some of them had smiles in the corner of their lips. Seungjae too barely suppressed his smile and asked.

"So what do you want to do when you become the Governor-General?"

"I want to receive a high salary, sir."

"How much do you want?"

"One hundred won . . . No, much more than that."

"What would you like to do with such a high salary?"

"Just spend as I wish, and then . . ."

The next boy who was called up was Jongswei. He was over twelve already, but still had a runny nose and was wearing grimy, tattered cotton clothes.

"What would you like to do when you grow up after studying?"

The boy kept his head lowered, just casting sideways glances at the other students around him. He'd always been a very gloomy boy, but today, he looked particularly downcast.

"Well, Jongswei, why don't you speak out?"

"Er . . ."

"Yes?"

"Er . . ."

"Yes, I'm listening."

"A policeman, that's what I want to be, sir."

"Police—man?"

A couple of boys in the back row began to giggle and Jongswei, who already felt timid, became even more intimidated and lowered his head further.

"So you want to become a policeman?"

"Yes."

"I wonder why you want that?"

"Er . . ."

"Yes?"

"Er, my father's . . ."

Unable to finish his words, Jongswei bit his finger.

"Is it that your father told you to become a policeman?"

"No, sir."

"What then?"

"I want my father not to be arrested."

Seungjae was more befuddled at this answer. The other boys in the class erupted into laughter. After scolding them, Seungjae asked,

"Jongswei, did the police arrest your father, is that it?"

"Ye-es."

"Oh no. How awful!"

His father, Mr. Jeon, lived in Sajaengi and worked at the pier as a porter with an A-frame, barely making a living, that is, living from hand-to-mouth. But a few days ago, he had sprained his ankle and came to Seungjae to get some iodine tincture. In addition he had a big family to support—four children, including an infant and his wife. Seungjae knew it all.

"Well, when did it happen?"

Seungjae came down to Jonswei's seat, gazing at his lowered face.

"Yesterday evening, sir."

"I see! . . . But for what? What did he do?"

"Er . . ."

"Did he fight with someone?"

"No, sir. It was because he stole some rice."

At this answer, Seungjae instantly regretted asking. He thought, Oh my! It's not a question to ask in front of other students. But it was too late. Unwittingly, he looked around at the other students with a fierce scowl. Intimidated by the teacher's fierce expression, they sat stock still, not daring to laugh or whisper among themselves.

Seungjae at last relaxed and went back to the teacher's platform, dejected, breathing a deep sigh.

"So, Jongswei, dear."

"Yes?"

"That's why you want to become a policeman? . . . Because you wouldn't arrest your father even if he stole rice?"

"That's right, sir."

"I see . . ., you want to become a policeman so that you wouldn't arrest your father?"

"Yes."

"Then you think your father, who stole and ate someone else's rice, is a good man?"

"No, sir."

"No?"

"That's right, sir."

"Then is he a bad father? When he did that because you and your siblings were starving to death?

"That's why I wouldn't arrest him, ever."

Seungjae couldn't continue his talk, choked by something that was rising in his throat. His eyes were smarting as well, as if he'd read a sad children's story.

THE PHARMACIST WHO'D coerced Seungjae into coming along to this bawdy saloon was already tipsy and was having fun holding two barmaids, one in each arm. Two barmaids were in the room, one to serve the pharmacist, the other for Seungjae, but both were playing with the pharmacist now. Seungjae, who'd never been in such a place in his life, abstained from touching anything in the room, let alone food or drinks, fearful of contracting syphilis.

The women's behavior was obnoxious, beyond imagination, almost animalistic. Seungjae couldn't look them in the eye. But the pharmacist was fondling the breasts of one of the women with one hand while with the other hand he was . . . The two women, however, didn't mind his caresses at all, as though he were merely touching their cheeks instead of those private parts. No, they were rather enjoying themselves, giggling all along. Seungjae, overwhelmed by abhorrence, kept his face turned sideways to avoid seeing them.

"Hey, Mr. Nam, Mr. Nam?"

The pharmacist, who was now rolling around on the floor with one woman, called Seungjae loudly, inviting him to join him with a fuzzy look. Seungjae pretended not to have heard him.

"Hey, Mr. Nam, aren't you also a bachelor? Come on, let's spend the night here. One won would be enough to cover everything. And it'll be my treat, for sure."

He openly encouraged Seungjae, while winking at the other woman, who had no partner now. Having understood the signal, the woman rushed at Seungjae to embrace him. Seungjae and the woman, who held onto his neck, fell down and tumbled together onto the floor. Seungjae, scared out of his wits, struggled to get out of the woman's grasp to no avail.

"This gentleman must be a eunuch?"

Making fun of Seungjae, the woman began to fumble around the lower part of his body, at which Seungjae pushed her away with all his might, stood up and was about to head toward his coat and hat in the corner of the room.

"Stop, stop a minute, Mr. Nam. You have to watch a really interesting show . . ."

The pharmacist raised his teetering body up and took out a fifty-jeon coin from his wallet, turning his head toward the woman who had been with Seungjae.

"You know what this is?"

"Pshaw, a mere fifty jeon!"

"In the Western world, they use gold coins, but in Korea, we don't have gold coins, do we? So please take this silver coin instead, won't you?"

"I wouldn't do it for a mere fifty jeon, ever!"

"All right, if you go all the way, I'll give you one won on top of that."

"Really?"

"I wouldn't lie to you, would I? Don't worry . . . just do it, dear. But remember you ought to . . . your bottom and all, right?"

"Sure, sure, no problem at all!"

"Come on, Mr. Nam, just watch the show. It's something you

can only see when you go overseas to Western countries. And then let's enjoy the night to the fullest, OK?"

The pharmacist put the coin on top of a matchbox and sat back. The woman, who was supposed to perform some rare feat, began to take off her skirt. Seungjae dashed out into the street before anyone could hold him back, barely putting on his shoes. Seungjae had waited because he assumed she was going to perform some sort of feat with her mouth using the silver coin. Seungjae, who had had no time to get his coat or hat, walked back toward his place, shivering all over with cold. He felt so sick at the lewd scene that he had to fight off fits of nausea time and time again, all the way back.

This had happened one night the previous winter when he accompanied the pharmacist to a bawdy saloon out of curiosity. That night the pharmacist had come over to his residence and urged him to come with him to visit a bar where women serve the customers. Persuaded by the pharmacist, Seungjae went along out of curiosity to observe the atmosphere of such a place, as well as its customs and manner of dealing with customers, though he ended up running away from the place as if he'd had a bucket of filthy water thrown in his face.

He couldn't have imagined the crazy extent of the bawdiness in such a place; he felt totally indignant at the obscenity wildly let loose there, wondering how humans (especially women) could degenerate to such a low level. Chewing over the memory of that night last winter, he was heading toward Gaemyeong-ok, a raunchy bar where Myeongnim was working. It was located up a hill in Gaebok-dong, an area where such bars clustered together.

He finished his class at around six o'clock and left the school after exchanging farewells with two other teachers, informing them that he would leave Gunsan the following night. Then he headed straight to this raunchy place.

At Gaemyeong-ok, no guests were to be seen, because the sun hadn't yet set. In the rooms, some women in groups of two or three were idly lying on the floor, humming songs, some others in their underwear were washing their faces making hissing sounds. To Seungjae's eyes, all the women, who were peeping out to see who was coming, looked as though they had distorted faces, or their foreheads, cheeks, and nose bridges were decaying, camouflaged with cosmetics.

In Seungjae's mind, this sort of place was a sewer through which insane humans reverted to behaving like animals. Unless they were insane, no humans could become so brazenly wanton, Seungjae thought.

Therefore, as he assumed that those women who were crazy enough "to revert to behaving like animals" were responsible for their own conduct, he felt no pity for them, and instead, despised them as filthy women.

Recognizing Seungjae's voice, Myeongnim, full of delight, rushed out of her room. But the moment she faced Seungjae, she stopped short, not smiling, her eyes welling with tears. She abruptly turned back, ran back to her room, and flopped down on the floor crying.

Myeongnim couldn't understand why she was crying. She wasn't feeling sad, nor did she have any accurate understanding of the nature of this place. She was rather apathetic about being here. The only thing that had bothered her was being away from her parents, placed among strangers. So perhaps she was crying like a child who came upon a familiar and friendly face in a strange place where she had felt lonesome.

Tears sprang to Seungjae's eyes as well, seeing Myeongnim's eyes welling with tears. He indeed was sorrowful for the right reason.

Throwing such an innocent and frail-looking girl into this

sewer, and leaving her to revert to behaving like an animal in company with crazy, wanton people, was something Seungjae couldn't bear. It was truly sad to see her in this environment, but it also made him more anxious and fretful.

Though Seungjae maintained that pity or charity was nothing but a means of consoling one's own troubled conscience in the face of others' misery, at present such a cynical opinion had no influence whatsoever on his determination to save Myeongnim from this pit at whatever cost.

For the last three days Seungjae had been running around like a madman, desperately seeking ways to make money. Seungjae being Seungjae, he didn't have much success. However, it must be acknowledged that no stone was left unturned.

Three days ago, Myeongnim came by at night to bid farewell to Seungjae, informing him that she had been sold at the price of two hundred won, and was due to move into Gaemyong-ok the following morning. He was absolutely stunned at the news, as he had continued admonishing her parents never to dare sell their daughter to such a degenerate place whenever he saw them. And they seemed to be listening to him. He had never expected the situation would take such a sudden turn for the worse.

The moment he heard about it, Seungjae jumped up, clenching his fists, ready to confront her parents. But Myeongnim said that her father, who wanted to become a retail merchant, had already left home early that morning to go to an island, carrying that two hundred won to purchase some dried fish. Hearing this, Seungjae plumped down on the floor with frustration.

All night long Seungjae racked his brains over ways to obtain that huge sum of money. The moment dawn broke, he ran to Yun Dalsik, the owner of his clinic, and asked him to lend him two hundred won in exchange for postponing his departure to Seoul and staying on in his employment for three or four months longer. Mr. Yun, who'd received a flat refusal from Seungjae a few days ago when he had asked him to remain at the clinic for two more years, was spiteful enough to say no point-blank to this appeal. In addition, he knew that Seungjae's staying on for three or four months more wouldn't make much difference, so there was nothing to be grateful about.

Seungjae, who'd been naively optimistic about this plan, was quite dismayed, having no recourse left. He at last decided to sell all his books, contacted a secondhand bookseller and asked him to bid a price. The dealer was rather reticent, saying that in this small city of Gunsan such medical books and natural science books weren't much in demand and that he would have a hard time selling them again. But he added reluctantly that if Seungjae had to sell them anyway, he could pay eighty won for the lot of them.

There were about four hundred books in his collection, the total price of which, when Seungjae purchased them, could easily amount to over one thousand won. Seungjae, however, begrudgingly accepted the price and sold them all. And then he made fifteen won more by selling most of the things he had in his room, including his desk, his clothes, and even kitchen utensils. So if he set aside five won for his travel expenses to Seoul, the total he could use for Myeongnim was only ninety won.

However hard he tried, he could come up with no other means of making more money. If he were a bit bolder, regardless of eventual failure or success, he might have sent a telegram asking for a loan to the man in Seoul who wanted to start a clinic with him. Yet he was too inexperienced, a man who had never been involved in lending or borrowing money, to think of such a recourse. Even if the thought had struck him, he would have given it up, because of the humiliation he had recently suffered on account of the owner of the Geumho Clinic.

Feeling helpless and frustrated, Seungjae could do nothing but belatedly regret that he hadn't saved a few won every month for such a contingency.

Having no other way to make more money, he decided to try his luck with the ninety won and headed for Gaemyong-ok. Even if he couldn't get Myeongnim out of the dreadful place, he would at least be able to bid her farewell, assuring her that he would come back later.

Seungjae felt quite uneasy; trying to suppress the tears that welled up at the sight of the crying Myeongnim, he nervously looked around without saying anything for some time. Then he left her alone, asking to see the owner of the place.

A corpulent woman came out, saying that she was the owner. She carried in her hand a fan with a full *Taegeuk* pattern on it, too early for the season. Seungjae was a bit daunted by her stout figure as well as her luxurious attire.

She seemed to be about fifty years of age; with her cheeks drooping down to her double chin, her complexion glowing rosily, her long ramie skirt trailing on the ground, and her gait upright and pompous—overall she looked genteel and big-hearted, and almost like a rich lady setting out on a pleasure outing. But the fact that she was wearing rings, gold or platinum, or some with gems sparkling on them, on each of her fingers made her look rather ostentatious. The vulgarity was quite out of tune with her gentle manners and gracious outfit.

The lady studied the appearance of Seungjae, looking him up and down, and asked,

"Who are you, please? What business do you want to see me about?"

She treated him as though he were one of those peddlers who sell cheap things such as gilt hairpins or cosmetics without brand names.

Seungjae could easily be mistaken for a peddler, as he was wearing dusty and shabby clothes while holding an old doctor's bag to his chest. He appeared to be about to pester her to buy his goods.

"Well, are you . . . the owner of the house?"

Seungjae started with a quite unnecessary question.

"I told you so already, didn't I? This place has no master. So if you have any business here, talk to me . . . What is it, please?"

"Ah, then . . . a girl named Myeongnim is here . . ."

"Myeongnim? Myeongnim?"

"Uh, she came here the day before yesterday . . . She's from the Yang family, living up over the other side of this hill . . ."

Seungjae was surprised at the audacity of the woman, who pretended not to know the girl whom he had just seen in the place. But he soon realized his mistake when the woman answered,

"Oh, you mean Hongdo, Mr. Yang's daughter! Yes, she's here. Well, are you here to meet her? Are you a relative?"

"I'm not a relative . . . I came to consult with the owner regarding her."

"You want to consult with me? I see . . . Who are you, by the way?"

"I'm uh . . . Nam Seungjae working at the Geumho Clinic . . ."

"Ah, indeed, you are!"

No sooner had he ended his words than the countenance of the mistress brightened up and she began to pour out exaggerated compliments.

"My, my, I didn't know that! Please come in and take a seat. It's my first time to meet you in person, but I've heard so much about you. I know well enough about your charitable activities and your benevolence is indeed something I do admire . . . Please come this way . . ."

Seungjae was at a loss for words as he was too embarrassed at her fuss. He silently followed her into the main room and sat on the silk cushion she offered.

The mistress continued with her fussing, offering cigarettes that he didn't smoke, and having her maid empty the ashtray. At last she took her seat and resumed her compliments for Seungjae's good deeds. Definitely her praises had no meaning—they were a sort of greeting of a woman who loves talking, and has a fluent tongue at that.

Seungjae felt it would be easier to bring up the matter as the mistress's attitude toward him had decidedly changed, from aloof and suspicious to friendly and trusting.

At length the mistress finished with her compliments and asked,

"Well, what about the girl, may I ask? Do you know her from before? Or is it that you're from the same village?"

Thus the mistress offered an apt opportunity for Seungjae to bring up his business. Seungjae began to explain the whole history of his relationship with Myeongnim, how he got to know her when he treated her as a patient, how for the past three years since then he had doted on her like a baby sister, how he was pained by the unexpected news that she had been sold to this place, and how he had tried all possible means to make the money to retrieve her, but could come up with only ninety won. And then he made a plea, acknowledging his temerity, that if she could release her, accepting that ninety won for the time being, he would send the remaining balance from Seoul within three months. He tried to persuade her with all sincerity, explaining everything carefully.

The lady listened to Seungjae's words, intermittently interjecting with words such as, "Ah, is that so?" or "Ah, I see." When Seungjae finished his talk, she at last let out a long exclamation,

"Hah-hah!" which could be taken either as a groan of pity or a sigh of admiration or both, and then lit a new cigarette.

"How commendable of you . . . what you're trying to do! . . . However . . ."

After puffing at her cigarette a couple of times, and having pretended to be in deep thought for a moment, she resumed,

". . . I don't think that's possible. I'm really sorry that I have to disappoint you, but . . ."

Seungjae had expected that his attempt would be in vain and had prepared himself for it, yet as he heard the response, he couldn't help but feel dejected. He remained silent with his head down.

". . . I wish I could do what you ask, considering your good intentions. But please think of my situation. Am I not in a business, whether good or bad? Haven't I obtained the girl to do business with, investing a lot of money despite my difficult financial situation?"

Seungjae remained silent.

"It would be regretful enough to let her go before having any business done by her. Then just think, how can I release her without having full reimbursement, when I've earned no money through her yet? The money I paid to Mr. Yang was what I squeezed out while I endured many adverse problems. Am I being unfair? Can you understand my situation?"

"Yes, I can . . ."

Seungjae reluctantly nodded his head.

"So, in appreciation of what you have kindly done for the girl, I'd be willing to release her without any objection, if I can recuperate the full amount I invested in her in one payment. That much I can concede, I say, to show my respect for you."

Engulfed by a sense of helplessness, Seungjae was speechless, even forgetting his other mission, that of pleading with her to take good care of Myeongnim for the time being.

"By the way, Mr. Nam, listen to me . . ."

The mistress of the house, perhaps because she felt she hadn't concluded the conversation properly, or simply because she wanted to talk more, resumed speaking with a serious face, but in a much softer voice. Seungjae raised his head, curious.

"I know this is a bit presumptuous, but I say what you're trying to do would be useless in the end. It's useless indeed . . ."

"What? . . . Why do you think so?"

"Huh-huh, I know you feel that girl is in an extremely pitiful position here, so you want to save her, don't you?"

"Pi—tiful? Uhm, right, that's true!"

"Right? However, if you knew the full extent of her situation, you'd see that it's much better for her to stay here! Surely much better!"

"Much better? . . . My goodness!"

"I say it again, much better without doubt, I assure you!"

"Much better, what nonsense . . ."

"Uh-uh! You don't know the reality . . ."

The lady shook her head so vigorously as to make her cheeks shake.

"Well, sir, you must know her family's financial situation, surely? They have to skip meals as often as not. I think even a meal a day is hard to maintain . . . What could be sadder than starving all the time! Their stomachs keep making growling sounds till they hurt, but they have nothing else to do but to grip their bellies and grieve over their poverty. What could be more sorrowful than that? Starving is the most difficult misery to endure and starving people are the most piteous of all, I think. Unless you yourself have experienced the pain of starvation firsthand, you couldn't know the extent of the agony. It's indeed something no human should be subjected to, and in addition . . ."

The lady's fervor grew even more heated and she moved closer to Seungjae, pushing up her sleeves.

"Damn it all, when even creatures like birds have their own portion of food in the world, how can a human be left with nothing to eat? Is it fair? You know that even wicked criminals are fed in prison, and when they execute a criminal, they feed him before the execution, don't they? Then is it just if an innocent person is left to starve to death? Answer me please, can anybody say it's acceptable for a human with all his limbs intact to starve to death?"

"Of course it's not all right. No one tells them to starve. Each person has to find a way and . . ."

As Seungjae stammered for a moment, the mistress cut in and reinforced her attack.

"Then, what are they supposed to do? Are they supposed to dig and eat soil as if they were moles?"

"If they dig like moles, carry burdens like ants, food would come along naturally."

Seungjae said this, but without any confidence.

He had witnessed so many cases that contradicted his theory while he was visiting the families of the night-school students. None of them was unwilling to work; they were simply either out of work or too ill to work.

Considering what he'd seen, he ought to agree with the lady. But Seungjae wouldn't and couldn't do that. Despite it being contrary to the "facts," agreeing with her would be diametrically opposed to the "standard of humanity" he maintained for himself. The truth, however, was that that "standard of humanity" wasn't something he'd attained through his own probing into reality, but a conclusion provided by others. He'd read about it, and adopted it as his own principle. It was nothing but an idol he took in and worshipped with the hope that it would solve all problems, giving no second thoughts about its viability.

In other words, Seungjae was upholding a conclusion whose provenance was unknown to him, blindly trusting its efficacy. Therefore, no matter how loudly he advocated it, it was merely ignorance.

"You don't need to explain yourself!"

The lady retreated a bit with an awkward smile, as if feeling embarrassed for her overzealous argument.

". . . I know that there are horrible people; some rogues and bitches make their daughters prostitutes simply to purchase their own comfort, and, from what I've heard, some are so depraved that they sell their daughters to a brothel or a bar to get opium. But most of them—nine out of ten—sell their daughters because they couldn't bear starvation any longer. I've been in this business many years, so I know these kinds of situations inside and out. Would a hungry tiger hesitate before attacking a magistrate? No, no. When there's no alternative but to starve to death or become a thief, which do you think people will choose? Do you really think stealing is a better choice than working in this kind of place?"

"Surely not!"

Seungjae in fact couldn't determine which was better.

"You see! Stealing is not an alternative, is it? Then should they sit with their hands tied and starve to death? My goodness, born into this world as a human being, how can anyone endure the fate of starving to death? Is there any worse fate than that in the whole world? Once they're born into this world, they're entitled to live regardless of whether their backgrounds are good or bad. They must find a way to live, whatever that may be. Can you blame them for that? Is the will to live wrong?"

Seungjae was at a loss for words, cornered in a dead-end alley. He just sat there silently, somewhat embarrassed.

"Listen, Mr. Nam, that's not all."

The lady of the house, who kept puffing out smoke, resumed her talk, but this time, in a low voice, casting a sideways glance at the room opposite.

"I'm not sure what you would do eventually, but I assure you that even if you take her out of this place, that wouldn't be a solution."

"Eh? . . . Why?"

"They would sell her again!"

"Again?"

"Yes, you wait and see."

"No way! How can that be!"

"They would . . . I say it because I've seen it happen many times, not just once or twice. How long would that mere two hundred won last? You don't imagine that money would enable them to live for long, do you? Doing business? Bah! If that business sustains them for one year, that would be long enough. If it fails, then what would they do? It wouldn't be the first time now. They'd find it easy to do it again, when they remembered the sweet taste of the easy money they got from selling the daughter the first time. They were hungry then, and they're hungry now. It's the same situation. Why would they hesitate now? If her parents were the kind of people who wouldn't sell her the second time, they wouldn't have sold her the first time. Just think, doesn't it make sense?"

"Indeed!"

Seungjae nodded his head repeatedly, consenting to the probability of what she was saying. And now it seemed to him that his plan of sending money from Seoul for Myeongnim's release might need to be reconsidered.

"Perhaps it could be arranged for her to be sent to a farmer's house in the countryside as a future daughter-in-law . . ."

Seungjae said this mostly to himself, as the idea suddenly popped into his head, but the lady of the house responded to it at once, shaking her head.

"That would be useless as well!"

"Why is that so?"

"Look, Mr. Nam. Do you have any clear idea about the real situation of those wives in the countryside? I'm sure you don't. So listen to me . . . They're also starving for most of the year except during the summer when they have enough barley rice to feed themselves. Do you think they have proper clothing to cover their bodies? During the scorching summer, they wrap their bodies in cotton clothes, unable to afford cool hemp clothes, while in the coldest winter they shiver all the time, wearing unlined clothes and walking barefoot. Yet they're driven to hard work day and night! They indeed live like horses and cows! They don't even look like humans . . . In addition they have mothers-in-law who without exception persecute them all the time, and even beat them often. Ten to one their husbands are also wife-beaters! I think even a dog's lot would be better. Their fate is worse than a dog's, I'm sure. So let me sum up their fate once again—they suffer from lack of food, lack of clothing, yet work as hard as animals until their backs are bent, only to be beaten day and night. Serving one husband, being legally married to a horrible bumpkin, is it anything to be proud of? For what great glory and honor do they have to live like that? The legendary Chunhyang, that beautiful emblem of faithful womanhood, persevered and endured all persecutions only because of her lover, Master Lee, but he was a nice guy of great ability whom she dearly loved. Just think, what girl would consider chastity such a high virtue as to hold onto an abusive country bumpkin husband despite all the hardships she suffers? The world is changing . . . I say this as I know you really care for the girl. Would you like to see her become such a farmer's wife? . . . If I were you, I'd rather leave her here than offering her such a fate!"

If women in the countryside really lived as miserably as the lady described, it would be saving Myeongnim from this depraved place only to relocate her to a different sort of bad place, he thought. It would be a shameful act, self-righteously imposing his ethical values upon her, disregarding her misery. Not only that, but he would also feel uneasy because of his affection for her if she had to live such a hard life. The woman was right, he wouldn't be able to bear such a pitiful fate for Myeongnim.

"Then, uh, would you do it this way?"

Seungjae, who had been pondering the matter for some time with his head down, at last spoke, raising his head.

"In what way? Do you have any good idea?"

"I'm leaving for Seoul by the night train tomorrow. I'll send the full amount as soon as possible, so . . ."

"Well, if you do, I will surely release her from here. But as I just said, her parents will soon sell . . ."

"No, don't send her back to her parents. I'll send you some more money for her fare, so send her to Seoul please . . ."

"Ah ah, I understand! . . . That wouldn't be difficult. But wouldn't her parents object to it?"

"I can take care of it. When I explain it to them, they won't object, I'm sure."

"If her parents have no objection, I can do as you wish. Then well . . ., it's all settled. She's still a young child, so I wouldn't make her do anything indecent for the time being. Don't worry about her. I'll take good care of her until she leaves this house. So do what you said at your earliest convenience, then I'll send her to you."

Seungjae was quite relieved at the lady's reasonable assurances and was grateful to her. The idea had suddenly struck him that he could bring Myeongnim to Seoul and give her the opportunity of apprenticing as a nurse under his guidance or even send her to a school when he could afford it.

He was quite happy with this idea, and regretted that he hadn't come up with it earlier. If he had, and told her father about it, he would have been more patient rather than selling her so rashly. Then he himself wouldn't have gone through all those unpleasant troubles.

Seungjae stood up to leave after asking her to take good care of Myeongnim one more time as well as reassuring her that he would send the money within two months.

The mistress of the house followed him to the gate and in turn asked him to settle the business without any problems. She added that if it were someone else, she would've asked for interest for the money as well as the costs of her lodging, but since Seungjae was such a generous young man, she was asking only for the original sum of two hundred won out of her gratitude for him. Seungjae was even more grateful to her, on seeing that a woman running a whorehouse could be so open-minded and sympathetic.

Myeongnim came out to see him off, smiling, but with her eyes all swollen. Seungjae without any words looked at her for some time, as she stood at the gate with her head lowered. She'd already begun developing the features of a young woman though she was only fifteen. Seungjae couldn't feel comfortable about leaving her behind in such a horrible place even for two months, despite all the assurances the lady had given him.

"Dear Myeongnim!"

Seungjae's voice was as tender as it could be. Myeongnim, instead of replying, raised her head.

"Endure the life here for two months at the longest . . . I promise I will bring you to Seoul within two months."

"To Seoul?"

Delighted at the news, Myeongnim's voice was bright, but tears welled up in her eyes at the same time. Her tears were tears of gratitude, but Seungjae took them for tears of sadness, and so he too was choked with tears.

"Yes, to Seoul . . . So you wait patiently for just a little while, won't you? Promise?"

"Yes, I will."

"I'll explain to your mother and father in advance. So when the lady buys you a ticket, you come to Seoul straight away, understood?"

"But how can I . . .?"

"You mean you can't come by yourself? . . . Don't worry . . . I'll ask the lady to send me a telegram in advance. When I receive the telegram, I'll come to meet you somewhere between Gunsan and Seoul. Or if I can make it, I can even come down to Gunsan . . . So don't worry, just take good care of yourself for the time being, and never cry, dear."

"Yes, I see."

"I understand your father's coming back today. Is he coming at night?"

"I'm not sure when . . . but I know it's definitely today . . ."

"All right . . . Then I'll drop by again tomorrow before I leave . . . Is there anything you want to have? I'll buy it and bring it tomorrow . . ."

"No, nothing at all . . ."

"It can't be true . . . Let me see, I'll think about it, and buy something for you on my way here tomorrow . . . Well, get back in now."

"Ye-s, I will."

Despite what she said, Myeongnim just stood there, biting

the tip of her skirt tie. Seungjae advised her one more time to stay well and endure her life without crying, and turned back very reluctantly to leave the house.

The scene was quite similar to that of two lovers unwilling to part.

Dusk was already descending and revealed their two shadows even more distinctly.

Chapter 16:
A Bouncy Morning

GYEBONG WAS BUSY in her room getting ready to go to work. Having just finished dressing, she stood in front of the mirror as usual, checking her teeth. Her teeth were as white as the inside of a gourd, neither too large nor too small, but quite even and shapely. She checked that nothing was stuck between them, neither scraps of red pepper nor rice grains.

Once she had confirmed this, she put her handkerchief into her sleeve, then gave a final look around the room. Her socks, skirt, and underwear, which she had just taken off, were scattered about. Her room hardly deserved a high grade as a room belonging to a grown-up girl. But Gyebong finished her inspection and muttered with satisfaction,

"*Neues Nichts*!"

She babbled the words although she barely knew even basic German. In fact the room was as untidy as always, showing "nothing unusual." But she muttered the German expression, meaning that her preparations for going out were satisfactory. Perhaps she should have said, "OK," but that expression seemed too common to her, so she used German instead, as it sounded more sophisticated.

She looked at her wristwatch. It was ten past eight. If she left now, she would arrive at the department store ten minutes earlier than the regular work hour, as it took only ten minutes to get there. Perhaps she could enjoy that extra ten minutes chatting with her colleagues.

"*Neues Nichts!*"

She muttered it one more time, and just as she was about to step out onto the maru through a small side door, she stopped on the doorstep. As if enchanted, she looked up at the sky, stretching her two arms wide.

The sky, which had been rather misty all through April as the flowers bloomed and faded, was now completely clear. Only a small portion of sky was visible between the eaves of her house and the roof of the house in front. Yet to her surprise, it was a vividly clear cobalt blue. It looked as though it had all been painted with one single color. Looking up at that uniform color could be rather dull and boring, but somehow she felt enchanted by it—the more she looked at it, the more she felt enlivened. In addition, there was just the right amount of soft breeze in the air. One could hardly notice the movement of the breeze, but it seemed to be carrying the pleasant fragrance of new buds sprouting somewhere unknown.

Standing on the threshold, she was fully absorbed in the scene. The weather was so good that she had looked out at it many times since she woke up this morning.

She chose bright clothes matching the fine weather. It was a brand new outfit that Chobong had finished sewing just last night, and as soon as she had inserted the last stitch and taken out her needle, Gyebong ironed it smooth, having the maid hold the other end. The top was made of cream-colored raw silk, and the skirt, of cool blue silk, which looked like a piece of that blue sky, cut out with scissors and draped around her waist.

As she was dressed in such gaily-colored clothes, she wished she could roam freely through lush, green woods, looking up at the sky, basking in the sunshine, feeling the soft breeze, instead of going to work in the dim department store. She was full of such urges.

Come to think of it, it was Sunday, and the next day would be the third Monday, the day she would be off work. That only made her more impatient. If that monthly day off were a week or two away, she could have calmed herself down more easily. But it was a torture for her to go to work on such a lovely day, while the very next day was a day off.

If Seungjae were around, perhaps she would be bold enough to skip work that day, have him take her somewhere nearby like Changgyeong Palace Garden, at least. With such thoughts, she missed Seungjae and wondered why there was no news from him when he must have come to Seoul already.

"Da—lala da-lala."

Gyebong finally opened the side door and went out onto the maru, humming "Gloomy Monday," not gloomily but cheerfully.

"Sister, I'm leaving now."

"All right dear, aren't you late for work?"

Chobong opened the sliding door of her room to answer the greeting, and her eyes opened wide, stunned by her sister's beauty.

". . . My goodness, look at you!"

"Why . . . ha ha ha, isn't it nice?"

Gyebong held up the hem of her skirt lightly and made a rhythmical spin like a dancer, then coyly stopped in front of her sister, who was looking up at her with a bright smile, sitting in her room and resting her hand on the doorsill.

". . . The weather is so nice that I fancied treating myself to a luxurious new outfit . . . ha ha ha, isn't it pretty, Sis?"

"Great! They match very well and look wonderful on you."

Chobong unreservedly expressed her delight, chiming in with her sister's mood. But as she observed the blooming body of her well-dressed sister, a shade of sadness fell over her face.

Gyebong had always been precocious. As she was now nineteen, her physique was fully developed, showing the full-blown beauty of young womanhood. Viewed from behind, her two straight legs stretched down under a round pelvis, firm and plump as if about to burst out of her silk stockings. The legs were so solidly planted on the ground that it seemed they wouldn't budge even if somebody pushed her suddenly from behind. The shoulders, though not square like a judo player's, looked strong. Her chest was noticeably bulging as her breasts had grown round.

She was at least one inch taller than Chobong. Her height was in perfect proportion to her full-blown physique. The chubbiness of her cheeks that had characterized Gyebong's face in her childhood was all gone—her face was now well balanced and handsome. Even without powder or blush, her face was healthy and glowed. She looked even healthier, having grown a little tanned under the spring sunlight. Her eyes, with no sign of sluggishness, sparkled with cleverness, yet her former temperament was still visible in them.

When she laughed heartily, she looked even more carefree than she had in her childhood. This vivacious, unreserved laughter and the soft line of her mouth gave an impression that she was easy-tempered and could accommodate anything or anybody. However the sharp line of her nose and the temperament visible in her eyes made her look obstinate and inaccessible at the same time. In other words, she somehow maintained a harmony of two opposing characteristics.

Although Gyebong wasn't very pretty in small details, she had a healthy and well-balanced physique and was attractive enough on the whole to draw attention—onlookers' eyes were easily drawn to her, especially when she was among other girls.

Chobong was proud of her charming sister. She enjoyed looking at her so much that she even wanted to show her off to others. Whenever possible, she chose to go out with her and enjoyed the opportunity of walking along with her on the streets.

Because of Hyeongbo's irksome complaints about her going out, Chobong couldn't enjoy such outings very often. But occasionally, especially on Gyebong's days off, when they walked the streets together, she could notice that not only young men but old ladies as well cast particular glances at her sister. As they were passing by, they usually muttered compliments,

"What a good-looking girl she is!"

On such occasions, Chobong was so delighted and proud of her sister that she felt inclined to carry her on her back and dance around. But on the other hand, she felt somewhat apprehensive about her being so attractive.

In Chobong's eyes, Gyebong seemed rather audacious, as she had no girlish shyness in either words or thoughts.

One day the two sisters had argued about female chastity—Chobong maintained that chastity must be considered as precious as life itself for a woman because once a woman lost her chastity, her life would be ruined as well, a claim based on her own bitter experience, but one to which Gyebong expressed strong opposition.

Gyebong maintained that a woman's chastity should be taken merely as an aspect of her physiology but it should never rule her life. The purity of chastity must be, according to her, a rather relative element. For instance, if a woman married ten times, she could be a "chaste" woman each time. In addition, she argued, even if a woman couldn't keep her chastity pure, if it was against her will or under irresistible circumstances, there could be absolutely no basis to declare her "disenfranchised."

This was an argument Gyebong had drawn based on the observance of her sister's misfortunes. Yet Chobong was apprehensive that her bold opinion might turn out to be the motivating factor for Gyebong's actions. She even felt her heart sink sometimes for fear that her sister might actually do something irreparable because of that opinion.

If Gyebong had gone to school as planned, Chobong would have been more at ease and less anxious about her. Whatever whim it was that had taken hold of her, Gyebong had decided not to go to school, and instead was working at a department store, where so many men flocked all the time. In Chobong's mind, Gyebong was like a child playing all alone next to a deep well.

Moreover, since the spring, Hyeongbo had begun casting lewd sidelong glances at Gyebong's body, which was fully blooming now. Having noticed this, Chobong shuddered with horror whenever Gyebong innocently played pranks on Hyeongbo, or exchanged jokes with him. Chobong's apprehension was growing more intense and serious.

As Gyebong was about to step down into the yard, the baby Songhui, her face covered with rice, pushed her mother away and shouted,

"Untie!"

Beaming with glee, Songhui tried to beckon to her auntie.

"Oh my goodness, my dearest Songhui!"

Gyebong ran toward Songhui, her two arms stretched wide.

"Oh, what is this! A respectable lady with rice all over her face . . ."

"Untie."

Songhui fell into Gyebong's arms, with a big, happy smile, baring her baby teeth, two upper ones and three lower ones.

"Oh dear, you'll spoil your new clothes!"

"It's all right, quite all right!"

Ignoring Chobong's warning, Gyebong kept cradling the baby in her arms.

"Isn't it, Songhui, dear?"

"Uh-huh."

Songhui jumped with happiness in her auntie's arms, and Gyebong kept kissing her making loud smacking sounds.

"What are clothes? My dear Songhui is more important, aren't you?"

"Uh-huh."

"Your mom is making a fuss over nothing, isn't she?"

"Uh-huh."

"Ha ha ha ha. Are you an errand boy? You keep saying Uh-huh Uh-huh all the time . . ."

"Uh-huh."

Chobong had known all along that Songhui really liked her auntie and Gyebong cared for her niece very dearly. But as she was watching the two having fun together, an idea suddenly struck her mind, *even if I'm not around, the two may make . . .*

"Gyebong, dear?"

"Ye-es?"

Gyebong turned around and approached her sister, while Songhui dug her head into her auntie's chest, as if she was worried that her auntie might leave her in her mother's hands rather than carry her outside.

"Would she be all right without me?" Chobong asked casually, smiling, though her heart was full of painful emotion.

"Without you, Sis? You mean Songhui?"

"Uh-huh."

"Sure!"

Not perceiving her sister's intention, Gyebong answered lightly, and turning to Songhui, said,

"Wouldn't you, Songhui?"

"Uh-huh."

"Even without your mom, you can eat with your auntie and sleep with your auntie, right?"

"Uh-huh."

"Ha ha ha ha, you see, Sis? I'm sure . . ."

As she was turning back, laughing aloud happily, Gyebong suddenly realized her thoughtlessness and silently clicked her tongue. She noticed a dark shadow flicker across her sister's face, which had been wearing a happy smile. She recognized it as an expression of her sister's sad sense of relief and resignation— Chobong seemed to think she could die and stop all her miseries now without worrying about her daughter.

"Oh, my my . . . I didn't mean it at all, you know . . . I can't imagine what Songhui would do if her mother weren't around!"

Gyebong quickly dismissed what she had said, and pretended to play with Songhui innocently.

"Don't you think so, Songhui, dear?"

"Uh-huh."

"Well, if your mother is planning to go out on an excursion, isn't it right that she should take Songhui with her?"

"Uh-huh."

"See what Songhui says . . . but your mother seems to be planning to go to Changgyeong Palace Garden alone, leaving Songhui behind. Right, Songhui, dear?"

"Uh-huh."

While making a fuss, babbling away, Gyebong was trying to read Chobong's mind at the same time. Chobong could see that the quick-witted Gyebong understood what was on her mind and was making such a fuss to hide her concern. Moved by her younger sister's affection for her, Chobong felt her eyes smarting as tears welled up.

At that moment loud noises of Hyeongbo spitting were heard—Hyeongbo was repeatedly clearing his throat as he came out of the toilet that was located at one corner of the yard.

Chobong was reminded of the brutal fact that Hyeongbo was still alive, and with this realization, her sad sense of relief crumbled to dust.

So long as Hyeongbo was alive, her death alone wouldn't put a stop to her misery. Perhaps she might free herself from his monstrous grip through her death, but it meant that she would leave Gyebong and Songhui to suffer at his hands. It would be nothing but an attempt to transfer her misery to innocent folk. Of course Gyebong's case was different to hers. In addition Gyebong was clever and had strong will power, so wouldn't be such easy prey to Hyeongbo as she herself had been. On the other hand, considering Hyeongbo's vicious, cunning nature, no one could tell what vile conspiracies he might cook up. Chobong couldn't think of death as an option so long as it meant that her loved ones, Gyebong and Songhui, would be left vulnerable to his horrendous scheming.

Then am I not entitled even to the freedom of death, let alone the right to live well?

Chobong unwittingly let out a deep sigh, tortured by a dismal sense of frustration.

"Well, well. How come her highness the queen is still dawdling here today . . .?"

Hyeongbo joked with Gyebong, as he sat on the edge of the *maru*, tightening the waistband of his baggy trousers.

"What is the attending officer doing now? Have you forgotten to get the shoes ready when the queen is about to go out?"

Gyebong arrogantly scolded at the protruding hunchback of Hyeongbo. Obsequiously responding to this, Hyeongbo said,

"Yes, your highness, I'm at your mercy. Please forgive my inattentiveness."

With these words, Hyeongbo promptly brought over Gyebong's flat shoes from the far end on the step and placed them right down in front of her.

"Look at the state of these shoes! If you're an attendant, shouldn't you have cleaned them in advance?"

"Huh-uh! That I wouldn't do, even if you killed me!"

"In that case, you're fired this instant!"

"My dear! Stop fooling around with useless prattling and just head off to work! What sort of antics are you playing at?"

Chobong frowned at her sister, scolding her with a stern voice.

"OK. But who dares to push out a queen like that? It's discourteous, isn't it, Songhui?"

"Uh huh."

"Ha ha ha ha, My Songhui is the best! . . . Oh, my darling . . ."

Gyebong kissed Songhui again, making a loud smacking sound, and put the baby into her sister's arms. Songhui clung to Gyebong, not wanting to be separated from her and once Gyebong had freed herself by force, she began to cry wildly, her limbs floundering in the air. Gyebong kept looking back, making gestures to soothe and lull her, until she finally got to the step.

"The queen's accoutrements are flagrantly luxurious but there's one item that falls short of the highest standard,"

Hyeongbo, who was eying the lower part of Gyebong's body, down to her stout legs, blurted out.

"You mean my shoes are shabby?"

"You hit the mark all right."

"You don't need to worry about that. If I really want a new pair of shoes, I can step over to the shoe department and pick a pair any time."

"How about if I go to a top-notch shoe store and have a fashionable pair made for you?"

"Hah! You know what they say about mothers-in-law? They say, if you live long enough, you can see your mother-in-law drowned in a bucket of water? I've never imagined the mouth of my brother-in-law would utter such words. Isn't it amazing?"

Gyebong rarely addressed Hyeongbo either with an honorific or with any title that indicated their relationship. But when she made a sarcastic remark to him, she called him "Mr. Brother-in-law."

However harshly Gyebong scorned him or made fun of him, Hyeongbo always took it lightly, smiling like a spineless man.

Gyebong, like an impertinent child, usually played nasty pranks on him, or provoked him to a quarrel whenever she felt like it. However it wasn't because she had any sisterly affection for him, nor because she considered him her brother-in-law. On the contrary, she teased this monstrous man for fun just as she would monkeys or bears in a zoo. Needless to say, she deeply despised him and harbored a deep-seated antipathy toward him.

Although she came up to Seoul in order to pursue further education at a technical school, medical or pharmaceutical, and was strongly encouraged to do so by her sister, she threw away that prized opportunity without a second thought, and instead took a job as a salesgirl at a department store for a salary of thirty won a month. She made that decision simply because she was ashamed to receive any benefits at the hands of that vile Hyeongbo or to become a parasite growing fat on the misery of her sister.

"Hey dear, my lord queen . . ."

Hyeongbo resumed his advances to Gyebong, who was about to put on her shoes.

"Why is a queen a lord? You really are an ignorant subject . . . Speak up this instant if you have anything to say."

"Please listen to me. You think I'm incapable of buying a pair of shoes for my sister? I'll come over to the place where you work later this afternoon. Just come along with me, and I'll get you a nice pair."

"I said, don't worry! I can take care of myself."

"My goodness, don't be so stubborn . . . I'll be there around nine o'clock when the department store closes, all right?"

"How dare you? If you come, I'll call the police and report you as a madman."

"Huh huh huh, that would be quite interesting! Getting me arrested for trying to buy you shoes . . . I'd enjoy a night in jail, wouldn't I?"

"Don't take it as an empty threat! I really mean it . . . If you come over and try to speak to me, I'll show you what I can do to punish you . . ."

Sharply rebuking him, Gyebong swiftly stepped out of the gate. Chobong, who'd been blankly watching the curious chit-chat between the two, forgetful of the need to lull the crying Songhui, at last turned back with a deep sigh.

Chobong saw that while Hyeongbo maintained a shamelessly playful facade from beginning to end, Gyebong couldn't oppose his abominable amiability and explode in anger, revealing her upright character. And in Chobong's eyes, this was a sign of Gyebong's vulnerability to Hyeongbo's skillful harassment in the future.

When a pliable person and an upright person clash often, the upright person may seem to triumph at first, but as the battle continues, the upright person suffers from repeated internal injuries and breaks in the end, yielding the final victory to the pliable one.

That was exactly what Chobong was worried about. She would rather her sister acted more flexibly and be more in control of her emotions, proving a match for Hyeongbo. For instance, when Hyeongbo said he would buy her a pair of shoes, she could have made light of it by responding, "Good, buy them for me." Or when he said he would visit the department store, she could have challenged him, saying, "Why not? With you there, I can give my colleagues some fun. Please come, I'll be waiting for you." If Gyebong could engage in that kind of light banter and repartee, Chobong would have felt more secure about her sister's future, even though it might look a bit unsafe at the present time.

Hyeongbo, who'd been staring at Gyebong's receding figure with his mouth open, at last walked into the room holding the waistband of his trousers in his hands.

"He-he, what a nice figure! Hee-hee."

Chobong understood his meaning, but pretended not to, and called in the maid to stop Hyeongbo's idle talk. The moment the maid finished clearing the room and carried the breakfast table away, Hyeongbo sat down in front of Chobong, still harboring a lewd grin.

"He-he-he-he . . ."

"Are you out of your mind? What's gotten into you? I can't stand the sight of you!" Chobong sharply reprimanded him, glaring.

"He-he. Adorable! I just love it, so very very much . . ."

"What on earth do you mean, babbling such a load of rubbish?"

"Just like a well-ripened peach! Isn't she?"

"Get away! You ugly thing!"

"If you took a bite, the juice would pour out, I reckon . . ."

Hyeongbo indeed was dribbling saliva, which he tried to swallow, and wiped the rest away with the back of his hand.

"So plump and blooming! My gosh, uh-huh, nineteen years of age! The prime of life!"

"Won't you stop that nonsense?"

"Hah, what's the big fuss! Haven't you heard how the wise king Yao in ancient China took two sisters, Ah-hwang and Yeoyoung, as his wives? He-he."

Chobong, who'd been staring at him fiercely, clenched her teeth, raised her fists, and punched his chest with all her might.

"Ouch!"

Hyeongbo fell back, hitting the floor, and rubbed his chest in pain, but as he saw Chobong about to attack him again, he rolled down to the far end of the room and sat up.

"He, he, he, he."

Hyeongbo rarely got upset over such minor attacks.

Chobong looked around the room to find something she could throw at him.

"He, he, he, he. No, I won't do it, I won't."

"Don't you ever dare say such things again!"

"No, I won't, I promise . . . He he."

"If you ever dare say such words again, I'll kill you . . ."

She didn't say, "I'll kill you," with any conscious intention. That expression was something that naturally followed a heated curse. But the moment she heard the expression emerge from her mouth, she suddenly felt a murderous desire, wishing that she could really kill the man. It was a strange, frightening discovery about herself.

As Chobong went out of the room to go to the toilet,

Songhui, whom she'd left behind, burst out crying again, still feeling cross.

"That damn thing is screaming again . . ."

Hyeongbo clicked his tongue, casting a malicious sideways glance at Songhui. Since Chobong wasn't around, he could hate the baby as much as he pleased.

"Damn! I hate the sound of crying! Where are the devils to carry away that wretched thing?"

Hyeongbo, glaring, made as if to hit the baby with his fist. He meant to frighten the baby to stop it crying, but the baby, being scared, cried even more fiercely.

"That little thing has such a bad temper, taking after her mother . . ."

Hyeongbo looked around the room until he located a toothbrush on the dresser, and put it in the baby's hand.

"Take it, and go to hell gobbling it, you damn thing!"

Songhui stopped crying, and after casting cautious glances at Hyeongbo a few times, sneakily put the brush into her mouth.

It was a toothbrush that had been used to clean a hairbrush, and had oily grime, dandruff, and strands of hair stuck to it. It must surely have had an obnoxious taste when Songhui sucked it. Songhui frowned, but kept chewing the brush, drooling grimy saliva down her chin.

". . . What an odd face it's making! My, I feel so good! That little urchin surely deserves that taste. You cry all the time and put everything that comes to hand into your gaping mouth! When you do that, you end up tasting that dirty thing!"

Hyeongbo, elated and gloating over the baby's mishap, kept cursing at the baby.

"Is it yummy? That wretched little thing! Were you born under the patronage of the starved demon, Heo Cheonbaek? . . . Whose seed is it after all, I wonder? Uh? . . . Why am I being so harassed to feed that thing, not even knowing who its father really is? I don't even have opportunities to relieve my anger like this. What a ridiculous situation I'm in, for goodness' sake."

Songhui, who was incapable of taking in curses, paid no attention to him, but kept enjoying herself chewing the odious-tasting toothbrush.

". . . If that thing would only drop dead, I would dance with delight. Are there any drugs that would kill it without leaving a trace? I wish I had some."

At the sound of Chobong stepping up onto the *maru*, Hyeongbo closed his mouth, and turned away as if he didn't notice what Songhui was doing.

"Oh, no, what is that, my baby!"

Chobong screamed as she entered the room, hastily snatching the toothbrush from Songhui's hand, and then glaring fiercely at Hyeongbo. Songhui began screaming to get it back, wriggling her legs on the floor.

"How come you pretend not to see when the child is sucking at such a thing!"

"If I took it away, she would've cried again, wouldn't she?"

"What a heartless rogue!"

"No, no, children grow up even stronger when they can eat anything."

"Shut up! You mean, cold-blooded villain!"

"Damn it . . . You must find your child a bother, I'm sure! Why don't you give it away to someone else, instead of bothering me like this?"

"You scoundrel, that's not something you can say to me, it's what I have to say to you. You're so brazen, you'll drive people to their deaths!"

"Don't quibble, you don't need to worry . . . I can put the child into the rucksack of a beggar monk, if you think it's a burden."

"Do you think I don't know what's going on inside you? I know well enough what you're hatching . . . You pretend the child is yours only because you don't want to lose me. You really want to kill her secretly but don't dare to because then you'd lose me too, wouldn't you? I know the dark intentions hidden in your heart."

"What the hell do you reckon you know? I can see that the child is an annoyance to you, as you can't figure out whose child it is! But as for me, I know that it's my own precious child."

"How shameless you are!"

"That's why people say that the woman who gives birth to a child whose father is unknown can never be a good mother!"

"What did you say?"

Stung in the most vulnerable spot of her heart, Chobong shouted at the top of her voice, thrashing her arms, overwhelmed by the rage that surged up. She was gasping, unable to continue speaking and a cascade of tears fell from her eyes.

"You, devil! You'll pay for this!"

It wasn't merely an empty threat that burst out in wrath, but an indicator that a resolution to kill Hyeongbo was at last distinctly taking shape in her heart. Or rather it was the declaration of such a resolution.

Even if she put aside her worries about the harm Hyeongbo could inflict on Songhui and Gyebong, she had reached the limit of her capacity to endure Hyeongbo—she knew that unless she killed either herself or Hyeongbo now, she would eventually die, totally worn out by Hyeongbo's incessant sexual drive.

Ever since the day she began to live with Hyeongbo the previous fall, Chobong had not only lost her peace of mind, but had withered away, harassed by Hyeongbo's untiring aggression. Hyeongbo, in the daytime, was docile enough to concede to Chobong whenever they had arguments over daily matters. The worst he did was to throw some sarcastic or sneering words at Chobong, even enduring her beating his back or her kicking without resistance.

However, should Chobong refuse his fickle nightly demands even once, he would suddenly turn into an angry wild beast, showing the whites of his eyes, raving like a madman. To start with he would pinch and bite her, or even punch Songhui, who was sleeping peacefully next to them, or grab the child and throw her down. If Chobong still refused him, he would fetch a knife and wildly brandish it with its tip pointing at the mother and the child.

In the end, Chobong would yield to him, grinding her teeth bitterly.

This pattern of behavior during the night wasn't purely due to his innate nature. It was rather a habit that had been initiated and cultivated by Chobong, albeit unintentionally.

From the start, whenever she was in bed with Hyeongbo, Chobong would act viciously, giving him as hard a time as she could. In order to subdue such a wild resistance, Hyeongbo had no other way than to become a "fierce dog."

It was true that Hyeongbo was detestable and obnoxious in the eyes of Chobong. But Chobong acted like that more out of her desire for revenge than her loathing of him. The consequence, however, turned out to be more harmful for Chobong herself.

The experience of obtaining the surrender of a woman by ferocious violence quite unexpectedly gave Hyeongbo a new sort of excitement. As it was repeated night after night, Hyeongbo began to enjoy it for its own sake, and in the end he became addicted to those sadistic rituals.

As a result, Chobong had to suffer doubly, not only being

frustrated psychologically, but having her physical health ruined as well.

In fact, Hyeongbo was giving her both the disease and the medicine. He went out of his way to find good medicines for Chobong, such as cod liver oil pills or many sorts of restorative herbal medicines. He even took the trouble to make tonics out of herbs, simmering them in an earthenware pot for a long time. Despite all his efforts, he couldn't stop Chobong's health deteriorating.

Within six months, Chobong had withered into an unsightly figure. Her cheeks were sunken and had dark shadows under them; dark circles formed around her eyes; her complexion grew dry and lost its firmness, seeming to rustle like an old, dried sheepskin; her limbs were flailing all the time, she was always looking for a place to lie down, day and night.

Chobong knew well enough that her life force was being eaten away, but she was at a loss as to what to do.

The thought that she could at least struggle to escape from Hyeongbo's strong grasp at whatever cost never even took shape in her mind. She never questioned herself about the causes of this groundless resignation, merely taking it as her fate.

Even when she threatened Hyeongbo in a fierce tone, that he would pay for his wickedness of the previous winter, as if she would avenge herself in some big way, she in fact gave up on what she said immediately after, sensing that she had no recourse whatsoever to make it happen.

In short, despair was the only passion she could summon up within herself all along. Maintaining the flickering flame of her ebbing life was a tediously painful business. She wished she could die. Death seemed to be a good way out of all these agonies.

But she couldn't kill herself, because of Songhui. Leaving that precious Songhui behind alone, only seeking her own comfort through death, was something too absurd for her to consider.

That morning, when she saw Gyebong playing with Songhui, however, Chobong suddenly experienced a sad sense of relief at the thought that she might die leaving Songhui in the hands of Gyebong. She saw that Gyebong would be able to take care of Songhui as well as she herself could. But such a "sad sense of relief" also lasted only for a short while, as she realized that so long as Hyeongbo was alive, that wouldn't work either.

In that moment of despair, a ray of hope reached her; a "satisfactory plan," to kill Hyeongbo first and then kill herself, struck her. If she could kill Hyeongbo first, she could die comfortably without any regrets or worries. It was true that once Hyeongbo was dead, there would be no need for her to die. She could have changed her plan either to go to prison or to live as a fugitive. But Chobong was too desperate to think reasonably or with flexibility. She simply thought that if she were to die soon, she should kill Hyeongbo first to eliminate the source of future mishaps.

Hyeongbo, destined to die at the hands of Chobong, even if he behaved himself and kept his mouth shut, inflamed her ire by uttering harsh, cruel words at mother and daughter. Therefore, if something terrible took place that day, it would all be his own doing, his life was being rushed to a sudden end.

THE COSMETICS COUNTER was located on the ground floor of the department store. The shop had glass display cases on three sides, to the left, the right, and the front, easily attracting the eyes of shoppers. The display cases were densely packed with all kinds of cosmetics contained in various colorful containers and boxes, which catered to the delicate and elegant tastes of women.

Within the boundary of the roughly seven-square-meter shop were four girls who looked as stylish and refined as the cosmetics they were selling. They all seemed to be of the same age group. In addition to Gyebong, there were three other girls; one had a round and pretty face with her hair cut short, the second had a distinctly high nose, with her eyes and mouth rather sunken, and the third one, sitting on a chair, was a cashier, who had a thin face sprinkled all over with freckles.

In the shop was also the imposing figure of a well-dressed man whose dark face seemed too rugged to harmonize with the four sleek girls. Some might envy him, standing there like an ugly rock among a flowerbed. Being the manager in charge of that counter, however, he was in fact exercising his authority by stamping a seal on the wrapping paper of each cosmetic item.

It was a little after nine o'clock in the morning. As the department store had just opened, there weren't many customers other than a few country people, who were peeping here and there, their hands behind their backs.

The shop being so quiet, the girls all gathered around the cashier.

"Hey, Gyebong, won't you go to the cinema with me after work?"

The girl with sunken eyes, who claimed to prefer movies to dating, coaxed Gyebong.

"Well, I'm not sure . . . unless it's a really good one . . ."

Gyebong, who was neither disinterested nor tempted, answered rather evasively. The sunken-eyed girl was about to retort, but the cashier with freckles mischievously cut in.

"How come that kid is so crazy about movies?"

"You busybody! You think I should rather be reading dull, musty novels like you?"

"Pah! Reading novels as a hobby is a good way to become refined and cultured!"

"But it's vulgar!" Gyebong commented to annoy the freckled one.

"Why, you silly, is reading novels vulgar?"

"No, I don't mean that. You've misunderstood, really!"

"Then, what do you mean is vulgar?"

"The novels you're reading . . ."

"Why is that so?"

"Can you tell me the novels of Gikuchi Gan aren't vulgar? Think of the one you've been reading lately. It's vulgar, beyond any doubt. Can anyone claim it as a work of art?"

"What has art got to do with the novel? Novels are simply novels . . ."

"Ha-ha, ha-ha. You're right. At least you don't read books like *Chulwolsaek* or *The Life of Yu Chung-ryeol*. For that I have to compliment you."

"You cheeky girl, are you making fun of me?"

"In appreciation of that, I give you sixty points for cultural refinement so that you won't flunk, OK? . . . And then, as for you . . ."

Gyebong, nudging at the sunken-eyed girl with her finger, began to address her, assuming the voice of a gentleman.

". . . You may say you're going to the movies to enjoy modern taste, but you should know that if a young girl like you goes to the movies so often, she's bound to be labeled 'no good.' Understood? You 'no good' girl . . ."

"Stop worrying about me, you naughty girl."

"You cocky girl!" Gyebong unwittingly shouted in a very loud voice.

The manager, looking back, flashed a smile as a warning.

Gyebong covered her mouth, turning around. The sunken-eyed girl and the freckled one gloated over her mishap and burst out laughing.

"What's so funny?" the shorthaired girl, who'd been away for a while to assist a customer, asked in an anxious voice as she rejoined the other girls. She seemed apprehensive in case she might have been the topic of their banter.

"Well, well, dear. What name should I give you?" Gyebong asked pulling the shorthaired girl's arm.

"What do you mean?"

"As for the other two, one is a bookworm, and the other is a movie fanatic. What title would you choose? . . . How about a romantic? Isn't that right?"

"Oh, my goodness! . . . What about you? . . . You should choose your title first!"

"Sure sure."

"That's right. She should do it first."

Both the sunken-eyed girl and the freckled one spoke at once, in support of the short-haired girl, who in turn began to press Gyebong, holding her arms.

"You're the one who's deep in romance, aren't you? . . . Inundated with love letters . . ."

"There's a boy covered with pimples . . ."

"A young and promising lawyer, too . . ."

"In addition, a dandy from a rich family . . ."

"Give us your answer!"

"Who is it you'll choose among them?"

"Nevertheless, you're indeed a seeker of romance, aren't you?"

The sunken-eyed, the freckled, and the shorthaired girl, as if in competition, kept pressing Gyebong for an answer without giving her a moment to reply.

"It's about time for the pimples to show up, I think . . ."

"How many letters have you received from that young lawyer in the meantime?"

"Ha-ha. Didn't he state the article number of the law of love at the heading of his letter?"

"Stop it girls, listen . . ."

Gyebong at last stopped the girls waving her hands, and said, "I'm the victim, you should know, the victim . . ."

The three girls looked at each other, confounded. Gyebong once again assumed the voice of a gentleman.

"Suppose that you've come out onto the street on a wet day . . . A car drives by you . . . It splashes muddy water on you . . .Your clothes get dirty all over . . . Hem hem, I'm in exactly the same situation. My being slandered as a seeker of romance by you is due to what the pimples, the lawyer, and the dandy did to me, not because of anything I did to them. In that sense, am I not a victim? I did nothing, but the car splashed and ruined my clothes. What those young men did was the same as running away after splashing muddy water on an innocent passerby. In other words, they are the "unpunished" gangsters who ran away after splashing mud on my new clothes. Therefore, all of you should also beware! If you're unlucky, it's quite easy to get hit by a car and die or be maimed, if not splashed by mud . . . Do you understand? Raise your hands if you understood!"

The girls, including Gyebong, all burst out laughing. The manager also grinned, unable to interfere with the girls' banter.

"Then what are you indeed? As you have such a sleek tongue, you must be a drug peddler, right?"

"Or a missionary of the Salvation Army?"

"Or a silent movie narrator?"

"Me? I'm an actionist, I've been an actionist for a long time . . ."

"What do you mean by 'an actionist?'" the freckled girl asked ahead of the others.

"You've never heard of an 'actionist?' People who act. You purport to be modern having read many novels, but you're in the dark!"

"Well, you slut, is there anyone who sits still day and night without taking any action?"

"You silly, do you think eating, going to the WC, or yawning are actions?"

"If they're not actions, are they nonsense?"

"They're merely things that dogs, pigs, or any beasts can do as well."

At that moment, the manager answered the phone and passed the receiver over to Gyebong. She promptly said into the phone,

"Is that you, Sis?"

Gyebong rarely received phone calls other than from her sister, so she always answered the phone in that way.

But today, from the other end of the line came a quite unexpected voice.

"It's me."

It was the deep, sonorous voice of a man. It was Seungjae calling, but Gyebong, who'd never talked to him on the phone, couldn't recognize the voice.

"You say me? Who is this 'me'?"

"It's me, Master Nam!"

"My goodness! I didn't recognize your voice!"

Gyebong was overwhelmed with delight, and expressed her gladness unaware of the people around her. The three girls standing behind her exchanged knowing looks, smiling.

"When did you come up?"

"I arrived the morning of the day before yesterday . . ."

"Yet you stayed silent all the time you've been in Seoul? Oh, my, my!"

"I'm sorry, my dear! I had so many things to take care of. I may stop by there, but . . ."

"No, it's all right. I'll come over to you. Is it in Ahyeon-dong?"

"Right, its location is . . ."

Seungjae gave her detailed directions to the clinic—take the streetcar to Mapo, get off at the Ahyeon Hill stop, walk along the road to Sinchon for a while, find an old two-story house on the right-hand side of the street with a sign that reads, "Ahyeon Clinic at Cost."

Gyebong hung up after saying she would be there around six-thirty or seven. As she turned back, her three friends, who were waiting, started to attack her all at once.

"You have one more admirer."

"Who is it?"

"Isn't he the car? The one that splashes muddy water . . ."

This last comment made by the shorthaired girl triggered loud laughter among them. Gyebong laughed along with them.

The girls, at the budding age of twenty or so, were gathered together prattling on and, once in a while, bursting into clear, resounding laughter—though the store itself was rather dim, the gay brightness of the atmosphere far exceeded the sparkling May sunshine that enlivened the streets outside.

When the laughter at last died down, the three girls laid into her straightaway.

"You slut, playing the innocent all along, how could you?"

"Who is he? Speak up at once!"

"That unpredictable girl has been so sly and secretive . . ."

"Is that what actionists usually do?"

"Do dogs and pigs also fall in love, I wonder?"

"Don't keep smiling, confess the whole truth now!"

"I'm sure she can no longer elude us!"

"Well, well, dear girls . . ."

When the attack slackened, Gyebong seized the opportunity to talk,

"Why on earth are you making such a fuss when you don't know who he is?"

"Who could it be but your liebe?" the girl with the freckles retorted.

"*Liebe?*"

"Of course!"

"He's the keeper of our forest. Ahem!"

All the girls once again split their sides with laughter.

"What does the animal look like? Give us a look at him!"

The shorthaired girl spoke as if jesting, but seemed really curious.

"If you took one look at him, you'd all fall backward with a thump!"

"Is he that handsome?"

"No, because he's so old-fashioned, both inside and out."

"You cursed girl! You're worried someone will snatch him away?"

"Do you want him?"

"No thank you!"

"The actionist's manner of loving is quite different. She gives away her liebe like a movie ticket to her friend . . . Is that a characteristic of the actionist's manner of behavior?"

The sunken-eyed girl chose an analogy that reflected her love of movies.

"You're certainly right! I'm willing because the man is too old-fashioned and never shows clearly what's inside . . ."

"Then that man isn't a man but a pig, to use your own word, isn't he?"

"Very close!"

"Look at the impertinent girl! . . . I'll tell him what you said."

"I wouldn't mind even if he were a fascist, or even a movie fanatic like you, so long as he's got something modern in common with me! He simply eats his meals, works all the time like a robot, goes to the toilet. And then when he does something other than everyday living, that's bound to be seen as being antiquated . . ."

"He must be a clerk in some company, right?"

"No, he's a so-called medical doctor by profession!"

"Indeed? I see why you've never glanced at those other admirers, the pimpled boy, the lawyer, or the dandy master!"

"Hey girls! Talk of the devil, and he's sure to appear. Look he's come, over there."

At the hint from Freckles, all the girls looked back toward the entrance. The man they called Pimples was indeed approaching the cosmetics counter, walking with a rather awkward gait.

The girls had given him the nickname because of the pimples that covered his face. His cap badge showed that he was a student of a certain high school, but his being at a department store to woo at this hour indicated that he must be a no-good student. He was nineteen at the most, or younger, still within the range of boyhood.

Last March, he had purchased an "almond papaya cream" for the first time, and since then he came over daily at around nine-thirty. No one noticed it at first until the girl with short hair pointed it out, and within a few days, it became evident that Gyebong was the target of his daily visits.

He usually loitered around in front of the display cases until a salesgirl approached him. If it was Gyebong, he always bought an item, but if it was someone else, he fiddled with this or that and just left. Since this pattern had been detected, the girls began to avoid him, pushing Gyebong forward instead.

Gyebong never avoided it, but deftly received him as a customer, even wheedling him to buy things at times. Thanks to that, Pimples became a daily provider of material for the girls' chitchat.

"Good morning! Can I help you?"

Gyebong, who'd been laughing, took some time before moving to the display cases in order to recover her normal face, and welcomed Pimples with the sort of courtesy befitting a salesgirl.

Pimples glanced up at Gyebong, his pimple-covered, half-red face becoming fully flushed, and soon dropped his head again. So far, there was nothing unusual about his behavior. And then, putting his hands into his jacket pockets, he seemed to become more timid and hesitant than usual.

After a while, his hands still in his pockets, he began to stroll along the display cases, slowly peering into them. Gyebong followed him along on the inner side of the display cases, while the other three girls watched amusedly to find out what item the boy would choose this time.

Pimples made a full round along the display cases and then turned back, seemingly to walk back to the center, but he stopped and pointed his finger at a spot on the glass top of a display case. Pointing his finger instead of saying something was one of his habits from his first visit.

Gyebong looked at the item he pointed at; it was a bottle of Coty perfume, priced at a full twenty-five won.

Gyebong suppressed a giggle, knowing that the student must have had bad luck when he randomly pointed at that item, but took out the perfume and handed it over to him. Pimples received it with his trembling hand. He pretended to read the label for some time and then looked up at Gyebong. This was his way of asking the price silently.

"It's twenty-five won."

Pimples flinched slightly, but then he fumbled in his pocket, produced three ten-won notes and placed them on top of the perfume bottle. He always used crisp ten-won bank notes, even when he purchased a mere ten-jeon soap. So it was no surprise that this time he produced three of them.

"Thank you very much!"

Gyebong picked up the money and the perfume, and walking to the register, winked at her friends, who were working hard to suppress their bubbling giggles. Gyebong put the perfume bottle into its box, wrapped it, and got it stamped by the manager. She returned to the student and handed him the perfume along with the change and the receipt she got from Freckles.

"Thank you," Gyebong said one more time, bowing lightly to the student.

Pimples stretched out his hands, which were shaking even more than before, to take the perfume and turned away immediately.

"Good bye!" Gyebong shouted at his back, and turned her face, which was beaming with laughter, toward her friends.

The shorthaired girl, as if she'd been waiting for the moment, rushed to the display case in front of which the student had been standing and took out a floral envelope that was stuck between the display case and the shelf on top of it. The envelope was small but rather bulky. The other two girls were full of glee as if they were about to clap.

Gyebong instantly recognized it as a letter left by Pimples for her. She swiftly snatched it from the shorthaired girl, and turning back, searched for the student.

"Hello! Hello, you, student!"

Pimples, who was about half a dozen steps away from the cosmetics counter, stopped in his tracks.

"Hey, student, look at me please!"

As though Gyebong really meant him to look at her, Pimples was standing where he was, only hesitantly turning back.

"Come over here for a moment, please."

Gyebong waved her hand to summon him nonchalantly. Pimples tottered back and stood in front of the display case, lowering his head.

"Shall I put this letter into a postbox?" she said, producing the letter she'd been holding behind her back. She noticed that the letter had no name or address on either side of the envelope.

Pimples stood motionless with his legs straight, close together, and his head hanging low like a student being scolded by his teacher. A deep blush spread to his ears.

"I can put a postage stamp on it for you, but since there's neither address nor name . . ."

Placing her chin on top of her palm and leaning on the display case, Gyebong, with her other hand, played with the envelope turning it back and forth. Her friends barely suppressed their giggles. Luckily for the student, no other customers were around at the moment, as it was still early in the morning; if not, it could have been a big spectacle, worth people gathering around.

"Please take it back, write the name and address clearly, stick a postage stamp right here, and then mail it in a postbox. OK?"

Pimples stretched out his hand to receive the envelope, but took his hand back on seeing that Gyebong was still holding it.

"Well, well, if you leave it in this sort of place, it'll cry like a lost child, won't it?"

This time Gyebong actually held out the envelope, but the student stood still, ignoring it.

"Here you are. Please take it."

When Gyebong held it out right before his nose, Pimples snatched it and hurried away from the place.

The four girls nearly gave vent to a burst of hysterical laughter, but the place being what it was, they struggled to maintain their composure.

Chapter 17:
Training an Old Bachelor in Love—A Journal

GYEBONG, WHO'D BEEN restless all day long after receiving Seungjae's call, obtained permission from her manager to leave work early at six o'clock. She knew that if she went straight to Seungjae's clinic in Ahyeon-dong, she wouldn't be able to get back home at the usual hour, which would cause Chobong to worry. But since she was anxious to see Seungjae, she was unwilling to lose precious time by dropping in at home first.

It was quite easy to find the place as she followed the directions Seungjae had given her. But she deliberately slowed her pace once she got near, as she wanted to calm herself first, and began to survey the house from outside.

Despite being a clinic, the two-story wooden house had none of the imposing appearance of a clinic that Gyebong expected. It was a rather dingy, tin-roofed building, well suited to Seungjae's humble character. Despite being disappointed by its appearance, Gyebong felt more affectionate and friendly toward the house, as if it were pervaded with the scent of Seungjae.

We will start offering consultations to patients from the fifteenth.

A note on a sheet of paper, handwritten in bold letters, probably by Seungjae, was attached to the door. The way it gave the information in such a wordy manner made Gyebong smile to herself, sensing that it carried Seungjae's unaffectedly kind but clumsy style.

The moment she opened the sliding glass door, each of whose four corners were slightly bent, she could tell instantly that it was a clinic because of the smell of chloroform that hung densely in the air. On the left-hand side of the entrance was a small windowed room with a wooden plaque that read "Free Consultation" placed on the windowsill. This must be the reception office, she thought.

There was a short hallway with a narrow staircase leading to the second floor. In the middle of the hallway on the right-hand side was a door with a frosted glass window and above it was a sign, "Consultation Room," its ink still vivid and fresh.

Though the outside looked quite shabby, the inside was clean and tidy, having been newly painted and plastered. It was very quiet, with no sign of any people. Gyebong knocked on the window of the reception office, but no one answered.

Gyebong stood there wondering how to summon Seungjae. Just then the door of the consultation room was opened roughly, and a man's head peeped out. It was Seungjae.

At the sight of Gyebong, Seungjae's face brightened with a smile, and he exclaimed,

"Oh! You've come!"

Unlike his usual cautious self, he rushed out to meet her. Having waited anxiously, he was overcome by delight, and ran toward her despite himself. He stopped in front of her, however, and stood there awkwardly, at a loss as to what to do next. Fortunately for Seungjae, Gyebong extended her hand and he grabbed it.

They looked into each other's eyes silently, their hearts wildly pounding with the passion that was surging up in them. They exchanged no words, nor was there any need for words. Their gasps alone were enough.

After a while, Gyebong, who couldn't withstand her strong emotions any longer, threw herself into Seungjae's arms. Her gestures were like those of a gentle, vibrant doe in springtime, whereas Seungjae resembled a heavy and guileless bear when he embraced her shoulders and softly pressed her to his chest.

In a moment, their lips met, leaving no space between them. The passion that had been rearing wildly in their hearts like a wild horse at last found an exit and was pacified.

A chick knows how to feed the moment it hatches from an egg. It doesn't need to learn from anyone. Seungjae was as innocent and inexperienced in matters of love as a brand new chick, but he could embrace and kiss the woman he loved naturally, just as chicks by instinct pick up the right grains.

No one else was in the clinic at that moment, giving them total privacy. However, if someone had suddenly walked into the house, they would have felt quite embarrassed. On the other hand, if Gyebong's mother had witnessed the scene, she would have been quite satisfied, though she might have frowned as well, rather displeased at the shabby appearance of the clinic . . .

And Chobong too would have been delighted, if she saw it. Perhaps she might have secretly shed a few tears behind the couple's back; yet still, she would have been excited about the love that had matured between them, and in a hurry for them to marry, volunteering to prepare the ceremony herself.

When the two separated, Gyebong, being a young woman, shyly stood to one side, looking away from him, and biting the tie of her dress. She was still visibly flushed to the roots of her ears. But Seungjae, being a man, showed no shyness at all.

"Please come in, won't you?"

"No, no!"

"Wait a bit."

Seungjae took out a pair of slippers from the shoe drawer, which was full of new slippers, placed them in front of Gyebong, and softly pressed her shoulders.

"Now, take off your shoes and put these on . . ."

"No, no! I must go home!"

"Hey, what's with you, dear?"

"Ha-ha-ha."

Gyebong quickly threw off her shoes, and she had barely put her feet into the slippers before she ran along the hallway toward the consultation room. As she got to the door, she looked back, asking,

"You mean here?"

"Right."

He responded by blinking his eyes as well as nodding his head, and picked up the shoes where she had let them fall, placing them neatly to one side of the porch.

As she was passing through the door of the consultation room, she looked back, and seeing that Seungjae was following her, closed the door in his face. Seungjae demanded that she open it, but she held onto the knob and wouldn't open.

"Open it, please? I want to get in!"

"No, you can't!"

"Am I in big trouble? What should I do then . . .?"

"You should admit you were wrong."

"Wrong?"

"Yes."

"What did I do wrong?"

"Well, uh . . ."

"Yes?"

"No, no. I don't know!"

"All right then. I did indeed do something wrong . . ."

"Ha-ha-ha-ha!"

Gyebong opened the door, and Seungjae walked into the room. It was about fifteen square meters in size, and well equipped with all the necessary amenities—an examination bed covered with a black rug, a bookcase, a chest for medical equipment, a desk for consultation, as well as a desk for study, a sink, and a gas burner. They were all perfectly placed and brand new.

Gyebong sat down on a swivel chair in front of the study desk, her feet dangling in the air. Seungjae brought over a stool from the far end of the room and sat beside the desk.

The two stared at each other, smiling constantly, not knowing why.

"Right."

"Uh-huh!"

Each said a meaningless word, and then smiled at each other again.

"Don't look at me like that!" Gyebong affectionately demanded, though she kept looking at him.

"Is it wrong to look at you?"

"Yep."

"What a predicament . . . Ha-ha!"

"Ha-ha-ha!"

"I thought you'd grown up into a lady, but you're still a mischievous girl, right?"

"No, I don't know!"

"You must act a bit more mature, right?"

"Why?"

"Because you'll soon become an adult . . ."

"An adult?"

"Yes. I think today you entered halfway into adulthood . . ."

"Ha-ha-ha . . . and then?"

"And then, soon . . ."

"Soon?"

"I mean, soon we will . . .," Seungjae faltered, and placed his hand on top of Gyebong's hand that was playing with a pen on the desk.

". . . When we get married, I mean, heh-he . . ."

"Married?"

Though she repeated the word rather mischievously, slowly pulling back her hand, there was also some serious determination in her face that couldn't be so easily dismissed as a playful gesture.

"Who says I will get married?" Gyebong asked earnestly, after staring at Seungjae's blinking eyes for a moment.

Seungjae was dumbfounded, and wanted to scratch the back of his head.

"Then, was what . . . happened earlier . . . merely a prank?" Seungjae stammered hesitantly, at which Gyebong retorted,

"A prank? Who said it was a prank?"

Seungjae felt he was being drawn into a conundrum.

Gyebong, who had jumped at the word marriage a moment ago, was now even more furious at the word prank. Seungjae wondered what could be in her mind. How could it be—how can the sort of love that has no prospect of marriage not be a prank? How can one refuse marriage yet still acknowledge love?

However hard he blinked his eyes or racked his brain, he couldn't come up with any solution, feeling he was bewitched by a fairy.

"Look at me, dear, uh?"

This time Gyebong pulled Seungjae's hand toward her, and holding it with her two hands, began to talk in a rather sweet voice.

"My, my, Master Nam. Ah, I shouldn't call you Master Nam. What should I call you? How about Dr. Nam?"

"Why doctor now? I like being called Master Nam as usual."

"Yet still . . . Oh, my gosh, no, no, I can't call you Master Nam, Ha-ha-ha . . . It really sounds like a forest keeper, no!"

"A forest keeper?"

"Ha-ha-ha! . . . You called me earlier this morning, didn't you?"

"Yes, I did."

"My friends caught me in the middle of speaking to you, and asked who it was. So I said, it's our forest keeper. Ha-ha-ha . . ."

"I like that. A forest keeper . . . Huh, huh, huh."

"Let me see, my, my, what shall I call you, uh?"

"How about Seungjae . . . ?"

"Seung? Jae? . . . Mr. Seungjae! Really? That sounds even more awkward, doesn't it?"

"Oh, don't bother. What does it matter whatever you call me? Do as you please, I don't care."

"Then until I find a good alternative, I'll keep calling you Master Nam, all right?"

"Sure."

"And now, listen to me carefully, please?"

"OK."

"You, Master Nam, you like me, don't you?"

"Like you?"

"Well, then you love me, don't you?"

"Hmm, but what about it?"

"Just answer me, Master Nam loves me, doesn't he?"

"Why do you need to ask that? It's all too obvious . . ."

"You do, right? And I also love you, Master Nam . . . You do know that I love you, don't you?"

"I do."

"That's true? . . . Then isn't that enough? Master Nam loves me, and I love Master Nam. We are indeed in love, aren't we?"

"Right."

"What I mean is, that's sufficient and we must be satisfied with that. But as for marriage, that's a different issue."

"How different?"

"Love is a passion, a game that's played with passion. In that sense, love allows you to remain an amateur, whereas marriage requires you to become a professional, entering into a sort of job."

"How could it be! My goodness."

"In other words, the two are as different as studying and getting a job. When we study, it's not necessarily to get a job, don't you think?"

Seungjae couldn't grasp her meaning at all. For him, a passion that didn't lead to marriage was definitely unstable and unsatisfactory, whatever others might say.

How open Seungjae's opinion might become in the future is something we will have to wait and see. Whether or not Gyebong may somehow succeed in harmonizing the "tremendous differences" between herself and Seungjae is also an issue no one can easily predict at this point. Nevertheless, based on what Seungjae thinks now, he doesn't seem to deserve a modern girl like Gyebong.

Having stared attentively at the disheartened Seungjae for some time, Gyebong stood up abruptly from the chair, went up behind him, and placing both her hands over his shoulders, leaned her whole body on his back. Seungjae pulled her hands to his chest and patted them.

"Master Na-am?"

A sweet voice whispered right next to his ear.

"Yes?"

"Are you mad at me?"

"No."

"Why are you so easily disheartened? Master Nam . . . answer me please!"

"Uh."

"Did I say I wouldn't marry you? . . . All I said was that I didn't say I would marry you."

" . . . "

"So now, I will do this . . ."

Gyebong was rubbing Seungjae's bristled cheek with her soft cheek, while muttering with her nasal voice.

"Isn't it good—just loving one another like this? And as for marrying, we can wait and see, I think. OK? Please hear me out. Love in principle has an instinct to move toward marriage, its destination . . . So if we get to the destination safely, we will be married, but if something happens on the way, we can't marry . . . Isn't it true?"

"That's true, of course, but . . ."

"You see now? If I die suddenly, say tomorrow, we won't be able to marry, right?"

"What an inauspicious thing to say!"

"Ha-ha-ha. Or what if I somehow grow to dislike you sometime later? . . . There's no guarantee that I would never dislike you, is there?"

"Well, I'm not sure . . ."

"No shilly-shallying please! What I'm saying is that if I don't like you, I wouldn't marry you, right? There would be no marriage if one of us doesn't want to."

"Of course, we wouldn't in that case . . ."

"See? Am I not right? And then . . ."

"What now?"

Seungjae tilted his head backward and smiled innocently with his eyes. His sulky feelings seemed to have faded away, as it turned out that Gyebong's reservations about marriage weren't based on any important issues.

The sun was about to set, throwing hazy beams of light through the window that faced west. The setting sun alone was producing changes in the room, which remained tranquil and cozy for the two lovers.

Gyebong didn't answer the question Seungjae asked, tilting his head, but simply stared into his eyes smiling.

It wasn't the first time that Gyebong had looked into his eyes, but this time, she was especially impressed by the way they were so candid and calm, like a deep lake in a remote mountain that would never make ripples regardless of the weather.

As she cherished his eyes so much, Gyebong didn't want to mention another hypothesis—what if Master Nam didn't like her anymore one day. She was about to bring up that possibility as something not absolutely impossible, but she forbore from saying it, perhaps because of her girlish wish to hang on to beautiful things, or because of her romantic instinct. She knew that saying it wouldn't affect their relationship in any way, yet still she didn't want to put that possibility into words. Nevertheless, she wasn't the sort of girl who believed that a man with such eyes would never betray his love, nor was she ready to argue for eternal love.

"Oh, by the way . . ."

Returning to her seat, Gyebong changed the topic.

"I expected you would have grown up a bit and matured in the meantime. But I find you the same as before."

"What do you mean?"

Seungjae, unable to catch the drift of her talk, blinked his eyes.

"I mean what you're doing here. Didn't I say this clinic would be useless? What stubbornness is this?"

"I know this could be futile in the end, but . . ."

"You know? How smart you've become. Ha-ha-ha . . . How did you realize that? Give me a lecture on that please."

"It's nothing much. As there are so many poor people, and so many sick people around, so . . ."

"You mean you can't help them all?"

"Yes . . . It seems that humanity as a whole suffers from the disease of poverty! Because of that damnable disease of poverty they're all oozing pus . . . Oh, blast it, it's all ugly and abominable . . ."

"But is it the poor's fault if they become poor?"

"Fault?"

"No one is poor because they want to be!"

"Isn't it up to them to be poor or not?"

"Do you know anyone who chooses to be poor?"

"Well, it's true everybody wishes to live as a rich man in his own way."

"I'm not sure about being rich, but I know people wouldn't be so poverty-stricken if only wealth were distributed more evenly."

"Distribution? Unfair distribution?"

Savoring his own words, Seungjae repeated them again and again, nodding his head. Yet at present, it was just like glimpsing the cover of a book. Although the cover seemed to be enticing enough, he couldn't determine the contents, not having read the book itself, nor did he know how to condense the ideas into one mouthful to swallow them easily. Like a few loose sheets from a dictionary, Gyebong's "Distribution Theory" had no head or tail, but merely piqued Seungjae's curiosity, offering no relevant information or rather leaving him more confused.

"Perhaps we need a teacher, ha-ha-ha."

Sensing her inability to explain any further, Gyebong tried to retreat.

"A teacher? Well, I was hatching an idea right now . . ."

"What idea? How would you cope with it?"

"Build a large chemical laboratory and then . . ."

"What for?"

"For research . . ."

"Research into what?"

"How to extract the most common and abundant chemical elements from the air . . ."

"And then?"

"And produce cheap, nutritious food or things like textiles that are essential for everyday living."

"Oh, my goodness! However cheap the artificial textiles might be, say like rayon, there are still many people who would wear only rags. Don't you see that?"

"Perhaps we can make it even cheaper than now . . . for instance, offer a suit at one or two jeon, how about that?"

"Stop daydreaming! It's nothing but a fantasy. Well well, if you know your efforts are bound to be futile, why are you starting again?"

"I can't stay put doing nothing when I see so much misery around. I know I won't be able to make much difference . . . Perhaps it's something I'm doing only to console myself . . ."

"I don't understand! What was on your mind when you were talking about marriage? I wonder how you would feed me. I don't want to be starving all the time! Please keep that in mind, dear."

Gyebong wiggled her shoulders coyly like a pampered child. Pleased with her affectionate gesture, Seungjae said, grinning,

"You don't need to worry. With this clinic, I can manage well enough even if I grant favors abundantly. I can make enough, for sure."

"I'm not so sure! You saw how my parents get by. Using poverty as an excuse, they shamelessly sold their daughter, you know. How despicable!"

Gyebong spat her words out bitterly as if she had bitten a lump of salt.

At that, Seungjae recalled his visit to Mr. Jeong's store and told her what he saw and heard there (excluding the squabble her parents had). He added that they seemed to be managing well enough not to have to worry about everyday living.

Although Gyebong had written to Seungjae asking him to stop by her parents' store at her sister's insistence, she herself had totally detached her mind from her "despicable" parents. So, it wasn't a matter of concern for her whether they lived well or not. She only listened halfheartedly to Seungjae's story in order to have something to report back to Chobong later.

What interested her instead was his story about Myeongnim—that he was planning to bring Myeongnim up to Seoul after paying off her debt, and train her as a nurse. At the word nurse, Gyebong felt a little jealous with the thought, "what about me?"

It wasn't simply that she felt uneasy about Myeongnim being beside Seungjae all the time; she was jealous more because she herself wanted to obtain an opportunity to become a professional. She had already cut off relations with her parents in her mind; she had no intention of sharing her life with them, or of becoming dependent on them as an unmarried girl, even if they became quite well off.

She was clever and had enough will power and confidence to stand on her own feet, but sometimes she couldn't help but feel a certain anxiety about her future, being a young girl who considered herself an orphan. Of course she tried to dismiss such feelings, never brooding on her situation or despairing about her future. Regardless of whether she herself was concerned about it or not, it was only natural for a nearly twenty-year-old unmarried girl to have vague misgivings about the days to come, and

Gyebong too could not be free from such misgivings from time to time.

It was true that her sister Chobong was doing everything for her out of unusual sisterly affection, yet she couldn't depend on her since Chobong herself didn't have any security for her own future. Anyway, Gyebong had never even considered depending on her sister, regardless of how Chobong fared. Not only did she refuse to go to school under her sponsorship, she even took a job as she didn't want to have free room and board at her sister's house.

The job she took, however, could offer no secure prospects for the future, being simply a way of killing time at the most. Most girls in such a situation would pursue marriage as a more secure alternative to a job, but she reacted quite negatively when Seungjae brought up marriage.

Gyebong had never considered marriage as a possible way of escaping from her insecure life. She wanted to enjoy her youth as an independent woman, without being indebted to anyone. This thought was firmly rooted in her mind, leaving no possibility for her to waver. Therefore, she needed a solid profession, as well as special skills to obtain such a profession.

"Let me be a nurse too, please, won't you?"

Gyebong, extending her hands, pleaded like a child asking for candies.

"A nurse?"

Seungjae just smiled back, taking it as a joke as Gyebong had spoken with a big smile.

"What? Am I no good?"

"There's no reason you can't be, but . . ."

"But what?"

"Why a nurse, out of all professions?"

"He-he . . . Then how about a pharmacist? Or a doctor? That would be even better . . . starting from tomorrow, I'll come in and you can teach me, all right?"

"No, that won't work."

"Why?"

"They're going to discontinue the examination system very soon, but . . ."

"Oh my goodness!"

"But my Gyebong doesn't need to worry."

"Really?"

"Sure, sure!"

"Why?"

"You can study and take exams to get into a medical school or a pharmaceutical school."

Excited, Gyebong began to smile widely, but then stopped and stared at Seungjae for some time before she blurted out,

"No, I don't like that idea!"

"You don't like it?"

"I don't want to."

"Is it that you'd feel ashamed if I paid for your schooling? Or is it too embarrassing?"

"I don't mean that."

"Then why? What's your objection?"

"I just don't want to."

"Why on earth don't you want to?"

"Because my indebtedness to you would interfere with our relationship, whether in love or marriage."

Gyebong, still smiling, studied Seungjae's expression. Seungjae was so dumbfounded he almost burst out laughing, but holding back, he became sullen and pouted.

"Stop talking nonsense. Am I not capable of sending you to school? Or would I force you to marry me in return for sending you to school? What nonsense!"

"I know you wouldn't. But what if I can't ignore that sense of obligation? What if I feel obliged to marry you even though I don't want to get married?"

"You shouldn't confuse two different things."

"I know I shouldn't in theory. Yet reality is far more imperative than theory, isn't it?"

Right at that moment, the room brightened up as the electricity came on. The additional light wasn't really needed yet. That change reminded Seungjae that it was dinnertime. Seungjae said, standing up,

"Well, well, let's leave it as a project, and have dinner now, how about that?"

"Let me see . . ."

"What shall I serve you? I can't take a lady to my regular chophouse, he-he."

"A chophouse? You haven't found a good inn yet?"

"There's nothing better at an inn! It could be even filthier . . . I live in the house behind this clinic, planning to take care of myself, and for the time being, I go to a chophouse for meals."

"You should quit living in such a deplorable way! Taking care of yourself, and going to a chophouse, what sort of life is that?"

"If you feel so bad about that, why don't you move in and stay with me?"

"Shall I? That sounds like fun!"

"We can hire a maid . . . Myeongnim will come up before long, so you can have a companion . . ."

"Ha-ha-ha, but people would think we're married."

"Heh, it will be all right if I tell them you're my sister."

"How can you marry me if I'm your sister?"

"Who cares? . . . Nevertheless, I'm not joking, but I really think you can move in even tomorrow. You've been saying you're uncomfortable living at your sister's."

"I can't move out and leave my sister behind in that place. If I could, I would have found a boarding house already."

Gyebong's face clouded with pity for her sister.

Seungjae too wasn't without some residue of emotion about Chobong, so he began pacing up and down behind Gyebong's chair, with his hands behind his back.

At last Gyebong turned back, and catching the skirt of his gown, said,

"Uh-uh, if you allow me to bring my sister along, perhaps I can . . ."

"With your sister?"

"Why? It wouldn't work?"

"No, no, I don't mean that, but . . ."

"Then why not?"

"No, it's quite all right with me, but . . ."

"If you do that instead of sending me to school, you'd become a really good and sweet Master Nam."

"That might be a good bargain, I think . . ."

Speaking rather carelessly, Seungjae was pacing up and down again, absorbed in his own thoughts.

Seungjae was as yet ignorant about the details of Chobong's situation—how she had suffered and endured the horrible vicissitudes of her life, let alone her desperate condition at present, in which she could choose neither life nor death.

Gyebong had sent a letter to him, explaining her sister's situation, but it was extremely cursory, containing no information that would allow him to imagine the extent of Chobong's misery. He merely guessed that she must be unhappy; he felt sorry for her and vaguely determined to help her in any way possible, when an opportunity arose, for instance, by encouraging her to pursue a new sort of life, and finding a way to make it possible for her.

Although he had been prepared to offer assistance to Chobong, he thought it would be untimely to bring her into his love nest with Gyebong, especially when they had only just confirmed each other's feelings that day and were about to move into a romantic relationship. It seemed inauspicious to him.

If the three of them lived together, ripples of subtle emotion would be generated, leading to delicate conflicts among them. As he thought of this possibility, he couldn't instantly welcome Gyebong's proposal.

If such conflicts took place among them, what he did to save her might end up causing her a new kind of grief and unhappiness. Not only that, his more urgent concern was that such conflicts might cause serious problems in his relationship with Gyebong.

But if he looked deeper into his mind, he would have found an intricate web of emotions circling around his somewhat selfish cautiousness. He hadn't completely erased the memories of his first love. Even though they were merely images imprinted in his heart, unable to evoke any passion or lingering affections, yet still, traces of one's first love could leave behind indelible scars, like pockmarks acquired in childhood.

And to be sure, they were also more than mere scars; even as his heart was burning intensely with fresh passion for his new love, faint shadows of sad nostalgia might arise from the scars, and linger in a corner of his heart.

It would be nothing but a "ghost of love," much like the ghosts that roam the outskirts of countryside villages. So Seungjae too would occasionally be a disciple of Hamlet, encountering the ghost of his first love as Hamlet did the ghost of his deceased father. Furthermore, based on how he felt, he assumed Chobong too would feel the same way.

This probability that both he and Chobong might not have completely forgotten each other loomed distinctly in his mind when Gyebong expressed her desire to bring along her sister. He became quite uneasy, imagining the most unpleasant result that might arise from the three of them living intimately together in the same house, that is to say, the revival of old love. In short, he was hesitant because he didn't want to expose himself to such danger.

Seungjae had always been sympathetic toward Chobong. That sympathy he meant to maintain in the future as well. But he had never dreamed of embracing her as his wife; she was an impure woman who had belonged to several men, and especially now he had Gyebong beside him. Perhaps most men experience mysophobia in relation to their women, but Seungjae, being a timid man, was more fastidious about women's purity than most men. So he retreated into himself like a frightened clam that tightly closes its shell.

Gyebong at last grabbed Seungjae, who was pacing restlessly, sat him down in a chair, and started to relate the full story of Chobong's miserable life in a calm voice.

"On her way to Seoul, she ran into Bak Jeho by chance, and . . ."

Beginning with this unlucky incident, Gyebong repeated the whole tale of her sister's misfortunes to Seungjae exactly as she had heard it told by her sister time and time again. And since the autumn of last year, Gyebong herself had been a witness to everything. So she could explain in more detail as well as more precisely than Chobong would have done—things like Jang Hyeongbo's wicked personality, the unnatural relationship between Hyeongbo and Chobong, her excessive attachment to Songhui, the recent intensity of her desperation, almost at the brink of death, her mental and physical deterioration, Hyeongbo's malicious threats and harm toward Songhui.

The account lasted almost one hour. Gyebong in the end added,

"I'm pretty sure that my sister intends to leave Songhui in my care to keep her away from the villain Jang's venomous grasp, and then kill herself."

In the end, Seungjae couldn't help but be stirred with indignation. The image of Chobong as a suffering, trembling lamb superseded all other images of her, and his self-protective wall at once crumbled like that of the Bastille, and the timid clam with its tightly closed shell was radically transformed into something quite different.

While listening to Gyebong, his reactions wavered; his face kept changing color, alternating from red to pale; at times he became quite moved while at others, clenching his fists, his nostrils flaring, he burned with fury; he often let out deep sighs, trembling. When Gyebong at last mentioned Chobong's intention to commit suicide, Seungjae could suppress his rage no longer, and shouted,

"What a damnable scoundrel!"

With this exclamation, large teardrops began to stream down his cheeks. He wiped away the tears with his big fist, muttering,

"Who could endure such a villain! I should thrash him or . . ."

Gyebong didn't feel as agitated as Seungjae. Rather amused by his excited reaction, she stared at him with a smile for some time, and then shaking her head, said,

"You know even such a villain is protected by the law. It protects his life as well as his property. And there's even a promissory notes act that allows him to prosper in the high-interest loan business. In a word, he's as much a full citizen in the eyes of the law as you and me, when in fact he's the most vicious devil in the whole world."

Seungjae placed his two arms on the table and, leaning his chin on them, stared intently ahead. Wrinkles lined his forehead, and he seemed engrossed in thought.

Gyebong's words, "protected by the law," were a fresh stimulus to his thoughts. Although it didn't convey as clear a message as "La Marseillaise," it somehow had a pungent flavor, as if he had drunk mint tea to the point of bitterness.

Filled with such strange pungency, which made him feel refreshed as well as stunned, Seungjae wondered why. He was frowning as he tried to figure out the true meaning of that effect.

Despite her curiosity, Gyebong left him to his pondering, and began to tap the center of the table with the tip of her finger, rocking her body to and fro.

The silence continued for quite some time. Gyebong at last pulled at Seungjae's arm, feeling bored. Seungjae started with a wince, and came to his senses to find Gyebong there. He smiled brightly.

"What are you thinking about so intently?"

"Oh, nothing important . . . By the way, we should bring your sister over here first, right?"

Seungjae sounded resolute, not even considering whether Hyeongbo would release Chobong so easily or not. The fire that had started to burn within hadn't as yet offered him a proper or viable way ahead; he was more like the knight-errant in a paper helmet who tilted at windmills, riding a lean donkey, wielding a broken wooden sword. Yet his determination to steal Chobong and vanquish Hyeongbo, and by that action to take further revenge on the law, was a definite indication that he was moving in the right direction.

"Really? Oh, thank you so much . . ."

Delighted, Gyebong jumped up and moved behind Seungjae, to embrace him from behind.

"You're truly my good Master Nam, ha-ha-ha."

"Well, let's proceed this way."

"Sure, how?"

"We should consult with your sister first about our plans."

"I'm sure she would accept the offer on the spot . . . Especially since it comes from you, not from anyone else . . . By the way . . . I think my sister hasn't forgotten you yet!"

"What idle talk!"

"No, whenever you come up in our conversation, her face really changes, I've seen it happen many times . . ."

"That can't be!"

Seungjae was suddenly reminded of his reservation, thinking it would be a big problem indeed. He became quite uneasy with worry. At that moment, shaking his shoulders, Gyebong blurted out,

"Oh, by the way, if, by any chance, you start a relationship with my sister, and make trouble for me, I won't tolerate it, you should be aware! Really, really, I mean it!"

"Why? Didn't you just say you're not sure whether you'd marry me or not?"

"What did you say?"

Although her voice wasn't sharp, it wasn't the same as before when she was playing with his affection like a baby.

Gyebong withdrew her arms that were around Seungjae's chest, and went back to her seat. Seungjae smiled awkwardly, regretting what he had just said. Yet he soon discovered that there were no signs of anger whatsoever in her face. There were only traces of a smile at the corners of her mouth, somewhat mischievous or rather pleased, but not at all disturbed.

"Do you really mean it?"

"No, no, don't misunderstand me, he-he."

"Shall I go home and send my sister to you right now?"

"No, no! I was just teasing you to see how you would respond."

"Look, Master Nam! I genuinely mean it; there's no cunning

in what I'm about to say. I beg you, do as you please, don't worry about me! It's obvious that my sister still has lingering affection for you, so if you're still carrying a flame for her, it would work out best for both of you. You needn't have a whit of concern for me . . ."

"I said I didn't mean it that way . . ."

"We'll wait and see if you meant it that way or not. Nevertheless, you should listen to me, even if it's only for future reference, all right? I'm saying that I will take all or nothing. Unless I can take the whole, I won't take anything at all. Bits of love, I have no business with that, do you get it? . . . It doesn't mean that I would feel jealous of my sister, not at all. I would quit before I felt that. Love divided, getting just a portion of it, I would absolutely refuse that. If it's love, it must be whole, otherwise, it would have no significance, and I won't be satisfied at all. Demanding the whole, that's my proud way of bookkeeping, my bookkeeping in love . . ."

Her tone of voice was neither cold nor angry; it wasn't without affability, nor was it a torrent of words thrown out as a result of heated emotions. She seemed to have proper control of her tongue, never giving free rein to her passions, she talked calmly all the way through, turning her speech into a rather interesting and friendly discourse.

Seungjae was now quite pleased; his wide nostrils flared, and the ends of his mouth curled upward in a smile despite himself. Although he had provoked it, the unexpected display of her passion for him, which he noticed in Gyebong's discourse, was quite satisfactory to him.

Maintaining her calm posture, Gyebong continued to talk, as if she were in a dream.

"It was three years ago! No, as it started in the winter the

year before, when I was fifteen years old, it was almost four
years ago, I think. I was merely a young girl then, still childish,
I could make neither head nor tail of anything! I just liked you
a lot. Perhaps a seed was planted then, unknown to me, maybe
unknown to you too. During the ensuing four years, I grew
taller, my mind grew more mature. The seed also grew; first
it sprouted, and put out leaves, then it took root, spread its
branches, and now it's become a distinctly visible, big tree . . .
When I think back over the gradual process of its growth, it's
quite amazing . . . Isn't it a marvel?"

Although Gyebong wasn't seeking consent, Seungjae kept
nodding his head, elated.

"But to tell the truth, love has nothing to do with 'the principle of the conservation of energy,' nor does it subscribe to
'the law of impenetrability.' Therefore, during that long period
of time, I could have forgotten you, or even if I hadn't forgotten you, I could have cultivated another love, or at least could
have had such an opportunity. Even if I did that, it couldn't be
deemed as a betrayal. Nevertheless, somehow I didn't do that,
and ended up loving you dearly and completely, I guess. I'm not
saying this to boast of my faithfulness, nor am I demanding a
reward from you. There's no basis to press you for a payback as
I've never lent you anything. Love attained through pleading is
not love, but merely pity . . ."

"I understand very well, my dearest . . ."

Seungjae affectionately patted her hands, which he had been
caressing all along, and added,

"And I'm now as certain as you are . . . You see what . . .?"

As she was studying Seungjae's beaming face, she too gave a
fleeting smile, struck by an odd thought.

It seemed to her that he was totally artless, being truthful and

ingenuous all the time, to be sure. But he also looked stupid as
his facial muscles were moving so awkwardly. Perhaps he might
be a good match for a homely old spinster who'd been fretting
for decades teaching children at a countryside primary school.
He seemed more suited to marrying such a woman through a
matchmaker, rather than to being in love with an urban girl.
Such a love might be too much for him, Gyebong thought,
smiling to herself.

Gyebong's nerves were as sound as her physical health. At
times, through her sturdy, pliable nervous system, she absorbed
modern wisdom as it was delivered, and at others, she accepted
it after having bent it to suit her. Her intelligence grew with this
discreet elasticity. On the other hand, if she were a consumptive,
oversensitive type of maiden, one who is apt to be overwhelmed
by so-called modern wisdom (in fact, there are no such maidens
here yet, though they can occasionally be found in the novels of
André Gide or Paul Valéry, therefore this is only hypothetical),
she wouldn't have seen Seungjae's awkward muscle movements as
merely a merry object of satirical jest. Such a morbid girl might
very well have tasted the odd excitement of her diseased nerves,
seeing Seungjae as a spectacle, rather like a hippopotamus in a
zoo, or even thrown him out of her house, loathing him as a
barbarian.

Neither did Gyebong belong to the opposite extreme, that
is, the conventional type of docile woman; for instance, imagine
a country bride who has just married a middle school student
with a buzz cut; she may even treasure his worn-out suit as much
as her new silk dress, and store them both carefully side by side
in her wardrobe. Such a rustic bride would adore her young
husband so much that she would say even his farts smell sweet.

Gyebong had no such blind adoration for Seungjae, neither

was she a victim of neurotic sensibility. She had normal, healthy senses that could see Seungjae's shortcomings for what they were.

To her eyes, Seungjae was rather antiquated, both inside and out; he was irresolute, tardy, sluggish, inept at using resources, unmindful of his shabbiness, and a bit childish. He was so naive that he had mentioned marriage the moment their romantic relationship had just started. Thus she couldn't be unaware of the deep chasm between herself and Seungjae, a chasm as wide as if they were living in different centuries. Despite all that, Seungjae was her first love, a puppy love, which had strong enough magic to make even rough walking socks look like silk stockings. Whatever people might say, the two lovers were quite happy with each other, gaily enjoying each other's company.

They stayed in the clinic until eight o'clock, discussing ways to help Chobong. Then they decided to go to Jongno to find a decent restaurant, and after dinner to head to Chobong's place, Jongno being halfway between the clinic and Chobong's home.

Their plan was first to have a meeting among the three of them, to hear Chobong's opinions, as well as to discuss a future course of action; secondly, Seungjae would meet up with Hyeongbo then and there or the following day, depending on the situation, and try to persuade him without resorting to harsh words. If Hyeongbo conceded to their plan, listening to reason, they would be lucky. But if not, they would seek other methods. That was what Seungjae and Gyebong roughly decided to do.

Their plan, however, was rather unrealistic. Asking Chobong's opinion was a matter of no consequence, but introducing Seungjae to Hyeongbo for a face-to-face negotiation would be far from beneficial. What kind of a man was Hyeongbo? Polite negotiation aside, even beseeching him on bended knee, begging for a hundred days, wouldn't sway him one bit. Even if they engaged in a violent wrestling match, the result would be no different. The only remaining option would be to kidnap Chobong and hide her in Seungjae's house. That too would be jeopardized, since Hyeongbo, having already been made aware of the existence of Seungjae, would no doubt locate him in the end. Hyeongbo would never rest until he found her, searching day and night, in a towering rage.

The plan was proposed by Gyebong, and accepted by Seungjae, who was too naive to imagine how horrendous Hyeongbo's character really was. Gyebong, who knew it better, wanted to come up with more discreet measures, but couldn't figure out anything better. She just let her worries rest, trusting Seungjae's strong fists to do what was necessary if things went wrong.

Suppressing the boastful mood that made his shoulders swell, Seungjae took off his doctor's gown, and changed into a black serge tsumeeri suit, the only suit he had.

Gyebong recognized the jacket and flashed a smile. Seungjae too smiled awkwardly, catching the meaning of her smile.

"When will you stop looking so shabby?"

"Oh, wait just a while, a way out is coming soon . . ."

Seungjae placed his hat on his head, while Gyebong, hanging on his arm, began to implore,

"What can that 'way out' be, I wonder! Please stop evading the issue, and listen to me."

"Yes, dear?"

"Now you've become a full doctor, you have to treat me to something!"

"Treat you? . . . Sure, why not?"

"Promise?"

"Of course!"

"You'll do as I command?"

"Yes."

"Good! Then while we're downtown tonight, let's go to a tailor's shop, and order a new suit for you, please?"

"Ah, is that what you want? I've already had a new suit made."

"Really? Then why aren't you wearing it?"

"It isn't finished yet . . . You know Mr. Gang who'll run this clinic with me, he wanted to give me a present, saying that I looked like an assistant rather than a doctor. He-he, he ordered a new suit for me to celebrate our partnership or something, ha-ha."

"That's very nice of him . . . Then I should buy you a present as well. What would you like? A necktie? Or a dress shirt?"

"No, that's quite all right. My Gyebong doesn't need to give me any present at all."

"Oh, why not?"

"Do you really have to? Then buy something cheap . . ."

"Then it will be a necktie. I'll choose a bright color . . . ha-ha-ha-ha. I can't wait to see you in that tie and a new suit. When will it be ready, the suit?"

"They said they would bring it early tomorrow morning . . ."

"Tomorrow morning? How wonderful!"

Gyebong was elated like a happy baby. Seungjae checked the windows before going out.

"Look, dear. Tomorrow is my day off, so let's make a plan, huh?"

"You want to go on an outing?"

"Right, you dress up in your new suit, and let's get away . . ."

"Where?"

"Anywhere outside the city . . ."

"That would be nice!"

"Ha-ha, wearing a new suit, accompanied by your amie, and going out into the suburbs on a fine May day. Ha-ha, Isn't that an extraordinary challenge for you, Master Nam?"

"Extraordinary challenge? Yes, it is a challenge all right . . .

But I'm not sure if we can really go out like that."

"Why not?"

"In case we have to hurry to take care of your sister's problem tonight or tomorrow . . ."

"In that case, we won't be able to go, for sure. But let's do it if there's nothing else we need to do tomorrow . . . Ah, right, we can take my sister with us, and Songhui too. I think you can carry Songhui on your back, ha-ha-ha-ha."

Gyebong almost split her sides with laughter, and Seungjae too laughed like a bull. They were in that period of a relationship when even a trivial thing could trigger laughter. Seungjae took some time to lock the door of the consultation room, and turning back, mumbled,

"Me, carry a baby on my back? . . . That would certainly make me look like a servant. He-he."

Seungjae was in fact thinking that he would look like Songhui's dad, married to Chobong, rather than a servant. To throw off that ominous foreboding, he turned it into a joke in his own inept way.

While he was diffident, Gyebong was broad-minded and indifferent to such trivial worries. So she retorted gaily,

"A servant? No, you would look like the baby's dad, ha-ha-ha."

As Gyebong openly mentioned that ominous word "dad," Seungjae too was released from constraint.

"If I look like the baby's dad, wouldn't it cause more trouble? Wouldn't someone cry?"

Seungjae's attempted retort was instantly returned by Gyebong.

"If you can make me cry, you'll be praised for that . . . I wish Songhui had a good dad like you!"

"Having said love is a sort of game, she must be playing it!"

Taking his shoes out of the shoe drawer, Seungjae mumbled

to himself, at which Gyebong squarely stared him in the face and said,

"Have you been caught in a sudden downpour? What are you mumbling about now?"

"You're making fun of me."

"No, I assure you I'm not, my Master Seungjae!"

"Then what is it?"

"I'm simply neither a calmotinist nor a conventist, that's it. Do you know what a calmotinist is? It's someone who relies on the sedative Calmotin when brokenhearted. And, well, a conventist is someone who goes into a convent to become a nun."

"How do you know all those things? How good you are at making up strange words! I wonder where you learned all that?"

Seungjae stood there, smiling at her in amazement.

"Ha-ha-ha . . . Let's put jesting aside. Regardless of what I said, I really hope my Songhui can find a good Papa like Master Nam! She's absolutely adorable, you'll see that when you meet her later."

"Is she?"

"Indeed! You too will fall for her when you see her."

"Do you also adore her that much?"

"More than that! . . . That pretty little girl is not only beautiful in appearance, but behaves so sweetly as well. How can I resist her!"

"Then do you mean that you'd dislike her if she weren't so pretty or not so sweetly behaved?"

"Of course I adore her because she looks so pretty and behaves sweetly. It's only natural, I think. You've seen my younger brother, Byeongju, haven't you? He looks like an ugly bull, and to match his appearance, every single thing he chooses to do is abominable. Did I ever adore him? I couldn't."

"That sounds a bit heartless! After all, he's your brother . . ."

"You're twisting the story around! Affection among siblings is a different matter, isn't it? Even if I don't like him, I still have some affection for him as my little brother. But in the case of the child of another family, I can adore him or her, without having familial affection . . ."

"Then how about that baby? Is her name Songhui?"

"Yes, Songhui . . . I adore her for herself, and feel strong familial affection for her at the same time. In both ways, I love her dearly. That's why my sister intends to die leaving Songhui in my care, I mean, because she knows how dearly I love the baby."

"Ah! How sad!"

Deeply moved again, Seungjae stood there blankly for a while, and said as if talking to himself,

"Tut, tut! . . . So a person can disregard her own life for the sake of her own child! Saving her child by sacrificing her own life! Well, well, is maternal love supposed to be so thorough and so desperate?"

"In addition, my sister's situation is unusually difficult. Incidentally, I think . . ."

Gyebong, an idea flashing into her mind, began a new topic.

"All parents, especially mothers—my mother is definitely an exception—have unbounded love for their children, but most people in the world don't deserve such precious maternal love, I think! Perhaps it's a matter of pearls before swine."

"What are you saying now?"

Seungjae, who was about to open the front door, turned back, and stared at Gyebong with an expression that seemed to say, "how do you keep saying such daring things?"

"Let's go now! We can talk while we're walking."

Gyebong pushed him out of the door as she opened it.

It was warmer outdoors, and a cozy night welcomed the couple into the crowded street.

On both sides of this narrow street small cottages were clustered, clearly revealing the poverty-stricken state of the residents
in Aeogae Pass. The street itself was jammed with people hur-
rying in and out.

Seungjae and Gyebong, emerging from the quiet, private
room into the street crowded with people, were having difficulty
in adapting to the new atmosphere. They walked in silence for
a while.

"By the way, uh . . . what should we . . ."

Seungjae broke the silence, stammering.

"I mean, what should we do about our relationship?"

"What do you mean?"

"I mean when we get to the house . . ."

"You mean to my sister? Telling her about our relationship?"

"Yes."

"Wouldn't it be improper? Having far more important things
to deal with . . ."

"Perhaps, you're right . . ."

Seungjae was also concerned about that, so he couldn't insist
on disclosing their relationship to Chobong. Yet still, he couldn't
help but feel uneasy.

If Chobong went along with their plan simply out of her
earnest desire to escape from Jang Hyeongbo, having no lingering emotions or hopes about Seungjae, there would be no
problem. However, in case Chobong, being ignorant about the
relationship between her sister and Seungjae, should misunderstand Seungjae's innocent good will as something more than
that, and begin to foster a hope for further developments, which
was not at all improbable, that could bring about a very unhappy
result, providing her with a futile hope only to be mercilessly
disappointed later. Seungjae was now really concerned about

Chobong, putting aside all self-centered concerns.

At that moment, a huge automobile intruded onto the path, shamelessly forcing its way down the narrow alley. Seungjae and Gyebong had to stand aside under the eaves of a shop along with other pedestrians, paying an imposed respect that wasn't respect at all. A car might be a product of civilization, but in this narrow street, it was nothing but a barbarous ruffian.

As they were about to step back onto the street, this time, a boy on a bike, perhaps an errand boy from a store, rode up the alley, steering a zigzag line among the packed passersby, as if he were in a circus. As he passed by the couple, he whistled and threw out a naughty exclamation, "Bravo, you two!"

Seungjae grinned awkwardly, while Gyebong, annoyed, cast a reproachful glance at the boy.

"That boy may also grow into a poisonous weed!"

Gyebong was reminded of the conversation discontinued earlier, and resumed the topic.

"By the way, I didn't finish my talk about maternal love, right? . . . Perhaps I should charge you a high tuition-fee for my lecture! Ha-ha."

"Well, I'll decide after hearing the whole theory . . ."

"Ha-ha, it doesn't deserve the title of a theory . . . Nevertheless, maternal love is sacred, and therefore the most valuable emotion, isn't it?"

"I agree . . ."

"You do? Then let's choose anyone at random to examine. Jang Hyeongbo might be a good example . . . Let's see, if we look back into his childhood, he too should have been beloved by his mother. However incapacitated or softheaded a child might be, mothers usually raise their children with wholehearted affection and devotion, don't they? I think mothers feel stronger compassion when the child has problems, or is incapacitated."

"That's true, indeed."

"Therefore, Jang Hyeongbo must have received very particular care and loving attention from his mother when he was a child, to be sure. But look at him at present. He's the most vicious rascal in the whole world, a completely useless human, therefore a poisonous weed, a poisonous weed that grew up sustained by the best fertilizer, maternal love. Just think about how many more such poisonous weeds there are in the world other than Hyeongbo. Don't you think maternal love is so often wasted on useless humans? What I'm going to say may be sinful, but I think no one can guarantee that even Songhui won't grow into a poisonous weed, that very Songhui to whom my sister is so devoted, willing to give up her life for her sake."

"You may not live long for what you just said!"

Seungjae said this to cut short Gyebong's horrible talk, using Songhui as an example, just as they arrived at the tram stop. Although he rebuked her, it was only for the part about Songhui, not about her insight itself that had introduced the concept of "poisonous weed" to characterize men like Hyeongbo. He indeed felt he had found a new perspective for his research on the law.

They got off the tram at the Jongno crossroad and walked into a restaurant located in a nearby building.

Gyebong was hungry, so hungry as to feel unable to stand upright. It had been a long while since they had last eaten together. When they were both in Gunsan, Gyebong had once cooked dinner at his place. But the rice ended up being only half-cooked. The two, however, enjoyed the almost raw rice along with the one side dish of pickled radish as if it were a sumptuous feast. That was half a year ago.

Recounting such memories, they relished each other's company as much as the meal itself. As both were quite hungry, they gobbled up their food merrily; Seungjae, especially, ate almost enough for two people. They had no reason to hurry, so they spent a long time at the restaurant, then came out onto the street at a leisurely pace.

They had full stomachs, and had nothing to worry about in their relationship, for they had confirmed each other's feelings. They didn't need to feel shy in the open street. Moreover, Jongno was quite different from Aeogae. People here unkindly pushed past them, making them hurry to get out of the way.

It was warm, but then there was no reason for it to be cooler, given that it was early May. It was a little past nine, yet since the days were long, it was still early evening. They were happy about everything. To avoid the side of the road where people flocked to do shopping at the night market, Seungjae and Gyebong crossed to the other side where Hwashin Department Store was standing tall, and began to stroll slowly toward Donggwan.

They admired the imposing power of the dark buildings soaring up into the sky and enjoyed the screeching sounds of trams on iron rails mixed with all sorts of other noises of the city. The more lively the atmosphere surrounding them, the more comfortable they felt together. The streetlights loomed tall over the paved street on which many people were coming and going, in front of the couple and behind them. It could have made them feel somewhat awkward, but as they were intoxicated by each other's presence, they felt as though they were walking through a fairyland.

When a couple walks down a street, the quality of their outfits is usually matched, neither one looking better or worse than the other does. But Seungjae and Gyebong looked quite mismatched, as Seungjae's clothes were so shabby. Regardless, the two walked proudly along the main street, unaware of that disparity, although Gyebong constantly drew the attention of the passersby.

They turned to the north at Pajugae in Donggwan, and it was around nine-thirty when they arrived at the alley leading to Chobong's home.

Gyebong led the way and entered the alley, where she found four people—their housemaid, the couple from next door, and the housewife from the house opposite—standing close together under the bright outdoor lamp of the gate, discussing something seriously.

People such as servants or live-in maids often get together and have fun chatting or sharing gossip about their masters and mistresses. So it wouldn't have been unusual for their maid to be one of them. However, that particular maid of Chobong's wasn't the type to go out in the evening unless she was forced to do an errand. She could go out during the day to chat, but not after sunset.

When serving the supper and washing the dishes were over, that is, by eight o'clock in the evening, the maid usually went back to her room, and fell asleep, snoring loudly. If she was needed for an errand, someone had to go to her room and wake her with much effort. So it was something really unprecedented that she was out talking at such a late hour.

Thinking it rather odd, Gyebong stopped, and at that moment the four people all turned their heads toward her at the same time, sensing someone approaching. There certainly was something wrong by the look on their faces, and the maid, obviously flurried, but glad to see her, ran toward Gyebong, and said in a muffled voice, almost crying,

"Oh, my, my, little Miss!"

"Yes, what is it?"

A dark premonition suddenly flashed into her mind. Gyebong was about to rush into the house, but stopped and turned toward the maid, inviting her with her eyes to say something. She was completely flabbergasted, not knowing what to do. They say when someone is in a desperate state, they often lose their mobility, just plump down on the ground, only able to move their bottom up and down. That certainly has some truth.

Gyebong was extremely agitated, looking this way and that, unable to move, because she believed that Chobong was dead, to be sure.

"Hurry up, Miss! You should go in and have a look. Something terrible has happened in the house!"

At this urging of the maid, Gyebong ran through the gate and was in the yard in a second. There she was astounded again on witnessing an utterly unexpected scene.

"Ah, Sis!"

Overwhelmed with joy, Gyebong ran into the room opposite the main room, shedding a flood of tears, almost falling on her face.

Her sister, who she assumed must be dead, was stepping out from the open door of the opposite room, dressed in new clothes, her hair tidily combed back. Songhui was sound asleep on the warm floor of the room.

"What, has something happened?"

Seungjae, instead of following Gyebong into the house, stopped in front of the gate, addressing the question to the others in general. Seungjae also had an ominous premonition about Chobong, but didn't rush into the house. The way he tried to get some information in advance might seem to suggest calm discretion, but the truth was that he was asking the question because he was equally confounded, and equally at a loss as to what to do.

The maid should have stepped forward and answered him, but since Seungjae was a stranger to her, she just sidled away, wary of him. Seungjae gave up expecting an answer and tried to summon up his courage to enter the house, when the only man in the group of people, the tenant of the servant's quarters of the house next door, stepped forward and asked bluntly,

"Who are you?"

The strange visitor to this house of disaster, whom he had never seen before in the neighborhood, seemed to have triggered his curiosity.

Instead of answering, Seungjae just turned his head toward the man, regretting his attempt to get some information, and feeling annoyed.

"Are you from the neighborhood office, perhaps?"

Moving a few steps nearer to Seungjae, the man addressed him again, this time in a more polite manner.

Coming from the neighborhood office was a polite way of asking if he'd come from the police. Seungjae was wearing a high-collared black suit studded with tarnished gold buttons as well as a hat, so he appeared to be either a policeman who had left behind his sword and police cap, or a plainclothes police-man. Even if they turned someone who wasn't a policeman into a policeman, they had nothing to lose, so long as they hadn't left their cart in the middle of a street, or created a drunken row in public.

Seungjae didn't catch the implied meaning of the word, "neighborhood office," but as he wasn't even a clerk of a local district office, he shook his head.

"I see. Then do you have any connections with this family?"

The man from next door, holding his hands behind his back, asked in a dignified manner.

"Yes, I'm from the same hometown."

"Then, please go into the house quickly . . . I think someone has been hurt inside."

"Someone! Has someone really got hurt?"

In spite of the premonition he had had earlier, Seungjae became utterly flustered, ready to rush into the house. Then he suddenly recalled that he was a doctor, but a doctor who didn't even have a stethoscope with him. Uncertain about what he should do, one moment he determined to take a taxi and drive back to his clinic to fetch medical equipment, and the next moment, thinking that the injured person would be left alone while he was gone, he decided to run into the house instantly. But then the next second his thoughts turned to the necessity of sending for a doctor from the nearest hospital. No, no, that may not be necessary, but what would be best? . . . Changing his mind every second, he wavered this way and that, unable to move in any direction.

Seungjae had misunderstood the man's words, "someone has been hurt," as literally meaning that a person had been injured.

The man from next door, not knowing what was going on in Seungjae's mind, repeated rather sluggishly,

"Yes, someone has definitely been hurt, definitely . . ."

Then casting a sideways glance at the maid, he added,

"The master of this house has perhaps definitely . . ."

"You mean that the master has hurt his wife, right?"

As Seungjae asked, gasping, the man slowly shook his head and said,

"No, no! . . . It was the mistress who did it to the master . . ."

"What?"

"She turned him into a corpse!"

"What!"

Seungjae couldn't even finish his scream, all the strength instantly draining out of his body. He murmured as if waking from a dream,

"You weren't talking about an injury? And the victim wasn't the mistress . . . but the husband, and he wasn't injured, but killed?"

"Yes! I think that's what happened! I don't know the details, but definitely that's what happened, it seems."

Seungjae stood there, blinking his eyes.

He could have nodded his head as at something probable, if, for instance, Chobong had committed suicide, or if, as he suspected earlier, Hyeongbo had injured Chobong, however shocking that might be. But the news that Chobong had killed Hyeongbo, that was beyond all imagination, something utterly incomprehensible.

Seungjae at last recovered his senses and ran into the house, and the three spectators who were standing in front of the gate pricked up their ears, suppressing their yawns.

Chapter 18:
An Angel Without, a Demon Within

Let's turn the clock back to about eight o'clock the same evening.

Chobong was preparing to go out shopping while Songhui was asleep; she combed her hair, which she hadn't touched for the past few days, and changed into a better dress.

Hyeongbo, who'd been checking bills at his desk in one corner of the room, furtively glancing sideways at Chobong, at last spoke up.

"So, what's the occasion, making such a fuss about your appearance?"

Though he couldn't control her going out in his absence, if he saw it happening, he always tried to interfere, and especially disliked her going out in the evening.

"Women aren't supposed to be exposed to the night dew, don't you know that? Ugh!"

As Chobong didn't respond, Hyeongbo raised his snakehead to irritate her. She winced a little at first, as there was something she wanted to hide, but she soon recovered her composure, tucked the sheet around Songhui one more time, patted her, and turned back, ready to go out without even a glance at Hyeongbo.

Hyeongbo quickly crawled to the door, placed himself in front of it to block her exit, and tilting his head back to look up at her, demanded,

"Where are you going? Where to, for God's sake?"

"I'm going out to buy a few things, why are you so anxious about nothing?"

"Let me have the list, I'll buy them for you!"

Hyeongbo relaxed a little, and with an awkward smile, stretched out his hand with his palm out to Chobong, like a beggar.

"Never mind!"

"Let me do it, please!"

"Why on earth are you bothering me! Won't you move away?"

"How about sending the nanny instead?"

"Why won't you get out of the way?" Chobong shouted, and, biting her lower lip, she raised her leg intending to kick Hyeongbo's back.

"Damn!"

Hyeongbo moved aside, grudgingly giving way. It wasn't that he didn't have enough stubbornness to defeat her, but he pretended to give in only to humor her. He tried to endure discomfort or suppress his temper, because he wanted to avoid any outright confrontation with her. He had a genuine desire to keep Chobong's mind at ease, although it was without doubt the desire of a cunning "snake" . . .

"I won't care even if the little thing wakes up and cries."

"If you make the baby cry, I'll slash your belly open!"

Chobong looked back at Songhui one more time and walked out onto the maru, with the hem of her long skirt sweeping the floor.

"Damn it! How often you've threatened to slash Jang Hyeongbo's belly! . . . Nevertheless, be sure to be back within twenty minutes."

"I won't come back, ever!"

"Pah! What about the hostage I have here?"

Curling his lip up, he looked back at Songhui with satisfaction.

ONCE UPON A time, there lived a couple. The wife eloped with her paramour, deserting her suckling baby. The baby kept crying all the time, seeking its mother, and at last starved to death. The husband removed the baby's intestines and salted its body like a fish. He procured a large padlock, and put it in a bag along with the baby's salt-cured body. Carrying the bag on his back, he set out to search for his wife. After wandering twelve years around the country, he found her. He pierced a hole through her breast, attached the salt-cured body to it with the padlock, and locked it. He then said, "Now, suck at it as much as you please," and turned back to go on his way.

Hyeongbo, with the pretense of telling an age-old story, had repeated this horrible story to Chobong many times. Each time, Chobong had shuddered, her lips turning pale, and covered her ears with her hands. Hyeongbo used to pretend not to notice Chobong's terrified reaction, and nonchalantly added in a louder voice,

"She could have eloped with the baby on her back, couldn't she?"

Without waiting for Chobong's answer, he would promptly offer an answer of his own.

"In that case, the baby would have been padlocked to her breast, alive, pah!"

Chobong was fully aware that this wasn't an empty threat, but something Hyeongbo certainly might do, considering his personality. She had never dreamed of the possibility of running away, leaving Songhui behind. But she dared not even consider the possibility of running away with Songhui because of such threats from Hyeongbo.

Hyeongbo knew her thoughts well enough, so he didn't worry about her leaving him. Most men dislike seeing their women go out, especially at night. Hyeongbo shared this common instinct. But in addition, Hyeongbo, who turns into a "fierce wolf on the prowl" at night, had peculiar, almost pathological symptoms. Whenever it was time to turn on the electric light, he had to have Chobong within his view. Having her around when it got dark appeased him. But if she wasn't around, he became fretful, a state almost approaching madness. It was the same that night. Although he generously allowed her to go out, once she was out of his sight, his temper grew vicious, as usual. Her retort that she wouldn't ever come back was still ringing in his ears, escalating the pressure of an ominous foreboding within him, and thereby inflating his temper until he was ready to explode.

Chobong went to a nearby pharmacy on the Donggwan Pajugae and purchased a whole bottle of potassium chlorate concentrate, containing a full five hundred grams. She also bought one hundred empty capsules.

She was finally in possession of a deadly drug. That morning she had come upon the idea of getting rid of Hyeongbo in such a way, opening a path to her own suicide.

Chobong could no longer endure her life by the side of the weird, frightful Hyeongbo, who harassed her endlessly with his insatiable sex drive. She felt as if she had been caught by a "canopy ghost" which, starting as small as a bean, grows to the size of a fist, then to that of a dog, that of a calf, that of a rice chest, until it finally unfurls into a canopy and devours the victim within its folds.

She felt like a victim enshrouded by a canopy ghost, having exhausted in the darkness all hope as well as the power to live on. Oppressed, she felt her life crumbling, and she herself was suffocating, yet she couldn't find any way out of this predicament.

For Chobong, driven to the very verge of death, life was nothing but constant agony. She almost yearned for death, which seemed to promise liberation from agony as well as rest. But once she determined to seek her own death, she could clearly foresee the evils Hyeongbo would inflict on Songhui and Gyebong. Hyeongbo was not only a canopy ghost to her, but in her absence would also become one to her beloved ones. So she wasn't free to choose even her own death, so long as Hyeongbo was alive.

Removing Hyeongbo was to remove the biggest obstacle to the suicide that she desperately desired at that moment. Unless she removed this obstacle first, her suicide would be neither a meaningful escape nor a perfect closure to her misery. That was her reasoning when she envisioned murder as her means to suicide, a suicide that had seemed so beyond her reach. Perhaps that was an arbitrary way of looking at things, or it was a precise calculation that produced the wrong answer. Perhaps she had adopted the wrong mathematical formula.

Some may say it was the product of a foolish female mind, but regardless of what onlookers might say, the person directly involved took it as the best answer, and moved on to the second stage. Chobong cracked the problem in the morning, and now in the evening, she had already purchased the deadly drug. Chobong was well aware that the drug wasn't really adequate to kill Hyeongbo, as a penultimate step before her own suicide. In order to kill effectively, she needed to get hold of a fatal poison like potassium cyanide, even a small portion of which would instantly bring about the desired result. Such a poison would be easy to mix secretly with Hyeongbo's food or drink.

She tried all day long to find a way of getting hold of cyanide, only to no avail. As it was a deadly poison, drug stores couldn't sell it to anyone. The only alternative was to steal it from a hospital or from Bak Jeho, approaching him with some pretense. Yet she could see no possible way to steal it without being noticed. So she purchased potassium chlorate instead, if only to appease her anxiety and to feel secure for the time being.

Chobong had had the experience of taking the drug when she attempted to abort Songhui the year before last. She could trust its efficacy to a certain extent. She had taken ten capsules, and it had nearly killed her. So she assumed that about thirty capsules would certainly do the job.

As for her own suicide, she could either take the same drug, or use any other means available to her, such as caustic soda, or a rope hung on a crossbeam. The point at issue was how to make Hyeongbo swallow those capsules. Thirty capsules would amount to over a fistful, a quantity that would need to be swallowed in three or four separate gulps at the least. It seemed it would be almost impossible to get Hyeongbo to take them without his catching on.

She might persuade him to take them as something good for his health. But it was highly unlikely for a man as cunning as Hyeongbo to be fooled like that. Perhaps she might become docile and act kindly toward him for about half a year to make him lower his guard, and then try it. But she couldn't even imagine putting up with him for such a long period of time, since even one moment was too long for her to endure at present.

She admitted that this potassium chlorate wasn't really what she needed, being nothing better than a backup. She resolved to quickly find a way to procure cyanide or something equally fatal.

If nothing came her way, she could, at the worst, take a sharp knife from the kitchen and use it while Hyeongbo was asleep . . . shuddering, she put her mind at rest.

They say even a woman who looks like an angel outwardly can be a demon inwardly. Whatever her complicated situation might have brought her to, no one would have imagined that such a frail and piteous-looking woman could hatch a plan to murder her so-called husband and actually purchase a deadly drug and be walking along the street in the center of the capital, carrying it with her.

Although her shopping was finished, she didn't want to go back to the house, recalling Hyeongbo's demand that she should get back within twenty minutes. She wanted to stroll around a bit longer, if only to provoke Hyeongbo. As Songhui wouldn't wake up for an hour or so, she had enough time to hang around, she thought. In addition, it was a beautiful May night, and the air was bracing enough to entice her to stay out.

The night air seemed to tickle her body delectably, passing through her thin clothes. She wanted to wander freely to enjoy this communion with the atmosphere. It was a charming night, even to those who came out often. For Chobong, who lived almost confined in the house, it was bound to be much more refreshing.

On the pavement, softly lit by street lamps, crowds of people were flowing like idle streams, crossing past each other; some moving toward her, while others passed by her, as she slowly walked all alone toward the Jongno intersection.

It was an enchanting night, for sure, but as she watched people coming and going, darkness began to permeate her mind, dampening her delight. All the faces seemed to be happy and carefree, and she couldn't see even one face that bore the marks of a miserably fading life like hers.

At last she found herself standing in front of the park. She encountered a young couple, holding the hand of a toddler between them. The child seemed a little taller than Songhui, and the young couple, looking down affectionately at the child, was laughing happily.

Filled with a surge of envy, she felt like squatting down on the spot and crying loudly. With much effort, she suppressed the urge and watched them pass by. As she blankly watched them, a vision emerged, overlapping the backs of the young couple—a dream taking the place of reality. The man was transformed into Seungjae, the woman into Chobong herself, the child toddling between her parents into Songhui . . .

Although she wasn't dreaming asleep in her bed, she intently pursued the phantom she had created, as if she really were the woman, and the woman were herself, forgetful of her own reality. In fact, even at home, she had often nourished such dreams of a happy family life with Songhui and Seungjae.

Of course, they were merely dreams, void of any hope of being able to fulfill them. She was like a lonely widow dreaming in front of wedding pictures, where she could only go back to the past in memories, but never bring it into the present. No one has that ability.

Even while she was living with Jeho, Chobong had never given up her lingering hopes regarding Seungjae. Although she had a tainted body, and thus was unworthy of Seungjae, she couldn't help secretly waiting for Seungjae to rescue her. But since she was trapped by Hyeongbo and both her body and mind had withered beyond help, she began to think that Seungjae must have forgotten her completely, considering her as no longer belonging to this world. Oddly enough, by utterly giving up thoughts of Seungjae, she began to dream as she pleased.

Gyebong occasionally passed along news of Seungjae—that he had acquired his full license as a medical doctor, or that he would open a clinic in Seoul before long. Those scraps of news had nourished her dreams.

Chobong sometimes questioned her sister to figure out how her relation with Seungjae was going, because she hoped that Gyebong and Seungjae would marry eventually. Perhaps it might seem odd and even sinful for her to want her sister to marry a man with whom she herself had had a relationship—even though it had gone no further than a vaguely romantic phase—and whom she had deserted for someone else. Furthermore, Seungjae was the man she still adored, although it was only in her dreams. Nevertheless, Gyebong's response always seemed to indicate that she and Seungjae had nothing more than friendship. Assuming it to be true, Chobong had more freely relished her own unrealistic dreams about Seungjae.

Earlier, when Gyebong had mentioned her sister's feelings toward Seungjae, it was based on what she had noticed in her conversations with her sister. Being rather guileful and secretive, she perfectly hid her own feelings while detecting her sister's feelings. Although it was highly unlikely, if Seungjae still had some lingering affection for Chobong and if Chobong found out about it, her dreams would no longer remain empty and hopeless; her almost extinguished embers of hope would rekindle and burn bright. Along with that, her withered spirit of life too would revive vigorously.

Chobong, who'd been standing in front of the park absentmindedly for quite a while, at last returned to herself. As she came back to reality, she suddenly let out a deep sigh. She felt all her energy drain out with the sigh.

She no longer wanted to wander around; her attempt to freely enjoy an evening out had proved futile, as no desire whatsoever was left within her. When she first started to walk toward Jongno, she intended to go as far as Jongno intersection, drop by the department store where Gyebong worked, stroll around inside it until it closed, and meet her sister to go home together. She also thought she would buy some tasty snacks on their way home. But as if some bad luck were following her, she encountered a happy couple walking with a child, which vividly reminded her of what was missing in her life. She now lost all interest in what was around her; she simply desired to go home, however hellish it might be, and lie down in her room.

Yet she hesitated a little because it was a rare opportunity to stay away, but she soon turned back, breathing out one more sigh, and started to walk languidly in the direction of her home.

While walking, she began to muse.

Have I not been living like a mere tree in the wood, or a nameless blade of grass in a hillside meadow, having nothing to show off nor any bad temper to fight with? I've never had any desire to stand high above others, or any need to bloom splendidly. I simply wanted to be as ordinary as anyone else, unnoticeable among people, neither doing any harm to others nor being harmed by others, carrying on quietly with an uneventful life.

Have I ever wanted any extraordinary happiness? Or luxury and comfort? Have I ever slandered anyone to profit myself? Have I ever harbored any ill will toward my parents or siblings?

My heart has never been hardened, my background has nothing grand. A mere soundless tree, a humble nameless blade of grass, I was. Despite all that, why have I been subject to such violent vicissitudes, a miserable life and horrendous persecutions? What am I going to do with this bottle? Why do I want to kill myself and even kill someone else?

What on earth has transformed me into such a frightening, wicked woman? What could it be but madness? I'm a lost soul, totally at a loss as to what to do. Some may say it's fate, but isn't life pointless after all? No matter how merciless fate could be, mine is far too obstinate and ruthless. Fate! Fate! Alas, what am I supposed to do?

She wanted to scream out, crying wildly, but she couldn't, only hot tears flooded down her cheeks. Startled by her tears, she looked around and found herself already on the wide Donggwan Street in the darkness.

Wiping away her tears with her sleeve, she listlessly walked the short remaining distance to her house. When she looked at her wristwatch under the dim streetlight, it was already eight-forty. She had hung around on the street for over forty minutes. It meant she had stayed away from home twice the length of time Hyeongbo had allotted to her. Still she didn't feel avenged at all.

She turned into the small alley leading to the house.

As she absentmindedly stepped into the alley, the shrill sound of a baby's crying reached her. It sounded as desperate as if the baby was about to faint. No doubt it was Songhui's voice; she gave a start and almost involuntarily froze, but the very next second, she frantically ran toward the house.

It wasn't time yet for Songhui to wake up on her own. Even if she woke up, she would be whimpering instead of crying so fiercely. The suspicion struck her that that evil rogue Hyeongbo must be hurting the child to vent his anger at her.

These thoughts flashed through her mind as she approached the house, which was only a few steps away once you stepped into the alley. Soon the west-facing window high up on the wall of the main bedroom fronting the alley came into view, and the sound of crying grew louder and more desperate; she wished she could break into the house through that window.

In the blink of an eye, she passed through the main gate, the inner gate, and the yard, unaware of what she was doing. She jumped up onto the maru, and violently pushed open the sliding door of the main room with a thundering sound. There, indeed, was a scene that nearly drove her out of her mind. The scene far exceeded her worst expectations, making her mind implode with rage.

Hyeongbo was dangling the child upside down, holding her in the air by the ankles with one hand, like he would do a chicken purchased for cooking. Songhui had turned blue, her hands wriggling in the air, almost choking on tears.

Hyeongbo had been checking the time ever since Chobong left home. When the twenty minutes he had allowed her went by and then nearly thirty minutes passed, and Chobong was still not back, his anxiety and irritation grew into a violent fury. Even more enraged by recalling Chobong's shrill voice threatening she would slash his belly open if he made Songhui cry, he determined to hurl the child at Chobong the moment she entered the room. But as if adding more fuel to his fury, the child woke up on her own and began to cry, aggravating his annoyance. So everything added together had triggered this "wolf on the prowl" to reveal his true, cruel nature.

He knew that either way Songhui would cry, whether he harassed her or left her alone. Either way he would get scolded by Chobong when she came home, so to vent his anger, he held Songhui upside down and kept raising her up and lowering her down repeatedly, with the intention of letting Chobong see that at whatever cost. Therefore, when he heard the sound of Chobong's footsteps, he maintained his posture holding Songhui upside down.

In a fit of rage, she glared at him, trembling violently, as if she would devour him alive, even forgetting that she should save the child first.

Casting a quick sidelong glance at Chobong, Hyeongbo threw the child onto her bedding, spitting out a curse,

"What a cursed thing; her crying made my ears sore . . ."

"You vile creature!"

With this exclamation, she dashed at Hyeongbo like an angry tigress defending its cub, and kicked him with all her might, aiming at his lower belly as he turned toward her. It was as merciless and swift a blow as that of a tigress, but it landed at a point lower than she had aimed; her foot sensed something harder than a belly, and Hyeongbo, with a loud cry, spun around a few times holding his groin tightly with both hands, then fell to the floor.

The misplaced kick luckily landed on Hyeongbo's vital spot and he had no time to avoid the sudden attack. A prostrate Hyeongbo writhed on the floor, covering his vital spot with his hands, his mouth opening and shutting repeatedly, like a catfish forced to drink water, unable to make any sounds. His eyes were all white, and he seemed about to breathe his final breath.

Looking down at Hyeongbo in agony, who seemed to be almost dying, Chobong felt a cold shiver run through her heart. Trembling with fear, she thought she should fetch some water and make him drink it while massaging the injured part. No, she should rather send for a doctor to save him, she thought the next moment. But after that, a sudden thought surged up, heating her whole body as if she had been plunged in hot water.

Right! I should kill him!

Although she didn't say it out loud, it was a bloodthirsty proclamation roaring from her very heart. She didn't even take the time to stop and reprimand herself for having thought about saving Hyeongbo's life. Perhaps she had just forgotten about that.

Anyone who saw her face at that moment would have shuddered at the resemblance between Chobong and a vicious predator; her face was flushed deep crimson, her facial muscles were twitching violently, blue veins were protruding from her neck, and her eyes were emitting a ferociously murderous glow.

"Ow, ow, I'm dying!"

Hyeongbo, in the meantime, must have recovered a little from the deadly pain, as he began to scream at the top of his voice.

Startled, Chobong bit her lips, rushed to Hyeongbo, and with her full force kicked at the spot he was attempting to cover with his hands. Chobong had guessed that that spot was lethal through his reaction. In a sense, Hyeongbo had taught her how to attack him.

Although she meant to aim at the same spot, this time it didn't work as well as the first kick. She kicked at the spot three times, but she hit the mark only once and even that wasn't effective because Hyeongbo's hands were covering it. Furthermore, knowing what she was aiming at, he dexterously dodged the attacks, turning his body this way and that, keeping his legs crossed, covering the spot with his two hands. No matter how hard her kicks might have been, they landed on his buttocks or anywhere other than the exact spot.

"Ow, this bitch is killing me!"

"Ugh, ow, ow!"

"Oh, look, this bitch is murdering me!"

"Ouch, ouch, ouch!"

"Ugh, just eat me up!"

At each of Chobong's kicks, he rejoined with a loud scream, rolling on the floor, although most of the kicks either missed completely or weren't at all painful. Even the shock of the first blow had almost receded by now, and he was merely pretending to be in pain to deceive Chobong.

Hyeongbo didn't notice Chobong's murderous intent at all. He understood the severity of what he had done to Songhui, so was expecting some outburst of wrath. But seeing her almost insane made him feel somewhat frightened. In the past, when she had gotten angry, she usually heaped abusive words on him, punching his back a few times. That was all. Never did she become so fierce and reckless.

Hyeongbo, who usually became more mellow when pushed to the extreme, simply thought that he shouldn't aggravate her anger, as she seemed to be at the peak of her venomous temper; he was afraid she might, in desperation, drink a bowl of caustic soda if he provoked her any further. So he determined not to confront her, while exaggerating his pain in response to her attacks, simply pretending to be an easy prey to her beating and kicking, until she had exhausted her anger on her own. The first attack on his vital spot he received when he was off guard, but now he was fully prepared, he knew he could withstand any of her kicks, which came from legs as slender as a bird's. Even if she kicked him tens of dozens of times, he knew he would be all right in the end, if only he protected the vital spot well enough, as he was doing right now. With such well thought-out calculation, Hyeongbo was slyly playing the role of an easy prey.

Chobong was becoming more desperate as she felt her strength draining from her with repeated kicking, while Hyeongbo seemed to be recovering despite her kicks. At that moment, an idea struck her; she had been standing in front of him while kicking him, but changing tactics, she moved to the side of him, pretending she would stop her attacks, then swiftly raised her heel and stomped on his belly with full force.

"Ow! Ow!"

This time Hyeongbo was in real pain, moving one of his hands that had been covering his vital spot to the place where he was kicked.

"Oh-h, I'm dying!"

Hyeongbo, shouting in a shrill voice, tried to dodge her attacks by rolling his body this way and that, but Chobong kept following him, repeatedly stomping on him from the side.

But one kick was quite misplaced, landing below the navel, giving a soft feel to her foot, at which Hyeongbo, even without finishing his scream, "yipe!" listlessly dropped his hand on the floor. The kick seemed to have been more deadly than the first one at his crotch. Below the navel was indeed one of the most vulnerable spots, of which neither Hyeongbo nor Chobong was aware.

Hyeongbo's eyes showed white as his eyelids rolled upward, his mouth was agape, and his twisted limbs were making no movements at all. He didn't seem to be breathing, and froth was bubbling around his lips like a crab.

"All right, take some more!"

Chobong, feeling new energy spring up within her, repeatedly kicked Hyeongbo on his lower belly, as if intending to make holes in it. One, two, three, four, and then five, six, seven, eight . . ., she kept kicking him, unaware of the number of her kicks.

She continued the fierce pounding with her foot on Hyeongbo's belly for some time, and then, as she happened to look down, she found him lying motionless, his four limbs stretched out. His eyes were almost closed, and he wasn't breathing at all.

For the first time, Chobong realized that he might be dead. She stopped her kicking, and gasping for breath, looked more closely at Hyeongbo's body stretched out at her feet. Chobong's appearance was even more macabre than the body lying down there.

Her long disheveled hair flowed down around her face, almost covering it. Her bloodshot eyes gleamed, shooting out frightening sparks. Dark crimson blood trickled from her lip. The high waist of her skirt had slipped down to her buttocks, revealing her white waist. With each gasping breath, the bare waist convulsed like a piece of meat.

Chobong was merely a mass of flesh, totally beyond any conscious control. She didn't care about either her disheveled hair or her bare waist. In fact she couldn't have cared as she was unaware of them. However much she gasped, she didn't know it. Although Songhui was crying desperately, floundering about on the floor, Chobong could hear nothing. The whole neighborhood was astir in alarm, but she didn't realize it.

She knew nothing, she could see nothing, other than the mere fact that Hyeongbo was lying on the floor, really dead at last.

It wasn't simply her senses that went numb, her consciousness too was half dead, severed from past and future, only capable of seeing the present alone. She was conscious only of the fact that Hyeongbo was lying dead now, at that very moment, at her feet. Her nervous system was akin to a lump of nerve tissue with severed ends preserved in a bottle of formaldehyde in a laboratory.

Chobong, in that horrible posture, had been silently looking down at the body of Hyeongbo for some time, then at last she knitted her brows, revealing her dismay at the scene. The fact that she had finally succeeded in killing Hyeongbo, her mortal enemy whom she had pledged to kill out of long accumulated hatred and vengeance, seemed to be something she regretted rather than something welcome or satisfactory.

Her sworn enemy was now lifeless, dead, not even able to know that he was dead; he would no longer feel pain even if she continued to kick and beat him. The enemy, who had utterly ruined her, devastating her life day after day in every conceivable aspect, was no longer a man in this world, she was now

deprived of the sole target on whom she could avenge herself.
He appeared to be comfortable. That tranquility! That invulner-
ability! That indifference! All those were his . . .

Chobong couldn't help but feel irritated and displeased with
what she saw.

She stood still only for a little while, then soon resumed tram-
pling on him with her heels, now more harshly and violently
than before, taking turns using both her feet, as if she were hard
at work to make holes in his belly. If she had indeed made a
hole and could touch the hard floor with her foot through the
hole, she might have felt relieved. But no matter how hard she
trampled on his belly, she could only feel the soft flesh giving
way like a deflated rubber ball. It was as insolent as Hyeongbo
used to be when he was alive. Exasperated by the unresponsive
body that could no longer feel any pain, Chobong began to shed
a flood of tears.

Overcome by her sense of frustration, she was ready to sink
down on the floor, but instead she began to look around, to see
if there were any tools she could use. If she had seen a knife, she
would have wielded it, slashing randomly at Hyeongbo's body. If
she had found a club or stick, she would have smashed the body
until it was totally mangled. If she had found a brazier filled
with burning charcoal, she would have tipped it onto the body.

But she could see nothing of the sort in the room. She looked
out at the maru through the open sliding door and saw a pair of
dark millstones sitting next to the rice chest. Without hesitation,
she instantly went out, picked up both of the millstones and
came back into the room. She usually had much difficulty in lifting even one millstone let alone the pair. But now she raised the
pair high up and threw them down right onto Hyeongbo's chest.

With a heavy thumping sound, the stones rolled down onto
the floor after smashing the chest, which was lying aslant because

of his hunched back. While throwing the stones down with her full force, Chobong lost her balance, almost falling forward onto the body, but with some effort, she managed to keep standing.

She then bent down to lift up the stones one more time, but stopped as she saw the blood seeping from his chest. The bloodstain on the thin undershirt that covered the chest mangled by the millstones was spreading widely; the tips of his fingers trembled slightly, almost invisibly. If Chobong noticed the slight movements, she would have thought Hyeongbo wasn't completely dead, and would have done something further. But the trembling was merely the convulsions that accompany death, the sort of twitch that can be seen in a chunk of meat. His head was flipped backward and from one corner of his mouth was flowing a thin stream of darkish red blood.

Chobong straightened up and blew out a deep sigh, having confirmed Hyeongbo's death once again from the blood flowing from his body. It was a sigh of relief, as she had at last fulfilled a mission, a mission that had seemed too difficult and formidable for her to handle, but somehow had been taken care of so easily.

As her scattered nerves began to function again, she couldn't help but see what she had done as a marvel, the outcome of a miracle, rather than the result of her own actions. As a matter of fact, she could never have succeeded in killing Hyeongbo in her normal state, even if she had got hold of an effective poison like potassium cyanide. It was purely the outcome of a series of unexpected contingencies that had taken place that night.

By and by Chobong recovered her senses, and the first thing she recognized was the sound of Songhui crying.

Although it seemed an age had passed since landing her first kick at Hyeongbo, it was actually only five minutes ago.

Chobong brushed back her disheveled hair, pulled up the waist of her skirt, then bent over to embrace Songhui, but she withdrew her hands with a start. She suddenly recalled that they were the hands that had murdered a man. She didn't want to hold her precious child with bloody hands. Regardless of her mother's uneasiness, Songhui crawled up to her and began to suck at her breast.

While feeding the child, Chobong pulled down a sheet and covered Hyeongbo's body with it. It might have been a customary act, springing from the instinctive wish to extend a final courtesy toward the dead, as well as to cover up a source of fear. But in this case, Chobong covered Hyeongbo's body out of a motherly instinct, to prevent Songhui's innocent eyes from taking in the horrible scene.

Then Chobong decided to clean up the mess. First of all, she looked up at the clock and confirmed that it was still only a quarter to nine. Gyebong usually came home at around nine-forty. So there was still plenty of time to have things under control before her sister's arrival.

Holding Songhui with one hand, Chobong began to clean up the room with the other, as though she were preparing to go out. As the bottle and the bag of capsules she had bought earlier were lying on the floor, she picked them up and put them away in the opposite room. She then took out all of Songhui's clothes that were stored in the bottom drawer of the dresser, and put them into a trunk, which she carried to the opposite room. Then she rummaged through the wardrobe and took out a new suit of clothes for herself, both the top and the skirt, as well as a new pair of socks. Finally, she cleaned up the mess scattered about the room and picked up her purse that was lying on top of the dressing table.

She had three rings—the one she was wearing was a platinum ring Hyeongbo had purchased for her, the other platinum one was given to her by Bak Jeho, and the third one was a gold ring studded with a sapphire. She put all three rings into her purse.

As she pulled off the platinum ring from her finger, she suddenly let out a deep sigh. She recalled the night she left Gunsan years ago, the night she pulled off the wedding ring Go Taesu had given her.

That she had to do it not just once but twice seemed to be a clear sign of her viciously warped fate. That mere ring stirred up various memories of her miserable life, filling her heart. She stood there blankly for some time, then breathing out a deep sigh once more, mumbled to herself,

"Back then, however, I was hopeful that I would somehow survive!"

As she was finally leaving the main room, she looked back. There were still things to be taken care of, but she decided that she couldn't waste any more time on it now.

Her gaze locked on Hyeongbo's body covered with a dark blue silk sheet, the corpse that no longer made any movements. She knew it was a corpse, but she felt neither horror nor fear.

After committing a murder, people usually feel vague dread, or a pang of conscience, or fright at the ensuing legal punishment, but Chobong felt none of these things. In her mind only two contrasting emotions alternated, satisfaction at the lucky outcome and jealousy of the peace her mortal enemy had attained.

She closed the sliding door of the main room behind her, and as she turned away, she frowned, bitterly muttering to herself,

"They say you're bound to encounter your enemy on a single log bridge! So am I supposed to go to the netherworld in his company?"

Filled with abomination at the idea, she wished she could rather go to the railroad or the Han-gang River to kill herself, instead of drinking poison in this damn house. Dying in this house would be shameful, she thought.

When she went into the opposite room, she put Songhui,

now asleep in her arms, on the floor. As she watched Songhui's sleeping face, a storm of sorrow surged up, and she burst into tears.

She wanted to abandon herself to grief, and cry endlessly, but she couldn't. There were things to take care of before her sister's arrival. Wiping away her tears, she pulled Gyebong's portable dresser toward her and began to brush her hair. She also tried to put on some makeup, but her tears kept messing it up. She then put on the new clothes. As she finished dressing, she felt somewhat refreshed.

Next, she began to write her farewell letters. Overwhelmed with sorrowful memories, her brush wouldn't flow very well. So she wrote a simple, short letter each to her father, Jeong Jusa, and her mother, Madam Yu, although many things crowded into her mind.

Her letter to Gyebong was a bit longer and more affectionate, as she had to entrust Songhui to her. She also mentioned her wish that Gyebong would eventually marry Seungjae.

She sealed each of the three letters, put them all in a larger envelope, and wrote on it "To My Respected Father."

It was nearly nine-thirty now. Gyebong would be back in about ten minutes. The moment her sister arrived, Chobong would hand her Songhui along with the purse, the envelope containing her letters, and the trunk, and send her away to the train station immediately.

She would say that she had received a telegram with the news that their mother was seriously ill, but Hyeongbo, being suspicious, wouldn't allow her to go down. Therefore if Gyebong went down to Gunsan with Songhui tonight by the eleven o'clock train, she would wait for her chance and join them in Gunsan tomorrow, if not tonight. Because she had that pretext in mind, she addressed the envelope to her father.

The pretext had not been in her mind in advance. It was

something she cooked up on the spot because she wanted to commit suicide after forcing both Songhui and Gyebong to leave the house. She didn't want to give them the burden of taking care of the aftermath of her murder and suicide. It was the last item of concern she had in this life.

Without such worries, she would have drunk the poison immediately, leaving her suicide notes at her bedside, rather than wait for Gyebong's return. Although she persuaded herself of the necessity to wait for Gyebong, it was also true that Chobong wanted to have a final meeting with her beloved sister before her death. Perhaps it would be the last meaningful moment of great pleasure she could enjoy in this life.

Having written the messages, she had completed all the preparations now.

She then thought she might pour the drug into the capsules while waiting for Gyebong. She set the bottle down in front of her, but the next moment she put it aside, sneering at her pathetic concern to cover the bitter taste of the drug with capsules, when she was ready to die.

She scolded herself for having forgotten the need to carry out her final motherly service to Songhui during the last ten minutes left to her. As she was turning away from the desk to move toward Songhui, Gyebong rushed into the house wildly, shouting out, "Sister, Sister!"

Gyebong stopped in front of the open door, unable to move, then said in a choked voice,

"S-sister!"

Large tears were falling down her cheeks, and with one sweep of her eyes she took in her sister's face, Songhui, the trunk, and the bottle of poison, then her eyes finally turned to her sister once again.

Chapter 19:
Prologue

AT FIRST CHOBONG was astounded on seeing her sister so flurried as she ran into the house calling her desperately, suspecting that her sister had somehow already discovered what had happened inside the house. However, she soon dismissed the suspicion as something improbable and tried to keep her normal composure as best she could.

But when Gyebong called her again in a sorrowful voice, standing on the threshold, facing her, (although her strained manner was quite extraordinary), Chobong was moved by the affection conveyed through her voice, even forgetful of her unusual manner. And on top of that, Gyebong's eyes were full of tears. Chobong's determination to stay calm fell apart at the moment, and she too began to shed large tears.

It was the sort of intense affection that could only arise between siblings. Chobong almost forgot everything else, overwhelmed by a genuine sense of communion with her sister. She was glad that she had waited for her, regardless of the consequences. The fact that she could meet her sister once more was more significant than anything else, she thought, even if it meant that she might fail in her plan to commit suicide because of her sister's intervention.

Gyebong shed tears of delight on finding her sister safe and well. Other than that, she couldn't figure out the meaning of the odd situation she saw in the room, feeling only confused.

Gyebong cautiously stepped into the room, studying her sister's expression, and called her name again, this time with a whimpering childlike tone, anxiously imploring her to give her an explanation.

"Sissy, dear!"

If someone had asked her why she was so anxious, she couldn't have come up with any answer. But Gyebong was indeed seriously worried.

Chobong, trying to give a big, warm smile, responded amiably, though her eyes were full of tears.

"My dearest, are you back now?"

Despite the strange situation, it momentarily occurred to Gyebong that her sister's mouth was still very pretty when she smiled.

The two sisters faced each other silently for a while. Gyebong longed to know what had happened but she couldn't ask any questions, unsure what to ask. Then she suddenly recalled that she had come home with Seungjae. Although she knew that the news wasn't important in this urgent situation, she just mentioned it in passing since she remembered it.

"Master Nam is here as well."

"What?"

Chobong was obviously surprised, and right at that moment, Seungjae came walking into the yard with big strides. Chobong instinctively leaned forward toward the door but when she saw Seungjae stop in the middle of the yard, she lowered her head.

Gyebong looked out over her sister's shoulder. The light was so dim that none of the three could see any changes in their expressions.

Seungjae hesitantly looked around while standing in the yard. But soon he boldly came walking into the house and stepped onto the maru. The sisters in the opposite room assumed he would enter the room where they were, but Seungjae, after wavering a little, walked toward the main room with a loud stomping sound.

Gyebong thought it strange, but Chobong, utterly astounded, lifted her head, with a muffled cry,

"My goodness, what's he doing!"

Seungjae was already in the main room, closing the sliding door behind him. Struck by a sudden idea, Gyebong glanced with wide-open eyes at Chobong. She was about to ask something, but swallowing it down, she rushed out to the maru. Chobong stood blankly, her shoulders slumped helplessly, while Gyebong hastily opened the door of the main room. She saw what she had expected, yet still her consternation was as extreme as if she hadn't expected it at all.

"Aargh!" Gyebong uttered a heavy but muffled exclamation.

"Close the door and stay out of the room!" Seungjae ordered Gyebong without raising his head. He was checking Hyeongbo's pulse after pulling off the sheet.

Intimidated by his command, Gyebong automatically closed the door, and just as automatically walked back to the opposite room. Chobong listlessly dropped her head when Gyebong stood facing her. Gyebong kept silent, looking at her sister's lowered head. She then turned her eyes to the bottle of poison and then back to her sister again. Gyebong's face was now full of sorrow, having recovered from her earlier shock.

Gyebong was experiencing the pain of her sister's unfortunate destiny, which was bound either to lead to suicide, as the bottle of the deadly drug suggested, or to the punishment the law would exact of her. Gyebong was feeling the pain, not as something that happened to someone else, but as something that was inflicted on the flesh of her own body.

"Sis!" Gyebong called out to her sister. As if forcing out an unconscious breath right before a seizure, the sound almost choked in her throat.

Chobong gently raised her head. A tearful smile emerged from total resignation to her fate. That too faded when she saw her sister's grief-stricken face.

"Gyebong, my dear!" Chobong called, her mouth twitching, ready to burst out crying again.

"Sis!"

Gyebong fell on her sister, embracing her waist, and soon Chobong too sank down and leaned her head upon Gyebong's shoulder. The sound of their crying, the younger sister's in a high pitch, and the older one's in a feeble tone, blended together, resounding as trembling echoes in the room.

"You should have waited a little longer, just a little bit . . .," Gyebong raised her head abruptly, shouting in agony, her shoulders shaking roughly.

"If you'd waited a little longer, Master Nam would have saved you and taken care of all the problems! I wish you'd been that little bit more patient! What shall we do now! Sis, Sis!"

Muttering her regrets, Gyebong embraced her sister again. She said this out of a sense of helplessness, not intending any other meaning than stating what could have been. But to Chobong's ears, it didn't sound so simple.

Something warm surged up in Chobong's heart, making her forget to weep over her situation. She sat blankly pondering over what could have happened to her.

Did she say Seungjae could have saved me and taken care of all my problems? Right! Does that mean that Seungjae still loves me and wishes to relieve me of my sufferings . . .?

As the thought struck her, she felt like new wings were sprouting from her arms. The next moment, however, she was filled with aching regrets.

If he really does, and if that's the real reason he came by with Gyebong . . . Alas! What have I done? I should have had more patience, if I'd waited for just one hour, just one hour . . .

Chobong felt she might go insane because of her mounting regrets. Gyebong didn't intend to give such a misunderstanding to her sister. Neither was it Chobong's fault. Leaning on her sister's shoulders again, Chobong began to cry pitifully, lamenting her hard fate.

Never had she been so happy, confirming Seungjae's love for her. But it was too late as she had already committed the irrevocable crime. It was vain to realize what could have been her happiness, the happiness she had lost for good because of a slight misplacement of timing. Could there be a worse fate than hers in the whole world?

Nevertheless, isn't it sweet and gratifying that Seungjae still loves me? But what's the use when I'm soon to die? Yet still . . . well . . . what shall I do? What am I going to do . . .?

Repeating these questions to herself, Chobong kept crying, unsure whether to be pleased or displeased.

At last Seungjae came out of the main room and stood silently facing the opposite room. Noticing Seungjae's movement, Chobong sat upright, covering her face with her hands. Gyebong too raised her head and looked up at Seungjae with swollen eyes. Understanding the question in her eyes, Seungjae shook his head. Hyeongbo was indeed dead from his fatal injuries.

Seungjae seemed to be having difficulty maintaining his standing posture, so Gyebong gave him a sign with her eyes to sit down where he was. All three were silent—the feeble sound of Chobong's intermittent crying was the only sound that filled the quiet room.

"Sister?"

Gyebong, who'd been pondering over what to do, having recovered her calmness, at last addressed her sister, moving closer to her. Chobong, instead of answering, took her hands from her face for a moment, and then covered it again.

"Um, listen, Sis . . ."

She couldn't continue, then after a little pause, said,

"Sis, listen to me . . . um . . . I think you'd better go to the police and turn yourself in. Can you do that, Sis? I don't know if you'll be able to go through with it, but perhaps, that's . . .," unable to finish the sentence, Gyebong let out a deep sigh.

Chobong was taken aback, and she raised her head to look at her sister. Indescribably complex expressions passed over her face. What her sister said was a welcome suggestion, but it was also cold advice.

"Turn myself in? . . . So I have to turn myself in!" Chobong uttered blankly, looking at her sister's face. She wasn't addressing her sister, but rather grumbling to herself, grieving over her own fate.

"If I turn myself in, you mean I have to go to prison? A death sentence would be welcome, but prison life . . . Do I have to add a new chapter of suffering to my life that's already full of all sorts of misery? No . . . I can't! I'd rather die, for I only did what I did planning to kill myself. I'd rather die, but no prison for me! What did I do to deserve it? Tell me, what wrong did I do? Jang Hyeongbo's life wasn't even worth the life of a fly. A fly doesn't harm people, but that vicious scoundrel, is it . . . is it a crime to kill the worst scoundrel in the world? Why on earth is it a crime? Beating a mad dog to death is a deed to be praised, isn't it? I killed a man worse than a mad dog, why is it a crime?

. . . I won't go to prison, because it's utterly unfair! Why, why should I live in a prison when I can die comfortably now with my two legs freely stretched out? Why should I take on such a woeful tribulation when I have an easy way out? Why? Why?"

Chobong felt like writhing and screaming on the floor, beating her chest. But she couldn't, she simply continued to cry, her face covered with her two hands. Tears dripped down between her fingers. Seungjae too had tears in his eyes, his nostrils were flaring, and he was gasping for breath like a bull.

As the unpleasant feelings he had experienced while face-to-face with the grotesque dead body faded, he was now beginning to feel full of sympathy for Chobong, who had been forced to commit murder. His indignation at "the poisonous weed," as well as the existing laws that had fostered and protected the weed, came flaring up in proportion to his growing sympathy with Chobong. He longed to go out onto the street, wielding a sword, but he couldn't think of anyone against whom he could wield it.

"What shall we do? Tell me please, Master Nam!"

Gyebong, turning her head toward Seungjae, demanded an answer. Seungjae, instead of answering, blurted out a curse,

"What a bloody, damned world!"

Seungjae, brushing away his tears with his fist, muttered, and then grinding his teeth, shouted,

"I won't let it go on, never!"

Seungjae glared up after uttering this threat.

"What an odd response!"

Gyebong cast a sideways glance at Seungjae, grumbling to herself, and turning to her sister, embraced her shoulders.

"Sis?"

"Gyebong, dear!"

Chobong, no longer able to sit still, laid her head on Gyebong's shoulder, and began to lament, crying intermittently.

"Gyebong, dear! What can I do now? What would be better, huh? I can't die, even if I want to . . . Even if I want to live, I can't live. What should I do, dear? Oh, my, my, Gyebong, dear!"

"Sis, Sis! We have no other options, do we? I don't think the punishment will be severe, considering the circumstances you were in and the fact that you turned yourself in . . . Perhaps ten years at the most, no, it might be only five to six years. If you serve that prison term, you'll be free, won't you? Everything will be fine then, I'm sure. Don't worry about Songhui, I'll take good care of her . . . Just endure a few years . . . But, how, how can my sister live through that! Confined in prison! . . . Oh, my goodness, what a disaster!"

Gyebong intended to console her sister, but ended up bursting into tears. As though a floodgate had been opened, the two sisters kept crying together, holding each other, while Seungjae sat next to them with his head lowered. Almost an hour passed, then Chobong suddenly stopped crying and raised her head toward Seungjae. Seungjae too raised his head, noticing Chobong had stopped crying, and their eyes met.

Chobong stared at him for quite some time, as if searching for something in his face, her eyes full of ardent imploring. In a raspy voice, she at last said,

"Shall I do that? If you tell me to do that, I'll do it. I will even serve a prison term and come back!"

She seemed to be pressing him for an answer. It was something Seungjae hadn't expected, but her attitude seemed very calm and determined.

Seungjae couldn't understand the meaning of her look, nor could he get the implied meaning of her words at first. When he finally figured out what she meant, he was at a loss as to what to say. However, he couldn't find the courage to say no on the spot to Chobong's ardent request for a "promise for tomorrow."

"Never worry about things left behind. Just come back safe after serving the term!"

Seungjae's voice was tender. Chobong unconsciously breathed out a sigh of relief, and said,

"Yes, I will."

With this docile reply, Chobong raised her head one more time to look at Seungjae. Seungjae couldn't miss the glow, accompanied by a faint smile that passed over her utterly sorrowful face.

CH'AE MAN-SIK (1902-1950) was a novelist best known for his satiric bent. His works, mostly written during the Japanese colonial period (1910-1945), employ a pungent, colloquial style, and evoke with sharp irony everyday life under Japanese rule. After graduating from Jung-ang High School in Seoul, he studied English literature at Waseda University for one year, then worked as a teacher, editor, and journalist before becoming a full-time writer in 1936. Among his works, the novels *Turbid Rivers*, *Peace Under Heaven*, and the short stories "A Ready-made Life" and "My Idiot Uncle" are widely admired by present-day readers of Korean literature.

KIM CHUNGHEE started her career as a reporter but later did her Ph.D. in English literature at Birkbeck College, University of London and taught at the Catholic University of Korea. In addition to several scholarly articles, she has also published a translation of Laurence Sterne's *Tristram Shandy* into Korean. At present she is teaching at LTI Korea Academy, while working on her own translation projects.

MICHAL AJVAZ, *The Golden Age.*
The Other City.

PIERRE ALBERT-BIROT, *Grabinoulor.*

YUZ ALESHKOVSKY, *Kangaroo.*

FELIPE ALFAU, *Chromos.*
Locos.

JOE AMATO, *Samuel Taylor's Last Night.*

IVAN ÂNGELO, *The Celebration.*
The Tower of Glass.

ANTÓNIO LOBO ANTUNES, *Knowledge of Hell.*
The Splendor of Portugal.

ALAIN ARIAS-MISSON, *Theatre of Incest.*

JOHN ASHBERY & JAMES SCHUYLER, *A Nest of Ninnies.*

ROBERT ASHLEY, *Perfect Lives.*

GABRIELA AVIGUR-ROTEM, *Heatwave and Crazy Birds.*

DJUNA BARNES, *Ladies Almanack.*
Ryder.

JOHN BARTH, *Letters.*
Sabbatical.

DONALD BARTHELME, *The King.*
Paradise.

SVETISLAV BASARA, *Chinese Letter.*

MIQUEL BAUÇÀ, *The Siege in the Room.*

RENÉ BELLETTO, *Dying.*

MAREK BIENCZYK, *Transparency.*

ANDREI BITOV, *Pushkin House.*

ANDREJ BLATNIK, *You Do Understand.*
Law of Desire.

LOUIS PAUL BOON, *Chapel Road.*
My Little War.
Summer in Termuren.

ROGER BOYLAN, *Killoyle.*

IGNÁCIO DE LOYOLA BRANDÃO, *Anonymous Celebrity.*
Zero.

BONNIE BREMSER, *Troia: Mexican Memoirs.*

CHRISTINE BROOKE-ROSE, *Amalgamemnon.*

BRIGID BROPHY, *In Transit.*
The Prancing Novelist.

GERALD L. BRUNS, *Modern Poetry and the Idea of Language.*

GABRIELLE BURTON, *Heartbreak Hotel.*

MICHEL BUTOR, *Degrees.*
Mobile.

G. CABRERA INFANTE, *Infante's Inferno.*
Three Trapped Tigers.

JULIETA CAMPOS, *The Fear of Losing Eurydice.*

ANNE CARSON, *Eros the Bittersweet.*

ORLY CASTEL-BLOOM, *Dolly City.*

LOUIS-FERDINAND CÉLINE, *North.*
Conversations with Professor Y.
London Bridge.

MARIE CHAIX, *The Laurels of Lake Constance.*

HUGO CHARTERIS, *The Tide Is Right.*

ERIC CHEVILLARD, *Demolishing Nisard.*
The Author and Me.

MARC CHOLODENKO, *Mordechai Schamz.*

JOSHUA COHEN, *Witz.*

EMILY HOLMES COLEMAN, *The Shutter of Snow.*

ERIC CHEVILLARD, *The Author and Me.*

ROBERT COOVER, *A Night at the Movies.*

STANLEY CRAWFORD, *Log of the S.S. The Mrs Unguentine.*
Some Instructions to My Wife.

RENÉ CREVEL, *Putting My Foot in It.*

RALPH CUSACK, *Cadenza.*

NICHOLAS DELBANCO, *Sherbrookes.*
The Count of Concord.

NIGEL DENNIS, *Cards of Identity.*

PETER DIMOCK, *A Short Rhetoric for Leaving the Family.*

ARIEL DORFMAN, *Konfidenz.*

COLEMAN DOWELL, *Island People.*
Too Much Flesh and Jabez.

ARKADII DRAGOMOSHCHENKO, *Dust.*

RIKKI DUCORNET, *Phosphor in Dreamland.*
The Complete Butcher's Tales.

RIKKI DUCORNET (cont.), *The Jade Cabinet.*
The Fountains of Neptune.

WILLIAM EASTLAKE, *The Bamboo Bed.*
Castle Keep.
Lyric of the Circle Heart.

JEAN ECHENOZ, *Chopin's Move.*

STANLEY ELKIN, *A Bad Man.*
Criers and Kibitzers, Kibitzers and Criers.
The Dick Gibson Show.
The Franchiser.
The Living End.
Mrs. Ted Bliss.

FRANÇOIS EMMANUEL, *Invitation to a Voyage.*

PAUL EMOND, *The Dance of a Sham.*

SALVADOR ESPRIU, *Ariadne in the Grotesque Labyrinth.*

LESLIE A. FIEDLER, *Love and Death in the American Novel.*

JUAN FILLOY, *Op Oloop.*

ANDY FITCH, *Pop Poetics.*

GUSTAVE FLAUBERT, *Bouvard and Pécuchet.*

KASS FLEISHER, *Talking out of School.*

JON FOSSE, *Aliss at the Fire.*
Melancholy.

FORD MADOX FORD, *The March of Literature.*

MAX FRISCH, *I'm Not Stiller.*
Man in the Holocene.

CARLOS FUENTES, *Christopher Unborn.*
Distant Relations.
Terra Nostra.
Where the Air Is Clear.

TAKEHIKO FUKUNAGA, *Flowers of Grass.*

WILLIAM GADDIS, JR., *The Recognitions.*

JANICE GALLOWAY, *Foreign Parts.*
The Trick Is to Keep Breathing.

WILLIAM H. GASS, *Life Sentences.*
The Tunnel.
The World Within the Word.
Willie Masters' Lonesome Wife.

GÉRARD GAVARRY, *Hoppla! 1 2 3.*

ETIENNE GILSON, *The Arts of the Beautiful.*
Forms and Substances in the Arts.

C. S. GISCOMBE, *Giscome Road.*
Here.

DOUGLAS GLOVER, *Bad News of the Heart.*

WITOLD GOMBROWICZ, *A Kind of Testament.*

PAULO EMÍLIO SALES GOMES, *P's Three Women.*

GEORGI GOSPODINOV, *Natural Novel.*

JUAN GOYTISOLO, *Count Julian.*
Juan the Landless.
Makbara.
Marks of Identity.

HENRY GREEN, *Blindness.*
Concluding.
Doting.
Nothing.

JACK GREEN, *Fire the Bastards!*

JIŘÍ GRUŠA, *The Questionnaire.*

MELA HARTWIG, *Am I a Redundant Human Being?*

JOHN HAWKES, *The Passion Artist.*
Whistlejacket.

ELIZABETH HEIGHWAY, ED., *Contemporary Georgian Fiction.*

AIDAN HIGGINS, *Balcony of Europe.*
Blind Man's Bluff.
Bornholm Night-Ferry.
Langrishe, Go Down.
Scenes from a Receding Past.

KEIZO HINO, *Isle of Dreams.*

KAZUSHI HOSAKA, *Plainsong.*

ALDOUS HUXLEY, *Antic Hay.*
Point Counter Point.
Those Barren Leaves.
Time Must Have a Stop.

NAOYUKI II, *The Shadow of a Blue Cat.*

DRAGO JANČAR, *The Tree with No Name.*

MIKHEIL JAVAKHISHVILI, *Kvachi.*

GERT JONKE, *The Distant Sound.*
Homage to Czerny.
The System of Vienna.

JACQUES JOUET, *Mountain R.*
Savage.
Upstaged.

MIEKO KANAI, *The Word Book.*

YORAM KANIUK, *Life on Sandpaper.*

ZURAB KARUMIDZE, *Dagny.*

JOHN KELLY, *From Out of the City.*

HUGH KENNER, *Flaubert, Joyce and Beckett: The Stoic Comedians.*
Joyce's Voices.

DANILO KIŠ, *The Attic.*
The Lute and the Scars.
Psalm 44.
A Tomb for Boris Davidovich.

ANITA KONKKA, *A Fool's Paradise.*

GEORGE KONRÁD, *The City Builder.*

TADEUSZ KONWICKI, *A Minor Apocalypse.*
The Polish Complex.

ANNA KORDZAIA-SAMADASHVILI,
Me, Margarita.

MENIS KOUMANDAREAS, *Koula.*

ELAINE KRAF, *The Princess of 72nd Street.*

JIM KRUSOE, *Iceland.*

AYSE KULIN, *Farewell: A Mansion in Occupied Istanbul.*

EMILIO LASCANO TEGUI, *On Elegance While Sleeping.*

ERIC LAURRENT, *Do Not Touch.*

VIOLETTE LEDUC, *La Bâtarde.*

EDOUARD LEVÉ, *Autoportrait.*
Newspaper.
Suicide.
Works.

MARIO LEVI, *Istanbul Was a Fairy Tale.*

DEBORAH LEVY, *Billy and Girl.*

JOSÉ LEZAMA LIMA, *Paradiso.*

ROSA LIKSOM, *Dark Paradise.*

OSMAN LINS, *Avalovara.*
The Queen of the Prisons of Greece.

FLORIAN LIPUŠ, *The Errors of Young Tjaž.*

GORDON LISH, *Peru.*

ALF MACLOCHLAINN, *Out of Focus.*
Past Habitual.

The Corpus in the Library.

RON LOEWINSOHN, *Magnetic Field(s).*

YURI LOTMAN, *Non-Memoirs.*

D. KEITH MANO, *Take Five.*

MINA LOY, *Stories and Essays of Mina Loy.*

MICHELINE AHARONIAN MARCOM,
A Brief History of Yes.
The Mirror in the Well.

BEN MARCUS, *The Age of Wire and String.*

WALLACE MARKFIELD, *Teitlebaum's Window.*

DAVID MARKSON, *Reader's Block.*
Wittgenstein's Mistress.

CAROLE MASO, *AVA.*

HISAKI MATSUURA, *Triangle.*

LADISLAV MATEJKA & KRYSTYNA POMORSKA, EDS., *Readings in Russian Poetics: Formalist & Structuralist Views.*

HARRY MATHEWS, *Cigarettes.*
The Conversions.
The Human Country.
The Journalist.
My Life in CIA.
Singular Pleasures.
The Sinking of the Odradek.
Stadium.
Tlooth.

HISAKI MATSUURA, *Triangle.*

DONAL MCLAUGHLIN, *beheading the virgin mary, and other stories.*

JOSEPH MCELROY, *Night Soul and Other Stories.*

ABDELWAHAB MEDDEB, *Talismano.*

GERHARD MEIER, *Isle of the Dead.*

HERMAN MELVILLE, *The Confidence-Man.*

AMANDA MICHALOPOULOU, *I'd Like.*

STEVEN MILLHAUSER, *The Barnum Museum.*
In the Penny Arcade.

RALPH J. MILLS, JR., *Essays on Poetry.*

MOMUS, *The Book of Jokes.*

CHRISTINE MONTALBETTI, *The Origin of Man.*
Western.

NICHOLAS MOSLEY, *Accident.*
Assassins.
Catastrophe Practice.
A Garden of Trees.
Hopeful Monsters.
Imago Bird.
Inventing God.
Look at the Dark.
Metamorphosis.
Natalie Natalia.
Serpent.

WARREN MOTTE, *Fables of the Novel:*
French Fiction since 1990.
Fiction Now: The French Novel in the
21st Century.
Mirror Gazing.
Oulipo: A Primer of Potential Literature.

GERALD MURNANE, *Barley Patch.*
Inland.

YVES NAVARRE, *Our Share of Time.*
Sweet Tooth.

DOROTHY NELSON, *In Night's City.*
Tar and Feathers.

ESHKOL NEVO, *Homesick.*

WILFRIDO D. NOLLEDO, *But for*
the Lovers.

BORIS A. NOVAK, *The Master of*
Insomnia.

FLANN O'BRIEN, *At Swim-Two-Birds.*
The Best of Myles.
The Dalkey Archive.
The Hard Life.
The Poor Mouth.
The Third Policeman.

CLAUDE OLLIER, *The Mise-en-Scène.*
Wert and the Life Without End.

PATRIK OUŘEDNÍK, *Europeana.*
The Opportune Moment, 1855.

BORIS PAHOR, *Necropolis.*

FERNANDO DEL PASO, *News from*
the Empire.
Palinuro of Mexico.

ROBERT PINGET, *The Inquisitory.*
Mahu or The Material.
Trio.

MANUEL PUIG, *Betrayed by Rita*
Hayworth.

The Buenos Aires Affair.
Heartbreak Tango.

RAYMOND QUENEAU, *The Last Days.*
Odile.
Pierrot Mon Ami.
Saint Glinglin.

ANN QUIN, *Berg.*
Passages.
Three.
Tripticks.

ISHMAEL REED, *The Free-Lance*
Pallbearers.
The Last Days of Louisiana Red.
Ishmael Reed: The Plays.
Juice!
The Terrible Threes.
The Terrible Twos.
Yellow Back Radio Broke-Down.

JASIA REICHARDT, *15 Journeys Warsaw*
to London.

JOÃO UBALDO RIBEIRO, *House of the*
Fortunate Buddhas.

JEAN RICARDOU, *Place Names.*

RAINER MARIA RILKE,
The Notebooks of Malte Laurids Brigge.

JULIÁN RÍOS, *The House of Ulysses.*
Larva: A Midsummer Night's Babel.
Poundemonium.

ALAIN ROBBE-GRILLET, *Project for a*
Revolution in New York.
A Sentimental Novel.

AUGUSTO ROA BASTOS, *I the Supreme.*

DANIËL ROBBERECHTS, *Arriving in*
Avignon.

JEAN ROLIN, *The Explosion of the*
Radiator Hose.

OLIVIER ROLIN, *Hotel Crystal.*

ALIX CLEO ROUBAUD, *Alix's Journal.*

JACQUES ROUBAUD, *The Form of*
a City Changes Faster, Alas, Than the
Human Heart.
The Great Fire of London.
Hortense in Exile.
Hortense Is Abducted.
Mathematics: The Plurality of Worlds of
Lewis.
Some Thing Black.

RAYMOND ROUSSEL, *Impressions of Africa.*

VEDRANA RUDAN, *Night.*

PABLO M. RUIZ, *Four Cold Chapters on the Possibility of Literature.*

GERMAN SADULAEV, *The Maya Pill.*

TOMAŽ ŠALAMUN, *Soy Realidad.*

LYDIE SALVAYRE, *The Company of Ghosts.*
The Lecture.
The Power of Flies.

LUIS RAFAEL SÁNCHEZ, *Macho Camacho's Beat.*

SEVERO SARDUY, *Cobra & Maitreya.*

NATHALIE SARRAUTE, *Do You Hear Them?*
Martereau.
The Planetarium.

STIG SÆTERBAKKEN, *Siamese.*
Self-Control.
Through the Night.

ARNO SCHMIDT, *Collected Novellas.*
Collected Stories.
Nobodaddy's Children.
Two Novels.

ASAF SCHURR, *Motti.*

GAIL SCOTT, *My Paris.*

DAMION SEARLS, *What We Were Doing and Where We Were Going.*

JUNE AKERS SEESE, *Is This What Other Women Feel Too?*

BERNARD SHARE, *Inish.*
Transit.

VIKTOR SHKLOVSKY, *Bowstring.*
Literature and Cinematography.
Theory of Prose.
Third Factory.
Zoo, or Letters Not about Love.

PIERRE SINIAC, *The Collaborators.*

KJERSTI A. SKOMSVOLD, *The Faster I Walk, the Smaller I Am.*

JOSEF ŠKVORECKÝ, *The Engineer of Human Souls.*

GILBERT SORRENTINO, *Aberration of Starlight.*
Blue Pastoral.
Crystal Vision.

Imaginative Qualities of Actual Things.
Mulligan Stew. Red the Fiend.
Steelwork.
Under the Shadow.

MARKO SOSIČ, *Ballerina, Ballerina.*

ANDRZEJ STASIUK, *Dukla.*
Fado.

GERTRUDE STEIN, *The Making of Americans.*
A Novel of Thank You.

LARS SVENDSEN, *A Philosophy of Evil.*

PIOTR SZEWC, *Annihilation.*

GONÇALO M. TAVARES, *A Man: Klaus Klump.*
Jerusalem.
Learning to Pray in the Age of Technique.

LUCIAN DAN TEODOROVICI, *Our Circus Presents...*

NIKANOR TERATOLOGEN, *Assisted Living.*

STEFAN THEMERSON, *Hobson's Island.*
The Mystery of the Sardine.
Tom Harris.

TAEKO TOMIOKA, *Building Waves.*

JOHN TOOMEY, *Sleepwalker.*

DUMITRU TSEPENEAG, *Hotel Europa.*
The Necessary Marriage.
Pigeon Post.
Vain Art of the Fugue.

ESTHER TUSQUETS, *Stranded.*

DUBRAVKA UGRESIC, *Lend Me Your Character.*
Thank You for Not Reading.

TOR ULVEN, *Replacement.*

MATI UNT, *Brecht at Night.*
Diary of a Blood Donor.
Things in the Night.

ÁLVARO URIBE & OLIVIA SEARS, EDS., *Best of Contemporary Mexican Fiction.*

ELOY URROZ, *Friction.*
The Obstacles.

LUISA VALENZUELA, *Dark Desires and the Others.*
He Who Searches.

PAUL VERHAEGHEN, *Omega Minor.*

BORIS VIAN, *Heartsnatcher.*

LLORENÇ VILLALONGA, *The Dolls' Room.*

TOOMAS VINT, *An Unending Landscape.*

ORNELA VORPSI, *The Country Where No One Ever Dies.*

AUSTRYN WAINHOUSE, *Hedyphagetica.*

CURTIS WHITE, *America's Magic Mountain.*
The Idea of Home.
Memories of My Father Watching TV.
Requiem.

DIANE WILLIAMS,
Excitability: Selected Stories.
Romancer Erector.

DOUGLAS WOOLF, *Wall to Wall.*
Ya! & John-Juan.

JAY WRIGHT, *Polynomials and Pollen.*
The Presentable Art of Reading Absence.

PHILIP WYLIE, *Generation of Vipers.*

MARGUERITE YOUNG, *Angel in the Forest.*
Miss MacIntosh, My Darling.

REYOUNG, *Unbabbling.*

VLADO ŽABOT, *The Succubus.*

ZORAN ŽIVKOVIĆ , *Hidden Camera.*

LOUIS ZUKOFSKY, *Collected Fiction.*

VITOMIL ZUPAN, *Minuet for Guitar.*

SCOTT ZWIREN, *God Head.*

AND MORE . . .